PENNY
DREADFULS

PENNY DREADFULS

DREADFULS

SENSATIONAL TALES OF TERROR

COMPILED BY STEFAN DZIEMIANOWICZ

New York

FALL RIVER PRESS

New York

An Imprint of Sterling Publishing Co., Inc.
1166 Avenue of the Americas
New York, NY 10036

ISBN 978-1-4351-5721-7

Manufactured in the United States of America

10

sterlingpublishing.com

The Fell Types are digitally reproduced by Igino Marini. www.iginomarini.com

Contents

Introduction

———◆———

P ENNY DREADFUL" IS USED AS A CATCH-ALL TERM TO DESCRIBE GRIM AND
gruesome tales of horror—an association that has gained considerable trac-
tion thanks to the popularity of the cable television program *Penny Dreadful*,
and its mash-up of characters and themes from supernatural horror stories of the nineteenth century. But the penny dreadful is an actual historical phenomenon. The term
came into vogue in the early decades of the nineteenth century to describe cheaply
priced publications that provided thrilling popular fiction, primarily for the British
working class. Between the 1830s and 1850s, scores of penny dreadfuls were published
weekly, and the entertainment they provided shines a glaring light on the tastes of the
public that bought them.

The literary origins of the penny dreadful can be traced back to the late eighteenth
century, and the heyday of the gothic novel. Launched in 1764 with the publication of
Horace Walpole's *The Castle of Otranto*, the gothic novel blended horror, suspense,
and romance in a wildly plotted tale that often featured a castle or monastery of medi-
eval origin as its setting. Gothic novels were conjured into being in direct opposition
to the rationalist spirit of the Age of Enlightenment. They were crude escapist fiction
that contrasted sharply with more sophisticated literary novels from that time, save in
one important regard: in nearly all of them, virtue was rewarded (albeit after many
trials and tribulations for the heroine) and villainy punished. Gothic novels found an
audience eager for the shocks and occasional supernatural thrills they offered, and several authors made their reputations writing them, among them Ann Radcliffe, whose
The Mysteries of Udolpho (1794) established a trend in gothic fiction for the rationaliza-
tion of seemingly supernatural phenomena, and Matthew Gregory Lewis, whose *The
Monk* (1796) is regarded as the most extravagant and outrageous of all gothic novels.

For every Radcliffe and Lewis, who at least showed modest literary talent, there
were scores of hacks eager to cash in on the popularity of gothic fiction. Toward the
end of the gothic era, the gothic bluebook—so named because of the cheap blue paper
covers most bore—emerged. These were chapbooks that ran thirty-six to seventy-two
pages long and sold for sixpence or a shilling—hence their nickname, the "shilling

shockers." The plots of most shilling shockers were usually a distillation of better-known gothic novels reduced to their essential thrills and chills, or occasionally a cross-stitch of plot elements from several novels, which sometimes meshed well but more often did not. The shilling shockers usually were published anonymously or pseudonymously—or sometimes spuriously as the work of the writer whose novel was being adapted—and they usually bore a frontispiece engraving depicting a lurid scene that sometimes did not even occur in the story.

The era of the gothic novel had come to its end by the 1820s, but it had popular-ized a number of sensational set pieces that were ripe for redeployment in the popular fiction that followed in its wake: the haunted ancestral castle with secret passageways and labyrinthine dungeons; the imperiled heroine; the brooding Byronic villain; the lecherous monk. The allure of gothic literature was eventually lampooned by Thomas Love Peacock, in his novel *Nightmare Abbey* (1818), and even by Jane Austen, whose *Northanger Abbey* (1818) had been written in the twilight years of the gothic era, and whose heroine, Catherine Morland, has a reading list of genuine gothic novels that have since become known as the "Northanger Horrids."

Enter the penny dreadful, which began less as a literary phenomenon than a business opportunity. In the earliest decades of the nineteenth century the publishing industry was revolutionized by the machine manufacture of paper (which previously had been made by hand) and the invention of the rotary steam printing press. The ability of printers to mass-produce publications relatively inexpensively dovetailed with improving rates of literacy among the working classes, who were increasingly better educated. Sensing an audience ripe for exploitation, enterprising publishers began publishing penny newspapers: pamphlets eight pages long that featured double columns of densely packed text. Some of these pamphlets featured self-contained sto-ries, but many offered a weekly installment—a chapter, or chapters—of a serial story meant to hook reader interest for the duration of its telling. (As added incentive, some publishers went so far as to give away several installments with the purchase of the first number.) The penny papers were cheap enough that they could be purchased with a workman's wages, and short enough that they could be read by those with little leisure time. They could be folded up for convenient transport in a shirt or pants pocket, passed around among friends, and in the case of serial installments disposed of by the time the next weekly number rolled off the presses. Although they were initially marketed to adults, by the middle of the nineteenth century the penny papers were catering mostly to the reading interests of young boys.

Writers for the penny papers ground out reams of copy for a pittance, and some-times for nothing at all, depending on how tight-fisted or unscrupulous the publishers were. It's not likely that they rigorously plotted out their stories in advance. By their nature, the stories in the penny papers were written to last as long as they were popular with readers. A story whose popularity was on the wane might conclude suddenly, loose ends left untied, with the next week's installment. A story that found a large audience, however, might run for a year or more and tally a significant number of chapters—for example, James Malcolm Rymer's *Varney the Vampire; or, The Feast of Blood* which, by the time it concluded, ran to 220 chapters totaling close to 900 pages. In order to achieve the length necessary to sustain a long story, writers resorted to a number of tricks to pad the narrative, including adding chapters of history not essential to the plot, lengthy character back-stories, subplots that went nowhere, and red herrings galore. They also added as many lines of short dialogue as they could fit. Strategies of this sort virtually ensured that even the best-written stories would not have very coherent plots—some-thing especially true for the stories that were written by a tag-team of different writers.

But readers didn't turn to penny dreadfuls for storytelling that met with high lit-erary standards. They read them for their crude thrills and shock value. The following passage, in which the title character of *Varney the Vampire* stalks his first victim, is typ-ical of the sort of sensationalized writing readers expected for their penny purchase:

> The figure turns half round, and the light falls upon the face. It is perfectly white—perfectly bloodless. The eyes look like polished tin; the lips are drawn back, and the principal feature next to those dreadful eyes is the teeth—the fearful looking teeth—projecting like those of some wild animal, hideously, glaringly white, and fang-like. It approaches the bed with a strange, gliding movement. It clashes together the long nails that literally appear to hang from the finger ends. No sound comes from its lips. Is she going mad— that young and beautiful girl exposed to so much terror? she has drawn up all her limbs; she cannot even now say help. The power of articulation is gone, but the power of movement has returned to her; she can draw herself slowly along to the other side of the bed from that towards which the hideous appearance is coming.

There was no limit to the outrageous extremes that penny dreadful writers would go when ratcheting up the thrills. In G. W. M. Reynolds's *The Mysteries of London*, a prisoner transported to Australia for hard labor escapes with a group of fellow convicts into the wilderness. When their provisions run out their leader, Blackley, murders one of their group to roast his flesh for food. The narrator, who along with another convict named Stephens resists the temptation to partake, describes the morning after the atrocity:

> "At length morning dawned upon that awful and never-to-be-forgotten night. The fire was now extinguished; but near the ashes lay the entrails and the head of the murdered man. The cannibals had completely anatomized the corpse, and had wrapped up in their shirts (which they took off for the purpose) all that they chose to carry away with them. Not a word was spoken among us. The last frail links of sympathy—if any had really existed— seemed to be broken by the incidents of the preceding night. Six men had partaken of the horrible repast; and they evidently looked on each other with loathing, and on Stephens and myself with suspicion. We all with one accord cut thick sticks, and advanced in the direction whence Blackley's cries had proceeded a few hours previously. His fate was that which we had suspected: an enormous snake was coiled around the wretch's corpse—licking it with its long tongue, to cover it with saliva for the purpose of deglutition. We attacked the monstrous reptile, and killed it. Its huge coils had actually squeezed our unfortunate comrade to death! Then—for the first time for many, many years—did a religious sentiment steal into my soul; and I murmured to myself, '*Surely, this was the judgment of God upon a man who had mediated murder.*' "

Some of the penny papers drew their content from gothic novels, or compendia of true crimes such as the *Newgate Calendar*, a monthly account of imprisonings and executions in England's Newgate Prison that was first published in book form in 1774, and *The Terrific Register* (1825), an anthology of exotic atrocities and gruesome crimes from around the world whose subtitle proclaimed it a "Record of Crimes, Judgments, Providences, and Calamities." Embellished with sensational details and related in purple prose, these stories found favor with a populace that still regularly attended public executions for entertainment and for whom the stomach-churning squalor described in *Report on the Sanitary Conditions of the Labouring Classes* (1842), *A Report on the Results of the Practice of Interment in Towns* (1843), and other journalistic tracts, was a daily reality. The better-known penny papers, however, were novel-length originals published in penny installments, among them Rymer's *Varney the Vampire* (1845–1847), G. W. M. Reynolds's *Wagner the Wehr-Wolf* (1846–1847), and Rymer's *The String of Pearls* (a possible collaboration with Thomas Peckett Prest) that relates the grisly history of Sweeney Todd, the demon barber of Fleet-street. It is hard to find a penny dreadful more lurid than *The String of Pearls,* with its account of a sinister barber who murders his wealthy customers, turns the citizens of London into unwitting cannibals when he gives the butchered corpses to a maker of popular meat pies, and deposits the unused remains in the vaults beneath St. Dunstan's church where they perfume the neighborhood with a suffocating, charnel stench.

Publication of the penny papers began in earnest in the 1830s, and by the 1840s publishers such as Reynolds, W. M. Clarke, and Edward Lloyd were getting wealthy off of them. Lloyd's *Calendar of Horrors,* published for ninety-one issues between 1835 and 1836 and edited by Prest, was a particularly successful and trendsetting penny paper that ran both horrid true crime stories and serial fiction and advertised itself as "An interesting collection of the romantic, wild and wonderful." Some of Lloyd's earliest penny papers were plagiarizations of the work of Charles Dickens, whose books were appearing serially in the popular press at the same time. It's estimated that over the span of twenty years, before he moved on to publishing more respectable papers such as the *Daily Chronicle,* Lloyd issued more than 200 penny dreadful serials.

It's not known exactly when the term "penny dreadful" was first used to describe these publications, but by the time they were primarily being read by young boys the term was certainly intended as a judgment on their dubious literary and moral merit. Penny dreadfuls also were sometimes called "penny bloods," a reference pertaining to their violence and gore, but also to the blood-and-thunder adventures they offered. Indeed, horror fiction was only one of several types of fare offered by the penny dreadfuls. Tales of highwaymen were extremely popular. Dick Turpin, the notorious highwayman executed in 1739, was the hero of a number of penny dreadfuls, among them *Black Bess; or, The Knight of the Road,* which ran for 254 installments. Spring-Heeled Jack, a leaping bandit who reportedly preyed on women in London in the 1830s, was the main character in several penny dreadfuls. In some, his horned head and batwings were presented as part of an elaborate disguise; in others, they were the stigmata of his supernatural pedigree. Pirates, outlaws, freebooters, revolutionaries, robbers, and cowboys put in appearances in the penny dreadfuls, as did folk heroes like Robin Hood and characters from real life, most notably Buffalo Bill. A look at the titles of some penny dreadfuls written by Rymer alone gives an idea of just how varied their subjects were: *The Black Monk; or, The Secret of the Grey Turret; The White Slave: A Romance for the Nineteenth Century; Amy or, Love and Madness; Ada the Betrayed; or, The Murder at the Smithy; Varney the Vampire; or, The Feast of Blood.*

Like the gothic novel, the penny dreadful enjoyed a brief but spectacular interval of popularity. By the 1850s, penny dreadfuls had given way to penny papers for boys, such as *The Boy's Own Paper*, *Boys of England*, and *The Young Gentleman's Journal*. Writers continued to produce serial stories for these penny papers, but the luridness of their content was greatly toned down, much to the relief of worried parents and protectors of public morality. The boy's papers were the forerunners of the nickel weeklies and dime novels popular at end of the nineteenth century. These more wholesome publications tended to feature stories with young heroes who triumph over circumstance through pluck and luck, as well as cowboys, crime-solvers, and real historical figures. Dime novels, in turn, paved the way in the early twentieth century for the pulp fiction magazines, in which the horror, science fiction, and detective fiction genres were shaped.

The stories chosen for *Penny Dreadfuls* were all first published in the nineteenth century, when penny dreadfuls were showing publishers and writers the public's tastes for popular fiction and helping to shape the state of the art of Victorian-era horror fiction. All were chosen for the resonance of their themes and plots with those of actual penny dreadfuls. Mary Shelley's *Frankenstein* and Washington Irving's "The Adventure of the German Student" are penny dreadful precursors, produced at the end of the era of the gothic novel. We have chosen to include the original 1818 edition of Shelley's novel rather than the better-known 1831 edition, in which she softened some of the tale's horrors. *The String of Pearls*, a genuine penny dreadful serial, is that era's best treatment of the Sweeney Todd theme. "The Apparition of Lord Tyrone to Lady Beresford" is reprinted from *The Terrific Register*, whose contents were regularly adapted for the penny dreadfuls. "Wake Not the Dead!; or, The Bride of the Grave"—which was first published anonymously but later attributed to influential German Romantic writer Johann Ludwig Tieck—and "A Night in the Grave; *or*, The Devil's Receipt," are both reprinted from *Legends of Terror! and Tales of the Wonderful and Wild* (1826), another source text for the penny dreadfuls composed of supernatural legends from throughout Europe and the east. "Sawney Beane: The Man Eater," is a chapter from *Lives and Exploits of the Most Noted Highwaymen, Robbers and Murderers, of All Nations*

(1836), many of whose subjects were featured in the penny bloods. "The Wehr-Wolf: A Legend of the Limousin" first appeared in Richard Thomson's *Tales of an Antiquary: Chiefly Illustrative of the Manners, Traditions, and Remarkable Localities of Ancient London* (1828), and its plot twist continued to appear in werewolf tales well into the twentieth century. Louisa May Alcott's "Lost in a Pyramid; or, The Mummy's Curse," was one of dozens of "sensation stories" that the author of *Little Women* contributed anonymously or pseudonymously to newspapers printed by American publisher Frank Leslie. Who is to say that the stories by the better-known authors—Edgar Allan Poe, Arthur Conan Doyle, Robert Louis Stevenson, Ralph Adams Cram, and Bram Stoker (whose *Dracula* was clearly influenced by *Varney the Vampire*)—that were published in more respectable venues are not the work of writers who were familiar with penny dreadfuls, breathed the atmosphere of the era in which they flourished, and found their imaginations fired by the thrills they offered?

—Stefan Dziemianowicz
New York, 2014

Frankenstein

OR, THE MODERN PROMETHEUS

Mary Shelley

———◆———

Did I request thee, Maker, from my clay
To mould Me man? Did I solicit thee
From darkness to promote me?—
Paradise Lost (x. 743–745)

LETTER I

To Mrs. SAVILLE, *England.*

St. Petersburgh, Dec. 11th, 17—.

You will rejoice to hear that no disaster has accompanied the commencement of an enterprise which you have regarded with such evil forebodings.
I arrived here yesterday; and my first task is to assure my dear sister of my
welfare, and increasing confidence in the success of my undertaking.

I am already far north of London; and as I walk in the streets of
Petersburgh, I feel a cold northern breeze play upon my cheeks, which braces
my nerves, and fills me with delight. Do you understand this feeling? This
breeze, which has travelled from the regions towards which I am advancing,
gives me a foretaste of those icy climes. Inspirited by this wind of promise,
my day dreams become more fervent and vivid. I try in vain to be persuaded
that the pole is the seat of frost and desolation; it ever presents itself to my
imagination as the region of beauty and delight. There, Margaret, the sun is
for ever visible; its broad disk just skirting the horizon, and diffusing a perpetual splendour. There—for with your leave, my sister, I will put some trust
in preceding navigators—there snow and frost are banished; and, sailing over

a calm sea, we may be wafted to a land surpassing in wonders and in beauty every region hitherto discovered on the habitable globe. Its productions and features may be without example, as the phænomena of the heavenly bodies undoubtedly are in those undiscovered solitudes. What may not be expected in a country of eternal light? I may there discover the wondrous power which attracts the needle; and may regulate a thousand celestial observations, that require only this voyage to render their seeming eccentricities consistent for ever. I shall satiate my ardent curiosity with the sight of a part of the world never before visited, and may tread a land never before imprinted by the foot of man. These are my enticements, and they are sufficient to conquer all fear of danger or death, and to induce me to commence this laborious voyage with the joy a child feels when he embarks in a little boat, with his holiday mates, on an expedition of discovery up his native river. But, supposing all these conjectures to be false, you cannot contest the inestimable benefit which I shall confer on all mankind to the last generation, by discovering a passage near the pole to those countries, to reach which at present so many months are requisite; or by ascertaining the secret of the magnet, which, if at all possible, can only be effected by an undertaking such as mine.

These reflections have dispelled the agitation with which I began my letter, and I feel my heart glow with an enthusiasm which elevates me to heaven; for nothing contributes so much to tranquillize the mind as a steady purpose,—a point on which the soul may fix its intellectual eye. This expedition has been the favourite dream of my early years. I have read with ardour the accounts of the various voyages which have been made in the prospect of arriving at the North Pacific Ocean through the seas which surround the pole. You may remember, that a history of all the voyages made for purposes of discovery composed the whole of our good uncle Thomas's library. My education was neglected, yet I was passionately fond of reading. These volumes were my study day and night, and my familiarity with them increased that regret which I had felt, as a child, on learning that my father's dying injunction had forbidden my uncle to allow me to embark in a sea-faring life.

These visions faded when I perused, for the first time, those poets whose effusions entranced my soul, and lifted it to heaven. I also became a poet, and for one year lived in a Paradise of my own creation; I imagined that I also might obtain a niche in the temple where the names of Homer and

Shakespeare are consecrated. You are well acquainted with my failure, and how heavily I bore the disappointment. But just at that time I inherited the fortune of my cousin, and my thoughts were turned into the channel of their earlier bent.

Six years have passed since I resolved on my present undertaking. I can, even now, remember the hour from which I dedicated myself to this great enterprise. I commenced by inuring my body to hardship. I accompanied the whale-fishers on several expeditions to the North Sea; I voluntarily endured cold, famine, thirst, and want of sleep; I often worked harder than the common sailors during the day, and devoted my nights to the study of mathematics, the theory of medicine, and those branches of physical science from which a naval adventurer might derive the greatest practical advantage. Twice I actually hired myself as an under-mate in a Greenland whaler, and acquitted myself to admiration. I must own I felt a little proud, when my captain offered me the second dignity in the vessel, and entreated me to remain with the greatest earnestness; so valuable did he consider my services.

And now, dear Margaret, do I not deserve to accomplish some great purpose. My life might have been passed in ease and luxury; but I preferred glory to every enticement that wealth placed in my path. Oh, that some encouraging voice would answer in the affirmative! My courage and my resolution is firm; but my hopes fluctuate, and my spirits are often depressed. I am about to proceed on a long and difficult voyage; the emergencies of which will demand all my fortitude: I am required not only to raise the spirits of others, but sometimes to sustain my own, when theirs are failing.

This is the most favourable period for travelling in Russia. They fly quickly over the snow in their sledges; the motion is pleasant, and, in my opinion, far more agreeable than that of an English stage-coach. The cold is not excessive, if you are wrapt in furs, a dress which I have already adopted; for there is a great difference between walking the deck and remaining seated motionless for hours, when no exercise prevents the blood from actually freezing in your veins. I have no ambition to lose my life on the post-road between St. Petersburgh and Archangel.

I shall depart for the latter town in a fortnight or three weeks; and my intention is to hire a ship there, which can easily be done by paying the insurance for the owner, and to engage as many sailors as I think necessary among those who are accustomed to the whale-fishing. I do not intend to sail until the month of June: and when shall I return? Ah, dear sister, how can I answer this question? If I succeed, many, many months, perhaps years, will pass before you and I may meet. If I fail, you will see me again soon, or never.

Farewell, my dear, excellent, Margaret. Heaven shower down blessings on you, and save me, that I may again and again testify my gratitude for all your love and kindness.

Your affectionate brother,

R. Walton.

LETTER II

To Mrs. SAVILLE, *England.*

Archangel, 28th March, 17—.

How slowly the time passes here, encompassed as I am by frost and snow; yet a second step is taken towards my enterprise. I have hired a vessel, and am occupied in collecting my sailors; those whom I have already engaged appear to be men on whom I can depend, and are certainly possessed of dauntless courage.

But I have one want which I have never yet been able to satisfy; and the absence of the object of which I now feel as a most severe evil. I have no friend, Margaret: when I am glowing with the enthusiasm of success, there will be none to participate my joy; if I am assailed by disappointment, no one will endeavour to sustain me in dejection. I shall commit my thoughts to paper, it is true; but that is a poor medium for the communication of feeling. I desire the company of a man who could sympathize with me; whose eyes would reply to mine. You may deem me romantic, my dear sister, but I bitterly feel the want of a friend. I have no one near me, gentle yet courageous, possessed of a cultivated as well as of a capacious mind, whose tastes are like my own, to approve or amend my plans. How would such a friend repair the faults of your poor brother! I am too ardent in execution, and too impatient of difficulties. But it is a still greater evil to me that I am self-educated: for the first fourteen years of my life I ran wild on a common, and read nothing but our uncle Thomas's books of voyages. At that age I became acquainted with the celebrated poets of our own country; but it was only when it had ceased to be in my power to derive its most important benefits from such a conviction, that I perceived the necessity of becoming acquainted with more languages than that of my native country. Now I am twenty-eight, and am in reality more illiterate than many school-boys of fifteen. It is true that I have thought more, and that my day dreams are more extended and magnificent; but they want (as the painters call it) *keeping*; and I greatly need a friend who would have sense enough not to despise me as romantic, and affection enough for me to endeavour to regulate my mind.

Well, these are useless complaints; I shall certainly find no friend on the wide ocean, nor even here in Archangel, among merchants and seamen. Yet some feelings, unallied to the dross of human nature, beat even in these rugged bosoms. My lieutenant, for instance, is a man of wonderful courage and enterprise; he is madly desirous of glory. He is an Englishman, and in the midst of national and professional prejudices, unsoftened by cultivation, retains some of the noblest endowments of humanity. I first became acquainted with him on board a whale vessel: finding that he was unemployed in this city, I easily engaged him to assist in my enterprise.

The master is a person of an excellent disposition, and is remarkable in the ship for his gentleness, and the mildness of his discipline. He is, indeed, of so amiable a nature, that he will not hunt (a favourite, and almost the only amusement here), because he cannot endure to spill blood. He is, moreover, heroically generous. Some years ago he loved a young Russian lady, of moderate fortune; and having amassed a considerable sum in prize-money, the father of the girl consented to the match. He saw his mistress once before the destined ceremony; but she was bathed in tears, and, throwing herself at his feet, entreated him to spare her, confessing at the same time that she loved another, but that he was poor, and that her father would never consent to the union. My generous friend reassured the suppliant, and on being informed of the name of her lover instantly abandoned his pursuit. He had already bought a farm with his money, on which he had designed to pass the remainder of his life; but he bestowed the whole on his rival, together with the remains of his prize-money to purchase stock, and then himself solicited the young woman's father to consent to her marriage with her lover. But the old man decidedly refused, thinking himself bound in honour to my friend; who, when he found the father inexorable, quitted his country, nor returned until he heard that his former mistress was married according to her inclinations. "What a noble fellow!" you will exclaim. He is so; but then he has passed all his life on board a vessel, and has scarcely an idea beyond the rope and the shroud.

But do not suppose that, because I complain a little, or because I can conceive a consolation for my toils which I may never know, that I am wavering in my resolutions. Those are as fixed as fate; and my voyage is only now delayed until the weather shall permit my embarkation. The winter has been dreadfully severe; but the spring promises well, and it is considered as a remarkably early season; so that, perhaps, I may sail sooner than I expected. I shall do nothing rashly; you know me sufficiently to confide in my prudence and considerateness whenever the safety of others is committed to my care.

I cannot describe to you my sensations on the near prospect of my undertaking. It is impossible to communicate to you a conception of the trembling sensation, half pleasurable and half fearful, with which I am preparing to depart. I am going to unexplored regions, to "the land of mist and snow"; but I shall kill no albatross, therefore do not be alarmed for my safety.

Shall I meet you again, after having traversed immense seas, and returned by the most southern cape of Africa or America? I dare not expect such success, yet I cannot bear to look on the reverse of the picture. Continue to write to me by every opportunity: I may receive your letters (though the chance is very doubtful) on some occasions when I need them most to support my spirits. I love you very tenderly. Remember me with affection, should you never hear from me again.

Your affectionate brother,
Robert Walton.

LETTER III

To Mrs. SAVILLE, *England.*

July 7th, 17—.

MY DEAR SISTER,

I write a few lines in haste, to say that I am safe, and well advanced on my voyage. This letter will reach England by a merchant-man now on its homeward voyage from Archangel; more fortunate than I, who may not see my native land, perhaps, for many years. I am, however, in good spirits: my men are bold, and apparently firm of purpose; nor do the floating sheets of ice that continually pass us, indicating the dangers of the region towards which we are advancing, appear to dismay them. We have already reached a very high latitude; but it is the height of summer, and although not so warm as in England, the southern gales, which blow us speedily towards those shores which I so ardently desire to attain, breathe a degree of renovating warmth which I had not expected.

No incidents have hitherto befallen us, that would make a figure in a letter. One or two stiff gales, and the breaking of a mast, are accidents which experienced navigators scarcely remember to record; and I shall be well content, if nothing worse happen to us during our voyage.

Adieu, my dear Margaret. Be assured, that for my own sake, as well as yours, I will not rashly encounter danger. I will be cool, persevering, and prudent.

Remember me to all my English friends.

Most affectionately yours,

R. W.

LETTER IV

To Mrs. SAVILLE, *England.*

August 5th, 17——.

So strange an accident has happened to us, that I cannot forbear recording it, although it is very probable that you will see me before these papers can come into your possession.

Last Monday (July 31st), we were nearly surrounded by ice, which closed in the ship on all sides, scarcely leaving her the sea room in which she floated. Our situation was somewhat dangerous, especially as we were compassed round by a very thick fog. We accordingly lay to, hoping that some change would take place in the atmosphere and weather.

About two o'clock the mist cleared away, and we beheld, stretched out in every direction, vast and irregular plains of ice, which seemed to have no end. Some of my comrades groaned, and my own mind began to grow watchful with anxious thoughts, when a strange sight suddenly attracted our attention, and diverted our solicitude from our own situation. We perceived

a low carriage, fixed on a sledge and drawn by dogs, pass on towards the
north, at the distance of half a mile: a being which had the shape of a man,
but apparently of gigantic stature, sat in the sledge, and guided the dogs. We
watched the rapid progress of the traveller with our telescopes, until he was
lost among the distant inequalities of the ice.

This appearance excited our unqualified wonder. We were, as we
believed, many hundred miles from any land; but this apparition seemed to
denote that it was not, in reality, so distant as we had supposed. Shut in, however, by ice, it was impossible to follow his track, which we had observed
with the greatest attention.

About two hours after this occurrence, we heard the ground sea, and
before night the ice broke, and freed our ship. We, however, lay to until the
morning, fearing to encounter in the dark those large loose masses which
float about after the breaking up of the ice. I profited of this time to rest for
a few hours.

In the morning, however, as soon as it was light, I went upon deck,
and found all the sailors busy on one side of the vessel, apparently talking
to some one in the sea. It was, in fact, a sledge, like that we had seen before,
which had drifted towards us in the night, on a large fragment of ice. Only
one dog remained alive; but there was a human being within it, whom the
sailors were persuading to enter the vessel. He was not, as the other traveller seemed to be, a savage inhabitant of some undiscovered island, but an
European. When I appeared on deck, the master said, "Here is our captain,
and he will not allow you to perish on the open sea."

On perceiving me, the stranger addressed me in English, although with
a foreign accent. "Before I come on board your vessel," said he, "will you
have the kindness to inform me whither you are bound?"

You may conceive my astonishment on hearing such a question
addressed to me from a man on the brink of destruction, and to whom I
should have supposed that my vessel would have been a resource which
he would not have exchanged for the most precious wealth the earth can
afford. I replied, however, that we were on a voyage of discovery towards
the northern pole.

Upon hearing this he appeared satisfied, and consented to come on board.
Good God! Margaret, if you had seen the man who thus capitulated for his

safety, your surprise would have been boundless. His limbs were nearly frozen, and his body dreadfully emaciated by fatigue and suffering. I never saw a man in so wretched a condition. We attempted to carry him into the cabin; but as soon as he had quitted the fresh air, he fainted. We accordingly brought him back to the deck, and restored him to animation by rubbing him with brandy, and forcing him to swallow a small quantity. As soon as he shewed signs of life, we wrapped him up in blankets, and placed him near the chimney of the kitchen-stove. By slow degrees he recovered, and ate a little soup, which restored him wonderfully.

Two days passed in this manner before he was able to speak; and I often feared that his sufferings had deprived him of understanding. When he had in some measure recovered, I removed him to my own cabin, and attended on him as much as my duty would permit. I never saw a more interesting creature: his eyes have generally an expression of wildness, and even madness; but there are moments when, if any one performs an act of kindness towards him, or does him any the most trifling service, his whole countenance is lighted up, as it were, with a beam of benevolence and sweetness that I never saw equalled. But he is generally melancholy and despairing; and sometimes he gnashes his teeth, as if impatient of the weight of woes that oppresses him.

When my guest was a little recovered, I had great trouble to keep off the men, who wished to ask him a thousand questions; but I would not allow him to be tormented by their idle curiosity, in a state of body and mind whose restoration evidently depended upon entire repose. Once, however, the lieutenant asked, Why he had come so far upon the ice in so strange a vehicle?

His countenance instantly assumed an aspect of the deepest gloom; and he replied, "To seek one who fled from me."

"And did the man whom you pursued travel in the same fashion?"

"Yes."

"Then I fancy we have seen him; for, the day before we picked you up, we saw some dogs drawing a sledge, with a man in it, across the ice."

This aroused the stranger's attention; and he asked a multitude of questions concerning the route which the dæmon, as he called him, had pursued. Soon after, when he was alone with me, he said, "I have, doubtless, excited your curiosity, as well as that of these good people; but you are too considerate to make inquiries."

"Certainly; it would indeed be very impertinent and inhuman in me to trouble you with any inquisitiveness of mine."

"And yet you rescued me from a strange and perilous situation; you have benevolently restored me to life."

Soon after this he inquired, if I thought that the breaking up of the ice had destroyed the other sledge? I replied, that I could not answer with any degree of certainty; for the ice had not broken until near midnight, and the traveller might have arrived at a place of safety before that time; but of this I could not judge.

From this time the stranger seemed very eager to be upon deck, to watch for the sledge which had before appeared; but I have persuaded him to remain in the cabin, for he is far too weak to sustain the rawness of the atmosphere. But I have promised that some one should watch for him, and give him instant notice if any new object should appear in sight.

Such is my journal of what relates to this strange occurrence up to the present day. The stranger has gradually improved in health, but is very silent, and appears uneasy when any one except myself enters his cabin. Yet his manners are so conciliating and gentle, that the sailors are all interested in him, although they have had very little communication with him. For my own part, I begin to love him as a brother; and his constant and deep grief fills me with sympathy and compassion. He must have been a noble creature in his better days, being even now in wreck so attractive and amiable.

I said in one of my letters, my dear Margaret, that I should find no friend on the wide ocean; yet I have found a man who, before his spirit had been broken by misery, I should have been happy to have possessed as the brother of my heart.

I shall continue my journal concerning the stranger at intervals, should I have any fresh incidents to record.

August 13th, 17——.

My affection for my guest increases every day. He excites at once my admiration and my pity to an astonishing degree. How can I see so noble a creature destroyed by misery without feeling the most poignant grief? He is so gentle, yet so wise; his mind is so cultivated; and when he speaks, although his words are culled with the choicest art, yet they flow with rapidity and unparalleled eloquence.

He is now much recovered from his illness, and is continually on the deck, apparently watching for the sledge that preceded his own. Yet, although unhappy, he is not so utterly occupied by his own misery, but that he interests himself deeply in the employments of others. He has asked me many questions concerning my design; and I have related my little history frankly to him. He appeared pleased with the confidence, and suggested several alterations in my plan, which I shall find exceedingly useful. There is no pedantry in his manner; but all he does appears to spring solely from the interest he instinctively takes in the welfare of those who surround him. He is often overcome by gloom, and then he sits by himself, and tries to overcome all that is sullen or unsocial in his humour. These paroxysms pass from him like a cloud from before the sun, though his dejection never leaves him. I have endeavoured to win his confidence; and I trust that I have succeeded. One day I mentioned to him the desire I had always felt of finding a friend who might sympathize with me, and direct me by his counsel. I said, I did not belong to that class of men who are offended by advice. "I am self-educated, and perhaps I hardly rely sufficiently upon my own powers. I wish therefore that my companion should be wiser and more experienced than myself, to confirm and support me; nor have I believed it impossible to find a true friend."

"I agree with you," replied the stranger, "in believing that friendship is not only a desirable, but a possible acquisition. I once had a friend, the most noble of human creatures, and am entitled, therefore, to judge respecting friendship. You have hope, and the world before you, and have no cause for despair. But I—I have lost every thing, and cannot begin life anew."

As he said this, his countenance became expressive of a calm settled grief, that touched me to the heart. But he was silent, and presently retired to his cabin.

Even broken in spirit as he is, no one can feel more deeply than he does the beauties of nature. The starry sky, the sea, and every sight afforded by these wonderful regions, seems still to have the power of elevating his soul from earth. Such a man has a double existence: he may suffer misery, and be overwhelmed by disappointments; yet when he has retired into himself, he will be like a celestial spirit, that has a halo around him, within whose circle no grief or folly ventures.

Will you laugh at the enthusiasm I express concerning this divine wanderer? If you do, you must have certainly lost that simplicity which was once your characteristic charm. Yet, if you will, smile at the warmth of my expressions, while I find every day new causes for repeating them.

August 19th, 17——.

Yesterday the stranger said to me, "You may easily perceive, Captain Walton, that I have suffered great and unparalleled misfortunes. I had determined, once, that the memory of these evils should die with me; but you have won me to alter my determination. You seek for knowledge and wisdom, as I once did; and I ardently hope that the gratification of your wishes may not be a serpent to sting you, as mine has been. I do not know that the relation of my misfortunes will be useful to you, yet, if you are inclined, listen to my tale. I believe that the strange incidents connected with it will afford a view of nature, which may enlarge your faculties and understanding. You will hear of powers and occurrences, such as you have been accustomed to believe impossible: but I do not doubt that my tale conveys in its series internal evidence of the truth of the events of which it is composed."

You may easily conceive that I was much gratified by the offered communication; yet I could not endure that he should renew his grief by a recital of his misfortunes. I felt the greatest eagerness to hear the promised narrative, partly from curiosity, and partly from a strong desire to ameliorate his fate, if it were in my power. I expressed these feelings in my answer.

"I thank you," he replied, "for your sympathy, but it is useless; my fate is nearly fulfilled. I wait but for one event, and then I shall repose in peace. I understand your feeling," continued he, perceiving that I wished to interrupt him; "but you are mistaken, my friend, if thus you will allow me to name you; nothing can alter my destiny: listen to my history, and you will perceive how irrevocably it is determined."

He then told me, that he would commence his narrative the next day when I should be at leisure. This promise drew from me the warmest thanks. I have resolved every night, when I am not engaged, to record, as nearly as possible in his own words, what he has related during the day. If I should be engaged, I will at least make notes. This manuscript will doubtless afford you the greatest pleasure: but to me, who know him, and who hear it from his own lips, with what interest and sympathy shall I read it in some future day!

CHAPTER I

I AM BY BIRTH A GENEVESE; AND MY FAMILY IS ONE OF THE MOST DISTINGUISHED OF that republic. My ancestors had been for many years counsellors and syndics; and my father had filled several public situations with honour and reputation. He was respected by all who knew him for his integrity and indefatigable attention to public business. He passed his younger days perpetually occupied by the affairs of his country; and it was not until the decline of life that he thought of marrying, and bestowing on the state sons who might carry his virtues and his name down to posterity.

As the circumstances of his marriage illustrate his character, I cannot refrain from relating them. One of his most intimate friends was a merchant, who, from a flourishing state, fell, through numerous mischances, into poverty. This man, whose name was Beaufort, was of a proud and unbending disposition, and could not bear to live in poverty and oblivion in the same country where he had formerly been distinguished for his rank and magnificence. Having paid his debts, therefore, in the most honourable manner, he retreated with his daughter to the town of Lucerne, where he lived unknown and in wretchedness. My father loved Beaufort with the truest friendship, and was deeply grieved by his retreat in these unfortunate circumstances. He grieved also for the loss of his society, and resolved to seek him out and endeavour to persuade him to begin the world again through his credit and assistance.

Beaufort had taken effectual measures to conceal himself; and it was ten months before my father discovered his abode. Overjoyed at this discovery, he hastened to the house, which was situated in a mean street, near the Reuss. But when he entered, misery and despair alone welcomed him. Beaufort had saved but a very small sum of money from the wreck of his fortunes; but it was sufficient to provide him with sustenance for some months, and in the mean time he hoped to procure some respectable employment in a merchant's house. The interval was consequently spent in inaction; his grief only became more deep and rankling, when he had leisure for reflection; and at length it took so fast hold of his mind, that at the end of three months he lay on a bed of sickness, incapable of any exertion.

His daughter attended him with the greatest tenderness; but she saw with despair that their little fund was rapidly decreasing, and that there was no other prospect of support. But Caroline Beaufort possessed a mind of an uncommon mould; and her courage rose to support her in her adversity. She procured plain work; she plaited straw; and by various means contrived to earn a pittance scarcely sufficient to support life.

Several months passed in this manner. Her father grew worse; her time was more entirely occupied in attending him; her means of subsistence decreased; and in the tenth month her father died in her arms, leaving her an orphan and a beggar. This last blow overcame her; and she knelt by Beaufort's coffin, weeping bitterly, when my father entered the chamber. He came like a protecting spirit to the poor girl, who committed herself to his care, and after the interment of his friend he conducted her to Geneva, and placed her under the protection of a relation. Two years after this event Caroline became his wife.

When my father became a husband and a parent, he found his time so occupied by the duties of his new situation, that he relinquished many of his public employments, and devoted himself to the education of his children. Of these I was the eldest, and the destined successor to all his labours and utility. No creature could have more tender parents than mine. My improvement and health were their constant care, especially as I remained for several years their only child. But before I continue my narrative, I must record an incident which took place when I was four years of age.

My father had a sister, whom he tenderly loved, and who had married early in life an Italian gentleman. Soon after her marriage, she had accompanied her husband into her native country, and for some years my father had very little communication with her. About the time I mentioned she died; and a few months afterwards he received a letter from her husband, acquainting him with his intention of marrying an Italian lady, and requesting my father to take charge of the infant Elizabeth, the only child of his deceased sister. "It is my wish," he said, "that you should consider her as your own daughter, and educate her thus. Her mother's fortune is secured to her, the documents of which I will commit to your keeping. Reflect upon this proposition; and decide whether you would prefer educating your niece yourself to her being brought up by a stepmother."

My father did not hestitate, and immediately went to Italy, that he might accompany the little Elizabeth to her future home. I have often heard my mother say, that she was at that time the most beautiful child she had ever seen, and shewed signs even then of a gentle and affectionate disposition. These indications, and a desire to bind as closely as possible the ties of domestic love, determined my mother to consider Elizabeth as my future wife; a design which she never found reason to repent.

From this time Elizabeth Lavenza became my playfellow, and, as we grew older, my friend. She was docile and good tempered, yet gay and playful as a summer insect. Although she was lively and animated, her feelings were strong and deep, and her disposition uncommonly affectionate. No one could better enjoy liberty, yet no one could submit with more grace than she did to constraint and caprice. Her imagination was luxuriant, yet her capability of application was great. Her person was the image of her mind; her hazel eyes, although as lively as a bird's, possessed an attractive softness. Her figure was light and airy; and, though capable of enduring great fatigue, she appeared the most fragile creature in the world. While I admired her understanding and fancy, I loved to tend on her, as I should on a favourite animal; and I never saw so much grace both of person and mind united to so little pretension.

Every one adored Elizabeth. If the servants had any request to make, it was always through her intercession. We were strangers to any species of disunion and dispute; for although there was a great dissimilitude in our characters, there was an harmony in that very dissimilitude. I was more calm and philosophical than my companion; yet my temper was not so yielding. My application was of longer endurance; but it was not so severe whilst it endured. I delighted in investigating the facts relative to the actual world; she busied herself in following the ærial creations of the poets. The world was to me a secret, which I desired to discover; to her it was a vacancy, which she sought to people with imaginations of her own.

My brothers were considerably younger than myself; but I had a friend in one of my schoolfellows, who compensated for this deficiency. Henry Clerval was the son of a merchant of Geneva, an intimate friend of my father. He was a boy of singular talent and fancy. I remember, when he was nine years old, he wrote a fairy tale, which was the delight and amazement of all his companions. His favourite study consisted in books of chivalry and romance; and when very young, I can remember, that we used to act plays composed by him out of these favourite books, the principal characters of which were Orlando, Robin Hood, Amadis, and St. George.

No youth could have passed more happily than mine. My parents were indulgent, and my companions amiable. Our studies were never forced; and by some means we always had an end placed in view, which excited us to ardour in the prosecution of them. It was by this method, and not by emulation, that we were urged to application. Elizabeth was not incited to apply herself to drawing, that her companions might not outstrip her; but through the desire of pleasing her aunt, by the representation of some favourite scene done by her own hand. We learned Latin and English, that we might read the writings in those languages; and so far from study being made odious to us through punishment, we loved application, and our amusements would have been the labours of other children. Perhaps we did not read so many books, or learn languages so quickly, as those who are disciplined according to the ordinary methods; but what we learned was impressed the more deeply on our memories.

In this description of our domestic circle I include Henry Clerval; for he was constantly with us. He went to school with me, and generally passed the afternoon at our house; for being an only child, and destitute of companions at home, his father was well pleased that he should find associates at our house; and we were never completely happy when Clerval was absent.

I feel pleasure in dwelling on the recollections of childhood, before misfortune had tainted my mind, and changed its bright visions of extensive usefulness into gloomy and narrow reflections upon self. But, in drawing the picture of my early days, I must not omit to record those events which led, by insensible steps to my after tale of misery: for when I would account to myself for the birth of that passion, which afterwards ruled my destiny, I find it arose, like a mountain river, from ignoble and almost forgotten sources; but, swelling as it proceeded, it became the torrent which, in its course, has swept away all my hopes and joys.

Natural philosophy is the genius that has regulated my fate; I desire therefore, in this narration, to state those facts which led to my predilection for that science. When I was thirteen years of age, we all went on a party of pleasure to the baths near Thonon: the inclemency of the weather obliged us to remain a day confined to the inn. In this house I chanced to find a volume of the works of Cornelius Agrippa. I opened it with apathy; the theory which he attempts to demonstrate, and the wonderful facts which he relates, soon changed this feeling into enthusiasm. A new light seemed to dawn upon my mind; and, bounding with joy, I communicated my discovery to my father. I cannot help remarking here the many opportunities instructors possess of directing the attention of their pupils to useful knowledge, which they utterly neglect. My father looked carelessly at the title-page of my book, and said, "Ah! Cornelius Agrippa! My dear Victor, do not waste your time upon this; it is sad trash."

If, instead of this remark, my father had taken the pains to explain to me, that the principles of Agrippa had been entirely exploded, and that a modern system of science had been introduced, which possessed much greater powers than the ancient, because the powers of the latter were chimerical, while those of the former were real and practical; under such circumstances, I should certainly have thrown Agrippa aside, and, with my imagination warmed as it was, should probably have applied myself to the more rational theory of chemistry which has resulted from modern discoveries. It is even possible, that the train of my ideas would never have received the fatal impulse that led to my ruin. But the cursory glance my father had taken of my volume by no means assured me that he was acquainted with its contents; and I continued to read with the greatest avidity.

When I returned home, my first care was to procure the whole works of this author, and afterwards of Paracelsus and Albertus Magnus. I read and studied the wild fancies of these writers with delight; they appeared to me treasures known to few beside myself; and although I often wished to communicate these secret stores of knowledge to my father, yet his indefinite censure of my favourite Agrippa always withheld me. I disclosed my discoveries to Elizabeth, therefore, under a promise of strict secrecy; but she did not interest herself in the subject, and I was left by her to pursue my studies alone.

It may appear very strange, that a disciple of Albertus Magnus should arise in the eighteenth century; but our family was not scientifical, and I had not attended any of the lectures given at the schools of Geneva. My dreams were therefore undisturbed by reality; and I entered with the greatest diligence into the search of the philosopher's stone and the elixir of life. But the latter obtained my most undivided attention: wealth was an inferior object; but what glory would attend the discovery, if I could banish disease from the human frame, and render man invulnerable to any but a violent death!

Nor were these my only visions. The raising of ghosts or devils was a promise liberally accorded by my favourite authors, the fulfilment of which I most eagerly sought; and if my incantations were always unsuccessful, I attributed the failure rather to my own inexperience and mistake, than to a want of skill or fidelity in my instructors.

The natural phenomena that take place every day before our eyes did not escape my examinations. Distillation, and the wonderful effects of steam, processes of which my favourite authors were utterly ignorant, excited my astonishment; but my utmost wonder was engaged by some experiments on an airpump, which I saw employed by a gentleman whom we were in the habit of visiting.

The ignorance of the early philosophers on these and several other points served to decrease their credit with me: but I could not entirely throw them aside, before some other system should occupy their place in my mind.

When I was about fifteen years old, we had retired to our house near Belrive, when we witnessed a most violent and terrible thunder-storm. It advanced from behind the mountains of Jura; and the thunder burst at once with frightful loudness from various quarters of the heavens. I remained, while the storm lasted, watching its progress with curiosity and delight. As I stood at the door, on a sudden I beheld a stream of fire issue from an old and beautiful oak, which stood about twenty yards from our house; and so soon as the dazzling light vanished, the oak had disappeared, and nothing remained but a blasted stump. When we visited it the next morning, we found the tree shattered in a singular manner. It was not splintered by the shock, but entirely reduced to thin ribbands of wood. I never beheld any thing so utterly destroyed.

The catastrophe of this tree excited my extreme astonishment; and I eagerly inquired of my father the nature and origin of thunder and lightning. He replied, "Electricity"; describing at the same time the various effects of that power. He constructed a small electrical machine, and exhibited a few experiments; he made also a kite, with a wire and string, which drew down that fluid from the clouds.

This last stroke completed the overthrow of Cornelius Agrippa, Albertus Magnus, and Paracelsus, who had so long reigned the lords of my imagination. But by some fatality I did not feel inclined to commence the study of any modern system; and this disinclination was influenced by the following circumstance.

My father expressed a wish that I should attend a course of lectures upon natural philosophy, to which I cheerfully consented. Some accident prevented my attending these lectures until the course was nearly finished. The lecture, being therefore one of the last, was entirely incomprehensible to me. The professor discoursed with the greatest fluency of potassium and boron, of sulphates and oxyds, terms to which I could affix no idea; and I became disgusted with the science of natural philosophy, although I still read Pliny and Buffon with delight, authors, in my estimation, of nearly equal interest and utility.

My occupations at this age were principally the mathematics, and most of the branches of study appertaining to that science. I was busily employed in learning languages; Latin was already familiar to me, and I began to read some of the easiest Greek authors without the help of a lexicon. I also perfectly understood English and German. This is the list of my accomplishments at the age of seventeen; and you may conceive that my hours were fully employed in acquiring and maintaining a knowledge of this various literature.

Another task also devolved upon me, when I became the instructor of my brothers. Ernest was six years younger than myself, and was my principal pupil. He had been afflicted with ill health from his infancy, through which Elizabeth and I had been his constant nurses: his disposition was gentle, but he was incapable of any severe application. William, the youngest of our family, was yet an infant, and the most beautiful little fellow in the world; his lively blue eyes, dimpled cheeks, and endearing manners, inspired the tenderest affection.

Such was our domestic circle, from which care and pain seemed for ever banished. My father directed our studies, and my mother partook of our enjoyments. Neither of us possessed the slightest pre-eminence over the other; the voice of command was never heard amongst us; but mutual affection engaged us all to comply with and obey the slightest desire of each other.

CHAPTER II

WHEN I HAD ATTAINED THE AGE OF SEVENTEEN, MY PARENTS RESOLVED THAT I should become a student at the university of Ingolstadt. I had hitherto attended the schools of Geneva; but my father thought it necessary, for the completion of my education, that I should be made acquainted with other customs than those of my native country. My departure was therefore fixed at an early date; but, before the day resolved upon could arrive, the first misfortune of my life occurred—an omen, as it were, of my future misery.

Elizabeth had caught the scarlet fever; but her illness was not severe, and she quickly recovered. During her confinement, many arguments had been urged to persuade my mother to refrain from attending upon her. She had, at first, yielded to our entreaties; but when she heard that her favourite was recovering, she could no longer debar herself from her society, and entered her chamber long before the danger of infection was past. The consequences of this imprudence were fatal. On the third day my mother sickened; her fever was very malignant, and the looks of her attendants prognosticated the worst event. On her death-bed the fortitude and benignity of this admirable woman did not desert her. She joined the hands of Elizabeth and myself: "My children," she said, "my firmest hopes of future happiness were placed on the prospect of your union. This expectation will now be the consolation of your father. Elizabeth, my love, you must supply my place to your younger cousins. Alas! I regret that I am taken from you; and, happy and beloved as I have been, is it not hard to quit you all? But these are not thoughts befitting me; I will endeavour to resign myself cheerfully to death, and will indulge a hope of meeting you in another world."

She died calmly; and her countenance expressed affection even in death. I need not describe the feelings of those whose dearest ties are rent by that most irreparable evil, the void that presents itself to the soul, and the despair that is exhibited on the countenance. It is so long before the mind can persuade itself that she, whom we saw every day, and whose very existence appeared a part of our own, can have departed for ever—that the brightness of a beloved eye can have been extinguished, and the sound of a voice so familiar, and dear to the ear, can be hushed, never more to be heard. These are the reflections of the first days; but when the lapse of time proves the reality of the evil, then the actual bitterness of grief commences. Yet from whom has not that rude hand rent away some dear connexion; and why should I describe a sorrow which all have felt, and must feel? The time at length arrives, when grief is rather an indulgence than a necessity; and the smile that plays upon the lips, although it may be deemed a sacrilege, is not banished. My mother was dead, but we had still duties which we ought to perform; we must continue our course with the rest, and learn to think ourselves fortunate, whilst one remains whom the spoiler has not seized.

My journey to Ingolstadt, which had been deferred by these events, was now again determined upon. I obtained from my father a respite of some weeks. This period was spent sadly; my mother's death, and my speedy departure, depressed our spirits; but Elizabeth endeavoured to renew the spirit of cheerfulness in our little society. Since the death of her aunt, her mind had acquired new firmness and vigour. She determined to fulfil her duties with the greatest exactness; and she felt that that most imperious duty, of rendering her uncle and cousins happy, had devolved upon her. She consoled me, amused her uncle, instructed my brothers; and I never beheld her so enchanting as at this time, when she was continually endeavouring to contribute to the happiness of others, entirely forgetful of herself.

The day of my departure at length arrived. I had taken leave of all my friends, excepting Clerval, who spent the last evening with us. He bitterly lamented that he was unable to accompany me: but his father could not be persuaded to part with him, intending that he should become a partner with him in business, in compliance with his favourite theory, that learning was superfluous in the commerce of ordinary life. Henry had a refined mind; he had no desire to be idle, and was well pleased to become his father's partner, but he believed that a man might be a very good trader, and yet possess a cultivated understanding.

We sat late, listening to his complaints, and making many little arrangements for the future. The next morning early I departed. Tears gushed from the eyes of Elizabeth; they proceeded partly from sorrow at my departure, and partly because she reflected that the same journey was to have taken place three months before, when a mother's blessing would have accompanied me.

I threw myself into the chaise that was to convey me away, and indulged in the most melancholy reflections. I, who had ever been surrounded by amiable companions, continually engaged in endeavouring to bestow mutual pleasure, I was now alone. In the university, whither I was going, I must form my own friends, and be my own protector. My life had hitherto been remarkably secluded and domestic; and this had given me invincible repugnance to new countenances. I loved my brothers, Elizabeth, and Clerval; these were "old familiar faces"; but I believed myself totally unfitted for the company of strangers. Such were my reflections as I commenced my journey; but as I proceeded, my spirits and hopes rose. I ardently desired the acquisition of knowledge. I had often, when at home, thought it hard to remain during my youth cooped up in one place, and had longed to enter the world, and take my station among other human beings. Now my desires were complied with, and it would, indeed, have been folly to repent.

I had sufficient leisure for these and many other reflections during my journey to Ingolstadt, which was long and fatiguing. At length the high white steeple of the town met my eyes. I alighted, and was conducted to my solitary apartment, to spend the evening as I pleased.

The next morning I delivered my letters of introduction, and paid a visit to some of the principal professors, and among others to M. Krempe, professor of natural philosophy. He received me with politeness, and asked me several questions concerning my progress in the different branches of science appertaining to natural philosophy. I mentioned, it is true, with fear and trembling, the only authors I had ever read upon those subjects. The professor stared: "Have you," he said, "really spent your time in studying such nonsense?"

I replied in the affirmative. "Every minute," continued M. Krempe with warmth, "every instant that you have wasted on those books is utterly and entirely lost. You have burdened your memory with exploded systems, and useless names. Good God! in what desert land have you lived, where no one was kind enough to inform you that these fancies, which you have so greedily imbibed, are a thousand years old, and as musty as they are ancient? I little expected in this enlightened and scientific age to find a disciple of Albertus Magnus and Paracelsus. My dear Sir, you must begin your studies entirely anew."

So saying, he stept aside, and wrote down a list of several books treating of natural philosophy, which he desired me to procure, and dismissed me, after mentioning that in the beginning of the following week he intended to commence a course of lectures upon natural philosophy in its general relations, and that M. Waldman, a fellow-professor, would lecture upon chemistry the alternate days that he missed.

I returned home, not disappointed, for I had long considered those authors useless whom the professor had so strongly reprobated; but I did not feel much inclined to study the books which I procured at his recommendation. M. Krempe was a little squat man, with a gruff voice and repulsive countenance; the teacher, therefore, did not prepossess me in favour of his doctrine. Besides, I had a contempt for the uses of modern natural philosophy. It was very different, when the masters of the science sought immortality and power; such views, although futile, were grand: but now the scene was changed. The ambition of the inquirer seemed to limit itself to the annihilation of those visions on which my interest in science was chiefly founded. I was required to exchange chimeras of boundless grandeur for realities of little worth.

Such were my reflections during the first two or three days spent almost in solitude. But as the ensuing week commenced, I thought of the information which M. Krempe had given me concerning the lectures. And although I could not consent to go and hear that little conceited fellow deliver sentences out of a pulpit, I recollected what he had said of M. Waldman, whom I had never seen, as he had hitherto been out of town.

Partly from curiosity, and partly from idleness, I went into the lecturing room, which M. Waldman entered shortly after. This professor was very unlike his colleague. He appeared about fifty years of age, but with an aspect expressive of the greatest benevolence; a few gray hairs covered his temples, but those at the back of his head were nearly black. His person was short, but remarkably erect; and his voice the sweetest I had ever heard. He began his lecture by a recapitulation of the history of chemistry and the various improvements made by different men of learning, pronouncing with fervour the names of the most distinguished discoverers. He then took a cursory view of the present state of the science, and explained many of its elementary terms. After having made a few preparatory experiments, he concluded with a panegyric upon modern chemistry, the terms of which I shall never forget:—

"The ancient teachers of this science," said he, "promised impossibilities, and performed nothing. The modern masters promise very little; they know that metals cannot be transmuted, and that the elixir of life is a chimera. But these philosophers, whose hands seem only made to dabble in dirt, and their eyes to pore over the microscope or crucible, have indeed performed miracles. They penetrate into the recesses of nature, and shew how she works in her hiding places. They ascend into the heavens; they have discovered how the blood circulates, and the nature of the air we breathe. They have acquired new and almost unlimited powers; they can command the thunders of heaven, mimic the earthquake, and even mock the invisible world with its own shadows."

I departed highly pleased with the professor and his lecture, and paid him a visit the same evening. His manners in private were even more mild and attractive than in public; for there was a certain dignity in his mien during his lecture, which in his own house was replaced by the greatest affability and kindness. He heard with attention my little narration concerning my studies, and smiled at the names of Cornelius Agrippa, and Paracelsus, but without the contempt that M. Krempe had exhibited. He said, that "these were men to whose indefatigable zeal modern philosophers were indebted for most of the foundations of their knowledge. They had left to us, as an easier task, to give new names, and arrange in connected classifications, the facts which they in a great degree had been the instruments of bringing to light. The labours of men of genius, however erroneously directed, scarcely ever fail in ultimately turning to the solid advantage of mankind." I listened to his statement, which was delivered without any presumption or affectation; and then added, that his lecture had removed my prejudices against modern chemists; and I, at the same time, requested his advice concerning the books I ought to procure.

"I am happy," said M. Waldman, "to have gained a disciple; and if your application equals your ability, I have no doubt of your success. Chemistry is that branch of natural philosophy in which the greatest improvements have been and may be made; it is on that account that I have made it my peculiar study; but at the same time I have not neglected the other branches of science. A man would make but a very sorry chemist, if he attended to that department of human knowledge alone. If your wish is to become really a man of science, and not merely a petty experimentalist, I should advise you to apply to every branch of natural philosophy, including mathematics."

He then took me into his laboratory, and explained to me the uses of his various machines; instructing me as to what I ought to procure, and promising me the use of his own, when I should have advanced far enough in the science not to derange their mechanism. He also gave me the list of books which I had requested; and I took my leave.

Thus ended a day memorable to me; it decided my future destiny.

CHAPTER III

FROM THIS DAY NATURAL PHILOSOPHY, AND PARTICULARLY CHEMISTRY, IN THE MOST comprehensive sense of the term, became nearly my sole occupation. I read with ardour those works, so full of genius and discrimination, which modern inquirers have written on these subjects. I attended the lectures, and cultivated the acquaintance, of the men of science of the university; and I found even in M. Krempe a great deal of sound sense and real information, combined, it is true, with a repulsive physiognomy and manners, but not on that account the less valuable. In M. Waldman I found a true friend. His gentleness was never tinged by dogmatism; and his instructions were given with an air of frankness and good nature, that banished every idea of pedantry. It was, perhaps, the amiable character of this man that inclined me more to that branch of natural philosophy which he professed, than an intrinsic love for the science itself. But this state of mind had place only in the first steps towards knowledge: the more fully I entered into the science, the more exclusively I pursued it for its own sake. That application, which at first had been a matter of duty and resolution, now became so ardent and eager, that the stars often disappeared in the light of morning whilst I was yet engaged in my laboratory.

As I applied so closely, it may be easily conceived that I improved rapidly. My ardour was indeed the astonishment of the students; and my proficiency, that of the masters. Professor Krempe often asked me, with a sly smile, how Cornelius Agrippa went on? whilst M. Waldman expressed the most heartfelt exultation in my progress. Two years passed in this manner, during which I paid no visit to Geneva, but was engaged, heart and soul, in the pursuit of some discoveries, which I hoped to make. None but those who have experienced them can conceive of the enticements of science. In other studies you go as far as others have gone before you, and there is nothing more to know; but in a scientific pursuit there is continual food for discovery and wonder. A mind of moderate capacity, which closely pursues one study, must infallibly arrive at great proficiency in that study; and I, who continually sought the attainment of one object of pursuit, and was solely wrapt up in this, improved so rapidly, that, at the end of two years, I made some discoveries in the improvement of some chemical instruments, which procured me great esteem and admiration at the university. When I had arrived at this point, and had become as well acquainted with the theory and practice of natural philosophy as depended on the lessons of any of the professors at Ingolstadt, my residence there being no longer conducive to my improvements,

I thought of returning to my friends and my native town, when an incident happened that protracted my stay.

One of the phænonema which had peculiarly attracted my attention was the structure of the human frame, and, indeed, any animal endued with life. Whence, I often asked myself, did the principle of life proceed? It was a bold question, and one which has ever been considered as a mystery; yet with how many things are we upon the brink of becoming acquainted, if cowardice or carelessness did not restrain our inquiries. I revolved these circumstances in my mind, and determined thenceforth to apply myself more particularly to those branches of natural philosophy which relate to physiology. Unless I had been animated by an almost supernatural enthusiasm, my application to this study would have been irksome, and almost intolerable. To examine the causes of life, we must first have recourse to death. I became acquainted with the science of anatomy: but this was not sufficient; I must also observe the natural decay and corruption of the human body. In my education my father had taken the greatest precautions that my mind should be impressed with no supernatural horrors. I do not ever remember to have trembled at a tale of superstition, or to have feared the apparition of a spirit. Darkness had no effect upon my fancy; and a church-yard was to me merely the receptacle of bodies deprived of life, which, from being the seat of beauty and strength, had become food for the worm. Now I was led to examine the cause and progress of this decay, and forced to spend days and nights in vaults and charnel houses. My attention was fixed upon every object the most insupportable to the delicacy of the human feelings. I saw how the fine form of man was degraded and wasted; I beheld the corruption of death succeed to the blooming cheek of life; I saw how the worm inherited the wonders of the eye and brain. I paused, examining and analysing all the minutiæ of causation, as exemplified in the change from life to death, and death to life, until from the midst of this darkness a sudden light broke in upon me—a light so brilliant and wondrous, yet so simple, that while I became dizzy with the immensity of the prospect which it illustrated, I was surprised that among so many men of genius, who had directed their inquiries towards the same science, that I alone should be reserved to discover so astonishing a secret.

Remember, I am not recording the vision of a madman. The sun does not more certainly shine in the heavens, than that which I now affirm is true. Some miracle might have produced it, yet the stages of the discovery were distinct and probable. After days and nights of incredible labour and fatigue, I succeeded in discovering the cause of generation and life; nay, more, I became myself capable of bestowing animation upon lifeless matter.

The astonishment which I had at first experienced on this discovery soon gave place to delight and rapture. After so much time spent in painful labour, to arrive at once at the summit of my desires, was the most gratifying consummation of my toils. But this discovery was so great and overwhelming, that all the steps by which I had been progressively led to it were obliterated, and I beheld only the result. What had been the study and desire of the wisest men since the creation of the world, was now within my grasp. Not that, like a magic scene, it all opened upon me at once: the information I had obtained was of a nature rather to direct my endeavours so soon as I should point them towards the object of my search, than to exhibit that object already accomplished. I was like the Arabian who had been buried with the dead, and found a passage to life aided only by one glimmering, and seemingly ineffectual, light.

I see by your eagerness, and the wonder and hope which your eyes express, my friend, that you expect to be informed of the secret with which I am acquainted; that cannot be: listen patiently until the end of my story, and you will easily perceive why I am reserved upon that subject. I will not lead you on, unguarded and ardent as I then was, to your destruction and infallible misery. Learn from me, if not by my precepts, at least by my example, how dangerous is the acquirement of knowledge, and how much happier that man is who believes his native town to be the world, than he who aspires to become greater than his nature will allow.

When I found so astonishing a power placed within my hands, I hesitated a long time concerning the manner in which I should employ it. Although I possessed the capacity of bestowing animation, yet to prepare a frame for the reception of it, with all its intricacies of fibres, muscles, and veins, still remained a work of inconceivable difficulty and labour. I doubted at first whether I should attempt the creation of a being like myself or one of simpler organization; but my imagination was too much exalted by my first success to permit me to doubt of my ability to give life to an animal as complex and wonderful as man. The materials at present within my command hardly appeared adequate to so arduous an undertaking; but I doubted not that I should ultimately succeed. I prepared myself for a multitude of reverses; my operations might be incessantly baffled, and at last my work be imperfect: yet, when I considered the improvement which every day takes place in science and mechanics, I was encouraged to hope my present attempts would at least lay the foundations of future success. Nor could I consider the magnitude and complexity of my plan as any argument of its impracticability. It was with these feelings that I began the creation of a human being. As the minuteness of the parts formed a great hindrance to my speed, I resolved, contrary to my first intention, to make the being of a gigantic stature; that is to say, about eight feet in height, and proportionably large. After having formed this determination, and having spent some months in successfully collecting and arranging my materials, I began.

No one can conceive the variety of feelings which bore me onwards, like a hurricane, in the first enthusiasm of success. Life and death appeared to me ideal bounds, which I should first break through, and pour a torrent of light into our dark world. A new species would bless me as its creator and source; many happy and excellent natures would owe their being to me. No father could claim the gratitude of his child so completely as I should deserve theirs. Pursuing these reflections, I thought, that if I could bestow animation upon lifeless matter, I might in process of time (although I now found it impossible) renew life where death had apparently devoted the body to corruption.

These thoughts supported my spirits, while I pursued my undertaking with unremitting ardour. My cheek had grown pale with study, and my person had become emaciated with confinement. Sometimes, on the very brink of certainty, I failed; yet still I clung to the hope which the next day or the next hour might realize. One secret which I alone possessed was the hope to which I had dedicated myself; and the moon gazed on my midnight labours, while, with unrelaxed and breathless eagerness, I pursued nature to her hiding places. Who shall conceive the horrors of my secret toil, as I dabbled among the unhallowed damps of the grave, or tortured the living animal to animate the lifeless clay? My limbs now tremble, and my eyes swim with the remembrance; but then a resistless, and almost frantic impulse, urged me forward; I seemed to have lost all soul or sensation but for this one pursuit. It was indeed but a passing trance, that only made me feel with renewed acuteness so soon as, the unnatural stimulus ceasing to operate, I had returned to my old habits. I collected bones from charnel houses; and disturbed, with profane fingers, the tremendous secrets of the human frame. In a solitary chamber, or rather cell, at the top of the house, and separated from all the other apartments by a gallery and staircase, I kept my workshop of filthy creation; my eyeballs were starting from their sockets in attending to the details of my employment. The dissecting room and the slaughterhouse furnished many of my materials; and often did my human nature turn with loathing from my occupation, whilst, still urged on by an eagerness which perpetually increased, I brought my work near to a conclusion.

The summer months passed while I was thus engaged, heart and soul, in one pursuit. It was a most beautiful season; never did the fields bestow a more plentiful harvest, or the vines yield a more luxuriant vintage: but my eyes were insensible to the charms of nature. And the same feelings which made me neglect the scenes around me caused me also to forget those friends who were so many miles absent, and whom I had not seen for so long a time. I knew my silence disquieted them; and I well remembered the words of my father: "I know that while you are pleased with yourself, you will think of us with affection, and we shall hear regularly from you. You must pardon me, if I regard any interruption in your correspondence as a proof that your other duties are equally neglected."

I knew well therefore what would be my father's feelings; but I could not tear my thoughts from my employment, loathsome in itself, but which had taken an irresistible hold of my imagination. I wished, as it were, to procrastinate all that related to my feelings of affection until the great object, which swallowed up every habit of my nature, should be completed.

I then thought that my father would be unjust if he ascribed my neglect to vice, or faultiness on my part; but I am now convinced that he was justified in conceiving that I should not be altogether free from blame. A human being in perfection ought always to preserve a calm and peaceful mind, and never to allow passion or a transitory desire to disturb his tranquillity. I do not think that the pursuit of knowledge is an exception to this rule. If the study to which you apply yourself has a tendency to weaken your affections, and to destroy your taste for those simple pleasures in which no alloy can possibly mix, then that study is certainly unlawful, that is to say, not befitting the human mind. If this rule were always observed; if no man allowed any pursuit whatsoever to interfere with the tranquillity of his domestic affections, Greece had not been enslaved; Cæsar would have spared his country; America would have been discovered more gradually; and the empires of Mexico and Peru had not been destroyed.

But I forget that I am moralizing in the most interesting part of my tale; and your looks remind me to proceed.

My father made no reproach in his letters; and only took notice of my silence by inquiring into my occupations more particularly than before. Winter, spring, and summer, passed away during my labours; but I did not watch the blossom or the expanding leaves—sights which before always yielded me supreme delight, so deeply was I engrossed in my occupation. The leaves of that year had withered before my work drew near to a close; and now every day shewed me more plainly how well I had succeeded. But my enthusiasm was checked by my anxiety, and I appeared rather like one doomed by slavery to toil in the mines, or any other unwholesome trade, than an artist occupied by his favourite employment. Every night I was oppressed by a slow fever, and I became nervous to a most painful degree; a disease that I regretted the more because I had hitherto enjoyed most excellent health, and had always boasted of the firmness of my nerves. But I believed that exercise and amusement would soon drive away such symptoms; and I promised myself both of these, when my creation should be complete.

CHAPTER IV

IT WAS ON A DREARY NIGHT OF NOVEMBER, THAT I BEHELD THE ACCOMPLISHMENT OF my toils. With an anxiety that almost amounted to agony, I collected the instruments of life around me, that I might infuse a spark of being into the lifeless thing that lay at my feet. It was already one in the morning; the rain pattered dismally against the panes, and my candle was nearly burnt out, when, by the glimmer of the half-extinguished light, I saw the dull yellow eye of the creature open; it breathed hard, and a convulsive motion agitated its limbs.

How can I describe my emotions at this catastrophe, or how delineate the wretch whom with such infinite pains and care I had endeavoured to form? His limbs were in proportion, and I had selected his features as beautiful. Beautiful!—Great God! His yellow skin scarcely covered the work of muscles and arteries beneath; his hair was of a lustrous black, and flowing; his teeth of a pearly whiteness; but these luxuriances only formed a more horrid contrast with his watery eyes, that seemed almost of the same colour as the dun white sockets in which they were set, his shrivelled complexion, and straight black lips.

The different accidents of life are not so changeable as the feelings of human nature. I had worked hard for nearly two years, for the sole purpose of infusing life into an inanimate body. For this I had deprived myself of rest and health. I had desired it with an ardour that far exceeded moderation; but now that I had finished, the beauty of the dream vanished, and breathless horror and disgust filled my heart. Unable to endure the aspect of the being I had created, I rushed out of the room, and continued a long time traversing my bed-chamber, unable to compose my mind to sleep. At length lassitude succeeded to the tumult I had before endured; and I threw myself on the bed in my clothes, endeavouring to seek a few moments of forgetfulness. But it was in vain: I slept indeed, but I was disturbed by the wildest dreams. I thought I saw Elizabeth, in the bloom of health, walking in the streets of Ingolstadt. Delighted and surprised,

I embraced her; but as I imprinted the first kiss on her lips, they became livid with the hue of death; her features appeared to change, and I thought that I held the corpse of my dead mother in my arms; a shroud enveloped her form, and I saw the grave-worms crawling in the folds of the flannel. I started from my sleep with horror; a cold dew covered my forehead, my teeth chattered, and every limb became convulsed; when, by the dim and yellow light of the moon, as it forced its way through the window-shutters, I beheld the wretch—the miserable monster whom I had created. He held up the curtain of the bed; and his eyes, if eyes they may be called, were fixed on me. His jaws opened, and he muttered some inarticulate sounds, while a grin wrinkled his cheeks. He might have spoken, but I did not hear; one hand was stretched out, seemingly to detain me, but I escaped, and rushed down stairs. I took refuge in the court-yard belonging to the house which I inhabited; where I remained during the rest of the night, walking up and down in the greatest agitation, listening attentively, catching and fearing each sound as if it were to announce the approach of the demoniacal corpse to which I had so miserably given life.

Oh! no mortal could support the horror of that countenance. A mummy again endued with animation could not be so hideous as that wretch. I had gazed on him while unfinished; he was ugly then; but when those muscles and joints were rendered capable of motion, it became a thing such as even Dante could not have conceived.

I passed the night wretchedly. Sometimes my pulse beat so quickly and hardly, that I felt the palpitation of every artery; at others, I nearly sank to the ground through languor and extreme weakness. Mingled with this horror, I felt the bitterness of disappointment: dreams that had been my food and pleasant rest for so long a space, were now become a hell to me; and the change was so rapid, the overthrow so complete!

Morning, dismal and wet, at length dawned, and discovered to my sleepless and aching eyes the church of Ingolstadt, its white steeple and clock, which indicated the sixth hour. The porter opened the gates of the court, which had that night been my asylum, and I issued into the streets, pacing them with quick steps, as if I sought to avoid the wretch whom I feared every turning of the street would present to my view. I did not dare return to the apartment which I inhabited, but felt impelled to hurry on, although wetted by the rain, which poured from a black and comfortless sky.

I continued walking in this manner for some time, endeavouring, by bodily exercise, to ease the load that weighed upon my mind. I traversed the streets, without any clear conception of where I was, or what I was doing. My heart palpitated in the sickness of fear; and I hurried on with irregular steps, not daring to look about me:

Like one who, on a lonely road,

Doth walk in fear and dread,

And, having once turn'd round, walks on,

And turns no more his head;

Because he knows a frightful fiend

Doth close behind him tread.

Continuing thus, I came at length opposite to the inn at which the various diligences and carriages usually stopped. Here I paused, I knew not why; but I remained some minutes with my eyes fixed on a coach that was coming towards me from the other end of the street. As it drew nearer, I observed that it was the Swiss diligence: it stopped just where I was standing; and, on the door being opened, I perceived Henry Clerval, who, on seeing me, instantly sprung out. "My dear Frankenstein," exclaimed he, "how glad I am to see you! how fortunate that you should be here at the very moment of my alighting!"

Nothing could equal my delight on seeing Clerval; his presence brought back to my thoughts my father, Elizabeth, and all those scenes of home so dear to my recollection. I grasped his hand, and in a moment forgot my horror and misfortune; I felt suddenly, and for the first time during many months, calm and serene joy. I welcomed my friend, therefore, in the most cordial manner, and we walked towards my college. Clerval continued talking for some time about our mutual friends, and his own good fortune in being permitted to come to Ingolstadt. "You may easily believe," said he, "how great was the difficulty to persuade my father that it was not absolutely necessary for a merchant not to understand any thing except book-keeping; and, indeed, I believe I left him incredulous to the last, for his constant answer to my unwearied entreaties was the same as that of the Dutch schoolmaster in the *Vicar of Wakefield*: 'I have ten thousand florins a year without Greek, I eat heartily without Greek.' But his affection for me at length overcame his dislike of learning, and he has permitted me to undertake a voyage of discovery to the land of knowledge."

"It gives me the greatest delight to see you; but tell me how you left my father, brothers, and Elizabeth."

"Very well, and very happy, only a little uneasy that they hear from you so seldom. By the bye, I mean to lecture you a little upon their account myself.—But, my dear Frankenstein," continued he, stopping short, and gazing full in my face, "I did not before remark how very ill you appear; so thin and pale; you look as if you had been watching for several nights."

"You have guessed right; I have lately been so deeply engaged in one occupation, that I have not allowed myself sufficient rest, as you see: but I hope, I sincerely hope, that all these employments are now at an end, and that I am at length free."

I trembled excessively; I could not endure to think of, and far less to allude to the occurrences of the preceding night. I walked with a quick pace, and we soon arrived at my college. I then reflected, and the thought made me shiver, that the creature whom I had left in my apartment might still be there, alive, and walking about. I dreaded to behold this monster; but I feared still more that Henry should see him. Entreating him therefore to remain a few minutes at the bottom of the stairs, I darted up towards my own room. My hand was already on the lock of the door before I recollected myself. I then paused; and a cold shivering came over me. I threw the door forcibly open, as children are accustomed to do when they expect a spectre to stand in waiting for them on the other side; but nothing appeared. I stepped fearfully in: the apartment was empty; and my bedroom was also freed from its hideous guest. I could hardly believe that so great a good-fortune could have befallen me; but when I became assured that my enemy had indeed fled, I clapped my hands for joy and ran down to Clerval.

We ascended into my room, and the servant presently brought breakfast; but I was unable to contain myself. It was not joy only that possessed me; I felt my flesh tingle with excess of sensitiveness, and my pulse beat rapidly. I was unable to remain for a single instant in the same place; I jumped over the chairs, clapped my hands, and laughed aloud. Clerval at first attributed my unusual spirits to joy on his arrival; but when he observed me more attentively, he saw a wildness in my eyes for which he could not account; and my loud, unrestrained, heartless laughter, frightened and astonished him.

"My dear Victor," cried he, "what, for God's sake, is the matter? Do not laugh in that manner. How ill you are! What is the cause of all this?"

"Do not ask me," cried I, putting my hands before my eyes, for I thought I saw the dreaded spectre glide into the room; "*he* can tell.—Oh, save me! save me!" I imagined that the monster seized me; I struggled furiously, and fell down in a fit.

Poor Clerval! what must have been his feelings? A meeting, which he anticipated with such joy, so strangely turned to bitterness. But I was not the witness of his grief; for I was lifeless, and did not recover my senses for a long, long time.

This was the commencement of a nervous fever, which confined me for several months. During all that time Henry was my only nurse. I afterwards learned that, knowing my father's advanced age, and unfitness for so long a journey, and how wretched my sickness would make Elizabeth, he spared them this grief by concealing the extent of my disorder. He knew that I could not have a more kind and attentive nurse than himself; and, firm in the hope he felt of my recovery, he did not doubt that, instead of doing harm, he performed the kindest action that he could towards them.

But I was in reality very ill; and surely nothing but the unbounded and unremitting attentions of my friend could have restored me to life. The form of the monster on whom I had bestowed existence was for ever before my eyes, and I raved incessantly concerning him. Doubtless my words surprised Henry: he at first believed them to be the wanderings of my disturbed imagination; but the pertinacity with which I continually recurred to the same subject persuaded him that my disorder indeed owed its origin to some uncommon and terrible event.

By very slow degrees, and with frequent relapses, that alarmed and grieved my friend, I recovered. I remember the first time I became capable of observing outward objects with any kind of pleasure, I perceived that the fallen leaves had disappeared, and that the young buds were shooting forth from the trees that shaded my window. It was a divine spring; and the season contributed greatly to my convalescence. I felt also sentiments of joy and affection revive in my bosom; my gloom disappeared, and in a short time I became as cheerful as before I was attacked by the fatal passion.

"Dearest Clerval," exclaimed I, "how kind, how very good you are to me. This whole winter, instead of being spent in study, as you promised yourself, has been consumed in my sick room. How shall I ever repay you? I feel the greatest remorse for the disappointment of which I have been the occasion; but you will forgive me."

"You will repay me entirely, if you do not discompose yourself, but get well as fast as you can; and since you appear in such good spirits, I may speak to you on one subject, may I not?"

I trembled. One subject! what could it be? Could he allude to an object on whom I dared not even think?

"Compose yourself," said Clerval, who observed my change of colour, "I will not mention it, if it agitates you; but your father and cousin would be very happy if they received a letter from you in your own hand-writing. They hardly know how ill you have been, and are uneasy at your long silence."

"Is that all? my dear Henry. How could you suppose that my first thought would not fly towards those dear, dear friends whom I love, and who are so deserving of my love."

"If this is your present temper, my friend, you will perhaps be glad to see a letter that has been lying here some days for you: it is from your cousin, I believe."

CHAPTER V

To V. FRANKENSTEIN.

MY DEAR COUSIN,

I cannot describe to you the uneasiness we have all felt concerning your health. We cannot help imagining that your friend Clerval conceals the extent of your disorder: for it is now several months since we have seen your hand-writing; and all this time you have been obliged to dictate your letters to Henry. Surely, Victor, you must have been exceedingly ill; and this makes us all very wretched, as much so nearly as after the death of your dear mother. My uncle was almost persuaded that you were indeed dangerously ill, and could hardly be restrained from undertaking a journey to Ingolstadt. Clerval always writes that you are getting better; I eagerly hope that you will confirm this intelligence soon in your own hand-writing; for indeed, indeed, Victor, we are all very miserable on this account. Relieve us from this fear, and we shall be the happiest creatures in the world. Your father's health is now so vigorous, that he appears ten years younger since last winter. Ernest also is so much improved, that you would hardly know him: he is now nearly sixteen, and has lost that sickly appearance which he had some years ago; he is grown quite robust and active.

My uncle and I conversed a long time last night about what profession Ernest should follow. His constant illness when young has deprived him of the habits of application; and now that he enjoys good health, he is continually in the open air, climbing the hills, or rowing on the lake. I therefore proposed that he should be a farmer; which you know, Cousin, is a favourite scheme of mine. A farmer's is a very healthy happy life; and the least hurtful, or rather the most beneficial profession of any. My uncle had an idea of his being educated as an advocate, that through his interest he might become a judge. But, besides that he is not at all fitted for such an occupation, it is certainly more creditable to cultivate the earth for the sustenance of man, than to be the confidant, and sometimes the accomplice, of his vices; which is the profession of a lawyer. I said, that the employments of a prosperous farmer, if they were not a more honourable, they were at least a happier species of occupation than that of a judge, whose misfortune it was always to meddle with the dark side of human nature. My uncle smiled, and said, that I ought to be an advocate myself, which put an end to the conversation on that subject.

"And now I must tell you a little story that will please, and perhaps amuse you. Do you not remember Justine Moritz? Probably you do not; I will relate her history, therefore, in a few words. Madame Moritz, her mother, was a widow with four children, of whom Justine was the third. This girl had always been the favourite of her father; but, through a strange perversity, her mother could not endure her, and, after the death of M. Moritz, treated her very ill. My aunt observed this; and, when Justine was twelve years of age, prevailed on her mother to allow her to live at her house. The republican institutions of our country have produced simpler and happier manners than those which prevail in the great monarchies that surround it. Hence there is less distinction between the several classes of its inhabitants; and the lower orders being neither so poor nor so despised, their manners are more refined and moral. A servant in Geneva does not mean the same thing as a servant in France and England. Justine, thus received in our family, learned the duties of a servant; a condition which, in our fortunate country, does not include the idea of ignorance, and a sacrifice of the dignity of a human being.

After what I have said, I dare say you well remember the heroine of my little tale: for Justine was a great favourite of yours; and I recollect you once remarked, that if you were in an ill humour, one glance from Justine could dissipate it, for the same reason that Ariosto gives concerning the beauty of Angelica—she looked so frank-hearted and happy. My aunt conceived a great attachment for her, by which she was induced to give her an education superior to that which she had at first intended. This benefit was fully repaid; Justine was the most grateful little creature in the world: I do not mean that she made any professions, I never heard one pass her lips; but you could see by her eyes that she almost adored her protectress. Although her disposition was gay, and in many respects inconsiderate, yet she paid the greatest attention to every gesture of my aunt. She thought her the model of all excellence, and endeavoured to imitate her phraseology and manners, so that even now she often reminds me of her.

When my dearest aunt died, every one was too much occupied in their own grief to notice poor Justine, who had attended her during her illness with the most anxious affection. Poor Justine was very ill; but other trials were reserved for her.

One by one, her brothers and sister died; and her mother, with the exception of her neglected daughter, was left childless. The conscience of the woman was troubled; she began to think that the deaths of her favourites was a judgment from heaven to chastise her partiality. She was a Roman Catholic; and I believe her confessor confirmed the idea which she had conceived. Accordingly, a few months after your departure for Ingolstadt, Justine was called home by her repentant mother. Poor girl! she wept when she quitted our house: she was much altered since the death of my aunt; grief had given softness and a winning mildness to her manners, which had before been remarkable for vivacity. Nor was her residence at her mother's house of a nature to restore her gaiety. The poor woman was very vacillating in her repentance. She sometimes begged Justine to forgive her unkindness, but much oftener accused her of having caused the deaths of her brothers and sister. Perpetual fretting at length threw Madame Moritz into a decline, which at first increased her irritability, but she is now at peace for ever. She died on the first approach of cold weather, at the beginning of this last winter. Justine has returned to us; and I assure you I love her tenderly. She is very clever and gentle, and extremely pretty; as I mentioned before, her mien and her expressions continually remind me of my dear aunt.

I must say also a few words to you, my dear cousin, of little darling William. I wish you could see him; he is very tall of his age, with sweet laughing blue eyes, dark eye-lashes, and curling hair. When he smiles, two little dimples appear on each cheek, which are rosy with health. He has already had one or two little *wives*, but Louisa Biron is his favourite, a pretty little girl of five years of age.

Now, dear Victor, I dare say you wish to be indulged in a little gossip concerning the good people of Geneva. The pretty Miss Mansfield has already received the congratulatory visits on her approaching marriage with a young Englishman, John Melbourne, Esq. Her ugly sister, Manon, married M. Duvillard, the rich banker, last autumn. Your favourite schoolfellow, Louis Manoir, has suffered several misfortunes since the departure of Clerval from Geneva. But he has already recovered his spirits, and is reported to be on the point of marrying a very lively pretty Frenchwoman,

Madame Tavernier. She is a widow, and much older than Manoir; but she is very much admired, and a favourite with every body.

I have written myself into good spirits, dear cousin; yet I cannot conclude without again anxiously inquiring concerning your health. Dear Victor, if you are not very ill, write yourself, and make your father and all of us happy; or—I cannot bear to think of the other side of the question; my tears already flow. Adieu, my dearest cousin.

ELIZABETH LAVENZA.

Geneva, March 18th, 17—.

"Dear, dear Elizabeth!" I exclaimed when I had read her letter, "I will write instantly, and relieve them from the anxiety they must feel." I wrote, and this exertion greatly fatigued me; but my convalescence had commenced, and proceeded regularly. In another fortnight I was able to leave my chamber.

One of my first duties on my recovery was to introduce Clerval to the several professors of the university. In doing this, I underwent a kind of rough usage, ill befitting the wounds that my mind had sustained. Ever since the fatal night, the end of my labours, and the beginning of my misfortunes, I had conceived a violent antipathy even to the name of natural philosophy. When I was otherwise quite restored to health, the sight of a chemical instrument would renew all the agony of my nervous symptoms. Henry saw this, and had removed all my apparatus from my view. He had also changed my apartment; for he perceived that I had acquired a dislike for the room which had previously been my laboratory. But these cares of Clerval were made of no avail when I visited the professors. M. Waldman inflicted torture when he praised, with kindness and warmth, the astonishing progress I had made in the sciences. He soon perceived that I disliked the subject; but, not guessing the real cause, he attributed my feelings to modesty, and changed the subject from my improvement to the science itself, with a desire, as I evidently saw, of drawing me out. What could I do? He meant to please, and he tormented me. I felt as if he had placed carefully, one by one, in my view those instruments which were to be afterwards used in putting me to a slow and cruel death. I writhed under his words, yet dared not exhibit the pain I felt. Clerval, whose eyes and feelings were always quick in discerning the sensations of others, declined the subject, alleging, in excuse, his total ignorance; and the conversation took a more general turn. I thanked my friend from my heart, but I did not speak. I saw plainly that he was surprised, but he never attempted to draw my secret from me; and although I loved him with a mixture of affection and reverence that knew no bounds, yet I could never persuade myself to confide to him that event which was so often present to my recollection, but which I feared the detail to another would only impress more deeply.

M. Krempe was not equally docile; and in my condition at that time, of almost insupportable sensitiveness, his harsh blunt encomiums gave me even more pain than the benevolent approbation of M. Waldman. "D—n the fellow!" cried he; "why, M. Clerval, I assure you he has outstript us all. Aye, stare if you please; but it is nevertheless true. A youngster who, but a few years ago, believed Cornelius Agrippa as firmly as the gospel, has now set himself at the head of the university; and if he is not soon pulled down, we shall all be out of countenance.—Aye, aye," continued he, observing my face expressive of suffering, "M. Frankenstein is modest; an excellent quality in a young man. Young men should be diffident of themselves, you know, M. Clerval; I was myself when young: but that wears out in a very short time."

M. Krempe had now commenced an eulogy on himself, which happily turned the conversation from a subject that was so annoying to me.

Clerval was no natural philosopher. His imagination was too vivid for the minutiæ of science. Languages were his principal study; and he sought, by acquiring their elements, to open a field for self-instruction on his return to Geneva. Persian, Arabic, and Hebrew, gained his attention, after he had made himself perfectly master of Greek and Latin. For my own part, idleness had ever been irksome to me; and now that I wished to fly from reflection, and hated my former studies, I felt great relief in being the fellow-pupil with my friend, and found not only instruction but consolation in the works of the orientalists. Their melancholy is soothing, and their joy elevating to a degree I never experienced in studying the authors of any other country. When you read their writings, life appears to consist in a warm sun and garden of roses,—in the smiles and frowns of a fair enemy, and the fire that consumes your own heart. How different from the manly and heroical poetry of Greece and Rome.

Summer passed away in these occupations, and my return to Geneva was fixed for the latter end of autumn; but being delayed by several accidents, winter and snow arrived, the roads were deemed impassable, and my journey was retarded until the ensuing spring. I felt this delay very bitterly; for I longed to see my native town, and my beloved friends. My return had only been delayed so long from an unwillingness to leave Clerval in a strange place, before he had become acquainted with any of its inhabitants. The winter, however, was spent cheerfully; and although the spring was uncommonly late, when it came, its beauty compensated for its dilatoriness.

The month of May had already commenced, and I expected the letter daily which was to fix the date of my departure, when Henry proposed a pedestrian tour in the environs of Ingolstadt that I might bid a personal farewell to the country I had so long inhabited. I acceded with pleasure to this proposition: I was fond of exercise, and Clerval had always been my favourite companion in the rambles of this nature that I had taken among the scenes of my native country.

We passed a fortnight in these perambulations: my health and spirits had long been restored, and they gained additional strength from the salubrious air I breathed, the natural incidents of our progress, and the conversation of my friend. Study had before secluded me from the intercourse of my fellow-creatures, and rendered me unsocial; but Clerval called forth the better feelings of my heart; he again taught me to love the aspect of nature, and the cheerful faces of children. Excellent friend! how sincerely did you love me, and endeavour to elevate my mind, until it was on a level with your own. A selfish pursuit had cramped and narrowed me, until your gentleness and affection warmed and opened my senses; I became the same happy creature who, a few years ago, loving and beloved by all, had no sorrow or care. When happy, inanimate nature had the power of bestowing on me the most delightful sensations. A serene sky and verdant fields filled me with ecstacy. The present season was indeed divine; the flowers of spring bloomed in the hedges, while those of summer were already in bud: I was undisturbed by thoughts which during the preceding year had pressed upon me, notwithstanding my endeavours to throw them off, with an invincible burden.

Henry rejoiced in my gaiety, and sincerely sympathized in my feelings: he exerted himself to amuse me, while he expressed the sensations that filled his soul. The resources of his mind on this occasion were truly astonishing: his conversation was full of imagination; and very often, in imitation of the Persian and Arabic writers, he invented tales of wonderful fancy and passion. At other times he repeated my favourite poems, or drew me out into arguments, which he supported with great ingenuity.

We returned to our college on a Sunday afternoon: the peasants were dancing, and every one we met appeared gay and happy. My own spirits were high, and I bounded along with feelings of unbridled joy and hilarity.

CHAPTER VI

On my return, I found the following letter from my father:—

To V. Frankenstein.

MY DEAR VICTOR,

You have probably waited impatiently for a letter to fix the date of your return to us; and I was at first tempted to write only a few lines, merely mentioning the day on which I should expect you. But that would be a cruel kindness, and I dare not do it. What would be your surprise, my son, when you expected a happy and gay welcome, to behold, on the contrary, tears and wretchedness? And how, Victor, can I relate our misfortune? Absence cannot have rendered you callous to our joys and griefs; and how shall I inflict pain on an absent child? I wish to prepare you for the woeful news, but I know it is impossible; even now your eye skims over the page, to seek the words which are to convey to you the horrible tidings.

William is dead!—that sweet child, whose smiles delighted and warmed my heart, who was so gentle, yet so gay! Victor, he is murdered!

I will not attempt to console you; but will simply relate the circumstances of the transaction.

Last Thursday (May 7th) I, my niece, and your two brothers, went to walk in Plainpalais. The evening was warm and serene, and we prolonged our walk farther than usual. It was already dusk before we thought of returning; and then we discovered that William and Ernest, who had gone on before, were not to be found. We accordingly rested on a seat until they should return. Presently Ernest came, and inquired if we had seen his brother: he said, that they had been playing together, that William had run away to hide himself, and that he vainly sought for him, and afterwards waited for him a long time, but that he did not return.

This account rather alarmed us, and we continued to search for him until night fell, when Elizabeth conjectured that he might have returned to the house. He was not there. We returned again, with torches; for I could not rest, when I thought that my sweet boy had lost himself, and was exposed to all the damps and dews of night: Elizabeth also suffered extreme anguish.

About five in the morning I discovered my lovely boy, whom the night before I had seen blooming and active in health, stretched on the grass livid and motionless: the print of the murderer's finger was on his neck.

He was conveyed home, and the anguish that was visible in my countenance betrayed the secret to Elizabeth. She was very earnest to see the corpse. At first I attempted to prevent her; but she persisted, and entering the room where it lay, hastily examined the neck of the victim, and clasping her hands exclaimed, "O God! I have murdered my darling infant!"

She fainted, and was restored with extreme difficulty. When she again lived, it was only to weep and sigh. She told me, that that same evening William had teazed her to let him wear a very valuable miniature that she possessed of your mother. This picture is gone, and was doubtless the temptation which urged the murderer to the deed. We have no trace of him at present, although our exertions to discover him are unremitted; but they will not restore my beloved William.

Come, dearest Victor; you alone can console Elizabeth. She weeps continually, and accuses herself unjustly as the cause of his death; her words pierce my heart. We are all unhappy; but will not that be an additional motive for you, my son, to return and be our comforter? Your dear mother! Alas, Victor! I now say, Thank God she did not live to witness the cruel, miserable death of her youngest darling!

Come, Victor; not brooding thoughts of vengeance against the assassin, but with feelings of peace and gentleness, that will heal, instead of festering the wounds of our minds. Enter the house of mourning, my friend, but with kindness and affection for those who love you, and not with hatred for your enemies.

Your affectionate and afflicted father,

ALPHONSE FRANKENSTEIN.

Geneva, May 12th, 17—.

Clerval, who had watched my countenance as I read this letter, was surprised to observe the despair that succeeded to the joy I at first expressed on receiving news from my friends. I threw the letter on the table, and covered my face with my hands.

"My dear Frankenstein," exclaimed Henry, when he perceived me weep with bitterness, "are you always to be unhappy? My dear friend, what has happened?"

I motioned to him to take up the letter, while I walked up and down the room in the extremest agitation. Tears also gushed from the eyes of Clerval, as he read the account of my misfortune.

"I can offer you no consolation, my friend," said he; "your disaster is irreparable. What do you intend to do?"

"To go instantly to Geneva: come with me, Henry, to order the horses."

During our walk, Clerval endeavoured to raise my spirits. He did not do this by common topics of consolation, but by exhibiting the truest sympathy. "Poor William!" said he, "that dear child; he now sleeps with his angel mother. His friends mourn and weep, but he is at rest: he does not now feel the murderer's grasp; a sod covers his gentle form, and he knows no pain. He can no longer be a fit subject for pity; the survivors are the greatest sufferers, and for them time is the only consolation. Those maxims of the Stoics, that death was no evil, and that the mind of man ought to be superior to despair on the eternal absence of a beloved object, ought not to be urged. Even Cato wept over the dead body of his brother."

Clerval spoke thus as we hurried through the streets; the words impressed themselves on my mind, and I remembered them afterwards in solitude. But now, as soon as the horses arrived, I hurried into a cabriole, and bade farewell to my friend.

My journey was very melancholy. At first I wished to hurry on, for I longed to console and sympathize with my loved and sorrowing friends; but when I drew near my native town, I slackened my progress. I could hardly sustain the multitude of feelings that crowded into my mind. I passed through scenes familiar to my youth, but which I had not seen for nearly six years. How altered every thing might be during that time? One sudden and desolating change had taken place; but a thousand little circumstances might have by degrees worked other alterations, which, although they were done more tranquilly, might not be the less decisive. Fear overcame me; I dared not advance, dreading a thousand nameless evils that made me tremble, although I was unable to define them.

I remained two days at Lausanne, in this painful state of mind. I contemplated the lake: the waters were placid; all around was calm, and the snowy mountains, "the palaces of nature," were not changed. By degrees the calm and heavenly scene restored me, and I continued my journey towards Geneva.

The road ran by the side of the lake, which became narrower as I approached my native town. I discovered more distinctly the black sides of Jura, and the bright summit of Mont Blanc; I wept like a child: "Dear mountains! my own beautiful lake! how do you welcome your wanderer? Your summits are clear; the sky and lake are blue and placid. Is this to prognosticate peace, or to mock at my unhappiness?"

I fear, my friend, that I shall render myself tedious by dwelling on these preliminary circumstances; but they were days of comparative happiness, and I think of them with pleasure. My country, my beloved country! who but a native can tell the delight I took in again beholding thy streams, thy mountains, and, more than all, thy lovely lake.

Yet, as I drew nearer home, grief and fear again overcame me. Night also closed around; and when I could hardly see the dark mountains, I felt still more gloomily. The picture appeared a vast and dim scene of evil, and I foresaw obscurely that I was destined to become the most wretched of human beings. Alas! I prophesied truly, and failed only in one single circumstance, that in all the misery I imagined and dreaded, I did not conceive the hundredth part of the anguish I was destined to endure.

It was completely dark when I arrived in the environs of Geneva; the gates of the town were already shut; and I was obliged to pass the night at Secheron, a village half a league to the east of the city. The sky was serene; and, as I was unable to rest, I resolved to visit the spot where my poor William had been murdered. As I could not pass through the town, I was obliged to cross the lake in a boat to arrive at Plainpalais. During this short voyage I saw the lightnings playing on the summit of Mont Blanc in the most beautiful figures. The storm appeared to approach rapidly; and, on landing, I ascended a low hill, that I might observe its progress. It advanced; the heavens were clouded, and I soon felt the rain coming slowly in large drops, but its violence quickly increased.

I quitted my seat, and walked on, although the darkness and storm increased every minute, and the thunder burst with a terrific crash over my head. It was echoed from Salêve, the Juras, and the Alps of Savoy; vivid flashes of lightning dazzled my eyes, illuminating the lake, making it appear like a vast sheet of fire; then for an instant every thing seemed of a pitchy darkness, until the eye recovered itself from the preceding flash. The storm, as is often the case in Switzerland, appeared at once in various parts of the heavens. The most violent storm hung exactly north of the town, over that part of the lake which lies between the promontory of Belrive and the village of Copêt. Another storm enlightened Jura with faint flashes; and another darkened and sometimes disclosed the Môle, a peaked mountain to the east of the lake.

While I watched the storm, so beautiful yet terrific, I wandered on with a hasty step. This noble war in the sky elevated my spirits; I clasped my hands, and exclaimed aloud, "William, dear angel! this is thy funeral, this thy dirge!" As I said these words,

I perceived in the gloom a figure which stole from behind a clump of trees near me; I stood fixed, gazing intently: I could not be mistaken. A flash of lightning illuminated the object, and discovered its shape plainly to me; its gigantic stature, and the deformity of its aspect, more hideous than belongs to humanity, instantly informed me that it was the wretch, the filthy dæmon to whom I had given life. What did he there? Could he be (I shuddered at the conception) the murderer of my brother? No sooner did that idea cross my imagination, than I became convinced of its truth; my teeth chattered, and I was forced to lean against a tree for support. The figure passed me quickly, and I lost it in the gloom. Nothing in human shape could have destroyed that fair child. *He* was the murderer! I could not doubt it. The mere presence of the idea was an irresistible proof of the fact. I thought of pursuing the devil; but it would have been in vain, for another flash discovered him to me hanging among the rocks of the nearly perpendicular ascent of Mont Saleve, a hill that bounds Plainpalais on the south. He soon reached the summit, and disappeared.

I remained motionless. The thunder ceased; but the rain still continued, and the scene was enveloped in an impenetrable darkness. I revolved in my mind the events which I had until now sought to forget: the whole train of my progress towards the creation; the appearance of the work of my own hands alive at my bed side; its departure. Two years had now nearly elapsed since the night on which he first received life; and was this his first crime? Alas! I had turned loose into the world a depraved wretch, whose delight was in carnage and misery; had he not murdered my brother?

No one can conceive the anguish I suffered during the remainder of the night, which I spent, cold and wet, in the open air. But I did not feel the inconvenience of the weather; my imagination was busy in scenes of evil and despair. I considered the being whom I had cast among mankind, and endowed with the will and power to effect purposes of horror, such as the deed which he had now done, nearly in the light of my own vampire, my own spirit let loose from the grave, and forced to destroy all that was dear to me.

Day dawned; and I directed my steps towards the town. The gates were open; and I hastened to my father's house. My first thought was to discover what I knew of the murderer, and cause instant pursuit to be made. But I paused when I reflected on the story that I had to tell. A being whom I myself had formed, and endued with life, had met me at midnight among the precipices of an inaccessible mountain. I remembered also the nervous fever with which I had been seized just at the time that I dated my creation, and which would give an air of delirium to a tale otherwise so utterly improbable. I well knew that if any other had communicated such a relation to me, I should have looked upon it as the ravings of insanity. Besides, the strange nature of the animal would elude all pursuit, even if I were so far credited as to persuade my relatives to commence it. Besides, of what use would be pursuit? Who could arrest a creature capable of scaling the overhanging sides of Mont Salève? These reflections determined me, and I resolved to remain silent.

It was about five in the morning when I entered my father's house. I told the servants not to disturb the family, and went into the library to attend their usual hour of rising.

Six years had elapsed, passed as a dream but for one indelible trace, and I stood in the same place where I had last embraced my father before my departure for Ingolstadt. Beloved and respectable parent! He still remained to me. I gazed on the picture of my mother, which stood over the mantlepiece. It was an historical subject, painted at my father's desire, and represented Caroline Beaufort in an agony of despair, kneeling by the coffin of her dead father. Her garb was rustic, and her cheek pale; but there was an air of dignity and beauty, that hardly permitted the sentiment of pity. Below this picture was a miniature of William; and my tears flowed when I looked upon it. While I was thus engaged, Ernest entered: he had heard me arrive, and hastened to welcome me. He expressed a sorrowful delight to see me: "Welcome, my dearest Victor," said he. "Ah! I wish you had come three months ago, and then you would have found us all joyous and delighted. But we are now unhappy; and, I am afraid, tears instead of smiles will be your welcome. Our father looks so sorrowful: this dreadful event seems to have revived in his mind his grief on the death of Mamma. Poor Elizabeth also is quite inconsolable." Ernest began to weep as he said these words.

"Do not," said I, "welcome me thus; try to be more calm, that I may not be absolutely miserable the moment I enter my father's house after so long an absence. But, tell me, how does my father support his misfortunes? and how is my poor Elizabeth?"

"She indeed requires consolation; she accused herself of having caused the death of my brother, and that made her very wretched. But since the murderer has been discovered—"

"The murderer discovered! Good God! how can that be? who could attempt to pursue him? It is impossible; one might as well try to overtake the winds, or confine a mountain-stream with a straw."

"I do not know what you mean; but we were all very unhappy when she was discovered. No one would believe it at first; and even now Elizabeth will not be convinced, notwithstanding all the evidence. Indeed, who would credit that Justine Moritz, who was so amiable, and fond of all the family, could all at once become so extremely wicked?"

"Justine Moritz! Poor, poor girl, is she the accused? But it is wrongfully; every one knows that; no one believes it, surely, Ernest?"

"No one did at first; but several circumstances came out, that have almost forced conviction upon us: and her own behaviour has been so confused, as to add to the evidence of facts a weight that, I fear, leaves no hope for doubt. But she will be tried to-day, and you will then hear all."

He related that, the morning on which the murder of poor William had been dis-covered, Justine had been taken ill, and confined to her bed; and, after several days, one of the servants, happening to examine the apparel she had worn on the night of the murder, had discovered in her pocket the picture of my mother, which had been judged to be the temptation of the murderer. The servant instantly shewed it to one of the oth-ers, who, without saying a word to any of the family, went to a magistrate; and, upon their deposition, Justine was apprehended. On being charged with the fact, the poor girl confirmed the suspicion in a great measure by her extreme confusion of manner.

This was a strange tale, but it did not shake my faith; and I replied earnestly, "You are all mistaken; I know the murderer. Justine, poor, good Justine is innocent."

At that instant my father entered. I saw unhappiness deeply impressed on his coun-tenance, but he endeavoured to welcome me cheerfully; and, after we had exchanged our mournful greeting, would have introduced some other topic than that of our disas-ter, had not Ernest exclaimed, "Good God, Papa! Victor says that he knows who was the murderer of poor William."

"We do also, unfortunately," replied my father; "for indeed I had rather have been for ever ignorant than have discovered so much depravity and ingratitude in one I valued so highly."

"My dear father, you are mistaken; Justine is innocent."

"If she is, God forbid that she should suffer as guilty. She is to be tried to-day, and I hope, I sincerely hope, that she will be acquitted."

This speech calmed me. I was firmly convinced in my own mind that Justine, and indeed every human being, was guiltless of this murder. I had no fear, therefore, that any circumstantial evidence could be brought forward strong enough to convict her; and, in this assurance, I calmed myself, expecting the trial with eagerness, but without prognosticating an evil result.

We were soon joined by Elizabeth. Time had made great alterations in her form since I had last beheld her. Six years before she had been a pretty, good-humoured girl, whom every one loved and caressed. She was now a woman in stature and expression of countenance, which was uncommonly lovely. An open and capacious forehead gave indications of a good understanding, joined to great frankness of disposition. Her eyes were hazel, and expressive of mildness, now through recent affliction allied to sadness. Her hair was of a rich dark auburn, her complexion fair, and her figure slight and graceful. She welcomed me with the greatest affection. "Your arrival, my dear cousin," said she, "fills me with hope. You perhaps will find some means to justify my poor guiltless Justine. Alas! who is safe, if she be convicted of crime? I rely on her innocence as certainly as I do upon my own. Our misfortune is doubly hard to us; we have not only lost that lovely darling boy, but this poor girl, whom I sincerely love, is to be torn away by even a worse fate. If she is condemned, I never shall know joy more. But she will not, I am sure she will not; and then I shall be happy again, even after the sad death of my little William."

"She is innocent, my Elizabeth," said I, "and that shall be proved; fear nothing, but let your spirits be cheered by the assurance of her acquittal."

"How kind you are! every one else believes in her guilt, and that made me wretched; for I knew that it was impossible: and to see every one else prejudiced in so deadly a manner, rendered me hopeless and despairing." She wept.

"Sweet niece," said my father, "dry your tears. If she is, as you believe, innocent, rely on the justice of our judges, and the activity with which I shall prevent the slightest shadow of partiality."

CHAPTER VII

WE PASSED A FEW SAD HOURS, UNTIL ELEVEN O'CLOCK, WHEN THE TRIAL WAS TO commence. My father and the rest of the family being obliged to attend as witnesses, I accompanied them to the court. During the whole of this wretched mockery of justice, I suffered living torture. It was to be decided, whether the result of my curiosity and lawless devices would cause the death of two of my fellow-beings: one a smiling babe, full of innocence and joy; the other far more dreadfully murdered, with every aggravation of infamy that could make the murder memorable in horror. Justine also was a girl of merit, and possessed qualities which promised to render her life happy: now all was to be obliterated in an ignominious grave; and I the cause! A thousand times rather would I have confessed myself guilty of the crime ascribed to Justine; but I was absent when it was committed, and such a declaration would have been considered as the ravings of a madman, and would not have exculpated her who suffered through me.

The appearance of Justine was calm. She was dressed in mourning; and her countenance, always engaging, was rendered, by the solemnity of her feelings, exquisitely beautiful. Yet she appeared confident in innocence, and did not tremble, although gazed on and execrated by thousands; for all the kindness which her beauty might otherwise have excited, was obliterated in the minds of the spectators by the imagination of the enormity she was supposed to have committed. She was tranquil, yet her tranquillity was evidently constrained; and as her confusion had before been adduced as a proof of her guilt, she worked up her mind to an appearance of courage. When she entered the court, she threw her eyes round it, and quickly discovered where we were seated. A tear seemed to dim her eye when she saw us; but she quickly recovered herself, and a look of sorrowful affection seemed to attest her utter guiltlessness.

The trial began; and after the advocate against her had stated the charge, several witnesses were called. Several strange facts combined against her, which might have staggered any one who had not such proof of her innocence as I had. She had been out the whole of the night on which the murder had been committed, and towards morning had been perceived by a market-woman not far from the spot where the body of the murdered child had been afterwards found. The woman asked her what she did there; but she looked very strangely, and only returned a confused and unintelligible answer. She returned to the house about eight o'clock; and when one inquired where she had passed the night, she replied, that she had been looking for the child, and demanded earnestly, if any thing had been heard concerning him. When shewn the body, she fell into violent hysterics, and kept her bed for several days. The picture was then produced, which the servant had found in her pocket; and when Elizabeth, in a faltering voice, proved that it was the same which, an hour before the child had been missed, she had placed round his neck, a murmur of horror and indignation filled the court.

Justine was called on for her defence. As the trial had proceeded, her countenance had altered. Surprise, horror, and misery, were strongly expressed. Sometimes she struggled with her tears; but when she was desired to plead, she collected her powers, and spoke in an audible although variable voice:—

"God knows," she said, "how entirely I am innocent. But I do not pretend that my protestations should acquit me: I rest my innocence on a plain and simple explanation of the facts which have been adduced against me; and I hope the character I have always borne will incline my judges to a favourable interpretation, where any circumstance appears doubtful or suspicious."

She then related that, by the permission of Elizabeth, she had passed the evening of the night on which the murder had been committed, at the house of an aunt at Chêne, a village situated at about a league from Geneva. On her return, at about nine o'clock, she met a man, who asked her if she had seen any thing of the child who was lost. She was alarmed by this account, and passed several hours in looking for him, when the gates of Geneva were shut, and she was forced to remain several hours of the night in a barn belonging to a cottage, being unwilling to call up the inhabitants, to whom she was well known. Unable to rest or sleep, she quitted her asylum early, that she might again endeavour to find my brother. If she had gone near the spot where his body lay, it was without her knowledge. That she had been bewildered when questioned by the market-woman, was not surprising, since she had passed a sleepless night, and the fate of poor William was yet uncertain. Concerning the picture she could give no account.

"I know," continued the unhappy victim, "how heavily and fatally this one circumstance weighs against me, but I have no power of explaining it; and when I have expressed my utter ignorance, I am only left to conjecture concerning the probabilities by which it might have been placed in my pocket. But here also I am checked. I believe that I have no enemy on earth, and none surely would have been so wicked as to destroy me wantonly. Did the murderer place it there? I know of no opportunity afforded him for so doing; or if I had, why should he have stolen the jewel, to part with it again so soon?

"I commit my cause to the justice of my judges, yet I see no room for hope. I beg permission to have a few witnesses examined concerning my character; and if their testimony shall not overweigh my supposed guilt, I must be condemned, although I would pledge my salvation on my innocence."

Several witnesses were called, who had known her for many years, and they spoke well of her; but fear, and hatred of the crime of which they supposed her guilty, rendered them timorous, and unwilling to come forward. Elizabeth saw even this last resource, her excellent dispositions and irreproachable conduct, about to fail the accused, when, although violently agitated, she desired permission to address the court.

"I am," said she, "the cousin of the unhappy child who was murdered, or rather his sister, for I was educated by and have lived with his parents ever since and even long before his birth. It may therefore be judged indecent in me to come forward on this occasion; but when I see a fellow-creature about to perish through the cowardice of her pretended friends, I wish to be allowed to speak, that I may say what I know of her character. I am well acquainted with the accused. I have lived in the same house with her, at one time for five, and at another for nearly two years. During all that period she appeared to me the most amiable and benevolent of human creatures. She nursed Madame Frankenstein, my aunt, in her last illness with the greatest affection and care; and afterwards attended her own mother during a tedious illness, in a manner that excited the admiration of all who knew her. After which she again lived in my uncle's house, where she was beloved by all the family. She was warmly attached to the child who is now dead, and acted towards him like a most affectionate mother. For my own part, I do not hesitate to say, that, notwithstanding all the evidence produced against her, I believe and rely on her perfect innocence. She had no temptation for such an action: as to the bauble on which the chief proof rests, if she had earnestly desired it, I should have willingly given it to her; so much do I esteem and value her."

Excellent Elizabeth! A murmur of approbation was heard; but it was excited by her generous interference, and not in favour of poor Justine, on whom the public indignation was turned with renewed violence, charging her with the blackest ingratitude. She herself wept as Elizabeth spoke, but she did not answer. My own agitation and anguish was extreme during the whole trial. I believed in her innocence; I knew it. Could the dæmon, who had (I did not for a minute doubt) murdered my brother, also in his hellish sport have betrayed the innocent to death and ignominy. I could not sustain the horror of my situation; and when I perceived that the popular voice, and the countenances of the judges, had already condemned my unhappy victim, I rushed out of the court in agony. The tortures of the accused did not equal mine; she was sustained by innocence, but the fangs of remorse tore my bosom, and would not forego their hold.

I passed a night of unmingled wretchedness. In the morning I went to the court; my lips and throat were parched. I dared not ask the fatal question; but I was known, and the officer guessed the cause of my visit. The ballots had been thrown; they were all black, and Justine was condemned.

I cannot pretend to describe what I then felt. I had before experienced sensations of horror; and I have endeavoured to bestow upon them adequate expressions, but words cannot convey an idea of the heart-sickening despair that I then endured. The person to whom I addressed myself added, that Justine had already confessed her guilt. "That evidence," he observed, "was hardly required in so glaring a case, but I am glad of it; and, indeed, none of our judges like to condemn a criminal upon circumstantial evidence, be it ever so decisive."

When I returned home, Elizabeth eagerly demanded the result.

"My cousin," replied I, "it is decided as you may have expected; all judges had rather that ten innocent should suffer, than that one guilty should escape. But she has confessed."

This was a dire blow to poor Elizabeth, who had relied with firmness upon Justine's innocence. "Alas!" said she, "how shall I ever again believe in human benevolence? Justine, whom I loved and esteemed as my sister, how could she put on those smiles of innocence only to betray; her mild eyes seemed incapable of any severity or ill-humour, and yet she has committed a murder."

Soon after we heard that the poor victim had expressed a wish to see my cousin. My father wished her not to go; but said, that he left it to her own judgment and feelings to decide. "Yes," said Elizabeth, "I will go, although she is guilty; and you, Victor, shall accompany me: I cannot go alone." The idea of this visit was torture to me, yet I could not refuse.

We entered the gloomy prison-chamber, and beheld Justine sitting on some straw at the further end; her hands were manacled, and her head rested on her knees. She rose on seeing us enter; and when we were left alone with her, she threw herself at the feet of Elizabeth, weeping bitterly. My cousin wept also.

"Oh, Justine!" said she, "why did you rob me of my last consolation. I relied on your innocence; and although I was then very wretched, I was not so miserable as I am now."

"And do you also believe that I am so very, very wicked? Do you also join with my enemies to crush me?" Her voice was suffocated with sobs.

"Rise, my poor girl," said Elizabeth, "why do you kneel, if you are innocent? I am not one of your enemies; I believed you guiltless, notwithstanding every evidence, until I heard that you had yourself declared your guilt. That report, you say, is false; and be assured, dear Justine, that nothing can shake my confidence in you for a moment, but your own confession."

"I did confess; but I confessed a lie. I confessed, that I might obtain absolution; but now that falsehood lies heavier at my heart than all my other sins. The God of heaven forgive me! Ever since I was condemned, my confessor has besieged me; he threatened and menaced, until I almost began to think that I was the monster that he said I was. He threatened excommunication and hell fire in my last moments, if I continued obdurate. Dear lady, I had none to support me; all looked on me as a wretch doomed to ignominy and perdition. What could I do? In an evil hour I subscribed to a lie; and now only am I truly miserable."

She paused, weeping, and then continued—"I thought with horror, my sweet lady, that you should believe your Justine, whom your blessed aunt had so highly honoured, and whom you loved, was a creature capable of a crime which none but the devil himself could have perpetrated. Dear William! dearest blessed child! I soon shall see you again in heaven, where we shall all be happy; and that consoles me, going as I am to suffer ignominy and death."

"Oh, Justine! forgive me for having for one moment distrusted you. Why did you confess? But do not mourn, my dear girl; I will every where proclaim your innocence, and force belief. Yet you must die; you, my playfellow, my companion, my more than sister. I never can survive so horrible a misfortune."

"Dear, sweet Elizabeth, do not weep. You ought to raise me with thoughts of a better life, and elevate me from the petty cares of this world of injustice and strife. Do not you, excellent friend, drive me to despair."

"I will try to comfort you; but this, I fear, is an evil too deep and poignant to admit of consolation, for there is no hope. Yet heaven bless thee, my dearest Justine, with resignation, and a confidence elevated beyond this world. Oh! how I hate its shews and mockeries! when one creature is murdered, another is immediately deprived of life in a slow torturing manner; then the executioners, their hands yet reeking with the blood of innocence, believe that they have done a great deed. They call this *retribution*. Hateful name! When that word is pronounced, I know greater and more horrid punishments are going to be inflicted than the gloomiest tyrant has ever invented to satiate his utmost revenge. Yet this is not consolation for you, my Justine, unless indeed that you may glory in escaping from so miserable a den. Alas! I would I were in peace with my aunt and my lovely William, escaped from a world which is hateful to me, and the visages of men which I abhor."

Justine smiled languidly. "This, dear lady, is despair, and not resignation. I must not learn the lesson that you would teach me. Talk of something else, something that will bring peace, and not increase of misery."

During this conversation I had retired to a corner of the prison-room, where I could conceal the horrid anguish that possessed me. Despair! Who dared talk of that? The poor victim, who on the morrow was to pass the dreary boundary between life and death, felt not as I did, such deep and bitter agony. I gnashed my teeth, and ground them together, uttering a groan that came from my inmost soul. Justine started. When she saw who it was, she approached me, and said, "Dear Sir, you are very kind to visit me; you, I hope, do not believe that I am guilty."

I could not answer. "No, Justine," said Elizabeth; "he is more convinced of your innocence than I was; for even when he heard that you had confessed, he did not credit it."

"I truly thank him. In these last moments I feel the sheerest gratitude towards those who think of me with kindness. How sweet is the affection of others to such a wretch as I am! It removes more than half my misfortune; and I feel as if I could die in peace, now that my innocence is acknowledged by you, dear lady, and your cousin."

Thus the poor sufferer tried to comfort others and herself. She indeed gained the resignation she desired. But I, the true murderer, felt the never-dying worm alive in my bosom, which allowed of no hope or consolation. Elizabeth also wept, and was unhappy; but hers also was the misery of innocence, which, like a cloud that passes over the fair moon, for a while hides, but cannot tarnish its brightness. Anguish and despair had penetrated into the core of my heart; I bore a hell within me, which nothing could extinguish. We staid several hours with Justine; and it was with great difficulty that Elizabeth could tear herself away. "I wish," cried she, "that I were to die with you; I cannot live in this world of misery."

Justine assumed an air of cheerfulness, while she with difficulty repressed her bitter tears. She embraced Elizabeth, and said, in a voice of half-suppressed emotion, "Farewell, sweet lady, dearest Elizabeth, my beloved and only friend; may heaven in its bounty bless and preserve you; may this be the last misfortune that you will ever suffer. Live, and be happy, and make others so."

As we returned, Elizabeth said, "You know not, my dear Victor, how much I am relieved, now that I trust in the innocence of this unfortunate girl. I never could again have known peace, if I had been deceived in my reliance on her. For the moment that I did believe her guilty, I felt an anguish that I could not have long sustained. Now my heart is lightened. The innocent suffers; but she whom I thought amiable and good has not betrayed the trust I reposed in her, and I am consoled."

Amiable cousin! such were your thoughts, mild and gentle as your own dear eyes and voice. But I—I was a wretch, and none ever conceived of the misery that I then endured.

CHAPTER VIII

NOTHING IS MORE PAINFUL TO THE HUMAN MIND, THAN, AFTER THE FEELINGS HAVE been worked up by a quick succession of events, the dead calmness of inaction and certainty which follows, and deprives the soul both of hope and fear. Justine died; she rested; and I was alive. The blood flowed freely in my veins, but a weight of despair and remorse pressed on my heart, which nothing could remove. Sleep fled from my eyes; I wandered like an evil spirit, for I had committed deeds of mischief beyond description horrible, and more, much more, (I persuaded myself) was yet behind. Yet my heart overflowed with kindness, and the love of virtue. I had begun life with benevolent intentions, and thirsted for the moment when I should put them in practice, and make myself useful to my fellow-beings. Now all was blasted: instead of that serenity of con- science, which allowed me to look back upon the past with self-satisfaction, and from thence to gather promise of new hopes, I was seized by remorse and the sense of guilt, which hurried me away to a hell of intense tortures, such as no language can describe.

This state of mind preyed upon my health, which had entirely recovered from the first shock it had sustained. I shunned the face of man; all sound of joy or complacency was torture to me; solitude was my only consolation—deep, dark, death-like solitude.

My father observed with pain the alteration perceptible in my disposition and hab- its, and endeavoured to reason with me on the folly of giving way to immoderate grief. "Do you think, Victor," said he, "that I do not suffer also? No one could love a child more than I loved your brother"; (tears came into his eyes as he spoke); "but is it not a duty to the survivors, that we should refrain from augmenting their unhappiness by an appearance of immoderate grief? It is also a duty owed to yourself; for excessive sorrow prevents improvement or enjoyment, or even the discharge of daily usefulness, without which no man is fit for society."

This advice, although good, was totally inapplicable to my case; I should have been the first to hide my grief, and console my friends, if remorse had not mingled its bitterness with my other sensations. Now I could only answer my father with a look of despair, and endeavour to hide myself from his view.

About this time we retired to our house at Belrive. This change was particularly agreeable to me. The shutting of the gates regularly at ten o'clock, and the impossi- bility of remaining on the lake after that hour, had rendered our residence within the walls of Geneva very irksome to me. I was now free. Often, after the rest of the fam- ily had retired for the night, I took the boat, and passed many hours upon the water.

Sometimes, with my sails set, I was carried by the wind; and sometimes, after rowing into the middle of the lake, I left the boat to pursue its own course, and gave way to my own miserable reflections. I was often tempted, when all was at peace around me, and I the only unquiet thing that wandered restless in a scene so beautiful and heavenly, if I except some bat, or the frogs, whose harsh and interrupted croaking was heard only when I approached the shore—often, I say, I was tempted to plunge into the silent lake, that the waters might close over me and my calamities for ever. But I was restrained, when I thought of the heroic and suffering Elizabeth, whom I tenderly loved, and whose existence was bound up in mine. I thought also of my father, and surviving brother: should I by my base desertion leave them exposed and unprotected to the malice of the fiend whom I had let loose among them?

At these moments I wept bitterly, and wished that peace would revisit my mind only that I might afford them consolation and happiness. But that could not be. Remorse extinguished every hope. I had been the author of unalterable evils; and I lived in daily fear, lest the monster whom I had created should perpetrate some new wickedness. I had an obscure feeling that all was not over, and that he would still commit some signal crime, which by its enormity should almost efface the recollection of the past. There was always scope for fear, so long as any thing I loved remained behind. My abhorrence of this fiend cannot be conceived. When I thought of him, I gnashed my teeth, my eyes became inflamed, and I ardently wished to extinguish that life which I had so thoughtlessly bestowed. When I reflected on his crimes and malice, my hatred and revenge burst all bounds of moderation. I would have made a pilgrimage to the highest peak of the Andes, could I, when there, have precipitated him to their base. I wished to see him again, that I might wreak the utmost extent of anger on his head, and avenge the deaths of William and Justine.

Our house was the house of mourning. My father's health was deeply shaken by the horror of the recent events. Elizabeth was sad and desponding; she no longer took delight in her ordinary occupations; all pleasure seemed to her sacrilege toward the dead; eternal woe and tears she then thought was the just tribute she should pay to innocence so blasted and destroyed. She was no longer that happy creature, who in earlier youth wandered with me on the banks of the lake, and talked with ecstacy of our future prospects. She had become grave, and often conversed of the inconstancy of fortune, and the instability of human life.

"When I reflect, my dear cousin," said she, "on the miserable death of Justine Moritz, I no longer see the world and its works as they before appeared to me. Before,

I looked upon the accounts of vice and injustice, that I read in books or heard from others, as tales of ancient days, or imaginary evils; at least they were remote, and more familiar to reason than to the imagination; but now misery has come home, and men appear to me as monsters thirsting for each other's blood. Yet I am certainly unjust. Every body believed that poor girl to be guilty; and if she could have committed the crime for which she suffered, assuredly she would have been the most depraved of human creatures. For the sake of a few jewels, to have murdered the son of her bene-factor and friend, a child whom she had nursed from its birth, and appeared to love as if it had been her own! I could not consent to the death of any human being; but cer-tainly I should have thought such a creature unfit to remain in the society of men. Yet she was innocent. I know, I feel she was innocent; you are of the same opinion, and that confirms me. Alas! Victor, when falsehood can look so like the truth, who can assure themselves of certain happiness? I feel as if I were walking on the edge of a precipice, towards which thousands are crowding, and endeavouring to plunge me into the abyss. William and Justine were assassinated, and the murderer escapes; he walks about the world free, and perhaps respected. But even if I were condemned to suffer on the scaf-fold for the same crimes, I would not change places with such a wretch."

I listened to this discourse with the extremest agony. I, not in deed, but in effect, was the true murderer. Elizabeth read my anguish in my countenance, and kindly tak-ing my hand said, "My dearest cousin, you must calm yourself. These events have affected me, God knows how deeply; but I am not so wretched as you are. There is an expression of despair, and sometimes of revenge, in your countenance, that makes me tremble. Be calm, my dear Victor; I would sacrifice my life to your peace. We surely shall be happy: quiet in our native country, and not mingling in the world, what can disturb our tranquillity?"

She shed tears as she said this, distrusting the very solace that she gave; but at the same time she smiled, that she might chase away the fiend that lurked in my heart. My father, who saw in the unhappiness that was painted in my face only an exaggera-tion of that sorrow which I might naturally feel, thought that an amusement suited to my taste would be the best means of restoring to me my wonted serenity. It was from this cause that he had removed to the country; and, induced by the same motive, he now proposed that we should all make an excursion to the valley of Chamounix. I had been there before, but Elizabeth and Ernest never had; and both had often expressed an earnest desire to see the scenery of this place, which had been described to them as so wonderful and sublime. Accordingly we departed from Geneva on this tour about the middle of the month of August, nearly two months after the death of Justine.

The weather was uncommonly fine; and if mine had been a sorrow to be chased away by any fleeting circumstance, this excursion would certainly have had the effect intended by my father. As it was, I was somewhat interested in the scene; it sometimes lulled, although it could not extinguish my grief. During the first day we travelled in a carriage. In the morning we had seen the mountains at a distance, towards which we gradually advanced. We perceived that the valley through which we wound, and which was formed by the river Arve, whose course we followed, closed in upon us by degrees; and when the sun had set, we beheld immense mountains and precipices overhanging us on every side, and heard the sound of the river raging among rocks, and the dashing of waterfalls around.

The next day we pursued our journey upon mules; and as we ascended still higher, the valley assumed a more magnificent and astonishing character. Ruined castles hanging on the precipices of piny mountains; the impetuous Arve, and cottages every here and there peeping forth from among the trees, formed a scene of singular beauty. But it was augmented and rendered sublime by the mighty Alps, whose white and shining pyramids and domes towered above all, as belonging to another earth, the habitations of another race of beings.

We passed the bridge of Pelissier, where the ravine, which the river forms, opened before us, and we began to ascend the mountain that overhangs it. Soon after we entered the valley of Chamounix. This valley is more wonderful and sublime, but not so beautiful and picturesque as that of Servox, through which we had just passed. The high and snowy mountains were its immediate boundaries; but we saw no more ruined castles and fertile fields. Immense glaciers approached the road; we heard the rumbling thunder of the falling avalanche, and marked the smoke of its passage. Mont Blanc, the supreme and magnificent Mont Blanc, raised itself from the surrounding *aiguilles*, and its tremendous *dome* overlooked the valley.

During this journey, I sometimes joined Elizabeth, and exerted myself to point out to her the various beauties of the scene. I often suffered my mule to lag behind, and indulged in the misery of reflection. At other times I spurred on the animal before my companions, that I might forget them, the world, and, more than all, myself. When at a distance, I alighted, and threw myself on the grass, weighed down by horror and despair. At eight in the evening I arrived at Chamounix. My father and Elizabeth were very much fatigued; Ernest, who accompanied us, was delighted, and in high spirits:

the only circumstance that detracted from his pleasure was the south wind, and the rain it seemed to promise for the next day.

We retired early to our apartments, but not to sleep; at least I did not. I remained many hours at the window, watching the pallid lightning that played above Mont Blanc, and listening to the rushing of the Arve, which ran below my window.

CHAPTER IX

The next day, contrary to the prognostications of our guides, was fine, although clouded. We visited the source of the Arveiron, and rode about the valley until evening. These sublime and magnificent scenes afforded me the greatest consolation that I was capable of receiving. They elevated me from all littleness of feeling; and although they did not remove my grief, they subdued and tranquillized it. In some degree, also, they diverted my mind from the thoughts over which it had brooded for the last month. I returned in the evening, fatigued, but less unhappy, and conversed with my family with more cheerfulness than had been my custom for some time. My father was pleased, and Elizabeth overjoyed. "My dear cousin," said she, "you see what happiness you diffuse when you are happy; do not relapse again!"

The following morning the rain poured down in torrents, and thick mists hid the summits of the mountains. I rose early, but felt unusually melancholy. The rain depressed me; my old feelings recurred, and I was miserable. I knew how disappointed my father would be at this sudden change, and I wished to avoid him until I had recovered myself so far as to be enabled to conceal those feelings that overpowered me. I knew that they would remain that day at the inn; and as I had ever inured myself to rain, moisture, and cold, I resolved to go alone to the summit of Montanvert. I remembered the effect that the view of the tremendous and ever-moving glacier had produced upon my mind when I first saw it. It had then filled me with a sublime ecstacy that gave wings to the soul, and allowed it to soar from the obscure world to light and joy. The sight of the awful and majestic in nature had indeed always the effect of solemnizing my mind, and causing me to forget the passing cares of life. I determined to go alone, for I was well acquainted with the path, and the presence of another would destroy the solitary grandeur of the scene.

The ascent is precipitous, but the path is cut into continual and short windings, which enable you to surmount the perpendicularity of the mountain. It is a scene terrifically desolate. In a thousand spots the traces of the winter avalanche may be perceived, where trees lie broken and strewed on the ground; some entirely destroyed, others bent, leaning upon the jutting rocks of the mountain, or transversely upon other trees. The path, as you ascend higher, is intersected by ravines of snow, down which stones continually roll from above; one of them is particularly dangerous, as the slightest sound, such as even speaking in a loud voice, produces a concussion of air sufficient to draw destruction upon the head of the speaker. The pines are not tall or luxuriant, but they are sombre, and add an air of severity to the scene. I looked on the valley beneath; vast mists were rising from the rivers which ran through it, and curling in thick wreaths around the opposite mountains, whose summits were hid in the uniform clouds, while rain poured from the dark sky, and added to the melancholy impression I received from the objects around me. Alas! why does man boast of sensibilities superior to those apparent in the brute; it only renders them more necessary beings. If our impulses were confined to hunger, thirst, and desire, we might be nearly free; but now we are moved by every wind that blows, and a chance word or scene that that word may convey to us.

> We rest; a dream has power to poison sleep.
>   We rise; one wand'ring thought pollutes the day.
> We feel, conceive, or reason; laugh, or weep,
>   Embrace fond woe, or cast our cares away;
> It is the same: for, be it joy or sorrow,
>   The path of its departure still is free.
> Man's yesterday may ne'er be like his morrow;
>   Nought may endure but mutability!

It was nearly noon when I arrived at the top of the ascent. For some time I sat upon the rock that overlooks the sea of ice. A mist covered both that and the surrounding mountains. Presently a breeze dissipated the cloud, and I descended upon the glacier. The surface is very uneven, rising like the waves of a troubled sea, descending low, and interspersed by rifts that sink deep. The field of ice is almost a league in width, but I spent nearly two hours in crossing it. The opposite mountain is a bare perpendicular rock. From the side where I now stood Montanvert was exactly opposite, at the distance of a league; and above it rose Mont Blanc, in awful majesty. I remained in a recess of the rock, gazing on this wonderful and stupendous scene. The sea, or rather the vast river of ice, wound among its dependent mountains, whose ærial summits hung over its recesses. Their icy and glittering peaks shone in the sunlight over the clouds. My heart, which was before sorrowful, now swelled with something like joy; I exclaimed—"Wandering spirits, if indeed ye wander, and do not rest in your narrow beds, allow me this faint happiness, or take me, as your companion, away from the joys of life."

As I said this, I suddenly beheld the figure of a man, at some distance, advancing towards me with superhuman speed. He bounded over the crevices in the ice, among which I had walked with caution; his stature also, as he approached, seemed to exceed that of man. I was troubled: a mist came over my eyes, and I felt a faintness seize me; but I was quickly restored by the cold gale of the mountains. I perceived, as the shape came nearer, (sight tremendous and abhorred!) that it was the wretch whom I had created. I trembled with rage and horror, resolving to wait his approach, and then close with him in mortal combat. He approached; his countenance bespoke bitter anguish, combined with disdain and malignity, while its unearthly ugliness rendered it almost too horrible for human eyes. But I scarcely observed this; anger and hatred had at first deprived me of utterance, and I recovered only to overwhelm him with words expressive of furious detestation and contempt.

"Devil!" I exclaimed, "do you dare approach me? and do not you fear the fierce vengeance of my arm wreaked on your miserable head? Begone, vile insect! or rather stay, that I may trample you to dust! and, oh, that I could, with the extinction of your miserable existence, restore those victims whom you have so diabolically murdered!"

"I expected this reception," said the dæmon. "All men hate the wretched; how then must I be hated, who am miserable beyond all living things! Yet you, my creator, detest and spurn me, thy creature, to whom thou art bound by ties only dissoluble by the annihilation of one of us. You purpose to kill me. How dare you sport thus with life? Do your duty towards me, and I will do mine towards you and the rest of mankind. If you will comply with my conditions, I will leave them and you at peace; but if you refuse, I will glut the maw of death, until it be satiated with the blood of your remaining friends."

"Abhorred monster! fiend that thou art! the tortures of hell are too mild a vengeance for thy crimes. Wretched devil! you reproach me with your creation; come on then, that I may extinguish the spark which I so negligently bestowed."

My rage was without bounds; I sprang on him, impelled by all the feelings which can arm one being against the existence of another.

He easily eluded me, and said,

"Be calm! I entreat you to hear me, before you give vent to your hatred on my devoted head. Have I not suffered enough, that you seek to increase my misery? Life, although it may only be an accumulation of anguish, is dear to me, and I will defend it. Remember, thou hast made me more powerful than thyself; my height is superior to thine; my joints more supple. But I will not be tempted to set myself in opposition to thee. I am thy creature, and I will be even mild and docile to my natural lord and king, if thou wilt also perform thy part, the which thou owest me. Oh, Frankenstein, be not equitable to every other, and trample upon me alone, to whom thy justice, and even thy clemency and affection, is most due. Remember, that I am thy creature: I ought to be thy Adam; but I am rather the fallen angel, whom thou drivest from joy for no misdeed. Every where I see bliss, from which I alone am irrevocably excluded. I was benevolent and good; misery made me a fiend. Make me happy, and I shall again be virtuous."

"Begone! I will not hear you. There can be no community between you and me; we are enemies. Begone, or let us try our strength in a fight, in which one must fall."

"How can I move thee? Will no entreaties cause thee to turn a favourable eye upon thy creature, who implores thy goodness and compassion. Believe me, Frankenstein: I was benevolent; my soul glowed with love and humanity: but am I not alone, miserably alone? You, my creator, abhor me; what hope can I gather from your fellow-creatures, who owe me nothing? they spurn and hate me. The desert mountains and dreary glaciers are my refuge. I have wandered here many days; the caves of ice, which I only do not fear, are a dwelling to me, and the only one which man does not grudge. These bleak skies I hail, for they are kinder to me than your fellow-beings. If the multitude of mankind knew of my existence, they would do as you do, and arm themselves for my destruction. Shall I not then hate them who abhor me? I will keep no terms with my enemies. I am miserable, and they shall share my wretchedness. Yet it is in your power to recompense me, and deliver them from an evil which it only remains for you to make so great, that not only you and your family, but thousands of others, shall be swallowed up in the whirlwinds of its rage. Let your compassion be moved, and do not disdain me. Listen to my tale: when you have heard that, abandon or commiserate me, as you shall judge that I deserve. But hear me. The guilty are allowed, by human laws, bloody as they may be, to speak in their own defence before they are condemned. Listen to me, Frankenstein. You accuse me of murder; and yet you would, with a satisfied conscience, destroy your own creature. Oh, praise the eternal justice of man! Yet I ask you not to spare me: listen to me; and then, if you can, and if you will, destroy the work of your hands."

"Why do you call to my remembrance circumstances of which I shudder to reflect, that I have been the miserable origin and author? Cursed be the day, abhorred devil, in which you first saw light! Cursed (although I curse myself) be the hands that formed you! You have made me wretched beyond expression. You have left me no power to consider whether I am just to you, or not. Begone! relieve me from the sight of your detested form."

"Thus I relieve thee, my creator," he said, and placed his hated hands before my eyes, which I flung from me with violence; "thus I take from thee a sight which you abhor. Still thou canst listen to me, and grant me thy compassion. By the virtues that I once possessed, I demand this from you. Hear my tale; it is long and strange, and the temperature of this place is not fitting to your fine sensations; come to the hut upon the mountain. The sun is yet high in the heavens; before it descends to hide itself behind yon snowy precipices, and illuminate another world, you will have heard my story, and can decide. On you it rests, whether I quit for ever the neighbourhood of man, and lead a harmless life, or become the scourge of your fellow-creatures, and the author of your own speedy ruin."

As he said this, he led the way across the ice: I followed. My heart was full, and I did not answer him; but, as I proceeded, I weighed the various arguments that he had used, and determined at least to listen to his tale. I was partly urged by curiosity, and compassion confirmed my resolution. I had hitherto supposed him to be the murderer of my brother, and I eagerly sought a confirmation or denial of this opinion. For the first time, also, I felt what the duties of a creator towards his creature were, and that I ought to render him happy before I complained of his wickedness. These motives urged me to comply with his demand. We crossed the ice, therefore, and ascended the opposite rock. The air was cold, and the rain again began to descend: we entered the hut, the fiend with an air of exultation, I with a heavy heart, and depressed spirits. But I consented to listen; and, seating myself by the fire which my odious companion had lighted, he thus began his tale.

CHAPTER X

"It is with considerable difficulty that I remember the original æra of my being: all the events of that period appear confused and indistinct. A strange multiplicity of sensations seized me, and I saw, felt, heard, and smelt, at the same time; and it was, indeed, a long time before I learned to distinguish between the operations of my various senses. By degrees, I remember, a stronger light pressed upon my nerves, so that I was obliged to shut my eyes. Darkness then came over me, and troubled me; but hardly had I felt this, when, by opening my eyes, as I now suppose, the light poured in upon me again. I walked, and, I believe, descended; but I presently found a great alteration in my sensations. Before, dark and opaque bodies had surrounded me, impervious to my touch or sight; but I now found that I could wander on at liberty, with no obstacles which I could not either surmount or avoid. The light became more and more oppressive to me; and, the heat wearying me as I walked, I sought a place where I could receive shade. This was the forest near Ingolstadt; and here I lay by the side of a brook resting from my fatigue, until I felt tormented by hunger and thirst. This roused me from my nearly dormant state, and I ate some berries which I found hanging on the trees, or lying on the ground. I slaked my thirst at the brook; and then lying down, was overcome by sleep.

"It was dark when I awoke; I felt cold also, and half-frightened as it were instinctively, finding myself so desolate. Before I had quitted your apartment, on a sensation of cold, I had covered myself with some clothes; but these were insufficient to secure me from the dews of night. I was a poor, helpless, miserable wretch; I knew, and could distinguish, nothing; but, feeling pain invade me on all sides, I sat down and wept.

"Soon a gentle light stole over the heavens, and gave me a sensation of pleasure. I started up, and beheld a radiant form rise from among the trees. I gazed with a kind of wonder. It moved slowly, but it enlightened my path; and I again went out in search of berries. I was still cold, when under one of the trees I found a huge cloak, with which I covered myself, and sat down upon the ground. No distinct ideas occupied my mind; all was confused. I felt light, and hunger, and thirst, and darkness; innumerable sounds rung in my ears, and on all sides various scents saluted me: the only object that I could distinguish was the bright moon, and I fixed my eyes on that with pleasure.

"Several changes of day and night passed, and the orb of night had greatly lessened when I began to distinguish my sensations from each other. I gradually saw plainly the clear stream that supplied me with drink, and the trees that shaded me with their foliage. I was delighted when I first discovered that a pleasant sound, which often saluted my ears, proceeded from the throats of the little winged animals who had often intercepted the light from my eyes. I began also to observe, with greater accuracy, the forms that surrounded me, and to perceive the boundaries of the radiant roof of light which canopied me. Sometimes I tried to imitate the pleasant songs of the birds, but was unable. Sometimes I wished to express my sensations in my own mode, but the uncouth and inarticulate sounds which broke from me frightened me into silence again.

"The moon had disappeared from the night, and again, with a lessened form, shewed itself, while I still remained in the forest. My sensations had, by this time, become distinct, and my mind received every day additional ideas. My eyes became accustomed to the light, and to perceive objects in their right forms; I distinguished the insect from the herb, and, by degrees, one herb from another. I found that the sparrow uttered none but harsh notes, whilst those of the blackbird and thrush were sweet and enticing.

"One day, when I was oppressed by cold, I found a fire which had been left by some wandering beggars, and was overcome with delight at the warmth I experienced from it. In my joy I thrust my hand into the live embers, but quickly drew it out again with a cry of pain. How strange, I thought, that the same cause should produce such opposite effects! I examined the materials of the fire, and to my joy found it to be composed of wood. I quickly collected some branches; but they were wet, and would not burn. I was pained at this, and sat still watching the operation of the fire. The wet wood which I had placed near the heat dried, and itself became inflamed. I reflected on this; and, by touching the various branches, I discovered the cause, and busied myself in collecting a great quantity of wood, that I might dry it, and have a plentiful supply of fire. When night came on, and brought sleep with it, I was in the greatest fear lest my fire should be extinguished. I covered it carefully with dry wood and leaves, and placed wet branches upon it; and then, spreading my cloak, I lay on the ground, and sunk into sleep.

"It was morning when I awoke, and my first care was to visit the fire. I uncovered it, and a gentle breeze quickly fanned it into a flame. I observed this also, and contrived a fan of branches, which roused the embers when they were nearly extinguished. When night came again, I found, with pleasure, that the fire gave light as well as heat; and that the discovery of this element was useful to me in my food; for I found some of the offals that the travellers had left had been roasted, and tasted much more savoury than the berries I gathered from the trees. I tried, therefore, to dress my food in the same manner, placing it on the live embers. I found that the berries were spoiled by this operation, and the nuts and roots much improved.

"Food, however, became scarce; and I often spent the whole day searching in vain for a few acorns to assuage the pangs of hunger. When I found this, I resolved to quit the place that I had hitherto inhabited, to seek for one where the few wants I experienced would be more easily satisfied. In this emigration, I exceedingly lamented the loss of the fire which I had obtained through accident, and knew not how to reproduce it. I gave several hours to the serious consideration of this difficulty; but I was obliged to relinquish all attempt to supply it; and, wrapping myself up in my cloak, I struck across the wood towards the setting sun. I passed three days in these rambles, and at length discovered the open country. A great fall of snow had taken place the night before, and the fields were of one uniform white; the appearance was disconsolate, and I found my feet chilled by the cold damp substance that covered the ground.

"It was about seven in the morning, and I longed to obtain food and shelter; at length I perceived a small hut, on a rising ground, which had doubtless been built for the convenience of some shepherd. This was a new sight to me; and I examined the structure with great curiosity. Finding the door open, I entered. An old man sat in it, near a fire, over which he was preparing his breakfast. He turned on hearing a noise; and, perceiving me, shrieked loudly, and, quitting the hut, ran across the fields with a speed of which his debilitated form hardly appeared capable. His appearance, different from any I had ever before seen, and his flight, somewhat surprised me. But I was enchanted by the appearance of the hut: here the snow and rain could not penetrate; the ground was dry; and it presented to me then as exquisite and divine a retreat as Pandæmonium appeared to the dæmons of hell after their sufferings in the lake of fire. I greedily devoured the remnants of the shepherd's breakfast, which consisted of bread, cheese, milk, and wine; the latter, however, I did not like. Then overcome by fatigue, I lay down among some straw, and fell asleep.

"It was noon when I awoke; and, allured by the warmth of the sun, which shone brightly on the white ground, I determined to recommence my travels; and, depositing the remains of the peasant's breakfast in a wallet I found, I proceeded across the fields for several hours, until at sunset I arrived at a village. How miraculous did this appear! the huts, the neater cottages, and stately houses, engaged my admiration by turns. The vegetables in the gardens, the milk and cheese that I saw placed at the windows of some of the cottages, allured my appetite. One of the best of these I entered; but I had hardly placed my foot within the door, before the children shrieked, and one of the women fainted. The whole village was roused; some fled, some attacked me, until, grievously bruised by stones and many other kinds of missile weapons, I escaped to the open country, and fearfully took refuge in a low hovel, quite bare, and making a wretched appearance after the palaces I had beheld in the village. This hovel, however, joined a cottage of a neat and pleasant appearance; but, after my late dearly-bought experience, I dared not enter it. My place of refuge was constructed of wood, but so low, that I could with difficulty sit upright in it. No wood, however, was placed on the earth, which formed the floor, but it was dry; and although the wind entered it by innumerable chinks, I found it an agreeable asylum from the snow and rain.

"Here then I retreated, and lay down, happy to have found a shelter, however miserable, from the inclemency of the season, and still more from the barbarity of man.

"As soon as morning dawned, I crept from my kennel, that I might view the adjacent cottage, and discover if I could remain in the habitation I had found. It was situated against the back of the cottage, and surrounded on the sides which were exposed by a pig-stye and a clear pool of water. One part was open, and by that I had crept in; but now I covered every crevice by which I might be perceived with stones and wood, yet in such a manner that I might move them on occasion to pass out: all the light I enjoyed came through the stye, and that was sufficient for me.

"Having thus arranged my dwelling, and carpeted it with clean straw, I retired; for I saw the figure of a man at a distance, and I remembered too well my treatment the night before, to trust myself in his power. I had first, however, provided for my sustenance for that day, by a loaf of coarse bread, which I purloined, and a cup with which I could drink, more conveniently than from my hand, of the pure water which flowed by my retreat. The floor was a little raised, so that it was kept perfectly dry, and by its vicinity to the chimney of the cottage it was tolerably warm.

"Being thus provided, I resolved to reside in this hovel, until something should occur which might alter my determination. It was indeed a paradise, compared to the bleak forest, my former residence, the rain-dropping branches, and dank earth. I ate my breakfast with pleasure, and was about to remove a plank to procure myself a little water, when I heard a step, and, looking through a small chink, I beheld a young creature, with a pail on her head, passing before my hovel. The girl was young and of gentle demeanour, unlike what I have since found cottagers and farm-house servants to be. Yet she was meanly dressed, a coarse blue petticoat and a linen jacket being her only garb; her fair hair was plaited, but not adorned; she looked patient, yet sad. I lost sight of her; and in about a quarter of an hour she returned, bearing the pail, which was now partly filled with milk. As she walked along, seemingly incommoded by the burden, a young man met her, whose countenance expressed a deeper despondence. Uttering a few sounds with an air of melancholy, he took the pail from her head, and bore it to the cottage himself. She followed, and they disappeared. Presently I saw the young man again, with some tools in his hand, cross the field behind the cottage; and the girl was also busied, sometimes in the house, and sometimes in the yard.

"On examining my dwelling, I found that one of the windows of the cottage had formerly occupied a part of it, but the panes had been filled up with wood. In one of these was a small and almost imperceptible chink, through which the eye could just penetrate. Through this crevice, a small room was visible, white-washed and clean, but very bare of furniture. In one corner, near a small fire, sat an old man, leaning his head on his hands in a disconsolate attitude. The young girl was occupied in arranging the cottage; but presently she took something out of a drawer, which employed her hands, and she sat down beside the old man, who, taking up an instrument, began to play, and to produce sounds, sweeter than the voice of the thrush or the nightingale. It was a lovely sight, even to me, poor wretch! who had never beheld aught beautiful before. The silver hair and benevolent countenance of the aged cottager, won my reverence; while the gentle manners of the girl enticed my love. He played a sweet mournful air, which I perceived drew tears from the eyes of his amiable companion, of which the old man took no notice, until she sobbed audibly; he then pronounced a few sounds, and the fair creature, leaving her work, knelt at his feet. He raised her, and smiled with such kindness and affection, that I felt sensations of a peculiar and overpowering nature: they were a mixture of pain and pleasure, such as I had never before experienced, either from hunger or cold, warmth or food; and I withdrew from the window, unable to bear these emotions.

"Soon after this the young man returned, bearing on his shoulders a load of wood. The girl met him at the door, helped to relieve him of his burden, and, taking some of the fuel into the cottage, placed it on the fire; then she and the youth went apart into a nook of the cottage, and he shewed her a large loaf and a piece of cheese. She seemed pleased; and went into the garden for some roots and plants, which she placed in water, and then upon the fire. She afterwards continued her work, whilst the young man went into the garden, and appeared busily employed in digging and pulling up roots. After he had been employed thus about an hour, the young woman joined him, and they entered the cottage together.

"The old man had, in the mean time, been pensive; but, on the appearance of his companions, he assumed a more cheerful air, and they sat down to eat. The meal was quickly dispatched. The young woman was again occupied in arranging the cottage; the old man walked before the cottage in the sun for a few minutes, leaning on the arm of the youth. Nothing could exceed in beauty the contrast between these two excellent creatures. One was old, with silver hairs and a countenance beaming with benevolence and love: the younger was slight and graceful in his figure, and his features were moulded with the finest symmetry; yet his eyes and attitude expressed the utmost sadness and despondency. The old man returned to the cottage; and the youth, with tools different from those he had used in the morning, directed his steps across the fields.

"Night quickly shut in; but, to my extreme wonder, I found that the cottagers had a means of prolonging light, by the use of tapers, and was delighted to find, that the setting of the sun did not put an end to the pleasure I experienced in watching my human neighbours. In the evening, the young girl and her companion were employed in various occupations which I did not understand; and the old man again took up the instrument, which produced the divine sounds that had enchanted me in the morning. So soon as he had finished, the youth began, not to play, but to utter sounds that were monotonous, and neither resembling the harmony of the old man's instrument or the songs of the birds; I since found that he read aloud, but at that time I knew nothing of the science of words or letters.

"The family, after having been thus occupied for a short time, extinguished their lights, and retired, as I conjectured, to rest."

CHAPTER XI

"I LAY ON MY STRAW, BUT I COULD NOT SLEEP. I THOUGHT OF THE OCCURRENCES OF the day. What chiefly struck me was the gentle manners of these people; and I longed to join them, but dared not. I remembered too well the treatment I had suffered the night before from the barbarous villagers, and resolved, whatever course of conduct I might hereafter think it right to pursue, that for the present I would remain quietly in my hovel, watching, and endeavouring to discover the motives which influenced their actions.

"The cottagers arose the next morning before the sun. The young woman arranged the cottage, and prepared the food; and the youth departed after the first meal.

"This day was passed in the same routine as that which preceded it. The young man was constantly employed out of doors, and the girl in various laborious occupations within. The old man, whom I soon perceived to be blind, employed his leisure hours on his instrument, or in contemplation. Nothing could exceed the love and respect which the younger cottagers exhibited towards their venerable companion.

They performed towards him every little office of affection and duty with gentleness; and he rewarded them by his benevolent smiles.

"They were not entirely happy. The young man and his companion often went apart, and appeared to weep. I saw no cause for their unhappiness; but I was deeply affected by it. If such lovely creatures were miserable, it was less strange that I, an imperfect and solitary being, should be wretched. Yet why were these gentle beings unhappy? They possessed a delightful house (for such it was in my eyes), and every luxury; they had a fire to warm them when chill, and delicious viands when hungry; they were dressed in excellent clothes; and, still more, they enjoyed one another's company and speech, interchanging each day looks of affection and kindness. What did their tears imply? Did they really express pain? I was at first unable to solve these questions; but perpetual attention, and time, explained to me many appearances which were at first enigmatic.

"A considerable period elapsed before I discovered one of the causes of the uneasiness of this amiable family; it was poverty: and they suffered that evil in a very distressing degree. Their nourishment consisted entirely of the vegetables of their garden, and the milk of one cow, who gave very little during the winter, when its masters could scarcely procure food to support it. They often, I believe, suffered the pangs of hunger very poignantly, especially the two younger cottagers; for several times they placed food before the old man, when they reserved none for themselves.

"This trait of kindness moved me sensibly. I had been accustomed, during the night, to steal a part of their store for my own consumption; but when I found that in doing this I inflicted pain on the cottagers, I abstained, and satisfied myself with berries, nuts, and roots, which I gathered from a neighbouring wood.

"I discovered also another means through which I was enabled to assist their labours. I found that the youth spent a great part of each day in collecting wood for the family fire; and, during the night, I often took his tools, the use of which I quickly discovered, and brought home firing sufficient for the consumption of several days.

"I remember, the first time that I did this, the young woman, when she opened the door in the morning, appeared greatly astonished on seeing a great pile of wood on the outside. She uttered some words in a loud voice, and the youth joined her, who also expressed surprise. I observed, with pleasure, that he did not go to the forest that day, but spent it in repairing the cottage and cultivating the garden.

"By degrees I made a discovery of still greater moment. I found that these people possessed a method of communicating their experience and feelings to one another by articulate sounds. I perceived that the words they spoke sometimes produced pleasure or pain, smiles or sadness, in the minds and countenances of the hearers. This was indeed a godlike science, and I ardently desired to become acquainted with it. But I was baffled in every attempt I made for this purpose. Their pronunciation was quick; and the words they uttered, not having any apparent connexion with visible objects, I was unable to discover any clue by which I could unravel the mystery of their reference. By great application, however, and after having remained during the space of several revolutions of the moon in my hovel, I discovered the names that were given to some of the most familiar objects of discourse: I learned and applied the words *fire*, *milk*, *bread*, and *wood*. I learned also the names of the cottagers themselves. The youth and his companion had each of them several names, but the old man had only one, which was *father*. The girl was called *sister*, or *Agatha*; and the youth *Felix*, *brother*, or *son*. I cannot describe the delight I felt when I learned the ideas appropriated to each of these sounds, and was able to pronounce them. I distinguished several other words, without being able as yet to understand or apply them; such as *good*, *dearest*, *unhappy*.

"I spent the winter in this manner. The gentle manners and beauty of the cottagers greatly endeared them to me: when they were unhappy, I felt depressed; when they rejoiced, I sympathized in their joys. I saw few human beings beside them; and if any other happened to enter the cottage, their harsh manners and rude gait only enhanced to me the superior accomplishments of my friends. The old man, I could perceive, often endeavoured to encourage his children, as sometimes I found that he called them, to cast off their melancholy. He would talk in a cheerful accent, with an expression of goodness that bestowed pleasure even upon me. Agatha listened with respect, her eyes sometimes filled with tears, which she endeavoured to wipe away unperceived; but I generally found that her countenance and tone were more cheerful after having listened to the exhortations of her father. It was not thus with Felix. He was always the saddest of the groupe; and, even to my unpractised senses, he appeared to have suffered more deeply than his friends. But if his countenance was more sorrowful, his voice was more cheerful than that of his sister, especially when he addressed the old man.

"I could mention innumerable instances, which, although slight, marked the dispositions of these amiable cottagers. In the midst of poverty and want, Felix carried with pleasure to his sister the first little white flower that peeped out from beneath the snowy ground. Early in the morning before she had risen, he cleared away the snow that obstructed her path to the milk-house, drew water from the well, and brought the wood from the outhouse, where, to his perpetual astonishment, he found his store always replenished by an invisible hand. In the day, I believe, he worked sometimes for a neighbouring farmer, because he often went forth, and did not return until dinner, yet brought no wood with him. At other times he worked in the garden; but, as there was little to do in the frosty season, he read to the old man and Agatha.

"This reading had puzzled me extremely at first; but, by degrees, I discovered that he uttered many of the same sounds when he read as when he talked. I conjectured, therefore, that he found on the paper signs for speech which he understood, and I ardently longed to comprehend these also; but how was that possible, when I did not even understand the sounds for which they stood as signs? I improved, however, sensibly in this science, but not sufficiently to follow up any kind of conversation, although I applied for my whole mind to the endeavour: for I easily perceived that, although I eagerly longed to discover myself to the cottagers, I ought not to make the attempt until I had first become master of their language; which knowledge might enable me to make them overlook the deformity of my figure; for with this also the contrast perpetually presented to my eyes had made me acquainted.

"I had admired the perfect forms of my cottagers—their grace, beauty, and delicate complexions: but how was I terrified, when I viewed myself in a transparent pool! At first I started back, unable to believe that it was indeed I who was reflected in the mirror; and when I became fully convinced that I was in reality the monster that I am, I was filled with the bitterest sensations of despondence and mortification. Alas! I did not yet entirely know the fatal effects of this miserable deformity.

"As the sun became warmer, and the light of day longer, the snow vanished, and I beheld the bare trees and the black earth. From this time Felix was more employed; and the heart-moving indications of impending famine disappeared. Their food, as I afterwards found, was coarse, but it was wholesome; and they procured a sufficiency of it. Several new kinds of plants sprung up in the garden, which they dressed; and these signs of comfort increased daily as the season advanced.

"The old man, leaning on his son, walked each day at noon, when it did not rain, as I found it was called when the heavens poured forth its waters. This frequently took place; but a high wind quickly dried the earth, and the season became far more pleasant than it had been.

"My mode of life in my hovel was uniform. During the morning I attended the motions of the cottagers; and when they were dispersed in various occupations, I slept: the remainder of the day was spent in observing my friends. When they had retired to rest, if there was any moon, or the night was starlight, I went into the woods, and

collected my own food and fuel for the cottage. When I returned, as often as it was necessary, I cleared their path from the snow, and performed those offices that I had seen done
by Felix. I afterwards found that these labours, performed by an invisible hand, greatly
astonished them; and once or twice I heard them, on these occasions, utter the words
good spirit, wonderful; but I did not then understand the signification of these terms.

"My thoughts now became more active, and I longed to discover the motives and
feelings of these lovely creatures; I was inquisitive to know why Felix appeared so miserable, and Agatha so sad. I thought (foolish wretch!) that it might be in my power to
restore happiness to these deserving people. When I slept, or was absent, the forms of
the venerable blind father, the gentle Agatha, and the excellent Felix, flitted before me.
I looked upon them as superior beings, who would be the arbiters of my future destiny.
I formed in my imagination a thousand pictures of presenting myself to them, and their
reception of me. I imagined that they would be disgusted, until, by my gentle demeanour and conciliating words, I should first win their favour, and afterwards their love.

"These thoughts exhilarated me, and led me to apply with fresh ardour to the
acquiring the art of language. My organs were indeed harsh, but supple; and although
my voice was very unlike the soft music of their tones, yet I pronounced such words as
I understood with tolerable ease. It was as the ass and the lap-dog; yet surely the gentle
ass, whose intentions were affectionate, although his manners were rude, deserved
better treatment than blows and execration.

"The pleasant showers and genial warmth of spring greatly altered the aspect of
the earth. Men, who before this change seemed to have been hid in caves, dispersed
themselves, and were employed in various arts of cultivation. The birds sang in more
cheerful notes, and the leaves began to bud forth on the trees. Happy, happy earth! fit
habitation for gods, which, so short a time before, was bleak, damp, and unwholesome.
My spirits were elevated by the enchanting appearance of nature; the past was blotted
from my memory, the present was tranquil, and the future gilded by bright rays of
hope, and anticipations of joy.

CHAPTER XII

"I now hasten to the more moving part of my story. I shall relate events
that impressed me with feelings which, from what I was, have made me what I am.

"Spring advanced rapidly; the weather became fine, and the skies cloudless. It surprised me, that what before was desert and gloomy should now bloom with the most

beautiful flowers and verdure. My senses were gratified and refreshed by a thousand scents of delight, and a thousand sights of beauty.

"It was on one of these days, when my cottagers periodically rested from labour—the old man played on his guitar, and the children listened to him—I observed that the countenance of Felix was melancholy beyond expression: he sighed frequently; and once his father paused in his music, and I conjectured by his manner that he inquired the cause of his son's sorrow. Felix replied in a cheerful accent, and the old man was recommencing his music, when some one tapped at the door.

"It was a lady on horseback, accompanied by a countryman as a guide. The lady was dressed in a dark suit, and covered with a thick black veil. Agatha asked a question; to which the stranger only replied by pronouncing, in a sweet accent, the name of Felix. Her voice was musical, but unlike that of either of my friends. On hearing this word, Felix came up hastily to the lady; who, when she saw him, threw up her veil, and I beheld a countenance of angelic beauty and expression. Her hair of a shining raven black, and curiously braided; her eyes were dark, but gentle, although animated; her features of a regular proportion, and her complexion wondrously fair, each cheek tinged with a lovely pink.

"Felix seemed ravished with delight when he saw her, every trait of sorrow vanished from his face, and it instantly expressed a degree of ecstatic joy, of which I could hardly have believed it capable; his eyes sparkled, as his cheek flushed with pleasure; and at that moment I thought him as beautiful as the stranger. She appeared affected by different feelings; wiping a few tears from her lovely eyes, she held out her hand to Felix, who kissed it rapturously, and called her, as well as I could distinguish, his sweet Arabian. She did not appear to understand him, but smiled. He assisted her to dismount, and, dismissing her guide, conducted her into the cottage. Some conversation took place between him and his father; and the young stranger knelt at the old man's feet, and would have kissed his hand, but he raised her, and embraced her affectionately.

"I soon perceived, that although the stranger uttered articulate sounds, and appeared to have a language of her own, she was neither understood by, or herself understood, the cottagers. They made many signs which I did not comprehend; but I saw that her presence diffused gladness through the cottage, dispelling their sorrow as the sun dissipates the morning mists. Felix seemed peculiarly happy, and with smiles of delight welcomed his Arabian. Agatha, the ever-gentle Agatha, kissed the hands of the lovely stranger; and, pointing to her brother, made signs which appeared to me to mean that he had been sorrowful until she came. Some hours passed thus, while they, by their countenances, expressed joy, the cause of which I did not comprehend. Presently I found, by the frequent recurrence of one sound which the stranger repeated after them, that she was endeavouring to learn their language; and the idea instantly occurred to me, that I should make use of the same instructions to the same end. The stranger learned about twenty words at the first lesson, most of them indeed were those which I had before understood, but I profited by the others.

"As night came on, Agatha and the Arabian retired early. When they separated, Felix kissed the hand of the stranger, and said, 'Good night, sweet Safie.' He sat up much longer, conversing with his father; and, by the frequent repetition of her name, I conjectured that their lovely guest was the subject of their conversation. I ardently desired to understand them, and bent every faculty towards that purpose, but found it utterly impossible.

"The next morning Felix went out to his work; and, after the usual occupations of Agatha were finished, the Arabian sat at the feet of the old man, and, taking his guitar, played some airs so entrancingly beautiful, that they at once drew tears of sorrow and delight from my eyes. She sang, and her voice flowed in a rich cadence, swelling or dying away, like a nightingale of the woods.

"When she had finished, she gave the guitar to Agatha, who at first declined it. She played a simple air, and her voice accompanied it in sweet accents, but unlike the wondrous strain of the stranger. The old man appeared enraptured, and said some words, which Agatha endeavoured to explain to Safie, and by which he appeared to wish to express that she bestowed on him the greatest delight by her music.

"The days now passed as peaceably as before, with the sole alteration, that joy had taken place of sadness in the countenances of my friends. Safie was always gay and happy; she and I improved rapidly in the knowledge of language, so that in two months I began to comprehend most of the words uttered by my protectors.

"In the meanwhile also the black ground was covered with herbage, and the green banks interspersed with innumerable flowers, sweet to the scent and the eyes, stars of pale radiance among the moonlight woods; the sun became warmer, the nights clear and balmy; and my nocturnal rambles were an extreme pleasure to me, although they were considerably shortened by the late setting and early rising of the sun; for I never ventured abroad during daylight, fearful of meeting with the same treatment as I had formerly endured in the first village which I entered.

"My days were spent in close attention, that I might more speedily master the language; and I may boast that I improved more rapidly than the Arabian, who understood very little, and conversed in broken accents, whilst I comprehended and could imitate almost every word that was spoken.

"While I improved in speech, I also learned the science of letters, as it was taught to the stranger; and this opened before me a wide field for wonder and delight.

"The book from which Felix instructed Safie was Volney's *Ruins of Empires*. I should not have understood the purport of this book, had not Felix, in reading it, given very minute explanations. He had chosen this work, he said, because the declamatory style was framed in imitation of the eastern authors. Through this work I obtained a cursory knowledge of history, and a view of the several empires at present existing in the world; it gave me an insight into the manners, governments, and religions of the different nations of the earth. I heard of the slothful Asiatics; of the stupendous genius and mental activity of the Grecians; of the wars and wonderful virtue of the early Romans—of their subsequent degeneration—of the decline of that mighty empire; of chivalry, christianity, and kings. I heard of the discovery of the American hemisphere, and wept with Safie over the hapless fate of its original inhabitants.

"These wonderful narrations inspired me with strange feelings. Was man, indeed, at once so powerful, so virtuous, and magnificent, yet so vicious and base? He appeared at one time a mere scion of the evil principle, and at another as all that can be conceived of noble and godlike. To be a great and virtuous man appeared the highest honour that can befall a sensitive being; to be base and vicious, as many on record have been, appeared the lowest degradation, a condition more abject than that of the blind mole or harmless worm. For a long time I could not conceive how one man could go forth to murder his fellow, or even why there were laws and governments; but when I heard details of vice and bloodshed, my wonder ceased, and I turned away with disgust and loathing.

"Every conversation of the cottagers now opened new wonders to me. While I listened to the instructions which Felix bestowed upon the Arabian, the strange system of human society was explained to me. I heard of the division of property, of immense wealth and squalid poverty; of rank, descent, and noble blood.

"The words induced me to turn towards myself. I learned that the possessions most esteemed by your fellow-creatures were, high and unsullied descent united with riches. A man might be respected with only one of these acquisitions; but without either he was considered, except in very rare instances, as a vagabond and a slave, doomed to waste his powers for the profit of the chosen few. And what was I? Of my creation and creator I was absolutely ignorant; but I knew that I possessed no money, no friends, no kind of property. I was, besides, endowed with a figure hideously deformed and loathsome; I was not even of the same nature as man. I was more agile than they, and could subsist upon coarser diet; I bore the extremes of heat and cold with less injury to my frame; my stature far exceeded theirs. When I looked around, I saw and heard of none like me. Was I then a monster, a blot upon the earth, from which all men fled, and whom all men disowned?

"I cannot describe to you the agony that these reflections inflicted upon me; I tried to dispel them, but sorrow only increased with knowledge. Oh, that I had for ever remained in my native wood, nor known or felt beyond the sensations of hunger, thirst, and heat!

"Of what a strange nature is knowledge! It clings to the mind, when it has once seized on it, like a lichen on the rock. I wished sometimes to shake off all thought and feeling; but I learned that there was but one means to overcome the sensation of pain, and that was death—a state which I feared yet did not understand. I admired virtue and good feelings, and loved the gentle manners and amiable qualities of my cottagers; but I was shut out from intercourse with them, except through means which I obtained by stealth, when I was unseen and unknown, and which rather increased than satisfied the desire I had of becoming one among my fellows. The gentle words of Agatha, and the animated smiles of the charming Arabian, were not for me. The mild exhortations of the old man, and the lively conversation of the loved Felix, were not for me. Miserable, unhappy wretch!

"Other lessons were impressed upon me even more deeply. I heard of the difference of sexes; of the birth and growth of children; how the father doated on the smiles of the infant, and the lively sallies of the older child; how all the life and cares of the mother were wrapt up in the precious charge; how the mind of youth expanded and gained knowledge; of brother, sister, and all the various relationships which bind one human being to another in mutual bonds.

"But where were my friends and relations? No father had watched my infant days, no mother had blessed me with smiles and caresses; or if they had, all my past life was now a blot, a blind vacancy in which I distinguished nothing. From my earliest remembrance I had been as I then was in height and proportion. I had never yet seen a being resembling me, or who claimed any intercourse with me. What was I? The question again recurred, to be answered only with groans.

"I will soon explain to what these feelings tended; but allow me now to return to the cottagers, whose story excited in me such various feelings of indignation, delight, and wonder, but which all terminated in additional love and reverence for my protectors (for so I loved, in an innocent, half painful self-deceit, to call them).

CHAPTER XIII

"SOME TIME ELAPSED BEFORE I LEARNED THE HISTORY OF MY FRIENDS. IT WAS ONE which could not fail to impress itself deeply on my mind, unfolding as it did a number of circumstances each interesting and wonderful to one so utterly inexperienced as I was.

"The name of the old man was De Lacey. He was descended from a good family in France, where he had lived for many years in affluence, respected by his superiors, and beloved by his equals. His son was bred in the service of his country; and Agatha had ranked with ladies of the highest distinction. A few months before my arrival, they had lived in a large and luxurious city, called Paris, surrounded by friends, and possessed of every enjoyment which virtue, refinement of intellect, or taste, accompanied by a moderate fortune, could afford.

"The father of Safie had been the cause of their ruin. He was a Turkish merchant, and had inhabited Paris for many years, when, for some reason which I could not learn, he became obnoxious to the government. He was seized and cast into prison the very day that Safie arrived from Constantinople to join him. He was tried, and condemned to death. The injustice of his sentence was very flagrant; all Paris was indignant; and it was judged that his religion and wealth, rather than the crime alleged against him, had been the cause of his condemnation.

"Felix had been present at the trial; his horror and indignation were uncontrollable, when he heard the decision of the court. He made, at that moment, a solemn vow to deliver him, and then looked around for the means. After many fruitless attempts to gain admittance to the prison, he found a strongly grated window in an unguarded part of the building, which lighted the dungeon of the unfortunate Mahometan; who, loaded with chains, waited in despair the execution of the barbarous sentence. Felix visited the grate at night, and made known to the prisoner his intentions in his favour. The Turk, amazed and delighted, endeavoured to kindle the zeal of his deliverer by promises of reward and wealth. Felix rejected his offers with contempt; yet when he saw the lovely Safie, who was allowed to visit her father, and who, by her gestures, expressed her lively gratitude, the youth could not help owning to his own mind, that the captive possessed a treasure which would fully reward his toil and hazard.

"The Turk quickly perceived the impression that his daughter had made on the heart of Felix, and endeavoured to secure him more entirely in his interests by the promise of her hand in marriage, so soon as he should be conveyed to a place of safety. Felix was too delicate to accept this offer; yet he looked forward to the probability of that event as to the consummation of his happiness.

"During the ensuing days, while the preparations were going forward for the escape of the merchant, the zeal of Felix was warmed by several letters that he received from this lovely girl, who found means to express her thoughts in the language of her lover by the aid of an old man, a servant of her father's, who understood French. She thanked him in the most ardent terms for his intended services towards her father; and at the same time she gently deplored her own fate.

"I have copies of these letters; for I found means, during my residence in the hovel, to procure the implements of writing; and the letters were often in the hands of Felix or Agatha. Before I depart, I will give them to you, they will prove the truth of my tale; but at present, as the sun is already far declined, I shall only have time to repeat the substance of them to you.

"Safie related, that her mother was a Christian Arab, seized and made a slave by the Turks; recommended by her beauty, she had won the heart of the father of Safie, who married her. The young girl spoke in high and enthusiastic terms of her mother, who, born in freedom spurned the bondage to which she was now reduced. She instructed her daughter in the tenets of her religion, and taught her to aspire to higher powers of intellect, and an independence of spirit, forbidden to the female followers of Mahomet. This lady died; but her lessons were indelibly impressed on the mind of Safie, who sickened at the prospect of again returning to Asia, and the being immured within the walls of a haram, allowed only to occupy herself with puerile amusements, ill suited to the temper of her soul, now accustomed to grand ideas and a noble emulation for virtue. The prospect of marrying a Christian, and remaining in a country where women were allowed to take a rank in society, was enchanting to her.

"The day for the execution of the Turk was fixed; but, on the night previous to it, he had quitted prison, and before morning was distant many leagues from Paris. Felix had procured passports in the name of his father, sister, and himself. He had previously communicated his plan to the former, who aided the deceit by quitting his house, under the pretence of a journey, and concealed himself, with his daughter, in an obscure part of Paris.

"Felix conducted the fugitives through France to Lyons, and across Mont Cenis to Leghorn, where the merchant had decided to wait a favourable opportunity of passing into some part of the Turkish dominions.

"Safie resolved to remain with her father until the moment of his departure, before which time the Turk renewed his promise that she should be united to his deliverer; and Felix remained with them in expectation of that event; and in the mean time he enjoyed the society of the Arabian, who exhibited towards him the simplest and tenderest affection. They conversed with one another through the means of an interpreter, and sometimes with the interpretation of looks; and Safie sang to him the divine airs of her native country.

"The Turk allowed this intimacy to take place, and encouraged the hopes of the youthful lovers, while in his heart he had formed far other plans. He loathed the idea that his daughter should be united to a Christian; but he feared the resentment of Felix if he should appear lukewarm; for he knew that he was still in the power of his deliverer, if he should choose to betray him to the Italian state which they inhabited. He revolved a thousand plans by which he should be enabled to prolong the deceit until it might be no longer necessary, and secretly to take his daughter with him when he departed. His plans were greatly facilitated by the news which arrived from Paris.

"The government of France were greatly enraged at the escape of their victim, and spared no pains to detect and punish his deliverer. The plot of Felix was quickly discovered, and De Lacey and Agatha were thrown into prison. The news reached Felix, and roused him from his dream of pleasure. His blind and aged father, and his gentle sister, lay in a noisome dungeon, while he enjoyed the free air, and the society of her whom he loved. This idea was torture to him. He quickly arranged with the Turk, that if the latter should find a favourable opportunity for escape before Felix could return to Italy, Safie should remain as a boarder at a convent at Leghorn; and then, quitting the lovely Arabian, he hastened to Paris, and delivered himself up to the vengeance of the law, hoping to free De Lacey and Agatha by this proceeding.

"He did not succeed. They remained confined for five months before the trial took place; the result of which deprived them of their fortune, and condemned them to a perpetual exile from their native country.

"They found a miserable asylum in the cottage in Germany, where I discovered them. Felix soon learned that the treacherous Turk, for whom he and his family endured such unheard-of oppression, on discovering that his deliverer was thus reduced to poverty and impotence, became a traitor to good feeling and honour, and had quitted Italy with his daughter, insultingly sending Felix a pittance of money to aid him, as he said, in some plan of future maintenance.

"Such were the events that preyed on the heart of Felix, and rendered him, when I first saw him, the most miserable of his family. He could have endured poverty, and when this distress had been the meed of his virtue, he would have gloried in it: but the ingratitude of the Turk, and the loss of his beloved Safie, were misfortunes more bitter and irreparable. The arrival of the Arabian now infused new life into his soul.

"When the news reached Leghorn, that Felix was deprived of his wealth and rank, the merchant commanded his daughter to think no more of her lover, but to prepare to return with him to her native country. The generous nature of Safie was outraged by this command; she attempted to expostulate with her father, but he left her angrily, reiterating his tyrannical mandate.

"A few days after, the Turk entered his daughter's apartment, and told her hastily, that he had reason to believe that his residence at Leghorn had been divulged, and that he should speedily be delivered up to the French government; he had, consequently, hired a vessel to convey him to Constantinople, for which city he should sail in a few hours. He intended to leave his daughter under the care of a confidential servant, to follow at her leisure with the greater part of his property, which had not yet arrived at Leghorn.

"When alone, Safie resolved in her own mind the plan of conduct that it would become her to pursue in this emergency. A residence in Turkey was abhorrent to her; her religion and feelings were alike adverse to it. By some papers of her father's, which fell into her hands, she heard of the exile of her lover, and learned the name of the spot where he then resided. She hesitated some time, but at length she formed her determination. Taking with her some jewels that belonged to her, and a small sum of money, she quitted Italy, with an attendant, a native of Leghorn, but who understood the common language of Turkey, and departed for Germany.

"She arrived in safety at a town about twenty leagues from the cottage of De Lacey, when her attendant fell dangerously ill. Safie nursed her with the most devoted affection; but the poor girl died, and the Arabian was left alone, unacquainted with the language of the country, and utterly ignorant of the customs of the world. She fell, however, into good hands. The Italian had mentioned the name of the spot for which they were bound; and, after her death, the woman of the house in which they had lived took care that Safie should arrive in safety at the cottage of her lover.

CHAPTER XIV

"SUCH WAS THE HISTORY OF MY BELOVED COTTAGERS. IT IMPRESSED ME DEEPLY. I learned, from the views of social life which it developed, to admire their virtues, and to deprecate the vices of mankind.

"As yet I looked upon crime as a distant evil; benevolence and generosity were ever present before me, inciting within me a desire to become an actor in the busy scene where so many admirable qualities were called forth and displayed. But, in giving an account of the progress of my intellect, I must not omit a circumstance which occurred in the beginning of the month of August of the same year.

"One night, during my accustomed visit to the neighbouring wood, where I collected my own food, and brought home firing for my protectors, I found on the ground a leathern portmanteau, containing several articles of dress and some books. I eagerly seized the prize, and returned with it to my hovel. Fortunately the books were written in the language the elements of which I had acquired at the cottage; they consisted of *Paradise Lost*, a volume of *Plutarch's Lives*, and the *Sorrows of Werter*. The possession of these treasures gave me extreme delight; I now continually studied and exercised my mind upon these histories, whilst my friends were employed in their ordinary occupations.

"I can hardly describe to you the effect of these books. They produced in me an infinity of new images and feelings, that sometimes raised me to ecstacy, but more frequently sunk me into the lowest dejection. In the *Sorrows of Werter*, besides the interest of its simple and affecting story, so many opinions are canvassed, and so many lights thrown upon what had hitherto been to me obscure subjects, that I found in it a never-ending source of speculation and astonishment. The gentle and domestic manners it described, combined with lofty sentiments and feelings, which had for their object something out of self, accorded well with my experience among my protectors, and with the wants which were for ever alive in my own bosom. But I thought Werter himself a more divine being than I had ever beheld or imagined; his character contained no pretension, but it sunk deep. The disquisitions upon death and suicide were calculated to fill me with wonder. I did not pretend to enter into the merits of the case, yet I inclined towards the opinions of the hero, whose extinction I wept, without precisely understanding it.

"As I read, however, I applied much personally to my own feelings and condition. I found myself similar, yet at the same time strangely unlike the beings concerning whom I read, and to whose conversation I was a listener. I sympathized with, and partly understood them, but I was unformed in mind; I was dependent on none, and related to none. "The path of my departure was free"; and there was none to lament my annihilation. My person was hideous, and my stature gigantic: what did this mean? Who was I? What was I? Whence did I come? What was my destination? These questions continually recurred, but I was unable to solve them.

"The volume of *Plutarch's Lives* which I possessed, contained the histories of the first founders of the ancient republics. This book had a far different effect upon me from the *Sorrows of Werter*. I learned from Werter's imaginations despondency and gloom: but Plutarch taught me high thoughts; he elevated me above the wretched sphere of my own reflections, to admire and love the heroes of past ages. Many things I read surpassed my understanding and experience. I had a very confused knowledge of kingdoms, wide extents of country, mighty rivers, and boundless seas. But I was perfectly unacquainted with towns, and large assemblages of men. The cottage of my protectors had been the only school in which I had studied human nature; but this book developed new and mightier scenes of action. I read of men concerned in public affairs governing or massacring their species. I felt the greatest ardour for virtue rise within me, and abhorrence for vice, as far as I understood the signification of those terms, relative as they were, as I applied them, to pleasure and pain alone. Induced by these feelings, I was of course led to admire peaceable law-givers, Numa, Solon, and Lycurgus, in preference to Romulus and Theseus. The patriarchal lives of my protectors caused these impressions to take a firm hold on my mind; perhaps, if my first introduction to humanity had been made by a young soldier, burning for glory and slaughter, I should have been imbued with different sensations.

"But *Paradise Lost* excited different and far deeper emotions. I read it, as I had read the other volumes which had fallen into my hands, as a true history. It moved every feeling of wonder and awe, that the picture of an omnipotent God warring with his creatures was capable of exciting. I often referred the several situations, as their similarity struck me, to my own. Like Adam, I was created apparently united by no link to any other being in existence; but his state was far different from mine in every other respect. He had come forth from the hands of God a perfect creature, happy and prosperous, guarded by the especial care of his Creator; he was allowed to converse with, and acquire knowledge from beings of a superior nature: but I was wretched, helpless, and alone. Many times I considered Satan as the fitter emblem of my condition; for often, like him, when I viewed the bliss of my protectors, the bitter gall of envy rose within me.

"Another circumstance strengthened and confirmed these feelings. Soon after my arrival in the hovel, I discovered some papers in the pocket of the dress which I had taken from your laboratory. At first I had neglected them; but now that I was able to decypher the characters in which they were written, I began to study them with diligence. It was your journal of the four months that preceded my creation. You minutely described in these papers every step you took in the progress of your work; this history was mingled with accounts of domestic occurrences. You, doubtless, recollect these papers. Here they are. Every thing is related in them which bears reference to my accursed origin; the whole detail of that series of disgusting circumstances which produced it is set in view; the minutest description of my odious and loathsome person is given, in language which painted your own horrors, and rendered mine ineffaceable. I sickened as I read. 'Hateful day when I received life!' I exclaimed in agony. 'Cursed creator! Why did you form a monster so hideous that even you turned from me in disgust? God in pity made man beautiful and alluring, after his own image; but my form is a filthy type of yours, more horrid from its very resemblance. Satan had his companions, fellow-devils, to admire and encourage him; but I am solitary and detested.'

"These were the reflections of my hours of despondency and solitude; but when I contemplated the virtues of the cottagers, their amiable and benevolent dispositions, I persuaded myself that when they should become acquainted with my admiration of their virtues, they would compassionate me, and overlook my personal deformity. Could they turn from their door one, however monstrous, who solicited their compassion and friendship? I resolved, at least, not to despair, but in every way to fit myself for an interview with them which would decide my fate. I postponed this attempt for some months longer; for the importance attached to its success inspired me with a dread lest I should fail. Besides, I found that my understanding improved so much with every day's experience, that I was unwilling to commence this undertaking until a few more months should have added to my wisdom.

"Several changes, in the mean time, took place in the cottage. The presence of Safie diffused happiness among its inhabitants; and I also found that a greater degree of plenty reigned there. Felix and Agatha spent more time in amusement and conversation, and were assisted in their labours by servants. They did not appear rich, but they were contented and happy; their feelings were serene and peaceful, while mine became every day more tumultuous. Increase of knowledge only discovered to me more clearly what a wretched outcast I was. I cherished hope, it is true; but it vanished, when I beheld my person reflected in water, or my shadow in the moon-shine, even as that frail image and that inconstant shade.

"I endeavoured to crush these fears, and to fortify myself for the trial which in a few months I resolved to undergo; and sometimes I allowed my thoughts, unchecked by reason, to ramble in the fields of Paradise, and dared to fancy amiable and lovely creatures sympathizing with my feelings and cheering my gloom; their angelic countenances breathed smiles of consolation. But it was all a dream: no Eve soothed my sorrows, or shared my thoughts; I was alone. I remembered Adam's supplication to his Creator; but where was mine? he had abandoned me, and, in the bitterness of my heart, I cursed him.

"Autumn passed thus. I saw, with surprise and grief, the leaves decay and fall, and nature again assume the barren and bleak appearance it had worn when I first beheld the woods and the lovely moon. Yet I did not heed the bleakness of the weather; I was better fitted by my conformation for the endurance of cold than heat. But my chief delights were the sight of the flowers, the birds, and all the gay apparel of summer; when those deserted me, I turned with more attention towards the cottagers. Their happiness was not decreased by the absence of summer. They loved, and sympathized with one another; and their joys, depending on each other, were not interrupted by the casualties that took place around them. The more I saw of them, the greater became my desire to claim their protection and kindness; my heart yearned to be known and loved by these amiable creatures: to see their sweet looks turned towards me with affection, was the utmost limit of my ambition. I dared not think that they would turn them from me with disdain and horror. The poor that stopped at their door were never driven away. I asked, it is true, for greater treasures than a little food or rest; I required kindness and sympathy; but I did not believe myself utterly unworthy of it.

"The winter advanced, and an entire revolution of the seasons had taken place since I awoke into life. My attention, at this time, was solely directed towards my plan of introducing myself into the cottage of my protectors. I revolved many projects; but that on which I finally fixed was, to enter the dwelling when the blind old man should be alone. I had sagacity enough to discover, that the unnatural hideousness of my person was the chief object of horror with those who had formerly beheld me. My voice, although harsh, had nothing terrible in it; I thought, therefore, that if, in the absence of his children, I could gain the good-will and mediation of the old De Lacey, I might, by his means, be tolerated by my younger protectors.

"One day, when the sun shone on the red leaves that strewed the ground, and diffused cheerfulness, although it denied warmth, Safie, Agatha, and Felix, departed on a long country walk, and the old man, at his own desire, was left alone in the cottage. When his children had departed, he took up his guitar, and played several mournful, but sweet airs, more sweet and mournful than I had ever heard him play before. At first his countenance was illuminated with pleasure, but, as he continued, thoughtfulness and sadness succeeded; at length, laying aside the instrument, he sat absorbed in reflection.

"My heart beat quick; this was the hour and moment of trial, which would decide my hopes, or realize my fears. The servants were gone to a neighbouring fair. All was silent in and around the cottage: it was an excellent opportunity; yet, when I proceeded to execute my plan, my limbs failed me, and I sunk to the ground. Again I rose; and, exerting all the firmness of which I was master, removed the planks which I had placed before my hovel to conceal my retreat. The fresh air revived me, and, with renewed determination, I approached the door of their cottage.

"I knocked. 'Who is there?' said the old man—'Come in.'

"I entered; 'Pardon this intrusion,' said I, 'I am a traveller in want of a little rest; you would greatly oblige me, if you would allow me to remain a few minutes before the fire.'

"'Enter,' said De Lacey; 'and I will try in what manner I can relieve your wants; but, unfortunately, my children are from home, and, as I am blind, I am afraid I shall find it difficult to procure food for you.'

"'Do not trouble yourself, my kind host, I have food; it is warmth and rest only that I need.'

"I sat down, and a silence ensued. I knew that every minute was precious to me, yet I remained irresolute in what manner to commence the interview; when the old man addressed me—

"'By your language, stranger, I suppose you are my countryman;—are you French?'

"'No; but I was educated by a French family, and understand that language only. I am now going to claim the protection of some friends, whom I sincerely love, and of whose favour I have some hopes.'

"'Are these Germans?'

"'No, they are French. But let us change the subject. I am an unfortunate and deserted creature; I look around, and I have no relation or friend upon earth. These amiable people to whom I go have never seen me, and know little of me. I am full of fears; for if I fail there, I am an outcast in the world for ever.'

" 'Do not despair. To be friendless is indeed to be unfortunate; but the hearts of men, when unprejudiced by any obvious self-interest, are full of brotherly love and charity. Rely, therefore, on your hopes; and if these friends are good and amiable, do not despair.'

" 'They are kind—they are the most excellent creatures in the world; but, unfortunately, they are prejudiced against me. I have good dispositions; my life has been hitherto harmless, and, in some degree, beneficial; but a fatal prejudice clouds their eyes, and where they ought to see a feeling and kind friend, they behold only a detestable monster.'

" 'That is indeed unfortunate; but if you are really blameless, cannot you undeceive them?'

" 'I am about to undertake that task; and it is on that account that I feel so many overwhelming terrors. I tenderly love these friends; I have, unknown to them, been for many months in the habits of daily kindness towards them; but they believe that I wish to injure them, and it is that prejudice which I wish to overcome.'

" 'Where do these friends reside?'

" 'Near this spot.'

"The old man paused, and then continued, 'If you will unreservedly confide to me the particulars of your tale, I perhaps may be of use in undeceiving them. I am blind, and cannot judge of your countenance, but there is something in your words which persuades me that you are sincere. I am poor, and an exile; but it will afford me true pleasure to be in any way serviceable to a human creature.'

" 'Excellent man! I thank you, and accept your generous offer. You raise me from the dust by this kindness; and I trust that, by your aid, I shall not be driven from the society and sympathy of your fellow-creatures.'

" 'Heaven forbid! even if you were really criminal; for that can only drive you to desperation, and not instigate you to virtue. I also am unfortunate; I and my family have been condemned, although innocent: judge, therefore, if I do not feel for your misfortunes.'

" 'How can I thank you, my best and only benefactor? from your lips first have I heard the voice of kindness directed towards me; I shall be for ever grateful; and your present humanity assures me of success with those friends whom I am on the point of meeting.'

" 'May I know the names and residence of those friends?'

"I paused. This, I thought, was the moment of decision, which was to rob me of, or bestow happiness on me for ever. I struggled vainly for firmness sufficient to answer him, but the effort destroyed all my remaining strength; I sank on the chair, and sobbed aloud. At that moment I heard the steps of my younger protectors. I had not a moment to lose; but, seizing the hand of the old man, I cried, 'Now is the time!—save and protect me! You and your family are the friends whom I seek. Do not you desert me in the hour of trial!'

"'Great God!' exclaimed the old man, 'who are you?'

"At that instant the cottage door was opened, and Felix, Safie, and Agatha entered. Who can describe their horror and consternation on beholding me? Agatha fainted; and Safie, unable to attend to her friend, rushed out of the cottage. Felix darted forward, and with supernatural force tore me from his father, to whose knees I clung: in a transport of fury, he dashed me to the ground, and struck me violently with a stick. I could have torn him limb from limb, as the lion rends the antelope. But my heart sunk within me as with bitter sickness, and I refrained. I saw him on the point of repeating his blow, when, overcome by pain and anguish, I quitted the cottage, and in the general tumult escaped unperceived to my hovel.

CHAPTER XV

"Cursed, cursed creator! Why did I live? Why, in that instant, did I not extinguish the spark of existence which you had so wantonly bestowed? I know not; despair had not yet taken possession of me; my feelings were those of rage and revenge. I could with pleasure have destroyed the cottage and its inhabitants, and have glutted myself with their shrieks and misery.

"When night came, I quitted my retreat, and wandered in the wood; and now, no longer restrained by the fear of discovery, I gave vent to my anguish in fearful howlings. I was like a wild beast that had broken the toils; destroying the objects that obstructed me, and ranging through the wood with a stag-like swiftness. Oh! what a miserable night I passed! the cold stars shone in mockery, and the bare trees waved their branches above me: now and then the sweet voice of a bird burst forth amidst the universal stillness. All, save I, were at rest or in enjoyment: I, like the arch fiend, bore a hell within me; and, finding myself unsympathized with, wished to tear up the trees, spread havoc and destruction around me, and then to have sat down and enjoyed the ruin.

"But this was a luxury of sensation that could not endure; I became fatigued with excess of bodily exertion, and sank on the damp grass in the sick impotence of despair.

There was none among the myriads of men that existed who would pity or assist me; and should I feel kindness towards my enemies? No: from that moment I declared everlasting war against the species, and, more than all, against him who had formed me, and sent me forth to this insupportable misery.

"The sun rose; I heard the voices of men, and knew that it was impossible to return to my retreat during that day. Accordingly I hid myself in some thick underwood, determining to devote the ensuing hours to reflection on my situation.

"The pleasant sunshine, and the pure air of day, restored me to some degree of tranquillity; and when I considered what had passed at the cottage, I could not help believing that I had been too hasty in my conclusions. I had certainly acted imprudently. It was apparent that my conversation had interested the father in my behalf, and I was a fool in having exposed my person to the horror of his children. I ought to have familiarized the old De Lacey to me, and by degrees have discovered myself to the rest of his family, when they should have been prepared for my approach. But I did not believe my errors to be irretrievable; and, after much consideration, I resolved to return to the cottage, seek the old man, and by my representations win him to my party.

"These thoughts calmed me, and in the afternoon I sank into a profound sleep; but the fever of my blood did not allow me to be visited by peaceful dreams. The horrible scene of the preceding day was for ever acting before my eyes; the females were flying, and the enraged Felix tearing me from his father's feet. I awoke exhausted; and, finding that it was already night, I crept forth from my hiding-place, and went in search of food.

"When my hunger was appeased, I directed my steps towards the well-known path that conducted to the cottage. All there was at peace. I crept into my hovel, and remained in silent expectation of the accustomed hour when the family arose. That hour past, the sun mounted high in the heavens, but the cottagers did not appear. I trembled violently, apprehending some dreadful misfortune. The inside of the cottage was dark, and I heard no motion; I cannot describe the agony of this suspence.

"Presently two countrymen passed by; but, pausing near the cottage, they entered into conversation, using violent gesticulations; but I did not understand what they said, as they spoke the language of the country, which differed from that of my protectors. Soon after, however, Felix approached with another man: I was surprised, as I knew that he had not quitted the cottage that morning, and waited anxiously to discover, from his discourse, the meaning of these unusual appearances.

"'Do you consider,' said his companion to him, 'that you will be obliged to pay three months' rent, and to lose the produce of your garden? I do not wish to take any unfair advantage, and I beg therefore that you will take some days to consider of your determination.'

"'It is utterly useless,' replied Felix, 'we can never again inhabit your cottage. The life of my father is in the greatest danger, owing to the dreadful circumstance that I have related. My wife and my sister will never recover their horror. I entreat you not to reason with me any more. Take possession of your tenement, and let me fly from this place.'

"Felix trembled violently as he said this. He and his companion entered the cottage, in which they remained for a few minutes, and then departed. I never saw any of the family of De Lacey more.

"I continued for the remainder of the day in my hovel in a state of utter and stupid despair. My protectors had departed, and had broken the only link that held me to the world. For the first time the feelings of revenge and hatred filled my bosom, and I did not strive to controul them; but, allowing myself to be borne away by the stream, I bent my mind towards injury and death. When I thought of my friends, of the mild voice of De Lacey, the gentle eyes of Agatha, and the exquisite beauty of the Arabian, these thoughts vanished, and a gush of tears somewhat soothed me. But again, when I reflected that they had spurned and deserted me, anger returned, a rage of anger; and, unable to injure any thing human, I turned my fury towards inanimate objects. As night advanced, I placed a variety of combustibles around the cottage; and, after having destroyed every vestige of cultivation in the garden, I waited with forced impatience until the moon had sunk to commence my operations.

"As the night advanced, a fierce wind arose from the woods, and quickly dispersed the clouds that had loitered in the heavens: the blast tore along like a mighty avalanche, and produced a kind of insanity in my spirits, that burst all bounds of reason and reflection. I lighted the dry branch of a tree, and danced with fury around the devoted cottage, my eyes still fixed on the western horizon, the edge of which the moon nearly touched. A part of its orb was at length hid, and I waved my brand; it sunk, and, with a loud scream, I fired the straw, and heath, and bushes, which I had collected. The wind fanned the fire, and the cottage was quickly enveloped by the flames, which clung to it, and licked it with their forked and destroying tongues.

"As soon as I was convinced that no assistance could save any part of the habitation, I quitted the scene, and sought for refuge in the woods.

"And now, with the world before me, whither should I bend my steps? I resolved to fly far from the scene of my misfortunes; but to me, hated and despised, every country must be equally horrible. At length the thought of you crossed my mind. I learned from your papers that you were my father, my creator; and to whom could I apply with more fitness than to him who had given me life? Among the lessons that Felix had bestowed upon Safie geography had not been omitted: I had learned from these the relative situations of the different countries of the earth. You had mentioned Geneva as the name of your native town; and towards this place I resolved to proceed.

"But how was I to direct myself? I knew that I must travel in a south-westerly direction to reach my destination; but the sun was my only guide. I did not know the names of the towns that I was to pass through, nor could I ask information from a single human being; but I did not despair. From you only could I hope for succour, although towards you I felt no sentiment but that of hatred. Unfeeling, heartless creator! you had endowed me with perceptions and passions, and then cast me abroad an object for the scorn and horror of mankind. But on you only had I any claim for pity and redress, and from you I determined to seek that justice which I vainly attempted to gain from any other being that wore the human form.

"My travels were long, and the sufferings I endured intense. It was late in autumn when I quitted the district where I had so long resided. I travelled only at night, fearful of encountering the visage of a human being. Nature decayed around me, and the sun became heatless; rain and snow poured around me; mighty rivers were frozen; the surface of the earth was hard, and chill, and bare, and I found no shelter. Oh, earth! how often did I imprecate curses on the cause of my being! The mildness of my nature had fled, and all within me was turned to gall and bitterness. The nearer I approached to your habitation, the more deeply did I feel the spirit of revenge enkindled in my heart. Snow fell, and the waters were hardened, but I rested not. A few incidents now and then directed me, and I possessed a map of the country; but I often wandered wide from my path. The agony of my feelings allowed me no respite: no incident occurred from which my rage and misery could not extract its food; but a circumstance that happened when I arrived on the confines of Switzerland, when the sun had recovered its warmth, and the earth again began to look green, confirmed in an especial manner the bitterness and horror of my feelings.

"I generally rested during the day, and travelled only when I was secured by night from the view of man. One morning, however, finding that my path lay through a deep wood, I ventured to continue my journey after the sun had risen; the day, which was one of the first of spring, cheered even me by the loveliness of its sunshine and the balminess of the air. I felt emotions of gentleness and pleasure, that had long appeared dead, revive within me. Half surprised by the novelty of these sensations, I allowed myself to be borne away by them; and, forgetting my solitude and deformity, dared to be happy. Soft tears again bedewed my cheeks, and I even raised my humid eyes with thankfulness towards the blessed sun which bestowed such joy upon me.

"I continued to wind among the paths of the wood, until I came to its boundary, which was skirted by a deep and rapid river, into which many of the trees bent their branches, now budding with the fresh spring. Here I paused, not exactly knowing what path to pursue, when I heard the sound of voices, that induced me to conceal myself under the shade of a cypress. I was scarcely hid, when a young girl came running towards the spot where I was concealed, laughing as if she ran from some one in sport. She continued her course along the precipitous sides of the river, when suddenly her foot slipt, and she fell into the rapid stream. I rushed from my hiding place, and, with extreme labour from the force of the current, saved her, and dragged her to shore. She was senseless; and I endeavoured, by every means in my power, to restore animation, when I was suddenly interrupted by the approach of a rustic, who was probably the person from whom she had playfully fled. On seeing me, he darted towards me, and, tearing the girl from my arms, hastened towards the deeper parts of the wood. I followed speedily, I hardly knew why; but when the man saw me draw near, he aimed a gun, which he carried, at my body, and fired. I sunk to the ground, and my injurer, with increased swiftness, escaped into the wood.

"This was then the reward of my benevolence! I had saved a human being from destruction, and, as a recompence, I now writhed under the miserable pain of a wound, which shattered the flesh and bone. The feelings of kindness and gentleness, which I had entertained but a few moments before, gave place to hellish rage and gnashing of teeth. Inflamed by pain, I vowed eternal hatred and vengeance to all mankind. But the agony of my wound overcame me; my pulses paused, and I fainted.

"For some weeks I led a miserable life in the woods, endeavouring to cure the wound which I had received. The ball had entered my shoulder, and I knew not whether it had remained there or passed through; at any rate I had no means of extracting it. My sufferings were augmented also by the oppressive sense of the injustice and ingratitude of their infliction. My daily vows rose for revenge—a deep and deadly revenge, such as would alone compensate for the outrages and anguish I had endured.

"After some weeks my wound healed, and I continued my journey. The labours I endured were no longer to be alleviated by the bright sun or gentle breezes of spring; all joy was but a mockery which insulted my desolate state, and made me feel more painfully that I was not made for the enjoyment of pleasure.

"But my toils now drew near a close; and, two months from this time, I reached the environs of Geneva.

"It was evening when I arrived, and I retired to a hiding-place among the fields that surround it, to meditate in what manner I should apply to you. I was oppressed by fatigue and hunger, and far too unhappy to enjoy the gentle breezes of evening, or the prospect of the sun setting behind the stupendous mountains of Jura.

"At this time a slight sleep relieved me from the pain of reflection, which was disturbed by the approach of a beautiful child, who came running into the recess I had chosen with all the sportiveness of infancy. Suddenly, as I gazed on him, an idea seized me, that this little creature was unprejudiced, and had lived too short a time to have imbibed a horror of deformity. If, therefore, I could seize him, and educate him as my companion and friend, I should not be so desolate in this peopled earth.

"Urged by this impulse, I seized on the boy as he passed, and drew him towards me. As soon as he beheld my form, he placed his hands before his eyes, and uttered a shrill scream: I drew his hand forcibly from his face, and said, 'Child, what is the meaning of this? I do not intend to hurt you; listen to me.'

"He struggled violently; 'Let me go,' he cried; 'monster! ugly wretch! you wish to eat me, and tear me to pieces—You are an ogre—Let me go, or I will tell my papa.'

"'Boy, you will never see your father again; you must come with me.'

"'Hideous monster! let me go; My papa is a Syndic—he is M. Frankenstein—he would punish you. You dare not keep me.'

"'Frankenstein! you belong then to my enemy—to him towards whom I have sworn eternal revenge; you shall be my first victim.'

"The child still struggled, and loaded me with epithets which carried despair to my heart: I grasped his throat to silence him, and in a moment he lay dead at my feet.

"I gazed on my victim, and my heart swelled with exultation and hellish triumph: clapping my hands, I exclaimed, 'I, too, can create desolation; my enemy is not impregnable; this death will carry despair to him, and a thousand other miseries shall torment and destroy him.'

"As I fixed my eyes on the child, I saw something glittering on his breast. I took it; it was a portrait of a most lovely woman. In spite of my malignity, it softened and attracted me. For a few moments I gazed with delight on her dark eyes fringed by deep lashes, and her lovely lips; but presently my rage returned: I remembered that I was for ever deprived of the delights that such beautiful creatures could bestow; and that she whose resemblance I contemplated would, in regarding me, have changed that air of divine benignity to one expressive of disgust and affright.

"Can you wonder that such thoughts transported me with rage? I only wonder that at that moment, instead of venting my sensations in exclamations and agony, I did not rush among mankind, and perish in the attempt to destroy them.

"While I was overcome by these feelings, I left the spot where I had committed the murder, and was seeking a more secluded hiding-place, when I perceived a woman passing near me. She was young, not indeed so beautiful as her whose portrait I held, but of an agreeable aspect, and blooming in the loveliness of youth and health. Here, I thought, is one of those whose smiles are bestowed on all but me; she shall not escape: thanks to the lessons of Felix, and the sanguinary laws of man, I have learned how to work mischief. I approached her unperceived, and placed the portrait securely in one of the folds of her dress.

"For some days I haunted the spot where these scenes had taken place; sometimes wishing to see you, sometimes resolved to quit the world and its miseries for ever. At length I wandered towards these mountains, and have ranged through their immense recesses, consumed by a burning passion which you alone can gratify. We may not part until you have promised to comply with my requisition. I am alone, and miserable; man will not associate with me; but one as deformed and horrible as myself would not deny herself to me. My companion must be of the same species, and have the same defects. This being you must create."

CHAPTER XVI

THE BEING FINISHED SPEAKING, AND FIXED HIS LOOKS UPON ME IN EXPECTATION OF a reply. But I was bewildered, perplexed, and unable to arrange my ideas sufficiently to understand the full extent of his proposition. He continued—

"You must create a female for me, with whom I can live in the interchange of those sympathies necessary for my being. This you alone can do; and I demand it of you as a right which you must not refuse."

The latter part of his tale had kindled anew in me the anger that had died away while he narrated his peaceful life among the cottagers, and, as he said this, I could no longer suppress the rage that burned within me.

"I do refuse it," I replied; "and no torture shall ever extort a consent from me. You may render me the most miserable of men, but you shall never make me base in my own eyes. Shall I create another like yourself, whose joint wickedness might desolate the world. Begone! I have answered you; you may torture me, but I will never consent."

"You are in the wrong," replied the fiend; "and, instead of threatening, I am content to reason with you. I am malicious because I am miserable; am I not shunned and hated by all mankind? You, my creator, would tear me to pieces, and triumph; remember that, and tell me why I should pity man more than he pities me? You would not call it murder, if you could precipitate me into one of those ice-rifts, and destroy my frame, the work of your own hands. Shall I respect man, when he contemns me? Let him live with me in the interchange of kindness, and, instead of injury, I would bestow every benefit upon him with tears of gratitude at his acceptance. But that cannot be; the human senses are insurmountable barriers to our union. Yet mine shall not be the submission of abject slavery. I will revenge my injuries: if I cannot inspire love, I will cause fear; and chiefly towards you my arch-enemy, because my creator, do I swear inextinguishable hatred. Have a care: I will work at your destruction, nor finish until I desolate your heart, so that you curse the hour of your birth."

A fiendish rage animated him as he said this; his face was wrinkled into contortions too horrible for human eyes to behold; but presently he calmed himself, and proceeded—

"I intended to reason. This passion is detrimental to me; for you do not reflect that you are the cause of its excess. If any being felt emotions of benevolence towards me, I should return them an hundred and an hundred fold; for that one creature's sake, I would make peace with the whole kind! But I now indulge in dreams of bliss that cannot be realized. What I ask of you is reasonable and moderate; I demand a creature of another sex, but as hideous as myself: the gratification is small, but it is all that I can receive, and it shall content me. It is true, we shall be monsters, cut off from all the world; but on that account we shall be more attached to one another. Our lives will not be happy, but they will be harmless, and free from the misery I now feel. Oh! my creator, make me happy; let me feel gratitude towards you for one benefit! Let me see that I excite the sympathy of some existing thing; do not deny me my request!"

I was moved. I shuddered when I thought of the possible consequences of my consent; but I felt that there was some justice in his argument. His tale, and the feelings he now expressed, proved him to be a creature of fine sensations; and did I not, as his maker, owe him all the portion of happiness that it was in my power to bestow? He saw my change of feeling, and continued —

"If you consent, neither you nor any other human being shall ever see us again: I will go to the vast wilds of South America. My food is not that of man; I do not destroy the lamb and the kid, to glut my appetite; acorns and berries afford me sufficient nourishment. My companion will be of the same nature as myself, and will be content with the same fare. We shall make our bed of dried leaves; the sun will shine on us as on man, and will ripen our food. The picture I present to you is peaceful and human, and you must feel that you could deny it only in the wantonness of power and cruelty. Pitiless as you have been towards me, I now see compassion in your eyes: let me seize the favourable moment, and persuade you to promise what I so ardently desire."

"You propose," replied I, "to fly from the habitations of man, to dwell in those wilds where the beasts of the field will be your only companions. How can you, who long for the love and sympathy of man, persevere in this exile? You will return, and again seek their kindness, and you will meet with their detestation; your evil passions will be renewed, and you will then have a companion to aid you in the task of destruction. This may not be; cease to argue the point, for I cannot consent."

"How inconstant are your feelings! but a moment ago you were moved by my representations, and why do you again harden yourself to my complaints? I swear to you, by the earth which I inhabit, and by you that made me, that, with the companion you bestow, I will quit the neighbourhood of man, and dwell, as it may chance, in the most savage of places. My evil passions will have fled, for I shall meet with sympathy; my life will flow quietly away, and, in my dying moments, I shall not curse my maker."

His words had a strange effect upon me. I compassionated him, and sometimes felt a wish to console him; but when I looked upon him, when I saw the filthy mass that moved and talked, my heart sickened, and my feelings were altered to those of horror and hatred. I tried to stifle these sensations; I thought, that as I could not sympathize with him, I had no right to withhold from him the small portion of happiness which was yet in my power to bestow.

"You swear," I said, "to be harmless; but have you not already shewn a degree of malice that should reasonably make me distrust you? May not even this be a feint that will increase your triumph by affording a wider scope for your revenge?"

"How is this? I thought I had moved your compassion, and yet you still refuse to bestow on me the only benefit that can soften my heart, and render me harmless. If I have no ties and no affections, hatred and vice must be my portion; the love of another will destroy the cause of my crimes, and I shall become a thing, of whose existence every one will be ignorant. My vices are the children of a forced solitude that I abhor; and my virtues will necessarily arise when I live in communion with an equal. I shall feel the affections of a sensitive being, and become linked to the chain of existence and events, from which I am now excluded."

I paused some time to reflect on all he had related, and the various arguments which he had employed. I thought of the promise of virtues which he had displayed on the opening of his existence, and the subsequent blight of all kindly feeling by the loathing and scorn which his protectors had manifested towards him. His power and threats were not omitted in my calculations: a creature who could exist in the ice caves of the glaciers, and hide himself from pursuit among the ridges of inaccessible precipices, was a being possessing faculties it would be vain to cope with. After a long pause of reflection, I concluded, that the justice due both to him and my fellow-creatures demanded of me that I should comply with his request. Turning to him, therefore, I said—

"I consent to your demand, on your solemn oath to quit Europe for ever, and every other place in the neighbourhood of man, as soon as I shall deliver into your hands a female who will accompany you in your exile."

"I swear," he cried, "by the sun, and by the blue sky of heaven, that if you grant my prayer, while they exist you shall never behold me again. Depart to your home, and commence your labours: I shall watch their progress with unutterable anxiety; and fear not but that when you are ready I shall appear."

Saying this, he suddenly quitted me, fearful, perhaps, of any change in my sentiments. I saw him descend the mountain with greater speed than the flight of an eagle, and quickly lost him among the undulations of the sea of ice.

His tale had occupied the whole day; and the sun was upon the verge of the horizon when he departed. I knew that I ought to hasten my descent towards the valley, as I should soon be encompassed in darkness; but my heart was heavy, and my steps slow. The labour of winding among the little paths of the mountains, and fixing my feet firmly as I advanced, perplexed me, occupied as I was by the emotions which the occurrences of the day had produced. Night was far advanced, when I came to the half-way resting-place, and seated myself beside the fountain. The stars shone at intervals, as the clouds passed from over them; the dark pines rose before me, and every here and there a broken tree lay on the ground: it was a scene of wonderful solemnity, and stirred strange thoughts within me. I wept bitterly; and, clasping my hands in agony, I exclaimed, "Oh! stars, and clouds, and winds, ye are all about to mock me: if ye really pity me, crush sensation and memory; let me become as nought; but if not, depart, depart and leave me in darkness."

These were wild and miserable thoughts; but I cannot describe to you how the eternal twinkling of the stars weighed upon me, and how I listened to every blast of wind, as if it were a dull ugly siroc on its way to consume me.

Morning dawned before I arrived at the village of Chamounix; but my presence, so haggard and strange, hardly calmed the fears of my family, who had waited the whole night in anxious expectation of my return.

The following day we returned to Geneva. The intention of my father in coming had been to divert my mind, and to restore me to my lost tranquillity; but the medicine had been fatal. And, unable to account for the excess of misery I appeared to suffer, he hastened to return home, hoping the quiet and monotony of a domestic life would by degrees alleviate my sufferings from whatsoever cause they might spring.

For myself, I was passive in all their arrangements; and the gentle affection of my beloved Elizabeth was inadequate to draw me from the depth of my despair. The promise I had made to the dæmon weighed upon my mind, like Dante's iron cowl on the heads of the hellish hypocrites. All pleasures of earth and sky passed before me like a dream, and that thought only had to me the reality of life. Can you wonder, that sometimes a kind of insanity possessed me, or that I saw continually about me a multitude of filthy animals inflicting on me incessant torture, that often extorted screams and bitter groans?

By degrees, however, these feelings became calmed. I entered again into the every-day scene of life, if not with interest, at least with some degree of tranquillity.

CHAPTER XVII

DAY AFTER DAY, WEEK AFTER WEEK, PASSED AWAY ON MY RETURN TO GENEVA; AND I could not collect the courage to recommence my work. I feared the vengeance of the disappointed fiend, yet I was unable to overcome my repugnance to the task which was enjoined me. I found that I could not compose a female without again devoting several months to profound study and laborious disquisition. I had heard of some discoveries having been made by an English philosopher, the knowledge of which was material to my success, and I sometimes thought of obtaining my father's consent to visit England for this purpose; but I clung to every pretence of delay, and could not resolve to interrupt my returning tranquillity. My health, which had hitherto declined, was now much restored; and my spirits, when unchecked by the memory of my unhappy promise, rose proportionably. My father saw this change with pleasure, and he turned his thoughts towards the best method of eradicating the remains of my melancholy, which every now and then would return by fits, and with a devouring blackness overcast the approaching sunshine. At these moments I took refuge in the most perfect solitude. I passed whole days on the lake alone in a little boat, watching the clouds, and listening to the rippling of the waves, silent and listless. But the fresh air and bright sun seldom failed to restore me to some degree of composure; and, on my return, I met the salutations of my friends with a readier smile and a more cheerful heart.

It was after my return from one of these rambles that my father, calling me aside, thus addressed me:—

"I am happy to remark, my dear son, that you have resumed your former pleasures, and seem to be returning to yourself. And yet you are still unhappy, and still avoid our society. For some time I was lost in conjecture as to the cause of this; but yesterday an idea struck me, and if it is well founded, I conjure you to avow it. Reserve on such a point would be not only useless, but draw down treble misery on us all."

I trembled violently at this exordium, and my father continued—

"I confess, my son, that I have always looked forward to your marriage with your cousin as the tie of our domestic comfort, and the stay of my declining years. You were attached to each other from your earliest infancy; you studied together, and appeared, in dispositions and tastes, entirely suited to one another. But so blind is the experience of man, that what I conceived to be the best assistants to my plan may have entirely destroyed it. You, perhaps, regard her as your sister, without any wish that she might become your wife. Nay, you may have met with another whom you may love; and, considering yourself as bound in honour to your cousin, this struggle may occasion the poignant misery which you appear to feel."

"My dear father, re-assure yourself. I love my cousin tenderly and sincerely. I never saw any woman who excited, as Elizabeth does, my warmest admiration and affection. My future hopes and prospects are entirely bound up in the expectation of our union."

"The expression of your sentiments on this subject, my dear Victor, gives me more pleasure than I have for some time experienced. If you feel thus, we shall assuredly be happy, however present events may cast a gloom over us. But it is this gloom, which appears to have taken so strong a hold of your mind, that I wish to dissipate. Tell me, therefore, whether you object to an immediate solemnization of the marriage. We have been unfortunate, and recent events have drawn us from that every-day tranquillity befitting my years and infirmities. You are younger; yet I do not suppose, possessed as you are of a competent fortune, that an early marriage would at all interfere with any future plans of honour and utility that you may have formed. Do not suppose, however, that I wish to dictate happiness to you, or that a delay on your part would cause me any serious uneasiness. Interpret my words with candour, and answer me, I conjure you, with confidence and sincerity."

I listened to my father in silence, and remained for some time incapable of offering any reply. I revolved rapidly in my mind a multitude of thoughts, and endeavoured to arrive at some conclusion. Alas! to me the idea of an immediate union with my cousin was one of horror and dismay. I was bound by a solemn promise, which I had not yet fulfilled, and dared not break; or, if I did, what manifold miseries might not impend over me and my devoted family! Could I enter into a festival with this deadly weight yet hanging round my neck, and bowing me to the ground. I must perform my engagement, and let the monster depart with his mate, before I allowed myself to enjoy the delight of an union from which I expected peace.

I remembered also the necessity imposed upon me of either journeying to England, or entering into a long correspondence with those philosophers of that country, whose knowledge and discoveries were of indispensable use to me in my present undertaking. The latter method of obtaining the desired intelligence was dilatory and unsatisfactory: besides, any variation was agreeable to me, and I was delighted with the idea of spending a year or two in change of scene and variety of occupation, in absence from my family; during which period some event might happen which would restore me to them in peace and happiness: my promise might be fulfilled, and the monster have departed; or some accident might occur to destroy him, and put an end to my slavery for ever.

These feelings dictated my answer to my father. I expressed a wish to visit England; but, concealing the true reasons of this request, I clothed my desires under the guise of wishing to travel and see the world before I sat down for life within the walls of my native town.

I urged my entreaty with earnestness, and my father was easily induced to comply; for a more indulgent and less dictatorial parent did not exist upon earth. Our plan was soon arranged. I should travel to Strasburgh, where Clerval would join me. Some short time would be spent in the towns of Holland, and our principal stay would be in England. We should return by France; and it was agreed that the tour should occupy the space of two years.

My father pleased himself with the reflection, that my union with Elizabeth should take place immediately on my return to Geneva. "These two years," said be, "will pass swiftly, and it will be the last delay that will oppose itself to your happiness. And, indeed, I earnestly desire that period to arrive, when we shall all be united, and neither hopes or fears arise to disturb our domestic calm."

"I am content," I replied, "with your arrangement. By that time we shall both have become wiser, and I hope happier, than we at present are." I sighed; but my father kindly forbore to question me further concerning the cause of my dejection. He hoped that new scenes, and the amusement of travelling, would restore my tranquillity.

I now made arrangements for my journey; but one feeling haunted me, which filled me with fear and agitation. During my absence I should leave my friends unconscious of the existence of their enemy, and unprotected from his attacks, exasperated as he might be by my departure. But he had promised to follow me wherever I might go; and would he not accompany me to England? This imagination was dreadful in itself, but soothing, inasmuch as it supposed the safety of my friends. I was agonized with the idea of the possibility that the reverse of this might happen. But through the whole period during which I was the slave of my creature, I allowed myself to be governed by the impulses of the moment; and my present sensations strongly intimated that the fiend would follow me, and exempt my family from the danger of his machinations.

It was in the latter end of August that I departed, to pass two years of exile. Elizabeth approved of the reasons of my departure, and only regretted that she had not the same opportunities of enlarging her experience, and cultivating her understanding. She wept, however, as she bade me farewell, and entreated me to return happy and tranquil. "We all," said she, "depend upon you; and if you are miserable, what must be our feelings?"

I threw myself into the carriage that was to convey me away, hardly knowing whither I was going, and careless of what was passing around. I remembered only, and it was with a bitter anguish that I reflected on it, to order that my chemical instruments should be packed to go with me: for I resolved to fulfil my promise while abroad, and return, if possible, a free man. Filled with dreary imaginations, I passed through many beautiful and majestic scenes; but my eyes were fixed and unobserving. I could only think of the bourne of my travels, and the work which was to occupy me whilst they endured.

After some days spent in listless indolence, during which I traversed many leagues, I arrived at Strasburgh, where I waited two days for Clerval. He came. Alas, how great was the contrast between us! He was alive to every new scene; joyful when he saw the beauties of the setting sun, and more happy when he beheld it rise, and recommence a new day. He pointed out to me the shifting colours of the landscape, and the appearances of the sky. "This is what it is to live;" he cried, "now I enjoy existence! But you, my dear Frankenstein, wherefore are you desponding and sorrowful?" In truth, I was occupied by gloomy thoughts, and neither saw the descent of the evening star, nor the golden sun-rise reflected in the Rhine.—And you, my friend, would be far more amused with the journal of Clerval, who observed the scenery with an eye of feeling and delight, than to listen to my reflections. I, a miserable wretch, haunted by a curse that shut up every avenue to enjoyment.

We had agreed to descend the Rhine in a boat from Strasburgh to Rotterdam, whence we might take shipping for London. During this voyage, we passed by many willowy islands, and saw several beautiful towns. We staid a day at Manheim, and, on the fifth from our departure from Strasburgh, arrived at Mayence. The course of the Rhine below Mayence becomes much more picturesque. The river descends rapidly, and winds between hills, not high, but steep, and of beautiful forms. We saw many ruined castles standing on the edges of precipices, surrounded by black woods, high and inaccessible. This part of the Rhine, indeed, presents a singularly variegated landscape. In one spot you view rugged hills, ruined castles overlooking tremendous precipices, with the dark Rhine rushing beneath; and, on the sudden turn of a promontory, flourishing vineyards, with green sloping banks, and a meandering river, and populous towns, occupy the scene.

We travelled at the time of the vintage, and heard the song of the labourers, as we glided down the stream. Even I, depressed in mind, and my spirits continually agitated by gloomy feelings, even I was pleased. I lay at the bottom of the boat, and, as I gazed on the cloudless blue sky, I seemed to drink in a tranquillity to which I had long been a stranger. And if these were my sensations, who can describe those of Henry? He felt as if he had been transported to Fairy-land, and enjoyed a happiness seldom tasted by man. "I have seen," he said, "the most beautiful scenes of my own country; I have visited the lakes of Lucerne and Uri, where the snowy mountains descend almost perpendicularly to the water, casting black and impenetrable shades, which would cause a gloomy and mournful appearance, were it not for the most verdant islands that relieve the eye by their gay appearance; I have seen this lake agitated by a tempest, when the wind tore up whirlwinds of water, and gave you an idea of what the water-spout must be on the great ocean, and the waves dash with fury the base of the mountain, where the priest and his mistress were overwhelmed by an avalanche, and where their dying voices are still said to be heard amid the pauses of the nightly wind; I have seen the mountains of La Valais, and the Pays de Vaud: but this country, Victor, pleases me more than all those wonders. The mountains of Switzerland are more majestic and strange; but there is a charm in the banks of this divine river, that I never before saw equalled. Look at that castle which overhangs yon precipice; and that also on the island, almost concealed amongst the foliage of those lovely trees; and now that group of labourers coming from among their vines; and that village half-hid in the recess of the mountain. Oh, surely, the spirit that inhabits and guards this place has a soul more in harmony with man, than those who pile the glacier, or retire to the inaccessible peaks of the mountains of our own country."

Clerval! beloved friend! even now it delights me to record your words, and to dwell on the praise of which you are so eminently deserving. He was a being formed in the "very poetry of nature." His wild and enthusiastic imagination was chastened by the sensibility of his heart. His soul overflowed with ardent affections, and his friendship was of that devoted and wondrous nature that the worldly-minded teach us to look for only in the imagination. But even human sympathies were not sufficient to satisfy his eager mind. The scenery of external nature, which others regard only with admiration, he loved with ardour:

> _____"The sounding cataract
> Haunted *him* like a passion: the tall rock,
> The mountain, and the deep and gloomy wood,
> Their colours and their forms, were then to him
> An appetite: a feeling, and a love,
> That had no need of a remoter charm,
> By thought supplied, or any interest
> Unborrowed from the eye."

And where does he now exist? Is this gentle and lovely being lost for ever? Has this mind so replete with ideas, imaginations fanciful and magnificent, which formed a world, whose existence depended on the life of its creator; has this mind perished? Does it now only exist in my memory? No, it is not thus; your form so divinely wrought, and beaming with beauty, has decayed, but your spirit still visits and consoles your unhappy friend.

Pardon this gush of sorrow; these ineffectual words are but a slight tribute to the unexampled worth of Henry, but they soothe my heart, overflowing with the anguish which his remembrance creates. I will proceed with my tale.

Beyond Cologne we descended to the plains of Holland; and we resolved to post the remainder of our way; for the wind was contrary, and the stream of the river was too gentle to aid us.

Our journey here lost the interest arising from beautiful scenery; but we arrived in a few days at Rotterdam, whence we proceeded by sea to England. It was on a clear morning, in the latter days of December, that I first saw the white cliffs of Britain. The banks of the Thames presented a new scene; they were flat, but fertile, and almost every town was marked by the remembrance of some story. We saw Tilbury Fort, and remembered the Spanish armada; Gravesend, Woolwich, and Greenwich, places which I had heard of even in my country.

At length we saw the numerous steeples of London, St. Paul's towering above all, and the Tower famed in English history.

CHAPTER XVIII

London was our present point of rest; we determined to remain several months in this wonderful and celebrated city. Clerval desired the intercourse of the men of genius and talent who flourished at this time; but this was with me a secondary object; I was principally occupied with the means of obtaining the information necessary for the completion of my promise, and quickly availed myself of the letters of introduction that I had brought with me, addressed to the most distinguished natural philosophers.

If this journey had taken place during my days of study and happiness, it would have afforded me inexpressible pleasure. But a blight had come over my existence, and I only visited these people for the sake of the information they might give me on the subject in which my interest was so terribly profound. Company was irksome to me; when alone, I could fill my mind with the sights of heaven and earth; the voice of Henry soothed me, and I could thus cheat myself into a transitory peace.

But busy uninteresting joyous faces brought back despair to my heart. I saw an insurmountable barrier placed between me and my fellow-men; this barrier was sealed with the blood of William and Justine; and to reflect on the events connected with those names filled my soul with anguish.

But in Clerval I saw the image of my former self; he was inquisitive, and anxious to gain experience and instruction. The difference of manners which he observed was to him an inexhaustible source of instruction and amusement. He was for ever busy; and the only check to his enjoyments was my sorrowful and dejected mien. I tried to conceal this as much as possible, that I might not debar him from the pleasures natural to one who was entering on a new scene of life, undisturbed by any care or bitter recollection. I often refused to accompany him, alleging another engagement, that I might remain alone. I now also began to collect the materials necessary for my new creation, and this was to me like the torture of single drops of water continually falling on the head. Every thought that was devoted to it was an extreme anguish, and every word that I spoke in allusion to it caused my lips to quiver, and my heart to palpitate.

After passing some months in London, we received a letter from a person in Scotland, who had formerly been our visitor at Geneva. He mentioned the beauties of his native country, and asked us if those were not sufficient allurements to induce us to prolong our journey as far north as Perth, where he resided. Clerval eagerly desired to accept this invitation; and I, although I abhorred society, wished to view again mountains and streams, and all the wondrous works with which Nature adorns her chosen dwelling-places.

We had arrived in England at the beginning of October, and it was now February. We accordingly determined to commence our journey towards the north at the expiration of another month. In this expedition we did not intend to follow the great road to Edinburgh, but to visit Windsor, Oxford, Matlock, and the Cumberland lakes, resolving to arrive at the completion of this tour about the end of July. I packed my chemical instruments, and the materials I had collected, resolving to finish my labours in some obscure nook in the northern highlands of Scotland.

We quitted London on the 27th of March, and remained a few days at Windsor, rambling in its beautiful forest. This was a new scene to us mountaineers; the majestic oaks, the quantity of game, and the herds of stately deer, were all novelties to us.

From thence we proceeded to Oxford. As we entered this city, our minds were filled with the remembrance of the events that had been transacted there more than a century and a half before. It was here that Charles I had collected his forces. This city had remained faithful to him, after the whole nation had forsaken his cause to join the standard of parliament and liberty. The memory of that unfortunate king, and his companions, the amiable Falkland, the insolent Gower, his queen, and son, gave a peculiar interest to every part of the city, which they might be supposed to have inhabited. The spirit of elder days found a dwelling here, and we delighted to trace its footsteps. If these feelings had not found an imaginary gratification, the appearance of the city had yet in itself sufficient beauty to obtain our admiration. The colleges are ancient and picturesque; the streets are almost magnificent; and the lovely Isis, which flows beside it through meadows of exquisite verdure, is spread forth into a placid expanse of waters, which reflects its majestic assemblage of towers, and spires, and domes, embosomed among aged trees.

I enjoyed this scene; and yet my enjoyment was embittered both by the memory of the past, and the anticipation of the future. I was formed for peaceful happiness. During my youthful days discontent never visited my mind; and if I was ever over-come by *ennui*, the sight of what is beautiful in nature, or the study of what is excellent and sublime in the productions of man, could always interest my heart, and communicate elasticity to my spirits. But I am a blasted tree; the bolt has entered my soul; and I felt then that I should survive to exhibit, what I shall soon cease to be—a miserable spectacle of wrecked humanity, pitiable to others, and abhorrent to myself.

We passed a considerable period at Oxford, rambling among its environs, and endeavouring to identify every spot which might relate to the most animating epoch of English history. Our little voyages of discovery were often prolonged by the successive objects that presented themselves. We visited the tomb of the illustrious Hampden, and the field on which that patriot fell. For a moment my soul was elevated from its debasing and miserable fears to contemplate the divine ideas of liberty and self-sacrifice, of which these sights were the monuments and the remembrancers. For an instant I dared to shake off my chains, and look around me with a free and lofty spirit; but the iron had eaten into my flesh, and I sank again, trembling and hopeless, into my miserable self.

We left Oxford with regret, and proceeded to Matlock, which was our next place of rest. The country in the neighbourhood of this village resembled, to a greater degree, the scenery of Switzerland; but every thing is on a lower scale, and the green hills want the crown of distant white Alps, which always attend on the piny mountains of my native country. We visited the wondrous cave, and the little cabi-nets of natural history, where the curiosities are disposed in the same manner as in the collections at Servox and Chamounix. The latter name made me tremble, when pronounced by Henry; and I hastened to quit Matlock, with which that terrible scene was thus associated.

From Derby still journeying northward, we passed two months in Cumberland and Westmoreland. I could now almost fancy myself among the Swiss mountains. The little patches of snow which yet lingered on the northern sides of the mountains, the lakes, and the dashing of the rocky streams, were all familiar and dear sights to me. Here also we made some acquaintances, who almost contrived to cheat me into happiness. The delight of Clerval was proportionably greater than mine; his mind expanded in the company of men of talent, and he found in his own nature greater capacities and resources than he could have imagined himself to have possessed while he associated with his inferiors. "I could pass my life here," said he to me; "and among these mountains I should scarcely regret Switzerland and the Rhine."

But he found that a traveller's life is one that includes much pain amidst its enjoyments. His feelings are for ever on the stretch; and when he begins to sink into repose, he finds himself obliged to quit that on which he rests in pleasure for something new, which again engages his attention, and which also he forsakes for other novelties.

We had scarcely visited the various lakes of Cumberland and Westmoreland, and conceived an affection for some of the inhabitants, when the period of our appointment with our Scotch friend approached, and we left them to travel on. For my own part I was not sorry. I had now neglected my promise for some time, and I feared the effects of the dæmon's disappointment. He might remain in Switzerland, and wreak his vengeance on my relatives. This idea pursued me, and tormented me at every moment from which I might otherwise have snatched repose and peace. I waited for my letters with feverish impatience: if they were delayed, I was miserable, and overcome by a thousand fears; and when they arrived, and I saw the superscription of Elizabeth or my father, I hardly dared to read and ascertain my fate. Sometimes I thought that the fiend followed me, and might expedite my remissness by murdering my companion. When these thoughts possessed me, I would not quit Henry for a moment, but followed him as his shadow, to protect him from the fancied rage of his destroyer. I felt as if I had committed some great crime, the consciousness of which haunted me. I was guiltless, but I had indeed drawn down a horrible curse upon my head, as mortal as that of crime.

I visited Edinburgh with languid eyes and mind; and yet that city might have interested the most unfortunate being. Clerval did not like it so well as Oxford; for the antiquity of the latter city was more pleasing to him. But the beauty and regularity of the new town of Edinburgh, its romantic castle, and its environs, the most delightful in the world, Arthur's Seat, St. Bernard's Well, and the Pentland Hills, compensated him for the change, and filled him with cheerfulness and admiration. But I was impatient to arrive at the termination of my journey.

We left Edinburgh in a week, passing through Coupar, St. Andrews, and along the banks of the Tay, to Perth, where our friend expected us. But I was in no mood to laugh and talk with strangers, or enter into their feelings or plans with the good humour expected from a guest; and accordingly I told Clerval that I wished to make the tour of Scotland alone. "Do you," said I, "enjoy yourself, and let this be our rendezvous. I may be absent a month or two; but do not interfere with my motions, I entreat you: leave me to peace and solitude for a short time; and when I return, I hope it will be with a lighter heart, more congenial to your own temper."

Henry wished to dissuade me; but, seeing me bent on this plan, ceased to remonstrate. He entreated me to write often. "I had rather be with you," he said, "in your solitary rambles, than with these Scotch people, whom I do not know: hasten then, my dear friend, to return, that I may again feel myself somewhat at home, which I cannot do in your absence."

Having parted from my friend, I determined to visit some remote spot of Scotland, and finish my work in solitude. I did not doubt but that the monster followed me, and would discover himself to me when I should have finished, that he might receive his companion.

With this resolution I traversed the northern highlands, and fixed on one of the remotest of the Orkneys as the scene of my labours. It was a place fitted for such a work, being hardly more than a rock, whose high sides were continually beaten upon by the waves. The soil was barren, scarcely affording pasture for a few miserable cows, and oatmeal for its inhabitants, which consisted of five persons, whose gaunt and scraggy limbs gave tokens of their miserable fare. Vegetables and bread, when they indulged in such luxuries, and even fresh water, was to be procured from the main land, which was about five miles distant.

On the whole island there were but three miserable huts, and one of these was vacant when I arrived. This I hired. It contained but two rooms, and these exhibited all the squalidness of the most miserable penury. The thatch had fallen in, the walls were unplastered, and the door was off its hinges. I ordered it to be repaired, bought some furniture, and took possession; an incident which would, doubtless, have occasioned some surprise, had not all the senses of the cottagers been benumbed by want and squalid poverty. As it was, I lived ungazed at and unmolested, hardly thanked for the pittance of food and clothes which I gave; so much does suffering blunt even the coarsest sensations of men.

In this retreat I devoted the morning to labour; but in the evening, when the weather permitted, I walked on the stony beach of the sea, to listen to the waves as they roared, and dashed at my feet. It was a monotonous, yet ever-changing scene. I thought of Switzerland; it was far different from this desolate and appalling landscape. Its hills are covered with vines, and its cottages are scattered thickly in the plains. Its fair lakes reflect a blue and gentle sky; and, when troubled by the winds, their tumult is but as the play of a lively infant, when compared to the roarings of the giant ocean.

In this manner I distributed my occupations when I first arrived; but, as I proceeded in my labour, it became every day more horrible and irksome to me. Sometimes I could not prevail on myself to enter my laboratory for several days; and at other times I toiled day and night in order to complete my work. It was indeed a filthy process in which I was engaged. During my first experiment, a kind of enthusiastic frenzy had blinded me to the horror of my employment; my mind was intently fixed on the sequel of my labour, and my eyes were shut to the horror of my proceedings. But now I went to it in cold blood, and my heart often sickened at the work of my hands.

Thus situated, employed in the most detestable occupation, immersed in a solitude where nothing could for an instant call my attention from the actual scene in which I was engaged, my spirits became unequal; I grew restless and nervous. Every moment I feared to meet my persecutor. Sometimes I sat with my eyes fixed on the ground, fearing to raise them lest they should encounter the object which I so much dreaded to behold. I feared to wander from the sight of my fellow-creatures, lest when alone he should come to claim his companion.

In the mean time I worked on, and my labour was already considerably advanced. I looked towards its completion with a tremulous and eager hope, which I dared not trust myself to question, but which was intermixed with obscure forebodings of evil, that made my heart sicken in my bosom.

CHAPTER XIX

I SAT ONE EVENING IN MY LABORATORY; THE SUN HAD SET, AND THE MOON WAS JUST rising from the sea; I had not sufficient light for my employment, and I remained idle, in a pause of consideration of whether I should leave my labour for the night, or hasten its conclusion by an unremitting attention to it. As I sat, a train of reflection occurred to me, which led me to consider the effects of what I was now doing. Three years before I was engaged in the same manner, and had created a fiend whose unparalleled barbarity had desolated my heart, and filled it for ever with the bitterest remorse. I was now about to form another being, of whose dispositions I was alike ignorant; she might become ten thousand times more malignant than her mate, and delight, for its own sake, in murder and wretchedness. He had sworn to quit the neighbourhood of man, and hide himself in deserts; but she had not; and she, who in all probability was to become a thinking and reasoning animal, might refuse to comply with a compact made before her creation. They might even hate each other; the creature who already lived loathed his own deformity, and might he not conceive a greater abhorence for it when it came before his eyes in the female form? She also might turn with disgust from him to the superior beauty of man; she might quit him, and he be again alone, exasperated by the fresh provocation of being deserted by one of his own species.

Even if they were to leave Europe, and inhabit the deserts of the new world, yet one of the first results of those sympathies for which the dæmon thirsted would be children, and a race of devils would be propagated upon the earth, who might make the very existence of the species of man a condition precarious and full of terror. Had I a right, for my own benefit, to inflict this curse upon everlasting generations? I had before been moved by the sophisms of the being I had created; I had been struck senseless by his fiendish threats: but now, for the first time, the wickedness of my promise burst upon me; I shuddered to think that future ages might curse me as their pest, whose selfishness had not hesitated to buy its own peace at the price perhaps of the existence of the whole human race.

I trembled, and my heart failed within me; when, on looking up, I saw, by the light of the moon, the dæmon at the casement. A ghastly grin wrinkled his lips as he gazed on me, where I sat fulfilling the task which he had allotted to me. Yes, he had followed me in my travels; he had loitered in forests, hid himself in caves, or taken refuge in wide and desert heaths; and he now came to mark my progress, and claim the fulfilment of my promise.

As I looked on him, his countenance expressed the utmost extent of malice and treachery. I thought with a sensation of madness on my promise of creating another like to him, and, trembling with passion, tore to pieces the thing on which I was engaged. The wretch saw me destroy the creature on whose future existence he depended for happiness, and, with a howl of devilish despair and revenge, withdrew.

I left the room, and, locking the door, made a solemn vow in my own heart never to resume my labours; and then, with trembling steps, I sought my own apartment. I was alone; none were near me to dissipate the gloom, and relieve me from the sickening oppression of the most terrible reveries.

Several hours past, and I remained near my window gazing on the sea; it was almost motionless, for the winds were hushed, and all nature reposed under the eye of the quiet moon. A few fishing vessels alone specked the water, and now and then the gentle breeze wafted the sound of voices, as the fishermen called to one another. I felt the silence, although I was hardly conscious of its extreme profundity, until my ear was suddenly arrested by the paddling of oars near the shore, and a person landed close to my house.

In a few minutes after, I heard the creaking of my door, as if some one endeavoured to open it softly. I trembled from head to foot; I felt a presentiment of who it was, and wished to rouse one of the peasants who dwelt in a cottage not far from mine; but I was overcome by the sensation of helplessness, so often felt in frightful dreams, when you in vain endeavour to fly from an impending danger, and was rooted to the spot.

Presently I heard the sound of footsteps along the passage; the door opened, and the wretch whom I dreaded appeared. Shutting the door, he approached me, and said, in a smothered voice—

"You have destroyed the work which you began; what is it that you intend? Do you dare to break your promise? I have endured toil and misery: I left Switzerland with you; I crept along the shores of the Rhine, among its willow islands, and over the summits of its hills. I have dwelt many months in the heaths of England, and among the deserts of Scotland. I have endured incalculable fatigue, and cold, and hunger; do you dare destroy my hopes?"

"Begone! I do break my promise; never will I create another like yourself, equal in deformity and wickedness."

"Slave, I before reasoned with you, but you have proved yourself unworthy of my condescension. Remember that I have power; you believe yourself miserable, but I can make you so wretched that the light of day will be hateful to you. You are my creator, but I am your master;—obey!"

"The hour of my weakness is past, and the period of your power is arrived. Your threats cannot move me to do an act of wickedness; but they confirm me in a resolution of not creating you a companion in vice. Shall I, in cool blood, set loose upon the earth a dæmon, whose delight is in death and wretchedness. Begone! I am firm, and your words will only exasperate my rage."

The monster saw my determination in my face, and gnashed his teeth in the impotence of anger. "Shall each man," cried he, "find a wife for his bosom, and each beast have his mate, and I be alone? I had feelings of affection, and they were requited by detestation and scorn. Man, you may hate; but beware! Your hours will pass in dread and misery, and soon the bolt will fall which must ravish from you your happiness for ever. Are you to be happy, while I grovel in the intensity of my wretchedness? You can blast my other passions; but revenge remains—revenge, henceforth dearer than light or food! I may die; but first you, my tyrant and tormentor, shall curse the sun that gazes on your misery. Beware; for I am fearless, and therefore powerful. I will watch with the wiliness of a snake, that I may sting with its venom. Man, you shall repent of the injuries you inflict."

"Devil, cease; and do not poison the air with these sounds of malice. I have declared my resolution to you, and I am no coward to bend beneath words. Leave me; I am inexorable."

"It is well. I go; but remember, I shall be with you on your wedding-night."

I started forward, and exclaimed, "Villain! before you sign my death-warrant, be sure that you are yourself safe."

I would have seized him; but he eluded me, and quitted the house with precipitation: in a few moments I saw him in his boat, which shot across the waters with an arrowy swiftness, and was soon lost amidst the waves.

All was again silent; but his words rung in my ears. I burned with rage to pursue the murderer of my peace, and precipitate him into the ocean. I walked up and down my room hastily and perturbed, while my imagination conjured up a thousand images to torment and sting me. Why had I not followed him, and closed with him in mortal strife? But I had suffered him to depart, and he had directed his course towards the main land. I shuddered to think who might be the next victim sacrificed to his insatiate revenge. And then I thought again of his words—*"I will be with you on your wedding-night."* That then was the period fixed for the fulfilment of my destiny. In that hour I should die, and at once satisfy and extinguish his malice. The prospect did not move me to fear; yet when I thought of my beloved Elizabeth,—of her tears and endless sorrow, when she should find her lover so barbarously snatched from her,—tears, the first I had shed for many months, streamed from my eyes, and I resolved not to fall before my enemy without a bitter struggle.

The night passed away, and the sun rose from the ocean; my feelings became calmer, if it may be called calmness, when the violence of rage sinks into the depths of despair. I left the house, the horrid scene of the last night's contention, and walked on the beach of the sea, which I almost regarded as an insuperable barrier between me and my fellow-creatures; nay, a wish that such should prove the fact stole across me. I desired that I might pass my life on that barren rock, wearily it is true, but uninterrupted by any sudden shock of misery. If I returned, it was to be sacrificed, or to see those whom I most loved die under the grasp of a dæmon whom I had myself created.

I walked about the isle like a restless spectre, separated from all it loved, and miserable in the separation. When it became noon, and the sun rose higher, I lay down on the grass, and was overpowered by a deep sleep. I had been awake the whole of the preceding night, my nerves were agitated, and my eyes inflamed by watching and misery. The sleep into which I now sunk refreshed me; and when I awoke, I again felt as if I belonged to a race of human beings like myself, and I began to reflect upon what had passed with greater composure; yet still the words of the fiend rung in my ears like a death-knell, they appeared like a dream, yet distinct and oppressive as a reality.

The sun had far descended, and I still sat on the shore, satisfying my appetite, which had become ravenous, with an oaten cake, when I saw a fishing-boat land close to me, and one of the men brought me a packet; it contained letters from Geneva, and one from Clerval, entreating me to join him. He said that nearly a year had elapsed since we had quitted Switzerland, and France was yet unvisited. He entreated me, therefore, to leave my solitary isle, and meet him at Perth, in a week from that time, when we might arrange the plan of our future proceedings. This letter in a degree recalled me to life, and I determined to quit my island at the expiration of two days.

Yet, before I departed, there was a task to perform, on which I shuddered to reflect: I must pack my chemical instruments; and for that purpose I must enter the room which had been the scene of my odious work, and I must handle those utensils, the sight of which was sickening to me. The next morning, at day-break, I summoned sufficient courage, and unlocked the door of my laboratory. The remains of the half-finished creature, whom I had destroyed, lay scattered on the floor, and I almost felt as if I had mangled the living flesh of a human being. I paused to collect myself, and then entered the chamber. With trembling hand I conveyed the instruments out of the room; but I reflected that I ought not to leave the relics of my work to excite the horror and suspicion of the peasants, and I accordingly put them into a basket, with a great quantity of stones, and laying them up, determined to throw them into the sea that very night; and in the mean time I sat upon the beach, employed in cleaning and arranging my chemical apparatus.

Nothing could be more complete than the alteration that had taken place in my feelings since the night of the appearance of the dæmon. I had before regarded my promise with a gloomy despair, as a thing that, with whatever consequences, must be fulfilled; but I now felt as if a film had been taken from before my eyes, and that I, for the first time, saw clearly. The idea of renewing my labours did not for one instant occur to me; the threat I had heard weighed on my thoughts, but I did not reflect that a voluntary act of mine could avert it. I had resolved in my own mind, that to create another like the fiend I had first made would be an act of the basest and most atrocious selfishness; and I banished from my mind every thought that could lead to a different conclusion.

Between two and three in the morning the moon rose; and I then, putting my basket aboard a little skiff, sailed out about four miles from the shore. The scene was perfectly solitary: a few boats were returning towards land, but I sailed away from them. I felt as if I was about the commission of a dreadful crime, and avoided with shuddering anxiety any encounter with my fellow-creatures. At one time the moon, which had before been clear, was suddenly overspread by a thick cloud, and I took advantage of the moment of darkness, and cast my basket into the sea; I listened to the gurgling sound as it sunk, and then sailed away from the spot. The sky became clouded; but the air was pure, although chilled by the north-east breeze that was then rising. But it refreshed me, and filled me with such agreeable sensations, that I resolved to prolong my stay on the water, and fixing the rudder in a direct position, stretched myself at the bottom of the boat. Clouds hid the moon, every thing was obscure, and I heard only the sound of the boat, as its keel cut through the waves; the murmur lulled me, and in a short time I slept soundly.

I do not know how long I remained in this situation, but when I awoke I found that the sun had already mounted considerably. The wind was high, and the waves continually threatened the safety of my little skiff. I found that the wind was north-east, and must have driven me far from the coast from which I had embarked. I endeavoured to change my course, but quickly found that if I again made the attempt the boat would be instantly filled with water. Thus situated, my only resource was to drive before the wind. I confess that I felt a few sensations of terror. I had no compass with me, and was so little acquainted with the geography of this part of the world that the sun was of little benefit to me. I might be driven into the wide Atlantic, and feel all the tortures of starvation, or be swallowed up in the immeasurable waters that roared and buffeted around me. I had already been out many hours, and felt the torment of a burning thirst, a prelude to my other sufferings. I looked on the heavens, which were covered by clouds that flew before the wind only to be replaced by others: I looked upon the sea, it was to be my grave. "Fiend," I exclaimed, "your task is already fulfilled!" I thought of Elizabeth, of my father, and of Clerval; and sunk into a reverie, so despairing and frightful, that even now, when the scene is on the point of closing before me for ever, I shudder to reflect on it.

Some hours passed thus; but by degrees, as the sun declined towards the horizon, the wind died away into a gentle breeze, and the sea became free from breakers. But these gave place to a heavy swell; I felt sick, and hardly able to hold the rudder, when suddenly I saw a line of high land towards the south.

Almost spent, as I was, by fatigue, and the dreadful suspense I endured for several hours, this sudden certainty of life rushed like a flood of warm joy to my heart, and tears gushed from my eyes.

How mutable are our feelings, and how strange is that clinging love we have of life even in the excess of misery! I constructed another sail with a part of my dress, and eagerly steered my course towards the land. It had a wild and rocky appearance; but as I approached nearer, I easily perceived the traces of cultivation. I saw vessels near the shore, and found myself suddenly transported back to the neighbourhood of civilized man. I eagerly traced the windings of the land, and hailed a steeple which I at length saw issuing from behind a small promontory. As I was in a state of extreme debility, I resolved to sail directly towards the town as a place where I could most easily procure nourishment. Fortunately I had money with me. As I turned the promontory, I perceived a small neat town and a good harbour, which I entered, my heart bounding with joy at my unexpected escape.

As I was occupied in fixing the boat and arranging the sails, several people crowded towards the spot. They seemed very much surprised at my appearance; but, instead of offering me any assistance, whispered together with gestures that at any other time might have produced in me a slight sensation of alarm. As it was, I merely remarked that they spoke English; and I therefore addressed them in that language: "My good friends," said I, "will you be so kind as to tell me the name of this town, and inform me where I am?"

"You will know that soon enough," replied a man with a gruff voice. "May be you are come to a place that will not prove much to your taste; but you will not be consulted as to your quarters, I promise you."

I was exceedingly surprised on receiving so rude an answer from a stranger; and I was also disconcerted on perceiving the frowning and angry countenances of his companions. "Why do you answer me so roughly?" I replied: "surely it is not the custom of Englishmen to receive strangers so inhospitably."

"I do not know," said the man, "what the custom of the English may be; but it is the custom of the Irish to hate villains."

While this strange dialogue continued, I perceived the crowd rapidly increase. Their faces expressed a mixture of curiosity and anger, which annoyed, and in some degree alarmed me. I inquired the way to the inn; but no one replied. I then moved forward, and a murmuring sound arose from the crowd as they followed and surrounded me; when an ill-looking man approaching, tapped me on the shoulder, and said, "Come, Sir, you must follow me to Mr. Kirwin's, to give an account of yourself."

"Who is Mr. Kirwin? Why am I to give an account of myself? Is not this a free country?"

"Aye, Sir, free enough for honest folks. Mr. Kirwin is a magistrate; and you are to give an account of the death of a gentleman who was found murdered here last night."

This answer startled me; but I presently recovered myself. I was innocent; that could easily be proved: accordingly I followed my conductor in silence, and was led to one of the best houses in the town. I was ready to sink from fatigue and hunger; but, being surrounded by a crowd, I thought it politic to rouse all my strength, that no physical debility might be construed into apprehension or conscious guilt. Little did I then expect the calamity that was in a few moments to overwhelm me, and extinguish in horror and despair all fear of ignominy or death.

I must pause here; for it requires all my fortitude to recall the memory of the frightful events which I am about to relate, in proper detail, to my recollection.

CHAPTER XX

I was soon introduced into the presence of the magistrate, an old benevolent man, with calm and mild manners. He looked upon me, however, with some degree of severity; and then, turning towards my conductors, he asked who appeared as witnesses on this occasion.

About half a dozen men came forward; and one being selected by the magistrate, he deposed, that he had been out fishing the night before with his son and brother-in-law,

Daniel Nugent, when, about ten o'clock, they observed a strong northerly blast rising, and they accordingly put in for port. It was a very dark night, as the moon had not yet risen; they did not land at the harbour, but, as they had been accustomed, at a creek about two miles below. He walked on first, carrying a part of the fishing tackle, and his companions followed him at some distance. As he was proceeding along the sands, he struck his foot against something, and fell all his length on the ground. His companions came up to assist him; and, by the light of their lantern, they found that he had fallen on the body of a man, who was to all appearance dead. Their first supposition was, that it was the corpse of some person who had been drowned, and was thrown on shore by the waves; but, upon examination, they found that the clothes were not wet, and even that the body was not then cold. They instantly carried it to the cottage of an old woman near the spot, and endeavoured, but in vain, to restore it to life. He appeared to be a hand-some young man, about five and twenty years of age. He had apparently been strangled; for there was no sign of any violence, except the black mark of fingers on his neck.

The first part of this deposition did not in the least interest me; but when the mark of the fingers was mentioned, I remembered the murder of my brother, and felt myself extremely agitated; my limbs trembled, and a mist came over my eyes, which obliged me to lean on a chair for support. The magistrate observed me with a keen eye, and of course drew an unfavourable augury from my manner.

The son confirmed his father's account: but when Daniel Nugent was called, he swore positively that, just before the fall of his companion, he saw a boat, with a single man in it, at a short distance from the shore; and, as far as he could judge by the light of a few stars, it was the same boat in which I had just landed.

A woman deposed, that she lived near the beach, and was standing at the door of her cottage, waiting for the return of the fishermen, about an hour before she heard of the discovery of the body, when she saw a boat, with only one man in it, push off from that part of the shore where the corpse was afterwards found.

Another woman confirmed the account of the fishermen having brought the body into her house; it was not cold. They put it into a bed, and rubbed it; and Daniel went to the town for an apothecary, but life was quite gone.

Several other men were examined concerning my landing; and they agreed, that, with the strong north wind that had arisen during the night, it was very probable that I had beaten about for many hours, and had been obliged to return nearly to the same spot from which I had departed. Besides, they observed that it appeared that I had brought the body from another place, and it was likely, that as I did not appear to know the shore, I might have put into the harbour ignorant of the distance of the town of —— from the place where I had deposited the corpse.

Mr. Kirwin, on hearing this evidence, desired that I should be taken into the room where the body lay for interment that it might be observed what effect the sight of it would produce upon me. This idea was probably suggested by the extreme agitation I had exhibited when the mode of the murder had been described. I was accordingly conducted, by the magistrate and several other persons, to the inn. I could not help being struck by the strange coincidences that had taken place during this eventful night; but, knowing that I had been conversing with several persons in the island I had inhabited about the time that the body had been found, I was perfectly tranquil as to the consequences of the affair.

I entered the room where the corpse lay, and was led up to the coffin. How can I describe my sensations on beholding it? I feel yet parched with horror, nor can I reflect on that terrible moment without shuddering and agony, that faintly reminds me of the anguish of the recognition. The trial, the presence of the magistrate and witnesses, passed like a dream from my memory, when I saw the lifeless form of Henry Clerval stretched before me. I gasped for breath; and, throwing myself on the body, I exclaimed, "Have my murderous machinations deprived you also, my dearest Henry, of life? Two I have already destroyed; other victims await their destiny: but you, Clerval, my friend, my benefactor"—

The human frame could no longer support the agonizing suffering that I endured, and I was carried out of the room in strong convulsions.

A fever succeeded to this. I lay for two months on the point of death: my ravings, as I afterwards heard, were frightful; I called myself the murderer of William, of Justine, and of Clerval. Sometimes I entreated my attendants to assist me in the destruction of the fiend by whom I was tormented; and, at others, I felt the fingers of the monster already grasping my neck, and screamed aloud with agony and terror. Fortunately, as I spoke my native language, Mr. Kirwin alone understood me; but my gestures and bitter cries were sufficient to affright the other witnesses.

Why did I not die? More miserable than man ever was before, why did I not sink into forgetfulness and rest? Death snatches away many blooming children, the only hopes of their doating parents: how many brides and youthful lovers have been one day in the bloom of health and hope, and the next a prey for worms and the decay of the tomb! Of what materials was I made, that I could thus resist so many shocks, which, like the turning of the wheel, continually renewed the torture.

But I was doomed to live; and, in two months, found myself as awaking from a dream, in a prison, stretched on a wretched bed, surrounded by gaolers, turnkeys, bolts, and all the miserable apparatus of a dungeon. It was morning, I remember, when I thus awoke to understanding: I had forgotten the particulars of what had happened, and only felt as if some great misfortune had suddenly overwhelmed me; but when I looked around, and saw the barred windows, and the squalidness of the room in which I was, all flashed across my memory, and I groaned bitterly.

This sound disturbed an old woman who was sleeping in a chair beside me. She was a hired nurse, the wife of one of the turnkeys, and her countenance expressed all those bad qualities which often characterize that class. The lines of her face were hard and rude, like that of persons accustomed to see without sympathizing in sights of misery. Her tone expressed her entire indifference; she addressed me in English, and the voice struck me as one that I had heard during my sufferings:

"Are you better now, Sir?" said she.

I replied in the same language, with a feeble voice, "I believe I am; but if it be all true, if indeed I did not dream, I am sorry that I am still alive to feel this misery and horror."

"For that matter," replied the old woman, "if you mean about the gentleman you murdered, I believe that it were better for you if you were dead, for I fancy it will go hard with you; but you will be hung when the next sessions come on. However, that's none of my business, I am sent to nurse you, and get you well; I do my duty with a safe conscience, it were well if every body did the same."

I turned with loathing from the woman who could utter so unfeeling a speech to a person just saved, on the very edge of death; but I felt languid, and unable to reflect on all that had passed. The whole series of my life appeared to me as a dream; I sometimes doubted if indeed it were all true, for it never presented itself to my mind with the force of reality.

As the images that floated before me became more distinct, I grew feverish; a darkness pressed around me; no one was near me who soothed me with the gentle voice of love; no dear hand supported me. The physician came and prescribed medicines, and the old woman prepared them for me; but utter carelessness was visible in the first, and the expression of brutality was strongly marked in the visage of the second. Who could be interested in the fate of a murderer, but the hangman who would gain his fee?

These were my first reflections; but I soon learned that Mr. Kirwin had shewn me extreme kindness. He had caused the best room in the prison to be prepared for me (wretched indeed was the best); and it was he who had provided a physician and a nurse. It is true, he seldom came to see me; for, although he ardently desired to relieve the sufferings of every human creature, he did not wish to be present at the agonies and miserable ravings of a murderer. He came, therefore, sometimes to see that I was not neglected; but his visits were short, and at long intervals.

One day, when I was gradually recovering, I was seated in a chair, my eyes half open, and my cheeks livid like those in death, I was overcome by gloom and misery, and often reflected I had better seek death than remain miserably pent up only to be let loose in a world replete with wretchedness. At one time I considered whether I should not declare myself guilty, and suffer the penalty of the law, less innocent than poor Justine had been. Such were my thoughts, when the door of my apartment was opened, and Mr. Kirwin entered. His countenance expressed sympathy and compassion; he drew a chair close to mine, and addressed me in French—

"I fear that this place is very shocking to you; can I do any thing to make you more comfortable?"

"I thank you; but all that you mention is nothing to me: on the whole earth there is no comfort which I am capable of receiving."

"I know that the sympathy of a stranger can be but of little relief to one borne down as you are by so strange a misfortune. But you will, I hope, soon quit this melancholy abode; for, doubtless, evidence can easily be brought to free you from the criminal charge."

"That is my least concern: I am, by a course of strange events, become the most miserable of mortals. Persecuted and tortured as I am and have been, can death be any evil to me?"

"Nothing indeed could be more unfortunate and agonizing than the strange chances that have lately occurred. You were thrown, by some surprising accident, on this shore, renowned for its hospitality: seized immediately, and charged with murder. The first sight that was presented to your eyes was the body of your friend, murdered in so unaccountable a manner, and placed, as it were, by some fiend across your path."

As Mr. Kirwin said this, notwithstanding the agitation I endured on this retrospect of my sufferings, I also felt considerable surprise at the knowledge he seemed to possess concerning me. I suppose some astonishment was exhibited in my countenance; for Mr. Kirwin hastened to say—

"It was not until a day or two after your illness that I thought of examining your dress, that I might discover some trace by which I could send to your relations an account of your misfortune and illness. I found several letters, and, among others, one which I discovered from its commencement to be from your father. I instantly wrote to Geneva: nearly two months have elapsed since the departure of my letter.—But you are ill; even now you tremble: you are unfit for agitation of any kind."

"This suspense is a thousand times worse than the most horrible event: tell me what new scene of death has been acted, and whose murder I am now to lament."

"Your family is perfectly well," said Mr. Kirwin, with gentleness; "and some one, a friend, is come to visit you."

I know not by what chain of thought the idea presented itself, but it instantly darted into my mind that the murderer had come to mock at my misery, and taunt me with the death of Clerval, as a new incitement for me to comply with his hellish desires. I put my hand before my eyes, and cried out in agony—

"Oh! take him away! I cannot see him; for God's sake, do not let him enter!"

Mr. Kirwin regarded me with a troubled countenance. He could not help regarding my exclamation as a presumption of my guilt, and said, in rather a severe tone—

"I should have thought, young man, that the presence of your father would have been welcome, instead of inspiring such violent repugnance."

"My father!" cried I, while every feature and every muscle was relaxed from anguish to pleasure. "Is my father, indeed, come? How kind, how very kind. But where is he, why does he not hasten to me?"

My change of manner surprised and pleased the magistrate; perhaps he thought that my former exclamation was a momentary return of delirium, and now he instantly resumed his former benevolence. He rose, and quitted the room with my nurse, and in a moment my father entered it.

Nothing, at this moment, could have given me greater pleasure than the arrival of my father. I stretched out my hand to him, and cried—

"Are you then safe—and Elizabeth—and Ernest?"

My father calmed me with assurances of their welfare, and endeavoured, by dwelling on these subjects so interesting to my heart, to raise my desponding spirits; but he soon felt that a prison cannot be the abode of cheerfulness. "What a place is this that you inhabit, my son!" said he, looking mournfully at the barred windows, and wretched appearance of the room. "You travelled to seek happiness, but a fatality seems to pursue you. And poor Clerval—"

The name of my unfortunate and murdered friend was an agitation too great to be endured in my weak state; I shed tears.

"Alas! yes, my father," replied I; "some destiny of the most horrible kind hangs over me, and I must live to fulfil it, or surely I should have died on the coffin of Henry."

We were not allowed to converse for any length of time, for the precarious state of my health rendered every precaution necessary that could insure tranquillity. Mr. Kirwin came in, and insisted that my strength should not be exhausted by too much exertion. But the appearance of my father was to me like that of my good angel, and I gradually recovered my health.

As my sickness quitted me, I was absorbed by a gloomy and black melancholy, that nothing could dissipate. The image of Clerval was for ever before me, ghastly and murdered. More than once the agitation into which these reflections threw me made my friends dread a dangerous relapse. Alas! why did they preserve so miserable and detested a life? It was surely that I might fulfil my destiny, which is now drawing to a close. Soon, oh, very soon, will death extinguish these throbbings, and relieve me from the mighty weight of anguish that bears me to the dust; and, in executing the award of justice, I shall also sink to rest. Then the appearance of death was distant, although the wish was ever present to my thoughts; and I often sat for hours motionless and speechless, wishing for some mighty revolution that might bury me and my destroyer in its ruins.

The season of the assizes approached. I had already been three months in prison; and although I was still weak, and in continual danger of a relapse, I was obliged to travel nearly a hundred miles to the county-town, where the court was held. Mr. Kirwin charged himself with every care of collecting witnesses, and arranging my defence. I was spared the disgrace of appearing publicly as a criminal, as the case was not brought before the court that decides on life and death. The grand jury rejected the bill, on its being proved that I was on the Orkney Islands at the hour the body of my friend was found, and a fortnight after my removal I was liberated from prison.

My father was enraptured on finding me freed from the vexations of a criminal charge, that I was again allowed to breathe the fresh atmosphere, and allowed to return to my native country. I did not participate in these feelings; for to me the walls of a dungeon or a palace were alike hateful. The cup of life was poisoned for ever; and although the sun shone upon me, as upon the happy and gay of heart, I saw around me nothing but a dense and frightful darkness, penetrated by no light but the glimmer of two eyes that glared upon me. Sometimes they were the expressive eyes of Henry, languishing in death, the dark orbs nearly covered by the lids, and the long black lashes that fringed them; sometimes it was the watery clouded eyes of the monster, as I first saw them in my chamber at Ingolstadt.

My father tried to awaken in me the feelings of affection. He talked of Geneva, which I should soon visit—of Elizabeth, and Ernest; but these words only drew deep groans from me. Sometimes, indeed, I felt a wish for happiness; and thought, with melancholy delight, of my beloved cousin; or longed, with a devouring *maladie du pays*, to see once more the blue lake and rapid Rhone, that had been so dear to me in early childhood: but my general state of feeling was a torpor, in which a prison was as welcome a residence as the divinest scene in nature; and these fits were seldom interrupted, but by paroxysms of anguish and despair. At these moments I often endeavoured to put an end to the existence I loathed; and it required unceasing attendance and vigilance to restrain me from committing some dreadful act of violence.

I remember, as I quitted the prison, I heard one of the men say, "He may be innocent of the murder, but he has certainly a bad conscience." These words struck me. A bad conscience! yes, surely I had one. William, Justine, and Clerval, had died through my infernal machinations; "And whose death," cried I, "is to finish the tragedy? Ah! my father, do not remain in this wretched country; take me where I may forget myself, my existence, and all the world."

My father easily acceded to my desire; and, after having taken leave of Mr. Kirwin, we hastened to Dublin. I felt as if I was relieved from a heavy weight, when the packet sailed with a fair wind from Ireland, and I had quitted for ever the country which had been to me the scene of so much misery.

It was midnight. My father slept in the cabin; and I lay on the deck, looking at the stars, and listening to the dashing of the waves. I hailed the darkness that shut Ireland from my sight, and my pulse beat with a feverish joy, when I reflected that I should soon see Geneva. The past appeared to me in the light of a frightful dream; yet the vessel in which I was, the wind that blew me from the detested shore of Ireland, and the sea which surrounded me, told me too forcibly that I was deceived by no vision, and that Clerval, my friend and dearest companion, had fallen a victim to me and the monster of my creation. I repassed, in my memory, my whole life; my quiet happiness while residing with my family in Geneva, the death of my mother, and my departure for Ingolstadt. I remembered shuddering at the mad enthusiasm that hurried me on to the creation of my hideous enemy, and I called to mind the night during which he first lived. I was unable to pursue the train of thought; a thousand feelings pressed upon me, and I wept bitterly.

Ever since my recovery from the fever I had been in the custom of taking every night a small quantity of laudanum; for it was by means of this drug only that I was enabled to gain the rest necessary for the preservation of life. Oppressed by the recollection of my various misfortunes, I now took a double dose, and soon slept profoundly. But sleep did not afford me respite from thought and misery; my dreams presented a thousand objects that scared me. Towards morning I was possessed by a kind of nightmare; I felt the fiend's grasp in my neck, and could not free myself from it; groans and cries rung in my ears. My father, who was watching over me, perceiving my restlessness, awoke me, and pointed to the port of Holyhead, which we were now entering.

CHAPTER XXI

We had resolved not to go to London, but to cross the country to Portsmouth, and thence to embark for Havre. I preferred this plan principally because I dreaded to see again those places in which I had enjoyed a few moments of tranquillity with my beloved Clerval. I thought with horror of seeing again those persons whom we had been accustomed to visit together, and who might make inquiries concerning an event, the very remembrance of which made me again feel the pang I endured when I gazed on his lifeless form in the inn at ——.

As for my father, his desires and exertions were bounded to the again seeing me restored to health and peace of mind. His tenderness and attentions were unremitting; my grief and gloom was obstinate, but he would not despair. Sometimes he thought that I felt deeply the degradation of being obliged to answer a charge of murder, and he endeavoured to prove to me the futility of pride.

"Alas! my father," said I, "how little do you know me. Human beings, their feelings and passions, would indeed be degraded, if such a wretch as I felt pride. Justine, poor unhappy Justine, was as innocent as I, and she suffered the same charge; she died for it; and I am the cause of this—I murdered her. William, Justine, and Henry—they all died by my hands."

My father had often, during my imprisonment, heard me make the same assertion; when I thus accused myself, he sometimes seemed to desire an explanation, and at others he appeared to consider it as caused by delirium, and that, during my illness, some idea of this kind had presented itself to my imagination, the remembrance of which I preserved in my convalescence. I avoided explanation, and maintained a continual silence concerning the wretch I had created. I had a feeling that I should be supposed mad, and this for ever chained my tongue, when I would have given the whole world to have confided the fatal secret.

Upon this occasion my father said, with an expression of unbounded wonder, "What do you mean, Victor? are you mad? My dear son, I entreat you never to make such an assertion again."

"I am not mad," I cried energetically; "the sun and the heavens, who have viewed my operations, can bear witness of my truth. I am the assassin of those most innocent victims; they died by my machinations. A thousand times would I have shed my own blood, drop by drop, to have saved their lives; but I could not, my father, indeed I could not sacrifice the whole human race."

The conclusion of this speech convinced my father that my ideas were deranged, and he instantly changed the subject of our conversation, and endeavoured to alter the course of my thoughts. He wished as much as possible to obliterate the memory of the scenes that had taken place in Ireland, and never alluded to them, or suffered me to speak of my misfortunes.

As time passed away I became more calm: misery had her dwelling in my heart, but I no longer talked in the same incoherent manner of my own crimes; sufficient for me was the consciousness of them. By the utmost self-violence, I curbed the imperious voice of wretchedness, which sometimes desired to declare itself to the whole world; and my manners were calmer and more composed than they had ever been since my journey to the sea of ice.

We arrived at Havre on the 8th of May, and instantly proceeded to Paris, where my father had some business which detained us a few weeks. In this city, I received the following letter from Elizabeth: ——

To VICTOR FRANKENSTEIn.

MY DEAREST FRIEND

It gave me the greatest pleasure to receive a letter from my uncle dated at Paris; you are no longer at a formidable distance, and I may hope to see you in less than a fortnight. My poor cousin, how much you must have suffered! I expect to see you looking even more ill than when you quitted Geneva. This winter has been passed most miserably, tortured as I have been by anxious suspense; yet I hope to see peace in your countenance, and to find that your heart is not totally devoid of comfort and tranquillity.

Yet I fear that the same feelings now exist that made you so miserable a year ago, even perhaps augmented by time. I would not disturb you at this period, when so many misfortunes weigh upon you; but a conversation that I had with my uncle previous to his departure renders some explanation necessary before we meet.

Explanation! you may possibly say; what can Elizabeth have to explain? If you really say this, my questions are answered, and I have no more to do than to sign myself your affectionate cousin. But you are distant from me, and it is possible that you may dread, and yet be pleased with this explanation; and, in a probability of this being the case, I dare not any longer postpone writing what, during your absence, I have often wished to express to you, but have never had the courage to begin.

You well know, Victor, that our union had been the favourite plan of your parents ever since our infancy. We were told this when young, and taught to look forward to it as an event that would certainly take place. We were affectionate playfellows during childhood, and, I believe, dear and valued friends to one another as we grew older. But as brother and sister often entertain a lively affection towards each other, without desiring a more intimate union, may not such also be our case? Tell me, dearest Victor. Answer me, I conjure you, by our mutual happiness, with simple truth—Do you not love another?

You have travelled; you have spent several years of your life at Ingolstadt; and I confess to you, my friend, that when I saw you last autumn so unhappy, flying to solitude, from the society of every creature, I could not help supposing that you might regret our connexion, and believe yourself bound in honour to fulfil the wishes of your parents, although they opposed themselves to your inclinations. But this is false reasoning. I confess to you, my cousin, that I love you, and that in my airy dreams of futurity you have been my constant friend and companion. But it is your happiness I desire as well as my own, when I declare to you, that our marriage would render me eternally miserable, unless it were the dictate of your own free choice. Even now I weep to think, that, borne down as you are by the cruelest misfortunes, you may stifle, by the word *honour*, all hope of that love and happiness which would alone restore you to yourself. I, who have so interested an affection for you, may increase your miseries ten-fold, by being an obstacle to your wishes. Ah, Victor, be assured that your cousin and playmate has too sincere a love for you not to be made miserable by this supposition. Be happy, my friend; and if you obey me in this one request, remain satisfied that nothing on earth will have the power to interrupt my tranquillity.

Do not let this letter disturb you; do not answer it tomorrow, or the next day, or even until you come, if it will give you pain. My uncle will send me news of your health; and if I see but one smile on your lips when we meet, occasioned by this or any other exertion of mine, I shall need no other happiness.

ELIZABETH LAVENZA.

Geneva, May 18th, 17——.

This letter revived in my memory what I had before forgotten, the threat of the fiend—"*I will be with you on your wedding-night!*" Such was my sentence, and on that night would the dæmon employ every art to destroy me, and tear me from the glimpse of happiness which promised partly to console my sufferings. On that night he had determined to consummate his crimes by my death. Well, be it so; a deadly struggle would then assuredly take place, in which if he was victorious, I should be at peace, and his power over me be at an end. If he were vanquished, I should be a free man. Alas! what freedom? such as the peasant enjoys when his family have been massacred before his eyes, his cottage burnt, his lands laid waste, and he is turned adrift, homeless, pennyless, and alone, but free. Such would be my liberty, except that in my Elizabeth I possessed a treasure; alas! balanced by those horrors of remorse and guilt, which would pursue me until death.

Sweet and beloved Elizabeth! I read and re-read her letter, and some softened feelings stole into my heart, and dared to whisper paradisaical dreams of love and joy; but the apple was already eaten, and the angel's arm bared to drive me from all hope. Yet I would die to make her happy. If the monster executed his threat, death was inevitable; yet, again, I considered whether my marriage would hasten my fate. My destruction might indeed arrive a few months sooner; but if my torturer should suspect that I postponed it, influenced by his menaces, he would surely find other, and perhaps more dreadful means of revenge. He had vowed *to be with me on my wedding-night*, yet he did not consider that threat as binding him to peace in the mean time; for, as if to shew me that he was not yet satiated with blood, he had murdered Clerval immediately after the enunciation of his threats. I resolved, therefore, that if my immediate union with my cousin would conduce either to hers or my father's happiness, my adversary's designs against my life should not retard it a single hour.

In this state of mind I wrote to Elizabeth. My letter was calm and affectionate. "I fear, my beloved girl," I said, "little happiness remains for us on earth; yet all that I may one day enjoy is concentered in you. Chase away your idle fears; to you alone do I consecrate my life, and my endeavours for contentment. I have one secret, Elizabeth, a dreadful one; when revealed to you, it will chill your frame with horror, and then, far from being surprised at my misery, you will only wonder that I survive what I have endured. I will confide this tale of misery and terror to you the day after our marriage shall take place; for, my sweet cousin, there must be perfect confidence between us. But until then, I conjure you, do not mention or allude to it. This I most earnestly entreat, and I know you will comply."

In about a week after the arrival of Elizabeth's letter, we returned to Geneva. My cousin welcomed me with warm affection; yet tears were in her eyes, as she beheld my emaciated frame and feverish cheeks. I saw a change in her also. She was thinner, and had lost much of that heavenly vivacity that had before charmed me; but her gentleness, and soft looks of compassion, made her a more fit companion for one blasted and miserable as I was.

The tranquillity which I now enjoyed did not endure. Memory brought madness with it; and when I thought on what had passed, a real insanity possessed me; sometimes I was furious, and burnt with rage, sometimes low and despondent. I neither spoke or looked, but sat motionless, bewildered by the multitude of miseries that overcame me.

Elizabeth alone had the power to draw me from these fits; her gentle voice would soothe me when transported by passion, and inspire me with human feelings when sunk in torpor. She wept with me, and for me. When reason returned, she would remonstrate, and endeavour to inspire me with resignation. Ah! it is well for the unfortunate to be resigned, but for the guilty there is no peace. The agonies of remorse poison the luxury there is otherwise sometimes found in indulging the excess of grief.

Soon after my arrival my father spoke of my immediate marriage with my cousin. I remained silent.

"Have you, then, some other attachment?"

"None on earth. I love Elizabeth, and look forward to our union with delight. Let the day therefore be fixed; and on it I will consecrate myself, in life or death, to the happiness of my cousin."

"My dear Victor, do not speak thus. Heavy misfortunes have befallen us; but let us only cling closer to what remains, and transfer our love for those whom we have lost to those who yet live. Our circle will be small, but bound close by the ties of affection and mutual misfortune. And when time shall have softened your despair, new and dear objects of care will be born to replace those of whom we have been so cruelly deprived."

Such were the lessons of my father. But to me the remembrance of the threat returned: nor can you wonder, that, omnipotent as the fiend had yet been in his deeds of blood, I should almost regard him as invincible; and that when he had pronounced the words, "*I shall be with you on your wedding-night*," I should regard the threatened fate as unavoidable. But death was no evil to me, if the loss of Elizabeth were balanced with it; and I therefore, with a contented and even cheerful countenance, agreed with my father, that if my cousin would consent, the ceremony should take place in ten days, and thus put, as I imagined, the seal to my fate.

Great God! if for one instant I had thought what might be the hellish intention of my fiendish adversary, I would rather have banished myself for ever from my native country, and wandered a friendless outcast over the earth, than have consented to this miserable marriage. But, as if possessed of magic powers, the monster had blinded me to his real intentions; and when I thought that I prepared only my own death, I hastened that of a far dearer victim.

As the period fixed for our marriage drew nearer, whether from cowardice or a prophetic feeling, I felt my heart sink within me. But I concealed my feelings by an appearance of hilarity, that brought smiles and joy to the countenance of my father, but hardly deceived the ever-watchful and nicer eye of Elizabeth. She looked forward to our union with placid contentment, not unmingled with a little fear, which past misfortunes had impressed, that what now appeared certain and tangible happiness, might soon dissipate into an airy dream, and leave no trace but deep and everlasting regret.

Preparations were made for the event; congratulatory visits were received; and all wore a smiling appearance. I shut up, as well as I could, in my own heart the anxiety that preyed there, and entered with seeming earnestness into the plans of my father, although they might only serve as the decorations of my tragedy. A house was purchased for us near Cologny, by which we should enjoy the pleasures of the country, and yet be so near Geneva as to see my father every day; who would still reside within the walls, for the benefit of Ernest, that he might follow his studies at the schools.

In the mean time I took every precaution to defend my person, in case the fiend should openly attack me. I carried pistols and a dagger constantly about me, and was ever on the watch to prevent artifice; and by these means gained a greater degree of tranquillity. Indeed, as the period approached, the threat appeared more as a delusion, not to be regarded as worthy to disturb my peace, while the happiness I hoped for in my marriage wore a greater appearance of certainty, as the day fixed for its solemnization drew nearer, and I heard it continually spoken of as an occurrence which no accident could possibly prevent.

Elizabeth seemed happy; my tranquil demeanour contributed greatly to calm her mind. But on the day that was to fulfil my wishes and my destiny, she was melancholy, and a presentiment of evil pervaded her; and perhaps also she thought of the dreadful secret, which I had promised to reveal to her the following day. My father was in the mean time overjoyed, and, in the bustle of preparation, only observed in the melancholy of his niece the diffidence of a bride.

After the ceremony was performed, a large party assembled at my father's; but it was agreed that Elizabeth and I should pass the afternoon and night at Evian, and return to Cologny the next morning. As the day was fair, and the wind favourable, we resolved to go by water.

Those were the last moments of my life during which I enjoyed the feeling of happiness. We passed rapidly along: the sun was hot, but we were sheltered from its rays by a kind of canopy, while we enjoyed the beauty of the scene, sometimes on one side of the lake, where we saw Mont Salêve, the pleasant banks of Montalègre, and at a distance, surmounting all, the beautiful Mont Blanc, and the assemblage of snowy mountains that in vain endeavour to emulate her; sometimes coasting the opposite banks, we saw the mighty Jura opposing its dark side to the ambition that would quit its native country, and an almost insurmountable barrier to the invader who should wish to enslave it.

I took the hand of Elizabeth: "You are sorrowful, my love. Ah! if you knew what I have suffered, and what I may yet endure, you would endeavour to let me taste the quiet, and freedom from despair, that this one day at least permits me to enjoy."

"Be happy, my dear Victor," replied Elizabeth; "there is, I hope, nothing to distress you; and be assured that if a lively joy is not painted in my face, my heart is contented. Something whispers to me not to depend too much on the prospect that is opened before us; but I will not listen to such a sinister voice. Observe how fast we move along, and how the clouds which sometimes obscure, and sometimes rise above the dome of Mont Blanc, render this scene of beauty still more interesting. Look also at the innumerable fish that are swimming in the clear waters, where we can distinguish every pebble that lies at the bottom. What a divine day! how happy and serene all nature appears!"

Thus Elizabeth endeavoured to divert her thoughts and mine from all reflection upon melancholy subjects. But her temper was fluctuating; joy for a few instants shone in her eyes, but it continually gave place to distraction and reverie.

The sun sunk lower in the heavens; we passed the river Drance, and observed its path through the chasms of the higher, and the glens of the lower hills. The Alps here come closer to the lake, and we approached the amphitheatre of mountains which forms its eastern boundary. The spire of Evian shone under the woods that surrounded it, and the range of mountain above mountain by which it was overhung.

The wind, which had hitherto carried us along with amazing rapidity, sunk at sunset to a light breeze; the soft air just ruffled the water, and caused a pleasant motion among the trees as we approached the shore, from which it wafted the most delightful scent of flowers and hay. The sun sunk beneath the horizon as we landed; and as I touched the shore, I felt those cares and fears revive, which soon were to clasp me, and cling to me for ever.

CHAPTER XXII

IT WAS EIGHT O'CLOCK WHEN WE LANDED; WE WALKED FOR A SHORT TIME ON THE shore, enjoying the transitory light, and then retired to the inn, and contemplated the lovely scene of waters, woods, and mountains, obscured in darkness, yet still displaying their black outlines.

The wind, which had fallen in the south, now rose with great violence in the west. The moon had reached her summit in the heavens, and was beginning to descend; the clouds swept across it swifter than the flight of the vulture, and dimmed her rays, while the lake reflected the scene of the busy heavens, rendered still busier by the restless waves that were beginning to rise. Suddenly a heavy storm of rain descended.

I had been calm during the day; but so soon as night obscured the shapes of objects, a thousand fears arose in my mind. I was anxious and watchful, while my right hand grasped a pistol which was hidden in my bosom; every sound terrified me; but I resolved that I would sell my life dearly, and not relax the impending conflict until my own life, or that of my adversary, were extinguished.

Elizabeth observed my agitation for some time in timid and fearful silence; at length she said, "What is it that agitates you, my dear Victor? What is it you fear?"

"Oh! peace, peace, my love," replied I, "this night, and all will be safe: but this night is dreadful, very dreadful."

I passed an hour in this state of mind, when suddenly I reflected how dreadful the combat which I momentarily expected would be to my wife, and I earnestly entreated her to retire, resolving not to join her until I had obtained some knowledge as to the situation of my enemy.

She left me, and I continued some time walking up and down the passages of the house, and inspecting every corner that might afford a retreat to my adversary. But I discovered no trace of him, and was beginning to conjecture that some fortunate chance had intervened to prevent the execution of his menaces; when suddenly I heard a shrill and dreadful scream. It came from the room into which Elizabeth had retired. As I heard it, the whole truth rushed into my mind, my arms dropped, the motion of every muscle and fibre was suspended; I could feel the blood trickling in my veins, and tingling in the extremities of my limbs. This state lasted but for an instant; the scream was repeated, and I rushed into the room.

Great God! why did I not then expire! Why am I here to relate the destruction of the best hope, and the purest creature of earth. She was there, lifeless and inanimate, thrown across the bed, her head hanging down, and her pale and distorted features half covered by her hair. Every where I turn I see the same figure—her bloodless arms and relaxed form flung by the murderer on its bridal bier. Could I behold this, and live? Alas! life is obstinate, and clings closest where it is most hated. For a moment only did I lose recollection; I fainted.

When I recovered, I found myself surrounded by the people of the inn; their countenances expressed a breathless terror: but the horror of others appeared only as a mockery, a shadow of the feelings that oppressed me. I escaped from them to the room where lay the body of Elizabeth, my love, my wife, so lately living, so dear, so worthy. She had been moved from the posture in which I had first beheld her; and now, as she lay, her head upon her arm, and a handkerchief thrown across her face and neck, I might have supposed her asleep. I rushed towards her, and embraced her with ardour; but the deathly languor and coldness of the limbs told me, that what I now held in my arms had ceased to be the Elizabeth whom I had loved and cherished. The murderous mark of the fiend's grasp was on her neck, and the breath had ceased to issue from her lips.

While I still hung over her in the agony of despair, I happened to look up. The windows of the room had before been darkened; and I felt a kind of panic on seeing the pale yellow light of the moon illuminate the chamber. The shutters had been thrown back; and, with a sensation of horror not to be described, I saw at the open window a figure the most hideous and abhorred. A grin was on the face of the monster; he seemed to jeer, as with his fiendish finger he pointed towards the corpse of my wife. I rushed towards the window, and drawing a pistol from my bosom, shot; but he eluded me, leaped from his station, and, running with the swiftness of lightning, plunged into the lake.

The report of the pistol brought a crowd into the room. I pointed to the spot where he had disappeared, and we followed the track with boats; nets were cast, but in vain. After passing several hours, we returned hopeless, most of my companions believing it to have been a form conjured by my fancy. After having landed, they proceeded to search the country, parties going in different directions among the woods and vines.

I did not accompany them; I was exhausted: a film covered my eyes, and my skin was parched with the heat of fever. In this state I lay on a bed, hardly conscious of what had happened; my eyes wandered round the room, as if to seek something that I had lost.

At length I remembered that my father would anxiously expect the return of Elizabeth and myself, and that I must return alone. This reflection brought tears into my eyes, and I wept for a long time; but my thoughts rambled to various subjects, reflecting on my misfortunes, and their cause. I was bewildered in a cloud of wonder and horror. The death of William, the execution of Justine, the murder of Clerval, and lastly of my wife; even at that moment I knew not that my only remaining friends were safe from the malignity of the fiend; my father even now might be writhing under his grasp, and Ernest might be dead at his feet. This idea made me shudder, and recalled me to action. I started up, and resolved to return to Geneva with all possible speed.

There were no horses to be procured, and I must return by the lake; but the wind was unfavourable, and the rain fell in torrents. However, it was hardly morning, and I might reasonably hope to arrive by night. I hired men to row, and took an oar myself, for I had always experienced relief from mental torment in bodily exercise. But the overflowing misery I now felt, and the excess of agitation that I endured, rendered me incapable of any exertion. I threw down the oar; and, leaning my head upon my hands, gave way to every gloomy idea that arose. If I looked up, I saw the scenes which were familiar to me in my happier time, and which I had contemplated but the day before in the company of her who was now but a shadow and a recollection. Tears streamed from my eyes. The rain had ceased for a moment, and I saw the fish play in the waters as they had done a few hours before; they had then been observed by Elizabeth. Nothing is so painful to the human mind as a great and sudden change. The sun might shine, or the clouds might lour; but nothing could appear to me as it had done the day before. A fiend had snatched from me every hope of future happiness: no creature had ever been so miserable as I was; so frightful an event is single in the history of man.

But why should I dwell upon the incidents that followed this last overwhelming event. Mine has been a tale of horrors; I have reached their *acme*, and what I must now relate can but be tedious to you. Know that, one by one, my friends were snatched away; I was left desolate. My own strength is exhausted; and I must tell, in a few words, what remains of my hideous narration.

I arrived at Geneva. My father and Ernest yet lived; but the former sunk under the tidings that I bore. I see him now, excellent and venerable old man! his eyes wandered in vacancy, for they had lost their charm and their delight—his niece, his more than daughter, whom he doated on with all that affection which a man feels, who, in the decline of life, having few affections, clings more earnestly to those that remain. Cursed, cursed be the fiend that brought misery on his grey hairs, and doomed him to waste in wretchedness! He could not live under the horrors that were accumulated around him; an apoplectic fit was brought on, and in a few days he died in my arms.

What then became of me? I know not; I lost sensation, and chains and darkness were the only objects that pressed upon me. Sometimes, indeed, I dreamt that I wandered in flowery meadows and pleasant vales with the friends of my youth; but awoke, and found myself in a dungeon. Melancholy followed, but by degrees I gained a clear conception of my miseries and situation, and was then released from my prison. For they had called me mad; and during many months, as I understood, a solitary cell had been my habitation.

But liberty had been a useless gift to me had I not, as I awakened to reason, at the same time awakened to revenge. As the memory of past misfortunes pressed upon me, I began to reflect on their cause—the monster whom I had created, the miserable dæmon whom I had sent abroad into the world for my destruction. I was possessed by a maddening rage when I thought of him, and desired and ardently prayed that I might have him within my grasp to wreak a great and signal revenge on his cursed head.

Nor did my hate long confine itself to useless wishes; I began to reflect on the best means of securing him; and for this purpose, about a month after my release, I repaired to a criminal judge in the town, and told him that I had an accusation to make; that I knew the destroyer of my family; and that I required him to exert his whole authority for the apprehension of the murderer.

The magistrate listened to me with attention and kindness: "Be assured, sir," said he, "no pains or exertions on my part shall be spared to discover the villain."

"I thank you," replied I; "listen, therefore, to the deposition that I have to make. It is indeed a tale so strange, that I should fear you would not credit it, were there not something in truth which, however wonderful, forces conviction. The story is too connected to be mistaken for a dream, and I have no motive for falsehood." My manner, as I thus addressed him, was impressive, but calm; I had formed in my own heart a resolution to pursue my destroyer to death; and this purpose quieted my agony, and provisionally reconciled me to life. I now related my history briefly, but with firmness and precision, marking the dates with accuracy, and never deviating into invective or exclamation.

The magistrate appeared at first perfectly incredulous, but as I continued he became more attentive and interested; I saw him sometimes shudder with horror, at others a lively surprise, unmingled with disbelief, was painted on his countenance.

When I had concluded my narration, I said, "This is the being whom I accuse, and for whose detection and punishment I call upon you to exert your whole power. It is your duty as a magistrate, and I believe and hope that your feelings as a man will not revolt from the execution of those functions on this occasion."

This address caused a considerable change in the physiognomy of my auditor. He had heard my story with that half kind of belief that is given to a tale of spirits and supernatural events; but when he was called upon to act officially in consequence, the whole tide of his incredulity returned. He, however, answered mildly, "I would willingly afford you every aid in your pursuit; but the creature of whom you speak appears to have powers which would put all my exertions to defiance. Who can follow an animal which can traverse the sea of ice, and inhabit caves and dens, where no man would venture to intrude? Besides, some months have elapsed since the commission of his crimes, and no one can conjecture to what place he has wandered, or what region he may now inhabit."

"I do not doubt that he hovers near the spot which I inhabit; and if he has indeed taken refuge in the Alps, he may be hunted like the chamois, and destroyed as a beast of prey. But I perceive your thoughts: you do not credit my narrative, and do not intend to pursue my enemy with the punishment which is his desert."

As I spoke, rage sparkled in my eyes; the magistrate was intimidated; "You are mistaken," said he, "I will exert myself; and if it is in my power to seize the monster, be assured that he shall suffer punishment proportionate to his crimes. But I fear, from what you have yourself described to be his properties, that this will prove impracticable, and that, while every proper measure is pursued, you should endeavour to make up your mind to disappointment."

"That cannot be; but all that I can say will be of little avail. My revenge is of no moment to you; yet, while I allow it to be a vice, I confess that it is the devouring and only passion of my soul. My rage is unspeakable, when I reflect that the murderer, whom I have turned loose upon society, still exists. You refuse my just demand: I have but one resource; and I devote myself, either in my life or death, to his destruction."

I trembled with excess of agitation as I said this; there was a phrenzy in my manner, and something, I doubt not, of that haughty fierceness, which the martyrs of old are said to have possessed. But to a Genevan magistrate, whose mind was occupied by far other ideas than those of devotion and heroism, this elevation of mind had much the appearance of madness. He endeavoured to soothe me as a nurse does a child, and reverted to my tale as the effects of delirium.

"Man," I cried, "how ignorant art thou in thy pride of wisdom! Cease; you know not what it is you say."

I broke from the house angry and disturbed, and retired to meditate on some other mode of action.

CHAPTER XXIII

MY PRESENT SITUATION WAS ONE IN WHICH ALL VOLUNTARY THOUGHT WAS swallowed up and lost. I was hurried away by fury; revenge alone endowed me with strength and composure; it modelled my feelings, and allowed me to be calculating and calm, at periods when otherwise delirium or death would have been my portion.

My first resolution was to quit Geneva for ever; my country, which, when I was happy and beloved, was dear to me, now, in my adversity, became hateful. I provided myself with a sum of money, together with a few jewels which had belonged to my mother, and departed.

And now my wanderings began, which are to cease but with life. I have traversed a vast portion of the earth, and have endured all the hardships which travellers, in deserts and barbarous countries, are wont to meet. How I have lived I hardly know; many times have I stretched my failing limbs upon the sandy plain, and prayed for death. But revenge kept me alive; I dared not die, and leave my adversary in being.

When I quitted Geneva, my first labour was to gain some clue by which I might trace the steps of my fiendish enemy. But my plan was unsettled; and I wandered many hours around the confines of the town, uncertain what path I should pursue. As night approached, I found myself at the entrance of the cemetery where William, Elizabeth, and my father, reposed. I entered it, and approached the tomb which marked their graves. Every thing was silent, except the leaves of the trees, which were gently agitated by the wind; the night was nearly dark; and the scene would have been solemn and affecting even to an uninterested observer. The spirits of the departed seemed to flit around, and to cast a shadow, which was felt but seen not, around the head of the mourner.

The deep grief which this scene had at first excited quickly gave way to rage and despair. They were dead, and I lived; their murderer also lived, and to destroy him I must drag out my weary existence. I knelt on the grass, and kissed the earth, and with quivering lips exclaimed, "By the sacred earth on which I kneel, by the shades that wander near me, by the deep and eternal grief that I feel, I swear; and by thee, O Night, and by the spirits that preside over thee, I swear to pursue the dæmon, who caused this misery, until he or I shall perish in mortal conflict. For this purpose I will preserve my life: to execute this dear revenge, will I again behold the sun, and tread the green herbage of earth, which otherwise should vanish from my eyes for ever. And I call on you, spirits of the dead; and on you, wandering ministers of vengeance, to aid and conduct me in my work. Let the cursed and hellish monster drink deep of agony; let him feel the despair that now torments me."

I had begun my adjuration with solemnity, and an awe which almost assured me that the shades of my murdered friends heard and approved my devotion; but the furies possessed me as I concluded, and rage choked my utterance.

I was answered through the stillness of night by a loud and fiendish laugh. It rung on my ears long and heavily; the mountains re-echoed it, and I felt as if all hell surrounded me with mockery and laughter. Surely in that moment I should have been possessed by phrenzy, and have destroyed my miserable existence, but that my vow was heard, and that I was reserved for vengeance. The laughter died away: when a well-known and abhorred voice, apparently close to my ear, addressed me in an audible whisper—"I am satisfied: miserable wretch! you have determined to live, and I am satisfied."

I darted towards the spot from which the sound proceeded; but the devil eluded my grasp. Suddenly the broad disk of the moon arose, and shone full upon his ghastly and distorted shape, as he fled with more than mortal speed.

I pursued him; and for many months this has been my task. Guided by a slight clue, I followed the windings of the Rhone, but vainly. The blue Mediterranean appeared; and, by a strange chance, I saw the fiend enter by night, and hide himself in a vessel bound for the Black Sea. I took my passage in the same ship; but he escaped, I know not how.

Amidst the wilds of Tartary and Russia, although he still evaded me, I have ever followed in his track. Sometimes the peasants, scared by this horrid apparition, informed me of his path; sometimes he himself, who feared that if I lost all trace I should despair and die, often left some mark to guide me. The snows descended on my head, and I saw the print of his huge step on the white plain. To you first entering on life, to whom care is new, and agony unknown, how can you understand what I have felt, and still feel? Cold, want, and fatigue, were the least pains which I was destined to endure; I was cursed by some devil, and carried about with me my eternal hell; yet still a spirit of good followed and directed my steps, and, when I most murmured, would suddenly extricate me from seemingly insurmountable difficulties. Sometimes, when nature, overcome by hunger, sunk under the exhaustion, a repast was prepared for me in the desert, that restored and inspirited me. The fare was indeed coarse, such as the peasants of the country ate; but I may not doubt that it was set there by the spirits that I had invoked to aid me. Often, when all was dry, the heavens cloudless, and I was parched by thirst, a slight cloud would bedim the sky, shed the few drops that revived me, and vanish.

I followed, when I could, the courses of the rivers; but the dæmon generally avoided these, as it was here that the population of the country chiefly collected. In other places human beings were seldom seen; and I generally subsisted on the wild animals that crossed my path. I had money with me, and gained the friendship of the villagers by distributing it, or bringing with me some food that I had killed, which, after taking a small part, I always presented to those who had provided me with fire and utensils for cooking.

My life, as it passed thus, was indeed hateful to me, and it was during sleep alone that I could taste joy. O blessed sleep! often, when most miserable, I sank to repose, and my dreams lulled me even to rapture. The spirits that guarded me had provided these moments, or rather hours, of happiness, that I might retain strength to fulfil my pilgrimage. Deprived of this respite, I should have sunk under my hardships. During the day I was sustained and inspirited by the hope of night: for in sleep I saw my friends, my wife, and my beloved country; again I saw the benevolent countenance of my father, heard the silver tones of my Elizabeth's voice, and beheld Clerval enjoying health and youth. Often, when wearied by a toilsome march, I persuaded myself that I was dreaming until night should come, and that I should then enjoy reality in the arms of my dearest friends. What agonizing fondness did I feel for them! how did I cling to their dear forms, as sometimes they haunted even my waking hours, and persuade myself that they still lived! At such moments vengeance, that burned within me, died in my heart, and I pursued my path towards the destruction of the dæmon, more as a task enjoined by heaven, as the mechanical impulse of some power of which I was unconscious, than as the ardent desire of my soul.

What his feelings were whom I pursued, I cannot know. Sometimes, indeed, he left marks in writing on the barks of the trees, or cut in stone, that guided me, and instigated my fury. "My reign is not yet over," (these words were legible in one of these inscriptions); "you live, and my power is complete. Follow me; I seek the everlasting ices of the north, where you will feel the misery of cold and frost, to which I am impassive. You will find near this place, if you follow not too tardily, a dead hare; eat, and be refreshed. Come on, my enemy; we have yet to wrestle for our lives; but many hard and miserable hours must you endure, until that period shall arrive."

Scoffing devil! Again do I vow vengeance; again do I devote thee, miserable fiend, to torture and death. Never will I omit my search, until he or I perish; and then with what ecstacy shall I join my Elizabeth, and those who even now prepare for me the reward of my tedious toil and horrible pilgrimage.

As I still pursued my journey to the northward, the snows thickened, and the cold increased in a degree almost too severe to support. The peasants were shut up in their hovels, and only a few of the most hardy ventured forth to seize the animals whom starvation had forced from their hiding-places to seek for prey. The rivers were covered with ice, and no fish could be procured; and thus I was cut off from my chief article of maintenance.

The triumph of my enemy increased with the difficulty of my labours. One inscription that he left was in these words: "Prepare! your toils only begin: wrap yourself in furs, and provide food, for we shall soon enter upon a journey where your sufferings will satisfy my everlasting hatred."

My courage and perseverance were invigorated by these scoffing words; I resolved not to fail in my purpose; and, calling on heaven to support me, I continued with unabated fervour to traverse immense deserts, until the ocean appeared at a distance, and formed the utmost boundary of the horizon. Oh! how unlike it was to the blue seas of the south! Covered with ice, it was only to be distinguished from land by its superior wildness and ruggedness. The Greeks wept for joy when they beheld the Mediterranean from the hills of Asia, and hailed with rapture the boundary of their toils. I did not weep; but I knelt down, and, with a full heart, thanked my guiding spirit for conducting me in safety to the place where I hoped, notwithstanding my adversary's gibe, to meet and grapple with him.

Some weeks before this period I had procured a sledge and dogs, and thus traversed the snows with inconceivable speed. I know not whether the fiend possessed the same advantages; but I found that, as before I had daily lost ground in the pursuit, I now gained on him; so much so, that when I first saw the ocean, he was but one day's journey in advance, and I hoped to intercept him before he should reach the beach. With new courage, therefore, I pressed on, and in two days arrived at a wretched hamlet on the seashore. I inquired of the inhabitants concerning the fiend, and gained accurate information. A gigantic monster, they said, had arrived the night before, armed with a gun and many pistols; putting to flight the inhabitants of a solitary cottage, through fear of his terrific appearance. He had carried off their store of winter food, and, placing it in a sledge, to draw which he had seized on a numerous drove of trained dogs, he had harnessed them, and the same night, to the joy of the horror-struck villagers, had pursued his journey across the sea in a direction that led to no land; and they conjectured that he must speedily be destroyed by the breaking of the ice, or frozen by the eternal frosts.

On hearing this information, I suffered a temporary access of despair. He had escaped me; and I must commence a destructive and almost endless journey across the mountainous ices of the ocean,—amidst cold that few of the inhabitants could long endure, and which I, the native of a genial and sunny climate, could not hope to survive. Yet at the idea that the fiend should live and be triumphant, my rage and vengeance returned, and, like a mighty tide, overwhelmed every other feeling. After a slight repose, during which the spirits of the dead hovered round, and instigated me to toil and revenge, I prepared for my journey.

I exchanged my land sledge for one fashioned for the inequalities of the frozen ocean; and, purchasing a plentiful stock of provisions, I departed from land.

I cannot guess how many days have passed since then; but I have endured misery, which nothing but the eternal sentiment of a just retribution burning within my heart could have enabled me to support. Immense and rugged mountains of ice often barred up my passage, and I often heard the thunder of the ground sea, which threatened my destruction. But again the frost came, and made the paths of the sea secure.

By the quantity of provision which I had consumed I should guess that I had passed three weeks in this journey; and the continual protraction of hope, return- ing back upon the heart, often wrung bitter drops of despondency and grief from my eyes. Despair had indeed almost secured her prey, and I should soon have sunk beneath this misery; when once, after the poor animals that carried me had with incredible toil gained the summit of a sloping ice mountain, and one sinking under his fatigue died, I viewed the expanse before me with anguish, when suddenly my eye caught a dark speck upon the dusky plain. I strained my sight to discover what it could be, and uttered a wild cry of ecstasy when I distinguished a sledge, and the distorted proportions of a well-known form within. Oh! with what a burning gush did hope revisit my heart! warm tears filled my eyes, which I hastily wiped away, that they might not intercept the view I had of the dæmon; but still my sight was dimmed by the burning drops, until, giving way to the emotions that oppressed me, I wept aloud.

But this was not the time for delay; I disencumbered the dogs of their dead com- panion, gave them a plentiful portion of food; and, after an hour's rest, which was absolutely necessary, and yet which was bitterly irksome to me, I continued my route. The sledge was still visible; nor did I again lose sight of it, except at the moments when for a short time some ice rock concealed it with its intervening crags. I indeed percep- tibly gained on it; and when, after nearly two days' journey, I beheld my enemy at no more than a mile distant, my heart bounded within me.

But now, when I appeared almost within grasp of my enemy, my hopes were sud- denly extinguished, and I lost all trace of him more utterly than I had ever done before. A ground sea was heard; the thunder of its progress, as the waters rolled and swelled beneath me, became every moment more ominous and terrific. I pressed on, but in vain. The wind arose; the sea roared; and, as with the mighty shock of an earthquake, it split, and cracked with a tremendous and overwhelming sound. The work was soon finished: in a few minutes a tumultuous sea rolled between me and my enemy, and I was left drifting on a scattered piece of ice, that was continually lessening, and thus preparing for me a hideous death.

In this manner many appalling hours passed; several of my dogs died; and I myself was about to sink under the accumulation of distress, when I saw your vessel riding at anchor, and holding forth to me hopes of succour and life. I had no conception that vessels ever came so far north, and was astounded at the sight. I quickly destroyed part of my sledge to construct oars; and by these means was enabled, with infinite fatigue, to move my ice-raft in the direction of your ship. I had determined, if you were going southward, still to trust myself to the mercy of the seas, rather than abandon my purpose. I hoped to induce you to grant me a boat with which I could still pursue my enemy. But your direction was northward. You took me on board when my vigour was exhausted, and I should soon have sunk under my multiplied hardships into a death, which I still dread,—for my task is unfulfilled.

Oh! when will my guiding spirit, in conducting me to the dæmon, allow me the rest I so much desire; or must I die, and he yet live? If I do, swear to me, Walton, that he shall not escape; that you will seek him, and satisfy my vengeance in his death. Yet, do I dare ask you to undertake my pilgrimage, to endure the hardships that I have undergone? No; I am not so selfish. Yet, when I am dead, if he should appear; if the ministers of vengeance should conduct him to you, swear that he shall not live—swear that he shall not triumph over my accumulated woes, and live to make another such a wretch as I am. He is eloquent and persuasive; and once his words had even power over my heart: but trust him not. His soul is as hellish as his form, full of treachery and fiend-like malice. Hear him not; call on the manes of William, Justine, Clerval, Elizabeth, my father, and of the wretched Victor, and thrust your sword into his heart. I will hover near, and direct the steel aright.

*   *   *

WALTON, *in continuation.*

August 26th, 17—.

You have read this strange and terrific story, Margaret; and do you not feel your blood congealed with horror, like that which even now curdles mine? Sometimes, seized with sudden agony, he could not continue his tale; at others, his voice broken, yet piercing, uttered with difficulty the words so replete with agony. His fine and lovely eyes were now lighted up with indignation, now subdued to downcast sorrow, and quenched in infinite wretchedness. Sometimes he commanded his countenance and tones, and related the most horrible incidents with a tranquil voice, suppressing every mark of agitation; then, like a volcano bursting forth, his face would suddenly change to an expression of the wildest rage, as he shrieked out imprecations on his persecutor.

His tale is connected, and told with an appearance of the simplest truth; yet I own to you that the letters of Felix and Safie, which he shewed me, and the apparition of the monster, seen from our ship, brought to me a greater conviction of the truth of his narrative than his asseverations, however earnest and connected. Such a monster has then really existence; I cannot doubt it; yet I am lost in surprise and admiration. Sometimes I endeavoured to gain from Frankenstein the particulars of his creature's formation; but on this point he was impenetrable.

"Are you mad, my friend?" said he, "or whither does your senseless curiosity lead you? Would you also create for yourself and the world a demoniacal enemy? Or to what do your questions tend? Peace, peace! learn my miseries, and do not seek to increase your own."

Frankenstein discovered that I made notes concerning his history: he asked to see them, and then himself corrected and augmented them in many places; but principally in giving the life and spirit to the conversations he held with his enemy. "Since you have preserved my narration," said he, "I would not that a mutilated one should go down to posterity."

Thus has a week passed away, while I have listened to the strangest tale that ever imagination formed. My thoughts, and every feeling of my soul, have been drunk up by the interest for my guest, which this tale, and his own elevated and gentle manners have created. I wish to soothe him; yet can I counsel one so infinitely miserable, so destitute of every hope of consolation, to live? Oh, no! the only joy that he can now know will be when he composes his shattered feelings to peace and death. Yet he enjoys one comfort, the offspring of solitude and delirium: he believes, that, when in dreams he holds converse with his friends, and derives from that communion consolation for his miseries, or excitements to his vengeance, that they are not the creations of his fancy, but the real beings who visit him from the regions of a remote world. This faith gives a solemnity to his reveries that render them to me almost as imposing and interesting as truth.

Our conversations are not always confined to his own history and misfortunes. On every point of general literature he displays unbounded knowledge, and a quick and piercing apprehension. His eloquence is forcible and touching; nor can I hear him, when he relates a pathetic incident, or endeavours to move the passions of pity or love, without tears. What a glorious creature must he have been in the days of his prosperity, when he is thus noble and godlike in ruin. He seems to feel his own worth, and the greatness of his fall.

"When younger," said he, "I felt as if I were destined for some great enterprise. My feelings are profound; but I possessed a coolness of judgment that fitted me for illustrious achievements. This sentiment of the worth of my nature supported me, when others would have been oppressed; for I deemed it criminal to throw away in useless grief those talents that might be useful to my fellow-creatures. When I reflected on the work I had completed, no less a one than the creation of a sensitive and rational animal, I could not rank myself with the herd of common projectors. But this feeling, which supported me in the commencement of my career, now serves only to plunge me lower in the dust. All my speculations and hopes are as nothing; and, like the archangel who aspired to omnipotence, I am chained in an eternal hell. My imagination was vivid, yet my powers of analysis and application were intense; by the union of these qualities I conceived the idea, and executed the creation of a man. Even now I cannot recollect, without passion, my reveries while the work was incomplete. I trod heaven in my thoughts, now exulting in my powers, now burning with the idea of their effects. From my infancy I was imbued with high hopes and a lofty ambition; but how am I sunk! Oh! my friend, if you had known me as I once was, you would not recognize me in this state of degradation. Despondency rarely visited my heart; a high destiny seemed to bear me on, until I fell, never, never again to rise."

Must I then lose this admirable being? I have longed for a friend; I have sought one who would sympathize with and love me. Behold, on these desert seas I have found such a one; but, I fear, I have gained him only to know his value, and lose him. I would reconcile him to life, but he repulses the idea.

"I thank you, Walton," he said, "for your kind intentions towards so miserable a wretch; but when you speak of new ties, and fresh affections, think you that any can replace those who are gone? Can any man be to me as Clerval was; or any woman another Elizabeth? Even where the affections are not strongly moved by any superior excellence, the companions of our childhood always possess a certain power over our minds, which hardly any later friend can obtain. They know our infantine dispositions, which, however they may be afterwards modified, are never eradicated; and they can judge of our actions with more certain conclusions as to the integrity of our motives. A sister or a brother can never, unless indeed such symptoms have been shewn early, suspect the other of fraud or false dealing, when another friend, however strongly he may be attached, may, in spite of himself, be invaded with suspicion. But I enjoyed friends, dear not only through habit and association, but from their own merits; and, wherever I am, the soothing voice of my Elizabeth, and the conversation of Clerval, will be ever whispered in my ear. They are dead; and but one feeling in such a solitude can persuade me to preserve my life. If I were engaged in any high undertaking or design, fraught with extensive utility to my fellow-creatures, then could I live to fulfil it. But such is not my destiny; I must pursue and destroy the being to whom I gave existence; then my lot on earth will be fulfilled, and I may die."

September 2d.

MY BELOVED SISTER,

I write to you, encompassed by peril, and ignorant whether I am ever doomed to see again dear England, and the dearer friends that inhabit it. I am surrounded by mountains of ice, which admit of no escape, and threaten every moment to crush my vessel. The brave fellows, whom I have persuaded to be my companions, look towards me for aid; but I have none to bestow. There is something terribly appalling in our situation, yet my courage and hopes do not desert me. We may survive; and if we do not, I will repeat the lessons of my Seneca, and die with a good heart.

Yet what, Margaret, will be the state of your mind? You will not hear of my destruction, and you will anxiously await my return. Years will pass, and you will have visitings of despair, and yet be tortured by hope. Oh! my beloved sister, the sickening failings of your heart-felt expectations are, in prospect, more terrible to me than my own death. But you have a husband, and lovely children; you may be happy: heaven bless you, and make you so!

My unfortunate guest regards me with the tenderest compassion. He endeavours to fill me with hope; and talks as if life were a possession which he valued. He reminds me how often the same accidents have happened to other navigators, who have attempted this sea, and, in spite of myself, he fills me with cheerful auguries. Even the sailors feel the power of his eloquence: when he speaks, they no longer despair; he rouses their energies, and, while they hear his voice, they believe these vast mountains of ice are mole-hills, which will vanish before the resolutions of man. These feelings are transitory; each day's expectation delayed fills them with fear, and I almost dread a mutiny caused by this despair.

September 5th.

A scene has just passed of such uncommon interest, that although it is highly probable that these papers may never reach you, yet I cannot forbear recording it.

We are still surrounded by mountains of ice, still in imminent danger of being crushed in their conflict. The cold is excessive, and many of my unfortunate comrades have already found a grave amidst this scene of desolation. Frankenstein has daily declined in health: a feverish fire still glimmers in his eyes; but he is exhausted, and, when suddenly roused to any exertion, he speedily sinks again into apparent lifelessness.

I mentioned in my last letter the fears I entertained of a mutiny. This morning, as I sat watching the wan countenance of my friend—his eyes half closed, and his limbs hanging listlessly,—I was roused by half a dozen of the sailors, who desired admission into the cabin. They entered; and their leader addressed me. He told me that he and his companions had been chosen by the other sailors to come in deputation to me, to make me a demand, which, in justice, I could not refuse. We were immured in ice, and should probably never escape; but they feared that if, as was possible, the ice should dissipate, and a free passage be opened, I should be rash enough to continue my voyage, and lead them into fresh dangers, after they might happily have surmounted this. They desired, therefore, that I should engage with a solemn promise, that if the vessel should be freed, I would instantly direct my course southward.

This speech troubled me. I had not despaired; nor had I yet conceived the idea of returning, if set free. Yet could I, in justice, or even in possibility, refuse this demand? I hesitated before I answered; when Frankenstein, who had at first been silent, and, indeed, appeared hardly to have force enough to attend, now roused himself; his eyes sparkled, and his cheeks flushed with momentary vigour. Turning towards the men, he said—

"What do you mean? What do you demand of your captain? Are you then so easily turned from your design? Did you not call this a glorious expedition? and wherefore was it glorious? Not because the way was smooth and placid as a southern sea, but because it was full of dangers and terror; because, at every new incident, your fortitude was to be called forth, and your courage exhibited; because danger and death surrounded, and these dangers you were to brave and overcome. For this was it a glorious, for this was it an honourable undertaking. You were hereafter to be hailed as the benefactors of your species; your name adored, as belonging to brave men who encountered death for honour and the benefit of mankind. And now, behold, with the first imagination of danger, or, if you will, the first mighty and terrific trial of your courage, you shrink away, and are content to be handed down as men who had not strength enough to endure cold and peril; and so, poor souls, they were chilly, and returned to their warm fire-sides. Why, that requires not this preparation; ye need not have come thus far, and dragged your captain to the shame of a defeat, merely to prove yourselves cowards. Oh! be men, or be more than men. Be steady to your purposes, and firm as a rock. This ice is not made of such stuff as your hearts might be; it is mutable, cannot withstand you, if you say that it shall not. Do not return to your families with the stigma of disgrace marked on your brows. Return as heroes who have fought and conquered, and who know not what it is to turn their backs on the foe."

He spoke this with a voice so modulated to the different feelings expressed in his speech, with an eye so full of lofty design and heroism, that can you wonder that these men were moved. They looked at one another, and were unable to reply. I spoke; I told them to retire, and consider of what had been said: that I would not lead them further north, if they strenuously desired the contrary; but that I hoped that, with reflection, their courage would return.

They retired, and I turned towards my friend; but he was sunk in languor, and almost deprived of life.

How all this will terminate, I know not; but I had rather die, than return shamefully,—my purpose unfulfilled. Yet I fear such will be my fate; the men, unsupported by ideas of glory and honour, can never willingly continue to endure their present hardships.

September 7th.

The die is cast; I have consented to return, if we are not destroyed. Thus are my hopes blasted by cowardice and indecision; I come back ignorant and disappointed. It requires more philosophy than I possess, to bear this injustice with patience.

September 12th.

It is past; I am returning to England. I have lost my hopes of utility and glory;—I have lost my friend. But I will endeavour to detail these bitter circumstances to you, my dear sister; and, while I am wafted towards England, and towards you, I will not despond.

September 9th, the ice began to move, and roarings like thunder were heard at a distance, as the islands split and cracked in every direction. We were in the most imminent peril; but, as we could only remain passive, my chief attention was occupied by my unfortunate guest, whose illness increased in such a degree, that he was entirely confined to his bed. The ice cracked behind us, and was driven with force towards the north; a breeze sprung from the west, and on the 11th the passage towards the south became perfectly free. When the sailors saw this, and that their return to their native country was apparently assured, a shout of tumultuous joy broke from them, loud and long-continued. Frankenstein, who was dozing, awoke, and asked the cause of the tumult. "They shout," I said, "because they will soon return to England."

"Do you then really return?"

"Alas! yes; I cannot withstand their demands. I cannot lead them unwillingly to danger, and I must return."

"Do so, if you will; but I will not. You may give up your purpose; but mine is assigned to me by heaven, and I dare not. I am weak; but surely the spirits who assist my vengeance will endow me with sufficient strength." Saying this, he endeavoured to spring from the bed, but the exertion was too great for him; he fell back, and fainted.

It was long before he was restored; and I often thought that life was entirely extinct. At length he opened his eyes, but he breathed with difficulty, and was unable to speak. The surgeon gave him a composing draught, and ordered us to leave him undisturbed. In the mean time he told me, that my friend had certainly not many hours to live.

His sentence was pronounced; and I could only grieve, and be patient. I sat by his bed watching him; his eyes were closed, and I thought he slept; but presently he called to me in a feeble voice, and, bidding me come near, said—"Alas! the strength I relied on is gone; I feel that I shall soon die, and he, my enemy and persecutor, may still be in being. Think not, Walton, that in the last moments of my existence I feel that burning hatred, and ardent desire of revenge, I once expressed, but I feel myself justified in desiring the death of my adversary. During these last days I have been occupied in examining my past conduct; nor do I find it blameable. In a fit of enthusiastic madness I created a rational creature, and was bound towards him, to assure, as far as was in my power, his happiness and well-being. This was my duty; but there was another still paramount to that. My duties towards my fellow-creatures had greater claims to my attention, because they included a greater proportion of happiness or misery. Urged by this view, I refused, and I did right in refusing, to create a companion for the first creature. He shewed unparalleled malignity and selfishness, in evil: he destroyed my friends; he devoted to destruction beings who possessed exquisite sensations, happiness, and wisdom; nor do I know where this thirst for vengeance may end. Miserable himself, that he may render no other wretched, he ought to die. The task of his destruction was mine, but I have failed. When actuated by selfish and vicious motives, I asked you to undertake my unfinished work; and I renew this request now, when I am only induced by reason and virtue.

"Yet I cannot ask you to renounce your country and friends, to fulfil this task; and now, that you are returning to England, you will have little chance of meeting with him. But the consideration of these points, and the well-balancing of what you may esteem your duties, I leave to you; my judgment and ideas are already disturbed by the near approach of death. I dare not ask you to do what I think right, for I may still be misled by passion.

"That he should live to be an instrument of mischief disturbs me; in other respects this hour, when I momentarily expect my release, is the only happy one which I have enjoyed for several years. The forms of the beloved dead flit before me, and I hasten to their arms. Farewell, Walton! Seek happiness in tranquillity, and avoid ambition, even if it be only the apparently innocent one of distinguishing yourself in science and discoveries. Yet why do I say this? I have myself been blasted in these hopes, yet another may succeed."

His voice became fainter as he spoke; and at length, exhausted by his effort, he sunk into silence. About half an hour afterwards he attempted again to speak, but was unable; he pressed my hand feebly, and his eyes closed for ever, while the irradiation of a gentle smile passed away from his lips.

Margaret, what comment can I make on the untimely extinction of this glorious spirit? What can I say, that will enable you to understand the depth of my sorrow? All that I should express would be inadequate and feeble. My tears flow; my mind is overshadowed by a cloud of disappointment. But I journey towards England, and I may there find consolation.

I am interrupted. What do these sounds portend? It is midnight; the breeze blows fairly, and the watch on deck scarcely stir. Again; there is a sound as of a human voice, but hoarser; it comes from the cabin where the remains of Frankenstein still lie. I must arise, and examine. Good night, my sister.

Great God! what a scene has just taken place! I am yet dizzy with the remembrance of it. I hardly know whether I shall have the power to detail it; yet the tale which I have recorded would be incomplete without this final and wonderful catastrophe.

I entered the cabin, where lay the remains of my ill-fated and admirable friend. Over him hung a form which I cannot find words to describe; gigantic in stature, yet uncouth and distorted in its proportions. As he hung over the coffin, his face was concealed by long locks of ragged hair; but one vast hand was extended, in colour and apparent texture like that of a mummy. When he heard the sound of my approach, he ceased to utter exclamations of grief and horror, and sprung towards the window. Never did I behold a vision so horrible as his face, of such loathsome, yet appalling hideousness. I shut my eyes involuntarily, and endeavoured to recollect what were my duties with regard to this destroyer. I called on him to stay.

He paused, looking on me with wonder; and, again turning towards the lifeless form of his creator, he seemed to forget my presence, and every feature and gesture seemed instigated by the wildest rage of some uncontrollable passion.

"That is also my victim!" he exclaimed; "in his murder my crimes are consummated; the miserable series of my being is wound to its close! Oh, Frankenstein! generous and self-devoted being! what does it avail that I now ask thee to pardon me? I, who irretrievably destroyed thee by destroying all thou lovedst. Alas! he is cold; he may not answer me."

His voice seemed suffocated; and my first impulses, which had suggested to me the duty of obeying the dying request of my friend, in destroying his enemy, were now suspended by a mixture of curiosity and compassion. I approached this tremendous being; I dared not again raise my looks upon his face, there was something so scaring and unearthly in his ugliness. I attempted to speak, but the words died away on my lips. The monster continued to utter wild and incoherent self-reproaches. At length I gathered resolution to address him, in a pause of the tempest of his passion: "Your repentance," I said, "is now superfluous. If you had listened to the voice of conscience, and heeded the stings of remorse, before you had urged your diabolical vengeance to this extremity, Frankenstein would yet have lived."

"And do you dream?" said the dæmon; "do you think that I was then dead to agony and remorse?—He," he continued, pointing to the corpse, "he suffered not more in the consummation of the deed;—oh! not the ten-thousandth portion of the anguish that was mine during the lingering detail of its execution. A frightful selfishness hurried me on, while my heart was poisoned with remorse. Think ye that the groans of Clerval were music to my ears? My heart was fashioned to be susceptible of love and sympathy; and, when wrenched by misery to vice and hatred, it did not endure the violence of the change without torture such as you cannot even imagine.

"After the murder of Clerval, I returned to Switzerland, heart-broken and overcome. I pitied Frankenstein; my pity amounted to horror: I abhorred myself. But when I discovered that he, the author at once of my existence and of its unspeakable torments, dared to hope for happiness; that while he accumulated wretchedness and despair upon me, he sought his own enjoyment in feelings and passions from the indulgence of which I was for ever barred, then impotent envy and bitter indignation filled me with an insatiable thirst for vengeance. I recollected my threat, and resolved that it should be accomplished. I knew that I was preparing for myself a deadly torture; but I was the slave, not the master of an impulse, which I detested, yet could not disobey. Yet when she died!—nay, then I was not miserable. I had cast off all feeling, subdued all anguish to riot in the excess of my despair. Evil thenceforth became my good. Urged thus far, I had no choice but to adapt my nature to an element which I had willingly chosen. The completion of my demoniacal design became an insatiable passion. And now it is ended; there is my last victim!"

I was at first touched by the expressions of his misery; yet when I called to mind what Frankenstein had said of his powers of eloquence and per-suasion, and when I again cast my eyes on the lifeless form of my friend, indignation was re-kindled within me. "Wretch!" I said, "it is well that you come here to whine over the desolation that you have made. You throw a torch into a pile of buildings, and when they are consumed you sit among the ruins, and lament the fall. Hypocritical fiend! if he whom you mourn still lived, still would he be the object, again would he become the prey of your accursed vengeance. It is not pity that you feel; you lament only because the victim of your malignity is withdrawn from your power."

"Oh, it is not thus—not thus," interrupted the being; "yet such must be the impression conveyed to you by what appears to be the purport of my actions. Yet I seek not a fellow-feeling in my misery. No sympathy may I ever find. When I first sought it, it was the love of virtue, the feelings of hap-piness and affection with which my whole being overflowed, that I wished to be participated. But now, that virtue has become to me a shadow, and that happiness and affection are turned into bitter and loathing despair, in what should I seek for sympathy? I am content to suffer alone, while my sufferings shall endure: when I die, I am well satisfied that abhorrence and opprobrium should load my memory. Once my fancy was soothed with dreams of virtue, of fame, and of enjoyment. Once I falsely hoped to meet with beings, who, pardoning my outward form, would love me for the excellent qualities which I was capable of bringing forth. I was nourished with high thoughts of hon-our and devotion. But now vice has degraded me beneath the meanest animal. No crime, no mischief, no malignity, no misery, can be found comparable to mine. When I call over the frightful catalogue of my deeds, I cannot believe that I am he whose thoughts were once filled with sublime and transcendant visions of the beauty and the majesty of goodness. But it is even so; the fallen angel becomes a malignant devil. Yet even that enemy of God and man had friends and associates in his desolation; I am quite alone.

"You, who call Frankenstein your friend, seem to have a knowledge of my crimes and his misfortunes. But, in the detail which he gave you of them, he could not sum up the hours and months of misery which I endured, wasting in impotent passions. For whilst I destroyed his hopes, I did not satisfy my own desires. They were for ever ardent and craving; still I desired love and fellowship, and I was still spurned. Was there no injustice in this? Am I to be thought the only criminal, when all human kind sinned against me? Why do you not hate Felix, who drove his friend from his door with contumely? Why do you not execrate the rustic who sought to destroy the saviour of his child? Nay, these are virtuous and immaculate beings! I, the miserable and the abandoned, am an abortion, to be spurned at, and kicked, and trampled on. Even now my blood boils at the recollection of this injustice.

"But it is true that I am a wretch. I have murdered the lovely and the helpless; I have strangled the innocent as they slept, and grasped to death his throat who never injured me or any other living thing. I have devoted my creator, the select specimen of all that is worthy of love and admiration among men, to misery; I have pursued him even to that irremediable ruin. There he lies, white and cold in death. You hate me; but your abhorrence cannot equal that with which I regard myself. I look on the hands which executed the deed; I think on the heart in which the imagination of it was conceived, and long for the moment when they will meet my eyes, when it will haunt my thoughts, no more.

"Fear not that I shall be the instrument of future mischief. My work is nearly complete. Neither your's nor any man's death is needed to consummate the series of my being, and accomplish that which must be done; but it requires my own. Do not think that I shall be slow to perform this sacrifice. I shall quit your vessel on the ice-raft which brought me hither, and shall seek the most northern extremity of the globe; I shall collect my funeral pile, and consume to ashes this miserable frame, that its remains may afford no light to any curious and unhallowed wretch, who would create such another as I have been. I shall die. I shall no longer feel the agonies which now consume me, or be the prey of feelings unsatisfied, yet unquenched. He is dead who called me into being; and when I shall be no more, the very remembrance of us both will speedily vanish. I shall no longer see the sun or stars, or feel the winds play on my cheeks. Light, feeling, and sense, will pass away; and in this condition must I find my happiness. Some years ago, when the images which this world affords first opened upon me, when I felt the cheering warmth of summer, and heard the rustling of the leaves and the chirping of the birds, and these were all to me, I should have wept to die; now it is my only consolation. Polluted by crimes, and torn by the bitterest remorse, where can I find rest but in death?

"Farewell! I leave you, and in you the last of human kind whom these eyes will ever behold. Farewell, Frankenstein! If thou wert yet alive, and yet cherished a desire of revenge against me, it would be better satiated in my life than in my destruction. But it was not so; thou didst seek my extinction, that I might not cause greater wretchedness; and if yet, in some mode unknown to me, thou hast not yet ceased to think and feel, thou desirest not my life for my own misery. Blasted as thou wert, my agony was still superior to thine; for the bitter sting of remorse may not cease to rankle in my wounds until death shall close them for ever.

"But soon," he cried, with sad and solemn enthusiasm, "I shall die, and what I now feel be no longer felt. Soon these burning miseries will be extinct. I shall ascend my funeral pile triumphantly, and exult in the agony of the torturing flames. The light of that conflagration will fade away; my ashes will be swept into the sea by the winds. My spirit will sleep in peace; or if it thinks, it will not surely think thus. Farewell."

He sprung from the cabin-window, as he said this, upon the ice-raft which lay close to the vessel. He was soon borne away by the waves, and lost in darkness and distance.

The Adventure of the German Student

Washington Irving

———◆———

O N A STORMY NIGHT, IN THE TEMPESTUOUS TIMES OF THE FRENCH Revolution, a young German was returning to his lodgings, at a late hour, across the old part of Paris. The lightning gleamed, and the loud claps of thunder rattled through the lofty narrow streets—but I should first tell you something about this young German.

Gottfried Wolfgang was a young man of good family. He had studied for some time at Gottingen, but being of a visionary and enthusiastic character, he had wandered into those wild and speculative doctrines which have so often bewildered German students. His secluded life, his intense application, and the singular nature of his studies, had an effect on both mind and body. His health was impaired; his imagination diseased. He had been indulging in fanciful speculations on spiritual essences, until, like Swedenborg, he had an ideal world of his own around him. He took up a notion, I do not know from what cause, that there was an evil influence hanging over him; an evil genius or spirit seeking to ensnare him and ensure his perdition. Such an idea working on his melancholy temperament, produced the most gloomy effects. He became haggard and desponding. His friends discovered the mental malady preying upon him, and determined that the best cure was a change of scene; he was sent, therefore, to finish his studies amidst the splendours and gaieties of Paris.

Wolfgang arrived at Paris at the breaking out of the revolution. The popular delirium at first caught his enthusiastic mind, and he was captivated by the political and philosophical theories of the day: but the scenes of blood which followed, shocked his sensitive nature; disgusted him with society and the world, and made him more than ever a recluse. He shut himself up in a solitary apartment in the *Pays Latin,* the quarter of students. There, in a gloomy street not far from the monastic walls of the Sorbonne, he pursued his favorite speculations. Sometimes he spent hours together in the great libraries of Paris, those catacombs of departed authors, rummaging among their hoards of dusty and obsolete works in quest of food for his unhealthy appetite. He was, in a manner, a literary ghoul, feeding in the charnel-house of decayed literature.

Wolfgang, though solitary and recluse, was of an ardent temperament, but for a time it operated merely upon his imagination. He was too shy and ignorant of the world to make any advances to the fair, but he was a passionate admirer of female beauty, and in his lonely chamber would often lose himself in reveries on forms and faces which he had seen, and his fancy would deck out images of loveliness far surpassing the reality.

While his mind was in this excited and sublimated state, a dream produced an extraordinary effect upon him. It was of a female face of transcendent beauty. So strong was the impression made, that he dreamt of it again and again. It haunted his thoughts by day, his slumbers by night; in fine, he became passionately enamoured of this shadow of a dream. This lasted so long that it became one of those fixed ideas which haunt the minds of melancholy men, and are at times mistaken for madness.

Such was Gottfried Wolfgang, and such his situation at the time I mentioned. He was returning home late one stormy night, through some of the old and gloomy streets of the *Marais*, the ancient part of Paris. The loud claps of thunder rattled among the high houses of the narrow streets. He came to the Place de Grève, the square where public executions are performed. The lightning quivered about the pinnacles of the ancient Hôtel de Ville, and shed flickering gleams over the open space in front. As Wolfgang was crossing the square, he shrank back with horror at finding himself close by the guillotine. It was the height of the reign of terror, when this dreadful instrument of death stood ever ready, and its scaffold was continually running with the blood of the virtuous and the brave. It had that very day been actively employed in the work of carnage, and there it stood in grim array, amidst a silent and sleeping city, waiting for fresh victims.

Wolfgang's heart sickened within him, and he was turning shuddering from the horrible engine, when he beheld a shadowy form, cowering as it were at the foot of the steps which led up to the scaffold. A succession of vivid flashes of lightning revealed it more distinctly. It was a female figure, dressed in black. She was seated on one of the lower steps of the scaffold, leaning forward, her face hid in her lap; and her long dishevelled tresses hanging to the ground, streaming with the rain which fell in torrents. Wolfgang paused. There was something awful in this solitary monument of woe. The female had the appearance of being above the common order. He knew the times to be full of vicissitude, and that many a fair head, which had once been pillowed on down, now wandered houseless. Perhaps this was some poor mourner whom the dreadful axe had rendered desolate, and who sat here heart-broken on the strand of existence, from which all that was dear to her had been launched into eternity.

He approached, and addressed her in the accents of sympathy. She raised her head and gazed wildly at him. What was his astonishment at beholding, by the bright glare of the lightning, the very face which had haunted him in his dreams. It was pale and disconsolate, but ravishingly beautiful.

Trembling with violent and conflicting emotions, Wolfgang again accosted her. He spoke something of her being exposed at such an hour of the night, and to the fury of such a storm, and offered to conduct her to her friends. She pointed to the guillotine with a gesture of dreadful signification.

"I have no friend on earth!" said she.

"But you have a home," said Wolfgang.

"Yes—in the grave!"

The heart of the student melted at the words.

"If a stranger dare make an offer," said he, "without danger of being misunderstood, I would offer my humble dwelling as a shelter; myself as a devoted friend. I am friendless myself in Paris, and a stranger in the land; but if my life could be of service, it is at your disposal, and should be sacrificed before harm or indignity should come to you."

There was an honest earnestness in the young man's manner that had its effect. His foreign accent, too, was in his favour; it showed him not to be a hackneyed inhabitant of Paris. Indeed, there is an eloquence in true enthusiasm that is not to be doubted. The homeless stranger confided herself implicitly to the protection of the student.

He supported her faltering steps across the Pont Neuf, and by the place where the statue of Henry the Fourth had been overthrown by the populace. The storm had abated, and the thunder rumbled at a distance. All Paris was quiet; that great volcano of human passion slumbered for a while, to gather fresh strength for the next day's eruption. The student conducted his charge through the ancient streets of the *Pays Latin*, and by the dusky walls of the Sorbonne, to the great dingy hotel which he inhabited. The old portress who admitted them stared with surprise at the unusual sight of the melancholy Wolfgang with a female companion.

On entering his apartment, the student, for the first time, blushed at the scantiness and indifference of his dwelling. He had but one chamber—an old-fashioned saloon—heavily carved, and fantastically furnished with the remains of former magnificence, for it was one of those hotels in the quarter of the Luxembourg palace which had once belonged to nobility. It was lumbered with books and papers, and all the usual apparatus of a student, and his bed stood in a recess at one end.

When lights were brought, and Wolfgang had a better opportunity of contemplating the stranger, he was more than ever intoxicated by her beauty. Her face was pale, but of a dazzling fairness, set off by a profusion of raven hair that hung clustering about it. Her eyes were large and brilliant, with a singular expression that approached almost to wildness. As far as her black dress permitted her shape to be seen, it was of perfect symmetry. Her whole appearance was highly striking, though she was dressed in the simplest style. The only thing approaching to an ornament which she wore, was a broad black band round her neck, clasped by diamonds.

The perplexity now commenced with the student how to dispose of the helpless being thus thrown upon his protection. He thought of abandoning his chamber to her, and seeking shelter for himself elsewhere. Still he was so fascinate by her charms, there seemed to be such a spell upon his thoughts and senses, that he could not tear himself from her presence. Her manner, too, was singular and unaccountable. She spoke no more of the guillotine. Her grief had abated. The attentions of the student had first won her confidence, and then, apparently, her heart. She was evidently an enthusiast like himself, and enthusiasts soon understand each other.

In the infatuation of the moment, Wolfgang avowed his passion for her. He told her the story of his mysterious dream, and how she had possessed his heart before he had even seen her. She was strangely affected by his recital, and acknowledged to have felt an impulse towards him equally unaccountable. It was the time for wild theory and wild actions. Old prejudices and superstitions were done away; everything was under the sway of the "Goddess of Reason." Among other rubbish of the old times, the forms and ceremonies of marriage began to be considered superfluous bonds for honorable minds. Social compacts were the vogue. Wolfgang was too much of a theorist not to be tainted by the liberal doctrines of the day.

"Why should we separate?" said he: "our hearts are united; in the eye of reason and honor we are as one. What need is there of sordid forms to bind high souls together?"

The stranger listened with emotion: she had evidently received illumination at the same school.

"You have no home nor family," continued he; "Let me be every thing to you, or rather let us be everything to one another. If form is necessary, form shall be observed—there is my hand. I pledge myself to you for ever."

"For ever?" said the stranger, solemnly.

"For ever!" repeated Wolfgang.

The stranger clasped the hand extended to her: "Then I am yours," murmured she, and sank upon his bosom.

The next morning the student left his bride sleeping, and sallied forth at an early hour to seek more spacious apartments, suitable to the change in his situation. When he returned, he found the stranger lying with her head hanging over the bed, and one arm thrown over it. He spoke to her, but received no reply. He advanced to awaken her from her uneasy posture. On taking her hand, it was cold—there was no pulsation— her face was pallid and ghastly.—In a word—she was a corpse.

Horrified and frantic, he alarmed the house. A scene of confusion ensued. The police was summoned. As the officer of police entered the room, he started back on beholding the corpse.

"Great heaven!" cried he, "how did this woman come here?"

"Do you know anything about her?" said Wolfgang, eagerly.

"Do I?" exclaimed the officer: "she was guillotined yesterday!" He stepped forward; undid the black collar round the neck of the corpse, and the head rolled on the floor!

The student burst into a frenzy. "The fiend! the fiend has gained possession of me!" shrieked he: "I am lost for ever."

They tried to soothe him, but in vain. He was possessed with the frightful belief that an evil spirit had reanimated the dead body to ensnare him. He went distracted, and died in a mad-house.

The Wehr-Wolf
A LEGEND OF THE LIMOUSIN

Richard Thomson

———— ◆ ————

The Wolf! the Wolf!
ÆSOP'S FABLES.

'Twas soothly said, in olden hours,
That men were oft with wondrous powers
Endow'd their wonted forms to change,
And Wehr-Wolves wild abroad to range!
So Garwal roams in savage pride,
    And hunts for blood and feeds on men,
Spreads dire destruction far and wide,
    And makes the forests broad his den.
MARIE'S LAI DU BISCLAVASET.

THE ANCIENT PROVINCE OF POICTOU, IN FRANCE, HAS LONG BEEN CELEBRATED in the annals of Romance, as one of the most famous haunts of those dreadful animals, whose species is between a phantom and a beast of prey; and which are called by the Germans, Wehr-Wolves, and by the French, Bisclavarets, or Loups Garoux. To the English, these midnight terrors are yet unknown, and almost without a name; but when they are spoken of in this country, they are called by way of eminence, Wild Wolves! The common superstition concerning them is, that they are men in compact with the Arch Enemy, who have the power of assuming the form and nature of wolves at certain periods. The hilly and woody district of the Upper Limousin, which now forms the Southern division of the Upper Vienne, was that particular part of the Province which the Wehr-Wolves were supposed to inhabit; whence,

like the animals which gave them their name, they would wander out by midnight, far
from their own hills and mountains, and run howling through the silent streets of the
nearest towns and villages, to the great terror of all the inhabitants; whose piety, however, was somewhat increased by these supernatural visitations.

There once stood in the suburbs of the Town of St. Yrieux, which is situate in those
dangerous parts of ancient Poictou, an old, but handsome, *Maison-de-Plaisance,* or, in
plain English, a country-house, belonging by ancient descent to the young Baroness
Louise Joliedame; who, out of a dread of the terrible Wehr-Wolves, a well-bred horror
at the *chambres à antique* which it contained, and a greater love for the gallant Court of
Francis I, let the Château to strangers; though they occupied but a very small portion
of it, whilst the rest was left unrepaired, and was rapidly falling to decay. One of the
parties by whom the old mansion was tenanted, was a country Chirurgeon, named
Antoine Du Pilon; who, according to his own account, was not only well acquainted
with the science of Galen and Hippocrates, but was also a profound adept in those
arts, for the learning of which some men toil their whole lives away, and are none the
wiser; such as Alchemy, converse with spirits, Magic, and so forth. Dr. Du Pilon had
abundant leisure to talk of his knowledge at the little Cabaret of St. Yrieux, which
bore the sign of the Chevalier Bayard's Arms, where he assembled round him many
of the idler members of the town, the chief of whom were Cuirbouilli, the Currier;
Malbois, the Joiner; La Jacquette, the Tailor, and Nicole Bonvarlet, his Host, together
with several other equally arrant gossips, who all swore roundly, at the end of each of
their parleys, that Doctor Antoine du Pilon was the best Doctor, and the wisest man
in the whole world! To remove, however, any wonder that may arise in the reader's
mind, how a professor of such skill and knowledge should be left to waste his abilities
so remote from the patronage of the great, it should be remarked, that in such cases as
had already come before him, he had not been quite so successful as could have been
expected, or desired; since old Genifréde Corbeau, who was frozen almost double with
age and ague, he kept cold and fasting, to preserve her from fever; and he would have
cut off the leg of Pierre Faucille, the reaper, when he wounded his right arm in harvest
time, to prevent the flesh from mortifying downwards!

In a retired apartment of the same deserted mansion where this mirror of
Chirurgeons resided, dwelt a peasant and his daughter, who had come to St. Yrieux
from a distant part of Normandy, and of whose history nothing was known, but that
they seemed to be in the deepest poverty; although they neither asked relief, nor
uttered a single complaint. Indeed they rather avoided all discourse with their gos-

siping neighbours, and even with their fellow inmates, excepting so far as the briefest courtesy required; and as they were able, on entering their abode, to place a reasonable security for payment in the hands of old Gervais, the Baroness Joliedame's Steward, they were permitted to live in the old Château with little questioning, and less sympathy. The father appeared in general to be a plain rude peasant, whom poverty had somewhat tinctured with misanthropy; though there were times when his bluntness towered into a haughtiness not accordant with his present station, but seemed like a relique of a higher sphere from which he had fallen. He strove, and the very endeavour increased the bitterness of his heart to mankind, to conceal his abject indigence, but that was too apparent to all, since he was rarely to be found at St. Yrieux, but led a wild life in the adjacent mountains and forests, occasionally visiting the town, to bring to his daughter Adéle a portion of the spoil, which, as a hunter, he indefatigably sought for the subsistence of both. Adéle, on the contrary, though she felt as deeply as her father the sad reverse of fortune to which they were exposed, had more gentleness in her sorrow, and more content in her humiliation. She would, when he returned to the cottage, worn with the fatigue of his forest labours, try, but many times in vain, to bring a smile to his face, and consolation to his heart. "My father," she would say, "quit, I beseech you, this wearisome hunting for some safer employment, nearer home. You depart, and I watch in vain for your return; days and nights pass away, and you come not! while my disturbed imagination will ever whisper the danger of a forest midnight, fierce howling wolves, and robbers still more cruel."

"Robbers! girl, sayest thou?" answered her father with a bitter laugh, "and what shall they gain from me, think ye? is there aught in this worn-out gaberdine to tempt them? Go to, Adéle! I am not now Count Gaspar de Marcanville, the friend of the royal Francis, and a Knight of the Holy Ghost; but plain Hubert, the Hunter of the Limousin; and wolves, thou trowest, will not prey upon wolves."

"But, dear my father," said Adéle, embracing him, "I would that thou would'st seek a safer occupation nearer to our dwelling, for I would be by your side."

"What wouldst have me to do, girl?" interrupted Gaspar impatiently; "would'st have me put this hand to the sickle, or the plough, which has so often grasped a sword in the battle, and a banner-lance in the tournament? or shall a companion of Le Saint-Esprit become a fellow-handworker with the low artizans of this miserable town? I tell thee Adéle, that but for thy sake I would never again quit the forest, but would remain there in a savage life, till I forgot my language and my species, and became a Wehr-wolf, or a wild-buck!"

Such was commonly the close of their conversation; for if Adéle dared to press her entreaties farther, Gaspar, half frenzied, would not fail to call to her mind all the unhappy circumstances of his fall, and work himself almost to madness by their repetition. He had in early life been introduced by the Count De Saintefleur to the Court of Francis I, where he had risen so high in the favour of his Sovereign, that he was continually in his society; and in the many wars which so embittered the reign of that excellent Monarch, De Marcanville's station was ever by his side. In these conflicts, Gaspar's bosom had often been the shield of Francis, even in moments of the most imminent danger; and the grateful King as often showered upon his deliverer those rewards, which, to the valiant and high-minded soldier, are far dearer than riches; the glittering jewels of knighthood, and the golden coronal of the peerage. To that friend who had fixed his feet so loftily and securely in the slippery paths of a Court, Gaspar felt all the ardour of youthful gratitude; and yet he sometimes imagined, that he could perceive an abatement in the favour of De Saintefleur, as that of Francis increased. The truth was, that the gold and rich promises of the King's great enemy, the Emperor Charles V, had induced De Saintefleur to swerve from his allegiance; and he now waited but for a convenient season to put the darkest designs in practice against his Sovereign. He also felt no slight degree of envy, even against that very person whom he had been the instrument of raising; and at length an opportunity occurred, when he might gratify both his ambition and his revenge, by the same blow. It was in one of those long wars in which the French Monarch was engaged, and in which De Saintefleur and De Marcanville were his most constant companions, that they were both watching near his couch whilst he slept, when the former, in a low tone of voice, thus began to sound the faith of the latter towards his royal master.

"What say'st thou, Gaspar, were not a prince's coronet and a king's revenue in Naples, better than thus ever toiling in a war that seems unending? Hearest thou, brave De Marcanville? we can close it with the loss of one life only!"

"Queen of Heaven!" ejaculated Gaspar, "what is it thou would'st say, De Saintefleur?"

"Say! why that there have been other Kings of France before this Francis, and will be, when he shall have gone to his place. Thinkest thou that He of the double-headed black eagle would not amply reward the sword that cut this fading lily from the earth?"

"No more, no more, De Saintefleur!" cried Gaspar; "even from you, who placed me where I might flourish beneath that lily's shade, will I not hear this treason. Rest secure that I will not betray thee to the King; my life shall sooner be given for thine; but I will watch thee with more vigilance than the wolf hath when he watcheth the night-fold, and your first step to the heart of Francis shall be over the body of Gaspar De Marcanville."

"Nay, then," said De Saintefleur aside, "he must be my first victim," and immediately drawing his sword, he cried aloud, "What, ho! guards! treason!"—whilst Gaspar stood immoveable with astonishment and horror. The event is soon related, for Francis was but too easily persuaded that De Marcanville was in reality guilty of the act about to have been perpetrated by De Saintefleur; and the magnanimity of Gaspar was such, that not one word which might criminate his former friend could be drawn from him, even to save his own life. The kind-hearted Francis, however, was unable to forget in a moment the favour with which for years he had been accustomed to look upon De Marcanville; and it was only at the earnest solicitation of the Courtiers, many of whom were rejoiced at the thought of a powerful rival's removal, that he could be prevailed on to pass upon him even the sentence of degradation and banishment.

Gaspar hastened to his Château, but the treasures which he was allowed to bear with him into exile were little more than his Rosalie and his daughter Adéle; with whom he immured himself in the dark and almost boundless recesses of the Hanoverian Harz, where his fatigues and his sorrows soon rendered his gaunt and attenuated form altogether unknown. In this savage retirement, he drew up a faithful narration of De Saintefleur's treachery; and in confirmation of its truth, procured a certificate from his Confessor, Father Ægidius,—one of those holy men who of old were dwellers in forests and deserts,—and directing it "To the King," placed it in the hands of his wife, that if, in any of those hazardous excursions in which he engaged to procure their daily subsistence, he should perish, it might be delivered to Francis, and his family thus be restored to their rank and estates, when his pledge to De Saintefleur could no longer be claimed. Years passed away, and, in the gloomy recesses of the Hercynian woods, Gaspar acquired considerable skill as a hunter: had it been to preserve his own life only, he had laid him calmly down upon the sod, and resigned that life to famine, or to the hungry wolf; but he had still two objects which bound him to existence, and therefore in the chase the wild-buck was too slow to escape his spear, and the bear too weak to resist his attacks.

His fate, notwithstanding, preyed heavily upon him, and often brake out in fits of vehement passion, and the most bitter lamentations; which at length so wrought upon the grief-worn frame of Rosalie de Marcanville, that about ten years after Gaspar's exile, her death left him a widower, when his daughter Adéle was scarcely eighteen years of age. It was then, with a mixture of desperation and distress, that De Marcanville determined to rush forth from his solitude into France, and, careless of the fate which might await him for returning from exile unrecalled, to advance even to the Court, and laying his papers at the foot of the throne, to demand the Ordeal of Combat with De Saintefleur; but when he had arrived at the woody Province of the Upper Limousin, his purpose failed him, as he saw in the broad day-light, which rarely entered the Harz Forest, the afflicting changes which ten years of the severest labour, and the most heartfelt sorrow, had made upon his form. He might, indeed, so far as it regarded all recollections of his person, have safely gone even into the Court of Francis; but Gaspar also saw, that in the retired forest surrounding St. Yrieux, he might still reside unknown in his beloved France; that under the guise of a hunter, he could still provide for the support of his gentle Adéle; and that, in the event of his death, she would be considerably nearer to her Sovereign's abode. It was, then, in consequence of these reasons, that De Marcanrille employed a part of his small remaining property, in securing a residence in the dilapidated Château, as it has been already mentioned.

It was some time after their arrival, that the inhabitants of the Town of St. Yrieux were alarmed by the intelligence, that a Wehr-Wolf, or perhaps a troop of them, certainly inhabited the woods of the Limousin. The most terrific howlings were heard in the night, and the wild rush of a chase swept through the deserted streets; yet the townspeople—according to the most approved rules for acting where Wehr-Wolves are concerned,—never once thought of sallying forth in a body, and with weapons, and lighted brands, to scare the monsters from their prey; but, adding a more secure fastening to every window, which is the Wehr-Wolf's usual entrance, they deserted such as had already fallen their victims, with one brief expression of pity for *them*, and many a *"Dieu me benit!"* for *themselves*. It was asserted, too, that some of the country people, whose dwellings came more immediately into contact with the Limousin forests, had lost their children, whose lacerated remains, afterwards discovered in the woods, only half devoured, plainly denoted them to have fallen the prey of some abandoned Wehr-Wolf!

It is not surprising, that in a retired town, where half the people were without employment, and all were thorough-bred gossips, and lovers of wonders, that the inroads of the Wehr-Wolves formed too important an epoch in their history, to be passed over without a due discussion. Under pretence, therefore, of being a protection to each other, many of the people of St. Yrieux, and especially the worthy conclave mentioned at the beginning of this history, were, almost eternally, convened at the Chevalier Bayard's Arms; talking over their nightly terrors, and filling each other with such affright, by the repetition of many a lying old tale upon the same subject, that, too much alarmed to part, they often agreed to pass the night over Nicole Bonvarlet's wine-flask and blazing fagots. Upon a theme so intimately connected with magical lore as is the history of Wehr-Wolves, Dr. Antoine Du Pilon discoursed like a Solomon; citing, to the great edification and wonder of his hearers, such hosts of authors, both sacred and profane, that he who should but have hinted, that the Wehr-Wolves of St. Yrieux were simply like other Wolves, would have found as little gentleness in his hearers, as he would have experienced from the animals themselves.

"Well, my masters!" began Bonvarlet, one evening when they were met, "I would not, for a tun of malmsey wine now, be in the Limousin forest to-night; for do ye hear how it blusters and pours? By the Ship of St. Mildred! in a wild night like this, there's no place in the world like your hearth-side in a goodly auberge, with a merry host and good liquor; both of which, neighbours, ye have to admiration."

"Aye, Nicole," replied Cuirbouilli, "it's a foul night, truly, either for man or cattle; and yet I'll warrant ye that the Wehr-Wolves will be out in't, for their skin is said to be the same as that the Fiend himself wears! and that would shut you out water, and storm, and wind, like a castle-wall. Mass, now! but it would be simply the making of my fortune, an' I could but get one of their hides!"

"Truly, for a churl," began Dr. Du Pilon, "an unlettered artizan, thy wish sheweth a pretty wit; for a cloak made from the skin of a Wehr-Wolf, would for ever defend its wearer from all other Wolves, and all animals that your Wolves feed upon: even, as Pythagoras writeth, that one holding the eye of a Wolf in his hand, shall scare away from him all weaker creatures; for like as the sight of a Wolf doth terrify—"

"Hark, neighbours! did ye hear that cry? it is a Wehr-Wolf's bark!" exclaimed Jerome Malbois, starting from his settle.

"Aye, by the Bull of St. Luke! did I, friend Jerome," returned Bonvarlet, "surely the great Fiend himself can make no worser a howling; I even thought 'twould split the very rafters last night, though I deem that they're of good seasoned fir."

"There thou errest again," said the Doctor in a pompous tone to the last speaker, "Oh! ye rustics, whom I live with as Orpheus did with the salvages of Thracia, whence is it that ye possess such boundless stupidity? Thou sayest, Jerome Malbois, that they bark, and, could I imagine, that shooting in the dark, thou had'st hit on the Greekish phrase which calls them Dogs of the Night, I could say thou had said wisely: but now

I declare that thou hast spoken full ignorantly, right woodenly, Jerome Malbois; thou art beyond thy square, friend joiner; thou hast overstepped thy rule, good Carpenter. Doth not the great Albertus bear testimony, Oh, most illiterate! that Wolves bark not, when he saith,—

'Ast Lupus ipse *vlulat,* frendit agrestis aper,'

which for thine edification is, in the vulgar tongue,—

But the Wolf doth loudly howl, and the boar his teeth doth grind,
Where the wildest plains are spread before, and forests rise behind.

Et idem Auctor, and the same Author also saith, which maketh yet more against thee, *O mentis inops!*

'Per noctem resonare Lupus, *vlulantibus* urbes.'

which in the common is

The Wolf by night through silent cities prowls,
And makes the streets resound with hideous howls.

"And doth not Servius say the like in a verse wherein I opine he hints at Wehr-Wolves? '*Vlulare,* canum est furiare'—to howl is the voice of dogs and furies:—thus findest thou, *Faber sciolus*! that here we have an agreement touching the voice of wolves, which is low and mournful, and therefore the word *Vlulatus* is fitly applied as an imitation thereof. Your Almaine says *Heulen*; the Frenchman saith *Hurler*; and the Englishman, with a conglomeration of sounds as bad as the Wolf's own, calleth it howling."

"By the holy Dog of Tobias!" ejaculated Bonvarlet, "and I think our Doctor speaketh all languages, as he had had his head broken with a brick from the Tower of Babel, and all the tongues had got in at once. But where think ye Monsieur, that these cursed Loups Garoux came from? Are they like unto other Wolves, or what breed be they?"

"Nicole Bonvarlet," again began the untired Doctor, after taking a long draught of the flask, "Nicole Bonvarlet, I perceive thou hast more of good literature than thy fellows; for not only dost thou mark erudition when it is set before thee, but thou also wisely distrustest thine own knowledge, and questionest of those who are more learned than thou. Touching thy demand of what breed are the Wehr-Wolves, be this mine answer. Thou knowest, that if ye ask of a shepherd how he can distinguish one sheep from another, he tells you that even in their faces he seeth a *distinctio secretio*, the which to a common observer is not visible; and thus, when the vulgar see a wolf, they can but say it is a wolf, and there endeth their cunning. But, by the Lion of St. Mark! if ye ask one skilled in the knowledge of four-footed animals, he shall presently discourse to you of the genus and species thereof; make known its haunts and history, display its occult properties, and give you a lection upon all that your ancient and modern authors have said concerning it."

"By the Mass now!" interrupted La Jaquette, "and I would fain know the habit in which your Loup Garoux vests him when he is not in his wolfish shape; whether he have slashed cuishes, and—."

"Peace, I pray you peace, good Tailleur," said Doctor Antoine; "it is but rarely that I speak, and even then my discourse is brief, and therefore I beseech you not to mar the words of wisdom which are seldom heard, with thy folly which men may listen to hourly. Touching your Wolves, honest friends, as I was saying, there are five kinds, as Oppianus noteth in his Admonition to Shepherds; of the which, two sorts that rove in the countries of Swecia and the Visigoths, are called *Acmonæ*, but of these I will not now speak, but turn me unto those of whose species is the Wehr-Wolf. The first is named the Shooter, for that he runneth fast, is very bold, howleth fearfully—"

"There is the cry again!" exclaimed Malbois, and as the sounds drew nearer, the Doctor's audience evinced symptoms of alarm, which were rapidly increasing, when a still louder shriek was heard close to the house.

"What, ho! within there!" cried a voice, evidently of one in an agony of terror, "an' ye be men, open the door!" and the next moment it was burst from its fastenings by the force of a human body falling against it, which dropped without motion upon the floor!

The confusion which this accident created may well be imagined; the Doctor, greatly alarmed, retreated into the fire-place, whence he cried out to the equally scared rustics, "It's a Wehr-Wolf in a human shape, don't touch him, I tell you, but strike him with a fire-fork between the eyes, and he 'll turn to a Wolf, and run away! You, Cuirbouilli, out with thy knife, and flay me a piece of his neck, and you 'll see the thick wolf-hide under it. For the love of the Saints, neighbours, take care of yourselves, and—"

"Peace, Master Doctor," said Bonvarlet, the only one of the party that had ventured near the stranger, "he breathes yet, for he's a Christian man, like as we are."

"Don't you be too sure of that," replied Du Pilon; "ask him to say his Creed, and his Pater-Noster in Latin."

"Nay, good my master," returned the humane host, pouring some wine down the stranger's throat, and bearing his reviving body to the hearth, "he can scarce speak his mother-tongue, and therefore he's no stomach for Latin, so come, thou prince of all Chirurgeons, and bleed me him; and when he comes too, why e'en school him yourself."

Doctor Antoine Du Pilon advanced from his retreat, with considerable reluctance, to attend upon his patient, who was richly habited in the luxuriant fashion of the Court of Francis, and appeared to be a middle-aged man, of handsome features, and commanding presence. As the Doctor, somewhat reassured, began to remove the short cloak to find out the stranger's arm, he started back with affright, and actually roared with pain at receiving a deep scratch from the huge paw of a Wolf, which apparently grew out from his shoulder! "Avaunt thee, Sathanas!" ejaculated Du Pilon, "I told ye how it would be, my masters, that this cursed Wehr-Wolf would bleed us first. By the Porker of St. Anthony! Blessed beast! and he hath clawed me from the *Biceps Flexor Cubiti*, down to the *Os Lunare*, even as a Peasant would plough up a furrow!"

"Ha, ha, ha!" laughed Bonvarlet, holding up the dreaded Wolf's paw, which was yet bleeding, as if it had been recently separated from the animal,—"Here's no Wehr-Wolf, but a brave Hunter, who hath cut off this goodly fore-hand in the forest, with his couteaude-chasse; but soft," he added, throwing it aside, "he recovers!"

"Pierre!—Henri!" said the stranger, recovering, "where are ye? How far is the King behind us?—Ha! what place is this? and who are ye?" he continued, looking round.

"This, your good worship, is the Chevalier Bayard's Arms, in the Town of St. Yrieux, where your Honour fell, through loss of blood, as I guess by this wound. We were fain to keep the door barred, for fear of the Wehr-Wolves; and we half deemed your Lordship to be one, at first sight of the great paw you carried, but I judge you brought it from the forest."

"Aye! yes, them art in the right on't," said the stranger, recollecting himself, "'twas in the forest! I tell thee, Host, that I have this night looked upon the Arch-Demon himself!"

"Apage, Lucifer!" ejaculated Du Pilon, devoutly crossing his breast, "and have I received a claw from his fore-foot! I feel the enchantment of Lycanthropy coming over me; I shall be a Wehr-Wolf myself shortly, for what saith Hornhoofius, in his Treatise De Diabolis, lib. xiv. cap. 23,—they who are torn by a Wehr-Wolf—Oh me! Oh me! *Libera nos Domine!* Look to yourselves, neighbours, or I shall raven upon ye all."

"I pray you, Master Doctor," said Bonvarlet, "to let his Lordship tell us his story first, and then we 'll hear yours. How was it, fair sir? but take another cup of wine first."

"My tale is brief," answered the stranger; "The King is passing to-night through the Limousin, and, with two of my attendants, I rode forward to prepare for his coming; when, in the darkness of the wood, we were separated, and as I galloped on alone, an enormous Wolf, with fiery flashing eyes, leaped out of a brake before me, with the most fearful howlings, and rushed on me with the speed of lightning."

"Aye," interrupted Du Pilon, "as I told ye, they are called, in the Greekish phrase, Dogs of the Night, because of their howlings, and the Shooter, for that they shoot along."

"Now I pray your honour to proceed, and heed not the Doctor," said Bonvarlet.

"As the Wolf leaped upon my horse," continued the stranger, "I drew my couteau-dechasse, and severed that huge paw which you found upon me; but as the violence of the blow made the weapon fall, I caught up a large forked branch of a tree, and struck the animal upon the forehead; upon which my horse began to rear and plunge, for where the Wolf stood, I saw, by a momentary glimpse of moonlight, the form of an ancient enemy, who had long since been banished from France, and whom I believe to have died of Famine in the Harz Forest!"

"Lo you there now!" cried Du Pilon, "a blow between the eyes with a forked stick;—said I not so from Philo-Daimones, lib. xcii? Oh! I'm condemned to be a Wehr-Wolf of a verity, and I shall eat those of my most intimate acquaintance the first.—Masters look to yourselves;—*Oh dies infelix!* Oh unhappy man that I am!" and with these words he rushed out of the cottage.

"I think the very Fiend's in Monsieur the Doctor to-night," cried the Host, "for here he 's gone off without dressing his honour's wound."

"Heed not that, friend, but do thou provide torches, and assistance, to meet the King; my hurt is but small; but when my horse saw the apparition I told you of, he bounded forward like a wild Russian colt, dragging me through all the briars of the forest, for there seemed a troop of a thousand wolves howling behind us; and at the verge of it he dropped lifeless, and left me, still pursued, to gain the town, weak and wounded as I was!"

"St. Denis be praised now!" said Bonvarlet, "you shewed a good heart, my Lord; but we'll at once set out to meet the King, so neighbours, take each of ye a good pine fagot off the hearth, and call up more help as you go; and Nicolette and Madelene will prepare for our return."

"But," asked the stranger, "whereas the Wolf's paw that I brought from the forest?"

"I cast it aside, my Lord," answered Bonvarlet, "till you had recovered, but I would fain beg it of you as a gift, for I will hang it over my fire-place, and have its story made into a song by Rowland the Minstrel, and—Mother of God! what is this?" continued he, putting into his guest's hand a human arm, cut off at the elbow, vested in the worn-out sleeve of a hunter's coat, and bleeding freshly at the part where it was dissevered!

"Holy St. Mary!" exclaimed the stranger, regarding the hand attentively, "this is the arm of Gaspar de Marcanville, yet bearing the executioner's brand burnt in the flesh! and he is a Wehr-Wolf!"

"Why," said Bonvarlet, "that's the habit worn by the melancholy Hunter, whose daughter lives at the ruined Château yonder. He rarely comes to St. Yrieux, but when he does, he brings more game than any ten of your gentlemen-huntsmen ever did. Come, we'll go seek the daughter of this Man-Wolf, and then on to the forest, for this fellow deserves a stake, and a bundle of fagots, as well as ever Jeanne d'Arc did, in my simple thinking."

They then proceeded to Adéle, at the dilapidated Château, and her distress at the foregoing story may better be conceived than described; yet she offered not the slightest assistance to accompanying them to the forest; though when one of the party mentioned their expected meeting with the King, her eyes became suddenly lighted up, and, retiring for a moment, she expressed herself in readiness to attend them. At the skirts of the forest they found an elderly man, of a strange quaint appearance, couching in the fern like a hare; who called out to them in a squeaking voice, that was at once familiar to all, "Take care of yourselves, good people, for I am a Wehr-Wolf, and shall speedily spring upon some of ye."

"Why that's our Doctor, as I am a sinful man," cried Bonvarlet, "let's try his own cure upon him. Neighbour Malbois, give me a tough forked branch, and I'll disenchant him, I warrant; and you, Cuirbouilli, out with your knife, as though you would skin him:"—and then he continued aloud,—"Oh! honest friend, you're a Wehr-Wolf, are you? why then I'll dispossess the Devil that's in you.—You shall be flayed, and then burned for a wizard."

With that the rustics of St. Yrieux, who enjoyed the jest, fell upon the unhappy Doctor, and, by a sound beating, and other rough usage, so convinced him that he was not a Wehr-Wolf, that he cried out,—"Praised be St. Gregory, I am a whole man again! Lo I am healed! but my bones feel wondrous sore. Who is he that hath cured me?—by the Mass I am grievously bruised!—thanks to the seraphical Father Francis, the Devil hath gone out of me!"

Whilst the peasants were engaged in searching for the King's party, and the mutilated Wolf, the stranger, who was left with Adéle de Marcanville, fainted through loss of blood; and, as she bent over him, and staunched his wounds with her scarf, he said, with a faint voice,—"Fair one! who is it thinkest thou whom thou art so blessedly attending?"

"I wot not," answered she, "but that thou art a man."

"Hear me then, and throw aside these bandages for my dagger, for I am thy father's ancient enemy, the Count de Saintefleur!"

"Heaven forgive you, then!" returned Adéle, "for the time of vengeance belongs to it only."

"And it is come," cried a loud hoarse voice, as a large Wolf, wounded by the loss of a forepaw, leaped upon the Count, and put an end to his existence. At the same moment, the royal train, which the peasants had discovered, rode up with flambeaux, and a Knight with a large partizan made a blow at the Wolf, whom Adéle vainly endeavoured to preserve, since the stroke was of sufficient power to destroy both. The Wolf gave one terrific howl, and fell backwards in the form of a tall gaunt man, in a hunter's dress; whilst Adéle, drawing a packet from her bosom, and offering it to the King, sank lifeless upon the body of her father, Gaspar de Marcanville, the Wehr-Wolf of Limousin.

The Pit and the Pendulum

Edgar Allan Poe

———◆———

Impia tortorum longas hic turba furores
Sanguinis innocui, non satiata, aluit.
Sospite nunc patria, fracto nunc funeris antro,
Mors ubi dira fuit vita salusque patent.

[*Quatrain composed for the gates of a market to be erected upon
the site of the Jacobin Club House at Paris.*]

I WAS SICK—SICK UNTO DEATH WITH THAT LONG AGONY; AND WHEN THEY AT length unbound me, and I was permitted to sit, I felt that my senses were leaving me. The sentence—the dread sentence of death—was the last of distinct accentuation which reached my ears. After that, the sound of the inquisitorial voices seemed merged in one dreamy indeterminate hum. It conveyed to my soul the idea of *revolution*—perhaps from its association in fancy with the burr of a mill-wheel. This only for a brief period; for presently I heard no more. Yet, for a while, I saw; but with how terrible an exaggeration! I saw the lips of the black-robed judges. They appeared to me white— whiter than the sheet upon which I trace these words—and thin even to grotesqueness; thin with the intensity of their expression of firmness—of immoveable resolution—of stern contempt of human torture. I saw that the decrees of what to me was Fate, were still issuing from those lips. I saw them writhe with a deadly locution. I saw them fashion the syllables of my name; and I shuddered because no sound succeeded. I saw, too, for a few moments of delirious horror, the soft and nearly imperceptible waving of the sable draperies which enwrapped the walls of the apartment. And then my vision fell upon the seven tall candles upon the table. At first they wore the aspect of charity, and seemed white slender angels who would save me; but then, all at once, there came a most deadly nausea over my spirit, and I felt every fibre in my frame thrill as if I had touched the wire of a galvanic battery, while the angel forms became meaningless spectres, with heads of flame, and I saw that from them there would be no help. And then there stole into my fancy, like a rich musical note, the thought of what sweet rest there must be in the grave. The thought came gently and stealthily, and it seemed long before it attained full appreciation; but just as my spirit came at length properly to feel and entertain it, the figures of the judges vanished, as if magically, from before me; the tall candles sank into nothingness; their flames went out utterly; the blackness of darkness supervened; all sensations appeared swallowed up in a mad rushing descent as of the soul into Hades. Then silence, and stillness, and night were the universe.

I had swooned; but still will not say that all of consciousness was lost. What of it there remained I will not attempt to define, or even to describe; yet all was not lost. In the deepest slumber—no! In delirium—no! In a swoon—no! In death—no! even in the grave all *is not* lost. Else there is no immortality for man. Arousing from the most profound of slumbers, we break the gossamer web of *some* dream. Yet in a second afterward, (so frail may that web have been) we remember not that we have dreamed. In the return to life from the swoon there are two stages; first, that of the sense of mental or spiritual; secondly, that of the sense of physical, existence. It seems probable that if, upon reaching the second stage, we could recall the impressions of the first, we should find these impressions eloquent in memories of the gulf beyond. And that gulf is—what? How at least shall we distinguish its shadows from those of the tomb? But if the impressions of what I have termed the first stage, are not, at will, recalled, yet, after long interval, do they not come unbidden, while we marvel whence they come? He who has never swooned, is not he who finds strange palaces and wildly familiar faces in coals that glow; is not he who beholds floating in mid-air the sad visions that the many may not view; is not he who ponders over the perfume of some novel flower—is not he whose brain grows bewildered with the meaning of some musical cadence which has never before arrested his attention.

Amid frequent and thoughtful endeavors to remember; amid earnest struggles to regather some token of the state of seeming nothingness into which my soul had lapsed, there have been moments when I have dreamed of success; there have been brief, very brief periods when I have conjured up remembrances which the lucid reason of a later epoch assures me could have had reference only to that condition of seeming unconsciousness. These shadows of memory tell, indistinctly, of tall figures that lifted and bore me in silence down—down—still down—till a hideous dizziness oppressed me at the mere idea of the interminableness of the descent. They tell also of a vague horror at my heart, on account of that heart's unnatural stillness.

Then comes a sense of sudden motionlessness throughout all things; as if those who bore me (a ghastly train!) had outrun, in their descent, the limits of the limitless, and paused from the wearisomeness of their toil. After this I call to mind flatness and dampness; and then all is *madness*—the madness of a memory which busies itself among forbidden things.

Very suddenly there came back to my soul motion and sound—the tumultuous motion of the heart, and, in my ears, the sound of its beating. Then a pause in which all is blank. Then again sound, and motion, and touch—a tingling sensation pervading my frame. Then the mere consciousness of existence, without thought—a condition which lasted long. Then, very suddenly, *thought*, and shuddering terror, and earnest endeavor to comprehend my true state. Then a strong desire to lapse into insensibility. Then a rushing revival of soul and a successful effort to move. And now a full memory of the trial, of the judges, of the sable draperies, of the sentence, of the sickness, of the swoon. Then entire forgetfulness of all that followed; of all that a later day and much earnestness of endeavor have enabled me vaguely to recall.

So far, I had not opened my eyes. I felt that I lay upon my back, unbound. I reached out my hand, and it fell heavily upon something damp and hard. There I suffered it to remain for many minutes, while I strove to imagine where and *what* I could be. I longed, yet dared not to employ my vision. I dreaded the first glance at objects around me. It was not that I feared to look upon things horrible, but that I grew aghast lest there should be *nothing* to see. At length, with a wild desperation at heart, I quickly unclosed my eyes. My worst thoughts, then, were confirmed. The blackness of eternal night encompassed me. I struggled for breath. The intensity of the darkness seemed to oppress and stifle me. The atmosphere was intolerably close. I still lay quietly, and made effort to exercise my reason. I brought to mind the inquisitorial proceedings, and attempted from that point to deduce my real condition. The sentence had passed; and it appeared to me that a very long interval of time had since elapsed. Yet not for a moment did I suppose myself actually dead. Such a supposition, notwithstanding what we read in fiction, is altogether inconsistent with real existence;—but where and in what state was I? The condemned to death, I knew, perished usually at the *auto-da-fes*, and one of these had been held on the very night of the day of my trial. Had I been remanded to my dungeon, to await the next sacrifice, which would not take place for many months? This I at once saw could not be. Victims had been in immediate demand. Moreover, my dungeon, as well as all the condemned cells at Toledo, had stone floors, and light was not altogether excluded.

A fearful idea now suddenly drove the blood in torrents upon my heart, and for a brief period, I once more relapsed into insensibility. Upon recovering, I at once started to my feet, trembling convulsively in every fibre. I thrust my arms wildly above and around me in all directions. I felt nothing; yet dreaded to move a step, lest I should be impeded by the walls of a *tomb*. Perspiration burst from every pore, and stood in cold big beads upon my forehead. The agony of suspense, grew at length intolerable, and I cautiously moved forward, with my arms extended, and my eyes straining from their sockets, in the hope of catching some faint ray of light. I proceeded for many paces; but still all was blackness and vacancy. I breathed more freely. It seemed evident that mine was not, at least, the most hideous of fates.

And now, as I still continued to step cautiously onward, there came thronging upon my recollection a thousand vague rumors of the horrors of Toledo. Of the dungeons there had been strange things narrated—fables I had always deemed them—but yet strange, and too ghastly to repeat, save in a whisper. Was I left to perish of starvation in this subterranean world of darkness; or what fate, perhaps even more fearful, awaited me? That the result would be death, and a death of more than customary bitterness, I knew too well the character of my judges to doubt. The mode and the hour were all that occupied or distracted me.

My outstretched hands at length encountered some solid obstruction. It was a wall, seemingly of stone masonry—very smooth slimy, and cold. I followed it up; stepping with all the careful distrust with which certain antique narratives had inspired me. This process, however, afforded me no means of ascertaining the dimensions of my dungeon; as I might make its circuit, and return to the point whence I set out, without being aware of the fact; so perfectly uniform seemed the wall. I therefore sought the knife which had been in my pocket, when led into the inquisitorial chamber; but it was gone; my clothes had been exchanged for a wrapper of coarse serge. I had thought of forcing the blade in some minute crevice of the masonry, so as to identify my point of departure. The difficulty, nevertheless, was but trivial; although, in the disorder of my fancy, it seemed at first insuperable. I tore a part of the hem from the robe and placed the fragment at full length, and at right angles to the wall. In groping my way around the prison, I could not fail to encounter this rag upon completing the circuit. So, at least I thought: but I had not counted upon the extent of the dungeon, or upon my own weakness. The ground was moist and slippery. I staggered onward for some time, when I stumbled and fell. My excessive fatigue induced me to remain prostrate; and sleep soon overtook me as I lay.

Upon awaking, and stretching forth an arm, I found beside me a loaf and a pitcher with water. I was too much exhausted to reflect upon this circumstance, but ate and drank with avidity. Shortly afterward, I resumed my tour around the prison, and with much toil, came at last upon the fragment of the serge. Up to the period when I fell, I had counted fifty-two paces, and, upon resuming my walk, I had counted forty-eight more—when I arrived at the rag. There were in all, then, a hundred paces; and, admitting two paces to the yard, I presumed the dungeon to be fifty yards in circuit. I had met, however, with many angles in the wall, and thus I could form no guess at the shape of the vault; for vault I could not help supposing it to be.

I had little object—certainly no hope—in these researches; but a vague curiosity prompted me to continue them. Quitting the wall, I resolved to cross the area of the enclosure. At first, I proceeded with extreme caution, for the floor, although seemingly of solid material, was treacherous with slime. At length, however, I took courage, and did not hesitate to step firmly—endeavoring to cross in as direct a line as possible. I had advanced some ten or twelve paces in this manner, when the remnant of the torn hem of my robe became entangled between my legs. I stepped on it, and fell violently on my face.

In the confusion attending my fall, I did not immediately apprehend a somewhat startling circumstance, which yet, in a few seconds afterward, and while I still lay prostrate, arrested my attention. It was this: my chin rested upon the floor of the prison, but my lips, and the upper portion of my head, although seemingly at a less elevation than the chin, touched nothing. At the same time, my forehead seemed bathed in a clammy vapor, and the peculiar smell of decayed fungus arose to my nostrils. I put forward my arm, and shuddered to find that I had fallen at the very brink of a circular pit, whose extent, of course, I had no means of ascertaining at the moment. Groping about the masonry just below the margin, I succeeded in dislodging a small fragment, and let it fall into the abyss. For many seconds I hearkened to its reverberations as it dashed against the sides of the chasm in its descent: at length, there was a sullen plunge into water, succeeded by loud echoes. At the same moment, there came a sound resembling the quick opening, and as rapid closing of a door overhead, while a faint gleam of light flashed suddenly through the gloom, and as suddenly faded away.

I saw clearly the doom which had been prepared for me, and congratulated myself upon the timely accident by which I had escaped. Another step before my fall, and the world had seen me no more. And the death just avoided, was of that very character which I had regarded as fabulous and frivolous in the tales respecting the Inquisition.

To the victims of its tyranny, there was the choice of death with its direst physical agonies, or death with its most hideous moral horrors. I had been reserved for the latter.
By long suffering my nerves had been unstrung, until I trembled at the sound of my
own voice, and had become in every respect a fitting subject for the species of torture
which awaited me.

Shaking in every limb, I groped my way back to the wall—resolving there to
perish rather than risk the terrors of the wells, of which my imagination now pictured
many in various positions about the dungeon. In other conditions of mind, I might
have had courage to end my misery at once, by a plunge into one of these abysses; but
now I was the veriest of cowards. Neither could I forget what I had read of these pits—
that the *sudden* extinction of life formed no part of their most horrible plan.

Agitation of spirit kept me awake for many long hours; but at length I again slumbered. Upon arousing, I found by my side, as before, a loaf and a pitcher of water. A
burning thirst consumed me, and I emptied the vessel at a draught. It must have been
drugged—for scarcely had I drunk, before I became irresistibly drowsy. A deep sleep
fell upon me—a sleep like that of death. How long it lasted, of course, I know not; but
when, once again, I unclosed my eyes, the objects around me were visible. By a wild,
sulphurous lustre, the origin of which I could not at first determine, I was enabled to
see the extent and aspect of the prison.

In its size I had been greatly mistaken. The whole circuit of its walls did not
exceed twenty-five yards. For some minutes this fact occasioned me a world of vain
trouble; vain indeed—for what could be of less importance, under the terrible circumstances which environed me, then the mere dimensions of my dungeon? But my
soul took a wild interest in trifles, and I busied myself in endeavors to account for the
error I had committed in my measurement. The truth at length flashed upon me. In
my first attempt at exploration I had counted fifty-two paces, up to the period when
I fell: I must then have been within a pace or two of the fragment of serge; in fact, I
had nearly performed the circuit of the vault. I then slept—and, upon awaking, I must
have returned upon my steps—thus supposing the circuit nearly double what it actually was. My confusion of mind prevented me from observing that I began my tour
with the wall to the left, and ended it with the wall to the right.

I had been deceived, too, in respect to the shape of the enclosure. In feeling my
way, I had found many angles, and thus deduced an idea of great irregularity; so potent
is the effect of total darkness upon one arousing from lethargy or sleep! The angles
were simply those of a few slight depressions, or niches, at odd intervals. The general

shape of the prison was square. What I had taken for masonry, seemed now to be iron, or some other metal, in huge plates, whose sutures or joints occasioned the depression. The entire surface of this metallic enclosure was rudely daubed in all the hideous and repulsive devices to which the charnel superstition of the monks has given rise. The figures of fiends in aspects of menace, with skeleton forms, and other more really fearful images, overspread and disfigured the walls. I observed that the outlines of these monstrosities were sufficiently distinct, but that the colors seemed faded and blurred, as if from the effects of a damp atmosphere. I now noticed the floor, too, which was of stone. In the centre yawned the circular pit from whose jaws I had escaped; but it was the only one in the dungeon.

All this I saw indistinctly and by much effort—for my personal condition had been greatly changed during slumber. I now lay upon my back, and at full length, on a species of low framework of wood. To this I was securely bound by a long strap resembling a surcingle. It passed in many convolutions about my limbs and body, leaving at liberty only my head, and my left arm to such extent, that I could, by dint of much exertion, supply myself with food from an earthen dish which lay by my side on the floor. I saw, to my horror, that the pitcher had been removed. I say, to my horror— for I was consumed with intolerable thirst. This thirst it appeared to be the design of my persecutors to stimulate—for the food in the dish was meat pungently seasoned.

Looking upward, I surveyed the ceiling of my prison. It was some thirty or forty feet overhead, and constructed much as the side walls. In one of its panels a very singular figure riveted my whole attention. It was the painted figure of Time as he is commonly represented, save that, in lieu of a scythe, he held what, at a casual glance, I supposed to be the pictured image of a huge pendulum, such as we see on antique clocks. There was something, however, in the appearance of this machine which caused me to regard it more attentively. While I gazed directly upward at it, (for its position was immediately over my own,) I fancied that I saw it in motion. In an instant afterward the fancy was confirmed. Its sweep was brief, and of course slow. I watched it for some minutes, somewhat in fear, but more in wonder. Wearied at length with observing its dull movement, I turned my eyes upon the other objects in the cell.

A slight noise attracted my notice, and, looking to the floor, I saw several enormous rats traversing it. They had issued from the well, which lay just within view to my right. Even then, while I gazed, they came up in troops, hurriedly, with ravenous eyes, allured by the scent of the meat. From this it required much effort and attention to scare them away.

It might have been half an hour, perhaps even an hour, (for I could take but imperfect note of time) before I again cast my eyes upward. What I then saw, confounded and amazed me. The sweep of the pendulum had increased in extent by nearly a yard. As a natural consequence, its velocity was also much greater. But what mainly disturbed me, was the idea that it had perceptibly *descended*. I now observed—with what horror it is needless to say—that its nether extremity was formed of a crescent of glittering steel, about a foot in length from horn to horn; the horns upward, and the under edge evidently as keen as that of a razor. Like a razor also, it seemed massy and heavy, tapering from the edge into a solid and broad structure above. It was appended to a weighty rod of brass, and the whole *hissed* as it swung through the air.

I could no longer doubt the doom prepared for me by monkish ingenuity in torture. My cognizance of the pit had become known to the inquisitorial agents—*the pit*, whose horrors had been destined for so bold a recusant as myself—*the pit*, typical of hell, and regarded by rumor as the Ultima Thule of all their punishments. The plunge into this pit I had avoided by the merest of accidents, and I knew that surprise, or entrapment into torment, formed an important portion of all the grotesquerie of these dungeon deaths. Having failed to fall, it was no part of the demon plan to hurl me into the abyss; and thus (there being no alternative) a different and a milder destruction awaited me. Milder! I half smiled in my agony as I thought of such application of such a term.

What boots it to tell of the long, long hours of horror more than mortal, during which I counted the rushing oscillations of the steel! Inch by inch—line by line—with a descent only appreciable at intervals that seemed ages—down and still down it came! Days passed—it might have been that many days passed—ere it swept so closely over me as to fan me with its acrid breath. The odor of the sharp steel forced itself into my nostrils. I prayed—I wearied heaven with my prayer for its more speedy descent. I grew frantically mad, and struggled to force myself upward against the sweep of the fearful scimitar. And then I fell suddenly calm, and lay smiling at the glittering death, as a child at some rare bauble.

There was another interval of utter insensibility; it was brief; for, upon again lapsing into life, there had been no perceptible descent in the pendulum. But it might have been long—for I knew there were demons who took note of my swoon, and who could have arrested the vibration at pleasure. Upon my recovery, too, I felt very—oh, inexpressibly—sick and weak, as if through long inanition. Even amid the agonies of that period, the human nature craved food. With painful effort I outstretched my left arm as far as my bonds permitted, and took possession of the small remnant which had been spared me by the rats. As I put a portion of it within my lips, there rushed to my mind a half-formed thought of joy—of hope. Yet what business had *I* with hope? It was, as I say, a half-formed thought—man has many such, which are never completed. I felt that it was of joy—of hope; but I felt also that it had perished in its formation. In vain I struggled to perfect—to regain it. Long suffering had nearly annihilated all my ordinary powers of mind. I was an imbecile—an idiot.

The vibration of the pendulum was at right angles to my length. I saw that the crescent was designed to cross the region of the heart. It would fray the serge of my robe—it would return and repeat its operations—again—and again. Notwithstanding its terrifically wide sweep, (some thirty feet or more,) and the hissing vigor of its descent, sufficient to sunder these very walls of iron, still the fraying of my robe would be all that, for several minutes, it would accomplish. And at this thought I paused. I dared not go farther than this reflection. I dwelt upon it with a pertinacity of attention—as if, in so dwelling, I could arrest *here* the descent of the steel. I forced myself to ponder upon the sound of the crescent as it should pass across the garment—upon the peculiar thrilling sensation which the friction of cloth produces on the nerves. I pondered upon all this frivolity until my teeth were on edge.

Down—steadily down it crept. I took a frenzied pleasure in contrasting its downward with its lateral velocity. To the right—to the left—far and wide—with the shriek of a damned spirit! to my heart, with the stealthy pace of the tiger! I alternately laughed and howled, as the one or the other idea grew predominant.

Down—certainly, relentlessly down! It vibrated within three inches of my bosom! I struggled violently—furiously—to free my left arm. This was free only from the elbow to the hand. I could reach the latter, from the platter beside me, to my mouth, with great effort, but no farther. Could I have broken the fastenings above the elbow, I would have seized and attempted to arrest the pendulum. I might as well have attempted to arrest an avalanche!

Down—still unceasingly—still inevitably down! I gasped and struggled at each vibration. I shrunk convulsively at its every sweep. My eyes followed its outward or upward whirls with the eagerness of the most unmeaning despair; they closed themselves spasmodically at the descent, although death would have been a relief, oh, how unspeakable! Still I quivered in every nerve to think how slight a sinking of the machinery would precipitate that keen, glistening axe upon my bosom. It was *hope* that prompted the nerve to quiver—the frame to shrink. It was *hope*—the hope that

triumphs on the rack—that whispers to the death-condemned even in the dungeons
of the Inquisition.

I saw that some ten or twelve vibrations would bring the steel in actual contact
with my robe—and with this observation there suddenly came over my spirit all the
keen, collected calmness of despair. For the first time during many hours—or perhaps
days—I *thought*. It now occurred to me, that the bandage, or surcingle, which enveloped me, was *unique*. I was tied by no separate cord. The first stroke of the razor-like
crescent athwart any portion of the band, would so detach it that it might be unwound
from my person by means of my left hand. But how fearful, in that case, the proximity
of the steel! The result of the slightest struggle, how deadly! Was it likely, moreover,
that the minions of the torturer had not foreseen and provided for this possibility?
Was it probable that the bandage crossed my bosom in the track of the pendulum?
Dreading to find my faint, and, as it seemed, my last hope frustrated, I so far elevated
my head as to obtain a distinct view of my breast. The surcingle enveloped my limbs
and body close in all directions—*save in the path of the destroying crescent.*

Scarcely had I dropped my head back into its original position, when there flashed
upon my mind what I cannot better describe than as the unformed half of that idea of
deliverance to which I have previously alluded, and of which a moiety only floated
indeterminately through my brain when I raised food to my burning lips. The whole
thought was now present—feeble, scarcely sane, scarcely definite—but still entire. I
proceeded at once, with the nervous energy of despair, to attempt its execution.

For many hours the immediate vicinity of the low framework upon which I lay,
had been literally swarming with rats. They were wild, bold, ravenous—their red eyes
glaring upon me as if they waited but for motionlessness on my part to make me their
prey. "To what food," I thought, "have they been accustomed in the well?"

They had devoured, in spite of all my efforts to prevent them, all but a small remnant of the contents of the dish. I had fallen into an habitual see-saw, or wave of the
hand about the platter; and, at length, the unconscious uniformity of the movement
deprived it of effect. In their voracity, the vermin frequently fastened their sharp fangs
in my fingers. With the particles of the oily and spicy viand which now remained, I
thoroughly rubbed the bandage wherever I could reach it; then, raising my hand from
the floor, I lay breathlessly still.

At first, the ravenous animals were startled and terrified at the change—at the
cessation of movement. They shrank alarmedly back; many sought the well. But this
was only for a moment. I had not counted in vain upon their voracity. Observing that I

remained without motion, one or two of the boldest leaped upon the frame-work, and smelt at the surcingle. This seemed the signal for a general rush. Forth from the well they hurried in fresh troops. They clung to the wood—they overran it, and leaped in hundreds upon my person. The measured movement of the pendulum disturbed them not at all. Avoiding its strokes, they busied themselves with the anointed bandage. They pressed—they swarmed upon me in ever accumulating heaps. They writhed upon my throat; their cold lips sought my own; I was half stifled by their thronging pressure; disgust, for which the world has no name, swelled my bosom, and chilled, with a heavy clamminess, my heart. Yet one minute, and I felt that the struggle would be over. Plainly I perceived the loosening of the bandage. I knew that in more than one place it must be already severed. With a more than human resolution I lay *still*.

Nor had I erred in my calculations—nor had I endured in vain. I at length felt that I was *free*. The surcingle hung in ribands from my body. But the stroke of the pendulum already pressed upon my bosom. It had divided the serge of the robe. It had cut through the linen beneath. Twice again it swung, and a sharp sense of pain shot through every nerve. But the moment of escape had arrived. At a wave of my hand my deliverers hurried tumultuously away. With a steady movement—cautious, sidelong, shrinking, and slow—I slid from the embrace of the bandage and beyond the reach of the scimitar. For the moment, at least, *I was free*.

Free!—and in the grasp of the Inquisition! I had scarcely stepped from my wooden bed of horror upon the stone floor of the prison, when the motion of the hellish machine ceased, and I beheld it drawn up, by some invisible force, through the ceiling. This was a lesson which I took desperately to heart. My every motion was undoubtedly watched. Free!—I had but escaped death in one form of agony, to be delivered unto worse than death in some other. With that thought I rolled my eyes nervously around on the barriers of iron that hemmed me in. Something unusual—some change which, at first, I could not appreciate distinctly—it was obvious, had taken place in the apartment. For many minutes of a dreamy and trembling abstraction, I busied myself in vain, unconnected conjecture. During this period, I became aware, for the first time, of the origin of the sulphurous light which illumined the cell. It proceeded from a fissure, about half an inch in width, extending entirely around the prison at the base of the walls, which thus appeared, and were completely separated from the floor. I endeavored, but of course in vain, to look through the aperture.

As I arose from the attempt, the mystery of the alteration in the chamber broke at once upon my understanding. I have observed that, although the outlines of the figures upon the walls were sufficiently distinct, yet the colors seemed blurred and indefinite. These colors had now assumed, and were momentarily assuming, a startling and most intense brilliancy, that gave to the spectral and fiendish portraitures an aspect that might have thrilled even firmer nerves than my own. Demon eyes, of a wild and ghastly vivacity, glared upon me in a thousand directions, where none had been visible before, and gleamed with the lurid lustre of a fire that I could not force my imagination to regard as unreal.

Unreal!—Even while I breathed there came to my nostrils the breath of the vapor of heated iron! A suffocating odor pervaded the prison! A deeper glow settled each moment in the eyes that glared at my agonies! A richer tint of crimson diffused itself over the pictured horrors of blood. I panted! I gasped for breath! There could be no doubt of the design of my tormentors—oh! most unrelenting! oh! most demoniac of men! I shrank from the glowing metal to the centre of the cell. Amid the thought of the fiery destruction that impended, the idea of the coolness of the well came over my soul like balm. I rushed to its deadly brink. I threw my straining vision below. The glare from the enkindled roof illumined its inmost recesses. Yet, for a wild moment, did my spirit refuse to comprehend the meaning of what I saw. At length it forced—it wrestled its way into my soul—it burned itself in upon my shuddering reason. Oh! for a voice to speak!—oh! horror!—oh! any horror but this! With a shriek, I rushed from the margin, and buried my face in my hands—weeping bitterly.

The heat rapidly increased, and once again I looked up, shuddering as with a fit of the ague. There had been a second change in the cell—and now the change was obviously in the *form*. As before, it was in vain that I at first endeavored to appreciate or understand what was taking place. But not long was I left in doubt. The Inquisitorial vengeance had been hurried by my two-fold escape, and there was to be no more dallying with the King of Terrors. The room had been square. I saw that two of its iron angles were now acute—two, consequently, obtuse. The fearful difference quickly increased with a low rumbling or moaning sound. In an instant the apartment had shifted its form into that of a lozenge. But the alteration stopped not here—I neither hoped nor desired it to stop. I could have clasped the red walls to my bosom as a garment of eternal peace. "Death," I said, "any death but that of the pit!" Fool! might I have not known that *into the pit* it was the object of the burning iron to urge me? Could I resist its glow? or if even that, could I withstand its pressure? And now, flatter and flatter grew the lozenge, with a rapidity that left me no time for contemplation. Its centre, and of course, its greatest width, came just over the yawning gulf. I shrank back—but the closing walls pressed me resistlessly onward. At length for my seared and writhing body there was no longer an inch of foothold on the firm floor of the prison. I struggled no more, but the agony of my soul found vent in one loud, long, and final scream of despair. I felt that I tottered upon the brink—I averted my eyes—

There was a discordant hum of human voices! There was a loud blast as of many trumpets! There was a harsh grating as of a thousand thunders! The fiery walls rushed back! An outstretched arm caught my own as I fell, fainting, into the abyss. It was that of General Lasalle. The French army had entered Toledo. The Inquisition was in the hands of its enemies.

Sawney Beane

THE MAN EATER

Charles Whitehead

———— ◆ ————

OUR NEXT NARRATIVE PRESENTS SUCH A PICTURE OF HUMAN BARBARITY, that, were it not attested by the most unquestionable historical evidence, it would be rejected as altogether fabulous and incredible, it is that of Sawney Beane.

This man was born in East Lothian, about eight miles east of Edinburgh, in the reign of James I of Scotland. His father was a hedger and ditcher, and brought up his son to the same laborious employment. Naturally idle and vicious, he abandoned that place in company with a young woman equally idle and profligate, and retired to the deserts of Galloway, where they took up their habitation by the sea-side. The place which they selected for their dwelling was a cave of about a mile in length, and of considerable breadth, so near the sea, that the tide often penetrated into the cave above two hundred yards. The entry had many intricate windings and turnings, leading to the extremity of the subterraneous dwelling, which was literally "the habitation of horrid cruelty."

In this cave they commenced their depredations, and to prevent the possibility of detection, they murdered every person they robbed. Destitute of the means of obtaining any other food, they resolved to live upon human flesh, and accordingly, when they had murdered any man, woman, or child, they carried them to their den, quartered them, salted the limbs, and dried them for food. In this manner they lived, carrying on their depredations and murder, until they had eight sons and six daughters, eighteen grandsons and fourteen grandaughters, all the offspring of incest.

But though they soon became numerous, yet such was the multitude which fell into their hands, that they had often superabundance of provisions, and would at a distance from their own habitation, throw legs and arms of dried human bodies into the sea by night. These were often cast out by the tide, and taken up by the country people, to the great dismay of all the surrounding inhabitants. Nor could any one discover what had befallen the many friends, relations, and neighbours who had unfortunately fallen into the hand of these merciless cannibals.

In proportion as Sawney's family increased, every one that was able acted his part in these horrid assassinations. They would sometimes attack four or six men on foot, but never more than two upon horseback. To prevent the possibility of escape, they would lie in ambush in every direction, so that if they escaped the attack of the first, they might be assailed with renewed fury by second party, and inevitably murdered. By this means they always secured their prey, and prevented detection. At last, however, the vast number who were slain raised the inhabitants of the country, and all the woods and lurking-places were carefully searched; yet, though they often passed by the mouth of the horrible den, it was never once suspected that any human being resided there. In this state of uncertainty and suspense concerning the authors of such frequent massacres, several innocent travellers and innkeepers were taken up on suspicion, because the persons who were missing had been seen last in their company, or had last resided at their houses. The effect of this well-meant and severe justice constrained the greater part of the innkeepers in those parts to abandon such employments, to the great inconvenience of those who travelled through that district.

Meanwhile, the country became depopulated, and the whole nation was at a loss to account for the numerous and unheard-of villanies and cruelties that were perpetrated, without the slightest clue to the discovery of the abominable actors. At length the horrible scene was terminated in the following manner. One evening, a man and wife were riding home upon the same horse from a fair which had been held in the neighbourhood, and being attacked, the husband made the most vigorous resistance; his wife, however, was dragged from behind him, carried to a little distance, and her entrails instantlly taken out. Struck with horror the husband redoubled his efforts to escape, and even trod some of the assassins down under his horse's feet. Fortunately for him, and the inhabitants of that part of the country, in the mean time, twenty or thirty in a company came riding home from the fair, but upon their approach, Sawney and his bloody crew fled into a thick wood, and hastened to their infernal den.

This man, who was the first that had ever escaped out of their hands, related to his neighbours what had happened, and showed them the mangled body of his wife lying at a distance, the bloodthirsty wretches not having time to carry it along with them. They were all struck with astonishment and horror, took him with them to Glasgow, and reported the whole adventure to the chief magistrate of the city, who, upon this information, instantly wrote to the king, informing him of the matter. In a few days, his majesty in person, accompanied by four hundred men, went in quest of the perpetrators of these horrid cruelties. The man, whose wife had been murdered before his eyes, went as their guide, with a great number of blood-hounds, that no possible means might be left unattempted to discover the haunt of such execrable villains.

They searched the woods, and traversed and examined the sea-shore; but as they passed by the entrance into their cave, some of the blood-hounds entered it, and raising an uncommon barking and noise, gave indication that they were about to seize their prey. The king and his men returned, but could scarcely conceive how any human beings could reside in a place of utter darkness, and where the entrance was difficult and narrow; but, as the bloodhounds increased in their vociferation, and refused to return, it occurred to all that the cave ought to be explored to the extremity. Accordingly, a sufficient number of torches was provided; the hounds were permitted to pursue their course; a great number of men penetrated through all the intricacies of the path, and at length arrived at the private entrance of the cannibals.

They were followed by all the band, who were shocked to behold a sight unequalled in Scotland if not in any part of the universe. Legs, arms, thighs, hands, and feet, of men, women, and children, were suspended in rows like dried beef, some limbs and other members were soaked in pickle; while a great mass of money, both of gold and silver, watches, rings, pistols, clothes, both linen and woollen, with an immense quantity of other articles, were either thrown together in heaps, or suspended upon the sides of the cave.

The whole cruel, brutal family, to the number formerly mentioned, were seized; the human flesh buried in the sand of the sea-shore; the immense booty carried away, and the king marched to Edinburgh with the prisoners. This new and wretched spectacle attracted the attention of the inhabitants, who flocked from all quarters to see, as they passed along, so bloody and unnatural a family which had increased, in the space of twenty-five years, to the number of twenty-seven men and twenty-one women. Arrived in the capital, they were all confined in the Tolbooth under a strong guard, and were next day conducted to the common place of execution in Leith Walk, and executed without any formal trial, it being deemed unnecessary to try those who were avowed enemies of all mankind and of all social order.

The enormity of their crimes dictated the severity of their death. The men had their entrails thrown into the fire, their hands and legs were severed from their bodies, and they were permitted to bleed to death. The wretched mother of the whole crew, the daughters, and grandchildnen, after being spectators of the death of the men, were cast into three separate fires, and consumed to ashes. Nor did they, in general, display any signs of repentance or regret but continued, with their last breath, to pour forth the most dreadful curses and imprecations upon all around.

Aurelia

OR, THE TALE OF A GHOUL

E. T. A. Hoffmann

———— ◆ ————

COUNT HYPPOLITUS HAD JUST RETURNED FROM A LONG TIME SPENT IN travelling to take possession of the rich inheritance which his father, recently dead, had left to him. The ancestral home was situated in the most beautiful and charming country imaginable, and the income from the property was amply sufficient to defray the cost of most extensive improvements. Whatever in the way of architecture and landscape gardening had struck the Count during his travels—particularly in England—as specially delightful and apposite, he was going to reproduce in his own demesne. Architects, landscape gardeners, and labourers of all sorts arrived on the scene as they were wanted, and there commenced at once a complete reconstruction of the place, whilst an extensive park was laid out on the grandest scale, which involved the including within its boundaries of the church, the parsonage, and the burial ground. All those improvements the Count, who possessed the necessary knowledge, superintended himself, devoting himself to this occupation body and soul; so that a year slipped away without its ever having occurred to him to take an old uncle's advice and let the light of his countenance shine in the Residenz before the eyes of the young ladies, so that the most beautiful, the best, and the most nobly born amongst them might fall to his share as wife. One morning, as he was sitting at his drawing table sketching the ground-plan of a new building, a certain elderly Baroness—distantly related to his father—was announced as having come to call. When Hyppolitus heard her name he remembered that his father had always spoken of her with the greatest indignation—nay, with absolute abhorrence, and had often warned people who were going to approach her to keep aloof, without explaining what the danger connected with her was. If he was questioned more closely, he said there were certain matters as to which it was better to keep silence. Thus much was certain, that there were rumours current in the Residenz of some most remarkable and unprecedented criminal trial in which the Baroness had been involved, which had led to her separation from her husband, driven her from her home—which was at some considerable distance—and for the suppression of the consequences of which she was indebted to the prince's forbearance. Hyppolitus felt a very painful and disagreeable impression at the coming of a person whom his father had so detested, although the reasons for this detestation were not known to him. But the laws of hospitality, more binding in the country than in town, obliged him to receive this visit.

Never had any one, without being at all ill-favoured in the usual acceptation of that term, made by her exterior such a disagreeable impression upon the Count as did this Baroness. When she came in she looked him through and through with a glance of fire, and then she cast her eyes down and apologized for her coming in terms which were almost over humble. She expressed her sorrow that his father, influenced by prejudices against her with which her enemies had impregnated his mind, had formed a mortal hatred to her, and though she was almost starving, in the depths of her poverty he had never given her the smallest help or support. As she had now, unexpectedly as she said, come into possession of a small sum of money she had found it possible to leave the Residenz and go to a small country town a short distance off. However, as she was engaged in this journey she had not found it possible to resist the desire to see the son of the man whom, notwithstanding his irreconcilable hatred, she had never ceased to regard with feelings of the highest esteem. The tone in which all this was spoken had the moving accents of sincerity, and the Count was all the more affected by it that, having turned his eyes away from her repulsive face, he had fixed them upon a marvellously charming and beautiful creature who was with her. The Baroness finished her speech. The Count did not seem to be aware that she had done so. He remained silent. She begged him to pardon—and attribute to her embarrassment at being where she was—her having neglected to explain that her companion was her daughter Aurelia. On this the Count found words, and blushing up to the eyes implored the Baroness, with the agitation of a young man overpowered by love, to let him atone in some degree for his father's shortcomings—the result of misunderstandings—and to favour him by paying him a long visit. In warmly enforcing this request he took her hand. But the words and the breath died away on his lips and his blood ran cold. For he felt his hand grasped as if in a vice by fingers cold and stiff as death, and the tall bony form of the Baroness, who was staring at him with eyes evidently deprived of the faculty of sight, seemed to him in its gay many tinted attire like some bedizened corpse.

"Oh, good heavens! how unfortunate just at this moment," Aurelia cried out, and went on to lament in a gentle heart-penetrating voice that her mother was now and then suddenly seized by a tetanic spasm, but that it generally passed off very quickly without its being necessary to take any measures with regard to it.

Hyppolitus disengaged himself with some difficulty from the Baroness, and all the glowing life of sweetest love delight came back to him as he took Aurelia's hand and pressed it warmly to his lips. Although he had almost come to man's estate it was the first time that he felt the full force of passion, so that it was impossible for him to hide what he felt, and the manner in which Aurelia received his avowal in a noble, simple, child-like delight, kindled the fairest of hopes within him. The Baroness recovered in a few minutes, and, seemingly quite unaware of what had been happening, expressed her gratitude to the Count for his invitation to pay a visit of some duration at the Castle, saying she would be but too happy to forget the injustice with which his father had treated her.

Thus the Count's household arrangements and domestic position were completely changed, and he could not but believe that some special favour of fortune had brought to him the only woman in all the world who, as a warmly beloved and deeply adored wife, was capable of bestowing upon him the highest conceivable happiness.

The Baroness's manner of conduct underwent little alteration. She continued to be silent, grave, much wrapped up in herself, and when opportunity offered, evinced a gentle disposition, and a heart disposed towards any innocent enjoyment. The Count had become accustomed to the death-like whiteness of her face, to the very remarkable network of wrinkles which covered it, and to the generally spectral appearance which she displayed; but all this he set down to the invalid condition of her health, and also, in some measure, to a disposition which she evinced to gloomy romanticism. The servants told him that she often went out for walks in the night-time, through the park to the churchyard. He was much annoyed that his father's prejudices had influenced him to the extent that they had; and the most earnest recommendations of his uncle that he should conquer the feeling which had taken possession of him, and give up a relationship which must sooner or later drive him to his ruin, had no effect upon him.

In complete certainty of Aurelia's sincere affection, he asked for her hand; and it may be imagined with what joy the Baroness received this proposal, which transferred her into the lap of luxury from a position of the deepest poverty. The pallor and the strange expression, which spoke of some invincible inward pain or trouble, had disappeared from Aurelia's face. The blissfulness of love beamed in her eyes, and shimmered in roses on her cheeks.

On the morning of the wedding-day a terrible event shattered the Count's hopes. The Baroness was found lying on her face dead, not far from the churchyard: and when the Count was looking out of his window on getting up, full of the bliss of the happiness which he had attained, her body was being brought back to the Castle. He supposed she was only in one of her usual attacks; but all efforts to bring her back to life were ineffectual. She was dead. Aurelia, instead of giving way to violent grief, seemed rather to be struck dumb and tearless by this blow, which appeared to have a paralyzing effect on her.

The Count was much distressed for her, and only ventured—most cautiously and most gently—to remind her that her orphaned condition rendered it necessary that conventionalities should be disregarded, and that the most essential matter in the circumstances was to hasten on the marriage as much as possible, notwithstanding the loss of her mother. At this Aurelia fell into the Count's arms, and, whilst a flood of tears ran down her cheeks, cried in a most eager manner, and in a voice which was shrill with urgency:

"Yes, yes! For the love of all the saints. For the sake of my soul's salvation—yes!"

The Count ascribed this burst of emotion to the bitter sense that, in her orphaned condition, she did not know whither to betake herself, seeing that she could not go on staying in the Castle. He took pains to procure a worthy matron as a companion for her, till in a few weeks, the wedding-day again came round. And this time no mischance interfered with it, and it crowned the bliss of Aurelia and Hyppolitus. But Aurelia had all this while been in a curiously strained and excited condition. It was not grief for her mother, but she seemed to be unceasingly, and without cessation, tortured by some inward anxiety. In the midst of the most delicious love-passage she would suddenly clasp the Count in her arms, pale as death, and like a person suddenly seized by some terror—just as if she were trying her very utmost to resist some extraneous power which was threatening to force her to destruction—and would cry, "Oh, no— no! Never, never!" Now that she was married, however, it seemed that this strange, overstrained, excited condition in which she had been, abated and left her, and the terrible inward anxiety and disturbance under which she had been labouring seemed to disappear.

The Count could not but suspect the existence of some secret evil mystery by which Aurelia's inner being was tormented, but he very properly thought it would be

unkind and unfeeling to ask her about it whilst her excitement lasted, and she herself
avoided any explanation on the subject. However, a time came when he thought he
might venture to hint gently, that perhaps it would be well if she indicated to him
the cause of the strange condition of her mind. She herself at once said it would be a
satisfaction to her to open her mind to him, her beloved husband. And great was his
amazement to learn that what was at the bottom of the mystery, was the atrociously
wicked life which her mother had led, that was so perturbing her mind.

"Can there be anything more terrible," she said, "than to have to hate, detest, and
abhor one's own mother?"

Thus the prejudices (as they were called) of his father and uncle had not been
unfounded, and the Baroness had deceived him in the most deliberate manner. He was
obliged to confess to himself—and he made no secret of it—that it was a fortunate circumstance that the Baroness had died on the morning of his wedding-day. But Aurelia
declared that as soon as her mother was dead she had been seized by dark and terrible
terrors, and could not help thinking that her mother would rise from her grave, and
drag her from her husband's arms into perdition.

She said she dimly remembered, one morning when she was a mere child, being
awakened by a frightful commotion in the house. Doors opened and shut; strangers'
voices cried out in confusion. At last, things becoming quieter, her nurse took her in
her arms, and carried her into a large room where there were many people, and the
man who had often played with her, and given her sweetmeats, lying stretched on a
long table. This man she had always called "Papa," and she stretched her hands out
to him, and wanted to kiss him. But his lips, always warm before, were cold as ice,
and Aurelia broke into violent weeping, without knowing why. The nurse took her
to a strange house, where she remained a long while, till at last a lady came and took
her away in a carriage. This was her mother, who soon after took her to the Residenz.

When Aurelia got to be about sixteen, a man came to the house whom her mother
welcomed joyfully, and treated with much confidentiality, receiving him with much
intimacy of friendship, as being a dear old friend. He came more and more frequently,
and the Baroness's style of existence was soon greatly altered for the better. Instead of
living in an attic, and subsisting on the poorest of fare, and wearing the most wretched
old clothes, she took a fine lodging in the most fashionable quarter, wore fine dresses,
ate and drank with this stranger of the best and most expensive food and drink daily
(he was her daily guest), and took her part in all the public pleasurings which the
Residenz had to offer.

Aurelia was the person upon whom this bettering of her mother's circumstances (evidently attributable solely to the stranger) exercised no influence whatever. She remained shut up in her room when her mother went out to enjoy herself in the stranger's company, and was obliged to live just as miserably as before. This man, though about forty, had a very fresh and youthful appearance, a tall, handsome person, and a face by no means devoid of a certain amount of manly good looks. Notwithstanding this, he was repugnant to Aurelia on account of his style of behaviour. He seemed to try to constrain himself, to conduct himself like a gentleman and person of some cultivation, but there was constantly, and most evidently, piercing through this exterior veneer the unmistakable evidence of his really being a totally uncultured person, whose manners and habit.s were those of the very lowest ranks of the people. And the way in which he began to look at Aurelia filled her with terror—nay, with an abhorrence of which she could not explain the reason to herself.

Up to this point the Baroness had never taken the trouble to say a single word to Aurelia about this stranger. But now she told her his name, adding that this Baron was a man of great wealth, and a distant relation. She lauded his good looks, and his various delightful qualities, and ended by asking Aurelia if she thought she could bring herself to take a liking to him. Aurelia made no secret of the inward detestation which she felt for him. The Baroness darted a glance of lightning at her, which terrified her excessively, and told her she was a foolish, ignorant creature. After this she was kinder to her than she had ever been before. She was provided with grand dresses in the height of the fashion, and taken to share in all the public pleasures. The man now strove to gain her favour in a manner which rendered him more and more abhorrent to her. But her delicate, maidenly instincts were wounded in the most mortal manner, when an unfortunate accident rendered her an unwilling, secret witness of an abominable atrocity between her abandoned and depraved mother and him. When, a few days after this, this man, after having taken a good deal of wine, clasped Aurelia in his arms in a way which left no doubt as to his intention, her desperation gave her strength, and she pushed him from her so that he fell down on his back. She rushed away and bolted herself in her own room. The Baroness told her, very calmly and deliberately, that, inasmuch as the Baron paid all the household expenses, and she had not the slightest intention of going back to the old poverty of their previous life, this was a case in which any absurd coyness would be both ludicrous and inconvenient, and that she would really have to make up her mind to comply with the Baron's wishes, because, if not, he had threatened to part company at once. Instead of being affected by Aurelia's bitter tears and agonized intreaties, the old woman, breaking into the most brazen and shameless laughter, talked in the most depraved manner of a state of matters which would cause Aurelia to bid, for ever, farewell to every feeling of enjoyment of life in such unrestrained and detestable depravity, defying and insulting all sense of ordinary propriety, so that her shame and terror were undescribable at what she was obliged to hear. In fact she gave herself up for lost, and her only means of salvation appeared to her to be immediate flight.

She had managed to possess herself of the key of the ball door, had got together the few little necessaries which she absolutely required, and, just after midnight, was moving softly through the dimly-lighted front hall, at a time when she thought her mother was sure to be fast asleep. She was on the point of stepping quietly out into the street, when the door opened with a clang, and heavy footsteps came noisily up the steps. The Baroness came staggering and stumbling into the hall, right up to Aurelia's feet, nothing upon her but a kind of miserable wrapper all covered with dirt, her breast and her arms naked, her grey hair all hanging down and dishevelled. And close after her came the stranger, who seized her by the hair, and dragged her into the middle of the hall, crying out in a yelling voice—

"Wait, you old devil, you witch of hell! I'll serve you up a wedding breakfast!" And with a good thick cudgel which he had in his hand he set to and belaboured and maltreated her in the most shameful manner. She made a terrible screaming and out-cry, whilst Aurelia, scarcely knowing what she was about, screamed aloud out of the window for help.

It chanced that there was a patrol of armed police just passing. The men came at once into the house.

"Seize him!" cried the Baroness, writhing in convulsions of rage and pain. "Seize him—hold him fast! Look at his bare back. He's—"

When the police sergeant heard the Baroness speak the name he shouted out in the greatest delight—

"Hoho! We've got you at last, Devil Alias, have we?" And in spite of his violent resistance, they marched him off.

But notwithstanding all this which had been happening, the Baroness had under-stood well enough what Aurelia's idea had been. She contented herself with taking her somewhat roughly by the arm, pushing her into her room, and locking her up in it, without saying a word. She went out early the next morning, and did not come back till late in the evening. And during this time Aurelia remained a prisoner in her room, never seeing nor hearing a creature, and having nothing to eat or drink. This went on for several days. The Baroness often glared at her with eyes flashing with anger, and seemed to be wrestling with some decision, until, one evening, letters came which seemed to cause her satisfaction.

"Silly creature! all this is your fault. However, it seems to be all coming right now, and all I hope is that the terrible punishment which the Evil Spirit was threatening you with may not come upon you." This was what the Baroness said to Aurelia, and then she became more kind and friendly, and Aurelia, no longer distressed by the presence of the horrible man, and having given up the idea of escaping, was allowed a little more freedom.

Some time had elapsed, when one day, as Aurelia was sitting alone in her room, she heard a great clamour approaching in the street. The maid came running in, and said that they were taking the hangman's son of —— to prison, that he had been branded on the back there for robbery and murder, and had escaped, and was now retaken.

Aurelia, full of anxious presentiment, tottered to the window. Her presentiment was not fallacious. It *was* the stranger (as we have styled him), and he was being brought along, firmly bound upon a tumbril, surrounded by a strong guard. He was being taken back to undergo his sentence. Aurelia, nearly fainting, sank back into her chair, as his frightfully wild look fell upon her, while he shook his clenched fist up at the window with the most threatening gestures.

After this the Baroness was still a great deal away from the house; but she never took Aurelia with her, so that the latter led a sorrowful, miserable existence—occupied in thinking many thoughts as to destiny, and the threatening future which might unexpectedly come upon her.

From the maidservant (who had only come into the house subsequently to the nocturnal adventure which has been described, and who had probably only quite recently heard about the intimacy of the terms in which the Baroness had been living with this criminal), Aurelia learned that the folks in the Residenz were very much grieved at the Baroness's having been so deceived and imposed upon by a scoundrel of this description. But Aurelia knew only too well how differently the matter had really stood; and it seemed to her impossible that, at all events, the men of the police, who had apprehended the fellow in the Baroness's very house, should not have known all about the intimacy of the relations between them, inasmuch as she herself had told them his name, and directed their attention to the brand-marks on his back, as proofs of his identity. Moreover, this loquacious maid sometimes talked in a very ambiguous way about that which people were, here and there, thinking and saying; and, for that matter, would like very much to know better about—as to the courts having been making careful investigations, and having gone so far as to threaten the Baroness with arrest, on account of strange disclosures which the hangman's son had made concerning her.

Aurelia was obliged to admit, in her own mind, that it was another proof of her mother's depraved way of looking at things that, even after this terrible affair, she should have found it possible to go on living in the Residenz. But at last she felt herself constrained to leave the place where she knew she was the object of but too well-founded, shameful suspicion, and fly to a more distant spot. On this journey she came to the Count's Castle, and there ensued what has been related.

Aurelia could not but consider herself marvellously fortunate to have got clear of all these troubles. But how profound was her horror when, speaking to her mother in this blessed sense of the merciful intervention of Heaven in her regard, the latter, with fires of hell in her eyes, cried out in a yelling voice—

"You are my misfortune, horrible creature that you are! But in the midst of your imagined happiness vengeance will overtake you, if I should be carried away by a sudden death. In those tetanic spasms, which your birth cost me, the subtle craft of the devil—"

Here Aurelia suddenly stopped. She threw herself upon her husband's breast, and implored him to spare her the complete recital of what the Baroness had said to her in the delirium of her insanity. She said she felt her inmost heart and soul crushed to pieces at the bare idea of the frightful threatenings—far beyond the wildest imagination's conception of the terrible—uttered to her by her mother, possessed, as she was at the time, by the most diabolical powers.

The Count comforted his bride to the best of his ability, although he felt himself permeated by the coldest and most deathly shuddering horror. Even when he had regained some calmness, he could not but confess to himself that the profound horribleness of the Baroness, even now that she was dead, cast a deep shadow over his life, sun-bright as it otherwise seemed to be.

In a very short time Aurelia began to alter very perceptibly. Whilst the deathly paleness of her face, and the fatigued appearance of her eyes, seemed to point to some bodily ailment, her mental state—confused, variable, restless, as if she were constantly frightened at something—led to the conclusion that there was some fresh mystery perturbing her system. She shunned her husband. She shut herself up in her rooms, sought the most solitary walks in the park. And when she then allowed herself to be seen, her eyes, red with weeping, her contorted features, gave unmistakable evidence of some terrible suffering which she had been undergoing. It was in vain that the Count took every possible pains to discover the cause of this condition of hers, and the only thing which had any effect in bringing him out of the hopeless state into which those remarkable symptoms of his wife's had plunged him, was the deliberate opinion of a celebrated doctor, that this strangely excited condition of the Countess was nothing other than the natural result of a bodily state which indicated the happy result of a fortunate marriage. This doctor, on one occasion when he was at table with the Count and Countess, permitted himself sundry allusions to this presumed state of what the German nation calls "good hope." The Countess seemed to listen to all this with indifference for some time. But suddenly her attention became vividly awakened when the doctor spoke of the wonderful longings which women in that condition become possessed by, and which they cannot resist without the most injurious effects supervening upon their own health, and even upon that of the child. The Countess overwhelmed the doctor with questions, and the latter did not weary of quoting the strangest and most entertaining cases of this description from his own practice and experience.

"Moreover," he said, "there are cases on record in which women have been led, by these strange, abnormal longings, to commit most terrible crimes. There was a certain blacksmith's wife, who had such an irresistible longing for her husband's flesh that, one night, when he came home the worse for liquor, she set upon him with a large knife, and cut him about so frightfully that he died in a few hours' time."

Scarcely had the doctor said these words, when the Countess fell back in her chair fainting, and was with much difficulty recovered from the succession of hysterical attacks which supervened. The doctor then saw that he had acted very thoughtlessly in alluding to such a frightful occurrence in the presence of a lady whose nervous system was in such a delicate condition.

However, this crisis seemed to have a beneficial effect upon her, for she became calmer; although, soon afterwards there came upon her a very remarkable condition of rigidity, as of benumbedness. There was a darksome fire in her eyes, and her death-like pallor increased to such an extent, that the Count was driven into new and most tormenting doubts as to her condition. The most inexplicable thing was that she never took the smallest morsel of anything to eat, evincing the utmost repugnance at the sight of all food, particularly meat. This repugnance was so invincible that she was constantly obliged to get up and leave the table, with the most marked indications of loathing. The doctor's skill was in vain, and the Count's most urgent and affectionate entreaties were powerless to induce her to take even a single drop of medicine of any kind. And, inasmuch as weeks, nay, months, had passed without her having taken so much as a morsel of food, and it had become an unfathomable mystery how she managed to keep alive, the doctor came to the conclusion that there was something in the case which lay beyond the domain of ordinary human science. He made some pretext for leaving the Castle, but the Count saw clearly enough that this doctor, whose skilfulness was well approved, and who had a high reputation to maintain, felt that the Countess's condition was too unintelligible, and, in fact, too strangely mysterious, for him to stay on there, witness of an illness impossible to be understood—as to which he felt he had no power to render assistance.

It may be readily imagined into what a state of mind all this put the Count. But there was more to come. Just at this juncture an old, privileged servant took an opportunity, when he found the Count alone, of telling him that the Countess went out every night, and did not come home till daybreak

The Count's blood ran cold. It struck him, as a matter which he had not quite realized before, that, for a short time back, there had fallen upon him, regularly about midnight, a curiously unnatural sleepiness, which he now believed to be caused by some narcotic administered to him by the Countess, to enable her to get away unobserved. The darkest suspicions and forebodings came into his mind. He thought of the diabolical mother, and that, perhaps, *her* instincts had begun to awake in her daughter. He thought of some possibility of a conjugal infidelity. He remembered the terrible hangman's son.

It was so ordained that the very next night was to explain this terrible mystery to him—that which alone could be the key to the Countess's strange condition.

She herself used, every evening, to make the tea which the Count always took before going to bed. This evening he did not take a drop of it, and when he went to bed he had not the slightest symptom of the sleepiness which generally came upon him as it got towards midnight. However, he lay back on his pillows, and had all the appearance of being fast asleep as usual.

And then the Countess rose up very quietly, with the utmost precautions, came up to his bedside, held a lamp to his eyes, and then, convinced that he was sound asleep, went softly out of the room.

His heart throbbed fast. He got up, put on a cloak, and went after the Countess. It was a fine moonlight night, so that, though Aurelia had got a considerable start of him, he could see her distinctly going along in the distance in her white dress. She went through the park, right on to the burying-ground, and there she disappeared at the wall. The Count ran quickly after her in through the gate of the burying-ground, which he found open. There, in the bright moonlight, he saw a circle of frightful, spectral-looking creatures. Old women, half naked, were cowering down upon the ground, and in the midst of them lay the corpse of a man, which they were tearing at with wolfish appetite.

Aurelia was amongst them.

The Count took flight in the wildest horror, and ran, without any idea where he was going or what he was doing, impelled by the deadliest terror, all about the walks in the park, till he found himself at the door of his own Castle as the day was breaking, bathed in cold perspiration. Involuntarily, without the capability of taking hold of a thought, he dashed up the steps, and went bursting through the passages and into his own bedroom. There lay the Countess, to all appearance in the deepest and sweetest of sleeps. And the Count would fain have persuaded himself that some deceptive dream-image, or (inasmuch as his cloak, wet with dew, was a proof, if any had been needed, that he had really been to the burying-ground in the night) some soul-deceiving phantom had been the cause of his deathly horror. He did not wait for Aurelia's waking, but left the room, dressed, and got on to a horse. His ride, in the exquisite morning, amid sweet-scented trees and shrubs, whence the happy songs of the newly-awakened birds greeted him, drove from his memory for a time the terrible images of the night. He went back to the Castle comforted and gladdened in heart.

But when he and the Countess sate down alone together at table, and, the dishes being brought and handed, she rose to hurry away, with loathing, at the sight of the food as usual, the terrible conviction that what he had seen was true, was reality, impressed itself irresistibly on his mind. In the wildest fury he rose from his seat, crying—

"Accursed misbirth of hell! I understand your hatred of the food of mankind. You get your sustenance out of the burying-ground, damnable creature that you are!"

As soon as those words had passed his lips, the Countess flew at him, uttering a sound between a snarl and a howl, and bit him on the breast with the fury of a hyena. He dashed her from him on to the ground, raving fiercely as she was, and she gave up the ghost in the most terrible convulsions.

The Count became a maniac.

Wake Not the Dead!

OR, THE BRIDE OF THE GRAVE

Johann Ludwig Tieck

———◆———

Wake not the dead:—they bring but gloomy night
    And cheerless desolation into day
    For in the grave who mouldering lay,
No more can feel the influence of light,
Or yield them to the sun's prolific might;
    Let them repose within their house of clay—
    Corruption, vainly wilt thou e'er essay
To quicken:—it sends forth a pest'lent blight;
And neither fiery sun, nor bathing dew,
Nor breath of spring the dead can e'er renew.
That which from life is pluck'd, becomes the foe
Of life, and whoso wakes it waketh woe.
Seek not the dead to waken from that sleep
In which from mortal eye they lie enshrouded deep.

WILT THOU FOR EVER SLEEP? WILT THOU NEVER MORE AWAKE, MY beloved, but henceforth repose for ever from thy short pilgrimage on earth? O yet once again return! and bring back with thee the vivifying dawn of hope to one whose existence hath, since thy departure, been obscured by the dunnest shades. What! dumb? for ever dumb? Thy friend lamenteth, and thou heedest him not? He sheds bitter, scalding tears, and thou reposest unregarding his affliction? He is in despair, and thou no longer openest thy arms to him as an asylum from his grief? Say then, doth the paly shroud become thee better than the bridal veil? Is the chamber of the grave a warmer bed than the couch of love? Is the spectre death more welcome to thy arms than thy enamoured consort? Oh! return, my beloved, return once again to this anxious disconsolate bosom." Such were the lamentations which Walter poured forth for his Brunhilda, the partner of his youthful, passionate love: thus did he bewail over her grave at the midnight hour, what time the spirit that presides in the troublous atmosphere, sends his legions of monsters through mid-air; so that their shadows, as they flit beneath the moon and across the earth, dart as wild, agitating thoughts that chase each other o'er the sinner's bosom:—thus did he lament under the tall linden trees by her grave, while his head reclined on the cold stone.

Walter was a powerful lord in Burgundy, who, in his earliest youth, had been smitten with the charms of the fair Brunhilda, a beauty far surpassing in loveliness all her rivals; for her tresses, dark as the raven face of night, streaming over her shoulders, set off to the utmost advantage the beaming lustre of her slender form, and the rich dye of a cheek whose tint was deep and brilliant as that of the western heaven: her eyes did not resemble those burning orbs whose pale glow gems the vault of night, and whose immeasurable distance fills the soul with deep thoughts of eternity, but rather as the sober beams which cheer this nether world, and which, while they enlighten, kindle the sons of earth to joy and love. Brunhilda became the wife of Walter, and both being equally enamoured and devoted, they abandoned themselves to the enjoyment of a passion that rendered them reckless of aught besides, while it lulled them in a fascinating dream. Their sole apprehension was lest aught should awaken them from a delirium which they prayed might continue for ever. Yet how vain is the wish that would arrest the decrees of destiny! as well might it seek to divert the circling planets from their eternal course. Short was the duration of this phrenzied passion; not that it gradually decayed and subsided into apathy, but death snatched away his blooming victim, and left Walter to a widowed couch. Impetuous, however, as was his first burst of grief, he was not inconsolable, for ere long another bride became the partner of the youthful nobleman.

Swanhilda also was beautiful; although nature had formed her charms on a very different model from those of Brunhilda. Her golden locks waved bright as the beams of morn: only when excited by some emotion of her soul did a rosy hue tinge the lily paleness of her cheek: her limbs were proportioned in the nicest symmetry, yet did they not possess that luxuriant fullness of animal life: her eye beamed eloquently, but it was with the milder radiance of a star, tranquillizing to tenderness rather than exciting to warmth. Thus formed, it was not possible that she should steep him in his former delirium, although she rendered happy his waking hours—tranquil and serious, yet cheerful, studying in all things her husband's pleasure, she restored order and comfort in his family, where her presence shed a general influence all around. Her mild benevolence tended to restrain the fiery, impetuous disposition of Walter: while at the same time her prudence recalled him in some degree from his vain, turbulent wishes, and his aspirings after unattainable enjoyments, to the duties and pleasures of actual life. Swanhilda bore her husband two children, a son and a daughter; the latter was mild and patient as her mother, well contented with her solitary sports, and even in these recreations displayed the serious turn of her character. The boy possessed his father's fiery, restless disposition, tempered, however, with the solidity of his mother. Attached by his offspring more tenderly towards their mother, Walter now lived for several years very happily: his thoughts would frequently, indeed, recur to Brunhilda, but without their former violence, merely as we dwell upon the memory of a friend of our earlier days, borne from us on the rapid current of time to a region where we know that he is happy.

But clouds dissolve into air, flowers fade, the sands of the hour-glass run imperceptibly away, and even so, do human feelings dissolve, fade, and pass away, and with them too, human happiness. Walter's inconstant breast again sighed for the extatic dreams of those days which he had spent with his equally romantic, enamoured Brunhilda—again did she present herself to his ardent fancy in all the glow of her bridal charms, and he began to draw a parallel between the past and the present; nor did imagination, as it is wont, fail to array the former in her brightest hues, while it proportionably obscured the latter; so that he pictured to himself, the one much more rich in enjoyment, and the other, much less so than they really were. This change in her husband did not escape Swanhilda; whereupon, redoubling her attentions towards him, and her cares towards their children, she expected, by this means, to re-unite the knot that was slackened; yet the more she endeavoured to regain his affections, the colder did he grow,—the more intolerable did her caresses seem, and the more continually did the image of Brunhilda haunt his thoughts. The children, whose endearments were now become indispensable to him, alone stood between the parents as genii eager to affect a reconciliation; and, beloved by them both, formed a uniting link between them. Yet, as evil can be plucked from the heart of man, only ere its root has yet struck deep, its fangs being afterwards too firm to be eradicated; so was Walter's diseased fancy too far affected to have its disorder stopped, for, in a short time, it completely tyrannized over him. Frequently of a night, instead of retiring to his consort's chamber, he repaired to Brunhilda's grave, where he murmured forth his discontent, saying: "Wilt thou sleep for ever?"

One night as he was reclining on the turf, indulging in his wonted sorrow, a sorcerer from the neighbouring mountains, entered into this field of death for the purpose of gathering, for his mystic spells, such herbs as grow only from the earth wherein the dead repose, and which, as if the last production of mortality, are gifted with a powerful and supernatural influence. The sorcerer perceived the mourner, and approached the spot where he was lying.

"Wherefore, fond wretch, dost thou grieve thus, for what is now a hideous mass of mortality—mere bones, and nerves, and veins? Nations have fallen unlamented; even worlds themselves, long ere this globe of ours was created, have mouldered into nothing; nor hath any one wept over them; why then should'st thou indulge this vain affliction for a child of the dust—a being as frail as thyself, and like thee the creature but of a moment?"

Walter raised himself up:—"Let yon worlds that shine in the firmament" replied he, "lament for each other as they perish. It is true, that I who am myself clay, lament for my fellow-clay: yet is this clay impregnated with a fire,—with an essence, that none of the elements of creation possess—with love: and this divine passion, I felt for her who now sleepeth beneath this sod."

"Will thy complaints awaken her: or could they do so, would she not soon upbraid thee for having disturbed that repose in which she is now hushed?"

"Avaunt, cold-hearted being: thou knowest not what is love. Oh! that my tears could wash away the earthy covering that conceals her from these eyes;—that my groan of anguish could rouse her from her slumber of death!—No, she would not again seek her earthy couch."

"Insensate that thou art, and couldst thou endure to gaze without shuddering on one disgorged from the jaws of the grave? Art thou too thyself the same from whom she parted; or hath time passed o'er thy brow and left no traces there? Would not thy love rather be converted into hate and disgust?"

"Say rather that the stars would leave yon firmament, that the sun will henceforth refuse to shed his beams through the heavens. Oh! that she stood once more before me;—that once again she reposed on this bosom!—how quickly should we then forget that death or time had ever stepped between us."

"Delusion! mere delusion of the brain, from heated blood, like to that which arises from the fumes of wine. It is not my wish to tempt thee;—to restore to thee thy dead; else wouldst thou soon feel that I have spoken truth."

"How! restore her to me," exclaimed Walter casting himself at the sorcerer's feet. "Oh! if thou art indeed able to effect that, grant it to my earnest supplication; if one throb of human feeling vibrates in thy bosom, let thy tears prevail with thee: restore to me my beloved; so shalt thou hereafter bless the deed, and see that it was a good work."

"A good work! a blessed deed!"—returned the sorcerer with a smile of scorn; "for me there exists nor good nor evil; since my will is always the same. Ye alone know evil, who will that which ye would not. It is indeed in my power to restore her to thee: yet, bethink thee well, whether it will prove thy weal. Consider too, how deep the abyss between life and death; across this, my power can build a bridge, but it can never fill up the frightful chasm."

Walter would have spoken, and have sought to prevail on this powerful being by fresh entreaties, but the latter prevented him, saying: "Peace! bethink thee well! and return hither to me tomorrow at midnight. Yet once more do I warn thee, 'Wake not the dead.' "

Having uttered these words, the mysterious being disappeared. Intoxicated with fresh hope, Walter found no sleep on his couch; for fancy, prodigal of her richest stores, expanded before him the glittering web of futurity; and his eye, moistened with the dew of rapture, glanced from one vision of happiness to another. During the next day he wandered through the woods, lest wonted objects by recalling the memory of later and less happier times, might disturb the blissful idea, that he should again behold her—again fold her in his arms, gaze on her beaming brow by day, repose on her bosom at night: and, as this sole idea filled his imagination, how was it possible that the least doubt should arise; or that the warning of the mysterious old man should recur to his thoughts.

No sooner did the midnight hour approach, than he hastened before the grave-field where the sorcerer was already standing by that of Brunhilda. "Hast thou maturely considered?" enquired he.

"Oh! restore to me the object of my ardent passion," exclaimed Walter with impetuous eagerness. "Delay not thy generous action, lest I die even this night, consumed with disappointed desire; and behold her face no more."

"Well then," answered the old man, "return hither again to-morrow at the same hour. But once more do I give thee this friendly warning, 'Wake not the dead.' "

All in the despair of impatience, Walter would have prostrated himself at his feet, and supplicated him to fulfill at once a desire now increased to agony; but the sorcerer had already disappeared. Pouring forth his lamentations more wildly and impetuously than ever, he lay upon the grave of his adored one, until the grey dawn streaked the east. During the day, which seemed to him longer than any he had ever experienced, he wandered to and fro, restless and impatient, seemingly without any object, and deeply buried in his own reflections, inquiet as the murderer who meditates his first deed of blood: and the stars of evening found him once more at the appointed spot. At midnight the sorcerer was there also.

"Hast thou yet maturely deliberated?" enquired he," as on the preceding night?"

"On what should I deliberate?" returned Walter impatiently. "I need not to deliberate: what I demand of thee, is that which thou hast promised me—that which will prove my bliss. Or dost thou but mock me? if so, hence from my sight, lest I be tempted to lay my hand on thee."

"Once more do I warn thee," answered the old man with undisturbed composure, "Wake not the dead'—let her rest."

"Aye, but not in the cold grave: she shall rather rest on this bosom which burns with eagerness to clasp her."

"Reflect, thou mayst not quit her until death, even though aversion and horror should seize thy heart. There would then remain only one horrible means."

"Dotard!" cried Walter, interrupting him, "how may I hate that which I love with such intensity of passion? how should I abhor that for which my every drop of blood is boiling?"

"Then be it even as thou wishest," answered the sorcerer; "step back."

The old man now drew a circle round the grave, all the while muttering words of enchantment. Immediately the storm began to howl among the tops of the trees; owls flapped their wings, and uttered their low voice of omen; the stars hid their mild, beaming aspect, that they might not behold so unholy and impious a spectacle; the stone then rolled from the grave with a hollow sound, leaving a free passage for the inhabitant of that dreadful tenement. The sorcerer scattered into the yawning earth, roots and herbs of most magic power, and of most penetrating odour, so that the worms crawling forth from the earth congregated together, and raised themselves in a fiery column over the grave: while rushing wind burst from the earth, scattering the mould before it, until at length the coffin lay uncovered. The moon-beams fell on it, and the lid burst open with a tremendous sound. Upon this the sorcerer poured upon it some blood from out of a human skull, exclaiming at the same time:—"Drink, sleeper, of this warm stream, that thy heart may again beat within thy bosom." And, after a short pause, shedding on her some other mystic liquid, he cried aloud with the voice of one inspired: "Yes, thy heart beats once more with the flood of life: thine eye is again opened to sight. Arise, therefore, from the tomb."

As an island suddenly springs forth from the dark waves of the ocean, raised upwards from the deep by the force of subterraneous fires, so did Brunhilda start from her earthy couch, borne forward by some invisible power. Taking her by the hand, the sorcerer led her towards Walter, who stood at some little distance, rooted to the ground with amazement.

"Receive again," said he, "the object of thy passionate sighs: mayest thou never more require my aid; should that, however, happen, so wilt thou find me, during the full of the moon, upon the mountains in that spot and where the three roads meet."

Instantly did Walter recognize in the form that stood before him, her whom he so ardently loved; and a sudden glow shot through his frame at finding her thus restored to him: yet the nightfrost had chilled his limbs and palsied his tongue. For a while he gazed upon her without either motion or speech, and during this pause, all was again become hushed and serene; and the stars shone brightly in the clear heavens.

"Walter!" exclaimed the figure; and at once the well-known sound, thrilling to his heart, broke the spell by which he was bound.

"Is it reality? Is it truth?" cried he, "or a cheating delusion?"

"No, it is no imposture: I am really living:—conduct me quickly to thy castle in the mountains."

Walter looked around: the old man had disappeared, but he perceived close by his side, a coal-black steed of fiery eye, ready equipped to conduct him thence; and on his back lay all proper attire for Brunhilda, who lost no time in arraying herself. This being done, she cried: "Haste, let us away ere the dawn breaks, for my eye is yet too weak to endure the light of day." Fully recovered from his stupor, Walter leaped into his saddle, and catching up, with a mingled feeling of delight and awe, the beloved being thus mysteriously restored from the power of the grave, he spurred on across the wild, towards the mountains, as furiously as if pursued by the shadows of the dead, hastening to recover from him their sister.

The castle to which Walter conducted his Brunhilda, was situated on a rock between other rocks rising up above it. Here they arrived, unseen by any, save one aged domestic, on whom Walter imposed secrecy by the severest threats.

"Here will we tarry," said Brunhilda, "until I can endure the light, and until thou canst look upon me without trembling: as if struck with a cold chill." They accordingly continued to make that place their abode: yet no one knew that Brunhilda existed, save only that aged attendant, who provided their meals. During seven entire days they had no light except that of tapers; during the next seven, the light was admitted through the lofty casements only while the rising or setting-sun faintly illumined the mountain-tops, the vallies being still enveloped in shade.

Seldom did Walter quit Brunhilda's side: a nameless spell seemed to attach him to her; even the shudder which he felt in her presence, and which would not permit him to touch her, was not unmixed with pleasure, like that thrilling awful emotion felt when strains of sacred music float under the vault of some temple; he rather sought, therefore, than avoided this feeling. Often too as he had indulged in calling to mind the beauties of Brunhilda, she had never appeared so fair, so fascinating, so admirable when depicted by his imagination, as when now beheld in reality. Never till now had her voice sounded with such tones of sweetness; never before did her language possess such eloquence as it now did, when she conversed with him on the subject of the past. And this was the magic fairy-land towards which her words constantly conducted him. Ever did she dwell upon the days of their first love, those hours of delight which they had partici-pated together when the one derived all enjoyment from the other: and so rapturous, so enchanting, so full of life did she recall to his imagination that blissful season, that he even doubted whether he had ever experienced with her so much felicity, or had been so truly happy. And, while she thus vividly portrayed their hours of past delight, she delineated in still more glowing, more enchanting colours, those hours of approaching bliss which now awaited them, richer in enjoyment than any preceding ones. In this manner did she charm her attentive auditor with enrapturing hopes for the future, and lull him into dreams of more than mortal ecstacy; so that while he listened to her syren strain, he entirely forgot how little blissful was the latter period of their union, when he had often sighed at her imperiousness, and at her harshness both to himself and all his household. Yet even had he recalled this to mind would it have disturbed him in his present delirious trance? Had she not now left behind in the grave all the frailty of mor-tality? Was she not cheerful as the morning hour of spring—affectionate and mild as the last beams of an autumnal sun? Was not her whole being refined and purified by that long sleep in which neither passion nor sin had approached her even in dreams? How different now was the subject of her discourse! Only when speaking of her affection for him, did she betray any thing of earthly feeling: at other times, she uniformly dwelt upon themes relating to the invisible and future world; when in descanting and declar-ing the mysteries of eternity, a stream of prophetic eloquence would burst from her lips.

In this manner had twice seven days elapsed, and, for the first time, Walter beheld the being now dearer to him than ever, in the full light of day. Every trace of the grave had disappeared from her countenance; a roseate tinge like the ruddy streaks of dawn again beamed on her pallid cheek; the faint, mouldering taint of the grave was changed into a delightful violet scent; the only sign of earth that never disappeared. He no longer felt either apprehension or awe, as he gazed upon her in the sunny light of day: it was not until now, that he seemed to have recovered her completely; and, glowing with all his former passion towards her, he would have pressed her to his bosom, but she gently repulsed him, saying:—"Not yet—spare your caresses until the moon has again filled her horn."

Spite of his impatience, Walter was obliged to await the lapse of another period of seven days: but, on the night when the moon was arrived at the full, he hastened to Brunhilda, whom he found more lovely than she had ever appeared before. Fearing no obstacles to his transports, he embraced her with all the fervour of a deeply enamoured and successful lover. Brunhilda, however, still refused to yield to his passion. "What!" exclaimed she, "is it fitting that I who have been purified by death from the frailty of mortality, should become thy concubine, while a mere daughter of the earth bears the title of thy wife: never shall it be. No, it must be within the walls of thy palace, within that chamber where I once reigned as queen, that thou obtainest the end of thy wishes,—and of mine also," added she, imprinting a glowing kiss on the lips, and immediately disappeared.

Heated with passion, and determined to sacrifice every thing to the accomplishment of his desires, Walter hastily quitted the apartment, and shortly after the castle itself. He travelled over mountain and across heath, with the rapidity of a storm, so that the turf was flung up by his horse's hoofs; nor once stopped until he arrived home.

Here, however, neither the affectionate caresses of Swanhilda, or those of his children could touch his heart, or induce him to restrain his furious desires. Alas! is the impetuous torrent to be checked in its devastating course by the beauteous flowers over which it rushes, when they exclaim:—"Destroyer, commiserate our helpless innocence and beauty, nor lay us waste?"—the stream sweeps over them unregarding, and a single moment annihilates the pride of a whole summer.

Shortly afterwards, did Walter begin to hint to Swanhilda, that they were ill-suited to each other; that he was anxious to taste that wild, tumultous life, so well according with the spirit of his sex, while she, on the contrary, was satisfied with the monotonous circle of household enjoyments:—that he was eager for whatever promised novelty, while she felt most attached to what was familiarized to her by habit; and lastly, that her cold disposition, bordering upon indifference, but ill assorted with his ardent temperament: it was therefore more prudent that they should seek apart from each other, that happiness which they could not find together. A sigh, and a brief acquiescence in his wishes was all the reply that Swanhilda made: and, on the following morning, upon his presenting her with a paper of separation, informing her that she was at liberty to return home to her father, she received it most submissively: yet, ere she departed, she gave him the following warning: "Too well do I conjecture to whom I am indebted for this our separation. Often have I seen thee at Brunhilda's grave, and beheld thee there even on that night when the face of the heavens was suddenly enveloped in a veil of clouds. Hast thou rashly dared to tear aside the awful veil that separates the mortality that dreams, from that which dreameth not? Oh! then woe to thee, thou wretched man, for thou hast attached to thyself that which will prove thy destruction." She ceased: nor did Walter attempt any reply, for the similar admonition uttered by the sorcerer flashed upon his mind, all obscured as it was by passion, just as the lightning glares momentarily through the gloom of night without dispersing the obscurity.

Swanhilda then departed, in order to pronounce to her children, a bitter farewell, for they, according to national custom, belonged to the father; and, having bathed them in her tears, and consecrated them with the holy water of maternal love, she quitted her husband's residence, and departed to the home of her father's.

Thus was the kind and benevolent Swanhilda, driven an exile from those halls, where she had presided with such grace;—from halls which were now newly decorated to receive another mistress. The day at length arrived, on which Walter, for the second time, conducted Brunhilda home, as a newlymade bride. And he caused it to be reported among his domestics, that his new consort had gained his affections by her extraordinary likeness to Brunhilda, their former mistress. How ineffably happy did he deem himself, as he conducted his beloved once more into the chamber which had often witnessed their former joys, and which was now newly gilded and adorned in a most costly style: among the other decorations were figures of angels scattering roses, which served to support the purple draperies, whose ample folds o'ershadowed the nuptial couch. With what impatience did he await the hour that was to put him in possession of those beauties, for which he had already paid so high a price, but, whose enjoyment was to cost him most dearly yet! Unfortunate Walter! revelling in bliss, thou beholdest not the abyss that yawns beneath thy feet, intoxicated with the luscious perfume of the flower thou hast plucked, thou little deemest how deadly is the venom with which it is fraught, although, for a short season, its potent fragrance bestows new energy on all thy feelings.

Happy, however, as Walter now was, his household were far from being equally so. The strange resemblance between their new lady and the deceased Brunhilda, filled them with a secret dismay,—an undefinable horror; for there was not a single difference of feature, of tone of voice, or of gesture. To add too to these mysterious circumstances, her female attendants discovered a particular mark on her back, exactly like one which Brunhilda had. A report was now soon circulated, that their lady was no other than Brunhilda herself, who had been recalled to life by the power of necromancy. How truly horrible was the idea of living under the same roof with one who had been an inhabitant of the tomb, and of being obliged to attend upon her, and acknowledge her as mistress! There was also in Brunhilda, much to increase this aversion, and favour their superstition: no ornaments of gold ever decked her person; all that others were wont to wear of this metal, she had formed of silver: no richly coloured and sparkling jewels glittered upon her; pearls alone, lent their pale lustre to adorn her bosom. Most carefully did she always avoid the cheerful light of the sun, and was wont to spend the brightest days in the most retired and gloomy apartments: only during the twilight of the commencing, or declining day did she ever walk abroad, but her favourite hour was, when the phantom light of the moon bestowed on all objects a shadowy appearance, and a sombre hue; always too at the crowing of the cock, an involuntary shudder was observed to seize her limbs. Imperious as before her death, she quickly imposed her iron yoke on every one around her, while she seemed even far more terrible than ever, since a dread of some supernatural power attached to her, appalled all who approached her. A malignant withering glance seemed to shoot from her eye on the unhappy object of her wrath, as if it would annihilate its victim. In short, those halls which, in the time of Swanhilda were the residence of cheerfulness and mirth, now resembled an extensive desert tomb. With fear imprinted on their pale countenances, the domestics glided through the apartments of the castle; and, in this abode of terror, the crowing of the cock caused the living to tremble, as if they were the spirits of the departed; for the sound always reminded them of their mysterious mistress. There was no one but who shuddered at meeting her in a lonely place, in the dusk of evening, or by the light of the moon, a circumstance that was deemed to be ominous of some evil: so great was the apprehension of her female attendants, they pined in continual disquietude, and, by degrees, all quitted her. In the course of time even others of the domestics fled, for an insupportable horror had seized them.

The art of the sorcerer had indeed bestowed upon Brunhilda an artificial life, and due nourishment had continued to support the restored body; yet, this body was not able of itself to keep up the genial glow of vitality, and to nourish the flame whence springs all the affections and passions, whether of love or hate; for death had for ever destroyed and withered it: all that Brunhilda now possessed was a chilled existence, colder than that of the snake. It was nevertheless necessary that she should love, and return with equal ardour the warm caresses of her spell-enthralled husband, to whose passion alone she was indebted for her renewed existence. It was necessary that a magic draught should animate the dull current in her veins, and awaken her to the glow of life and the flame of love—a potion of abomination—one not even to be named without a curse—human blood, imbibed whilst yet warm, from the veins of youth. This was the hellish drink for which she thirsted: possessing no sympathy with the purer feelings of humanity; deriving no enjoyment from aught that interests in life, and occupies its varied hours; her existence was a mere blank, unless when in the arms of her paramour husband, and therefore was it that she craved incessantly after the horrible draught. It was even with the utmost effort that she could forbear sucking even the blood of Walter himself, as he reclined beside her. Whenever she beheld some innocent child, whose lovely face denoted the exuberance of infantine health and vigour, she would entice it by soothing words and fond caresses into her most secret apartment, where, lulling it to sleep in her arms, she would suck from its bosom the warm, purple tide of life. Nor were youths of either sex safe from her horrid attack: having first breathed upon her unhappy victim, who never failed immediately to sink into a lengthened sleep, she would then in a similar manner drain his veins of the vital juice. Thus children, youths, and maidens quickly faded away, as flowers gnawn by the cankering worm: the fullness of their limbs disappeared; a sallow hue succeeded to the rosy freshness of their cheeks, the liquid lustre of the eye was deadened, even as the sparkling stream when arrested by the touch of frost; and their locks became thin and grey, as if already ravaged by the storm of life. Parents beheld with horror this desolating pestilence devouring their offspring; nor could simple or charm, potion or amulet avail aught against it: The grave swallowed up one after the other; or did the miserable victim survive, he became cadaverous and wrinkled even in the very morn of existence. Parents observed with horror, this devastating pestilence snatch away their offspring—a pestilence which, nor herb however potent, nor charm, nor holy taper, nor exorcism could avert. They either beheld their children sink one after the other into the grave, or their youthful forms withered by the unholy, vampire embrace of Brunhilda assume the decrepitude of sudden age.

At length strange surmises and reports began to prevail; it was whispered that Brunhilda herself was the cause of all these horrors; although no one could pretend to tell in what manner she destroyed her victims, since no marks of violence were discernable. Yet when young children confessed that she had frequently lulled them asleep in her arms, and elder ones said that a sudden slumber had come upon them whenever she began to converse with them, suspicion became converted into certainty, and those whose offspring had hitherto escaped unharmed, quitted their hearths and home—all their little possessions—the dwellings of their fathers and the inheritance of their children, in order to rescue from so horrible a fate those who were dearer to their simple affections than aught else the world could give.

Thus daily did the castle assume a more desolate appearance; daily did its environs become more deserted; none but a few aged decrepit old women and grey-headed menials were to be seen remaining of the once numerous retinue. Such will in the latter days of the earth, be the last generation of mortals, when child-bearing shall have ceased, when youth shall no more be seen, nor any arise to replace those who shall await their fate in silence.

Walter alone noticed not, or heeded not, the desolation around him; he apprehended not death, lapped as he was in a glowing elysium of love. Far more happy than formerly did he now seem in the possession of Brunhilda. All those caprices and frowns which had been wont to overcloud their former union had now entirely disappeared. She even seemed to doat on him with a warmth of passion that she had never exhibited even during the happy season of bridal love; for the flame of that youthful blood, of which she drained the veins of others, rioted in her own. At night, as soon as he closed his eyes, she would breathe on him till he sank into delicious dreams, from which he awoke only to experience more rapturous enjoyment. By day she would continually discourse with him on the bliss experienced by happy spirits beyond the grave, assuring him that, as his affection had recalled her from the tomb, they were now irrevocably united. Thus fascinated by a continual spell, it was not possible that he should perceive what was taking place around him. Brunhilda, however, foresaw with savage grief that the source of her youthful ardour was daily decreasing, for, in a short time, there remained nothing gifted with youth, save Walter and his children, and these latter she resolved should be her next victims.

On her first return to the castle, she had felt an aversion towards the offspring of another, and therefore abandoned them entirely to the attendants appointed by Swanhilda. Now, however, she began to pay considerable attention to them, and caused them to be frequently admitted into her presence. The aged nurses were filled with dread at perceiving these marks of regard from her towards their young charges, yet dared they not to oppose the will of their terrible and imperious mistress. Soon did Brunhilda gain the affection of the children, who were too unsuspecting of guile to apprehend any danger from her; on the contrary, her caresses won them completely to her. Instead of ever checking their mirthful gambols, she would rather instruct them in new sports; often too did she recite to them tales of such strange and wild inter- est as to exceed all the stories of their nurses. Were they wearied either with play or with listening to her narratives, she would take them on her knees and lull them to slumber. Then did visions of the most surpassing magnificence attend their dreams: they would fancy themselves in some garden where flowers of every hue rose in rows one above the other, from the humble violet to the tall sun-flower, forming a party- coloured broidery of every hue, sloping upwards towards the golden clouds, where little angels, whose wings sparkled with azure and gold, descended to bring them delicious cates, or splendid jewels; or sung to them soothing melodious hymns. So delightful did these dreams in short time become to the children, that they longed for nothing so eagerly as to slumber on Brunhilda's lap, for never did they else enjoy such visions of heavenly forms. Thus were they most anxious for that which was to prove their destruction:—yet do we not all aspire after that which conducts us to the grave— after the enjoyment of life? These innocents stretched out their arms to approaching death, because it assumed the mask of pleasure; for, while they were lapped in these ecstatic slumbers, Brunhilda sucked the life-stream from their bosoms. On waking, indeed, they felt themselves faint and exhausted, yet did no pain, nor any mark betray the cause. Shortly, however, did their strength entirely fail, even as the summer brook is gradually dried up: their sports became less and less noisy; their loud, frolicsome laughter was converted into a faint smile; the full tones of their voices died away into a mere whisper. Their attendants were filled with horror and despair; too well did they conjecture the horrible truth, yet dared not to impart their suspicions to Walter, who was so devotedly attached to his horrible partner. Death had already smote his prey: the children were but the mere shadows of their former selves, and even this shadow quickly disappeared.

The anguished father deeply bemoaned their loss, for, notwithstanding his appar- ent neglect, he was strongly attached to them, nor until he had experienced their loss, was he aware that his love was so great. His affliction could not fail to excite the dis- pleasure of Brunhilda: "Why dost thou lament so fondly," said she, "for these little ones? What satisfaction could such unformed beings yield to thee, unless thou wert still attached to their mother? Thy heart then is still hers? Or dost thou now regret her and them, because thou art satiated with my fondness, and weary of my endearments? Had these young ones grown up, would they not have attached thee, thy spirit and thy affections more closely to this earth of clay—to this dust, and have alienated thee from that sphere to which I, who have already passed the grave, endeavour to raise thee? Say is thy spirit so heavy, or thy love so weak, or thy faith so hollow, that the hope of being mine for ever is unable to touch thee?" Thus did Brunhilda express her indignation at her consort's grief, and forbade him her presence. The fear of offending her beyond forgiveness, and his anxiety to appease her soon dried up his tears; and he again abandoned himself to his fatal passion, until approaching destruction, at length awakened him from his delusion.

Neither maiden, nor youth, was any longer to be seen, either within the dreary walls of the castle, or the adjoining territory:—all had disappeared; for those whom the grave had not swallowed up, had fled from the region of death. Who, therefore, now remained to quench the horrible thirst of the female vampire, save Walter himself? and his death she dared to contemplate unmoved; for that divine sentiment that unites two beings in one joy and one sorrow was unknown to her bosom. Was he in his tomb, so was she free to search out other victims, and glut herself with destruction, until she herself should, at the last day, be consumed with the earth itself: such is the fatal law, to which the dead are subject, when awoke by the arts of necromancy from the sleep of the grave.

She now began to fix her bloodthirsty lips on Walter's breast, when cast into a profound sleep by the odour of her violet breath, he reclined beside her quite unconscious of his impending fate: yet soon did his vital powers begin to decay; and many a grey hair peeped through his raven locks. With his strength, his passion also declined; and he now frequently left her in order to pass the whole day in the sports of the chase, hoping thereby, to regain his wonted vigour. As he was reposing one day in a wood beneath the shade of an oak, he perceived, on the summit of a tree, a bird of strange appearance, and quite unknown to him; but, before he could take aim at it with his bow, it flew away into the clouds; at the same time, letting fall a rose-coloured root which dropped at Walter's feet, who immediately took it up, and, although he was well acquainted with almost every plant, he could not remember to have seen any at all resembling this. Its delightfully odoriferous scent induced him to try its flavour, but ten times more bitter than wormwood, it was even as gall in his mouth; upon which, impatient of the disappointment, he flung it away with violence. Had he, however, been aware of its miraculous quality, and that it acted as a counter charm against the opiate perfume of Brunhilda's breath, he would have blessed it in spite of its bitterness: thus do mortals often blindly cast away in displeasure, the unsavoury remedy that would otherwise work their weal.

When Walter returned home in the evening, and laid him down to repose as usual by Brunhilda's side, the magic power of her breath produced no effect upon him; and for the first time during many months did he close his eyes in a natural slumber. Yet hardly had he fallen asleep, ere a pungent smarting pain disturbed him from his dreams; and, opening his eyes, he discerned, by the gloomy rays of a lamp, that glimmered in the apartment, what for some moments transfixed him quite aghast, for it was Brunhilda, drawing with her lips, the warm blood from his bosom. The wild cry of horror which at length escaped him, terrified Brunhilda, whose mouth was besmeared with the warm blood. "Monster!" exclaimed he, springing from the couch, "is it thus that you love me?

"Aye, even as the dead love," replied she, with a malignant coldness.

"Creature of blood!" continued Walter, "the delusion which has so long blinded me is at an end: thou art the fiend who hast destroyed my children—who hast murdered the offspring of my vassals." Raising herself upwards, and, at the same time, casting on him a glance that froze him to the spot with dread, she replied. "It is not I who have murdered them:—I was obliged to pamper myself with warm youthful blood, in order that I might satisfy thy furious desires—thou art the murderer!"— These dreadful words summoned, before Walter's terrified conscience, the threatening shades of all those who had thus perished; while despair choked his voice. "Why," continued she, in a tone that increased his horror, "why dost thou make mouths at me like a puppet? Thou who hadst the courage to love the dead—to take into thy bed, one who had been sleeping in the grave, the bedfellow of the worm—who hast clasped in thy lustful arms, the corruption of the tomb—dost thou, unhallowed as thou art, now raise this hideous cry for the sacrifice of a few lives?—They are but leaves swept from their branches by a storm.—Come, chase these idiot fancies, and taste the bliss thou hast so dearly purchased." So saying, she extended her arms towards him; but this motion served only to increase his terror, and exclaiming: "Accursed Being,"—he rushed out of the apartment.

All the horrors of a guilty, upbraiding conscience became his companions, now that he was awakened from the delirium of his unholy pleasures. Frequently did he curse his own obstinate blindness, for having given no heed to the hints and admonitions of his children's nurses, but treating them as vile calumnies. But his sorrow was now too late, for, although repentance may gain pardon for the sinner, it cannot alter the immutable decrees of fate—it cannot recall the murdered from the tomb. No sooner did the first break of dawn appear, than he set out for his lonely castle in the mountains, determined no longer to abide under the same roof with so terrific a being; yet vain was his flight, for, on waking the following morning, he perceived himself in Brunhilda's arms, and quite entangled in her long raven tresses, which seemed to involve him, and bind him in the fetters of his fate; the powerful fascination of her breath held him still more captivated, so that, forgetting all that had passed, he returned her caresses, until awakening as if from a dream he recoiled in unmixed horror from her embrace. During the day he wandered through the solitary wilds of the mountains, as a culprit seeking an asylum from his pursuers; and, at night, retired to the shelter of a cave; fearing less to couch himself within such a dreary place, than to expose himself to the horror of again meeting Brunhilda; but, alas! it was in vain that he endeavoured to flee her. Again, when he awoke, he found her the partner of his miserable bed. Nay, had he sought the centre of the earth as his hiding place; had he even imbedded himself beneath rocks, or formed his chamber in the recesses of the ocean, still had he found her his constant companion; for, by calling her again into existence, he had rendered himself inseparably hers; so fatal were the links that united them.

Struggling with the madness that was beginning to seize him, and brooding incessantly on the ghastly visions that presented themselves to his horror-stricken mind, he lay motionless in the gloomiest recesses of the woods, even from the rise of sun till the shades of eve. But, no sooner was the light of day extinguished in the west, and the woods buried in impenetrable darkness, than the apprehension of resigning himself to sleep drove him forth among the mountains. The storm played wildly with the fantastic clouds, and with the rattling leaves, as they were caught up into the air, as if some dread spirit was sporting with these images of transitoriness and decay: it roared among the summits of the oaks as if uttering a voice of fury, while its hollow sound rebounding among the distant hills, seemed as the moans of a departing sinner, or as the faint cry of some wretch expiring under the murderer's hand: the owl too, uttered its ghastly cry as if foreboding the wreck of nature. Walter's hair flew disorderly in the wind, like black snakes wreathing around his temples and shoulders; while each sense was awake to catch fresh horror. In the clouds he seemed to behold the forms of the murdered; in the howling wind to hear their laments and groans; in the chilling blast itself he felt the dire kiss of Brunhilda; in the cry of the screeching bird he heard her voice; in the mouldering leaves he scented the charnel-bed out of which he had awakened her. "Murderer of thy own offspring," exclaimed he in a voice making night, and the conflict of the element still more hideous, par-amour of a blood-thirsty vampire, "reveller with the corruption of the tomb!" while in his despair he rent the wild locks from his head. Just then the full moon darted from beneath the bursting clouds; and the sight recalled to his remembrance the advice of the sorcerer, when he trembled at the first apparition of Brunhilda rising from her sleep of death;—namely, to seek him, at the season of the full moon, in the mountains, where three roads met. Scarcely had this gleam of hope broke in on his bewildered mind, than he flew to the appointed spot.

On his arrival, Walter found the old man seated there upon a stone, as calmly as though it had been a bright sunny day, and completely regardless of the uproar around. "Art thou come then?" exclaimed he to the breathless wretch, who, flinging himself at his feet, cried in a tone of anguish:—"Oh save me—succour me—rescue me from the monster that scattereth death and desolation around her."

"I am acquainted with all," returned the sorcerer, "thou now perceivest how wholesome was the advice—'Wake not the dead.' "

"And wherefore a mysterious warning? why didst thou not rather disclose to me, at once, all the horrors that awaited my sacrilegious profanation of the grave?"

"Wert thou able to listen to any other voice than that of thy impetuous passions? Did not thy eager impatience shut my mouth at the very moment I would have cau-tioned thee?"

"True, true:—thy reproof is just: but what does it avail now;—I need the prompt-est aid."

"Well," replied the old man, "there remains even yet a means of rescuing thyself, but it is fraught with horror, and demands all thy resolution."

"Utter it then, utter it; for what can be more appalling, more hideous than the misery I now endure?"

"Know then," continued the sorcerer, "that only on the night of the new moon, does she sleep the sleep of mortals; and then all the supernatural power which she inherits from the grave totally fails her. 'Tis then that thou must murder her."

"How! murder her!" echoed Walter.

"Aye," returned the old man calmly, "pierce her bosom with a sharpened dagger, which I will furnish thee with; at the same time renounce her memory for ever, swearing never to think of her intentionally, and that, if thou dost involuntarily, thou wilt repeat the curse."

"Most horrible! yet what can be more horrible than she herself is?— I'll do it."

"Keep then this resolution until the next new moon."

"What, must I wait until then?" cried Walter, "alas ere then, either her savage thirst for blood will have forced me into the night of the tomb, or horror will have driven me into the night of madness."

"Nay," replied the sorcerer, "that I can prevent"; and, so saying, he conducted him to a cavern further among the mountains. "Abide here twice seven days," said he; "so long can I protect thee against her deadly caresses. Here wilt thou find all due provision for thy wants; but take heed that nothing tempt thee to quit this place. Farewell, when the moon renews itself, then do I repair hither again." So saying, the sorcerer drew a magic circle around the cave, and then immediately disappeared.

Twice seven days did Walter continue in this solitude, where his companions were his own terrifying thoughts, and his bitter repentance. The present was all desolation and dread; the future presented the image of a horrible deed, which he must perforce commit; while the past was empoisoned by the memory of his guilt. Did he think on his former happy union with Brunhilda, her horrible image presented itself to his imagination with her lips defiled with dropping blood: or, did he call to mind the peaceful days he had passed with Swanhilda, he beheld her sorrowful spirit, with the shadows of her murdered children. Such were the horrors that attended him by day: those of night were still more dreadful, for then he beheld Brunhilda herself, who, wandering round the magic circle which she could not pass, called upon his name, till the cavern re-echoed the horrible sound. "Walter, my beloved," cried she, "wherefore dost thou avoid me? art thou not mine? for ever mine—mine here, and mine hereafter? And dost thou seek to murder me?—ah! commit not a deed which hurls us both to perdition— thyself as well as me." In this manner did the horrible visitant torment him each night, and, even when she departed, robbed him of all repose.

The night of the new moon at length arrived, dark as the deed it was doomed to bring forth. The sorcerer entered the cavern; "Come," said he, to Walter, "let us depart hence, the hour is now arrived": and he forthwith conducted him in silence from the grave, to a coal-black steed, the sight of which recalled to Walter's remembrance the fatal night. He then related to the old man Brunhilda's nocturnal visits, and anxiously enquired whether her apprehensions of eternal perdition would be fulfilled or not. "Mortal eye," exclaimed the sorcerer, "may not pierce the dark secrets of another world, or penetrate the deep abyss that separates earth from heaven." Walter hesitated to mount the steed. "Be resolute," exclaimed his companion, "but this once is it granted to thee to make the trial, and, should thou fail now, nought can rescue thee from her power."

"What can be more horrible than she herself?—I am determined": and he leaped on the horse, the sorcerer mounting also behind him.

Carried with a rapidity equal to that of the storm that sweeps across the plain, they in brief space arrived at Walter's castle. All the doors flew open at the bidding of his companion, and they speedily reached Brunhilda's chamber, and stood beside her couch. Reclining in a tranquil slumber; she reposed in all her native loveliness, every trace of horror had disappeared from her countenance; she looked so pure, meek and innocent that all the sweet hours of their endearments rushed to Walter's memory, like interceding angels pleading in her behalf. His unnerved hand could not take the dagger which the sorcerer presented to him. "The blow must be struck even now": said the latter, "shouldst thou delay but an hour, she will lie at day-break on thy bosom, suck-ing the warm life-drops from thy heart."

"Horrible! most horrible!" faultered the trembling Walter, and turning away his face, he thrust the dagger into her bosom, exclaiming—"I curse thee for ever!"—and the cold blood gushed upon his hand. Opening her eyes once more, she cast a look of ghastly horror on her husband, and, in a hollow dying accent said—"Thou too art doomed to perdition."

"Lay now thy hand upon her corse," said the sorcerer, "and swear the oath."—Walter did as commanded, saying—"Never will I think of her with love, never recall her to mind intentionally, and, should her image recur to my mind involuntarily, so will I exclaim to it: be thou accursed."

"Thou hast now done everything," returned the sorcerer;—"restore her there-fore to the earth, from which thou did'st so foolishly recall her; and be sure to recollect thy oath: for, shouldst thou forget it but once, she would return, and thou wouldst be inevitably lost. Adieu—we see each other no more." Having uttered these words he quitted the apartment, and Walter also fled from this abode of horror, having first given directions that the corse should be speedily interred.

Again did the terrific Brunhilda repose within her grave; but her image con-tinually haunted Walter's imagination, so that his existence was one continued martyrdom, in which he continually struggled, to dismiss from his recollection the hideous phantoms of the past; yet, the stronger his effort to banish them, so much the more frequently and the more vividly did they return; as the night-wanderer, who is enticed by a fire-wisp into quagmire or bog, sinks the deeper into his damp grave the more he struggles to escape. His imagination seemed incapable of admitting any other image than that of Brunhilda: now he fancied he beheld her expiring, the blood streaming from her beautiful bosom: at others he saw the lovely bride of his youth, who reproached him with having disturbed the slumbers of the tomb; and to both he was compelled to utter the dreadful words, "I curse thee for ever." The terrible imprecation was constantly passing his lips; yet was he in incessant terror lest he should forget it, or dream of her without being able to repeat it, and then, on awaking, find himself in her arms. Else would he recall her expiring words, and, appalled at their terrific import, imagine that the doom of his perdition was irrecoverably passed. Whence should he fly from himself? or how erase from his brain these images and forms of horror? In the din of combat, in the tumult of war and its incessant pour of victory to defeat; from the cry of anguish to the exultation of victory—in these he hoped to find at least the relief of distraction: but here too he was disappointed. The giant fang of apprehension now seized him who had never before known fear; each drop of blood that sprayed upon him seemed the cold blood that had gushed from Branhilda's wound; each dying wretch that fell beside him looked like her, when expiring, she exclaimed:—"Thou too art doomed to perdition"; so that the aspect of death seemed more full of dread to him than aught beside, and this unconquerable terror compelled him to abandon the battle-field. At length, after many a weary and fruitless wandering, he returned to his castle. Here all was deserted and silent, as if the sword, or a still more deadly pestilence had laid every thing waste: for the few inhabitants that still remained, and even those servants who had once shewn themselves the most attached, now fled from him, as though he had been branded with the mark of Cain. With horror he perceived that, by uniting himself as he had done with the dead, he had cut himself off from the living, who refused to hold any intercourse with him. Often, when he stood on the battlements of his castle, and looked down upon desolate fields, he compared their present solitude with the lively activity they were wont to exhibit, under the strict but benevolent discipline of Swanhilda. He now felt that she alone could reconcile him to life, but durst he hope that one, whom he had so deeply agrieved, could pardon him, and receive him again? Impatience at length got the better of fear; he sought Swanhilda, and, with the deepest contrition, acknowledged his complicated guilt; embracing her knees he beseeched her to pardon him, and to return to his desolate castle, in order that it might again become the abode of contentment and peace. The pale form which she beheld at her feet, the shadow of the lately blooming youth, touched Swanhilda. "Thy folly," said she gently, "though it has caused me much sorrow, has never excited my resentment or my anger. But say, where are my children?" To this dreadful interrogation the agonized father could for a while frame no reply: at length he was obliged to confess the dreadful truth. "Then we are sundered for ever," returned Swanhilda; nor could all his tears or supplications prevail upon her to revoke the sentence she had given.

Stripped of his last earthly hope, bereft of his last consolation, and thereby rendered as poor as mortal can possibly be on this side of the grave, Walter returned homewards; when, as he was riding through the forest in the neighbourhood of his castle, absorbed in his gloomy meditations, the sudden sound of a horn roused him from his reverie. Shortly after he saw appear a female figure clad in black, and mounted on a steed of the same colour: her attire was like that of a huntress, but, instead of a falcon, she bore a raven in her hand; and she was attended by a gay troop of cavaliers and dames. The first salutations being passed, he found that she was proceeding the same road as himself; and, when she found that Walter's castle was close at hand, she requested that he would lodge her for that night, the evening being far advanced. Most willingly did he comply with this request, since the appearance of the beautiful stranger had struck him greatly; so wonderfully did she resemble Swanhilda, except that her locks were brown, and her eye dark and full of fire. With a sumptuous banquet did he entertain his guests, whose mirth and songs enlivened the lately silent halls. Three days did this revelry continue, and so exhilirating did it prove to Walter, that he seemed to have forgotten his sorrows and his fears; nor could he prevail upon himself to dismiss his visitors, dreading lest, on their departure, the castle would seem a hundred times more desolate than before, and his grief be proportionably increased. At his earnest request, the stranger consented to stay seven days, and again another seven days. Without being requested, she took upon herself the superintendance of the household, which she regulated as discreetly and cheerfully as Swanhilda had been wont to do, so that the castle, which had so lately been the abode of melancholy and horror, became the residence of pleasure and festivity, and Walter's grief disappeared altogether in the midst of so much gaiety. Daily did his attachment to the fair unknown increase; he even made her his confidant; and, one evening as they were walking together apart from any of her train, he related to her his melancholy and frightful history. "My dear friend," returned she, as soon as he had finished his tale, "it ill beseems a man of thy discretion to afflict thyself, on account of all this. Thou hast awakened the dead from the sleep of the grave, and afterwards found,—what might have been anticipated, that the dead possess no sympathy with life. What then? thou wilt not commit this error a second time. Thou hast however murdered the being whom thou had'st thus recalled again to existence—but it was only in appearance, for thou couldst not deprive that of life, which properly had none. Thou hast, too, lost a wife and two children: but, at thy years, such a loss is most easily repaired. There are beauties who will gladly share thy couch, and make thee again a father. But thou dread'st the reckoning of hereafter:—go, open the graves and ask the sleepers there whether that hereafter disturbs them." In such manner would she frequently exhort and cheer him, so that, in a short time, his melancholy entirely disappeared. He now ventured to declare to the unknown the passion with which she had inspired him, nor did she refuse him her hand. Within seven days afterwards the nuptials were celebrated, and the very foundations of the castle seemed to rock from the wild tumultuous uproar of unrestrained riot. The wine streamed in abundance; the goblets circled incessantly: intemperance reached its utmost bounds, while shouts of laughter, almost resembling madness, burst from the numerous train belonging to the unknown. At length Walter, heated with wine and love, conducted his bride into the nuptial chamber: but, oh! horror! scarcely had he clasped her in his arms, ere she transformed herself into a monstrous serpent, which entwining him in its horrid folds, crushed him to death. Flames crackled on every side of the apartment; in a few minutes after, the whole castle was enveloped in a blaze that consumed it entirely: while, as the walls fell in with a tremendous crash, a voice exclaimed aloud—"Wake not the dead!"

The Dream-Woman

Wilkie Collins

———— ◆ ————

CHAPTER I

I HAD NOT BEEN SETTLED MUCH MORE THAN SIX WEEKS IN MY COUNTRY PRACTICE when I was sent for to a neighboring town, to consult with the resident medical man there on a case of very dangerous illness.

My horse had come down with me at the end of a long ride the night before, and had hurt himself, luckily, much more than he had hurt his master. Being deprived of the animal's services, I started for my destination by the coach (there were no railways at that time), and I hoped to get back again, toward the afternoon, in the same way.

After the consultation was over, I went to the principal inn of the town to wait for the coach. When it came up it was full inside and out. There was no resource left me but to get home as cheaply as I could by hiring a gig. The price asked for this accommodation struck me as being so extortionate, that I determined to look out for an inn of inferior pretensions, and to try if I could not make a better bargain with a less prosperous establishment.

I soon found a likely-looking house, dingy and quiet, with an old-fashioned sign, that had evidently not been repainted for many years past. The landlord, in this case, was not above making a small profit, and as soon as we came to terms he rang the yard-bell to order the gig.

"Has Robert not come back from that errand?" asked the landlord, appealing to the waiter who answered the bell.

"No, sir, he hasn't."

"Well, then, you must wake up Isaac."

"Wake up Isaac!" I repeated; "that sounds rather odd. Do your ostlers go to bed in the daytime?"

"This one does," said the landlord, smiling to himself in rather a strange way.

"And dreams too," added the waiter; "I sha'n't forget the turn it gave me the first time I heard him."

"Never you mind about that," retorted the proprietor; "you go and rouse Isaac up. The gentleman's waiting for his gig."

The landlord's manner and the waiter's manner expressed a great deal more than they either of them said. I began to suspect that I might be on the trace of something professionally interesting to me as a medical man, and I thought I should like to look at the ostler before the waiter awakened him.

"Stop a minute," I interposed; "I have rather a fancy for seeing this man before you wake him up. I'm a doctor; and if this queer sleeping and dreaming of his comes from anything wrong in his brain, I may be able to tell you what to do with him."

"I rather think you will find his complaint past all doctoring, sir," said the landlord; "but, if you would like to see him, you're welcome, I'm sure."

He led the way across a yard and down a passage to the stables, opened one of the doors, and, waiting outside himself, told me to look in.

I found myself in a two-stall stable. In one of the stalls a horse was munching his corn; in the other an old man was lying asleep on the litter.

I stooped and looked at him attentively. It was a withered, woe-begone face. The eyebrows were painfully contracted; the mouth was fast set, and drawn down at the corners. The hollow wrinkled cheeks, and the scanty grizzled hair, told their own tale of some past sorrow or suffering. He was drawing his breath convulsively when I first looked at him, and in a moment more he began to talk in his sleep.

"Wake up!" I heard him say, in a quick whisper, through his clenched teeth. "Wake up there! Murder!"

He moved one lean arm slowly till it rested over his throat, shuddered a little, and turned on his straw. Then the arm left his throat, the hand stretched itself out, and clutched at the side toward which he had turned, as if he fancied himself to be grasping at the edge of something. I saw his lips move, and bent lower over him. He was still talking in his sleep.

"Light gray eyes," he murmured, "and a droop in the left eyelid; flaxen hair, with a gold-yellow streak in it—all right, mother—fair white arms, with a down on them—little lady's hand, with a reddish look under the finger nails. The knife—always the cursed knife—first on one side, then on the other. Aha! you she-devil, where's the knife?"

At the last word his voice rose, and he grew restless on a sudden. I saw him shudder on the straw; his withered face became distorted, and he threw up both his hands with a quick hysterical gasp. They struck against the bottom of the manger under which he lay, and the blow awakened him. I had just time to slip through the door and close it before his eyes were fairly open, and his senses his own again.

"Do you know anything about that man's past life?" I said to the landlord.

"Yes, sir, I know pretty well all about it," was the answer, "and an uncommon queer story it is. Most people don't believe it. It's true, though, for all that. Why, just look at him," continued the landlord, opening the stable door again. "Poor devil! he's so worn out with his restless nights that he's dropped back into his sleep already."

"Don't wake him," I said; "I'm in no hurry for the gig. Wait till the other man comes back from his errand; and, in the mean time, suppose I have some lunch and a bottle of sherry, and suppose you come and help me to get through it?"

The heart of mine host, as I had anticipated, warmed to me over his own wine. He soon became communicative on the subject of the man asleep in the stable, and by little and little I drew the whole story out of him. Extravagant and incredible as the events must appear to every body, they are related here just as I heard them and just as they happened.

CHAPTER II

SOME YEARS AGO THERE LIVED IN THE SUBURBS OF A LARGE SEA-PORT TOWN ON the west coast of England a man in humble circumstances, by name Isaac Scatchard. His means of subsistence were derived from any employment that he could get as an ostler, and occasionally, when times went well with him, from temporary engagements in service as stable-helper in private houses. Though a faithful, steady, and honest man, he got on badly in his calling. His ill luck was proverbial among his neighbors. He was always missing good opportunities by no fault of his own, and always living longest in service with amiable people who were not punctual payers of wages. "Unlucky Isaac" was his nickname in his own neighborhood, and no one could say that he did not richly deserve it.

With far more than one man's fair share of adversity to endure, Isaac had but one consolation to support him, and that was of the dreariest and most negative kind. He had no wife and children to increase his anxieties and add to the bitterness of his various failures in life. It might have been from mere insensibility, or it might have been from generous unwillingness to involve another in his own unlucky destiny; but the fact undoubtedly was, that he had arrived at the middle term of life without marrying, and, what is much more remarkable, without once exposing himself, from eighteen to eight-and-thirty, to the genial imputation of ever having had a sweetheart.

When he was out of service he lived alone with his widowed mother. Mrs. Scatchard was a woman above the average in her lowly station as to capacity and manners. She had seen better days, as the phrase is, but she never referred to them in the presence of curious visitors; and, though perfectly polite to every one who approached her, never cultivated any intimacies among her neighbors. She contrived to provide, hardly enough, for her simple wants by doing rough work for the tailors, and always managed to keep a decent home for her son to return to whenever his ill luck drove him out helpless into the world.

One bleak autumn, when Isaac was getting on fast toward forty, and when he was, as usual, out of place through no fault of his own, he set forth from his mother's cottage on a long walk inland to a gentleman's seat where he had heard that a stable-helper was required.

It wanted then but two days of his birthday; and Mrs. Scatchard, with her usual fondness, made him promise, before he started, that he would be back in time to keep that anniversary with her, in as festive a way as their poor means would allow. It was easy for him to comply with this request, even supposing he slept a night each way on the road.

He was to start from home on Monday morning, and, whether he got the new place or not, he was to be back for his birthday dinner on Wednesday at two o'clock.

Arriving at his destination too late on the Monday night to make application for the stable-helper's place, he slept at the village inn, and in good time on the Tuesday morning presented himself at the gentleman's house to fill the vacant situation. Here again his ill luck pursued him as inexorably as ever. The excellent written testimonials to his character which he was able to produce availed him nothing; his long walk had been taken in vain: only the day before the stable-helper's place had been given to another man.

Isaac accepted this new disappointment resignedly and as a matter of course. Naturally slow in capacity, he had the bluntness of sensibility and phlegmatic patience of disposition which frequently distinguish men with sluggishly-working mental powers. He thanked the gentleman's steward with his usual quiet civility for granting him an interview, and took his departure with no appearance of unusual depression in his face or manner.

Before starting on his homeward walk, he made some inquiries at the inn, and ascertained that he might save a few miles on his return by following a new road.

Furnished with full instructions, several times repeated, as to the various turnings he was to take, he set forth on his homeward journey, and walked on all day with only one stoppage for bread and cheese. Just as it was getting toward dark, the rain came on and the wind began to rise, and he found himself, to make matters worse, in a part of the country with which he was entirely unacquainted, though he knew himself to be some fifteen miles from home. The first house he found to inquire at was a lonely roadside inn, standing on the outskirts of a thick wood. Solitary as the place looked, it was welcome to a lost man who was also hungry, thirsty, footsore, and wet. The landlord was civil and respectable-looking, and the price he asked for a bed was reasonable enough. Isaac therefore decided on stopping comfortably at the inn for that night.

He was constitutionally a temperate man. His supper consisted of two rashers of bacon, a slice of home-made bread, and a pint of ale. He did not go to bed immediately after this moderate meal, but sat up with the landlord, talking about his bad prospects and his long run of ill luck, and diverging from these topics to the subjects of horse-flesh and racing. Nothing was said either by himself, his host, or the few laborers who strayed into the tap-room, which could, in the slightest degree, excite the very small and very dull imaginative faculty which Isaac Scatchard possessed.

At a little after eleven the house was closed. Isaac went round with the land-lord and held the candle while the doors and lower windows were being secured. He noticed with surprise the strength of the bolts and bars, and iron-sheathed shutters.

"You see, we are rather lonely here," said the landlord. "We never have had any attempts made to break in yet, but it's always as well to be on the safe side. When nobody is sleeping here, I am the only man in the house. My wife and daughter are timid, and the servant-girl takes after her missuses. Another glass of ale before you turn in? No! Well, how such a sober man as you comes to be out of place is more than I can make out, for one. Here's where you're to sleep. You're our only lodger to-night, and I think you'll say my missus has done her best to make you comfortable. You're quite sure you won't have another glass of ale? Very well. Good-night."

It was half past eleven by the clock in the passage as they went up stairs to the bedroom, the window of which looked on to the wood at the back of the house.

Isaac locked the door, set his candle on the chest of drawers, and wearily got ready for bed. The bleak autumn wind was still blowing, and the solemn, monotonous, surging moan of it in the wood was dreary and awful to hear through the night-silence. Isaac felt strangely wakeful. He resolved, as he lay down in bed, to keep the candle alight until he began to grow sleepy, for there was something unendurably depressing in the bare idea of lying awake in the darkness, listening to the dismal, ceaseless moaning of the wind in the wood.

Sleep stole on him before he was aware of it. His eyes closed, and he fell off insensibly to rest without having so much as thought of extinguishing the candle.

The first sensation of which he was conscious after sinking into slumber was a strange shivering that ran through him suddenly from head to foot, and a dreadful sinking pain at the heart, such as he had never felt before. The shivering only disturbed his slumbers; the pain woke him instantly. In one moment he passed from a state of sleep to a state of wakefulness—his eyes wide open—his mental perceptions cleared on a sudden, as if by a miracle.

The candle had burnt down nearly to the last morsel of tallow, but the top of the unsnuffed wick had just fallen off, and the light in the little room was, for the moment, fair and full.

Between the foot of his bed and the closed door there stood a woman with a knife in her hand, looking at him.

He was stricken speechless with terror, but he did not lose the preternatural clearness of his faculties, and he never took his eyes off the woman. She said not a word as they stared each other in the face, but she began to move slowly toward the left-hand side of the bed.

His eyes followed her. She was a fair, fine woman, with yellowish flaxen hair and light gray eyes, with a droop in the left eyelid. He noticed those things and fixed them on his mind before she was round at the side of the bed. Speechless, with no expression in her face, with no noise following her footfall, she came closer and closer—stopped—and slowly raised the knife. He laid his right arm over his throat to save it; but, as he saw the knife coming down, threw his hand across the bed to the right side, and jerked his body over that way just as the knife descended on the mattress within an inch of his shoulder.

His eyes fixed on her arm and hand as she slowly drew her knife out of the bed: a white, well-shaped arm, with a pretty down lying lightly over the fair skin—a delicate lady's hand, with the crowning beauty of a pink flush under and round the finger nails.

She drew the knife out, and passed back again slowly to the foot of the bed; stopped there for a moment looking at him; then came on—still speechless, still with no expression on the blank, beautiful face, still with no sound following the stealthy footfalls—came on to the right side of the bed, where he now lay.

As she approached she raised the knife again, and he drew himself away to the left side. She struck, as before, right into the mattress, with a deliberate, perpendicularly-downward action of the arm. This time his eyes wandered from her to the knife. It was like the large clasp-knives which he had often seen laboring men use to cut their bread and bacon with. Her delicate little fingers did not conceal more than two thirds of the handle: he noticed that it was made of buck-horn, clean and shining as the blade was, and looking like new.

For the second time she drew the knife out, concealed it in the wide sleeve of her gown, then stopped by the bedside, watching him. For an instant he saw her standing in that position, then the wick of the spent candle fell over into the socket; the flame diminished to a little blue point, and the room grew dark.

A moment, or less, if possible, passed so, and then the wick flamed up, smokingly, for the last time. His eyes were still looking eagerly over the right-hand side of the bed when the final flash of light came, but they discerned nothing. The fair woman with the knife was gone.

The conviction that he was alone again weakened the hold of the terror that had struck him dumb up to this time. The preternatural sharpness which the very intensity of his panic had mysteriously imparted to his faculties left them suddenly. His brain grew confused—his heart beat wildly—his ears opened for the first time since the appearance of the woman to a sense of the woeful ceaseless moaning of the wind among the trees. With the dreadful conviction of the reality of what he had seen still strong within him, he leaped out of bed, and screaming "Murder! Wake up, there! wake up!" dashed headlong through the darkness to the door.

It was fast locked, exactly as he had left it on going to bed.

His cries on starting up had alarmed the house. He heard the terrified, confused exclamations of women; he saw the master of the house approaching along the passage with his burning rush-candle in one hand and his gun in the other.

"What is it?" asked the landlord, breathlessly.

Isaac could only answer in a whisper. "A woman, with a knife in her hand," he gasped out. "In my room—a fair, yellow-haired woman; she jobbed at me with the knife twice over."

The landlord's pale cheeks grew paler. He looked at Isaac eagerly by the flickering light of his candle, and his face began to get red again; his voice altered, too, as well as his complexion.

"She seems to have missed you twice," he said.

"I dodged the knife as it came down," Isaac went on, in the same scared whisper. "It struck the bed each time."

The landlord took his candle into the bedroom immediately. In less than a minute he came out again into the passage in a violent passion.

"The devil fly away with you and your woman with the knife! There isn't a mark in the bedclothes any where. What do you mean by coming into a man's place, and frightening his family out of their wits about a dream?"

"I'll leave your house," said Isaac, faintly. "Better out on the road, in rain and dark, on my road home, than back again in that room, after what I've seen in it. Lend me a light to get my clothes by, and tell me what I'm to pay."

"Pay!" cried the landlord, leading the way with his light sulkily into the bedroom. "You'll find your score on the slate when you go down stairs. I wouldn't have taken you in for all the money you've got about you if I'd known your dreaming, screeching ways beforehand. Look at the bed. Where's the cut of a knife in it? Look at the window—is the lock bursted? Look at the door (which I heard you fasten yourself)—is it broke in? A murdering woman with a knife in my house! You ought to be ashamed of yourself!"

Isaac answered not a word. He huddled on his clothes, and then they went down stairs together.

"Nigh on twenty minutes past two!" said the landlord, as they passed the clock. "A nice time in the morning to frighten honest people out of their wits!"

Isaac paid his bill, and the landlord let him out at the front door, asking, with a grin of contempt, as he undid the strong fastenings, whether "the murdering woman got in that way."

They parted without a word on either side. The rain had ceased, but the night was dark, and the wind bleaker than ever. Little did the darkness, or the cold, or the uncertainty about the way home matter to Isaac. If he had been turned out into a wilderness in a thunder-storm, it would have been a relief after what he had suffered in the bedroom of the inn.

What was the fair woman with the knife? The creature of a dream, or that other creature from the unknown world called among men by the name of ghost? He could make nothing of the mystery—had made nothing of it, even when it was midday on Wednesday, and when he stood, at last, after many times missing his road, once more on the doorstep of home.

CHAPTER III

HIS MOTHER CAME OUT EAGERLY TO RECEIVE HIM. HIS FACE TOLD HER IN A MOMENT that something was wrong.

"I've lost the place; but that's my luck. I dreamed an ill dream last night, mother— or maybe I saw a ghost. Take it either way, it scared me out of my senses, and I'm not my own man again yet."

"Isaac, your face frightens me. Come in to the fire—come in, and tell mother all about it."

He was as anxious to tell as she was to hear; for it had been his hope, all the way home, that his mother, with her quicker capacity and superior knowledge, might be able to throw some light on the mystery which he could not clear up for himself. His memory of the dream was still mechanically vivid, though his thoughts were entirely confused by it.

His mother's face grew paler and paler as he went on. She never interrupted him by so much as a single word; but when he had done, she moved her chair close to his, put her arm round his neck, and said to him,

"Isaac, you dreamed your ill dream on this Wednesday morning. What time was it when you saw the fair woman with the knife in her hand?"

Isaac reflected on what the landlord had said when they had passed by the clock on his leaving the inn; allowed as nearly as he could for the time that must have elapsed between the unlocking of his bedroom door and the paying of his bill just before going away, and answered,

"Somewhere about two o'clock in the morning."

His mother suddenly quitted her hold of his neck, and struck her hands together with a gesture of despair.

"This Wednesday is your birthday, Isaac, and two o'clock in the morning was the time when you were born."

Isaac's capacities were not quick enough to catch the infection of his mother's superstitious dread. He was amazed, and a little startled also, when she suddenly rose from her chair, opened her old writing-desk, took pen, ink, and paper, and then said to him.

"Your memory is but a poor one, Isaac, and, now I'm an old woman, mine's not much better. I want all about this dream of yours to be as well known to both of us, years hence, as it is now. Tell me over again all you told me a minute ago, when you spoke of what the woman with the knife looked like."

Isaac obeyed, and marveled much as he saw his mother carefully set down on paper the very words that he was saying.

"Light gray eyes," she wrote, as they came to the descriptive part, "with a droop in the left eyelid; flaxen hair, with a gold-yellow streak in it; white arms, with a down upon them; little lady's hand, with a reddish look about the finger nails; clasp-knife with a buck-horn handle, that seemed as good as new." To these particulars Mrs. Scatchard added the year, month, day of the week, and time in the morning when the woman of the dream appeared to her son. She then locked up the paper carefully in her writing-desk.

Neither on that day nor on any day after could her son induce her to return to the matter of the dream. She obstinately kept her thoughts about it to herself, and even refused to refer again to the paper in her writing-desk. Ere long Isaac grew weary of attempting to make her break her resolute silence; and time, which sooner or later wears out all things, gradually wore out the impression produced on him by the dream. He began by thinking of it carelessly, and he ended by not thinking of it at all.

The result was the more easily brought about by the advent of some important changes for the better in his prospects which commenced not long after his terrible night's experience at the inn. He reaped at last the reward of his long and patient suffering under adversity by getting an excellent place, keeping it for seven years, and leaving it, on the death of his master, not only with an excellent character, but also with a comfortable annuity bequeathed to him as a reward for saving his mistress's life in a carriage accident. Thus it happened that Isaac Scatchard returned to his old mother, seven years after the time of the dream at the inn, with an annual sum of money at his disposal sufficient to keep them both in ease and independence for the rest of their lives.

The mother, whose health had been bad of late years, profited so much by the care bestowed on her and by freedom from money anxieties, that when Isaac's birthday came round she was able to sit up comfortably at table and dine with him.

On that day, as the evening drew on, Mrs. Scatchard discovered that a bottle of tonic medicine which she was accustomed to take, and in which she had fancied that a dose or more was still left, happened to be empty. Isaac immediately volunteered to go to the chemist's and get it filled again. It was as rainy and bleak an autumn night as on the memorable past occasion when he lost his way and slept at the road-side inn.

On going into the chemist's shop he was passed hurriedly by a poorly-dressed woman coming out of it. The glimpse he had of her face struck him, and he looked back after her as she descended the door-steps.

"You're noticing that woman?" said the chemist's apprentice behind the counter. "It's my opinion there's something wrong with her. She's been asking for laudanum to put to a bad tooth. Master's out for half an hour, and I told her I wasn't allowed to sell poison to strangers in his absence. She laughed in a queer way, and said she would come back in half an hour. If she expects master to serve her, I think she'll be disappointed. It's a case of suicide, sir, if ever there was one yet."

These words added immeasurably to the sudden interest in the woman which Isaac had felt at the first sight of her face. After he had got the medicine-bottle filled, he looked about anxiously for her as soon as he was out in the street. She was walking slowly up and down on the opposite side of the road. With his heart, very much to his own surprise, beating fast, Isaac crossed over and spoke to her.

He asked if she was in any distress. She pointed to her torn shawl, her scanty dress, her crushed, dirty bonnet; then moved under a lamp so as to let the light fall on her stern, pale, but still most beautiful face.

"I look like a comfortable, happy woman, don't I?" she said, with a bitter laugh.

She spoke with a purity of intonation which Isaac had never heard before from other than ladies' lips. Her slightest actions seemed to have the easy, negligent grace of a thorough-bred woman. Her skin, for all its poverty-stricken paleness, was as delicate as if her life had been passed in the enjoyment of every social comfort that wealth can purchase. Even her small, finely-shaped hands, gloveless as they were, had not lost their whiteness.

Little by little, in answer to his questions, the sad story of the woman came out. There is no need to relate it here; it is told over and over again in police reports and paragraphs about attempted suicides.

"My name is Rebecca Murdoch," said the woman, as she ended. "I have ninepence left, and I thought of spending it at the chemist's over the way in securing a passage to the other world. Whatever it is, it can't be worse to me than this, so why should I stop here?"

Besides the natural compassion and sadness moved in his heart by what he heard, Isaac felt within him some mysterious influence at work all the time the woman was speaking which utterly confused his ideas and almost deprived him of his powers of speech. All that he could say in answer to her last reckless words was that he would prevent her from attempting her own life, if he followed her about all night to do it. His rough, trembling earnestness seemed to impress her.

"I won't occasion you that trouble," she answered, when he repeated his threat. "You have given me a fancy for living by speaking kindly to me. No need for the mockery of protestations and promises. You may believe me without them. Come to Fuller's Meadow tomorrow at twelve, and you will find me alive, to answer for myself—No!— no money. My ninepence will do to get me as good a night's lodging as I want."

She nodded and left him. He made no attempt to follow—he felt no suspicion that she was deceiving him.

"It's strange, but I can't help believing her," he said to himself, and walked away, bewildered, toward home.

On entering the house, his mind was still so completely absorbed by its new subject of interest that he took no notice of what his mother was doing when he came in with the bottle of medicine. She had opened her old writing-desk in his absence, and was now reading a paper attentively that lay inside it. On every birthday of Isaac's since she had written down the particulars of his dream from his own lips, she had been accustomed to read that same paper, and ponder over it in private.

The next day he went to Fuller's Meadow.

He had done only right in believing her so implicitly. She was there, punctual to a minute, to answer for herself. The last-left faint defenses in Isaac's heart against the fascination which a word or look from her began inscrutably to exercise over him sank down and vanished before her forever on that memorable morning.

When a man previously insensible to the influence of women forms an attachment in middle life, the instances are rare indeed, let the warning circumstances be what they may, in which he is found capable of freeing himself from the tyranny of the new ruling passion. The charm of being spoken to familiarly, fondly, and gratefully by a woman whose language and manners still retained enough of their early refinement to hint at the high social station that she had lost, would have been a dangerous luxury to a man of Isaac's rank at the age of twenty. But it was far more than that—it was certain ruin to him—now that his heart was opening unworthily to a new influence at that middle time of life when strong feelings of all kinds, once implanted, strike root most stubbornly in a man's moral nature. A few more stolen interviews after that first morning in Fuller's Meadow completed his infatuation. In less than a month from the time when he first met her, Isaac Scatchard had consented to give Rebecca Murdoch a new interest in existence, and a chance of recovering the character she had lost by promising to make her his wife.

She had taken possession, not of his passions only, but of his faculties as well. All the mind he had he put into her keeping. She directed him on every point—even instructing him how to break the news of his approaching marriage in the safest manner to his mother.

"If you tell her how you met me and who I am at first," said the cunning woman, "she will move heaven and earth to prevent our marriage. Say I am the sister of one of your fellow-servants—ask her to see me before you go into any more particulars—and leave it to me to do the rest. I mean to make her love me next best to you, Isaac, before she knows any thing of who I really am."

The motive of the deceit was sufficient to sanctify it to Isaac. The stratagem proposed relieved him of his one great anxiety, and quieted his uneasy conscience on the subject of his mother. Still, there was something wanting to perfect his happiness, something that he could not realize, something mysteriously untraceable, and yet something that perpetually made itself felt; not when he was absent from Rebecca Murdoch, but, strange to say, when he was actually in her presence! She was kindness itself with him. She never made him feel his inferior capacities and inferior manners. She showed the sweetest anxiety to please him in the smallest trifles; but, in spite of all these attractions, he never could feel quite at his ease with her. At their first meeting, there had mingled with his admiration, when he looked in her face, a faint, involuntary feeling of doubt whether that face was entirely strange to him. No after familiarity had the slightest effect on this inexplicable, wearisome uncertainty.

Concealing the truth as he had been directed, he announced his marriage engagement precipitately and confusedly to his mother on the day when he contracted it. Poor Mrs. Scatchard showed her perfect confidence in her son by flinging her arms round his neck, and giving him joy of having found at last, in the sister of one of his fellow-servants, a woman to comfort and care for him after his mother was gone. She was all eagerness to see the woman of her son's choice, and the next day was fixed for the introduction.

It was a bright sunny morning, and the little cottage parlor was full of light as Mrs. Scatchard, happy and expectant, dressed for the occasion in her Sunday gown, sat waiting for her son and her future daughter-in-law.

Punctual to the appointed time, Isaac hurriedly and nervously led his promised wife into the room. His mother rose to receive her—advanced a few steps, smiling—looked Rebecca full in the eyes, and suddenly stopped. Her face, which had been flushed the moment before, turned white in an instant; her eyes lost their expression of softness and kindness, and assumed a blank look of terror; her outstretched hands fell to her sides, and she staggered back a few steps with a low cry to her son.

"Isaac," she whispered, clutching him fast by the arm when he asked alarmedly if she was taken ill, "Isaac, does that woman's face remind you of nothing?"

Before he could answer—before he could look round to where Rebecca stood, astonished and angered by her reception, at the lower end of the room, his mother pointed impatiently to her writing-desk, and gave him the key.

"Open it," she said, in a quick, breathless whisper.

"What does this mean? Why am I treated as if I had no business here? Does your mother want to insult me?" asked Rebecca, angrily.

"Open it, and give me the paper in the left-hand drawer. Quick! quick, for Heaven's sake!" said Mrs. Scatchard, shrinking farther back in terror.

Isaac gave her the paper. She looked it over eagerly for a moment, then followed Rebecca, who was now turning away haughtily to leave the room, and caught her by the shoulder—abruptly raised the long, loose sleeve of her gown, and glanced at her hand and arm. Something like fear began to steal over the angry expression of Rebecca's face as she shook herself free from the old woman's grasp. "Mad!" she said to herself; "and Isaac never told me." With these few words she left the room.

Isaac was hastening after her when his mother turned and stopped his farther progress. It wrung his heart to see the misery and terror in her face as she looked at him.

"Light gray eyes," she said, in low, mournful, awestruck tones, pointing toward the open door; "a droop in the left eyelid; flaxen hair, with a gold-yellow streak in it; white arms, with a down upon them; little lady's hand, with a reddish look under the finger nails—*The Dream-Woman*, Isaac, the Dream-Woman!"

That faint cleaving doubt which he had never been able to shake off in Rebecca Murdoch's presence was fatally set at rest forever. He *had* seen her face, then, before— seven years before, on his birthday, in the bedroom of the lonely inn.

"Be warned! oh, my son, be warned! Isaac, Isaac, let her go, and do you stop with me!"

Something darkened the parlor window as those words were said. A sudden chill ran through him, and he glanced sidelong at the shadow. Rebecca Murdoch had come back. She was peering in curiously at them over the low window-blind.

"I have promised to marry, mother," he said, "and marry I must."

The tears came into his eyes as he spoke and dimmed his sight, but he could just discern the fatal face outside moving away again from the window.

His mother's head sank lower.

"Are you faint?" he whispered.

"Broken-hearted, Isaac."

He stooped down and kissed her. The shadow, as he did so, returned to the window, and the fatal face peered in curiously once more.

CHAPTER IV

THREE WEEKS AFTER THAT DAY ISAAC AND REBECCA WERE MAN AND WIFE. ALL THAT was hopelessly dogged and stubborn in the man's moral nature seemed to have closed round his fatal passion, and to have fixed it unassailably in his heart.

After that first interview in the cottage parlor no consideration would induce Mrs. Scatchard to see her son's wife again, or even to talk of her when Isaac tried hard to plead her cause after their marriage.

This course of conduct was not in any degree occasioned by a discovery of the degradation in which Rebecca had lived. There was no question of that between mother and son. There was no question of any thing but the fearfully-exact resemblance between the living, breathing woman, and the spectre-woman of Isaac's dream.

Rebecca, on her side, neither felt nor expressed the slightest sorrow at the estrangement between herself and her mother-in-law. Isaac, for the sake of peace, had never contradicted her first idea that age and long illness had affected Mrs. Scatchard's mind. He even allowed his wife to upbraid him for not having confessed this to her at the time of their marriage engagement, rather than risk any thing by hinting at the truth. The sacrifice of his integrity before his one all-mastering delusion seemed but a small thing, and cost his conscience but little after the sacrifices he had already made.

The time of waking from this delusion—the cruel and the rueful time—was not far off. After some quiet months of married life, as the summer was ending, and the year was getting on toward the month of his birthday, Isaac found his wife altering toward him. She grew sullen and contemptuous; she formed acquaintances of the most dangerous kind in defiance of his objections, his entreaties, and his commands; and, worst of all, she learned, ere long, after every fresh difference with her husband, to seek the deadly self-oblivion of drink. Little by little, after the first miserable discovery that his wife was keeping company with drunkards, the shocking certainty forced itself on Isaac that she had grown to be a drunkard herself.

He had been in a sadly desponding state for some time before the occurrence of these domestic calamities. His mother's health, as he could but too plainly discern every time he went to see her at the cottage, was failing fast, and he upbraided himself in secret as the cause of the bodily and mental suffering she endured. When to his remorse on his mother's account was added the shame and misery occasioned by the discovery of his wife's degradation, he sank under the double trial—his face began to alter fast, and he looked what he was, a spirit-broken man.

His mother, still struggling bravely against the illness that was hurrying her to the grave, was the first to notice the sad alteration in him, and the first to hear of his last worst trouble with his wife. She could only weep bitterly on the day when he made his humiliating confession, but on the next occasion when he went to see her she had taken a resolution in reference to his domestic afflictions which astonished and even alarmed him. He found her dressed to go out, and on asking the reason received this answer:

"I am not long for this world, Isaac," she said, "and I shall not feel easy on my death-bed unless I have done my best to the last to make my son happy. I mean to put my own fears and my own feelings out of the question, and to go with you to your wife, and try what I can do to reclaim her. Give me your arm, Isaac, and let me do the last thing I can in this world to help my son before it is too late."

He could not disobey her, and they walked together slowly toward his miserable home.

It was only one o'clock in the afternoon when they reached the cottage where he lived. It was their dinner-hour, and Rebecca was in the kitchen. He was thus able to take his mother quietly into the parlor, and then prepare his wife for the interview. She had fortunately drunk but little at that early hour, and she was less sullen and capricious than usual.

He returned to his mother with his mind tolerably at ease. His wife soon followed him into the parlor, and the meeting between her and Mrs. Scatchard passed off better than he had ventured to anticipate, though he observed with secret apprehension that his mother, resolutely as she controlled herself in other respects, could not look his wife in the face when she spoke to her. It was a relief to him, therefore, when Rebecca began to lay the cloth.

She laid the cloth, brought in the bread-tray, and cut a slice from the loaf for her husband, then returned to the kitchen. At that moment, Isaac, still anxiously watching his mother, was startled by seeing the same ghastly change pass over her face which had altered it so awfully on the morning when Rebecca and she first met. Before he could say a word, she whispered, with a look of horror,

"Take me back—home, home again, Isaac. Come with me, and never go back again."

He was afraid to ask for an explanation; he could only sign to her to be silent, and help her quickly to the door. As they passed the bread-tray on the table she stopped and pointed to it.

"Did you see what your wife cut your bread with?" she asked, in a low whisper.

"No, mother—I was not noticing—what was it?"

"Look!"

He did look. A new clasp-knife, with a buck-horn handle, lay with the loaf in the bread-tray. He stretched out his hand shudderingly to possess himself of it; but, at the same time, there was a noise in the kitchen, and his mother caught at his arm.

"The knife of the dream! Isaac, I'm faint with fear. Take me away before she comes back."

He was hardly able to support her. The visible, tangible reality of the knife struck him with a panic, and utterly destroyed any faint doubts that he might have entertained up to this time in relation to the mysterious dream-warning of nearly eight years before. By a last desperate effort, he summoned self-possession enough to help his mother out of the house—so quietly that the "Dream-woman" (he thought of her by that name now) did not hear them departing from the kitchen.

"Don't go back, Isaac—don't go back!" implored Mrs. Scatchard, as he turned to go away, after seeing her safely seated again in her own room.

"I must get the knife," he answered, under his breath. His mother tried to stop him again, but he hurried out without another word.

On his return he found that his wife had discovered their secret departure from the house. She had been drinking, and was in a fury of passion. The dinner in the kitchen was flung under the grate; the cloth was off the parlor table. Where was the knife?

Unwisely, he asked for it. She was only too glad of the opportunity of irritating him which the request afforded her. "He wanted the knife, did he? Could he give her a reason why? No! Then he should not have it—not if he went down on his knees to ask for it." Farther recriminations elicited the fact that she had bought it a bargain, and that she considered it her own especial property. Isaac saw the uselessness of attempting to get the knife by fair means, and determined to search for it, later in the day, in secret.

The search was unsuccessful. Night came on, and he left the house to walk about the streets. He was afraid now to sleep in the same room with her.

Three weeks passed. Still sullenly enraged with him, she would not give up the knife; and still that fear of sleeping in the same room with her possessed him. He walked about at night, or dozed in the parlor, or sat watching by his mother's bedside. Before the expiration of the first week in the new month his mother died. It wanted then but ten days of her son's birthday. She had longed to live till that anniversary. Isaac was present at her death, and her last words in this world were addressed to him:

"Don't go back, my son, don't go back!"

He was obliged to go back, if it were only to watch his wife. Exasperated to the last degree by his distrust of her, she had revengefully sought to add a sting to his grief, during the last days of his mother's illness, by declaring that she would assert her right to attend the funeral. In spite of all that he could do or say, she held with wicked pertinacity to her word, and on the day appointed for the burial forced herself—inflamed and shameless with drink—into her husband's presence, and declared that she would walk in the funeral procession to his mother's grave.

This last worst outrage, accompanied by all that was most insulting in word and look, maddened him for the moment. He struck her.

The instant the blow was dealt he repented it. She crouched down, silent, in a corner of the room, and eyed him steadily; it was a look that cooled his hot blood and made him tremble. But there was no time now to think of a means of making atonement. Nothing remained but to risk the worst till the funeral was over. There was but one way of making sure of her. He locked her into her bedroom.

When he came back some hours after, he found her sitting, very much altered in look and bearing, by the bedside, with a bundle on her lap. She rose, and faced him quietly, and spoke with a strange stillness in her voice, a strange repose in her eyes, a strange composure in her manner.

"No man has ever struck me twice," she said, "and my husband shall have no second opportunity. Set the door open and let me go. From this day forth we see each other no more."

Before he could answer she passed him and left the room. He saw her walk away up the street.

Would she return?

All that night he watched and waited, but no footstep came near the house. The next night, overpowered by fatigue, he lay down in bed in his clothes, with the door locked, the key on the table, and the candle burning. His slumber was not disturbed. The third night, the fourth, the fifth, the sixth passed, and nothing happened. He lay down on the seventh, still in his clothes, still with the door locked, the key on the table, and the candle burning, but easier in his mind.

Easier in his mind, and in perfect health of body when he fell off to sleep. But his rest was disturbed. He woke twice without any sensation of uneasiness. But the third time it was that never-to-be-forgotten shivering of the night at the lonely inn, that dreadful sinking pain at the heart, which once more aroused him in an instant.

His eyes opened toward the left-hand side of the bed, and there stood—

The Dream-Woman again? No! His wife; the living reality, with the dream-spectre's face, in the dream-spectre's attitude; the fair arm up, the knife clasped in the delicate white hand.

He sprang upon her almost at the instant of seeing her, and yet not quickly enough to prevent her from hiding the knife. Without a word from him—without a cry from her—he pinioned her in a chair. With one hand he felt up her sleeve, and there, where the Dream-Woman had hidden the knife, his wife had hidden it—the knife with the buck-horn handle, that looked like new.

In the despair of that fearful moment his brain was steady, his heart was calm. He looked at her fixedly with the knife in his hand, and said these last words:

"You told me we should see each other no more, and you have come back. It is my turn now to go, and to go forever. I say that we shall see each other no more, and *my* word shall not be broken."

He left her, and set forth into the night. There was a bleak wind abroad, and the smell of recent rain was in the air. The distant church-clocks chimed the quarter as he walked rapidly beyond the last houses in the suburb. He asked the first policeman he met what hour that was of which the quarter past had just struck.

The man referred sleepily to his watch, and answered, "Two o'clock." Two in the morning. What day of the month was this day that had just begun? He reckoned it up from the date of his mother's funeral. The fatal parallel was complete: it was his birthday!

Had he escaped the mortal peril which his dream foretold? or had he only received a second warning?

As that ominous doubt forced itself on his mind, he stopped, reflected, and turned back again toward the city. He was still resolute to hold to his word, and never to let her see him more; but there was a thought now in his mind of having her watched and followed. The knife was in his possession; the world was before him; but a new distrust of her—a vague, unspeakable, superstitious dread had overcome him.

"I must know where she goes, now she thinks I have left her," he said to himself, as he stole back wearily to the precincts of his house.

It was still dark. He had left the candle burning in the bedchamber; but when he looked up to the window of the room now, there was no light in it. He crept cautiously to the house door. On going away, he remembered to have closed it; on trying it now, he found it open.

He waited outside, never losing sight of the house, till daylight. Then he ventured in-doors—listened, and heard nothing—looked into kitchen, scullery, parlor, and found nothing; went up, at last, into the bedroom—it was empty. A picklock lay on the floor, betraying how she had gained entrance in the night, and that was the only trace of her.

Whither had she gone? That no mortal tongue could tell him. The darkness had covered her flight; and when the day broke, no man could say where the light found her.

Before leaving the house and the town forever, he gave instructions to a friend and neighbor to sell his furniture for any thing that it would fetch, and apply the proceeds to employing the police to trace her. The directions were honestly followed, and the money was all spent, but the inquiries led to nothing. The picklock on the bedroom floor remained the one last useless trace of the Dream-Woman.

At this point of the narrative the landlord paused, and, turning toward the window of the room in which we were sitting, looked in the direction of the stable-yard.

"So far," he said, "I tell you what was told to me. The little that remains to be added lies within my own experience. Between two and three months after the events I have just been relating, Isaac Scatchard came to me, withered and old-looking before his time, just as you saw him to-day. He had his testimonials to character with him, and he asked for employment here. Knowing that my wife and he were distantly related, I gave him a trial in consideration of that relationship, and liked him in spite of his queer habits. He is as sober, honest, and willing a man as there is in England. As for his restlessness at night, and his sleeping away his leisure time in the day, who can wonder at it after hearing his story? Besides, he never objects to being roused up when he's wanted, so there's not much inconvenience to complain of, after all."

"I suppose he is afraid of a return of that dreadful dream, and of waking out of it in the dark ?" said I.

"No," returned the landlord. "The dream comes back to him so often that he has got to bear with it by this time resignedly enough. It's his wife keeps him waking at night, as he has often told me."

"What! Has she never been heard of yet?"

"Never. Isaac himself has the one perpetual thought about her, that she is alive and looking for him. I believe he wouldn't let himself drop off to sleep toward two in the morning for a king's ransom. Two in the morning, he says, is the time she will find him, one of these days. Two in the morning is the time all the year round when he likes to be most certain that he has got that clasp-knife safe about him. He does not mind being alone as long as he is awake, except on the night before his birthday, when he firmly believes himself to be in peril of his life. The birthday has only come round once since he has been here, and then he sat up along with the night-porter. 'She's looking for me,' is all he says when any body speaks to him about the one anxiety of his life; 'she's looking for me.' He may be right. She *may* be looking for him. Who can tell?"

"Who can tell?" said I.

A Night in the Grave

OR, THE DEVIL'S RECEIPT

Anonymous

———————◆———————

YE MAUN HAVE HEARD OF SIR ROBERT REDGAUNTLET OF THAT ILK, WHO lived in these parts before the dear years. The country will lang mind him; and our fathers used to draw breath thick if ever they heard him named. He was out wi' the Hielandmen in Montrose's time; and again he was in the hills wi' Glencairn in the year saxteen hundred and fifty-twa; and sae when King Charles the Second came in, wha was in sic favour as the Laird of Redgauntlet? He was knighted at Lonon court, wi' the king's ain sword; and being a red-hot prelatist, he came down here, rampauging like a lion, with commissions of lieutenancy, and of lunacy for what I ken, to put down a' the Whigs and Covenanters in the country. Wild wark they made of it; for the Whigs were as dour as the Cavaliers were fierce, and it was which should first tire the other. Redgauntlet was aye for the strong hand; and his name is kenn'd as wide in the country as Claverhouse's or Tam Dalywell's. Glen, nor dargle, nor mountain, nor cave, could hide the puir hill-folk when Redgauntlet was out with bugle and bloodhound after them, as if they had been sae mony deer. And troth when 'they found them, they didna mak muckle mair ceremony than a Hieland man wi' a roe-buck— It was just, "Will ye tak the test?"—if not, "Make ready—present—fire!"—and there lay the recusant.

Far and wide was Sir Robert hated and feared. Men thought he had a direct compact with Satan—that he was proof against steel—and that bullets hopped off his buff-coat like hail-stones from a hearth—that he had a mear that would turn a hare on the side of Carrifragawns—and muckle to the same purpose, of whilk mair anon. The best lessing they wared on him was, "De'il scowp wi' Redgauntlet!" He wasn't a bad master to his ain folk though, and was weel aneugh liked by his tenants; and as for the lackies and troopers that raid out wi' him to the persecutions, as the Whigs ca'ad these killing times, they wad hae drunken themsels blind to his health at ony time.

Now ye are to ken that my gudesire lived on Redgauntlet's grund—they ca' the place Primrose-Knowe. We had lived on the grund, and under the Redgauntlets, since the riding days, and lang before. It was a pleasant bit; and I think the air is callerer and fresher there than onywhere else in the country. It's a' deserted now; and I sat on the broken door-cheek three days since, and was glad I couldna see the plight the place was in; but that's a wide o' the mark. There dwelt my gudesire, Steenie Steenson, a rambling, rattling chiel' he had been in his young days, and could play weel on the pipes; he was famous at "Hoopers and Girders"—a' Cumberland couldna touch him at "Jockie Lattin," and he had the finest finger for the back-lill between Berwick and Carlisle. The like o' Steenie wasna the sort that they made Whigs o'. And so he became a Tory, as they ca' it, which we now ca' Jacobites, just out of a kind of needcessity, that he might belang to some side or other. He had nae ill-will to the Whig bodies, and likedna to see the blude rin, though, being obliged to follow Sir Robert in hunting and hosting, watching and warding, he saw muckle mischief, and maybe did some, that he couldna avoid.

Now Steenie was a kind of favourite with his master, and kenn'd a' the folks about the castle, and was often sent for to play the pipes when they were at their merriment. Auld Dougal Mac Callum, the butler, that had followed Sir Robert through gude and ill, thick and thin, pool and stream, was specially fond of the pipes, and aye gae my gudesire his gude word wi' the Laird; for Dougal could turn his master round his finger.

Weel, round came the Revolution, and it like to have broken the hearts baith of Dougal and his master. But the change was not a'thegether sae great as they feared, and other folk thought for. The Whigs made an unca crawing what they wad do with their auld enemies, and in special wi' Sir Robert Redgauntlet. But there were ower mony great folks dipped in the same doings, to make a spick and span new warld. So Parliament passed it a' ower easy; and Sir Robert, bating that he was held to hunting foxes instead of Covenanters, remained just the man he was. His revel was as loud, and his hall as weel lighted, as ever it had been, though maybe he lacked the fines of the nonconformists, that used to come to stock larder and cellar; for it is certain he began to be keener about the rents than his tenants used to find him before, and it behoved them to be prompt to the rent-day, or else the laird wasna pleased. And he was sic an awsome body, that naebody cared to anger him; for the oaths he swore, and the rage that he used to get into, and the looks that he put on, made men sometimes think him a devil incarnate.

Weel, my gudesire was nae manager—no that he was a very great misguider—but he hadna the saving gift, and he got two terms rent in arrear. He got the first brash at Whitsunday put ower wi' fair words and piping; but when Martinmas came, there was a summons from the grand-officer to come wi' the rent on a day precese, or else Steenie behoved to flitt. Sair wark he had to get the siller; but he was weel-freended, and at last he got the whole scraped thegether—a thousand merks— the maist of it was from a neighbour they ca'ad Laurie Lapraik—a sly tod. Laurie had walth o' gear—could hunt wi' the hound and rin wi' the hare—and be Whig or Tory, saunt or sinner, as the wind stood. He was a professor of religious music in this Revolution warld, but he liked another sound and a tune on the pipes weel aneugh at a bye-time; and abune a', he thought he had gude security for the siller he lent my gudesire over the stocking at Primrose-Knowe.

Away trots my gudesire to Redgauntlet Castle wi' a heavy purse and a light heart, glad to be out of the Laird's danger. Weel, the first thing he learned at the castle was, that Sir Robert had fretted himself into a fit of the gout, because he did not appear before twelve o'clock. It wasna a'thegether for the sake of the money, Dougal thought; but because he didna like to part wi' my gudesire off the grund. Dougal was glad to see Steenie, and brought him into the great oak parlour, and there sat the Laird his lee-some lane, excepting that he had beside him a great, ill-favoured jack-an-ape, that was a special pet of his; a cankered beast it was, and many an ill-natured trick it played—ill to please it was, and easily angered—ran about the whole castle, chattering and yowl-ing, and pinching, and biting folk, especially before ill-weather, or disturbances in the state. Sir Robert ca'ad it Major Weir, after the warlock that was burned; and few folk liked either the name or the conditions of the creature—they thought there was something in it by ordinar—and my gudesire was not just easy in mind when the door shut on him, and he saw himself in the room wi' naebody but the Laird, Dougal Mac Callum, and the Major, a thing that hadna chanced to him before.

Sir Robert sat, or, I should say, lay, in a great armed chair, wi' his grand velvet gown, and his feet on a cradle; for he had baith gout and gravel, and his face looked as gash and ghastly as Satan's. Major Weir sat opposite to him, in a red laced coat, and the Laird's wig on his head; and aye as Sir Robert grinned wi' pain the jack-an-ape grinned too, like a sheep's-head between a pair of tongs—an ill-faur'd, fearsome couple they were. The Laird's buff-coat was hung on a pin behind him, and his broadsword and his pistols within reach; for he keepit up the old fashion of having the weapons ready, and a horse saddled day and night, just as he used to do when he was able to leap on horseback, and sway after any of the hill-folk he could get speerings of. Some said it was for fear of the Whigs taking vengeance, but I judge it was just his auld custom— he wasna gien to fear onything. The rental-book wi' its black cover and brass clasps, was lying beside him; and a book of sculduddry songs was put betwixt the leaves, to keep it open at the place where it bore evidence against the Goodman of Primrose-Knowe, as behind the hand with his mails and duties. Sir Robert gave my gudesire a look, as if he would have withered his heart in his bosom. Ye maun ken he had a way of bending his brows, that men saw the visible mark of a horse-shoe in his forehead, deep-dinted, as if it had been stamped there.

"Are ye come light-handed, ye son of a toom whistle?" said Sir Robert. "Zounds! if ye are—"

My gudesire, with as gude a countenance as he could put on, made a leg, and placed the bag of money on the table wi' a dash, like a man that does something clever. The Laird drew it to him hastily—"Is it all here, Steenie, man?"

"Your honour will find it right," said my gudesire.

"Here, Dougal," said the Laird, "gie Steenie a tass of brandy down stairs, till I count the siller and write the receipt."

But they werena weel out of the room, when Sir Robert gied a yelloch that shook the castle rock. Back ran Dougal—in flew the livery-men—yell on yell gied the Laird, ilk ane mair awfu' than the ither. My gudesire knew not whether to stand or flee, but he ventured back into the parlour, where a' was gaun hirdy-girdie—naebody to say "come in," or "gae out." Terribly the Laird roared for cauld water to his feet, and wine to cool his throat; and Hell, hell, hell, and its flames, was aye the word in his mouth. They brought him water, and when they plunged his swoln feet into the tub, he cried out it was burning; and folks say that it did bubble and sparkle like a seething cauldron. He flung the cup at Dougal's head, and said he had given him blood instead of burgundy ; and sure aneugh, the lass washed clottered blood off the carpet the next day. The jack-an-ape they ca'ad Major Weir, it jibbered and cried as if it was mocking its master; my gudesire's head was like to turn—he forgot baith siller and receipt, and down stairs he banged; but as he ran, the shrieks came faint and fainter; there was a deep-drawn shivering groan, and word gaed through the castle, that the Laird was dead.

Weel, away came my gudesire, wi' his finger in his mouth, and his best hope was, that Dougal had seen the money-bag, and heard the Laird speak of writing the receipt. The young Laird, now Sir John, came from Edinburgh, to see things put to rights. Sir

John and his father never gree'd weel—he had been bred an advocate, and afterwards sat in the last Scots Parliament and voted for the Union, having gotten, it was thought, a rug of the compensations—if his father could have come out of his grave, he would have brained him for it on his own hearth-stone. Some thought it was easier counting with the auld rough Knight than the fair-spoken young ane—but mair of that anon.

Dougal Mac Callum, poor body, neither great nor graned, but gaed about the house looking like a corpse, and directing, as was his duty, a' the order of the grand funeral. Now, Dougal looked aye waur and waur when night was coming, and was aye the last to gang to his bed, whilk was in a little round just opposite the chamber of dais, whilk his master occupied while he was living, and where he now lay ina state as they ca'ad it, well-a-day! The night before the funeral, Dougul could keep his awn counsel nae langer; he came doun with his proud spirit, and fairly asked auld Hatcheon to sit in his room with him for an hour. When they were in the round, Dougal took ae tass of brandy to himsel, and gave another to Hutcheon, and wished him all health and lang life, and said that, for himsel, he wasna lang for this world; for that, every night since Sir Robert's death, his silver call had sounded from the state chamber, just as it used to do at nights in his lifetime, to call Dougal to help to turn him in his bed. Dougal said, that being alone with the dead on that floor of the tower, (for nae body cared to wake Sir Robert Redgauntlet like another corpse,) he had never daured to answer the call, but that now his conscience checked him for neglecting his duty; for "though death breaks service," said Mac Callum, "it shall never break my service to Sir Robert; and I will answer his next whistle, so be you will stand by me, Hutcheon."

Hutcheon had nae will to the wark, but he had stood by Dougal in battle and broil, and he wad not fail him at this pinch; so down the carles sat over a stoup of brandy, and Hutcheon, who was something of a clerk, would have read a chapter of the Bible; but Dougal would hear naething but a song of Davie Lindsay, whilk was the waur preparation.

When midnight came, and the house was quiet as the grave, sure aneugh the silver whistle sounded as sharp and shrill as if Sir Robert was blowing it, and up got the two auld serving-men, and tottered into the room where the dead man lay. Hutcheon saw aneugh at the first glance; for there were torches in the room, which shewed him the foul fiend, in his ain shape, sitting on the Laird's coffin! Over he cowped as if he had been dead. He could not tell how lang he lay in a trance at the door, but when he gathered himself, he cried on his neighbour, and getting no answer, raised the house, when Dougal was found lying dead within two steps of the bed where his master's coffin was placed. As for the whistle, it was given anes and aye; but many a time was it heard on the top of the house in the bartizan, and amang the auld chimnies and turrets, where the howlets have their nests. Sir John hushed the matter up, and the funeral passed over without mair bogle-wark.

But when a' was over, and the Laird was beginning to settle his affairs, every tenant was called up for his arrears, and my gudesire for the full sum that appeared against him in the rental-book. Weel, away he trots to the Castle, to tell his story, and there he is introduced to Sir John, sitting in his father's chair, in deep mourning, with weepers and hanging cravat, and a small walking rapier by his side, instead of the auld broadsword that had a hundred-weight of steel about it, what with blade, chape, and basket-hilt. I have heard their communing so often tauld ower, that I almost think I was there myself, though I couldna be born at the time. However my grandfather in a half flattering, half conciliating tone, addressed the Laird, who, during the commencement of the conversation, often sighed deeply, and hypocritically lifted his napkin to his eyes. My grandfather had, while he spoke, his eye fixed on the rental-book, as if it were a mastiff-dog that he was afraid would spring up and bite him.

"I wuss ye joy, Sir, of the headseat, and the white loaf and the braid lairdship. Your father was a kind man to friends and followers; muckle grace to you, Sir John, to fill his shoon—his boots, I suld say, for he seldom wore shoon, unless it were muils when he had the gout.'

"Aye, Steenie," quoth the Laird, sighing deeply, and putting his napkin to his face, "his was a sudden call, and he will be missed in the country; no time to set his house in order—weel prepared God-ward, no doubt, which is the root of the matter—but left us behind a tangled hesp to wind, Steenie.—Hem! hem! We maun go to business, Steenie; much to do, and little time to do it in."

Here he opened the fatal volume; I have heard of a thing they call Doomsday-book—I am clear it has been a rental of back-ganging tenants.

"Stephen," said Sir John, still in the same soft, sleekit tone of voice—"Stephen Stevenson, or Steenson, ye are down here for a year's rent behind the hand—due at last term."

Stephen. "Please your honour. Sir John, I paid it to your father."

Sir John. "Ye took a receipt then, doubtless, Stephen; and can produce it?"

Stephen. "Indeed I hadna time, an it like your honour; for nae sooner had I set doun the siller, and just as his honour, Sir Robert, that's gaen, drew it to him to count it, and write out the receipt, he was ta'en wi' the pains that removed him."

"That was unlucky," said Sir John, after a pause. "But ye maybe paid it in the presence of somebody. I want but a talis qualis evidence, Stephen. I would go ower strictly to work with no poor man."

Stephen. "Troth, Sir John, there was naebody in the room but Dougal Mac Callum the butler. But, as your honour kens, he has e'en followed his auld master."

"Very unlucky again, Stephen," said Sir John, without altering his voice a single note. "The man to whom ye paid the money is dead—and the man who witnessed the payment is dead too—and the siller, which should have been to the fore, is neither seen nor heard tell of in the repositories. How am I to believe a' this?"

Stephen. "I didna ken, your honour; but there is a bit memorandum note of the very coins; for, God help me! I had to borrow out of twenty purses; and I am sure that ilk man there set down will take his grit oath for what purpose I borrowed the money."

Sir John. "I have little doubt ye borrowed the money, Steenie. It is the payment that I want to have some proof of."

Stephen. "The siller maun be about the house, Sir John. And since your honour never got it, and his honour that was canna have taen it wi' him, maybe some of the family may have seen it."

Sir John. "We will examine the servants, Stephen; that is but reasonable."

But lackey and lass, and page and groom, all denied stoutly that they had ever seen such a bag of money as my gudesire described. What was waur, he had unluckily not mentioned to any living soul of them his purpose of paying his rent. One quean had noticed something under his arm, but she took it for the pipes.

Sir John Redgauntlet ordered the servants out of the room, and then said to my gudesire, "Now, Steenie, ye see you have fair play; and as I have little doubt ye ken better where to find the siller than any other body, I beg, in fair terms, and for your own sake, that you will end this fasherie; for, Stephen, ye maun pay or flitt."

"The Lord forgie your opinion," said Stephen, driven almost to his wits' end—"I am an honest man."

"So am I, Stephen," said his honour; "and so are all the folks in the house, I hope. But if there be a knave amongst us, it must be he that tells the story he cannot prove." He paused, and then added, mair sternly, "If I understand your trick, Sir, you want to take advantage of some malicious reports concerning things in this family, and particularly respecting my father's sudden death, thereby to cheat me out of the money, and perhaps take away my character, by insinuating that I have received the rent I am demanding.—Where do you suppose this money to be?—I insist upon knowing."

My gudesire saw every thing look so muckle against him, that he grew nearly desperate—however, he shifted from one foot to another, looked to every corner of the room, and made no answer.

"Speak out, Sirrah," said the Laird, assuming a look of his father's, a very particular one, which he had when he was angry—it seemed as if the wrinkles of his frown made that self-same fearful shape of a horse's shoe in the middle of his brow;—"Speak out, Sir! I will know your thoughts;—do you suppose that I have this money?"

"Far be it frae me to say so," said Stephen.

"Do you charge any of my people with having taken it?"

"I wad be laith to charge them that may be innocent," said my gudesire; "and if there be any one that is guilty, I have nae proof."

"Somewhere the money must be, if there is a word of truth in your story," said Sir John; "I ask where you think it is—and demand a correct answer?"

"In hell, if you will have my thoughts of it," said my gudesire, driven to extremity,—"in hell! with your father and his silver whistle."

Down the stairs he ran, (for the parlour was nae place for him after such a word,) and he heard the Laird swearing blood and wounds behind him, as fast as ever did Sir Robert, and roaring for the baillie and the baron-officer.

Away rode my gudesire to his chief creditor, (him they ca'ad Laurie Lapraik,) to try if he could make onything out of him; but when he tauld his story, he got but the worst word in his mouth—thief, beggar, and dyvour, were the softest terms; and to the boot of these hard terms, Laurie brought up the auld story of his dipping his hand in the blood of God's saints, just as if a tenant could have helped riding with the Laird, and that a Laird like Sir Robert Redgauntlet. My gudesire was, by this time, far beyond the bounds of patience, and, while he and Laurie were at de'il speed the liars, he was wanchancie aneugh to abuse his doctrine as weel as the man, and said things that gar'd folks flesh grew that heard them; he wasna just himsell, and he had lived wi' a wild set in his day.

At last they parted, and my gudesire was to ride hame through the wood of Pitmarkie, that is all full of black firs, as they say. I ken the wood, but the firs may be black or white for what I can tell.—At the entry of the wood there is a wild common, and on the edge of the common, a little lonely change-house that was keepit then by an ostler-wife, they suld hae ca'd her Tibbie Faw, and there puir Steenie cried for a mutchkin of brandy, for he had had no refreshment the whole day. Tibbie was earnest wi' him to take a bite of meat, but he couldna think o't, nor would he take his foot out of the stirrup, and took aff the brandy, wholey, at twa draughts, and named a toast at each:—the first was, The memory of Sir Robert Redgauntlet, and might he never lie quiet in his grave till he had righted his poor bond-tenant; and the second was, A health to Man's Enemy, if he would but get him back the pock of siller, or tell him what came o't, for he saw the whole world was like to regard him as a thief and a cheat, and he took that waur than even the ruin of his house and hauld.

On he rode, little caring where. It was a dark night turned, and the trees made it yet darker, and he let the beast take its ain road through the wood; when, all of a sudden, from tired and wearied that it was before, the nag began to spring, and flee, and stend, that my gudesire could hardly keep the saddle— Upon the whilk, a horseman, suddenly riding up beside him, said, "That's a mettle beast of yours, friend; will you sell him?"—So saying, he touched the horse's neck with his riding-wand, and it fell into its auld heigh-ho of a stumbling trot; "But his spunk's soon out of him, I think," continued the stranger, "and that is like many a man's courage, that thinks he wad do great things till he come to the proof."

My gudesire scarce listened to this, but spurred his horse, with 'Gude e'en to you, friend."

But it's like the stranger was ane that does na lightly yield his point; for, ride as Steenie liked, he was aye beside him at the self-same place. At last my gudesire, Steenie Steenson, grew half angry; and, to say the truth, half feared.

"What is it that ye want with me, friend?" he said. "If ye be a robber, I have nae money; if ye be a leal man, wanting company, I have nae heart to mirth or speaking; and if ye want to ken the road, I scarce ken it mysell."

"If you will tell me your grief," said the stranger, "I am one that, though I have been sair misca'ad in the world, am the only hand for helping my freends."

So my gudesire, to ease his ain heart, mair than from any hope of help, told him the story from beginning to end.

"It's a hard pinch,"' said the stranger; "but I think I can help you."

"If you could lend the money, Sir, and take a lang day—I ken nae other help on earth," said my gudesire.

"But there may be some under the earth," said the stranger. "Come, I'll be frank wi' you; I could lend you the money on bond, but you would, maybe, scruple my terms. Now, I can tell you, that your auld Laird is disturbed in his grave by your curses, and the wailing of your family, and—if ye dare venture to go to see him, he will give you the receipt."

My gudesire's hair stood on end at this proposal, but he thought his companion might be some humoursome chield that was trying to frighten him, and might end with lending him the money. Besides, he was bold wi' brandy, and desperate wi' distress; and he said, he had courage to go to the gate of hell, and a step farther, for that receipt.—The stranger laughed.

Weel, they rode on through the thickest of the wood, when, all of a sudden, the horse stopped at the door of a great house; and, but that he knew the place was ten miles off, my father would have thought he was at Redgauntlet Castle. They rode into the outer court-yard, through the muckle folding gates, and aneath the auld portcullis; and the whole front of the house was lighted, and there were pipes and fiddles, and as much dancing and deray within as used to be in Sir Robert's house at Pace and Yule, and such high seasons. They lap off, and my gudesire, as seemed to him, fastened his horse to the very ring he had tied him to that morning, when he gaed to wait on the young Sir John.

"God!" said my father, "if Sir Robert's death be but a dream!"

He knocked at the ha' door, just as he was wont, and his auld acquaintance, Dougal MacCallum, just after his wont, too,—came to open the door, and said, "Piper Steenie, are ye there, lad? Sir Robert has been crying for you."

My gudesire was like a man in a dream—he looked for the stranger, but he was gaen for the time. At last, he just tried to say, "Ha! Dougal Driveower, are ye living? I thought ye had been dead."

"Never fash yoursell wi' me," said Dougal, "but look to yoursell; and see ye tak naething free onybody here, neither meat, drink, or siller, except just the receipt that is your ain."

So saying, he led the way out through halls and trances that were weel kenn'd to my gudesire, and into the auld oak parlour; and there was as much singing of profane songs, and birling of red wine, and speaking blasphemy and sculduddry, as had ever been in Redgauntlet Castle when it was at the blythest.

But, Lord, take us in keeping! what a set of ghastly revellers they were that sat round that table!—My gudesire kenn'd many that had long before gone to their place. There was the fierce Middleton, and the dissolute Rothes, and the crafty Lauderdale; and Dalyell, with his bald head and a beard to his girdle; and Earlshall, with Cameron's blude on his hand; and wild Bonshaw, that tied blessed Mr. Cargill's limbs till the blude sprung; and Dumbarton Douglas, the twice-turned traitor baith to country and king. There was the Bluidy Advocate Mac Kenyie, who, for his worldly wit and wisdom, had been to the rest as a god. And there was Claverhouse, as beautiful as when he lived, with his long, dark, curled locks, streaming down to his laced buff-coat, and his left hand always on his right spule-blade, to hide the wound that the silver bullet had made. He sat apart from them all, and looked at them with a melancholy, haughty countenance; while the rest hallooed, and sung, and laughed, that the room rang. But their smiles were fearfully contorted from time to time; and their laughter passed into such wild sounds, as made my gudesire's very nails grow blue, and chilled the marrow in his bones.

They that waited at the table were jast the wicked serving-men and troopers, that had done their work and wicked bidding on earth. There was the Lang Lad of the Nethertown, that helped to take Argyll; and the Bishop's summoner, that they called the Deil's Rattle-bag; and the wicked guardsmen, in their laced coats; and the savage Highland Amorites, that shed blood like water; and many a proud servingman, haughty of heart and bloody of hand, cringing to the rich, and making them wickeder than they would be; grinding the poor to powder, when the rich had broken them to fragments. And many, many mair were coming and ganging, a' as busy in their vocation as if they had been alive.

Sir Robert Redgauntlet, in the midst of a' this fearful riot, cried, wi' a voice like thunder, on Steenie Piper, to come to the hoard-bead where he was sitting; his legs stretched out before him, and swathed up with flannel, with his holster pistols aside him, and great broad-sword rested against his chair, just as my gudesire had seen him the last time upon earth—the very cushion for the jack-an-ape was close to him, but the creature itsell was not there—it wasna its hour, it's likely; for he heard them say as he came forward, "Is not the Major come yet?" And another answered, "The jack-an-ape will be here be times in the morn." And when my gudesire came forward, Sir Robert or his ghost, or the devil in his likeness, said, "Weel, Piper, hae ye settled wi' my son for the year's rent?"

With much ado my father got breath to say, that Sir John would not settle without his honour's receipt.

"Ye shall hae that for a tune of the pipes, Steenie," said the appearance of Sir Robert—"Play us up 'Weel hoddled, Luckie.' "

"Now this was a tune my gudesire learned frae a warlock, that heard it when they were worshipping Satan at their meetings; and my gudesire had sometimes play it at the ranting suppers in Redgauntlet Castle, but never very willingly; and now he grew could at the very name of it, and said for excuse, he hadna his pipes wi' him.

"Mac Callum, ye limb of Beelzebub," said the fearfu' Sir Robert, "bring Steenie the pipes that I am keeping for him!"

Mac Callum brought a pair of pipes might have served the piper of Donald and of Isles. But he gave my gudesire a nudge as he offered them; and looking secretly and closely, Steenie saw that the chanter was of steel, and heated to a white heat; so he had fair warning not to trust his fingers with it. So he excused himself again, and said, he was faint and frightened, and had not wind aneugh to fill the bag.

"Then ye maun eat and drink, Steenie," said the figure; "for we do little else here; and it's ill speaking between a full man and a fasting."

Now these were the very words that the bloody Earl of Douglas said to keep the king's messenger in hand, while he cut the head off Mac Lellan of Bombie, at the Threave Castle; and that put Steenie mair and mair on his guard. So he spoke up like a man, and said he came neither to eat or drink, or make minstrelsy; but simply for his ain—to ken what was come o' the money he had paid, and to get a discharge for it, and he was so stout-hearted by this time, that he charged Sir Robert for conscience-sake—(he had no power to say the holy name)—and as he hoped for peace and rest, to spread no snares for him, but just to give him his ain.

The appearance gnashed its teeth and laughed, but it took from a large pocket-book the receipt, and handed it to Steenie. "Here is your receipt, ye pitiful cur; and for the money, my dog-whelp of a son may go look for it in the Cat's Cradle."

My gudesire uttered mony thanks, and was about to retire, when Sir Robert roared aloud, "Stop though, thou sack-doudling son of a whore! I am not done with thee. Here we do nothing for nothing; and you must return on this very day twelvemonth, to pay your master the homage that you owe me for my protection."

My father's tongue was loosed of a suddenty, and he said aloud, "I refer myself to God's pleasure, and not to yours."

He had no sooner uttered the word than all was dark around him; and he sunk on the earth with such a sudden shock, that he lost both breath and sense.

How lang Steenie lay there he could not tell; but when he came to himself, he was lying in the auld kirkyard of Redgauntlet parishine, just at the door of the family aisle, and the scutcheon of the auld knight, Sir Robert, hanging over his head. There was a deep morning fog on grass and gravestone around him, and his horse was feeding quietly beside the minister's twa cows. Steenie would have thought the whole was a dream, but he had the receipt in his hand, fairly written and signed by the auld Laird;

only the last letters of his name were a little disorderly, written like one seized with sudden pain.

Sorely troubled in his mind, he left that dreary place, rode through the mist to Redgauntlet Castle, and with much ado he got speech of the Laird. "Well, you dyvour bankrupt," was the first word, "have you brought me my rent?"

"No," answered my gudesire, "I have not; but I have brought your honour Sir Robert's receipt for it."

"How, Sirrah?—Sir Robert's receipt!—You told me he had not given you one."

"Will your honour please to see if that bit line is right?"

Sir John looked at every line, and at every letter, with much attention; and at last, at the date, which my gudesire had not observed,—"*From my appointed place,*" he read "*this twenty-fifth of November.* "What! —That is yesterday!—Villain, thou must have gone to hell for this!'

"I got it from your honour's father—whether he be in heaven or hell, I know not," said Steenie.

"I will debate you for a warlock to the Privy Council!" said Sir John. "I will send you to your master, the devil, with the help of a tar-barrel and a torch!"

"I intend to delate mysell to the Presbytery," said Steenie, "and tell them all I have seen last night, whilk are things fitter for them to judge of than a borrel man like me."

Sir John paused, composed himself, and desired to hear the full history; and my gudesire told it him from point to point, as I have told it you—word for word, neither more nor less.

Sir John was silent again for a long time, and at last he said, very composedly, "Steenie, this story of yours concerns the honour of many a noble family besides mine and if it be a leasing-making, to keep yourself out of my danger, the least you can expect is to have a red-hot iron driven through your tongue, and that will be as bad as scauding your fingers wi' a red-hot chanter. But yet it may be true, Steenie; and if the money cast up, I will not know what to think of it.—But where shall we find the Cat's Cradle? There are cats enough about the old house, but I think they kitten without the ceremony of bed or cradle."

"We were best ask Hutcheon," said my gudesire; "he kens a' the odd corners about as weel as—another servingman that is now gane, and that I wad not like to name."

Aweel, Hutcheon, when he was asked, told them, that a ruinous turret, lang dis-used, next to the clock-house, only accessible by a ladder, for the opening was on the outside, and far above the battlements, was called of old the Cat's Cradle.

"There will I go immediately," said Sir John; and he took (with what purpose, heaven kens,) one of his father's pistols from the hall-table, where they had lain since the night he died, and hastened to the battlements.

It was a dangerous place to climb, for the ladder was auld and frail, and wanted ane or twa rounds. However, up got Sir John, and entered at the turret door, where his body stopped the only little light that was in the bit turret. Something flees at him wi' a vengeance, maist dang him back ower—bang gaed the knight's pistol, and Hutcheon, that held the ladder, and my gudesire that stood beside him, hears a loud skelloch. A minute after Sir John flings the body of the jack-an-ape down to them, and cries that the siller is found, and that they should come up and help him. And there was the bag of siller sure aneugh, and many other things besides, that had been missing for many a day. And Sir John, when he had riped the turret weel, led my gudesire into the dining-parlour, and took him by the hand, and spoke kindly to him, and said he was sorry he should have doubted his word, and that he would hereafter be a good master to him, to make amends.

"And now, Steenie," said Sir John, "although this vision of yours tends, on the whole, to my father's credit, as an honest man, that he should, even after his death, desire to see justice done to a poor man like you, yet you are sensible that ill-dispositioned men might make bad constructions upon it, concerning his soul's health. So, I think, we had better lay the whole dirdum on that ill-deedie creature, Major Weir, and say naething about your dream in the wood of Pitmurkie. You had taken ower mickle brandy to be very certain about anything; and, Steenie, this receipt, (his hand shook while he held it out)—it's but a queer document, and we will do best, I think, to put it quietly in the fire."

"Od, but for as queer as it is, it's a' the voucher I have for my rent," said my gude-sire, who was afraid, it may be, of losing the benefit of Sir Robert's discharge.

"I will bear the contents to your credit in the rental-book, and give you a dis-charge under my own hand," said Sir John, "and that on the spot. And, Steenie, if you can hold your tongue about this matter, you shall sit, from this term downward, at an easier rent."

"Many thanks to your honour," said Steenie, who saw easily in what corner the wind sat; "doubtless I will be conformable to all your honour's commands; only I would willingly speak wi' some powerful minister on the subject, for I do not like the sort of summons of appointment whilk your honour's father—"

"Do not call the phantom my father!" said Sir John, interrupting him.

"Weel then, the thing that was so like him,"—said my gudesire; "he spoke of my coming back to him this time twelvemonth, and it's weight on my conscience.—" "Aweel, then," said Sir John, "if you be so much distressed in mind, you may speak to our minister of the parish; he is a douce man, regards the honour of our family, and the mair that he may look for some patronage from me."

Wi' that, my father readily agreed that the receipt should be burnt, and the Laird threw it into the fire with his ain hand. Burn it would not for them, though; but away it flew up the chimney, wi' a long train of sparks at his tail, and a hissing noise like a squib.

My gudesire gaed down to the Manse, and the minister, when he had heard the story, said, it was his real opinion, that though my gudesire had gaen very far in tampering with dangerous matters, yet, as he had refused the devil's arles, (for such was the offer of meat and drink,) and had refused to do homage by piping at his bidding, he hoped, that if he held a circumspect walk hereafter, Satan could take little advantage by what was come and gane. And, indeed, my gudesire, of his ain accord, lang forswore baith the pipes and the brandy—it was not even till the year was out, and the fatal day passed, that he would as much as take the fiddle, or drink usquebaugh or tippenny.

Sir John made up his story about the jack-an-ape as he liked himself; and some believe till this day there was no more in the matter than the filching nature of the brute. Indeed ye'll no hinder some to threap, that it was nane o' the Auld Enemy that Dougal and my gudesire saw in the Laird's room, but only that wanchancy creature, the Major, capering on the coffin; and that, as to the blowing on the Laird's whistle that was heard after he was dead, the filthy brute could do that as weel as the Laird himself, if no better. But heaven kens the truth, whilk first came out by the minister's wife, after Sir John and her ain gudeman were baith in the moulds. And then my gudesire, who was failed in his limbs, but not in his judgment or memory—at least nothing to speak of—was obliged to tell the real narrative to his friends, for the credit of his gude name. He might else have been charged for a warlock.

The Case of Lady Sannox

Arthur Conan Doyle

———◆———

HE RELATIONS BETWEEN DOUGLAS STONE AND THE NOTORIOUS LADY Sannox were very well known both among the fashionable circles of which she was a brilliant member, and the scientific bodies which numbered him among their most illustrious *confrères*. There was naturally, therefore, a very widespread interest when it was announced one morning that the lady had absolutely and for ever taken the veil, and that the world would see her no more. When, at the very tail of this rumour, there came the assurance that the celebrated operating surgeon, the man of steel nerves, had been found in the morning by his valet, seated on one side of his bed, smiling pleasantly upon the universe, with both legs jammed into one side of his breeches and his great brain about as valuable as a cap full of porridge, the matter was strong enough to give quite a little thrill of interest to folk who had never hoped that their jaded nerves were capable of such a sensation.

Douglas Stone in his prime was one of the most remarkable men in England. Indeed, he could hardly be said to have ever reached his prime, for he was but nine-and-thirty at the time of this little incident. Those who knew him best were aware that famous as he was as a surgeon, he might have succeeded with even greater rapidity in any of a dozen lines of life. He could have cut his way to fame as a soldier, struggled to it as an explorer, bullied for it in the courts, or built it out of stone and iron as an engineer. He was born to be great, for he could plan what another man dare not do, and he could do what another man dare not plan. In surgery none could follow him. His nerve, his judgment, his intuition, were things apart. Again and again his knife cut away death, but grazed the very springs of life in doing it, until his assistants were as white as the patient. His energy, his audacity, his full-blooded self-confidence—does not the memory of them still linger to the south of Marylebone Road and the north of Oxford Street?

His vices were as magnificent as his virtues, and infinitely more picturesque. Large as was his income, and it was the third largest of all professional men in London, it was far beneath the luxury of his living. Deep in his complex nature lay a rich vein of sensualism, at the sport of which he placed all the prizes of his life. The eye, the ear, the touch, the palate, all were his masters. The bouquet of old vintages, the scent of rare exotics, the curves and tints of the daintiest potteries of Europe, it was to these that the quick-running stream of gold was transformed. And then there came his sudden mad passion for Lady Sannox, when a single interview with two challenging glances and a whispered word set him ablaze. She was the loveliest woman in London and the only one to him. He was one of the handsomest men in London, but not the only one to her. She had a liking for new experiences, and was gracious to most men who wooed her. It may have been cause or it may have been effect that Lord Sannox looked fifty, though he was but six-and-thirty.

He was a quiet, silent, neutral-tinted man, this lord, with thin lips and heavy eyelids, much given to gardening, and full of home-like habits. He had at one time been fond of acting, had even rented a theatre in London, and on its boards had first seen Miss Marion Dawson, to whom he had offered his hand, his title, and the third of a county. Since his marriage his early hobby had become distasteful to him. Even in private theatricals it was no longer possible to persuade him to exercise the talent which he had often showed that he possessed. He was happier with a spud and a watering-can among his orchids and chrysanthemums.

It was quite an interesting problem whether he was absolutely devoid of sense, or miserably wanting in spirit. Did he know his lady's ways and condone them, or was he a mere blind, doting fool? It was a point to be discussed over the teacups in snug little drawing-rooms, or with the aid of a cigar in the bow windows of clubs. Bitter and plain were the comments among men upon his conduct. There was but one who had a good word to say for him, and he was the most silent member in the smoking-room. He had seen him break in a horse at the University, and it seemed to have left an impression upon his mind.

But when Douglas Stone became the favourite all doubts as to Lord Sannox's knowledge or ignorance were set for ever at rest. There was no subterfuge about Stone. In his high-handed, impetuous fashion, he set all caution and discretion at defiance. The scandal became notorious. A learned body intimated that his name had been struck from the list of its vice-presidents. Two friends implored him to consider his professional credit. He cursed them all three, and spent forty guineas on a bangle to take with him to the lady. He was at her house every evening, and she drove in his carriage in the afternoons. There was not an attempt on either side to conceal their relations; but there came at last a little incident to interrupt them.

It was a dismal winter's night, very cold and gusty, with the wind whooping in the chimneys and blustering against the window-panes. A thin spatter of rain tinkled on the glass with each fresh sough of the gale, drowning for the instant the dull gurgle and drip from the eaves. Douglas Stone had finished his dinner, and sat by his fire in the study, a glass of rich port upon the malachite table at his elbow. As he raised it to his lips, he held it up against the lamplight, and watched with the eye of a connoisseur the tiny scales of beeswing which floated in its rich ruby depths. The fire, as it spurted up, threw fitful lights upon his bald, clear-cut face, with its widely-opened grey eyes, its thick and yet firm lips, and the deep, square jaw, which had something Roman in its strength and its animalism. He smiled from time to time as he nestled back in his luxurious chair. Indeed, he had a right to feel well pleased, for, against the advice of six colleagues, he had performed an operation that day of which only two cases were on record, and the result had been brilliant beyond all expectation. No other man in London would have had the daring to plan, or the skill to execute, such a heroic measure.

But he had promised Lady Sannox to see her that evening and it was already half-past eight. His hand was outstretched to the bell to order the carriage when he heard the dull thud of the knocker. An instant later there was the shuffling of feet in the hall, and the sharp closing of a door.

"A patient to see you, sir, in the consulting room," said the butler.

"About himself?"

"No, sir; I think he wants you to go out."

"It is too late," cried Douglas Stone peevishly. "I won't go."

"This is his card, sir."

The butler presented it upon the gold salver which had been given to his master by the wife of a Prime Minister.

" 'Hamil Ali, Smyrna.' Hum! The fellow is a Turk, I suppose."

"Yes, sir. He seems as if he came from abroad, sir. And he's in a terrible way."

"Tut, tut! I have an engagement. I must go somewhere else. But I'll see him. Show him in here, Pim."

A few moments later the butler swung open the door and ushered in a small and decrepit man, who walked with a bent back and with the forward push of the face and blink of the eyes which goes with extreme short sight. His face was swarthy, and his hair and beard of the deepest black. In one hand he held a turban of white muslin striped with red, in the other a small chamois leather bag.

"Good evening," said Douglas Stone, when the butler had closed the door. "You speak English, I presume?"

"Yes, sir. I am from Asia Minor, but I speak English when I speak slow."

"You wanted me to go out, I understand?"

"Yes, sir. I wanted very much that you should see my wife."

"I could come in the morning, but I have an engagement which prevents me from seeing your wife tonight."

The Turk's answer was a singular one. He pulled the string which closed the mouth of the chamois leather bag, and poured a flood of gold on to the table.

"There are one hundred pounds there," said he, "and I promise you that it will not take you an hour. I have a cab ready at the door."

Douglas Stone glanced at his watch. An hour would not make it too late to visit Lady Sannox. He had been there later. And the fee was an extraordinarily high one. He had been pressed by his creditors lately, and he could not afford to let such a chance pass. He would go.

"What is the case?" he asked.

"Oh, it is so sad a one! So sad a one! You have not, perhaps heard of the daggers of the Almohades?"

"Never."

"Ah, they are Eastern daggers of a great age and of a singular shape, with the hilt like what you call a stirrup. I am a curiosity dealer, you understand, and that is why I have come to England from Smyrna, but next week I go back once more. Many things I brought with me, and I have a few things left, but among them, to my sorrow, is one of these daggers."

"You will remember that I have an appointment, sir," said the surgeon, with some irritation; "pray confine yourself to the necessary details."

"You will see that it is necessary. To-day my wife fell down in a faint in the room in which I keep my wares, and she cut her lower lip upon this cursed dagger of Almohades."

"I see," said Douglas Stone, rising. "And you wish me to dress the wound?"

"No, no, it is worse than that."

"What then?"

"These daggers are poisoned."

"Poisoned!"

"Yes, and there is no man, East or West, who can tell now what is the poison or what the cure. But all that is known I know, for my father was in this trade before me, and we have had much to do with these poisoned weapons."

"What are the symptoms?"

"Deep sleep, and death in thirty hours."

"And you say there is no cure. Why then should you pay me this considerable fee?"

"No drug can cure, but the knife may."

"And how?"

"The poison is slow of absorption. It remains for hours in the wound."

"Washing, then, might cleanse it?"

"No more than in a snake bite. It is too subtle and too deadly."

"Excision of the wound, then?"

"That is it. If it be on the finger, take the finger off. So said my father always. But think of where this wound is, and that it is my wife. It is dreadful!"

But familiarity with such grim matters may take the finer edge from a man's sympathy. To Douglas Stone this was already an interesting case, and he brushed aside as irrelevant the feeble objections of the husband.

"It appears to be that or nothing," said he brusquely. "It is better to lose a lip than a life."

"Ah, yes, I know that you are right. Well, well, it is kismet, and it must be faced. I have the cab, and you will come with me and do this thing."

Douglas Stone took his case of bistouries from a drawer, and placed it with a roll of bandage and a compress of lint in his pocket. He must waste no more time if he were to see Lady Sannox.

"I am ready," said he, pulling on his overcoat. "Will you take a glass of wine before you go out into this cold air?"

His visitor shrank away, with a protesting hand upraised.

"You forget that I am a Mussulman, and a true follower of the Prophet," said he. "But tell me what is the bottle of green glass which you have placed in your pocket?"

"It is chloroform."

"Ah, that also is forbidden to us. It is a spirit, and we make no use of such things."

"What! You would allow your wife to go through an operation without an anæsthetic?"

"Ah! she will feel nothing, poor soul. The deep sleep has already come on, which is the first working of the poison. And then I have given her of our Smyrna opium. Come, sir, for already an hour has passed."

As they stepped out into the darkness, a sheet of rain was driven in upon their faces, and the hall lamp, which dangled from the arm of a marble Caryatid, went out with a fluff. Pim, the butler, pushed the heavy door to, straining hard with his shoulder against the wind, while the two men groped their way towards the yellow glare which showed where the cab was waiting. An instant later they were rattling upon their journey.

"Is it far?" asked Douglas Stone.

"Oh, no. We have a very little quiet place off the Euston Road."

The surgeon pressed the spring of his repeater and listened to the little tings which told him the hour. It was a quarter past nine. He calculated the distances, and the short time which it would take him to perform so trivial an operation. He ought to reach Lady Sannox by ten o'clock. Through the fogged windows he saw the blurred gas lamps dancing past, with occasionally the broader glare of a shop front. The rain was pelting and rattling upon the leathern top of the carriage, and the wheels swashed as they rolled through puddle and mud. Opposite to him the white headgear of his companion gleamed faintly through the obscurity. The surgeon felt in his pockets and arranged his needles, his ligatures and his safety-pins, that no time might be wasted when they arrived. He chafed with impatience and drummed his foot upon the floor.

But the cab slowed down at last and pulled up. In an instant Douglas Stone was out, and the Smyrna merchant's toe was at his very heel.

"You can wait," said he to the driver.

It was a mean-looking house in a narrow and sordid street. The surgeon, who knew his London well, cast a swift glance into the shadows, but there was nothing distinctive—no shop, no movement, nothing but a double line of dull, flat-faced houses, a double stretch of wet flagstones which gleamed in the lamplight, and a double rush of water in the gutters which swirled and gurgled towards the sewer gratings. The door which faced them was blotched and discoloured, and a faint light in the fan pane above it served to show the dust and the grime which covered it. Above in one of the bedroom windows, there was a dull yellow glimmer. The merchant knocked loudly, and, as he turned his dark face towards the light, Douglas Stone could see that it was contracted with anxiety. A bolt was drawn, and an elderly woman with a taper stood in the doorway, shielding the thin flame with her gnarled hand.

"Is all well?" gasped the merchant.

"She is as you left her, sir."

"She has not spoken?"

"No, she is in a deep sleep."

The merchant closed the door, and Douglas Stone walked down the narrow passage, glancing about him in some surprise as he did so. There was no oil-cloth, no mat, no hat-rack. Deep grey dust and heavy festoons of cobwebs met his eyes everywhere. Following the old woman up the winding stair, his firm footfall echoed harshly through the silent house. There was no carpet.

The bedroom was on the second landing. Douglas Stone followed the old nurse into it, with the merchant at his heels. Here, at least, there was furniture and to spare. The floor was littered and the corners piled with Turkish cabinets, inlaid tables, coats of chain mail, strange pipes, and grotesque weapons. A single small lamp stood upon a bracket on the wall. Douglas Stone took it down, and picking his way among the lumber, walked over to a couch in the corner, on which lay a woman dressed in the Turkish fashion, with yashmak and veil. The lower part of the face was exposed, and the surgeon saw a jagged cut which zigzagged along the border of the under lip.

"You will forgive the yashmak," said the Turk. "You know our views about women in the East."

But the surgeon was not thinking about the yashmak. This was no longer a woman to him. It was a case. He stooped and examined the wound carefully.

"There are no signs of irritation," said he. "We might delay the operation until local symptoms develop."

The husband wrung his hands in uncontrollable agitation.

"Oh! sir, sir," he cried. "Do not trifle. You do not know. It is deadly. I know, and I give you my assurance that an operation is absolutely necessary. Only the knife can save her."

"And yet I am inclined to wait," said Douglas Stone.

"That is enough," the Turk cried, angrily. "Every minute is of importance, and I cannot stand here and see my wife allowed to sink. It only remains for me to give you my thanks for having come, and to call in some other surgeon before it is too late."

Douglas Stone hesitated. To refund that hundred pounds was no pleasant matter. But of course if he left the case he must return the money. And if the Turk were right and the woman died, his position before a coroner might be an embarrassing one.

"You have had personal experience of this poison?" he asked.

"I have."

"And you assure me that an operation is needful."

"I swear it by all that I hold sacred."

"The disfigurement will be frightful."

"I can understand that the mouth will not be a pretty one to kiss."

Douglas Stone turned fiercely upon the man. The speech was a brutal one. But the Turk has his own fashion of talk and of thought, and there was no time for wrangling. Douglas Stone drew a bistoury from his case, opened it and felt the keen straight edge with his forefinger. Then he held the lamp closer to the bed. Two dark eyes were gazing up at him through the slit in the yashmak. They were all iris, and the pupil was hardly to be seen.

"You have given her a very heavy dose of opium."

"Yes, she has had a good dose."

He glanced again at the dark eyes which looked straight at his own. They were dull and lustreless, but, even as he gazed, a little shifting sparkle came into them, and the lips quivered.

"She is not absolutely unconscious," said he.

"Would it not be well to use the knife while it will be painless?"

The same thought had crossed the surgeon's mind. He grasped the wounded lip with his forceps, and with two swift cuts he took out a broad V-shaped piece. The woman sprang up on the couch with a dreadful gurgling scream. Her covering was torn from her face. It was a face that he knew. In spite of that protruding upper lip and that slobber of blood, it was a face that he knew. She kept on putting her hand up to the gap and screaming. Douglas Stone sat down at the foot of the couch with his knife and his forceps. The room was whirling round, and he had felt something go like a ripping seam behind his ear. A bystander would have said that his face was the more ghastly of the two. As in a dream, or as if he had been looking at something at the play, he was conscious that the Turk's hair and beard lay upon the table, and that Lord Sannox was leaning against the wall with his hand to his side, laughing silently. The screams had died away now, and the dreadful head had dropped back again upon the pillow, but Douglas Stone still sat motionless, and Lord Sannox still chuckled quietly to himself.

"It was really very necessary for Marion, this operation," said he, "not physically, but morally, you know, morally."

Douglas Stone stooped for yards and began to play with the fringe of the coverlet. His knife tinkled down upon the ground, but he still held the forceps and something more.

"I had long intended to make a little example," said Lord Sannox, suavely. "Your note of Wednesday miscarried, and I have it here in my pocket-book. I took some pains in carrying out my idea. The wound, by the way, was from nothing more dangerous than my signet ring."

He glanced keenly at his silent companion and cocked the small revolver which he held in his coat pocket. But Douglas Stone was still picking at the coverlet.

"You see you have kept your appointment after all," said Lord Sannox.

And at that Douglas Stone began to laugh. He laughed long and loudly. But Lord Sannox did not laugh now. Something like fear sharpened and hardened his features. He walked from the room, and he walked on tiptoe. The old woman was waiting outside.

"Attend to your mistress when she awakes," said Lord Sannox.

Then he went down to the street. The cab was at the door, and the driver raised his hand to his hat.

"John," said Lord Sannox, "you will take the doctor home first. He will want leading down-stairs, I think. Tell his butler that he has been taken ill at a case."

"Very good, sir."

"Then you can take Lady Sannox home."

"And how about yourself, sir?"

"Oh, my address for the next few months will be Hotel di Roma, Venice. Just see that the letters are sent on. And tell Stevens to exhibit all the purple chrysanthemums next Monday, and to wire me the result."

The Diary of a Madman

Guy de Maupassant

———◆———

H<small>E WAS DEAD—THE HEAD OF A HIGH TRIBUNAL, THE UPRIGHT MAGISTRATE,</small> whose irreproachable life was a proverb in all the courts of France. Advocates, young counsellors, judges had greeted him at sight of his large, thin, pale face lighted up by two sparkling deep-set eyes, bowing low in token of respect.

He had passed his life in pursuing crime and in protecting the weak. Swindlers and murderers had no more redoubtable enemy, for he seemed to read the most secret thoughts of their minds.

He was dead, now, at the age of eighty-two, honored by the homage and followed by the regrets of a whole people. Soldiers in red trousers had escorted him to the tomb and men in white cravats had spoken words and shed tears that seemed to be sincere beside his grave.

But here is the strange paper found by the dismayed notary in the desk where he had kept the records of great criminals! It was entitled:

WHY?

20th June, 1851. I have just left court. I have condemned Blondel to death! Now, why did this man kill his five children? Frequently one meets with people to whom the destruction of life is a pleasure. Yes, yes, it should be a pleasure, the greatest of all, perhaps, for is not killing the next thing to creating? To make and to destroy! These two words contain the history of the universe, all the history of worlds, all that is, all! Why is it not intoxicating to kill?

25th June. To think that a being is there who lives, who walks, who runs. A being? What is a being? That animated thing, that bears in it the principle of motion and a will ruling that motion. It is attached to nothing, this thing. Its feet do not belong to the ground. It is a grain of life that moves on the earth, and this grain of life, coming I know not whence, one can destroy at one's will. Then nothing—nothing more. It perishes, it is finished.

26th June. Why then is it a crime to kill? Yes, why? On the contrary, it is the law of nature. The mission of every being is to kill; he kills to live, and he kills to kill. The beast kills without ceasing, all day, every instant of his existence. Man kills without ceasing, to nourish himself; but since he needs, besides, to kill for pleasure, he has invented hunting! The child kills the insects he finds, the little birds, all the little animals that come in his way. But this does not suffice for the irresistible need to massacre that is in us. It is not enough to kill beasts; we must kill man too. Long ago this need was satisfied by human sacrifices. Now the requirements of social life have made murder a crime. We condemn and punish the assassin! But as we cannot live without yielding to this natural and imperious instinct of death, we relieve ourselves, from time to time, by wars. Then a whole nation slaughters another nation. It is a feast of blood, a feast that maddens armies and that intoxicates civilians, women and children, who read, by lamplight at night, the feverish story of massacre.

One might suppose that those destined to accomplish these butcheries of men would be despised! No, they are loaded with honors. They are clad in gold and in resplendent garments; they wear plumes on their heads and ornaments on their breasts, and they are given crosses, rewards, titles of every kind. They are proud, respected, loved by women, cheered by the crowd, solely because their mission is to shed human blood. They drag through the streets their instruments of death, that the passer-by, clad in black, looks on with envy. For to kill is the great law set by nature in the heart of existence! There is nothing more beautiful and honorable than killing!

30th June. To kill is the law, because nature loves eternal youth. She seems to cry in all her unconscious acts: "Quick! quick! quick!" The more she destroys, the more she renews herself.

2d July. A human being—what is a human being? Through thought it is a reflection of all that is; through memory and science it is an abridged edition of the universe whose history it represents, a mirror of things and of nations, each human being becomes a microcosm in the macrocosm.

3d July. It must be a pleasure, unique and full of zest, to kill; to have there before one the living, thinking being; to make therein a little hole, nothing but a little hole, to see that red thing flow which is. the blood, which makes life; and to have before one only a heap of limp flesh, cold, inert, void of thought!

5th August. I, who have passed my life in judging, condemning, killing by the spoken word, killing by the guillotine those who had killed by the knife, I, I, if I should do as all the assassins have done whom I have smitten, I—I—who would know it?

10th August. Who would ever know? Who would ever suspect me, me, me, especially if I should choose a being I had no interest in doing away with?

15th August. The temptation has come to me. It pervades my whole being; my hands tremble with the desire to kill.

22d August. I could resist no longer. I killed a little creature as an experiment, for a beginning. Jean, my servant, had a goldfinch in a cage hung in the office window. I sent him on an errand, and I took the little bird in my hand, in my hand where I felt its heart beat. It was warm. I went up to my room. From time to time I squeezed it tighter; its heart beat faster; this was atrocious and delicious. I was near choking it. But I could not see the blood.

Then I took scissors, short-nail scissors, and I cut its throat with three slits, quite gently. It opened its bill, it struggled to escape me, but I held it, oh! I held it—I could have held a mad dog—and I saw the blood trickle.

And then I did as assassins do—real ones. I washed the scissors, I washed my hands. I sprinkled water and took the body, the corpse, to the garden to hide it. I buried it under a strawberry-plant. It will never be found. Every day I shall eat a strawberry from that plant. How one can enjoy life when one knows how!

My servant cried; he thought his bird flown. How could he suspect me? Ah! ah!

25th August. I must kill a man! I must!

30th August. It is done. But what a little thing! I had gone for a walk in the forest of Vernes. I was thinking of nothing, literally nothing. A child was in the road, a little child eating a slice of bread and butter.

He stops to see me pass and says, "Good-day, Mr. President."

And the thought enters my head, "Shall I kill him?"

I answer: "You are alone, my boy?"

"Yes, sir."

"All alone in the wood?"

"Yes, sir."

The wish to kill him intoxicated me like wine. I approached him quite softly, persuaded that he was going to run away. And, suddenly, I seized him by the throat. He looked at me with terror in his eyes—such eyes! He held my wrists in his little hands and his body writhed like a feather over the fire. Then he moved no more. I threw the body in the ditch, and some weeds on top of it. I returned home, and dined well. What a little thing it was! In the evening I was very gay, light, rejuvenated; I passed the evening at the Prefect's. They found me witty. But I have not seen blood! I am tranquil.

31st August. The body has been discovered. They are hunting for the assassin. Ah! ah!

1st September. Two tramps have been arrested. Proofs are lacking.

2d September. The parents have been to see me. They wept! Ah! ah!

6th October. Nothing has been discovered. Some strolling vagabond must have done the deed. Ah! ah! If I had seen the blood flow, it seems to me I should be tranquil now! The desire to kill is in my blood; it is like the passion of youth at twenty.

20th October. Yet another. I was walking by the river, after breakfast. And I saw, under a willow, a fisherman asleep. It was noon. A spade was standing in a potato-field near by, as if expressly for me.

I took it. I returned; I raised it like a club, and with one blow of the edge I cleft the fisherman's head. Oh! he bled, this one! Rose-colored blood. It flowed into the water, quite gently. And I went away with a grave step. If I had been seen! Ah! ah! I should have made an excellent assassin.

25th October. The affair of the fisherman makes a great stir. His nephew, who fished with him, is charged with the murder.

26th October. The examining magistrate affirms that the nephew is guilty. Everybody in town believes it. Ah! ah!

27th October. The nephew makes a very poor witness. He had gone to the village to buy bread and cheese, he declared. He swore that his uncle had been killed in his absence! Who would believe him?

28th October. The nephew has all but confessed, they have badgered him so. Ah! ah! Justice!

15th November. There are overwhelming proofs against the nephew, who was his uncle's heir. I shall preside at the sessions.

25th January. To death! to death! to death! I have had him condemned to death! Ah! ah! The advocate-general spoke like an angel! Ah! ah! Yet another! I shall go to see him executed!

10th March. It is done. They guillotined him this morning. He died very well! very well! That gave me pleasure! How fine it is to see a man's head cut off!

Now, I shall wait, I can wait. It would take such a little thing to let myself be caught.

The manuscript contained yet other pages, but without relating any new crime.

Alienist physicians to whom the awful story has been submitted declare that there are in the world many undiscovered madmen as adroit and as much to be feared as this monstrous lunatic.

George Dobson's Expedition to Hell

James Hogg

———◆———

THERE IS NO PHENOMENON IN NATURE LESS UNDERSTOOD, AND ABOUT which greater nonsense is written than dreaming. It is a strange thing. For my part I do not understand it, nor have I any desire to do so; and I firmly believe that no philosopher that ever wrote knows a particle more about it than I do, however elaborate and subtle the theories he may advance concerning it. He knows not even what sleep is, nor can he define its nature, so as to enable any common mind to comprehend him; and how, then, can he define that ethereal part of it, wherein the soul holds intercourse with the external world?—how, in that state of abstraction, some ideas force themselves upon us, in spite of all our efforts to get rid of them; while others, which we have resolved to bear about with us by night as well as by day, refuse us their fellowship, even at periods when we most require their aid?

No, no; the philosopher knows nothing about either; and if he says he does, I entreat you not to believe him. He does not know what mind is; even his own mind, to which one would think he has the most direct access: far less can he estimate the operations and powers of that of any other intelligent being. He does not even know, with all his subtlety, whether it be a power distinct from his body, or essentially the same, and only incidentally and temporarily endowed with different qualities. He sets himself to discover at what period of his existence the union was established. He is baffled; for Consciousness refuses the intelligence, declaring, that she cannot carry him far enough back to ascertain it. He tries to discover the precise moment when it is dissolved, but on this Consciousness is altogether silent; and all is darkness and mystery; for the origin, the manner of continuance, and the time and mode of breaking up of the union between soul and body, are in reality undiscoverable by our natural faculties—are not patent, beyond the possibility of mistake: but whosoever can read his Bible, and solve a dream, can do either, without being subjected to any material error.

It is on this ground that I like to contemplate, not the theory of dreams, but the dreams themselves; because they prove to the unlettered man, in a very forcible manner, a distinct existence of the soul, and its lively and rapid intelligence with external nature, as well as with a world of spirits with which it has no acquaintance, when the body is lying dormant, and the same to the soul as if sleeping in death.

I account nothing of any dream that relates to the actions of the day; the person is not sound asleep who dreams about these things; there is no division between matter and mind, but they are mingled together in a sort of chaos—what a farmer would call compost—fermenting and disturbing one another. I find that in all dreams of that kind, men of every profession have dreams peculiar to their own occupations; and, in the country, at least, their import is generally understood. Every man's body is a barometer. A thing made up of the elements must be affected by their various changes and convulsions; and so the body assuredly is. When I was a shepherd, and all the comforts of my life depended so much on good or bad weather, the first thing I did every morning was strictly to overhaul the dreams of the night; and I found that I could calculate better from them than from the appearance and changes of the sky. I know a keen sportsman who pretends that his dreams never deceive him. If he dream of angling, or pursuing salmon in deep waters, he is sure of rain; but if fishing on dry ground, or in waters so low that the fish cannot get from him, it forebodes drought; hunting or shooting hares is snow, and moorfowl wind, &c. But the most extraordinary professional dream on record is, without all doubt, that well-known one of George Dobson, coach-driver in Edinburgh, which I shall here relate; for though it did not happen in the shepherd's cot, it has often been recited there.

George was part proprietor and driver of a hackneycoach in Edinburgh, when such vehicles were scarce; and one day a gentleman, whom he knew, came to him and said:—"George, you must drive me and my son here out to ——," a certain place that he named, somewhere in the vicinity of Edinburgh.

"Sir," said George, "I never heard tell of such a place, and I cannot drive you to it unless you give me very particular directions."

"It is false," returned the gentleman; "there is no man in Scotland who knows the road to that place better than you do. You have never driven on any other road all your life; and I insist on you taking us."

"Very well, sir," said George, " I'll drive you to hell, if you have a mind; only you are to direct me on the road."

"Mount and drive on, then," said the other; "and no fear of the road."

George did so, and never in his life did he see his horses go at such a noble rate; they snorted, they pranced, and they flew on; and as the whole road appeared to lie down-hill, he deemed that he should soon come to his journey's end. Still he drove on at the same rate, far, far down-hill,—and so fine an open road he never travelled,—till by degrees it grew so dark that he could not see to drive any farther. He called to the gentleman, inquiring what he should do; who answered that this was the place they were bound to, so he might draw up, dismiss them, and return. He did so, alighted from the dickie, wondered at his foaming horses, and forthwith opened the coach-door, held the rim of his hat with the one hand, and with the other demanded his fare.

"You have driven us in fine style, George," said the elder gentleman, "and deserve to be remembered; but it is needless for us to settle just now, as you must meet us here again to-morrow precisely at twelve o'clock."

"Very well, sir," said George; "there is likewise an old account, you know, and some toll-money"; which indeed there was.

"It shall be all settled to-morrow, George, and moreover, I fear there will be some toll-money to-day."

"I perceived no tolls to-day, your honour," said George.

"But I perceived one, and not very far back neither, which I suspect you will have difficulty in repassing without a regular ticket. What a pity I have no change on me!"

"I never saw it otherwise with your honour," said George, jocularly; "what a pity it is you should always suffer yourself to run short of change!"

"I will give you that which is as good, George," said the gentleman; and he gave him a ticket written with red ink, which the honest coachman could not read. He, however, put it into his sleeve, and inquired of his employer where that same toll was which he had not observed, and how it was that they did not ask toll from him as he came through? The gentleman replied, by informing George that there was no road out of that domain, and that whoever entered it must either remain in it, or return by the same path; so they never asked any toll till the person's return, when they were at times highly capricious; but that the ticket he had given him would answer his turn. And he then asked George if he did not perceive a gate, with a number of men in black standing about it.

"Oho! Is yon the spot?" says George; "then, I assure your honour, yon is no toll-gate, but a private entrance into a great man's mansion; for do not I know two or three of the persons yonder to be gentlemen of the law, whom I have driven often and often? and as good fellows they are too as any I know—men who never let them-selves run short of change! Good day.—Twelve o'clock to-morrow?"

"Yes, twelve o'clock noon, precisely"; and with that, George's employer vanished in the gloom, and left him to wind his way out of that dreary labyrinth the best way he could. He found it no easy matter, for his lamps were not lighted, and he could not see an ell before him—he could not even perceive his horses' ears; and what was worse, there was a rushing sound, like that of a town on fire, all around him, that stunned his senses, so that he could not tell whether his horses were moving or standing still. George was in the greatest distress imaginable, and was glad when he perceived the gate before him, with his two identical friends, men of the law, still standing. George drove boldly up, accosted them by their names, and asked what they were doing there; they made him no answer, but pointed to the gate and the keeper. George was terrified to look at this latter personage, who now came up and seized his horses by the reins, refusing to let him pass. In order to introduce himself, in some degree, to this austere toll-man, George asked him, in a jocular manner, how he came to employ his two emi-nent friends as assistant gate-keepers.

"Because they are among the last comers," replied the ruffian, churlishly. "You will be an assistant here to-morrow."

"The devil I will, sir!"

"Yes, the devil you will, sir."

"I'll be d——d if I do then—that I will!"

"Yes, you'll be d——d if you do—that you will."

"Let my horses go in the mean time, then, sir, that I may proceed on my journey."

"Nay."

"Nay!—Dare you say nay to me, sir? My name is George Dobson, of the Pleasance, Edinburgh, coach-driver, and coach-proprietor too; and no man shall say *nay* to me, as long as I can pay my way. I have his Majesty's license, and I'll go and come as I choose—and that I will. Let go my horses there, and tell me what is your demand."

"Well, then, I'll let your horses go," said the keeper. "But I'll keep yourself for a pledge." And with that he let go the horses, and seized honest George by the throat, who struggled in vain to disengage himself, and swore, and threatened, according to his own confession, most bloodily. His horses flew off like the wind, so swift, that the coach seemed flying in the air, and scarcely bounding on the earth once in a quarter of a mile. George was in furious wrath, for he saw that his grand coach and harness would all be broken to pieces, and his gallant pair of horses maimed or destroyed; and how was his family's bread now to be won!—He struggled, threatened, and prayed in vain;—the intolerable toll-man was deaf to all remonstrances. He once more appealed to his two genteel acquaintances of the law, reminding them how he had of late driven them to Roslin on a Sunday, along with two ladies, who, he supposed, were their sisters, from their familiarity, when not another coachman in town would engage with them. But the gentlemen, very ungenerously, only shook their heads, and pointed to the gate. George's circumstances now became desperate, and again he asked the hideous toll-man what right he had to detain him, and what were his charges.

"What right have I to detain you, sir, say you? Who are you that make such a demand here? Do you know where you are, sir?"

"No, faith, I do not," returned George; "I wish I did. But I *shall* know, and make you repent your insolence too. My name, I told you, is George Dobson, licensed coach-hirer in Pleasance, Edinburgh; and to get full redress of you for this unlawful interruption, I only desire to know where I am."

"Then, sir, if it can give you so much satisfaction to know where you are," said the keeper, with a malicious grin, "you *shall* know, and you may take instruments by the hands of your two friends there, instituting a legal prosecution. Your redress, you may be assured, will be most ample, when I inform you that you are in HELL! and out at this gate you pass no more."

This was rather a damper to George, and he began to perceive that nothing would be gained in such a place by the strong hand, so he addressed the inexorable toll-man, whom he now dreaded more than ever, in the following terms: "But I must go home at all events, you know, sir, to unyoke my two horses, and put them up, and to inform Chirsty Halliday, my wife, of my engagement. And, bless me! I never recollected till this moment, that I am engaged to be back here to-morrow at twelve o'clock, and see, here is a free ticket for my passage this way."

The keeper took the ticket with one hand, but still held George with the other. "Oho! were you in with our honourable friend, Mr. R—— of L——y?" said he. "He has been on our books for a long while;—however, this will do, only you must put your name to it likewise; and the engagement is this—You, by this instrument, engage your soul, that you will return here by to-morrow at noon."

"Catch me there, billy!" says George. "I'll engage no such thing, depend on it;—that I will not."

"Then remain where you are," said the keeper, "for there is no other alternative. We like best for people to come here in their own way,—in the way of their business";

and with that he flung George backwards, heels-over-head down hill, and closed the gate.

George finding all remonstrance vain, and being desirous once more to see the open day, and breathe the fresh air, and likewise to see Chirsty Halliday, his wife, and set his house and stable in some order, came up again, and in utter desperation, signed the bond, and was suffered to depart. He then bounded away on the track of his horses, with more than ordinary swiftness, in hopes to overtake them; and always now and then uttered a loud Wo! in hopes they might hear and obey, though he could not come in sight of them. But George's grief was but beginning; for at a well-known and dangerous spot, where there was a tan-yard on the one hand, and a quarry on the other, he came to his gallant steeds overturned, the coach smashed to pieces, Dawtie with two of her legs broken, and Duncan dead. This was more than the worthy coachman could bear, and many degrees worse than being in hell. There, his pride and manly spirit bore him up against the worst of treatment; but here his heart entirely failed him, and he laid himself down, with his face on his two hands, and wept bitterly, bewailing, in the most deplorable terms, his two gallant horses, Dawtie and Duncan.

While lying in this inconsolable state, some one took hold of his shoulder, and shook it; and a well-known voice said to him, "Geordie! what is the matter wi' ye, Geordie?" George was provoked beyond measure at the insolence of the question, for he knew the voice to be that of Chirsty Halliday, his wife. " I think you needna ask that, seeing what you see," said George. "O, my poor Dawtie, where are a' your jinkings and prancings now, your moopings and your wincings? I'll ne'er be a proud man again—bereaved o' my bonny pair!"

"Get up, George; get up, and bestir yourself," said Chirsty Halliday, his wife. "You are wanted directly, to bring in the Lord President to the Parliament House. It is a great storm, and he must be there by nine o' clock.—Get up—rouse yourself, and make ready—his servant is waiting for you."

"Woman, you are demented!" cried George. "How can I go and bring in the Lord President, when my coach is broken in pieces, my poor Dawtie lying with twa of her legs broken, and Duncan dead? And, moreover, I have a previous engagement, for I am obliged, to be in hell before twelve o clock."

Chirsty Halliday now laughed outright, and continued long in a fit of laughter; but George never moved his head from the pillow, but lay and groaned,—for, in fact, he was all this while lying snug in his bed; while the tempest without was roaring with great violence, and which circumstance may perhaps account for the rushing and deafening sound which astounded him so much in hell. But so deeply was he impressed with the idea of the reality of his dream, that he would do nothing but lie and moan, persisting and believing in the truth of all he had seen. His wife now went and informed her neighbours of her husband's plight, and of his singular engagement with Mr. R—— of L——y at twelve o'clock. She persuaded one friend to harness the horses, and go for the Lord President; but all the rest laughed immoderately at poor coachy's predicament. It was, however, no laughing to him; he never raised his head, and his wife becoming at last uneasy about the frenzied state of his mind, made him repeat every circumstance of his adventure to her, (for he would never believe or admit that it was a dream,) which he did in the terms above narrated; and she perceived or dreaded that he was becoming somewhat feverish. She went out, and told Dr. Wood of her husband's malady, and of his solemn engagement to be in hell at twelve o'clock.

"He maunna keep it, dearie. He maunna keep that engagement at no rate," said Dr. Wood. "Set back the clock an hour or twa, to drive him past the time, and I'll ca' in the course of my rounds. Are ye sure he hasna been drinking hard?"—She assured him he had not.—"Weel, weel, ye maun tell him that he maunna keep that engagement at no rate. Set back the clock, and I'll come and see him. It is a frenzy that maunna be trifled with. Ye maunna laugh at it, dearie,—maunna laugh at it. Maybe a nervish fever, wha kens."

The Doctor and Chirsty left the house together, and as their road lay the same way for a space, she fell a telling him of the two young lawyers whom George saw standing at the gate of hell, and whom the porter had described as two of the last comers. When the Doctor heard this, he stayed his hurried, stooping pace in one moment, turned full round on the woman, and fixing his eyes on her, that gleamed with a deep unstable lustre, he said, "What's that ye were saying, dearie? What's that ye were saying? Repeat it again to me, every word." She did so. On which the Doctor held up his hands, as if palsied with astonishment, and uttered some fervent ejaculations. "I'll go with you straight," said he, "before I visit another patient. This is wonderfu'! it is terrible! The young gentlemen are both at rest—both lying corpses at this time! Fine young men—I attended them both—died of the same exterminating disease—Oh, this is wonderful; this is wonderful!"

The Doctor kept Chirsty half running all the way down the High Street and St Mary's Wynd, at such a pace did he walk, never lifting his eyes from the pavement, but always exclaiming now and then, "It is wonderfu'! most wonderfu'!" At length, prompted by woman's natural curiosity, Chirsty inquired at the Doctor if he knew any thing of their friend Mr. R—— of L——y. But he shook his head, and replied, "Na, na, dearie,—ken naething about him. He and his son are baith in London,—ken naething about him; but the tither is awfu'—it is perfectly awfu'!"

When Dr. Wood reached his patient he found him very low, but only a little feverish; so he made all haste to wash his head with vinegar and cold water, and then he covered the crown with a treacle plaster, and made the same application to the soles of his feet, awaiting the issue. George revived a little, when the Doctor tried to cheer him up by joking him about his dream; but on mention of that he groaned, and shook his head. "So you are convinced, dearie, that it is nae dream?" said the Doctor.

"Dear sir, how could it be a dream?" said the patient. "I was there in person, with Mr. R—— and his son; and see, here are the marks of the porter's fingers on my throat."—Dr. Wood looked, and distinctly saw two or three red spots on one side of his throat, which confounded him not a little.—"I assure you, sir," continued George, "it was no dream, which I know to my sad experience. I have lost my coach and horses,—and what more have I?—signed the bond with my own hand, and in person entered into the most solemn and terrible engagement."

"But ye're no to keep it, I tell ye," said Dr. Wood; "ye're no to keep it at no rate. It is a sin to enter into a compact wi' the deil, but it is a far greater ane to keep it. Sae let Mr. R—— and his son bide where they are yonder, for ye sanna stir a foot to bring them out the day."

"Oh, oh, Doctor!" groaned the poor fellow, "this is not a thing to be made a jest o'! I feel that it is an engagement that I cannot break. Go I must, and that very shortly. Yes, yes, go I must, and go I will, although I should borrow David Barclay's pair." With that he turned his face towards the wall, groaned deeply, and fell into a lethargy, while Dr. Wood caused them to let him alone, thinking if he would sleep out the appointed time, which was at hand, he would be safe; but all the time he kept feeling his pulse, and by degrees showed symptoms of uneasiness. His wife ran for a clergyman of famed abilities, to pray and converse with her husband, in hopes by that means to bring him to his senses; but after his arrival, George never spoke more, save calling to his horses, as if encouraging them to run with great speed; and thus in imagination driving at full career to keep his appointment, he went off in a paroxysm, after a terrible struggle, precisely within a few minutes of twelve o'clock.

A circumstance not known at the time of George's death made this singular professional dream the more remarkable and unique in all its parts. It was a terrible storm on the night of the dream, as has been already mentioned, and during the time of the hurricane, a London smack went down off Wearmouth about three in the morning. Among the sufferers were the Hon. Mr. R—— of L——y, and his son! George could not know aught of this at break of day, for it was not known in Scotland till the day of his interment; and as little knew he of the deaths of the two young lawyers, who both died of the small-pox the evening before.

Strange Case of Dr. Jekyll and Mr. Hyde

Robert Louis Stevenson

———◆———

STORY OF THE DOOR

MR. UTTERSON THE LAWYER WAS A MAN OF A RUGGED COUNTENANCE, THAT WAS never lighted by a smile; cold, scanty and embarrassed in discourse; backward in sentiment; lean, long, dusty, dreary and yet somehow lovable. At friendly meetings, and when the wine was to his taste, something eminently human beaconed from his eye; something indeed which never found its way into his talk, but which spoke not only in these silent symbols of the after-dinner face, but more often and loudly in the acts of his life. He was austere with himself; drank gin when he was alone, to mortify a taste for vintages; and though he enjoyed the theater, had not crossed the doors of one for twenty years. But he had an approved tolerance for others; sometimes wondering, almost with envy, at the high pressure of spirits involved in their misdeeds; and in any extremity inclined to help rather than to reprove. "I incline to Cain's heresy," he used to say quaintly: "I let my brother go to the devil in his own way." In this character, it was frequently his fortune to be the last reputable acquaintance and the last good influence in the lives of down-going men. And to such as these, so long as they came about his chambers, he never marked a shade of change in his demeanour.

No doubt the feat was easy to Mr. Utterson; for he was undemonstrative at the best, and even his friendships seemed to be founded in a similar catholicity of good-nature. It is the mark of a modest man to accept his friendly circle ready-made from the hands of opportunity; and that was the lawyer's way. His friends were those of his own blood or those whom he had known the longest; his affections, like ivy, were the growth of time, they implied no aptness in the object. Hence, no doubt the bond that united him to Mr. Richard Enfield, his distant kinsman, the well-known man about town. It was a nut to crack for many, what these two could see in each other, or what subject they could find in common. It was reported by those who encountered them in their Sunday walks, that they said nothing, looked singularly dull and would hail with obvious relief the appearance of a friend. For all that, the two men put the greatest store by these excursions, counted them the chief jewel of each week, and not only set aside occasions of pleasure, but even resisted the calls of business, that they might enjoy them uninterrupted.

It chanced on one of these rambles that their way led them down a by-street in a busy quarter of London. The street was small and what is called quiet, but it drove a thriving trade on the week-days. The inhabitants were all doing well, it seemed, and all emulously hoping to do better still, and laying out the surplus of their grains in coquetry; so that the shop fronts stood along that thoroughfare with an air of invitation, like rows of smiling saleswomen. Even on Sunday, when it veiled its more florid charms and lay comparatively empty of passage, the street shone out in contrast to its dingy neighbourhood, like a fire in a forest; and with its freshly painted shutters, well-polished brasses, and general cleanliness and gaiety of note, instantly caught and pleased the eye of the passenger.

Two doors from one corner, on the left hand going east the line was broken by the entry of a court; and just at that point, a certain sinister block of building thrust forward its gable on the street. It was two storeys high; showed no window, nothing but a door on the lower storey and a blind forehead of discoloured wall on the upper; and bore in every feature, the marks of prolonged and sordid negligence. The door which was equipped with neither bell nor knocker, was blistered and distained. Tramps slouched into the recess and struck matches on the panels; children kept shop upon the steps; the schoolboy had tried his knife on the mouldings; and for close on a generation, no one had appeared to drive away these random visitors or to repair their ravages.

Mr. Enfield and the lawyer were on the other side of the by-street; but when they came abreast of the entry, the former lifted up his cane and pointed.

"Did you ever remark that door?" he asked; and when his companion had replied in the affirmative. "It is connected in my mind," added he, "with a very odd story."

"Indeed?" said Mr. Utterson, with a slight change of voice, "and what was that?"

"Well, it was this way," returned Mr. Enfield: "I was coming home from some place at the end of the world, about three o'clock of a black winter morning, and my way lay through a part of town where there was literally nothing to be seen but lamps. Street after street and all the folks asleep—street after street, all lighted up as if for a procession and all as empty as a church—till at last I got into that state of mind when a man listens and listens and begins to long for the sight of a policeman. All at once, I saw two figures: one a little man who was stumping along eastward at a good walk, and the other a girl of maybe eight or ten who was running as hard as she was able down a cross street. Well, sir, the two ran into one another naturally enough at the corner; and then came the horrible part of the thing; for the man trampled calmly over the child's body and left her screaming on the ground. It sounds nothing to hear, but it was hellish to see. It wasn't like a man; it was like some damned Juggernaut. I gave a few halloa, took to my heels, collared my gentleman, and brought him back to where there was already quite a group about the screaming child. He was perfectly cool and made no resistance, but gave me one look, so ugly that it brought out the sweat on me like running. The people who had turned out were the girl's own family; and pretty soon, the doctor, for whom she had been sent, put in his appearance. Well, the child was not much the worse, more frightened, according to the Sawbones; and there you might have supposed would be an end to it. But there was one curious circumstance. I had taken a loathing to my gentleman at first sight. So had the child's family, which was only natural. But the doctor's case was what struck me. He was the usual cut and dry apothecary, of no particular age and colour, with a strong Edinburgh accent, and about as emotional as a bagpipe. Well, sir, he was like the rest of us; every time he looked at my prisoner, I saw that Sawbones turn sick and white with desire to kill him. I knew what was in his mind, just as he knew what was in mine; and killing being out of the question, we did the next best. We told the man we could and would make such a scandal out of this as should make his name stink from one end of London to the other. If he had any friends or any credit, we undertook that he should lose them. And all the time, as we were pitching it in red hot, we were keeping the women off him as best we could, for they were as wild as harpies. I never saw a circle of such hateful faces; and there was the man in the middle, with a kind of black, sneering coolness—frightened too, I could see that—but carrying it off, sir, really like Satan. 'If you choose to make capital out of this accident,' said he, 'I am naturally helpless. No gentleman but wishes to avoid a scene,' says he. 'Name your figure.' Well, we screwed him up to a hundred pounds for the child's family; he would have clearly liked to stick out; but there was something about the lot of us that meant mischief, and at last he struck. The next thing was to get the money; and where do you think he carried us but to that place with the door?—whipped out a key, went in, and presently came back with the matter of ten pounds in gold and a cheque for the balance on Coutts's, drawn payable to bearer and signed with a name that I can't mention, though it's one of the points of my story, but it was a name at least very well known and often printed. The figure was stiff; but the signature was good for more than that, if it was only genuine. I took the liberty of pointing out to my gentleman that the whole business looked apocryphal, and that a man does not, in real life, walk into a cellar door at four in the morning and come out of it with another man's cheque for close upon a hundred pounds. But he was quite easy and sneering. 'Set your mind at rest,' says he, 'I will stay with you till the banks open and cash the cheque myself.' So we all set off, the doctor, and the child's father, and our friend and myself, and passed the rest of the night in my chambers; and next day, when we had breakfasted, went in a body to the bank. I gave in the cheque myself, and said I had every reason to believe it was a forgery. Not a bit of it. The cheque was genuine."

"Tut-tut," said Mr. Utterson.

"I see you feel as I do," said Mr. Enfield. "Yes, it's a bad story. For my man was a fellow that nobody could have to do with; a really damnable man; and the person that drew the cheque is the very pink of the proprieties, celebrated too, and (what makes it worse) one of your fellows who do what they call good. Black mail, I suppose; an honest man paying through the nose for some of the capers of his youth. Black Mail House is what I call the place with the door, in consequence. Though even that, you know, is far from explaining all," he added, and with the words fell into a vein of musing.

From this he was recalled by Mr. Utterson asking rather suddenly: "And you don't know if the drawer of the cheque lives there?"

"A likely place isn't it?" returned Mr. Enfield. "But I happen to have noticed his address; he lives in some square or other."

"And you never asked about— the place with the door?" said Mr. Utterson.

"No, sir: I had a delicacy," was the reply. "I feel very strongly about putting questions; it partakes too much of the style of the day of judgment. You start a question, and it's like starting a stone. You sit quietly on the top of a hill; and away the stone goes, starting others; and presently some bland old bird (the last you would have thought of) is knocked on the head in his own back garden and the family have to change their name. No, sir, I make it a rule of mine: the more it looks like Queer Street, the less I ask."

"A very good rule, too," said the lawyer.

"But I have studied the place for myself," continued Mr. Enfield. "It seems scarcely a house. There is no other door, and nobody goes in or out of that one but, once in a great while, the gentleman of my adventure. There are three windows looking on the court on the first floor; none below; the windows are always shut but they're clean. And then there is a chimney which is generally smoking; so somebody must live there. And yet it's not so sure; for the buildings are so packed together about the court, that it's hard to say where one ends and another begins."

The pair walked on again for a while in silence; and then "Enfield," said Mr. Utterson, "that's a good rule of yours."

"Yes, I think it is," returned Enfield.

"But for all that," continued the lawyer, "there's one point I want to ask: I want to ask the name of that man who walked over the child."

"Well," said Mr. Enfield, "I can't see what harm it would do. It was a man of the name of Hyde."

"Hm," said Mr. Utterson. "What sort of a man is he to see?"

"He is not easy to describe. There is something wrong with his appearance; something displeasing, something downright detestable. I never saw a man I so disliked, and yet I scarce know why. He must be deformed somewhere; he gives a strong feeling of deformity, although I couldn't specify the point. He's an extraordinary looking man, and yet I really can name nothing out of the way. No, sir; I can make no hand of it; I can't describe him. And it's not want of memory; for I declare I can see him this moment."

Mr. Utterson again walked some way in silence and obviously under a weight of consideration. "You are sure he used a key?" he inquired at last.

"My dear sir . . ." began Enfield, surprised out of himself.

"Yes, I know," said Utterson; "I know it must seem strange. The fact is, if I do not ask you the name of the other party, it is because I know it already. You see, Richard, your tale has gone home. If you have been inexact in any point you had better correct it."

"I think you might have warned me," returned the other with a touch of sullenness. "But I have been pedantically exact, as you call it. The fellow had a key; and what's more, he has it still. I saw him use it not a week ago."

Mr. Utterson sighed deeply but said never a word; and the young man presently resumed. "Here is another lesson to say nothing," said he. "I am ashamed of my long tongue. Let us make a bargain never to refer to this again."

"With all my heart," said the lawyer. "I shake hands on that, Richard."

SEARCH FOR MR. HYDE

THAT EVENING, MR. UTTERSON CAME HOME TO HIS BACHELOR HOUSE IN SOMBRE spirits and sat down to dinner without relish. It was his custom of a Sunday, when this meal was over, to sit close by the fire, a volume of some dry divinity on his reading desk, until the clock of the neighbouring church rang out the hour of twelve, when he would go soberly and gratefully to bed. On this night, however, as soon as the cloth was taken away, he took up a candle and went into his business room. There he opened his safe, took from the most private part of it a document endorsed on the envelope as Dr. Jekyll's Will, and sat down with a clouded brow to study its contents. The will was holograph, for Mr. Utterson, though he took charge of it now that it was made, had refused to lend the least assistance in the making of it; it provided not only that, in case of the decease of Henry Jekyll, M.D., D.C.L., LL.D., F.R.S., etc., all his possessions were to pass into the hands of his "friend and benefactor Edward Hyde," but that in case of Dr. Jekyll's "disappearance or unexplained absence for any period exceeding three calendar months," the said Edward Hyde should step into the said Henry Jekyll's shoes without further delay and free from any burthen or obligation, beyond the payment of a few small sums to the members of the doctor's household. This document had long been the lawyer's eyesore. It offended him both as a lawyer and as a lover of the sane and customary sides of life, to whom the fanciful was the immodest. And hitherto it was his ignorance of Mr. Hyde that had swelled his indignation; now, by a sudden turn, it was his knowledge. It was already bad enough when the name was but a name of which he could learn no more. It was worse when it began to be clothed upon with detestable attributes; and out of the shifting, insubstantial mists that had so long baffled his eye, there leaped up the sudden, definite presentment of a fiend.

"I thought it was madness," he said, as he replaced the obnoxious paper in the safe, "and now I begin to fear it is disgrace."

With that he blew out his candle, put on a great coat, and set forth in the direction of Cavendish Square, that citadel of medicine, where his friend, the great Dr. Lanyon, had his house and received his crowding patients. "If anyone knows, it will be Lanyon," he had thought.

The solemn butler knew and welcomed him; he was subjected to no stage of delay, but ushered direct from the door to the dining-room where Dr. Lanyon sat alone over his wine. This was a hearty, healthy, dapper, red-faced gentleman, with a shock of hair prematurely white, and a boisterous and decided manner. At sight of Mr. Utterson, he sprang up from his chair and welcomed him with both hands. The geniality, as was the way of the man, was somewhat theatrical to the eye; but it reposed on genuine feeling. For these two were old friends, old mates both at school and college, both thorough respecters of themselves and of each other, and, what does not always follow, men who thoroughly enjoyed each other's company.

After a little rambling talk, the lawyer led up to the subject which so disagreeably preoccupied his mind.

"I suppose, Lanyon," said he, "you and I must be the two oldest friends that Henry Jekyll has?"

"I wish the friends were younger," chuckled Dr. Lanyon. "But I suppose we are. And what of that? I see little of him now."

"Indeed?" said Utterson. "I thought you had a bond of common interest."

"We had," was the reply. "But it is more than ten years since Henry Jekyll became too fanciful for me. He began to go wrong, wrong in mind; and though of course I continue to take an interest in him for old sake's sake as they say, I see and I have seen devilish little of the man. Such unscientific balderdash," added the doctor, flushing suddenly purple, "would have estranged Damon and Pythias."

This little spirit of temper was somewhat of a relief to Mr. Utterson. "They have only differed on some point of science," he thought; and being a man of no scientific passions (except in the matter of conveyancing) he even added: "It is nothing worse than that!" He gave his friend a few seconds to recover his composure, and then approached the question he had come to put. "Did you ever come across a protégé of his—one Hyde?" he asked.

"Hyde?" repeated Lanyon. "No. Never heard of him. Since my time."

That was the amount of information that the lawyer carried back with him to the great, dark bed on which he tossed to and fro, until the small hours of the morning began to grow large. It was a night of little ease to his toiling mind, toiling in mere darkness and besieged by questions.

Six o'clock struck on the bells of the church that was so conveniently near to Mr. Utterson's dwelling, and still he was digging at the problem. Hitherto it had touched him on the intellectual side alone; but now his imagination also was engaged or rather enslaved; and as he lay and tossed in the gross darkness of the night and the curtained room, Mr. Enfield's tale went by before his mind in a scroll of lighted pictures. He would be aware of the great field of lamps of a nocturnal city; then of the figure of a man walking swiftly; then of a child running from the doctor's; and then these met, and that human Juggernaut trod the child down and passed on regardless of her screams. Or else he would see a room in a rich house, where his friend lay asleep, dreaming and smiling at his dreams; and then the door of that room would be opened, the curtains of the bed plucked apart, the sleeper recalled, and lo! there would stand by his side a figure to whom power was given, and even at that dead hour, he must rise and do its bidding. The figure in these two phases haunted the lawyer all night; and if at any time he dozed over, it was but to see it glide more stealthily through sleeping houses, or move the more swiftly and still the more swiftly, even to dizziness, through wider labyrinths of lamplighted city, and at every street corner crush a child and leave her screaming. And still the figure had no face by which he might know it; even in his dreams, it had no face, or one that baffled him and melted before his eyes; and thus it was that there sprang up and grew apace in the lawyer's mind a singularly strong, almost an inordinate, curiosity to behold the features of the real Mr. Hyde. If he could but once set eyes on him, he thought the mystery would lighten and perhaps roll altogether away, as was the habit of mysterious things when well examined. He might see a reason for his friend's strange preference or bondage (call it which you please) and even for the startling clause of the will. At least it would be a face worth seeing: the face of a man who was without bowels of mercy: a face which had but to show itself to raise up, in the mind of the unimpressionable Enfield, a spirit of enduring hatred.

From that time forward, Mr. Utterson began to haunt the door in the bystreet of shops. In the morning before office hours, at noon when business was plenty and time scarce, at night under the face of the fogged city moon, by all lights and at all hours of solitude or concourse, the lawyer was to be found on his chosen post.

"If he be Mr. Hyde," he had thought, "I shall be Mr. Seek."

And at last his patience was rewarded. It was a fine dry night; frost in the air; the streets as clean as a ballroom floor; the lamps, unshaken by any wind, drawing a regular pattern of light and shadow. By ten o'clock, when the shops were closed, the bystreet was very solitary and, in spite of the low growl of London from all round, very silent. Small sounds carried far; domestic sounds out of the houses were clearly audible on either side of the roadway; and the rumour of the approach of any passenger preceded him by a long time. Mr. Utterson had been some minutes at his post, when he was aware of an odd, light footstep drawing near. In the course of his nightly patrols, he had long grown accustomed to the quaint effect with which the footfalls of a single person, while he is still a great way off, suddenly spring out distinct from the vast hum and clatter of the city. Yet his attention had never before been so sharply and decisively arrested; and it was with a strong, superstitious prevision of success that he withdrew into the entry of the court.

The steps drew swiftly nearer, and swelled out suddenly louder as they turned the end of the street. The lawyer, looking forth from the entry, could soon see what manner of man he had to deal with. He was small and very plainly dressed, and the look of him, even at that distance, went somehow strongly against the watcher's inclination. But he made straight for the door, crossing the roadway to save time; and as he came, he drew a key from his pocket like one approaching home.

Mr. Utterson stepped out and touched him on the shoulder as he passed. "Mr. Hyde, I think?"

Mr. Hyde shrank back with a hissing intake of the breath. But his fear was only momentary; and though he did not look the lawyer in the face, he answered coolly enough: "That is my name. What do you want?"

"I see you are going in," returned the lawyer. "I am an old friend of Dr. Jekyll's— Mr. Utterson of Gaunt Street—you must have heard of my name; and meeting you so conveniently, I thought you might admit me."

"You will not find Dr. Jekyll; he is from home," replied Mr. Hyde, blowing in the key. And then suddenly, but still without looking up, "How did you know me?" he asked.

"On your side," said Mr. Utterson "will you do me a favour?"

"With pleasure," replied the other. "What shall it be?"

"Will you let me see your face?" asked the lawyer.

Mr. Hyde appeared to hesitate, and then, as if upon some sudden reflection, fronted about with an air of defiance; and the pair stared at each other pretty fixedly for a few seconds. "Now I shall know you again," said Mr. Utterson. "It may be useful."

"Yes," returned Mr. Hyde, "it is as well we have met; and à propos, you should have my address." And he gave a number of a street in Soho.

"Good God!" thought Mr. Utterson, "can he too have been thinking of the will?" But he kept his feelings to himself and only grunted in acknowledgment of the address.

"And now," said the other, "how did you know me?"

"By description," was the reply.

"Whose description?"

"We have common friends," said Mr. Utterson.

"Common friends," echoed Mr. Hyde, a little hoarsely. "Who are they?"

"Jekyll, for instance," said the lawyer.

"He never told you," cried Mr. Hyde, with a flush of anger. "I did not think you would have lied."

"Come," said Mr. Utterson, "that is not fitting language."

The other snarled aloud into a savage laugh; and the next moment, with extraordinary quickness, he had unlocked the door and disappeared into the house.

The lawyer stood awhile when Mr. Hyde had left him, the picture of disquietude. Then he began slowly to mount the street, pausing every step or two and putting his hand to his brow like a man in mental perplexity. The problem he was thus debating as he walked, was one of a class that is rarely solved. Mr. Hyde was pale and dwarfish, he gave an impression of deformity without any nameable malformation, he had a displeasing smile, he had borne himself to the lawyer with a sort of murderous mixture of timidity and boldness, and he spoke with a husky, whispering and somewhat broken voice; all these were points against him, but not all of these together could explain the hitherto unknown disgust, loathing and fear with which Mr. Utterson regarded him. "There must be something else," said the perplexed gentleman. "There *is* something more, if I could find a name for it. God bless me, the man seems hardly human! Something troglodytic, shall we say? or can it be the old story of Dr. Fell? or is it the mere radiance of a foul soul that thus transpires through, and transfigures, its clay continent? The last, I think; for, O my poor old Harry Jekyll, if ever I read Satan's signature upon a face, it is on that of your new friend."

Round the corner from the bystreet, there was a square of ancient, handsome houses, now for the most part decayed from their high estate and let in flats and chambers to all sorts and conditions of men: map-engravers, architects, shady lawyers and the agents of obscure enterprises. One house, however, second from the corner, was still occupied entire; and at the door of this, which wore a great air of wealth and comfort, though it was now plunged in darkness except for the fan-light, Mr. Utterson stopped and knocked. A well-dressed, elderly servant opened the door.

"Is Dr. Jekyll at home, Poole?" asked the lawyer.

"I will see, Mr. Utterson," said Poole, admitting the visitor, as he spoke, into a large, low-roofed, comfortable hall, paved with flags, warmed (after the fashion of a country house) by a bright, open fire, and furnished with costly cabinets of oak. "Will you wait here by the fire, sir? or shall I give you a light in the dining-room?"

"Here, thank you," said the lawyer, and he drew near and leaned on the tall fender. This hall, in which he was now left alone, was a pet fancy of his friend the doctor's; and Utterson himself was wont to speak of it as the pleasantest room in London. But to-night there was a shudder in his blood; the face of Hyde sat heavy on his memory; he felt (what was rare with him) a nausea and distaste of life; and in the gloom of his spirits, he seemed to read a menace in the flickering of the firelight on the polished cabinets and the uneasy starting of the shadow on the roof. He was ashamed of his relief, when Poole presently returned to announce that Dr. Jekyll was gone out.

"I saw Mr. Hyde go in by the old dissecting room, Poole," he said. "Is that right, when Dr. Jekyll is from home?"

"Quite right, Mr. Utterson, sir," replied the servant. "Mr. Hyde has a key."

"Your master seems to repose a great deal of trust in that young man, Poole," resumed the other musingly.

"Yes, sir, he do indeed," said Poole. "We have all orders to obey him."

"I do not think I ever met Mr. Hyde?" asked Utterson.

"O, dear no, sir. He never *dines* here," replied the butler. "Indeed we see very little of him on this side of the house; he mostly comes and goes by the laboratory."

"Well, goodnight, Poole."

"Goodnight, Mr. Utterson."

And the lawyer set out homeward with a very heavy heart. "Poor Harry Jekyll," he thought, "my mind misgives me he is in deep waters! He was wild when he was young; a long while ago to be sure; but in the law of God, there is no statute of limitations. Ay, it must be that; the ghost of some old sin, the cancer of some concealed disgrace: punish-ment coming, *pede claudo,* years after memory has forgotten and self-love condoned the fault." And the lawyer, scared by the thought, brooded awhile on his own past, groping in all the corners of memory, lest by chance some Jack-in-the-Box of an old iniquity should leap to light there. His past was fairly blameless; few men could read the rolls of their life with less apprehension; yet he was humbled to the dust by the many ill things he had done, and raised up again into a sober and fearful gratitude by the many that he had come so near to doing, yet avoided. And then by a return on his former subject, he conceived a spark of hope. "This Master Hyde, if he were studied," thought he, "must have secrets of his own: black secrets, by the look of him; secrets compared to which poor Jekyll's worst would be like sunshine. Things cannot continue as they are. It turns me cold to think of this creature stealing like a thief to Harry's bedside; poor Harry, what a wakening! And the danger of it; for if this Hyde suspects the existence of the will, he may grow impatient to inherit. Ay, I must put my shoulder to the wheel—if Jekyll will but let me," he added, "if Jekyll will only let me." For once more he saw before his mind's eye, as clear as transparency, the strange clauses of the will.

DR. JEKYLL WAS QUITE AT EASE

A FORTNIGHT LATER, BY EXCELLENT GOOD FORTUNE, THE DOCTOR GAVE ONE OF HIS pleasant dinners to some five or six old cronies, all intelligent, reputable men and all judges of good wine; and Mr. Utterson so contrived that he remained behind after the others had departed. This was no new arrangement, but a thing that had befallen many scores of times. Where Utterson was liked, he was liked well. Hosts loved to detain the dry lawyer, when the light-hearted and loose-tongued had already their foot on the threshold; they liked to sit a while in his unobtrusive company, practising for solitude, sobering their minds in the man's rich silence after the expense and strain of gaiety. To this rule, Dr. Jekyll was no exception; and as he now sat on the opposite side of the fire—a large, well-made, smooth-faced man of fifty, with something of a slyish cast perhaps, but every mark of capacity and kindness—you could see by his looks that he cherished for Mr. Utterson a sincere and warm affection.

"I have been wanting to speak to you, Jekyll," began the latter. "You know that will of yours?"

A close observer might have gathered that the topic was distasteful; but the doctor carried it off gaily. "My poor Utterson," said he, "you are unfortunate in such a client. I never saw a man so distressed as you were by my will; unless it were that hide-bound pedant, Lanyon, at what he called my scientific heresies. O, I know he's a good fellow—you needn't frown—an excellent fellow, and I always mean to see more of him; but a hide-bound pedant for all that; an ignorant, blatant pedant. I was never more disappointed in any man than Lanyon."

"You know I never approved of it," pursued Utterson, ruthlessly disregarding the fresh topic.

"My will? Yes, certainly, I know that," said the doctor, a trifle sharply. "You have told me so."

"Well, I tell you so again," continued the lawyer. "I have been learning something of young Hyde."

The large handsome face of Dr. Jekyll grew pale to the very lips, and there came a blackness about his eyes. "I do not care to hear more," said he. "This is a matter I thought we had agreed to drop."

"What I heard was abominable," said Utterson.

"It can make no change. You do not understand my position," returned the doctor, with a certain incoherency of manner. "I am painfully situated, Utterson; my position is a very strange—a very strange one. It is one of those affairs that cannot be mended by talking."

"Jekyll," said Utterson, "you know me: I am a man to be trusted. Make a clean breast of this in confidence; and I make no doubt I can get you out of it."

"My good Utterson," said the doctor, "this is very good of you, this is downright good of you, and I cannot find words to thank you in. I believe you fully; I would trust you before any man alive, ay, before myself, if I could make the choice; but indeed it isn't what you fancy; it is not as bad as that; and just to put your good heart at rest, I will tell you one thing: the moment I choose, I can be rid of Mr. Hyde. I give you my hand upon that; and I thank you again and again; and I will just add one little word, Utterson, that I'm sure you'll take in good part: this is a private matter, and I beg of you to let it sleep."

Utterson reflected a little looking in the fire.

"I have no doubt you are perfectly right," he said at last, getting to his feet.

"Well, but since we have touched upon this business, and for the last time I hope," continued the doctor, "there is one point I should like you to understand. I have really a very great interest in poor Hyde. I know you have seen him; he told me so; and I fear he was rude. But I do sincerely take a great, a very great interest in that young man; and if I am taken away, Utterson, I wish you to promise me that you will bear with him and get his rights for him. I think you would, if you knew all; and it would be a weight off my mind if you would promise."

"I can't pretend that I shall ever like him," said the lawyer.

"I don't ask that," pleaded Jekyll, laying his hand upon the other's arm; "I only ask for justice; I only ask you to help him for my sake, when I am no longer here."

Utterson heaved an irrepressible sigh. "Well," said he, "I promise."

THE CAREW MURDER CASE

NEARLY A YEAR LATER, IN THE MONTH OF OCTOBER, 18—, LONDON WAS STARTLED BY a crime of singular ferocity and rendered all the more notable by the high position of the victim. The details were few and startling. A maid servant living alone in a house not far from the river, had gone upstairs to bed about eleven. Although a fog rolled over the city in the small hours, the early part of the night was cloudless, and the lane, which the maid's window overlooked, was brilliantly lit by the full moon. It seems she was romantically given, for she sat down upon her box, which stood immediately under the window, and fell into a dream of musing. Never (she used to say, with streaming tears, when she narrated that experience) never had she felt more at peace with all men or thought more kindly of the world. And as she so sat she became aware of an aged beautiful gentleman with white hair, drawing near along the lane; and advancing to meet him, another and very small gentleman, to whom at first she paid less attention. When they had come within speech (which was just under the maid's eyes) the older man bowed and accosted the other with a very pretty manner of politeness. It did not seem as if the subject of his address were of great importance; indeed, from his pointing, it some times appeared as if he were only inquiring his way; but the moon shone on his face as he spoke, and the girl was pleased to watch it, it seemed to breathe such an innocent and old-world kindness of disposition, yet with something high too, as of a well-founded self-content. Presently her eye wandered to the other, and she was surprised to recognise in him a certain Mr. Hyde, who had once visited her master and for whom she had conceived a dislike. He had in his hand a heavy cane, with which he was trifling; but he answered never a word, and seemed to listen with an ill-contained impatience. And then all of a sudden he broke out in a great flame of anger, stamping with his foot, brandishing the cane, and carrying on (as the maid described it) like a madman. The old gentleman took a step back, with the air of one very much surprised and a trifle hurt; and at that Mr. Hyde broke out of all bounds and clubbed him to the earth. And next moment, with ape-like fury, he was trampling his victim under foot, and hailing down a storm of blows, under which the bones were audibly shattered and the body jumped upon the roadway. At the horror of these sights and sounds, the maid fainted.

It was two o'clock when she came to herself and called for the police. The murderer was gone long ago; but there lay his victim in the middle of the lane, incredibly mangled. The stick with which the deed had been done, although it was of some rare and very tough and heavy wood, had broken in the middle under the stress of this insensate cruelty; and one splintered half had rolled in the neighbouring gutter—the other, without doubt, had been carried away by the murderer. A purse and a gold watch were found upon the victim; but no cards or papers, except a sealed and stamped envelope, which he had been probably carrying to the post, and which bore the name and address of Mr. Utterson.

This was brought to the lawyer the next morning, before he was out of bed; and he had no sooner seen it and been told the circumstances, than he shot out a solemn lip. "I shall say nothing till I have seen the body," said he; "this may be very serious. Have the kindness to wait while I dress." And with the same grave countenance he hurried through his breakfast and drove to the police station, whither the body had been carried. As soon as he came into the cell, he nodded.

"Yes," said he, "I recognise him. I am sorry to say that this is Sir Danvers Carew."

"Good God, sir," exclaimed the officer, "is it possible?" And the next moment his eye lighted up with professional ambition. "This will make a deal of noise," he said. "And perhaps you can help us to the man." And he briefly narrated what the maid had seen, and showed the broken stick.

Mr. Utterson had already quailed at the name of Hyde; but when the stick was laid before him, he could doubt no longer: broken and battered as it was, he recognized it for one that he had himself presented many years before to Henry Jekyll.

"Is this Mr. Hyde a person of small stature?" he inquired.

"Particularly small and particularly wicked-looking, is what the maid calls him," said the officer.

Mr. Utterson reflected; and then, raising his head, "If you will come with me in my cab," he said, "I think I can take you to his house."

It was by this time about nine in the morning, and the first fog of the season. A great chocolate-coloured pall lowered over heaven, but the wind was continually charging and routing these embattled vapours; so that as the cab crawled from street to street, Mr. Utterson beheld a marvelous number of degrees and hues of twilight; for here it would be dark like the back-end of evening; and there would be a glow of a rich, lurid brown, like the light of some strange conflagration; and here, for a moment, the fog would be quite broken up, and a haggard shaft of daylight would glance in between the swirling wreaths. The dismal quarter of Soho seen under these changing glimpses, with its muddy ways, and slatternly passengers, and its lamps, which had never been extinguished or had been kindled afresh to combat this mournful reïnvasion of darkness, seemed, in the lawyer's eyes, like a district of some city in a nightmare. The thoughts of his mind, besides, were of the gloomiest dye; and when he glanced at the companion of his drive, he was conscious of some touch of that terror of the law and the law's officers, which may at times assail the most honest.

As the cab drew up before the address indicated, the fog lifted a little and showed him a dingy street, a gin palace, a low French eating house, a shop for the retail of penny numbers and twopenny salads, many ragged children huddled in the doorways, and many women of many different nationalities passing out, key in hand, to have a morning glass; and the next moment the fog settled down again upon that part, as brown as umber, and cut him off from his blackguardly surroundings. This was the home of Henry Jekyll's favourite; of a man who was heir to a quarter of a million sterling.

An ivory-faced and silvery-haired old woman opened the door. She had an evil face, smoothed by hypocrisy: but her manners were excellent. Yes, she said, this was

Mr. Hyde's, but he was not at home; he had been in that night very late, but he had gone away again in less than an hour; there was nothing strange in that; his habits were very irregular, and he was often absent; for instance, it was nearly two months since she had seen him till yesterday.

"Very well then, we wish to see his rooms," said the lawyer; and when the woman began to declare it was impossible, "I had better tell you who this person is," he added. "This is Inspector Newcomen of Scotland Yard."

A flash of odious joy appeared upon the woman's face. "Ah!" said she, "he is in trouble! What has he done?"

Mr. Utterson and the inspector exchanged glances. "He don't seem a very popular character," observed the latter. "And now, my good woman, just let me and this gentleman have a look about us."

In the whole extent of the house, which but for the old woman remained otherwise empty, Mr. Hyde had only used a couple of rooms; but these were furnished with luxury and good taste. A closet was filled with wine; the plate was of silver, the napery elegant; a good picture hung upon the walls, a gift (as Utterson supposed) from Henry Jekyll, who was much of a connoisseur; and the carpets were of many plies and agreeable in colour. At this moment, however, the rooms bore every mark of having been recently and hurriedly ransacked; clothes lay about the floor, with their pockets inside out; lockfast drawers stood open; and on the hearth there lay a pile of grey ashes, as though many papers had been burned. From these embers the inspector disinterred the butt end of a green cheque book, which had resisted the action of the fire; the other half of the stick was found behind the door; and as this clinched his suspicions, the officer declared himself delighted. A visit to the bank, where several thousand pounds were found to be lying to the murderer's credit, completed his gratification.

"You may depend upon it, sir," he told Mr. Utterson: "I have him in my hand. He must have lost his head, or he never would have left the stick or, above all, burned the cheque book. Why, money's life to the man. We have nothing to do but wait for him at the bank, and get out the handbills."

This last, however, was not so easy of accomplishment; for Mr. Hyde had numbered few familiars—even the master of the servant maid had only seen him twice; his family could nowhere be traced; he had never been photographed; and the few who could describe him differed widely, as common observers will. Only on one point, were they agreed; and that was the haunting sense of unexpressed deformity with which the fugitive impressed his beholders.

INCIDENT OF THE LETTER

IT WAS LATE IN THE AFTERNOON, WHEN MR. UTTERSON FOUND HIS WAY TO DR. Jekyll's door, where he was at once admitted by Poole, and carried down by the kitchen offices and across a yard which had once been a garden, to the building which was indifferently known as the laboratory or dissecting rooms. The doctor had bought the house from the heirs of a celebrated surgeon; and his own tastes being rather chemical than anatomical, had changed the destination of the block at the bottom of the garden. It was the first time that the lawyer had been received in that part of his friend's quarters; and he eyed the dingy windowless structure with curiosity, and gazed round with a distasteful sense of strangeness as he crossed the theatre, once crowded with eager students and now lying gaunt and silent, the tables laden with chemical apparatus, the floor strewn with crates and littered with packing straw, and the light falling dimly through the foggy cupola. At the further end, a flight of stairs mounted to a door covered with red baize; and through this, Mr. Utterson was at last received into the doctor's cabinet. It was a large room, fitted round with glass presses, furnished, among other things, with a cheval-glass and a business table, and looking out upon the court by three dusty windows barred with iron. The fire burned in the grate; a lamp was set lighted on the chimney shelf, for even in the houses the fog began to lie thickly; and there, close up to the warmth, sat Dr. Jekyll, looking deathly sick. He did not rise to meet his visitor, but held out a cold hand and bade him welcome in a changed voice.

"And now," said Mr. Utterson, as soon as Poole had left them, "you have heard the news?"

The doctor shuddered. "They were crying it in the square," he said. "I heard them in my dining room."

"One word," said the lawyer. "Carew was my client, but so are you, and I want to know what I am doing. You have not been mad enough to hide this fellow?"

"Utterson, I swear to God," cried the doctor, "I swear to God I will never set eyes on him again. I bind my honour to you that I am done with him in this world. It is all at an end. And indeed he does not want my help; you do not know him as I do; he is safe, he is quite safe; mark my words, he will never more be heard of."

The lawyer listened gloomily; he did not like his friend's feverish manner. "You seem pretty sure of him," said he; "and for your sake, I hope you may be right. If it came to a trial, your name might appear."

"I am quite sure of him," replied Jekyll; "I have grounds for certainty that I cannot share with any one. But there is one thing on which you may advise me. I have—I have received a letter; and I am at a loss whether I should show it to the police. I should like to leave it in your hands, Utterson; you would judge wisely I am sure; I have so great a trust in you."

"You fear, I suppose, that it might lead to his detection?" asked the lawyer.

"No," said the other. "I cannot say that I care what becomes of Hyde; I am quite done with him. I was thinking of my own character, which this hateful business has rather exposed."

Utterson ruminated awhile; he was surprised at his friend's selfishness, and yet relieved by it. "Well," said he, at last, "let me see the letter."

The letter was written in an odd, upright hand and signed "Edward Hyde": and it signified, briefly enough, that the writer's benefactor, Dr. Jekyll, whom he had long so unworthily repaid for a thousand generosities, need labour under no alarm for his safety, as he had means of escape on which he placed a sure dependence. The lawyer liked this letter well enough; it put a better colour on the intimacy than he had looked for; and he blamed himself for some of his past suspicions.

"Have you the envelope?" he asked.

"I burned it," replied Jekyll, "before I thought what I was about. But it bore no postmark. The note was handed in."

"Shall I keep this and sleep upon it?" asked Utterson.

"I wish you to judge for me entirely," was the reply. "I have lost confidence in myself."

"Well, I shall consider," returned the lawyer. "And now one word more: it was Hyde who dictated the terms in your will about that disappearance?"

The doctor seemed seized with a qualm of faintness; he shut his mouth tight and nodded.

"I knew it," said Utterson. "He meant to murder you. You had a fine escape."

"I have had what is far more to the purpose," returned the doctor solemnly: "I have had a lesson—O God, Utterson, what a lesson I have had!" And he covered his face for a moment with his hands.

On his way out, the lawyer stopped and had a word or two with Poole. "By the by," said he, "there was a letter handed in to-day: what was the messenger like?" But Poole was positive nothing had come except by post; "and only circulars by that," he added.

This news sent off the visitor with his fears renewed. Plainly the letter had come by the laboratory door; possibly, indeed, it had been written in the cabinet; and if that were so, it must be differently judged, and handled with the more caution. The newsboys, as he went, were crying themselves hoarse along the footways: "Special edition. Shocking murder of an M.P." That was the funeral oration of one friend and client; and he could not help a certain apprehension lest the good name of another should be sucked down in the eddy of the scandal. It was, at least, a ticklish decision that he had to make; and self-reliant as he was by habit, he began to cherish a longing for advice. It was not to be had directly; but perhaps, he thought, it might be fished for.

Presently after, he sat on one side of his own hearth, with Mr. Guest, his head clerk, upon the other, and midway between, at a nicely calculated distance from the fire, a bottle of a particular old wine that had long dwelt unsunned in the foundations of his house. The fog still slept on the wing above the drowned city, where the lamps glimmered like carbuncles; and through the muffle and smother of these fallen clouds, the procession of the town's life was still rolling in through the great arteries with a sound as of a mighty wind. But the room was gay with firelight. In the bottle the acids were long ago resolved; the imperial dye had softened with time, as the colour grows richer in stained windows; and the glow of hot autumn afternoons on hillside vineyards, was ready to be set free and to disperse the fogs of London. Insensibly the lawyer melted. There was no man from whom he kept fewer secrets than Mr. Guest; and he was not always sure that he kept as many as he meant. Guest had often been on business to the doctor's; he knew Poole; he could scarce have failed to hear of Mr. Hyde's familiarity about the house; he might draw conclusions: was it not as well, then, that he should see a letter which put that mystery to rights? and above all since Guest, being a great student and critic of handwriting, would consider the step natural and obliging? The clerk, besides, was a man of counsel; he could scarce read so strange a document without dropping a remark; and by that remark Mr. Utterson might shape his future course.

"This is a sad business about Sir Danvers," he said.

"Yes, sir, indeed. It has elicited a great deal of public feeling," returned Guest. "The man, of course, was mad."

"I should like to hear your views on that," replied Utterson. "I have a document here in his handwriting; it is between ourselves, for I scarce know what to do about it; it is an ugly business at the best. But there it is; quite in your way: a murderer's autograph."

Guest's eyes brightened, and he sat down at once and studied it with passion. "No sir," he said: "not mad; but it is an odd hand."

"And by all accounts a very odd writer," added the lawyer.

Just then the servant entered with a note.

"Is that from Dr. Jekyll, sir?" inquired the clerk. "I thought I knew the writing. Anything private, Mr. Utterson?"

"Only an invitation to dinner. Why? Do you want to see it?"

"One moment. I thank you, sir"; and the clerk laid the two sheets of paper alongside and sedulously compared their contents. "Thank you, sir," he said at last, returning both; "it's a very interesting autograph."

There was a pause, during which Mr. Utterson struggled with himself. "Why did you compare them, Guest?" he inquired suddenly.

"Well, sir," returned the clerk, "there's a rather singular resemblance; the two hands are in many points identical: only differently sloped."

"Rather quaint," said Utterson.

"It is, as you say, rather quaint," returned Guest.

"I wouldn't speak of this note, you know," said the master.

"No, sir," said the clerk. "I understand."

But no sooner was Mr. Utterson alone that night, than he locked the note into his safe where it reposed from that time forward. "What!" he thought. "Henry Jekyll forge for a murderer!" And his blood ran cold in his veins.

REMARKABLE INCIDENT OF DR. LANYON

TIME RAN ON; THOUSANDS OF POUNDS WERE OFFERED IN REWARD, FOR THE DEATH of Sir Danvers was resented as a public injury; but Mr. Hyde had disappeared out of the ken of the police as though he had never existed. Much of his past was unearthed, indeed, and all disreputable: tales came out of the man's cruelty, at once so callous and violent, of his vile life, of his strange associates, of the hatred that seemed to have surrounded his career; but of his present whereabouts, not a whisper. From the time he had left the house in Soho on the morning of the murder, he was simply blotted out; and gradually, as time drew on, Mr. Utterson began to recover from the hotness of his alarm, and to grow more at quiet with himself. The death of Sir Danvers was, to his way of thinking, more than paid for by the disappearance of Mr. Hyde. Now that that evil influence had been withdrawn, a new life began for Dr. Jekyll. He came out of his seclusion, renewed relations with his friends, became once more their familiar guest and entertainer; and whilst he had always been known for charities, he was now no less distinguished for religion. He was busy, he was much in the open air, he did good; his face seemed to open and brighten, as if with an inward consciousness of service; and for more than two months, the doctor was at peace.

On the 8th of January Utterson had dined at the doctor's with a small party; Lanyon had been there; and the face of the host had looked from one to the other as in the old days when the trio were inseparable friends. On the 12th, and again on the 14th, the door was shut against the lawyer. "The doctor was confined to the house," Poole said, "and saw no one." On the 15th, he tried again, and was again refused; and having now been used for the last two months to see his friend almost daily, he found this return of solitude to weigh upon his spirits. The fifth night, he had in Guest to dine with him; and the sixth he betook himself to Doctor Lanyon's.

There at least he was not denied admittance; but when he came in, he was shocked at the change which had taken place in the doctor's appearance. He had his death-warrant written legibly upon his face. The rosy man had grown pale; his flesh had fallen away; he was visibly balder and older; and yet it was not so much these tokens of a swift physical decay that arrested the lawyer's notice, as a look in the eye and quality of manner that seemed to testify to some deep-seated terror of the mind. It was unlikely that the doctor should fear death; and yet that was what Utterson was tempted to suspect. "Yes," he thought; "he is a doctor, he must know his own state and that his days are counted; and the knowledge is more than he can bear." And yet when Utterson remarked on his ill-looks, it was with an air of great firmness that Lanyon declared himself a doomed man.

"I have had a shock," he said, "and I shall never recover. It is a question of weeks. Well, life has been pleasant; I liked it; yes, sir, I used to like it. I sometimes think if we knew all, we should be more glad to get away."

"Jekyll is ill, too," observed Utterson. "Have you seen him?"

But Lanyon's face changed, and he held up a trembling hand. "I wish to see or hear no more of Doctor Jekyll," he said in a loud, unsteady voice. "I am quite done with that person; and I beg that you will spare me any allusion to one whom I regard as dead."

"Tut-tut," said Mr. Utterson; and then after a considerable pause, "Can't I do anything?" he inquired. "We are three very old friends, Lanyon; we shall not live to make others."

"Nothing can be done," returned Lanyon; "ask himself."

"He will not see me," said the lawyer.

"I am not surprised at that," was the reply. "Some day, Utterson, after I am dead, you may perhaps come to learn the right and wrong of this. I cannot tell you. And in the meantime, if you can sit and talk with me of other things, for God's sake, stay and do so; but if you cannot keep clear of this accursed topic, then in God's name, go, for I cannot bear it."

As soon as he got home, Utterson sat down and wrote to Jekyll, complaining of his exclusion from the house, and asking the cause of this unhappy break with Lanyon; and the next day brought him a long answer, often very pathetically worded, and sometimes darkly mysterious in drift. The quarrel with Lanyon was incurable. "I do not blame our old friend," Jekyll wrote, "but I share his view that we must never meet. I mean from henceforth to lead a life of extreme seclusion; you must not be surprised, nor must you doubt my friendship, if my door is often shut even to you. You must suffer me to go my own dark way. I have brought on myself a punishment and a danger that I cannot name. If I am the chief of sinners, I am the chief of sufferers also. I could not think that this earth contained a place for sufferings and terrors so unmanning; and you can do but one thing, Utterson, to lighten this destiny, and that is to respect my silence." Utterson was amazed; the dark influence of Hyde had been withdrawn, the doctor had returned to his old tasks and amities; a week ago, the prospect had smiled with every promise of a cheerful and an honoured age; and now in a moment, friendship, and peace of mind and the whole tenor of his life were wrecked. So great and unprepared a change pointed to madness; but in view of Lanyon's manner and words, there must lie for it some deeper ground.

A week afterwards Dr. Lanyon took to his bed, and in something less than a fortnight he was dead. The night after the funeral, at which he had been sadly affected, Utterson locked the door of his business room, and sitting there by the light of a melancholy candle, drew out and set before him an envelope addressed by the hand and sealed with the seal of his dead friend. "PRIVATE: for the hands of G. J. Utterson ALONE and in case of his predecease *to be destroyed unread,*" so it was emphatically superscribed; and the lawyer dreaded to behold the contents. "I have buried one friend to-day," he thought: "what if this should cost me another?" And then he condemned the fear as a disloyalty, and broke the seal. Within there was another enclosure, likewise sealed, and marked upon the cover as "not to be opened till the death or disappearance of Dr. Henry Jekyll." Utterson could not trust his eyes. Yes, it was disappearance; here again, as in the mad will which he had long ago restored to its author, here again were the idea of a disappearance and the name of Henry Jekyll bracketed. But in the will, that idea had sprung from the sinister suggestion of the man Hyde; it was set there with a purpose all too plain and horrible. Written by the hand of Lanyon, what should it mean? A great curiosity came on the trustee, to disregard the prohibition and dive at once to the bottom of these mysteries; but professional honour and faith to his dead friend were stringent obligations; and the packet slept in the inmost corner of his private safe.

It is one thing to mortify curiosity, another to conquer it; and it may be doubted if, from that day forth, Utterson desired the society of his surviving friend with the same eagerness. He thought of him kindly; but his thoughts were disquieted and fearful. He went to call indeed; but he was perhaps relieved to be denied admittance; perhaps, in his heart, he preferred to speak with Poole upon the doorstep and surrounded by the air and sounds of the open city, rather than to be admitted into that house of voluntary bondage, and to sit and speak with its inscrutable recluse. Poole had, indeed, no very pleasant news to communicate. The doctor, it appeared, now more than ever confined himself to the cabinet over the laboratory, where he would sometimes even sleep; he was out of spirits, he had grown very silent, he did not read; it seemed as if he had something on his mind. Utterson became so used to the unvarying character of these reports, that he fell off little by little in the frequency of his visits.

INCIDENT AT THE WINDOW

It chanced on Sunday, when Mr. Utterson was on his usual walk with Mr. Enfield, that their way lay once again through the bystreet; and that when they came in front of the door, both stopped to gaze on it.

"Well," said Enfield, "that story's at an end at least. We shall never see more of Mr. Hyde."

"I hope not," said Utterson. "Did I ever tell you that I once saw him, and shared your feeling of repulsion?"

"It was impossible to do the one without the other," returned Enfield. "And by the way what an ass you must have thought me, not to know that this was a back way to Dr. Jekyll's! It was partly your own fault that I found it out, even when I did."

"So you found it out, did you?" said Utterson. "But if that be so, we may step into the court and take a look at the windows. To tell you the truth, I am uneasy about poor Jekyll; and even outside, I feel as if the presence of a friend might do him good."

The court was very cool and a little damp, and full of premature twilight, although the sky, high up overhead, was still bright with sunset. The middle one of the three windows was halfway open; and sitting close beside it, taking the air with an infinite sadness of mien, like some disconsolate prisoner, Utterson saw Dr. Jekyll.

"What! Jekyll!" he cried. "I trust you are better."

"I am very low, Utterson," replied the doctor drearily, "very low. It will not last long, thank God."

"You stay too much indoors," said the lawyer. "You should be out, whipping up the circulation like Mr. Enfield and me. (This is my cousin—Mr. Enfield—Dr. Jekyll.) Come now; get your hat and take a quick turn with us."

"You are very good," sighed the other. "I should like to very much; but no, no, no, it is quite impossible; I dare not. But indeed, Utterson, I am very glad to see you; this is really a great pleasure; I would ask you and Mr. Enfield up, but the place is really not fit."

"Why, then," said the lawyer, good-naturedly, "the best thing we can do is to stay down here and speak with you from where we are."

"That is just what I was about to venture to propose," returned the doctor with a smile. But the words were hardly uttered, before the smile was struck out of his face and succeeded by an expression of such abject terror and despair, as froze the very blood of the two gentlemen below. They saw it but for a glimpse, for the window was instantly thrust down; but that glimpse had been sufficient, and they turned and left the court without a word. In silence, too, they traversed the bystreet; and it was not until they had come into a neighbouring thoroughfare, where even upon a Sunday there were still some stirrings of life, that Mr. Utterson at last turned and looked at his companion. They were both pale; and there was an answering horror in their eyes.

"God forgive us, God forgive us," said Mr. Utterson.

But Mr. Enfield only nodded his head very seriously, and walked on once more in silence.

THE LAST NIGHT

MR. UTTERSON WAS SITTING BY HIS FIRESIDE ONE EVENING AFTER DINNER, WHEN he was surprised to receive a visit from Poole.

"Bless me, Poole, what brings you here?" he cried; and then taking a second look at him, "What ails you?" he added, "is the doctor ill?"

"Mr. Utterson," said the man, "there is something wrong."

"Take a seat, and here is a glass of wine for you," said the lawyer. "Now, take your time, and tell me plainly what you want."

"You know the doctor's ways, sir," replied Poole, "and how he shuts himself up. Well, he's shut up again in the cabinet; and I don't like it, sir—I wish I may die if I like it. Mr. Utterson, sir, I'm afraid."

"Now, my good man," said the lawyer, "be explicit. What are you afraid of?"

"I've been afraid for about a week," returned Poole, doggedly disregarding the question, "and I can bear it no more."

The man's appearance amply bore out his words; his manner was altered for the worse; and except for the moment when he had first announced his terror, he had not once looked the lawyer in the face. Even now, he sat with the glass of wine untasted on his knee, and his eyes directed to a corner of the floor. "I can bear it no more," he repeated.

"Come," said the lawyer, "I see you have some good reason, Poole; I see there is something seriously amiss. Try to tell me what it is."

"I think there's been foul play," said Poole, hoarsely.

"Foul play!" cried the lawyer, a good deal frightened and rather inclined to be irritated in consequence. "What foul play! What does the man mean?"

"I daren't say, sir," was the answer; "but will you come along with me and see for yourself?"

Mr. Utterson's only answer was to rise and get his hat and great coat; but he observed with wonder the greatness of the relief that appeared upon the butler's face, and perhaps with no less, that the wine was still untasted when he set it down to follow.

It was a wild, cold, seasonable night of March, with a pale moon, lying on her back as though the wind had tilted her, and a flying wrack of the most diaphanous and lawny texture. The wind made talking difficult, and flecked the blood into the face. It seemed to have swept the streets unusually bare of passengers, besides; for Mr. Utterson thought he had never seen that part of London so deserted. He could have wished it otherwise; never in his life had he been conscious of so sharp a wish to see and touch his fellow-creatures; for struggle as he might, there was borne in upon his mind a crushing anticipation of calamity. The square, when they got there, was all full of wind and dust, and the thin trees in the garden were lashing themselves along the railing. Poole, who had kept all the way a pace or two ahead, now pulled up in the middle of the pavement, and in spite of the biting weather, took off his hat and mopped his brow with a red pocket-handkerchief. But for all the hurry of his coming, these were not the dews of exertion that he wiped away, but the moisture of some strangling anguish; for his face was white and his voice, when he spoke, harsh and broken.

"Well, sir," he said, "here we are, and God grant there be nothing wrong."

"Amen, Poole," said the lawyer.

Thereupon the servant knocked in a very guarded manner; the door was opened on the chain; and a voice asked from within, "Is that you, Poole?"

"It's all right," said Poole. "Open the door."

The hall, when they entered it, was brightly lighted up; the fire was built high; and about the hearth the whole of the servants, men and women, stood huddled together like a flock of sheep. At the sight of Mr. Utterson, the housemaid broke into hysterical whimpering; and the cook, crying out "Bless God! it's Mr. Utterson," ran forward as if to take him in her arms.

"What, what? Are you all here?" said the lawyer peevishly. "Very irregular, very unseemly; your master would be far from pleased."

"They're all afraid," said Poole.

Blank silence followed, no one protesting; only the maid lifted her voice and now wept loudly.

"Hold your tongue!" Poole said to her, with a ferocity of accent that testified to his own jangled nerves; and indeed, when the girl had so suddenly raised the note of her lamentation, they had all started and turned towards the inner door with faces of dreadful expectation. "And now," continued the butler, addressing the knife-boy, "reach me a candle, and we'll get this through hands at once." And then he begged Mr. Utterson to follow him, and led the way to the back garden.

"Now, sir," said he, "you come as gently as you can. I want you to hear, and I don't want you to be heard. And see here, sir, if by any chance he was to ask you in, don't go."

Mr. Utterson's nerves, at this unlooked-for termination, gave a jerk that nearly threw him from his balance; but he re-collected his courage and followed the butler into the laboratory building through the surgical theatre, with its lumber of crates and bottles, to the foot of the stair. Here Poole motioned him to stand on one side and listen; while he himself, setting down the candle and making a great and obvious call on his resolution, mounted the steps and knocked with a somewhat uncertain hand on the red baize of the cabinet door.

"Mr. Utterson, sir, asking to see you," he called; and even as he did so, once more violently signed to the lawyer to give ear.

A voice answered from within: "Tell him I cannot see anyone," it said complainingly.

"Thank you, sir," said Poole, with a note of something like triumph in his voice; and taking up his candle, he led Mr. Utterson back across the yard and into the great kitchen, where the fire was out and the beetles were leaping on the floor.

"Sir," he said, looking Mr. Utterson in the eyes, "was that my master's voice?"

"It seems much changed," replied the lawyer, very pale, but giving look for look.

"Changed? Well, yes, I think so," said the butler. "Have I been twenty years in this man's house, to be deceived about his voice? No, sir; master's made away with; he was made away with, eight days ago, when we heard him cry out upon the name of God; and *who's* in there instead of him, and *why* it stays there, is a thing that cries to Heaven, Mr. Utterson!"

"This is a very strange tale, Poole; this is rather a wild tale, my man," said Mr. Utterson, biting his finger. "Suppose it were as you suppose, supposing Dr. Jekyll to have been—well, murdered, what could induce the murderer to stay? That won't hold water; it doesn't commend itself to reason."

"Well, Mr. Utterson, you are a hard man to satisfy, but I'll do it yet," said Poole. "All this last week (you must know) him, or it, whatever it is that lives in that cabinet, has been crying night and day for some sort of medicine and cannot get it to his mind. It was sometimes his way—the master's, that is—to write his orders on a sheet of paper and throw it on the stair. We've had nothing else this week back; nothing but papers, and a closed door, and the very meals left there to be smuggled in when nobody was looking. Well, sir, every day, ay, and twice and thrice in the same day, there have been orders and complaints, and I have been sent flying to all the wholesale chemists in town. Every time I brought the stuff back, there would be another paper telling me to return it, because it was not pure, and another order to a different firm. This drug is wanted bitter bad, sir, whatever for."

"Have you any of these papers?" asked Mr. Utterson.

Poole felt in his pocket and handed out a crumpled note, which the lawyer, bending nearer to the candle, carefully examined. Its contents ran thus: "Dr. Jekyll presents his compliments to Messrs. Maw. He assures them that their last sample is impure and quite useless for his present purpose. In the year 18—, Dr. J. purchased a somewhat large quantity from Messrs. M. He now begs them to search with most sedulous care, and should any of the same quality be left, to forward it to him at once. Expense is no consideration. The importance of this to Dr. J. can hardly be exaggerated." So far the letter had run composedly enough, but here with a sudden splutter of the pen, the writer's emotion had broken loose. "For God's sake," he added, "find me some of the old."

"This is a strange note," said Mr. Utterson; and then sharply, "How do you come to have it open?"

"The man at Maw's was main angry, sir, and he threw it back to me like so much dirt," returned Poole.

"This is unquestionably the doctor's hand, do you know?" resumed the lawyer.

"I thought it looked like it," said the servant rather sulkily; and then, with another voice, "But what matters hand of write," he said. "I've seen him!"

"Seen him?" repeated Mr. Utterson. "Well?"

"That's it!" said Poole. "It was this way. I came suddenly into the theater from the garden. It seems he had slipped out to look for this drug or whatever it is; for the cabinet door was open, and there he was at the far end of the room digging among the crates. He looked up when I came in, gave a kind of cry, and whipped upstairs into the cabinet. It was but for one minute that I saw him, but the hair stood upon my head like quills. Sir, if that was my master, why had he a mask upon his face? If it was my master, why did he cry out like a rat, and run from me? I have served him long enough. And then . . ." the man paused and passed his hand over his face.

"These are all very strange circumstances," said Mr. Utterson, "but I think I begin to see daylight. Your master, Poole, is plainly seized with one of those maladies that both torture and deform the sufferer; hence, for aught I know, the alteration of his voice; hence the mask and the avoidance of his friends; hence his eagerness to find this drug, by means of which the poor soul retains some hope of ultimate recovery—God grant that he be not deceived! There is my explanation; it is sad enough, Poole, ay, and appalling to consider; but it is plain and natural, hangs well together and delivers us from all exorbitant alarms."

"Sir," said the butler, turning to a sort of mottled pallor, "that thing was not my master, and there's the truth. My master"—here he looked round him and began to whisper—"is a tall fine build of a man, and this was more of a dwarf." Utterson attempted to protest. "O, sir," cried Poole, "do you think I do not know my master after twenty years? Do you think I do not know where his head comes to in the cabinet door, where I saw him every morning of my life? No, sir, that thing in the mask was never Dr. Jekyll—God knows what it was, but it was never Dr. Jekyll; and it is the belief of my heart that there was murder done."

"Poole," replied the lawyer, "if you say that, it will become my duty to make certain. Much as I desire to spare your master's feelings, much as I am puzzled by this note which seems to prove him to be still alive, I shall consider it my duty to break in that door."

"Ah, Mr. Utterson, that's talking!" cried the butler.

"And now comes the second question," resumed Utterson: "Who is going to do it?"

"Why, you and me, sir," was the undaunted reply.

"That's very well said," returned the lawyer; "and whatever comes of it, I shall make it my business to see you are no loser."

"There is an axe in the theatre," continued Poole; "and you might take the kitchen poker for yourself."

The lawyer took that rude but weighty instrument into his hand, and balanced it. "Do you know, Poole," he said, looking up, "that you and I are about to place ourselves in a position of some peril?"

"You may say so, sir, indeed," returned the butler.

"It is well, then, that we should be frank," said the other. "We both think more than we have said; let us make a clean breast. This masked figure that you saw, did you recognise it?"

"Well, sir, it went so quick, and the creature was so doubled up, that I could hardly swear to that," was the answer. "But if you mean, was it Mr. Hyde?—why, yes, I think it was! You see, it was much of the same bigness; and it had the same quick light way with it; and then who else could have got in by the laboratory door? You have not forgot, sir, that at the time of the murder he had still the key with him? But that's not all. I don't know, Mr. Utterson, if you ever met this Mr. Hyde?"

"Yes," said the lawyer, "I once spoke with him."

"Then you must know as well as the rest of us that there was something queer about that gentleman—something that gave a man a turn—I don't know rightly how to say it, sir, beyond this: that you felt it in your marrow kind of cold and thin."

"I own I felt something of what you describe," said Mr. Utterson.

"Quite so, sir," returned Poole. "Well, when that masked thing like a monkey jumped from among the chemicals and whipped into the cabinet, it went down my spine like ice. O, I know it's not evidence, Mr. Utterson; I'm book-learned enough for that; but a man has his feelings, and I give you my bible-word it was Mr. Hyde!"

"Ay, ay," said the lawyer. "My fears incline to the same point. Evil, I fear, founded—evil was sure to come—of that connection. Ay truly, I believe you; I believe poor Harry is killed; and I believe his murderer (for what purpose, God alone can tell) is still lurking in his victim's room. Well, let our name be vengeance. Call Bradshaw."

The footman came at the summons, very white and nervous.

"Put yourself together, Bradshaw," said the lawyer. "This suspense, I know, is telling upon all of you; but it is now our intention to make an end of it. Poole, here, and I are going to force our way into the cabinet. If all is well, my shoulders are broad enough to bear the blame. Meanwhile, lest anything should really be amiss, or any malefactor seek to escape by the back, you and the boy must go round the corner with a pair of good sticks, and take your post at the laboratory door. We give you ten minutes, to get to your stations."

As Bradshaw left, the lawyer looked at his watch. "And now, Poole, let us get to ours," he said; and taking the poker under his arm, led the way into the yard. The scud had banked over the moon, and it was now quite dark. The wind, which only broke in puffs and draughts into that deep well of building, tossed the light of the candle to and fro about their steps, until they came into the shelter of the theatre, where they sat down silently to wait. London hummed solemnly all around; but nearer at hand, the stillness was only broken by the sounds of a footfall moving to and fro along the cabinet floor.

"So it will walk all day, sir," whispered Poole; "ay, and the better part of the night. Only when a new sample comes from the chemist, there's a bit of a break. Ah, it's an ill-conscience that's such an enemy to rest! Ah, sir, there's blood foully shed in every step of it! But hark again, a little closer—put your heart in your ears, Mr. Utterson, and tell me, is that the doctor's foot?"

The steps fell lightly and oddly, with a certain swing, for all they went so slowly; it was different indeed from the heavy creaking tread of Henry Jekyll. Utterson sighed. "Is there never anything else?" he asked.

Poole nodded. "Once," he said. "Once I heard it weeping!"

"Weeping? how that?" said the lawyer, conscious of a sudden chill of horror.

"Weeping like a woman or a lost soul," said the butler. "I came away with that upon my heart, that I could have wept too."

But now the ten minutes drew to an end. Poole disinterred the axe from under a stack of packing straw; the candle was set upon the nearest table to light them to the attack; and they drew near with bated breath to where that patient foot was still going up and down, up and down, in the quiet of the night.

"Jekyll," cried Utterson, with a loud voice, "I demand to see you." He paused a moment, but there came no reply. "I give you fair warning, our suspicions are aroused, and I must and shall see you," he resumed; "if not by fair means, then by foul—if not of your consent, then by brute force!"

"Utterson," said the voice, "for God's sake, have mercy!"

"Ah, that's not Jekyll's voice—it's Hyde's!" cried Utterson. "Down with the door, Poole."

Poole swung the axe over his shoulder; the blow shook the building, and the red baize door leaped against the lock and hinges. A dismal screech, as of mere animal terror, rang from the cabinet. Up went the axe again, and again the panels crashed and the frame bounded; four times the blow fell; but the wood was tough and the fittings were of excellent workmanship; and it was not until the fifth, that the lock burst in sunder and the wreck of the door fell inwards on the carpet.

The besiegers, appalled by their own riot and the stillness that had succeeded, stood back a little and peered in. There lay the cabinet before their eyes in the quiet lamplight, a good fire glowing and chattering on the hearth, the kettle singing its thin strain, a drawer or two open, papers neatly set forth on the business table, and nearer the fire, the things laid out for tea; the quietest room, you would have said, and, but for the glazed presses full of chemicals, the most commonplace that night in London.

Right in the middle there lay the body of a man sorely contorted and still twitching. They drew near on tiptoe, turned it on its back and beheld the face of Edward Hyde. He was dressed in clothes far too large for him, clothes of the doctor's bigness; the cords of his face still moved with a semblance of life, but life was quite gone; and by the crushed phial in the hand and the strong smell of kernels that hung upon the air, Utterson knew that he was looking on the body of a self-destroyer.

"We have come too late," he said sternly, "whether to save or punish. Hyde is gone to his account; and it only remains for us to find the body of your master."

The far greater proportion of the building was occupied by the theatre, which filled almost the whole ground story and was lighted from above, and by the cabinet, which formed an upper story at one end and looked upon the court. A corridor joined the theatre to the door on the bystreet; and with this, the cabinet communicated separately by a second flight of stairs. There were besides a few dark closets and a spacious cellar. All these they now thoroughly examined. Each closet needed but a glance, for all were empty, and all, by the dust that fell from their doors, had stood long unopened. The cellar, indeed, was filled with crazy lumber, mostly dating from the times of the surgeon who was Jekyll's predecessor; but even as they opened the door, they were advertised of the uselessness of further search, by the fall of a perfect mat of cobweb which had for years sealed up the entrance. No where was there any trace of Henry Jekyll, dead or alive.

Poole stamped on the flags of the corridor. "He must be buried here," he said, hearkening to the sound.

"Or he may have fled," said Utterson, and he turned to examine the door in the bystreet. It was locked; and lying near by on the flags, they found the key, already stained with rust.

"This does not look like use," observed the lawyer.

"Use!" echoed Poole. "Do you not see, sir, it is broken? much as if a man had stamped on it."

"Ay," continued Utterson, "and the fractures, too, are rusty." The two men looked at each other with a scare. "This is beyond me, Poole," said the lawyer. "Let us go back to the cabinet."

They mounted the stair in silence, and still with an occasional awestruck glance at the dead body, proceeded more thoroughly to examine the contents of the cabinet. At one table, there were traces of chemical work, various measured heaps of some white salt being laid on glass saucers, as though for an experiment in which the unhappy man had been prevented.

"That is the same drug that I was always bringing him," said Poole; and even as he spoke, the kettle with a startling noise boiled over.

This brought them to the fireside, where the easy chair was drawn cosily up, and the tea things stood ready to the sitter's elbow, the very sugar in the cup. There were several books on a shelf; one lay beside the tea things open, and Utterson was amazed to find it a copy of a pious work, for which Jekyll had several times expressed a great esteem, annotated, in his own hand, with startling blasphemies.

Next, in the course of their review of the chamber, the searchers came to the cheval glass, into whose depths they looked with an involuntary horror. But it was so turned as to show them nothing but the rosy glow playing on the roof, the fire sparkling in a hundred repetitions along the glazed front of the presses, and their own pale and fearful countenances stooping to look in.

"This glass has seen some strange things, sir," whispered Poole.

"And surely none stranger than itself," echoed the lawyer in the same tones. "For what did Jekyll"—he caught himself up at the word with a start, and then conquering the weakness—"what could Jekyll want with it?" he said.

"You may say that!" said Poole.

Next they turned to the business table. On the desk among the neat array of papers, a large envelope was uppermost, and bore, in the doctor's hand, the name of Mr. Utterson. The lawyer unsealed it, and several enclosures fell to the floor. The first was a will, drawn in the same eccentric terms as the one which he had returned six months before, to serve as a testament in case of death and as a deed of gift in case of disappearance; but in place of the name of Edward Hyde, the lawyer, with indescribable amazement, read the name of Gabriel John Utterson. He looked at Poole, and then back at the paper, and last of all at the dead malefactor stretched upon the carpet.

"My head goes round," he said. "He has been all these days in possession; he had no cause to like me; he must have raged to see himself displaced; and he has not destroyed this document."

He caught up the next paper; it was a brief note in the doctor's hand and dated at the top. "O Poole!" the lawyer cried, "he was alive and here this day. He cannot have been disposed of in so short a space; he must be still alive, he must have fled! And then, why fled? and how? and in that case, can we venture to declare this suicide? O, we must be careful. I foresee that we may yet involve your master in some dire catastrophe."

"Why don't you read it, sir?" asked Poole.

"Because I fear," replied the lawyer solemnly. "God grant I have no cause for it!" And with that he brought the paper to his eyes and read as follows:

My dear Utterson,—When this shall fall into your hands, I shall have disappeared, under what circumstances I have not the penetration to foresee, but my instinct and all the circumstances of my nameless situation tell me that the end is sure and must be early. Go then, and first read the narrative which Lanyon warned me he was to place in your hands; and if you care to hear more, turn to the confession of

Your unworthy and unhappy friend,
HENRY JEKYLL

"There was a third enclosure?" asked Utterson.

"Here, sir," said Poole, and gave into his hands a considerable packet sealed in several places.

The lawyer put it in his pocket. "I would say nothing of this paper. If your master has fled or is dead, we may at least save his credit. It is now ten; I must go home and read these documents in quiet; but I shall be back before midnight, when we shall send for the police."

They went out, locking the door of the theatre behind them; and Utterson, once more leaving the servants gathered about the fire in the hall, trudged back to his office to read the two narratives in which this mystery was now to be explained.

DOCTOR LANYON'S NARRATIVE

ON THE NINTH OF JANUARY, NOW FOUR DAYS AGO, I RECEIVED BY THE EVENING delivery a registered envelope, addressed in the hand of my colleague and old school-companion, Henry Jekyll. I was a good deal surprised by this; for we were by no means in the habit of correspondence; I had seen the man, dined with him, indeed, the night before; and I could imagine nothing in our intercourse that should justify the formality of registration. The contents increased my wonder; for this is how the letter ran:

10th DECEMBER, 18—

Dear Lanyon,—You are one of my oldest friends; and although we may have differed at times on scientific questions, I cannot remember, at least on my side, any break in our affection. There was never a day when, if you had said to me, "Jekyll, my life, my honour, my reason, depend upon you," I would not have sacrificed my fortune or my left hand to help you. Lanyon, my life, my honour, my reason, are all at your mercy; if you fail me to-night, I am lost. You might suppose, after this preface, that I am going to ask you for something dishonourable to grant. Judge for yourself.

I want you to postpone all other engagements for to-night—ay, even if you were summoned to the bedside of an emperor; to take a cab, unless your carriage should be actually at the door; and with this letter in your hand for consultation, to drive straight to my house. Poole, my butler, has his orders; you will find him waiting your arrival with a locksmith. The door of my cabinet is then to be forced; and you are to go in alone; to open the glazed press (letter E) on the left hand, breaking the lock if it be shut; and to draw out, *with all its contents as they stand,* the fourth drawer from the top or (which is the same thing) the third from the bottom. In my extreme distress of mind, I have a morbid fear of misdirecting you; but even if I am in error, you may know the right drawer by its contents: some powders, a phial and a paper book. This drawer I beg of you to carry back with you to Cavendish Square exactly as it stands.

That is the first part of the service: now for the second. You should be back, if you set out at once on the receipt of this, long before midnight; but I will leave you that amount of margin, not only in the fear of one of those obstacles that can neither be prevented nor foreseen, but because an hour when your servants are in bed is to be preferred for what will then remain to do. At midnight, then, I have to ask you to be alone in your consulting room, to admit with your own hand into the house a man who will present himself in my name, and to place in his hands the drawer that you will have brought with you from my cabinet. Then you will have played your part and earned my gratitude completely. Five minutes, afterwards, if you insist upon an explanation, you will have understood that these arrangements are of capital importance; and that by the neglect of one of them, fantastic as they must appear, you might have charged your conscience with my death or the shipwreck of my reason.

Confident as I am that you will not trifle with this appeal, my heart sinks and my hand trembles at the bare thought of such a possibility. Think of me at this hour, in a strange place, labouring under a blackness of distress that no fancy can exaggerate, and yet well aware that, if you will but punctually serve me, my troubles will roll away like a story that is told. Serve me, my dear Lanyon, and save

Your friend,

H.J.

P.S.—I had already sealed this up when a fresh terror struck upon my soul. It is possible that the post office may fail me, and this letter not come into your hands until to-morrow morning. In that case, dear Lanyon, do my errand when it shall be most convenient for you in the course of the day; and once more expect my messenger at midnight. It may then already be too late; and if that night passes without event, you will know that you have seen the last of Henry Jekyll.

Upon the reading of this letter, I made sure my colleague was insane; but till that was proved beyond the possibility of doubt, I felt bound to do as he requested. The less I understood of this farrago, the less I was in a position to judge of its importance; and an appeal so worded could not be set aside without a grave responsibility. I rose accordingly from table, got into a hansom, and drove straight to Jekyll's house. The butler was awaiting my arrival; he had received by the same post as mine a registered letter of instruction, and had sent at once for a locksmith and a carpenter. The tradesmen came while we were yet speaking; and we moved in a body to old Dr. Denman's surgical theatre, from which (as you are doubtless aware) Jekyll's private cabinet is most conveniently entered. The door was very strong, the lock excellent; the carpenter avowed he would have great trouble and have to do much damage, if force were to be used; and the locksmith was near despair. But this last was a handy fellow, and after two hours' work, the door stood open. The press marked E was unlocked; and I took out the drawer, had it filled up with straw and tied in a sheet, and returned with it to Cavendish Square.

Here I proceeded to examine its contents. The powders were neatly enough made up, but not with the nicety of the dispensing chemist; so that it was plain they were of Jekyll's private manufacture; and when I opened one of the wrappers, I found what seemed to me a simple, crystalline salt of a white colour. The phial, to which I next turned my attention, might have been about half-full of a blood-red liquor, which was highly pungent to the sense of smell and seemed to me to contain phosphorus and some volatile ether. At the other ingredients, I could make no guess. The book was an ordinary version book and contained little but a series of dates. These covered a period of many years, but I observed that the entries ceased nearly a year ago and quite abruptly. Here and there a brief remark was appended to a date, usually no more than a single word: "double" occurring perhaps six times in a total of several hundred entries; and once very early in the list and followed by several marks of exclamation, "total failure!!!" All this, though it whetted my curiosity, told me little that was definite. Here were a phial of some salt, and the record of a series of experiments that had led (like too many of Jekyll's investigations) to no end of practical usefulness. How could the presence of these articles in my house affect either the honour, the sanity, or the life of my flighty colleague? If his messenger could go to one place, why could he not go to another? And even granting some impediment, why was this gentleman to be received by me in secret? The more I reflected, the more convinced I grew that I was dealing with a case of cerebral disease; and though I dismissed my servants to bed, I loaded an old revolver that I might be found in some posture of self-defence.

Twelve o'clock had scarce rung out over London, ere the knocker sounded very gently on the door. I went myself at the summons, and found a small man crouching against the pillars of the portico.

"Are you come from Dr. Jekyll?" I asked.

He told me "yes" by a constrained gesture; and when I had bidden him enter, he did not obey me without a searching backward glance into the darkness of the square. There was a policeman not far off, advancing with his bull's eye open; and at the sight, I thought my visitor started and made greater haste.

These particulars struck me, I confess, disagreeably; and as I followed him into the bright light of the consulting room, I kept my hand ready on my weapon. Here, at last, I had a chance of clearly seeing him. I had never set eyes on him before, so much was certain. He was small, as I have said; I was struck besides with the shocking expression of his face, with his remarkable combination of great muscular activity and great apparent debility of constitution, and—last but not least—with the odd, subjective disturbance caused by his neighbourhood. This bore some resemblance to incipient rigor, and was accompanied by a marked sinking of the pulse. At the time, I set it down to some idio-syncratic, personal distaste, and merely wondered at the acuteness of the symptoms; but I have since had reason to believe the cause to lie much deeper in the nature of man, and to turn on some nobler hinge than the principle of hatred.

This person (who had thus, from the first moment of his entrance, struck in me what I can only describe as a disgustful curiosity) was dressed in a fashion that would have made an ordinary person laughable; his clothes, that is to say, although they were of rich and sober fabric, were enormously too large for him in every measurement— the trousers hanging on his legs and rolled up to keep them from the ground, the waist of the coat below his haunches, and the collar sprawling wide upon his shoulders. Strange to relate, this ludicrous accoutrement was far from moving me to laughter. Rather, as there was something abnormal and misbegotten in the very essence of the creature that now faced me—something seizing, surprising and revolting—this fresh disparity seemed but to fit in with and to reïnforce it; so that to my interest in the man's nature and character, there was added a curiosity as to his origin, his life, his fortune and status in the world.

These observations, though they have taken so great a space to be set down in, were yet the work of a few seconds. My visitor was, indeed, on fire with sombre excitement.

"Have you got it?" he cried. "Have you got it?" And so lively was his impatience that he even laid his hand upon my arm and sought to shake me.

I put him back, conscious at his touch of a certain icy pang along my blood. "Come, sir," said I. "You forget that I have not yet the pleasure of your acquaintance.

Be seated, if you please." And I showed him an example, and sat down myself in my customary seat and with as fair an imitation of my ordinary manner to a patient, as the lateness of the hour, the nature of my prëoccupations, and the horror I had of my visitor, would suffer me to muster.

"I beg your pardon, Dr. Lanyon," he replied civilly enough. "What you say is very well founded; and my impatience has shown its heels to my politeness. I come here at the instance of your colleague, Dr. Henry Jekyll, on a piece of business of some moment; and I understood . . ." he paused and put his hand to his throat, and I could see, in spite of his collected manner, that he was wrestling against the approaches of the hysteria—"I understood, a drawer . . ."

But here I took pity on my visitor's suspense, and some perhaps on my own growing curiosity.

"There it is, sir," said I, pointing to the drawer, where it lay on the floor behind a table and still covered with the sheet.

He sprang to it, and then paused, and laid his hand upon his heart: I could hear his teeth grate with the convulsive action of his jaws; and his face was so ghastly to see that I grew alarmed both for his life and reason.

"Compose yourself," said I.

He turned a dreadful smile to me, and as if with the decision of despair, plucked away the sheet. At sight of the contents, he uttered one loud sob of such immense relief that I sat petrified. And the next moment, in a voice that was already fairly well under control, "Have you a graduated glass?" he asked.

I rose from my place with something of an effort and gave him what he asked.

He thanked me with a smiling nod, measured out a few minims of the red tincture and added one of the powders. The mixture, which was at first of a reddish hue, began, in proportion as the crystals melted, to brighten in colour, to effervesce audibly, and to throw off small fumes of vapour. Suddenly and at the same moment, the ebullition ceased and the compound changed to a dark purple, which faded again more slowly to a watery green. My visitor, who had watched these metamorphoses with a keen eye, smiled, set down the glass upon the table, and then turned and looked upon me with an air of scrutiny.

"And now," said he, "to settle what remains. Will you be wise? will you be guided? will you suffer me to take this glass in my hand and to go forth from your house without further parley? or has the greed of curiosity too much command of you? Think before you answer, for it shall be done as you decide. As you decide, you shall be left as you were before, and neither richer nor wiser, unless the sense of service rendered to a man in mortal distress may be counted as a kind of riches of the soul. Or, if you shall so prefer to choose, a new province of knowledge and new avenues to fame and power shall be laid open to you, here, in this room, upon the instant; and your sight shall be blasted by a prodigy to stagger the unbelief of Satan."

"Sir," said I, affecting a coolness that I was far from truly possessing, "you speak enigmas, and you will perhaps not wonder that I hear you with no very strong impression of belief. But I have gone too far in the way of inexplicable services to pause before I see the end."

"It is well," replied my visitor. "Lanyon, you remember your vows: what follows is under the seal of our profession. And now, you who have so long been bound to the most narrow and material views, you who have denied the virtue of transcendental medicine, you who have derided your superiors—behold!"

He put the glass to his lips and drank at one gulp. A cry followed; he reeled, staggered, clutched at the table and held on, staring with injected eyes, gasping with open mouth; and as I looked there came, I thought, a change—he seemed to swell—his face became suddenly black and the features seemed to melt and alter—and the next moment, I had sprung to my feet and leaped back against the wall, my arms raised to shield me from that prodigy, my mind submerged in terror.

"O God!" I screamed, and "O God!" again and again; for there before my eyes—pale and shaken, and half fainting, and groping before him with his hands, like a man restored from death—there stood Henry Jekyll!

What he told me in the next hour, I cannot bring my mind to set on paper. I saw what I saw, I heard what I heard, and my soul sickened at it; and yet now when that sight has faded from my eyes, I ask myself if I believe it, and I cannot answer. My life is shaken to its roots; sleep has left me; the deadliest terror sits by me at all hours of the day and night; and I feel that my days are numbered, and that I must die; and yet I shall die incredulous. As for the moral turpitude that man unveiled to me, even with tears of penitence, I cannot, even in memory, dwell on it without a start of horror. I will say but one thing, Utterson, and that (if you can bring your mind to credit it) will be more than enough. The creature who crept into my house that night was, on Jekyll's own confession, known by the name of Hyde and hunted for in every corner of the land as the murderer of Carew.

HASTIE LANYON

Henry Jekyll's Full Statement of the Case

I was born in the year 18— to a large fortune, endowed besides with excellent parts, inclined by nature to industry, fond of the respect of the wise and good among my fellow-men, and thus, as might have been supposed, with every guarantee of an honourable and distinguished future. And indeed the worst of my faults was a certain impatient gaiety of disposition, such as has made the happiness of many, but such as I found it hard to reconcile with my imperious desire to carry my head high, and wear a more than commonly grave countenance before the public. Hence it came about that I concealed my pleasures; and that when I reached years of reflection, and began to look round me and take stock of my progress and position in the world, I stood already committed to a profound duplicity of life. Many a man would have even blazoned such irregularities as I was guilty of; but from the high views that I had set before me, I regarded and hid them with an almost morbid sense of shame. It was thus rather the exacting nature of my aspirations than any particular degradation in my faults, that made me what I was, and, with even a deeper trench than in the majority of men, severed in me those provinces of good and ill which divide and compound man's dual nature. In this case, I was driven to reflect deeply and inveterately on that hard law of life, which lies at the root of religion and is one of the most plentiful springs of distress. Though so profound a double-dealer, I was in no sense a hypocrite; both sides of me were in dead earnest; I was no more myself when I laid aside restraint and plunged in shame, than when I laboured, in the eye of day, at the furtherance of knowledge or the relief of sorrow and suffering. And it chanced that the direction of my scientific studies, which led wholly towards the mystic and the transcendental, rëacted and shed a strong light on this consciousness of the perennial war among my members. With every day, and from both sides of my intelligence, the moral and the intellectual, I thus drew steadily nearer to that truth, by whose partial discovery I have been doomed to such a dreadful shipwreck: that man is not truly one, but truly two. I say two, because the state of my own knowledge does not pass beyond that point. Others will follow, others will outstrip me on the same lines; and I hazard the guess that man will be ultimately known for a mere polity of multifarious, incongruous and independent denizens. I for my part, from the nature of my life, advanced infallibly in one direction and in one direction only. It was on the moral side, and in my own person, that I learned to recognise the thorough and primitive duality of man; I saw that, of the two natures that contended in the field of my consciousness, even if I could rightly be said to be either, it was only because I was radically both; and from an early date, even before the course of my scientific discoveries had begun to suggest the most naked possibility of such a miracle, I had learned to dwell with pleasure, as a beloved daydream, on the thought of the separation of these elements. If each, I told myself, could be housed in separate identities, life would be relieved of all that was unbearable; the unjust might go his way, delivered from the aspirations and remorse of his more upright twin; and the just could walk steadfastly and securely on his upward path, doing the good things in which he found his pleasure, and no longer exposed to disgrace and penitence by the hands of this extraneous evil. It was the curse of mankind that these incongruous faggots were thus bound together—that in the agonised womb of consciousness, these polar twins should be continuously struggling. How, then, were they dissociated?

I was so far in my reflections when, as I have said, a side light began to shine upon the subject from the laboratory table. I began to perceive more deeply than it has ever yet been stated, the trembling immateriality, the mist-like transience, of this seemingly so solid body in which we walk attired. Certain agents I found to have the power to shake and pluck back that fleshly vestment, even as a wind might toss the curtains of a pavilion. For two good reasons, I will not enter deeply into this scientific branch of my confession. First, because I have been made to learn that the doom and burthen of our life is bound for ever on man's shoulders, and when the attempt is made to cast it off, it but returns upon us with more unfamiliar and more awful pressure. Second, because, as my narrative will make alas! too evident, my discoveries were incomplete. Enough, then, that I not only recognised my natural body from the mere aura and effulgence of certain of the powers that made up my spirit, but managed to compound a drug by which these powers should be dethroned from their supremacy, and a second form and countenance substituted, none the less natural to me because they were the expression, and bore the stamp, of lower elements in my soul.

I hesitated long before I put this theory to the test of practice. I knew well that I risked death; for any drug that so potently controlled and shook the very fortress of identity, might by the least scruple of an overdose or at the least inopportunity in the moment of exhibition, utterly blot out that immaterial tabernacle which I looked to it to change. But the temptation of a discovery so singular and profound, at last overcame the suggestions of alarm. I had long since prepared my tincture; I purchased at once, from a firm of wholesale chemists, a large quantity of a particular salt which I knew, from my experiments, to be the last ingredient required; and late one accursed night, I compounded the elements, watched them boil and smoke together in the glass, and when the ebullition had subsided, with a strong glow of courage, drank off the potion.

The most racking pangs succeeded: a grinding in the bones, deadly nausea, and a horror of the spirit that cannot be exceeded at the hour of birth or death. Then these agonies began swiftly to subside, and I came to myself as if out of a great sickness. There was something strange in my sensations, something indescribably new and, from its very novelty, incredibly sweet. I felt younger, lighter, happier in body; within I was conscious of a heady recklessness, a current of disordered sensual images running like a mill race in my fancy, a solution of the bonds of obligation, an unknown but not an innocent freedom of the soul. I knew myself, at the first breath of this new life, to be more wicked, tenfold more wicked, sold a slave to my original evil; and the thought, in that moment, braced and delighted me like wine. I stretched out my hands, exulting in the freshness of these sensations; and in the act, I was suddenly aware that I had lost in stature.

There was no mirror, at that date, in my room; that which stands beside me as I write, was brought there later on and for the very purpose of these transformations. The night, however, was far gone into the morning—the morning, black as it was, was nearly ripe for the conception of the day—the inmates of my house were locked in the most rigorous hours of slumber; and I determined, flushed as I was with hope and triumph, to venture in my new shape as far as to my bedroom. I crossed the yard, wherein the constellations looked down upon me, I could have thought, with wonder, the first creature of that sort that their unsleeping vigilance had yet disclosed to them; I stole through the corridors, a stranger in my own house; and coming to my room, I saw for the first time the appearance of Edward Hyde.

I must here speak by theory alone, saying not that which I know, but that which I suppose to be most probable. The evil side of my nature, to which I had now transferred the stamping efficacy, was less robust and less developed than the good which I had just deposed. Again, in the course of my life, which had been, after all, nine tenths a life of effort, virtue and control, it had been much less exercised and much less exhausted. And hence, as I think, it came about that Edward Hyde was so much smaller, slighter and younger than Henry Jekyll. Even as good shone upon the countenance of the one, evil was written broadly and plainly on the face of the other. Evil besides (which I must still believe to be the lethal side of man) had left on that body an imprint of deformity and decay. And yet when I looked upon that ugly idol in the glass, I was conscious of no repugnance, rather of a leap of welcome. This, too, was myself. It seemed natural and human. In my eyes it bore a livelier image of the spirit, it seemed more express and single, than the imperfect and divided countenance, I had been hitherto accustomed to call mine. And in so far I was doubtless right. I have observed that when I wore the semblance of Edward Hyde, none could come near to me at first without a visible misgiving of the flesh. This, as I take it, was because all human beings, as we meet them, are commingled out of good and evil: and Edward Hyde, alone in the ranks of mankind, was pure evil.

I lingered but a moment at the mirror: the second and conclusive experiment had yet to be attempted; it yet remained to be seen if I had lost my identity beyond redemption and must flee before daylight from a house that was no longer mine; and hurrying back to my cabinet, I once more prepared and drank the cup, once more suffered the pangs of dissolution, and came to myself once more with the character, the stature and the face of Henry Jekyll.

That night I had come to the fatal cross roads. Had I approached my discovery in a more noble spirit, had I risked the experiment while under the empire of generous or pious aspirations, all must have been otherwise, and from these agonies of death and birth, I had come forth an angel instead of a fiend. The drug had no discriminating action; it was neither diabolical nor divine; it but shook the doors of the prisonhouse of my disposition; and like the captives of Philippi, that which stood within ran forth. At that time my virtue slumbered; my evil, kept awake by ambition, was alert and swift to seize the occasion; and the thing that was projected was Edward Hyde. Hence, although I had now two characters as well as two appearances, one was wholly evil, and the other was still the old Henry Jekyll, that incongruous compound of whose reformation and improvement I had already learned to despair. The movement was thus wholly toward the worse.

Even at that time, I had not conquered my aversions to the dryness of a life of study. I would still be merrily disposed at times; and as my pleasures were (to say the least) undignified, and I was not only well known and highly considered, but growing towards the elderly man, this incoherency of my life was daily growing more unwelcome. It was on this side that my new power tempted me until I fell in slavery. I had but to drink the cup, to doff at once the body of the noted professor, and to assume, like a thick cloak, that of Edward Hyde. I smiled at the notion; it seemed to me at the time to be humorous; and I made my preparations with the most studious care. I took and furnished that house in Soho, to which Hyde was tracked by the police; and engaged as housekeeper a creature whom I knew well to be silent and unscrupulous.

On the other side, I announced to my servants that a Mr. Hyde (whom I described) was to have full liberty and power about my house in the square; and to parry mishaps, I even called and made myself a familiar object, in my second character. I next drew up that will to which you so much objected; so that if anything befell me in the person of Doctor Jekyll, I could enter on that of Edward Hyde without pecuniary loss. And thus fortified, as I supposed, on every side, I began to profit by the strange immunities of my position.

Men have before hired bravos to transact their crimes, while their own person and reputation sat under shelter. I was the first that ever did so for his pleasures. I was the first that could plod in the public eye with a load of genial respectability, and in a moment, like a schoolboy, strip off these lendings and spring headlong into the sea of liberty. But for me, in my impenetrable mantle, the safety was complete. Think of it—I did not even exist! Let me but escape into my laboratory door, give me but a second or two to mix and swallow the draught that I had always standing ready; and whatever he had done, Edward Hyde would pass away like the stain of breath upon a mirror; and there in his stead, quietly at home, trimming the midnight lamp in his study, a man who could afford to laugh at suspicion, would be Henry Jekyll.

The pleasures which I made haste to seek in my disguise were, as I have said, undignified; I would scarce use a harder term. But in the hands of Edward Hyde, they soon began to turn towards the monstrous. When I would come back from these excursions, I was often plunged into a kind of wonder at my vicarious depravity. This familiar that I called out of my own soul, and sent forth alone to do his good pleasure, was a being inherently malign and villainous; his every act and thought centered on self; drinking pleasure with bestial avidity from any degree of torture to another; relentless like a man of stone. Henry Jekyll stood at times aghast before the acts of Edward Hyde; but the situation was apart from ordinary laws, and insidiously relaxed the grasp of conscience. It was Hyde, after all, and Hyde alone, that was guilty. Jekyll was no worse; he woke again to his good qualities seemingly unimpaired; he would even make haste, where it was possible, to undo the evil done by Hyde. And thus his conscience slumbered.

Into the details of the infamy at which I thus connived (for even now I can scarce grant that I committed it) I have no design of entering; I mean but to point out the warnings and the successive steps with which my chastisement approached. I met with one accident which, as it brought on no consequence, I shall no more than mention. An act of cruelty to a child aroused against me the anger of a passerby, whom I recognised the other day in the person of your kinsman; the doctor and the child's family joined him; there were moments when I feared for my life; and at last, in order to pacify their too just resentment, Edward Hyde had to bring them to the door, and pay them in a cheque drawn in the name, of Henry Jekyll. But this danger was easily eliminated from the future, by opening an account at another bank in the name of Edward Hyde himself; and when, by sloping my own hand backward, I had supplied my double with a signature, I thought I sat beyond the reach of fate.

Some two months before the murder of Sir Danvers, I had been out for one of my adventures, had returned at a late hour, and woke the next day in bed with somewhat odd sensations. It was in vain I looked about me; in vain I saw the decent furniture and tall proportions of my room in the square; in vain that I recognised the pattern of the bed curtains and the design of the mahogany frame; something still kept insisting that I was not where I was, that I had not wakened where I seemed to be, but in the little room in Soho where I was accustomed to sleep in the body of Edward Hyde. I smiled to myself, and, in my psychological way, began lazily to inquire into the elements of this illusion, occasionally, even as I did so, dropping back into a comfortable morning doze. I was still so engaged when, in one of my more wakeful moments, my eye fell upon my hand. Now the hand of Henry Jekyll (as you have often remarked) was professional in shape and size: it was large, firm, white and comely. But the hand which I now saw, clearly enough, in the yellow light of a mid-London morning, lying half shut on the bed clothes, was lean, corded, knuckly, of a dusky pallor and thickly shaded with a swart growth of hair. It was the hand of Edward Hyde.

I must have stared upon it for near half a minute, sunk as I was in the mere stupidity of wonder, before terror woke up in my breast as sudden and startling as the crash of cymbals; and bounding from my bed, I rushed to the mirror. At the sight that met my eyes, my blood was changed into something exquisitely thin and icy. Yes, I had gone to bed Henry Jekyll, I had awakened Edward Hyde. How was this to be explained? I asked myself; and then, with another bound of terror—how was it to be remedied? It was well on in the morning; the servants were up; all my drugs were in the cabinet—a long journey, down two pair of stairs, through the back passage, across the open court and through the anatomical theatre, from where I was then standing horror-struck. It might indeed be possible to cover my face; but of what use was that, when I was unable to conceal the alteration in my stature? And then with an overpow-ing sweetness of relief, it came back upon my mind that the servants were already to the coming and going of my second self. I had soon dressed, as well as I was able, in clothes of my own size: had soon passed through the house, where Bradshaw stared and drew back at seeing Mr. Hyde at such an hour and in such a strange array; and ten minutes later, Dr. Jekyll had returned to his own shape and was sitting down, with a darkened brow, to make a feint of breakfasting.

Small indeed was my appetite. This inexplicable incident, this reversal of my previous experience, seemed, like the Babylonian finger on the wall, to be spelling out the letters of my judgment; and I began to reflect more seriously than ever before on the issues and possibilities of my double existence. That part of me which I had the power of projecting, had lately been much exercised and nourished; it had seemed to me of late as though the body of Edward Hyde had grown in stature, as though (when I wore that form) I were conscious of a more generous tide of blood; and I began to spy a danger that, if this were much prolonged, the balance of my nature might be permanently overthrown, the power of voluntary change be forfeited, and the character of Edward Hyde become irrevocably mine. The power of the drug had not been always equally displayed. Once, very early in my career, it had totally failed me; since then I had been obliged on more than one occasion to double, and once, with infinite risk of death, to treble the amount; and these rare uncertainties had cast hitherto the sole shadow on my contentment. Now, however, and in the light of that morning's accident, I was led to remark that whereas, in the beginning, the difficulty had been to throw off the body of Jekyll, it had of late, gradually but decidedly transferred itself to the other side. All things therefore seemed to point to this: that I was slowly losing hold of my original and better self, and becoming slowly incorporated with my second and worse.

Between these two, I now felt I had to choose. My two natures had memory in common, but all other faculties were most unequally shared between them. Jekyll (who was composite) now with the most sensitive apprehensions, now with a greedy gusto, projected and shared in the pleasures and adventures of Hyde; but Hyde was indifferent to Jekyll, or but remembered him as the mountain bandit remembers the cavern in which he conceals himself from pursuit. Jekyll had more than a father's interest; Hyde had more than a son's indifference. To cast in my lot with Jekyll, was to die to those appetites which I had long secretly indulged and had of late begun to pamper. To cast it in with Hyde, was to die to a thousand interests and aspirations, and to become, at a blow and forever, despised and friendless. The bargain might appear unequal; but there was still another consideration in the scales; for while Jekyll would suffer smartingly in the fires of abstinence, Hyde would be not even conscious of all that he had lost. Strange as my circumstances were, the terms of this debate are as old and commonplace as man; much the same inducements and alarms cast the die for any tempted and trembling sinner; and it fell out with me, as it falls with so vast a majority of my fellows, that I chose the better part and was found wanting in the strength to keep to it.

Yes, I preferred the elderly and discontented doctor, surrounded by friends and cherishing honest hopes; and bade a resolute farewell to the liberty, the comparative youth, the light step, leaping impulses and secret pleasures, that I had enjoyed in the disguise of Hyde. I made this choice perhaps with some unconscious reservation, for I neither gave up the house in Soho, nor destroyed the clothes of Edward Hyde, which still lay ready in my cabinet. For two months, however, I was true to my determination; for two months, I led a life of such severity as I had never before attained to, and enjoyed the compensations of an approving conscience. But time began at last to obliterate the freshness of my alarm; the praises of conscience began to grow into a thing of course; I began to be tortured with throes and longings, as of Hyde struggling after freedom; and at last, in an hour of moral weakness, I once again compounded and swallowed the transforming draught.

I do not suppose that, when a drunkard reasons with himself upon his vice, he is once out of five hundred times affected by the dangers that he runs through his brutish, physical insensibility; neither had I, long as I had considered my position, made enough allowance for the complete moral insensibility and insensate readiness to evil, which were the leading characters of Edward Hyde. Yet it was by these that I was punished. My devil had been long caged, he came out roaring. I was conscious, even when I took the draught, of a more unbridled, a more furious propensity to ill. It must have been this, I suppose, that stirred in my soul that tempest of impatience with which I listened to the civilities of my unhappy victim; I declare at least, before God, no man morally sane could have been guilty of that crime upon so pitiful a provocation; and that I struck in no more reasonable spirit than that in which a sick child may break a plaything. But I had voluntarily stripped myself of all those balancing instincts, by which even the worst of us continues to walk with some degree of steadiness among temptations; and in my case, to be tempted, however slightly, was to fall.

Instantly the spirit of hell awoke in me and raged. With a transport of glee, I mauled the unresisting body, tasting delight from every blow; and it was not till weariness had begun to succeed, that I was suddenly, in the top fit of my delirium, struck through the heart by a cold thrill of terror. A mist dispersed; I saw my life to be forfeit; and fled from the scene of these excesses, at once glorying and trembling, my lust of evil gratified and stimulated, my love of life screwed to the topmost peg. I ran to the house in Soho, and (to make assurance doubly sure) destroyed my papers; thence I set out through the lamplit streets, in the same divided ecstasy of mind, gloating on my crime, light-headedly devising others in the future, and yet still hastening and still hearkening in my wake for the steps of the avenger. Hyde had a song upon his lips as he compounded the draught, and as he drank it, pledged the dead man. The pangs of transformation had not done tearing him, before Henry Jekyll, with streaming tears of gratitude and remorse, had fallen upon his knees and lifted his clasped hands to God. The veil of self-indulgence was rent from head to foot. I saw my life as a whole: I followed it up from the days of childhood, when I had walked with my father's hand, and through the self-denying toils of my professional life, to arrive again and again, with the same sense of unreality, at the damned horrors of the evening. I could have screamed aloud; I sought with tears and prayers to smother down the crowd of hideous images and sounds with which my memory swarmed against me; and still, between the petitions, the ugly face of my iniquity stared into my soul. As the acuteness of this remorse began to die away, it was succeeded by a sense of joy. The problem of my conduct was solved. Hyde was thenceforth impossible; whether I would or not, I was now confined to the better part of my existence; and O, how I rejoiced to think of it! with what willing humility, I embraced anew the restrictions of natural life! with what sincere renunciation I locked the door by which I had so often gone and come, and ground the key under my heel!

The next day, came the news that the murder had not been overlooked, that the guilt of Hyde was patent to the world, and that the victim was a man high in public estimation. It was not only a crime, it had been a tragic folly. I think I was glad to know it; I think I was glad to have my better impulses thus buttressed and guarded by the terrors of the scaffold. Jekyll was now my city of refuge; let but Hyde peep out an instant, and the hands of all men would be raised to take and slay him.

I resolved in my future conduct to redeem the past; and I can say with honesty that my resolve was fruitful of some good. You know yourself how earnestly, in the last months of the last year, I laboured to relieve suffering; you know that much was done for others, and that the days passed quietly, almost happily for myself. Nor can I truly say that I wearied of this beneficent and innocent life; I think instead that I daily enjoyed it more completely; but I was still cursed with my duality of purpose; and as the first edge of my penitence wore off, the lower side of me, so long indulged, so recently chained down, began to growl for licence. Not that I dreamed of resuscitating

Hyde; the bare idea of that would startle me to frenzy: no, it was in my own person that I was once more tempted to trifle with my conscience; and it was as an ordinary secret sinner, that I at last fell before the assaults of temptation.

There comes an end to all things; the most capacious measure is filled at last; and this brief condescension to my evil finally destroyed the balance of my soul. And yet I was not alarmed; the fall seemed natural, like a return to the old days before I had made my discovery. It was a fine, clear, January day, wet under foot where the frost had melted, but cloudless overhead; and the Regent's park was full of winter chirruppings and sweet with Spring odours. I sat in the sun on a bench; the animal within me licking the chops of memory; the spiritual side a little drowsed, promising subsequent penitence, but not yet moved to begin. After all, I reflected I was like my neighbours; and then I smiled, comparing myself with other men, comparing my active goodwill with the lazy cruelty of their neglect. And at the very moment of that vainglorious thought, a qualm came over me, a horrid nausea and the most deadly shuddering. These passed away, and left me faint; and then as in its turn faintness subsided, I began to be aware of a change in the temper of my thoughts, a greater boldness, a contempt of danger, a solution of the bonds of obligation. I looked down; my clothes hung formlessly on my shrunken limbs; the hand that lay on my knee was corded and hairy. I was once more Edward Hyde. A moment before I had been safe of all men's respect, wealthy, beloved—the cloth laying for me in the dining room at home; and now I was the common quarry of mankind, hunted, houseless, a known murderer, thrall to the gallows.

My reason wavered, but it did not fail me utterly. I have more than once observed that in my second character, my faculties seemed sharpened to a point and my spirits more tensely elastic; thus it came about that, where Jekyll perhaps might have succumbed, Hyde rose to the importance of the moment. My drugs were in one of the presses of my cabinet; how was I to reach them? That was the problem that (crushing my temples in my hands) I set myself to solve. The laboratory door I had closed. If I sought to enter by the house, my own servants would consign me to the gallows. I saw I must employ another hand, and thought of Lanyon. How was he to be reached? how persuaded? Supposing that I escaped capture in the streets, how was I to make my way into his presence? and how should I, an unknown and displeasing visitor, prevail on the famous physician to rifle the study of his colleague, Dr. Jekyll? Then I remembered that of my original character, one part remained to me: I could write my own hand; and once I had conceived that kindling spark, the way that I must follow became lighted up from end to end.

Thereupon, I arranged my clothes as best I could, and summoning a passing hansom, drove to an hotel in Portland street, the name of which I chanced to remember. At my appearance (which was indeed comical enough, however tragic a fate these garments covered) the driver could not conceal his mirth. I gnashed my teeth upon him with a gust of devilish fury; and the smile withered from his face—happily for him—yet more happily for myself, for in another instant I had certainly dragged him from his perch. At the inn, as I entered, I looked about me with so black a countenance as made the attendants tremble; not a look did they exchange in my presence; but obsequiously took my orders, led me to a private room, and brought me wherewithal to write. Hyde in danger of his life was a creature new to me: shaken with inordinate anger, strung to the pitch of murder, lusting to inflict pain. Yet the creature was astute; mastered his fury with a great effort of the will; composed his two important letters, one to Lanyon and one to Poole; and that he might receive actual evidence of their being posted, sent them out with directions that they should be registered.

Thenceforward, he sat all day over the fire in the private room, gnawing his nails; there he dined, sitting alone with his fears, the waiter visibly quailing before his eye; and thence, when the night was fully come, he set forth in the corner of a closed cab, and was driven to and fro about the streets of the city. He, I say—I cannot say, I. That child of Hell had nothing human; nothing lived in him but fear and hatred. And when at last, thinking the driver had begun to grow suspicious, he discharged the cab and ventured on foot, attired in his misfitting clothes, an object marked out for observation, into the midst of the nocturnal passengers, these two base passions raged within him like a tempest. He walked fast, hunted by his fears, chattering to himself, skulking through the less frequented thoroughfares, counting the minutes that still divided him from midnight. Once a woman spoke to him, offering, I think, a box of lights. He smote her in the face, and she fled.

When I came to myself at Lanyon's, the horror of my old friend perhaps affected me somewhat: I do not know; it was at least but a drop in the sea to the abhorrence with which I looked back upon these hours. A change had come over me. It was no longer the fear of the gallows, it was the horror of being Hyde that racked me. I received Lanyon's condemnation partly in a dream; it was partly in a dream that I came home to my own house and got into bed. I slept after the prostration of the day, with a stringent and profound slumber which not even the nightmares that wrung me could avail to break. I awoke in the morning shaken, weakened, but refreshed. I still hated and feared the thought of the brute that slept within me, and I had not of course forgotten the appalling dangers of the day before; but I was once more at home, in my own house and close to my drugs; and gratitude for my escape shone so strong in my soul that it almost rivalled the brightness of hope.

I was stepping leisurely across the court after breakfast, drinking the chill of the air with pleasure, when I was seized again with those indescribable sensations that heralded the change; and I had but the time to gain the shelter of my cabinet, before I was once again raging and freezing with the passions of Hyde. It took on this occasion a double dose to recall me to myself; and alas, six hours after, as I sat looking sadly in the fire, the pangs returned, and the drug had to be re-administered. In short, from that day forth it seemed only by a great effort as of gymnastics, and only under the immediate stimulation of the drug, that I was able to wear the countenance of Jekyll. At all hours of the day and night, I would be taken with the premonitory shudder; above all, if I slept, or even dozed for a moment in my chair, it was always as Hyde that I awakened. Under the strain of this continually impending doom and by the sleeplessness to which I now condemned myself, ay, even beyond what I had thought possible to man, I became, in my own person, a creature eaten up and emptied by fever, languidly weak both in body and mind, and solely occupied by one thought: the horror of my other self. But when I slept, or when the virtue of the medicine wore off, I would leap almost without transition (for the pangs of transformation grew daily less marked) into the possession of a fancy brimming with images of terror, a soul boiling with causeless hatreds, and a body that seemed not strong enough to contain the raging energies of life. The powers of Hyde seemed to have grown with the sickliness of Jekyll. And certainly the hate that now divided them was equal on each side. With Jekyll, it was a thing of vital instinct. He had now seen the full deformity of that creature that shared with him some of the phenomena of consciousness, and was co-heir with him to death: and beyond these links of community, which in themselves made the most poignant part of his distress, he thought of Hyde, for all his energy of life, as of something not only hellish but inorganic. This was the shocking thing; that the slime of the pit seemed to utter cries and voices; that the amorphous dust gesticulated and sinned; that what was dead, and had no shape, should usurp the offices of life. And this again, that that insurgent horror was knit to him closer than a wife, closer than an eye; lay caged in his flesh, where he heard it mutter and felt it struggle to be born; and at every hour of weakness, and in the confidence of slumber, prevailed against him, and deposed him out of life. The hatred of Hyde for Jekyll, was of a different order. His terror of the gallows drove him continually to commit temporary suicide, and return to his subordinate station of a part instead of a person; but he loathed the necessity, he loathed the despondency into which Jekyll was now fallen, and he resented the dislike with which he was himself regarded. Hence the apelike tricks that he would play me, scrawling in my own hand blasphemies on the pages of my books, burning the letters and destroying the portrait of my father; and indeed, had it not been for his fear of death, he would long ago have ruined himself in order to involve me in the ruin. But his love of me is wonderful; I go further: I, who sicken and freeze at the mere thought of him, when I recall the abjection and passion of this attachment, and when I know how he fears my power to cut him off by suicide, I find it in my heart to pity him.

It is useless, and the time awfully fails me, to prolong this description; no one has ever suffered such torments, let that suffice; and yet even to these, habit brought—no, not alleviation—but a certain callousness of soul, a certain acquiescence of despair; and my punishment might have gone on for years, but for the last calamity which has now fallen, and which has finally severed me from my own face and nature. My provision of the salt, which had never been renewed since the date of the first experiment, began to run low. I sent out for a fresh supply and mixed the draught; the ebullition followed, and the first change of colour, not the second; I drank it and it was without efficiency. You will learn from Poole how I have had London ransacked; it was in vain; and I am now persuaded that my first supply was impure, and that it was that unknown impurity which lent efficacy to the draught.

About a week has passed, and I am now finishing this statement under the influence of the last of the old powders. This, then, is the last time, short of a miracle, that Henry Jekyll can think his own thoughts or see his own face (now how sadly altered!) in the glass. Nor must I delay too long to bring my writing to an end; for if my narrative has hitherto escaped destruction, it has been by a combination of great prudence and great good luck. Should the throes of change take me in the act of writing it, Hyde will tear it in pieces; but if some time shall have elapsed after I have laid it by, his wonderful selfishness and circumscription to the moment will probably save it once again from the action of his apelike spite. And indeed the doom that is closing on us both, has already changed and crushed him. Half an hour from now, when I shall again and forever reindue that hated personality, I know how I shall sit shuddering and weeping in my chair, or continue, with the most strained and fearstruck ecstasy of listening, to pace up and down this room (my last earthly refuge) and give ear to every sound of menace. Will Hyde die upon the scaffold? or will he find courage to release himself at the last moment? God knows; I am careless; this is my true hour of death, and what is to follow concerns another than myself. Here then, as I lay down the pen and proceed to seal up my confession, I bring the life of that unhappy Henry Jekyll to an end.

The Apparition of Lord Tyrone to Lady Beresford

Anonymous

———— ◆ ————

L ORD TYRONE AND MISS ———— WERE BORN IN IRELAND, AND WERE LEFT orphans in their infancy to the care of the same person, by whom they were both educated in the principles of deism.

Their guardian dying when they were each of them about fourteen years of age, they fell into very different hands. The persons on whom the care of them now devolved used every means to eradicate the erroneous principles they had imbibed, and to persuade them to embrace revealed religion, but in vain. Their arguments were insufficient to convince, though they were strong enough to stagger their former faith. Though separated from each other, their friendship was unalterable, and they continued to regard each other with a sincere and fraternal affection. After some years were elapsed, and both were grown up, they made a solemn promise to each other that whichever should die first, would, if permitted, appear to the other, to declare what religion was most approved by the Supreme Being. Miss ———— was shortly after addressed by Sir Martin Beresford, to whom she was, after a few years, married, but a change of condition had no power to alter their friendship The families visited each other, and often for some weeks together. A short time after one of these visits, Sir Martin remarked, that when his lady came down to breakfast, her countenance was disturbed, and inquired of her health. She assured him she was quite well. He then asked her if she had hurt her wrist: "Have you sprained it?" said he, observing a black ribbon round it. She answered to the negative, and added, "Let me conjure you, Sir Martin, never to inquire the cause of my wearing this ribbon; you will never see me without it. If it concerned you as a husband to know, I would not for a moment conceal it: I never in my life denied you a request, but of this I entreat you to forgive me the refusal, and never to urge me further on the subject." "Very well," said he, smiling, " since you beg me so earnestly, I will inquire no more." The conversation here ended;

but breakfast was scarce over when Lady Beresford eagerly inquired if the post was come; she was told it was not. In a few minutes she ran again and repeated the inquiry. She was again answered as at first. "Do you expect letters?" said Sir Martin, "that you are so anxious for the arrival of the post?" "I do," she answered, "I expect to hear that Lord Tyrone is dead; he died last Tuesday at four o'clock." "I never in my life," said Sir Martin, "believed you superstitious; some idle dream has surely thus alarmed you." At that instant the servant entered and delivered to them it letter sealed with black. "It is as I expected," exclaimed Lady Beresford, "Lord Tyrone is dead." Sir Martin opened the letter; it came from Lord Tyrone's steward, and contained the melancholy intelligence of his master's death, and on the very day and hour Lady Beresford had before specified. Sir Martin begged Lady Beresford to compose herself, and she assured him she felt much easier than she had done for a long time; and added, "I can communicate intelligence to you which I know will prove welcome; I can assure you, beyond the possibility of a doubt, that I shall in some months present you with a son." Sir Martin received this news with the greatest joy. After some months, Lady Beresford was delivered of a son; she had before been the mother of only two daughters. Sir Martin survived the birth of his son little more than four years. After his decease his widow seldom left home; she visited no family but that of a clergyman who resided in the same village; with them she frequently passed a few hours every day; the rest of her time was spent in solitude, and she appeared determined for ever to banish all other society. The clergyman's family consisted of himself, his wife, and one son, who, at the time of Sir Martin's death, was quite a youth; to this son, however, she was after a few years married, notwithstanding the disparity of years, and the manifest imprudence of a connection so unequal in every point of view. Lady Beresford was treated by her young husband with contempt and cruelty, while at the same time his conduct evinced him the most abandoned libertine, utterly destitute of every principle of virtue and humanity. By this, her second husband, she had two daughters; after which, such was the baseness of his conduct, that she insisted on a separation. They parted for a few years, when so great was the contrition he expressed for his former conduct, that, won over by his supplications, promises, and entreaties, she was induced to pardon, and once more to reside with him, and was in time the mother of a son.

The day on which she had lain-in a month, being the anniversary of her birth-day, she sent for Lady Betty Cobb (of whose friendship she had long been possessed), and a few other friends to request them to spend the day with her. About seven, the clergyman by whom she had been christened, and with whom she had all her life been intimate, came into the room to inquire after her health. She told him she was perfectly well, and requested him to spend the day with them; "For," said she, " this is my birth-day. I am forty-eight to-day." "No, madam," answered the clergyman, "you are mistaken; your mother and myself have had many disputes concerning your age, and I have at last discovered that I was right. I happened to go last week into the parish where you were born; I was resolved to put an end to the dispute; I searched the register, and find that you are but forty-seven this day." "You have signed my death warrant," she exclaimed; "I have but a few hours to live. I must, therefore, entreat you to leave me immediately, as I have something of importance to settle before I die." When the cler-gyman had left her, Lady Beresford sent to forbid the company coming, and at the same time to request Lady Betty Cobb, and her son (of whom Sir Martin was the father, and was then about twenty-two years of age), to come to her apartment immediately. Upon their arrival, having ordered the attendants to quit the room, "I have some-thing," she said, "of the greatest importance to communicate to you both before I die, a period which is not far distant. You, Lady Betty, are no stranger to the friendship which subsisted between Lord Tyrone and myself: we were educated under the same roof, and in the same principles of deism. When the friends, into whose hands we after-wards fell, endeavoured to persuade us to embrace revealed religion, their arguments, though insufficient to convince, were powerful enough to stagger our former feelings, and to leave us wavering between the two opinions: in this perplexing state of doubt and uncertainty, we made a solemn promise to each other, that which died first should (if permitted) appear to the other, and declare what religion was most acceptable to God: accordingly, one night, while Sir Martin and myself were in bed, I suddenly awoke and discovered Lord Tyrone sitting by my bedside. I screamed out and endeav-oured to awake Sir Martin; 'For heaven's sake,' I exclaimed, 'Lord Tyrone, by what means, or for what reason, came you hither at this time of night?' 'Have you then forgotten our promise?' said he. 'I died last Tuesday at four o'clock, and have been permitted by the Supreme Being to appear to you, to assure you that the revealed reli-gion is true, and the only religion by which we can be saved. I am further suffered to inform you that you will soon produce a son; who, it is decreed, will marry my daugh-ter: not many years after his birth Sir Martin will die, and you will marry again, and to a man by whose ill treatment you will be rendered miserable: you will have two daugh-ters, and afterwards a son, in child-birth of whom you will die in the forty-seventh year of your age.', 'Just Heavens!' I exclaimed, 'and cannot I prevent this?' 'Undoubtedly you may,' returned the spectre; 'you are a free agent, and may prevent it all by resisting every temptation to a second marriage; but your passions are strong, you know not their power; hitherto you have had no trials. More I am not permitted to reveal, but if after this warning you persist in your infidelity, your lot in another world will be miserable indeed!' 'May I not ask,' said I, 'if you are happy?' 'Had I been otherwise,' he replied, 'I should not be permitted to appear to you.' 'I may then infer that you are happy?' He smiled. 'But how,' said I, 'when morning comes, shall I know that your appearance to me has been real, and not the mere representation of my own imagination?' 'Will not the news of my death be sufficient to convince you?' 'No,' I returned, 'I might have had such a dream, and that dream accidentally come to pass. I will have some stronger proofs of its reality.' 'You shall,' said he, and waving his hand, the bed-curtains, which were of crimson velvet, were instantly drawn through a large iron hoop by which the tester of the bed was suspended. 'In that,' said he, 'you cannot be mistaken; no mortal arm could have performed this.' 'True,' said I, 'but sleeping we are often of far more strength than when awake; though waking I could not have done it, asleep I might; and I shall still doubt.' 'Here is a pocket-book,' said he; 'in it I will write my name: you know my hand-writing.' I replied, 'Yes.' He wrote with a pencil on one side of the leaves. 'Still,' said I, 'in the morning I may doubt; though waking I could not imitate your hand, asleep I might.' 'You are hard of belief,' said he: 'it would injure you irreparably; it is not for spirits to touch mortal flesh.' 'I do not,' said I, 'regard a light blemish.' 'You are a woman of courage,' replied he, 'hold out your hand.' I did: he touched my wrist: his hand was cold as marble: in a moment the sinews shrunk up, every nerve withered. 'Now,' said he, 'while you live, let no mortal eye behold that wrist: to see it is sacrilege.' He stopped; I turned to him again; he was gone. During the time I had conversed with him my thoughts were perfectly calm and collected, but the moment he was gone, I felt chilled with horror, the very bed moved under me. I endeavoured, but in vain, to wake Sir Martin, all my attempts were ineffectual, and in this state of agitation and terror I lay for some time, when a shower of tears came to my relief, and I dropped asleep. In the morning, Sir Martin arose and dressed himself as usual, without perceiving the state the curtains remained in. When I awoke I found Sir Martin gone down; I arose, and having put on my clothes, went to the gallery adjoining the apartment, and took from thence a long broom (such as cornices are swept with), by the help of this I took down with some difficulty the curtains, as I imagined their extraordinary position might excite suspicion in the family. I then went to the bureau, took up my pocket-book, and bound a piece of black ribbon round my wrist. When I came down, the agitation of my mind had left an impression on my countenance too visible to pass unobserved by my husband. He instantly remarked it and asked the cause; I informed him Lord Tyrone was no more, that he died at the hour of four on the preceding Tuesday, and desired him never to question me more respecting the black ribbon; which he kindly desisted from after. You, my son, as had been foretold, I afterwards brought into the world, and in a little time after your birth your lamented father expired in my arms. After this melancholy event, I determined as the only probable chance to avoid the sequel of the prediction, for ever to abandon all society; to give up every pleasure resulting from it, and pass the remainder of my days in solitude and retirement. But few can long endure to exist in a state of perfect sequestration: I began an intimacy with a family, and one alone; nor could I then foresee the fatal consequences which afterwards resulted from it. Little did I think their son, their only son, then a mere youth, would form the person destined by fate to prove my destruction, in a very few years I ceased to regard him with indifference; I endeavoured by every possible way to conquer a passion the fatal effects of which I too well knew. I had fondly imagined I had overcome its influence, when the evening of one fatal day terminated my fortitude, and plunged me in a moment down that abyss I had so long been meditating to shun. He had often solicited his parents for leave to go into the army, and at last obtained permission, and came to bid adieu before his departure. The instant he entered the room he fell upon his knees at his feet, told me he was miserable, and that I alone was the cause. At that moment my fortitude forsook me, I gave myself up for lost, and regarding my fate as inevitable, without further hesitation consented to an union, the immediate result of which I knew to be misery, and its end death. The conduct of my husband, after a few years, amply justified a separation, and I hoped by this means to avoid the fatal sequel of the prophecy; but won over by his reiterated entreaties, I was prevailed upon to pardon, and once more reside with him, though not till after I had, as I thought, passed my forty-seventh year. But alas! I have this day heard from undisputable authority, that I have hitherto lain under a mistake with regard to my age, and that I am but forty-seven to-day. Of the near approach of my death then I entertain not the slightest doubt; but I do not dread its arrival; armed with the sacred precepts of Christianity, I can meet the King of Terrors without dismay, and without fear bid adieu to mortality for ever. When I am dead, as the necessity of concealment closes with my life, I could wish that you, Lady Betty, would unbind my wrist, take from thence the black ribbon, and let my son with yourself behold it."

Lady Beresford here paused for some time, but resuming the conversation she entreated her son would behave himself so as to merit the high honour he would in future receive from an union with the daughter of Lord Tyrone. Lady B. then expressed a wish to lay down on the bed and endeavour to compose herself to sleep. Lady Betty Cobb and her son immediately called her domestics, and quitted the room, having first desired them to watch their mistress attentively, and if they observed the smallest change in her, to call instantly.

An hour passed, and all was quiet in the room. They listened at the door and every thing remained still, but in half an hour more a bell rang violently; they flew to her apartment, but before they reached the door, they heard the servants exclaim, "Oh, she is dead!" Lady Betty then bade the servants for a few minutes to quit the room, and herself with Lady Beresford's son approached the bed of his mother; they knelt down by the side of it; Lady Betty then lifted up her hand and untied the ribbon; the wrist was found exactly as Lady Beresford had described it, every sinew shrunk, every nerve withered.

Lady Beresford's son, as had been predicted, is since married to Lord Tyrone's daughter. The black ribbon and pocket-book were formerly in the possession of Lady Betty Cobb, Marlborough Buildings, Bath, who, during her long life, was ever ready to attest the truth of this narration, as are, to the present hour, the whole of the Tyrone and Beresford families.

Lost in a Pyramid

OR, THE MUMMY'S CURSE

Louisa May Alcott

———— ◆ ————

I

"AND WHAT ARE THESE, PAUL?" ASKED EVELYN, OPENING A TARNISHED GOLD BOX and examining its contents curiously.

"Seeds of some unknown Egyptian plant," replied Forsyth, with a sudden shadow on his dark face, as he looked down at the three scarlet grains lying in the white hand lifted to him.

"Where did you get them?" asked the girl.

"That is a weird story, which will only haunt you if I tell it," said Forsyth, with an absent expression that strongly excited the girl's curiosity.

"Please tell it, I like weird tales, and they never trouble me. Ah, do tell it; your stories are always so interesting," she cried, looking up with such a pretty blending of entreaty and command in her charming face, that refusal was impossible.

"You'll be sorry for it, and so shall I, perhaps; I warn you beforehand, that harm is foretold to the possessor of those mysterious seeds," said Forsyth, smiling, even while he knit his black brows, and regarded the blooming creature before him with a fond yet foreboding glance.

"Tell on, I'm not afraid of these pretty atoms," she answered, with an imperious nod.

"To hear is to obey. Let me read the facts, and then I will begin," returned Forsyth, pacing to and fro with the far-off look of one who turns the pages of the past.

Evelyn watched him a moment, and then returned to her work, or play, rather, for the task seemed well suited to the vivacious little creature, half-child, half-woman.

"While in Egypt," commenced Forsyth, slowly, "I went one day with my guide and Professor Niles, to explore the Cheops. Niles had a mania for antiquities of all sorts, and forgot time, danger and fatigue in the ardor of his pursuit. We rummaged up and down the narrow passages, half choked with dust and close air; reading inscriptions on the walls, stumbling over shattered mummy-cases, or coming face to face with some shriveled specimen perched like a hobgoblin on the little shelves where the dead used to be stowed away for ages. I was desperately tired after a few hours of it, and begged the professor to return. But he was bent on exploring certain places, and would not desist. We had but one guide, so I was forced to stay; but Jumal, my man, seeing how weary I was, proposed to us to rest in one of the larger passages, while he went to procure another guide for Niles. We consented, and assuring us that we were perfectly safe, if we did not quit the spot, Jumal left us, promising to return speedily. The professor sat down to take notes of his researches, and stretching my self on the soft sand, I fell asleep.

"I was roused by that indescribable thrill which instinctively warns us of danger, and springing up, I found myself alone. One torch burned faintly where Jumal had struck it, but Niles and the other light were gone. A dreadful sense of loneliness oppressed me for a moment; then I collected myself and looked well about me. A bit of paper was pinned to my hat, which lay near me, and on it, in the professor's writing were these words:

"'I've gone back a little to refresh my memory on certain points. Don't follow me till Jumal comes. I can find my way back to you, for I have a clue. Sleep well, and dream gloriously of the Pharaohs.'

"I laughed at first over the old enthusiast, then felt anxious then restless, and finally resolved to follow him, for I discovered a strong cord fastened to a fallen stone, and knew that this was the clue he spoke of. Leaving a line for Jumal, I took my torch and retraced my steps, following the cord along the winding ways. I often shouted, but received no reply, and pressed on, hoping at each turn to see the old man poring over some musty relic of antiquity. Suddenly the cord ended, and lowering my torch, I saw that the footsteps had gone on.

"'Rash fellow, he'll lose himself, to a certainty,' I thought, really alarmed now.

"As I paused, a faint call reached me, and I answered it, waited, shouted again, and a still fainter echo replied.

"Niles was evidently going on, misled by the reverberations of the low passages. No time was to be lost, and, forgetting myself, I stuck my torch in the deep sand to guide me back to the clue, and ran down the straight path before me, whooping like a madman as I went. I did not mean to lose sight of the light, but in my eagerness to find

Niles I turned from the main passage, and, guided by his voice, hastened on. His torch soon gladdened my eyes, and the clutch of his trembling hands told me what agony he had suffered.

"'Let us get out of this horrible place at once,' he said, wiping the great drops off his forehead.

"'Come, we're not far from the clue. I can soon reach it, and then we are safe'; but as I spoke, a chill passed over me, for a perfect labyrinth of narrow paths lay before us.

"Trying to guide myself by such land-marks as I had observed in my hasty passage, I followed the tracks in the sand till I fancied we must be near my light. No glimmer appeared, however, and kneeling down to examine the footprints nearer, I discovered, to my dismay, that I had been following the wrong ones, for among those marked by a deep boot-heel, were prints of bare feet; we had had no guide there, and Jumal wore sandals.

"Rising, I confronted Niles, with the one despairing word, 'Lost!' as I pointed from the treacherous sand to the fast-waning light.

"I thought the old man would be overwhelmed but, to my surprise, he grew quite calm and steady, thought a moment, and then went on, saying, quietly:

"'Other men have passed here before us; let us follow their steps, for, if I do not greatly err, they lead toward great passages, where one's way is easily found.'

"On we went, bravely, till a misstep threw the professor violently to the ground with a broken leg, and nearly extinguished the torch. It was a horrible predicament, and I gave up all hope as I sat beside the poor fellow, who lay exhausted with fatigue, remorse and pain, for I would not leave him.

"'Paul,' he said suddenly, 'if you will not go on, there is one more effort we can make. I remember hearing that a party lost as we are, saved themselves by building a fire. The smoke penetrated further than sound or light, and the guide's quick wit understood the unusual mist; he followed it, and rescued the party. Make a fire and trust to Jumal.'

"'A fire without wood?' I began; but he pointed to a shelf behind me, which had escaped me in the gloom; and on it I saw a slender mummy-case. I understood him, for these dry cases, which lie about in hundreds, are freely used as firewood. Reaching up, I pulled it down, believing it to be empty, but as it fell, it burst open, and out rolled a mummy. Accustomed as I was to such sights, it startled me a little, for danger had unstrung my nerves. Laying the little brown chrysalis aside, I smashed the case, lit the pile with my torch, and soon a light cloud of smoke drifted down the three passages which diverged from the cell-like place where we had paused.

"While busied with the fire, Niles, forgetful of pain and peril, had dragged the mummy nearer, and was examining it with the interest of a man whose ruling passion was strong even in death.

" 'Come and help me unroll this. I have always longed to be the first to see and secure the curious treasures put away among the folds of these uncanny winding-sheets. This is a woman, and we may find something rare and precious here,' he said, beginning to unfold the outer coverings, from which a strange aromatic odor came.

"Reluctantly I obeyed, for to me there was something sacred in the bones of this unknown woman. But to beguile the time and amuse the poor fellow, I lent a hand, wondering as I worked, if this dark, ugly thing had ever been a lovely, soft-eyed Egyptian girl.

"From the fibrous folds of the wrappings dropped precious gums and spices, which half intoxicated us with their potent breath, antique coins, and a curious jewel or two, which Niles eagerly examined.

"All the bandages but one were cut off at last, and a small head laid bare, round which still hung great plaits of what had once been luxuriant hair. The shriveled hands were folded on the breast, and clasped in them lay that gold box."

"Ah!" cried Evelyn, dropping it from her rosy palm with a shudder.

"Nay; don't reject the poor little mummy's treasure. I never have quite forgiven myself for stealing it, or for burning her," said Forsyth, painting rapidly, as if the recollection of that experience lent energy to his hand.

"Burning her! Oh, Paul, what do you mean?" asked the girl, sitting up with a face full of excitement.

"I'll tell you. While busied with Madame la Momie, our fire had burned low, for the dry case went like tinder. A faint, far-off sound made our hearts leap, and Niles cried out: 'Pile on the wood; Jumal is tracking us; don't let the smoke fail now or we are lost!'

" 'There is no more wood; the case was very small, and is all gone,' I answered, tearing off such of my garments as would burn readily, and piling them upon the embers.

"Niles did the same, but the light fabrics were quickly consumed, and made no smoke.

" 'Burn that!' commanded the professor, pointing to the mummy.

"I hesitated a moment. Again came the faint echo of a horn. Life was dear to me. A few dry bones might save us, and I obeyed him in silence.

"A dull blaze sprung up, and a heavy smoke rose from the burning mummy, rolling in volumes through the low passages, and threatening to suffocate us with its fragrant mist. My brain grew dizzy, the light danced before my eyes, strange phantoms seemed to people the air, and, in the act of asking Niles why he gasped and looked so pale, I lost consciousness."

Evelyn drew a long breath, and put away the scented toys from her lap as if their odor oppressed her.

Forsyth's swarthy face was all aglow with the excitement of his story, and his black eyes glittered as he added, with a quick laugh:

"That's all; Jumal found and got us out, and we both forswore pyramids for the rest of our days."

"But the box: how came you to keep it?" asked Evelyn, eyeing it askance as it lay gleaming in a streak of sunshine.

"Oh, I brought it away as a souvenir, and Niles kept the other trinkets."

"But you said harm was foretold to the possessor of those scarlet seeds," persisted the girl, whose fancy was excited by the tale, and who fancied all was not told.

"Among his spoils, Niles found a bit of parchment, which he deciphered, and this inscription said that the mummy we had so ungallantly burned was that of a famous sorceress who bequeathed her curse to whoever should disturb her rest. Of course I don't believe that curse has anything to do with it, but it's a fact that Niles never prospered from that day. He says it's because he has never recovered from the fall and fright and I dare say it is so; but I sometimes wonder if I am to share the curse, for I've a vein of superstition in me, and that poor little mummy haunts my dreams still."

A long silence followed these words. Paul painted mechanically and Evelyn lay regarding him with a thoughtful face. But gloomy fancies were as foreign to her nature as shadows are to noonday, and presently she laughed a cheery laugh, saying as she took up the box again:

"Why don't you plant them, and see what wondrous flower they will bear?"

"I doubt if they would bear anything after lying in a mummy's hand for centuries," replied Forsyth, gravely.

"Let me plant them and try. You know wheat has sprouted and grown that was taken from a mummy's coffin; why should not these pretty seeds? I should so like to watch them grow; may I, Paul?"

"No, I'd rather leave that experiment untried. I have a queer feeling about the matter, and don't want to meddle myself or let anyone I love meddle with these seeds.

They may be some horrible poison, or possess some evil power, for the sorceress evidently valued them, since she clutched them fast even in her tomb."

"Now, you are foolishly superstitious, and I laugh at you. Be generous; give me one seed, just to learn if it will grow. See I'll pay for it," and Evelyn, who now stood beside him, dropped a kiss on his forehead as she made her request, with the most engaging air.

But Forsyth would not yield. He smiled and returned the embrace with lover-like warmth, then flung the seeds into the fire, and gave her back the golden box, saying, tenderly:

"My darling, I'll fill it with diamonds or bonbons, if you please, but I will not let you play with that witch's spells. You've enough of your own, so forget the 'pretty seeds' and see what a Light of the Harem I've made of you."

Evelyn frowned, and smiled, and presently the lovers were out in the spring sunshine reveling in their own happy hopes, untroubled by one foreboding fear.

II

"I HAVE A LITTLE SURPRISE FOR YOU, LOVE," SAID FORSYTH, AS HE GREETED HIS cousin three months later on the morning of his wedding day.

"And I have one for you," she answered, smiling faintly.

"How pale you are, and how thin you grow! All this bridal bustle is too much for you, Evelyn." he said, with fond anxiety, as he watched the strange pallor of her face, and pressed the wasted little hand in his.

"I am so tired," she said, and leaned her head wearily on her lover's breast. "Neither sleep, food, nor air gives me strength, and a curious mist seems to cloud my mind at times. Mamma says it is the heat, but I shiver even in the sun, while at night I burn with fever. Paul, dear, I'm glad you are going to take me away to lead a quiet, happy life with you, but I'm afraid it will be a very short one."

"My fanciful little wife! You are tired and nervous with all this worry, but a few weeks of rest in the country will give us back our blooming Eve again. Have you no curiosity to learn my surprise?" he asked, to change her thoughts.

The vacant look stealing over the girl's face gave place to one of interest, but as she listened it seemed to require an effort to fix her mind on her lover's words.

"You remember the day we rummaged in the old cabinet?"

"Yes," and a smile touched her lips for a moment.

"And how you wanted to plant those queer red seeds I stole from the mummy?"

"I remember," and her eyes kindled with sudden fire.

"Well, I tossed them into the fire, as I thought, and gave you the box. But when I went back to cover up my picture, and found one of those seeds on the rug, a sudden fancy to gratify your whim led me to send it to Niles and ask him to plant and report on its progress. Today I hear from him for the first time, and he reports that the seed has grown marvelously, has budded, and that he intends to take the first flower, if it blooms in time, to a meeting of famous scientific men, after which he will send me its true name and the plant itself. From his description, it must be very curious, and I'm impatient to see it."

"You need not wait; I can show you the flower in its bloom," and Evelyn beckoned with the méchant smile so long a stranger to her lips.

Much amazed, Forsyth followed her to her own little boudoir, and there, standing in the sunshine, was the unknown plant. Almost rank in their luxuriance were the vivid green leaves on the slender purple stems, and rising from the midst, one ghostly-white flower, shaped like the head of a hooded snake, with scarlet stamens like forked tongues, and on the petals glittered spots like dew.

"A strange, uncanny flower! Has it any odor?" asked Forsyth, bending to examine it, and forgetting, in his interest, to ask how it came there.

"None, and that disappoints me, I am so fond of perfumes," answered the girl, caressing the green leaves which trembled at her touch, while the purple stems deepened their tint.

"Now tell me about it," said Forsyth, after standing silent for several minutes.

"I had been before you, and secured one of the seeds, for two fell on the rug. I planted it under a glass in the richest soil I could find, watered it faithfully, and was amazed at the rapidity with which it grew when once it appeared above the earth. I told no-one, for I meant to surprise you with it; but this bud has been so long in blooming, I have had to wait. It is a good omen that it blossoms today, and as it is nearly white, I mean to wear it, for I've learned to love it, having been my pet for so long."

"I would not wear it, for, in spite of its innocent color, it is an evil-looking plant, with its adder's tongue and unnatural dew. Wait till Niles tells us what it is, then pet it if it is harmless.

"Perhaps my sorceress cherished it for some symbolic beauty—those old Egyptians were full of fancies. It was very sly of you to turn the tables on me in this way. But I forgive you, since in a few hours, I shall chain this mysterious hand forever. How cold it is! Come out into the garden and get some warmth and color for tonight, my love."

But when night came, no-one could reproach the girl with her pallor, for she glowed like a pomegranate-flower, her eyes were full of fire, her lips scarlet, and all her old vivacity seemed to have returned. A more brilliant bride never blushed under a misty veil, and when her lover saw her, he was absolutely startled by the almost unearthly beauty which transformed the pale, languid creature of the morning into this radiant woman.

They were married, and if love, many blessings, and all good gifts lavishly showered upon them could make them happy, then this young pair were truly blest. But even in the rapture of the moment that made her his, Forsyth observed how icy cold was the little hand he held, how feverish the deep color on the soft cheek he kissed, and what a strange fire burned in the tender eyes that looked so wistfully at him.

Blithe and beautiful as a spirit, the smiling bride played her part in all the festivities of that long evening, and when at last light, life and color began to fade, the loving eyes that watched her thought it but the natural weariness of the hour. As the last guest departed, Forsyth was met by a servant, who gave him a letter marked "Haste." Tearing it open, he read these lines, from a friend of the professor's:

DEAR SIR—Poor Niles died suddenly two days ago, while at the Scientific Club, and his last words were: "Tell Paul Forsyth to beware of the Mummy's Curse, for this fatal flower has killed me." The circumstances of his death were so peculiar, that I add them as a sequel to this message. For several months, as he told us, he had been watching an unknown plant, and that evening he brought us the flower to examine. Other matters of interest absorbed us till a late hour, and the plant was forgotten. The professor wore it in his buttonhole—a strange white, serpent-headed blossom, with pale glittering spots, which slowly changed to a glittering scarlet, till the leaves looked as if sprinkled with blood. It was observed that instead of the pallor and feebleness which had recently come over him, that the professor was unusually animated, and seemed in an almost unnatural state of high spirits. Near the close of the meeting, in the midst of a lively discussion, he suddenly dropped, as if smitten with apoplexy. He was conveyed home insensible, and after one lucid interval, in which he gave me the message I have recorded above, he died in great agony, raving of mummies, pyramids, serpents, and some fatal curse which had fallen upon him.

After his death, livid scarlet spots, like those on the flower, appeared upon his skin, and he shriveled like a withered leaf. At my desire, the mysterious plant was examined, and pronounced by the best authority one of the most deadly poisons known to the Egyptian sorceresses. The plant slowly absorbs the vitality of whoever cultivates it, and the blossom, worn for two or three hours, produces either madness or death.

Down dropped the paper from Forsyth's hand; he read no further, but hurried back into the room where he had left his young wife. As if worn out with fatigue, she had thrown herself upon a couch, and lay there motionless, her face half-hidden by the light folds of the veil, which had blown over it.

"Evelyn, my dearest! Wake up and answer me. Did you wear that strange flower today?" whispered Forsyth, putting the misty screen away.

There was no need for her to answer, for there, gleaming spectrally on her bosom, was the evil blossom, its white petals spotted now with flecks of scarlet, vivid as drops of newly spilt blood.

But the unhappy bridegroom scarcely saw it, for the face above it appalled him by its utter vacancy. Drawn and pallid, as if with some wasting malady, the young face, so lovely an hour ago, lay before him aged and blighted by the baleful influence of the plant which had drunk up her life. No recognition in the eyes, no word upon the lips, no motion of the hand—only the faint breath, the fluttering pulse, and wide-opened eyes, betrayed that she was alive.

Alas for the young wife! The superstitious fear at which she had smiled had proved true: the curse that had bided its time for ages was fulfilled at last, and her own hand wrecked her happiness for ever. Death in life was her doom, and for years Forsyth secluded himself to tend with pathetic devotion the pale ghost, who never, by word or look, could thank him for the love that outlived even such a fate as this.

In Kropfsberg Keep

Ralph Adams Cram

———◆———

To the traveller from Innsbrück to Munich, up the lovely valley of the silver Inn, many castles appear, one after another, each on its beetling cliff or gentle hill,—appear and disappear, melting into the dark fir trees that grow so thickly on every side,—Laneck, Lichtwer, Ratholtz, Tratzberg, Matzen, Kropfsberg, gathering close around the entrance to the dark and wonderful Zillerthal.

But to us—Tom Rendel and myself—there are two castles only: not the gorgeous and princely Ambras, nor the noble old Tratzberg, with its crowded treasures of solemn and splendid mediævalism; but little Matzen, where eager hospitality forms the new life of a never-dead chivalry, and Kropfsberg, ruined, tottering, blasted by fire and smitten with grievous years,—a dead thing, and haunted,—full of strange legends, and eloquent of mystery and tragedy.

We were visiting the von C——s at Matzen, and gaining our first wondering knowledge of the courtly, cordial castle life in the Tyrol,—of the gentle and delicate hospitality of noble Austrians. Brixleg had ceased to be but a mark on a map, and had become a place of rest and delight, a home for homeless wanderers on the face of Europe, while Schloss Matzen was a synonym for all that was gracious and kindly and beautiful in life. The days moved on in a golden round of riding and driving and shooting: down to Landl and Thiersee for chamois, across the river to the magic Achensee, up the Zillerthal, across the Schmerner Joch, even to the railway station at Steinach. And in the evenings after the late dinners in the upper hall where the sleepy hounds leaned against our chairs looking at us with suppliant eyes, in the evenings when the fire was dying away in the hooded fireplace in the library, stories. Stories, and legends, and fairy tales, while the stiff old portraits changed countenance constantly under the flickering firelight, and the sound of the drifting Inn came softly across the meadows far below.

If ever I tell the Story of Schloss Matzen, then will be the time to paint the too inadequate picture of this fair oasis in the desert of travel and tourists and hotels; but just now it is Kropfsberg the Silent that is of greater importance, for it was only in Matzen that the story was told by Fräulein E——, the gold-haired niece of Frau von C——, one hot evening in July, when we were sitting in the great west window of the drawing-room after a long ride up the Stallenthal. All the windows were open to catch the faint wind, and we had sat for a long time watching the Otzethaler Alps turn rose-color over distant Innsbrück, then deepen to violet as the sun went down and the white mists rose slowly until Lichtwer and Laneck and Kropfsberg rose like craggy islands in a silver sea.

And this is the story as Fräulein E—— told it to us,—the Story of Kropfsberg Keep.

A great many years ago, soon after my grandfather died, and Matzen came to us, when I was a little girl, and so young that I remember nothing of the affair except as something dreadful that frightened me very much, two young men who had studied painting with my grandfather came down to Brixleg from Munich, partly to paint, and partly to amuse themselves,—"ghost-hunting" as they said, for they were very sensible young men and prided themselves on it, laughing at all kinds of "superstition," and particularly at that form which believed in ghosts and feared them. They had never seen a real ghost, you know, and they belonged to a certain set of people who believed nothing they had not seen themselves,—which always seemed to me *very* conceited. Well, they knew that we had lots of beautiful castles here in the "lower valley," and they assumed, and rightly, that every castle has at least *one* ghost story connected with it, so they chose this as their hunting ground, only the game they sought was ghosts, not chamois. Their plan was to visit every place that was supposed to be haunted, and to meet every reputed ghost, and prove that it really was no ghost at all.

There was a little inn down in the village then, kept by an old man named Peter Rosskopf, and the two young men made this their headquarters. The very first night they began to draw from the old innkeeper all that he knew of legends and ghost stories connected with Brixleg and its castles, and as he was a most garrulous old gentleman he filled them with the wildest delight by his stories of the ghosts of the castles about the mouth of the Zillerthal. Of course the old man believed every word he said, and you can imagine his horror and amazement when, after telling his guests the particularly blood-curdling story of Kropfsberg and its haunted keep, the elder of the two boys, whose surname I have forgotten, but whose Christian name was

Rupert, calmly said, "Your story is most satisfactory: we will sleep in Kropfsberg Keep to-morrow night, and you must provide us with all that we may need to make ourselves comfortable."

The old man nearly fell into the fire. "What for a blockhead are you?" he cried, with big eyes. "The keep is haunted by Count Albert's ghost, I tell you!"

"That is why we are going there to-morrow night; we wish to make the acquaintance of Count Albert."

"But there was a man stayed there once, and in the morning he was dead."

"Very silly of him; there are two of us, and we carry revolvers."

"But it's a *ghost*, I tell you," almost screamed the innkeeper; "are ghosts afraid of firearms?"

"Whether they are or not, we are *not* afraid of *them*."

Here the younger boy broke in,—he was named Otto von Kleist. I remember the name, for I had a music teacher once by that name. He abused the poor old man shamefully; told him that they were going to spend the night in Kropfsberg in spite of Count Albert and Peter Rosskopf, and that he might as well make the most of it and earn his money with cheerfulness.

In a word, they finally bullied the old fellow into submission, and when the morning came he set about preparing for the suicide, as he considered it, with sighs and mutterings and ominous shakings of the head.

You know the condition of the castle now,—nothing but scorched walls and crumbling piles of fallen masonry. Well, at the time I tell you of, the keep was still partially preserved. It was finally burned out only a few years ago by some wicked boys who came over from Jenbach to have a good time. But when the ghost hunters came, though the two lower floors had fallen into the crypt, the third floor remained. The peasants said it *could* not fall, but that it would stay until the Day of Judgment, because it was in the room above that the wicked Count Albert sat watching the flames destroy the great castle and his imprisoned guests, and where he finally hung himself in a suit of armor that had belonged to his mediæval ancestor, the first Count Kropfsberg.

No one dared touch him, and so he hung there for twelve years, and all the time venturesome boys and daring men used to creep up the turret steps and stare awfully through the chinks in the door at that ghostly mass of steel that held within itself the body of a murderer and suicide, slowly returning to the dust from which it was made. Finally it disappeared, none knew whither, and for another dozen years the room stood empty but for the old furniture and the rotting hangings.

So, when the two men climbed the stairway to the haunted room, they found a very different state of things from what exists now. The room was absolutely as it was left the night Count Albert burned the castle, except that all trace of the suspended suit of armor and its ghastly contents had vanished.

No one had dared to cross the threshold, and I suppose that for forty years no living thing had entered that dreadful room.

On one side stood a vast canopied bed of black wood, the damask hangings of which were covered with mould and mildew. All the clothing of the bed was in perfect order, and on it lay a book, open, and face downward. The only other furniture in the room consisted of several old chairs, a carved oak chest, and a big inlaid table covered with books and papers, and on one corner two or three bottles with dark solid sediment at the bottom, and a glass, also dark with the dregs of wine that had been poured out almost half a century before. The tapestry on the walls was green with mould, but hardly torn or otherwise defaced, for although the heavy dust of forty years lay on everything the room had been preserved from further harm. No spider web was to be seen, no trace of nibbling mice, not even a dead moth or fly on the sills of the diamond-paned windows; life seemed to have shunned the room utterly and finally.

The men looked at the room curiously, and, I am sure, not without some feelings of awe and unacknowledged fear; but, whatever they may have felt of instinctive shrinking, they said nothing, and quickly set to work to make the room passably inhabitable. They decided to touch nothing that had not absolutely to be changed, and therefore they made for themselves a bed in one corner with the mattress and linen from the inn. In the great fireplace they piled a lot of wood on the caked ashes of a fire dead for forty years, turned the old chest into a table, and laid out on it all their arrangements for the evening's amusement: food, two or three bottles of wine, pipes and tobacco, and the chess-board that was their inseparable travelling companion.

All this they did themselves: the innkeeper would not even come within the walls of the outer court; he insisted that he had washed his hands of the whole affair, the silly dunderheads might go to their death their own way. *He* would not aid and abet them. One of the stable boys brought the basket of food and the wood and the bed up the winding stone stairs, to be sure, but neither money nor prayers nor threats would bring him within the walls of the accursed place, and he stared fearfully at the hare-brained boys as they worked around the dead old room preparing for the night that was coming so fast.

At length everything was in readiness, and after a final visit to the inn for dinner Rupert and Otto started at sunset for the Keep. Half the village went with them, for

Peter Rosskopf had babbled the whole story to an open-mouthed crowd of wondering men and women, and as to an execution the awe-struck crowd followed the two boys dumbly, curious to see if they surely would put their plan into execution. But none went farther than the outer doorway of the stairs, for it was already growing twilight. In absolute silence they watched the two foolhardy youths with their lives in their hands enter the terrible Keep, standing like a tower in the midst of the piles of stones that had once formed walls joining it with the mass of the castle beyond. When a moment later a light showed itself in the high windows above, they sighed resignedly and went their ways, to wait stolidly until morning should come and prove the truth of their fears and warnings.

In the mean time the ghost hunters built a huge fire, lighted their many candles, and sat down to await developments. Rupert afterwards told my uncle that they really felt no fear whatever, only a contemptuous curiosity, and they ate their supper with good appetite and an unusual relish. It was a long evening. They played many games of chess, waiting for midnight. Hour passed after hour, and nothing occurred to interrupt the monotony of the evening. Ten, eleven, came and went,—it was almost midnight. They piled more wood in the fireplace, lighted new candles, looked to their pistols—and waited. The clocks in the village struck twelve; the sound coming muffled through the high, deep-embrasured windows. Nothing happened, nothing to break the heavy silence; and with a feeling of disappointed relief they looked at each other and acknowledged that they had met another rebuff.

Finally they decided that there was no use in sitting up and boring themselves any longer, they had much better rest; so Otto threw himself down on the mattress, falling almost immediately asleep. Rupert sat a little longer, smoking, and watching the stars creep along behind the shattered glass and the bent leads of the lofty windows; watching the fire fall together, and the strange shadows move mysteriously on the mouldering walls. The iron hook in the oak beam, that crossed the ceiling midway, fascinated him, not with fear, but morbidly. So, it was from that hook that for twelve years, twelve long years of changing summer and winter, the body of Count Albert, murderer and suicide, hung in its strange casing of mediæval steel; moving a little at first, and turning gently while the fire died out on the hearth, while the ruins of the castle grew cold, and horrified peasants sought for the bodies of the score of gay, reckless, wicked guests whom Count Albert had gathered in Kropfsberg for a last debauch, gathered to their terrible and untimely death. What a strange and fiendish idea it was, the young, handsome noble who had ruined himself and his family in the society of the splendid debauchees, gathering them all together, men and women who had known only love and pleasure, for a glorious and awful riot of luxury, and then, when they were all dancing in the great ballroom, locking the doors and burning the whole castle about them, the while he sat in the great keep listening to their screams of agonized fear, watching the fire sweep from wing to wing until the whole mighty mass was one enormous and awful pyre, and then, clothing himself in his great-great-grandfather's armor, hanging himself in the midst of the ruins of what had been a proud and noble castle. So ended a great family, a great house.

But that was forty years ago.

He was growing drowsy; the light flickered and flared in the fireplace; one by one the candles went out; the shadows grew thick in the room. Why did that great iron hook stand out so plainly? why did that dark shadow dance and quiver so mockingly behind it?—why— But he ceased to wonder at anything. He was asleep.

It seemed to him that he woke almost immediately; the fire still burned, though low and fitfully on the hearth. Otto was sleeping, breathing quietly and regularly; the shadows had gathered close around him, thick and murky; with every passing moment the light died in the fireplace; he felt stiff with cold. In the utter silence he heard the clock in the village strike two. He shivered with a sudden and irresistible feeling of fear, and abruptly turned and looked towards the hook in the ceiling.

Yes, It was there. He knew that It would be. It seemed quite natural, he would have been disappointed had he seen nothing; but now he knew that the story was true, knew that he was wrong, and that the dead *do* sometimes return to earth, for there, in the fast-deepening shadow, hung the black mass of wrought steel, turning a little now and then, with the light flickering on the tarnished and rusty metal. He watched it quietly; he hardly felt afraid; it was rather a sentiment of sadness and fatality that filled him, of gloomy forebodings of something unknown, unimaginable. He sat and watched the thing disappear in the gathering dark, his hand on his pistol as it lay by him on the great chest. There was no sound but the regular breathing of the sleeping boy on the mattress.

It had grown absolutely dark; a bat fluttered against the broken glass of the window. He wondered if he was growing mad, for—he hesitated to acknowledge it to himself—he heard music; far, curious music, a strange and luxurious dance, very faint, very vague, but unmistakable.

Like a flash of lightning came a jagged line of fire down the blank wall opposite him, a line that remained, that grew wider, that let a pale cold light into the room, showing him now all its details,—the empty fireplace, where a thin smoke rose in a spiral from a bit of charred wood, the mass of the great bed, and, in the very middle, black against the curious brightness, the armored man, or ghost, or devil, standing, not suspended, beneath the rusty hook. And with the rending of the wall the music grew more distinct, though sounding still very, very far away.

Count Albert raised his mailed hand and beckoned to him; then turned, and stood in the riven wall.

Without a word, Rupert rose and followed him, his pistol in hand. Count Albert passed through the mighty wall and disappeared in the unearthly light. Rupert followed mechanically. He felt the crushing of the mortar beneath his feet, the roughness of the jagged wall where he rested his hand to steady himself.

The keep rose absolutely isolated among the ruins, yet on passing through the wall Rupert found himself in a long, uneven corridor, the floor of which was warped and sagging, while the walls were covered on one side with big faded portraits of an inferior quality, like those in the corridor that connects the Pitti and Uffizzi in Florence. Before him moved the figure of Count Albert,—a black silhouette in the ever-increasing light. And always the music grew stronger and stranger, a mad, evil, seductive dance that bewitched even while it disgusted.

In a final blaze of vivid, intolerable light, in a burst of hellish music that might have come from Bedlam, Rupert stepped from the corridor into a vast and curious room where at first he saw nothing, distinguished nothing but a mad, seething whirl of sweeping figures, white, in a white room, under white light, Count Albert standing before him, the only dark object to be seen. As his eyes grew accustomed to the fearful brightness, he knew that he was looking on a dance such as the damned might see in hell, but such as no living man had ever seen before.

Around the long, narrow hall, under the fearful light that came from nowhere, but was omnipresent, swept a rushing stream of unspeakable horrors, dancing insanely, laughing, gibbering hideously; the dead of forty years. White, polished skeletons, bare of flesh and vesture, skeletons clothed in the dreadful rags of dried and rattling sinews, the tags of tattering grave-clothes flaunting behind them. These were the dead of many years ago. Then the dead of more recent times, with yellow bones showing only here and there, the long and insecure hair of their hideous heads writhing in the beating air. Then green and gray horrors, bloated and shapeless, stained with earth or dripping with spattering water; and here and there white, beautiful things, like chiselled ivory, the dead of yesterday, locked it may be, in the mummy arms of rattling skeletons.

Round and round the cursed room, a swaying, swirling maelstrom of death, while the air grew thick with miasma, the floor foul with shreds of shrouds, and yellow parchment, clattering bones, and wisps of tangled hair.

And in the very midst of this ring of death, a sight not for words nor for thought, a sight to blast forever the mind of the man who looked upon it: a leaping, writhing dance of Count Albert's victims, the score of beautiful women and reckless men who danced to their awful death while the castle burned around them, charred and shapeless now, a living charnel-house of nameless horror.

Count Albert, who had stood silent and gloomy, watching the dance of the damned, turned to Rupert, and for the first time spoke.

"We are ready for you now; dance!"

A prancing horror, dead some dozen years, perhaps, flaunted from the rushing river of the dead, and leered at Rupert with eyeless skull.

"Dance!"

Rupert stood frozen, motionless.

"Dance!"

His hard lips moved. "Not if the devil came from hell to make me."

Count Albert swept his vast two-handed sword into the fœtid air while the tide of corruption paused in its swirling, and swept down on Rupert with gibbering grins.

The room, and the howling dead, and the black portent before him circled dizzily around, as with a last effort of departing consciousness he drew his pistol and fired full in the face of Count Albert.

Perfect silence, perfect darkness; not a breath, not a sound: the dead stillness of a long-sealed tomb. Rupert lay on his back, stunned, helpless, his pistol clenched in his frozen hand, a smell of powder in the black air. Where was he? Dead? In hell? He reached his hand out cautiously; it fell on dusty boards. Outside, far away, a clock struck three. Had he dreamed? Of course; but how ghastly a dream! With chattering teeth he called softly,—

"Otto!"

There was no reply, and none when he called again and again. He staggered weakly to his feet, groping for matches and candles. A panic of abject terror came on him; the matches were gone! He turned towards the fireplace: a single coal glowed in the white ashes. He swept a mass of papers and dusty books from the table, and with trembling hands cowered over the embers, until he succeeded in lighting the dry tinder. Then he piled the old books on the blaze, and looked fearfully around.

No: It was gone,—thank God for that; the hook was empty.

But why did Otto sleep so soundly; why did he not awake?

He stepped unsteadily across the room in the flaring light of the burning books, and knelt by the mattress.

So they found him in the morning, when no one came to the inn from Kropfsberg Keep, and the quaking Peter Rosskopf arranged a relief party;—found him kneeling beside the mattress where Otto lay, shot in the throat and quite dead.

The Buried Alive

John Galt

———————◆———————

I HAD BEEN FOR SOME TIME ILL OF A LOW AND LINGERING FEVER. MY STRENGTH gradually wasted, but the sense of life seemed to become more and more acute as my corporeal powers became weaker. I could see by the looks of the doctor that he despaired of my recovery; and the soft and whispering sorrow of my friends, taught me that I had nothing to hope.

One day towards the evening, the crisis took place.—I was seized with a strange and indescribable quivering,—a rushing sound was in my ears,—I saw around my couch innumerable strange faces; they were bright and visionary, and without bodies. There was light and solemnity, and I tried to move, but could not.—For a short time a terrible confusion overwhelmed me,—and when it passed off, all my recollection returned with the most perfect distinctness, but the power of motion had departed.— I heard the sound of weeping at my pillow—and the voice of the nurse say, "He is dead."—I cannot describe what I felt at these words.—I exerted my utmost power of volition to stir myself, but I could not move even an eyelid. After a short pause my friend drew near; and, sobbing and convulsed with grief, drew his hand over my face, and closed my eyes. The world was then darkened, but I could still hear, and feel, and suffer.

When my eyes were closed, I heard by the attendants that my friend had left the room, and I soon after found the undertakers were preparing to habit me in the garments of the grave. Their thoughtlessness was more awful than the grief of my friends.— They laughed at one another as they turned me from side to side, and treated what they believed a corpse, with the most appalling ribaldry.

When they had laid me out, these wretches retired, and the degrading formality of affected mourning commenced. For three days a number of friends called to see me.—I heard them, in low accents, speak of what I was; and more than one touched me with his finger. On the third day some of them talked of the smell of corruption in the room.

The coffin was procured—I was lifted and laid in—My friend placed my head on what was deemed its last pillow, and I felt his tears drop on my face.

When all who had any peculiar interest in me, had for a short time looked at me in the coffin, I heard them retire; and the undertaker's men placed the lid on the coffin, and screwed it down. There were two of them present—one had occasion to go away before the task was done. I heard the fellow who was left begin to whistle as he turned the screw-nails; but he checked himself, and completed the work in silence.

I was then left alone,—every one shunned the room.—I knew, however, that I was not yet buried; and though darkened and motionless, I had still hope, but this was not permitted long. The day of interment arrived—I felt the coffin lifted and borne away—I heard and felt it placed in the hearse.—There was a crowd of people around; some of them spoke sorrowfully of me. The hearse began to move—I knew that it carried me to the grave. It halted, and the coffin was taken out—I felt myself carried on the shoulders of men, by the inequality of the motion—A pause ensued—I heard the cords of the coffin moved—I felt it swing as dependent by them—It was lowered and rested on the bottom of the grave—the cords were dropped upon the lid—I heard them fall—Dreadful was the effort I then made to exert the power of action, but my whole frame was immovable.

Soon after, a few handfuls of earth were thrown upon the coffin—then there was another pause—after which the shovel was employed, and the sound of the rattling mould, as it covered me, was far more tremendous than thunder. But I could make no effort. The sound gradually became less and less, and by a surging reverberation in the coffin, I knew that the grave was filled up, and that the sexton was treading in the earth, slapping the grave with the flat of his spade.—This too ceased, and then all was silent.

I had no means of knowing the lapse of time; and the silence continued. This is death, thought I, and I am doomed to remain in the earth till the resurrection. Presently the body will fall into corruption, and the epicurean worm, that is only satisfied with the flesh of man, will come to partake of the banquet that has been prepared for him with so much solicitude and care. In the contemplation of this hideous thought, I heard a low and undersound in the earth over me, and I fancied that the worms and the reptiles of death were coming—that the mole and the rat of the grave would soon be upon me. The sound continued to grow louder and nearer. Can it be possible, I thought, that my friends suspect they have buried me too soon? The hope was truly like light bursting through the gloom of death.

The sound ceased, and presently I felt the hands of some dreadful being working about my throat. They dragged me out of the coffin by the head. I felt again the living air, but it was piercingly cold; and I was carried swiftly away—I thought to judgment, perhaps perdition.

When borne to some distance, I was then thrown down like a clod—it was not upon the ground. A moment after, I found myself on a carriage; and, by the interchange of two or three brief sentences, I discovered that I was in the hands of two of those robbers who live by plundering the grave, and selling the bodies of parents, and children, and friends. One of the men sung snatches and scraps of obscene songs, as the cart rattled over the pavement of the streets.

When it halted, I was lifted out, and I soon perceived, by the closeness of the air, and the change of temperature, that I was carried into a room, and, being rudely stripped of my shroud, was placed naked on a table. By the conversation of the two fellows with the servant who admitted them, I learnt that I was that night to be dissected.

My eyes were still shut, I saw nothing; but in a short time I heard, by the bustle in the room, that the students of anatomy were assembling. Some of them came round the table, and examined me minutely. They were pleased to find that so good a subject had been procured. The demonstrator himself at last came in.

Previous to beginning the dissection, he proposed to try on me some galvanic experiment—and an apparatus was arranged for that purpose The first shock vibrated through all my nerves; they rung and jangled like the strings of a harp. The students expressed their admiration at the convulsive effect. The second shock threw my eyes open, and the first person I saw was the doctor who had attended me. But still I was as dead; I could, however, discover among the students the faces of many with whom I was familiar; and when my eyes were opened, I heard my name pronounced by several of the students, with an accent of awe and compassion, and a wish that it had been some other subject.

When they had satisfied themselves with the galvanic phenomena, the demonstrator took the knife, and pierced me on the bosom with the point. I felt a dreadful crackling, as it were, throughout my whole frame—a convulsive shuddering instantly followed, and a shriek of horror rose from all present. The ice of death was broken up—my trance ended. The utmost exertions were made to restore me, and in the course of an hour I was in the full possession of all my faculties.

The Dualitists

OR, THE DEATH-DOOM OF THE DOUBLE-BORN

Bram Stoker

———◆———

CHAPTER I

Bis dat qui non cito dat.

THERE WAS JOY IN THE HOUSE OF BUBB.

For ten long years had Ephraim and Sophonisba Bubb mourned in vain the loneliness of their life. Unavailingly had they gazed into the emporia of baby-linen, and fixed their searching glances on the basket-makers' warehouses where the cradles hung in tempting rows. In vain had they prayed, and sighed, and groaned, and wished, and waited, and wept, but never had even a ray of hope been held out by the family physician.

But now at last the wished-for moment had arrived. Month after month had flown by on leaden wings, and the destined days had slowly measured their course. The months had become weeks; the weeks had dwindled down to days; the days had been attenuated to hours; the hours had lapsed into minutes, the minutes had slowly died away, and but seconds remained.

Ephraim Bubb sat cowering on the stairs, and tried with high-strung ears to catch the strain of blissful music from the lips of his first-born. There was silence in the house—silence as of the deadly calm before the cyclone. Ah! Ephraim Bubb, little thinkest thou that another moment may for ever destroy the peaceful, happy course of thy life, and open to thy too craving eyes the portals of that wondrous land where Childhood reigns supreme, and where the tyrant infant with the wave of his tiny hand and the imperious treble of his tiny voice sentences his parent to the deadly vault beneath the castle moat. As the thought strikes thee thou becomest pale. How thou tremblest as thou findest thyself upon the brink of the abyss! Wouldst that thou could recall the past!

But hark! the die is cast for good or ill. The long years of praying and hoping have found an end at last. From the chamber within comes a sharp cry, which shortly after is repeated. Ahl Ephraim, that cry is the feeble effort of childish lips as yet unused to the rough, worldly form of speech to frame the word Father. In the glow of thy transport all doubts are forgotten; and when the doctor cometh forth as the harbinger of joy he findeth thee radiant with new found delight.

"My dear sir, allow me to congratulate you—to offer twofold felicitations. Mr. Bubb, sir, you are the father of Twins!"

CHAPTER II
Halcyon Days

THE TWINS WERE THE FINEST CHILDREN THAT EVER WERE SEEN—SO AT LEAST SAID the *cognoscenti*, and the parents were not slow to believe. The nurse's opinion was in itself a proof.

It was not, ma'am, that they was fine for twins, but they was fine for singles, and she had ought to know, for she had nussed a many in her time, both twins *and* singles. All they wanted was to have their dear little legs cut off and little wings on their dear little shoulders, for to be put one on each side of a white marble tombstone, cut beautiful, sacred to the relic of Ephraim Bubb, that they might, sir, if so be that missus was to survive the father of two such lovely twins—although she would make bold to say, and no offence intended, that a handsome gentleman, though a trifle or two older than his good lady, though for the matter of that she heerd that gentlemen was never too old at all, and for her own part she liked them the better for it: not like bits of boys that didn't know their own minds—that a gentleman what was the father of two such 'eavenly twins (God bless them!) couldn't be called anything but a boy; though for the matter of that she never knowed in her experience—which it was much—of a boy as had such twins, or any twins at all so much for the matter of that.

The twins were the idols of their parents, and at the same time their pleasure and their pain. Did Zerubbabel cough, Ephraim would start from his balmy slumbers with an agonised cry of consternation, for visions of innumerable twins black in the face from croup haunted his nightly pillow. Did Zacariah rail at æthereal expansion,

Sophonisba with pallid hue and dishevelled locks would fly to the cradle of her off-spring. Did pins torture or strings afflict, or flannel or flies tickle, or light dazzle, or darkness affright, or hunger or thirst assail the synchronous productions, the house-hold of Bubb would be roused from quiet slumbers or the current of its manifold workings changed.

The twins grew apace; were weaned; teethed; and at length arrived at the stage of three years!

"They grew in beauty side by side,
They filled one home," etc.

CHAPTER III
Rumours of Wars

HARRY MERFORD AND TOMMY SANTON LIVED IN THE SAME RANGE OF VILLAS AS Ephraim Bubb. Harry's parents had taken up their abode in No.25, No. 27 was happy in the perpetual sunshine of Tommy's smiles, and between these two residences Ephraim Bubb reared his blossoms, the number of his mansion being 26. Harry and Tommy had been accustomed from the earliest times to meet each other daily. Their primal method of communication had been by the housetops, till their respective sires had been obliged to pay compensation to Bubb for damages to his roof and dormer windows; and from that time they had been forbidden by the home authorities to meet, whilst their mutual neighbour had taken the precaution of having his garden walls pebble-dashed and topped with broken glass to prevent their incursions. Harry and Tommy, however, being gifted with daring souls, lofty ambitious, impetuous natures, and strong seats to their trousers, defied the rugged walls of Bubb and continued to meet in secret.

Compared with these two youths, Castor and Pollux, Damon and Pythias, Eloisa and Abelard are but tame examples of duality or constancy and friendship. All the poets from Hyginus to Schiller might sing of noble deeds done and desperate dangers held as naught for friendship's sake, but they would have been mute had they but known of the mutual affection of Harry and Tommy. Day by day, and often night by night, would these two brave the perils of nurse, and father, and mother, of whip and imprisonment, and hunger and thirst, and solitude and darkness to meet together.

What they discussed in secret none other knew. What deeds of darkness were perpe-trated in their symposia none could tell. Alone they met, alone they remained, and alone they departed to their several abodes. There was in the garden of Bubb a sum-mer house overgrown with trailing plants, and surrounded by young poplars which the fond father had planted on his children's natal day, and whose rapid growth he had proudly watched. These trees quite obscured the summerhouse, and here Harry and Tommy, knowing after a careful observation that none ever entered the place, held their conclaves. Time after time they met in full security and followed their custom-ary pursuit of pleasure. Let us raise the mysterious veil and see what was the great Unknown at whose shrine they bent the knee.

Harry and Tommy had each been given as a Christmas box a new knife; and for a long time—nearly a year—these knives, similar in size and pattern, were their chief delights. With them they cut and hacked in their respective homes all things which would not be likely to be noticed; for the young gentlemen were wary and had no wish that their moments of pleasure should be atoned for by moments of pain. The insides of drawers, and desks, and boxes, the underparts of tables and chairs, the backs of picture frames, even the floors, where corners of the carpets could surreptitiously be turned up, all bore marks of their craftsmanship; and to compare notes on these artistic triumphs was a source of joy. At length, however, a critical time came, some new field of action should be opened up, for the old appetites were sated, and the old joys had begun to pall. It was absolutely necessary that the existing schemes of destruction should be enlarged; and yet this could hardly be done without a terrible risk of discovery, for the limits of safety had long since been reached and passed. But, be the risk great or small, some new ground should be broken—some new joy found, for the old earth was barren, and the craving for pleasure was growing fiercer with each successive day.

The crisis had come: who could tell the issue?

CHAPTER IV
The Tucket Sounds

THEY MET IN THE ARBOUR, DETERMINED TO DISCUSS THIS GRAVE QUESTION. THE heart of each was big with revolution, the head of each was full of scheme and strat-egy, and the pocket of each was full of sweet-stuff, the sweeter for being stolen. After having despatched the sweets, the conspirators proceeded to explain their respective views with regard to the enlargement of their artistic operations. Tommy unfolded with much pride a scheme which he had in contemplation of cutting a series of holes in the sounding board of the piano, so as to destroy its musical properties. Harry was in no wise behindhand in his ideas of reform. He had conceived the project of cutting the canvas at the back of his great grandfather's portrait, which his father held in high regard among his lares and penates, so that in time when the picture should be moved the skin of paint would be broken, the head fall bodily out from the frame.

At this point of the council a brilliant thought occurred to Tommy. "Why should not the enjoyment be doubled, and the musical instruments and family pictures of both establishments be sacrificed on the altar of pleasure?" This was agreed to *nem. con.*; and then the meeting adjourned for dinner. When they next met it was evident that there was a screw loose somewhere—that there was "something rotten in the state of Denmark." After a little fencing on both sides, it came out that all the schemes of domestic reform had been foiled by maternal vigilance, and that so sharp had been the reprimand consequent on a partial discovery of the schemes that they would have to be abandoned—till such time, at least, as increased physical strength would allow the reformers to laugh to scorn parental threats and injunctions.

Sadly the two forlorn youths took out their knives and regarded them; sadly, sadly they thought, as erst did Othello, of all the fair chances of honour and triumph and glory gone for ever. They compared knives with almost the fondness of doting parents. There they were—so equal in size and strength and beauty—dimmed by no corrosive rust, tarnished by no stain, and with unbroken edges of the keenness of Saladin's sword.

So like were the knives that but for the initials scratched in the handles neither boy could not have been sure which was his own. After a little while they began mutually to brag of the superior excellence of their respective weapons. Tommy insisted that his was the sharper, Harry asserted that his was the stronger of the two. Hotter and hotter grew the war of words. The tempers of Harry and Tommy got inflamed, and their boyish bosoms glowed with manly thoughts of daring and of hate. But there was abroad in that hour a spirit of a bygone age—one that penetrated even to that dim arbour in the grove of Bubb. The world-old scheme of ordeal was whispered by the spirit in the ear of each, and suddenly the tumult was allayed. With one impulse the boys suggested that they should test the quality of their knives by the ordeal of the Hach.

No sooner said than done. Harry held out his knife edge uppermost; and Tommy, grasping his firmly by the handle, brought down the edge of the blade crosswise on Harry's. The process was then reversed, and Harry became in turn the aggressor. Then they paused and eagerly looked for the result. It was not hard to see; in each knife were two great dents of equal depth; and so it was necessary to renew the contest, and seek a further proof.

What needs it to relate *seriatim* the details of that direful strife? The sun had long since gone down, and the moon with fair, smiling face had long risen over the roof of Bubb, when, wearied and jaded, Harry and Tommy sought their respective homes. Alas! the splendour of the knives was gone for ever. Ichabod!—Ichabod! the glory had departed and naught remained but two useless wrecks, with keen edges destroyed, and now like unto nothing save the serried hills of Spain.

But though they mourned for their fondly cherished weapons, the hearts of the boys were glad; for the bygone day had opened to their gaze a prospect of pleasure as boundless as the limits of the world.

CHAPTER V
The First Crusade

FROM THAT DAY A NEW ERA DAWNED IN THE LIVES OF HARRY AND TOMMY. SO LONG AS the resources of the parental establishments could hold out so long would their new amusement continue. Subtly they obtained surreptitious possession of articles of family cutlery not in general use, and brought them one by one to their rendezvous. These came fair and spotless from the sanctity of the butlers' pantry. Alas! they returned not as they came.

But in course of time the stock of available cutlery became exhausted, and again the inventive faculties of the youths were called into requisition. They reasoned thus: "The knife game, it is true, is played out, but the excitement of the Hack is not to be dispensed with. Let us carry, then, this Great Idea into new worlds; let us still live in the sunshine of pleasure; let us continue to hack, but with objects other than knives."

It was done. Not knives now engaged the attention of the ambitious youths. Spoons and forks were daily flattened and beaten out of shape; pepper castor met pepper castor in combat, and both were borne dying from the field; candlesticks met in fray to part no more on this side of the grave; even épergnes were used as weapons in the crusade of Hack.

At last all the resources of the butler's pantry became exhausted, and then began a system of miscellaneous destruction that proved in a little time ruinous to the furniture of the respective homes of Harry and Tommy. Mrs. Santon and Mrs. Merford began to notice that the wear and tear in their households became excessive. Day after day some new domestic calamity seemed to have occurred. To-day a valuable edition of some book whose luxurious binding made it an object for public display would appear to have suffered some dire misfortune, for the edges were frayed and broken and the back loose if not altogether displaced; to-morrow the same awful fate would seem to have followed some miniature frame; the day following the legs of some chair or spider-table would show signs of extraordinary hardship. Even in the nursery the sounds of lamentation were heard. It was a thing of daily occurrence for the little girls to state that when going to bed at night they had laid their dear dollies in their beds with tender care, but that when again seeking them in the period of recess they had found them with all their beauty gone, with legs and arms amputated and faces beaten from all semblance of human form.

Then articles of crockery began to be missed. The thief could in no case be discovered, and the wages. of the servants, from constant stoppages, began to be nominal rather than real. Mrs. Merford and Mrs. Santon mourned their losses, but Harry and Tommy gloated day after day over their spoils, which lay in an ever-increasing heap in the hidden grove of Bubb. To such an extent had the fondness of the Hack now grown that with both youths it was an infatuation—a madness—a frenzy.

At length one awful day arrived. The butlers of the houses of Merford and Santon, harassed by constant losses and complaints, and finding that their breakage account was in excess of their wages, determined to seek some sphere of occupation where, if they did not meet with a suitable reward or recognition of their services, they would, at least, not lose whatever fortune and reputation they had already acquired. Accordingly, before rendering up their keys and the goods entrusted to their charge, they proceeded to take a preliminary stock of their own accounts, to make sure of their accredited accuracy. Dire indeed was their distress when they knew to the full the havoc which had been wrought; terrible their anguish of the present, bitter their thoughts of the future. Their hearts, bowed down with weight of woe, failed them quite; reeled the strong brains that had erst overcome foes of deadlier spirit than grief; and fell their stalwart forms prone on the floors of their respective *sancta sanctorum*.

Late in the day when their services were required they were sought for in bower and hall, and at length discovered where they lay.

But alas for justice! They were accused of being drunk and for having, whilst in that degraded condition, deliberately injured all the property on which they could lay hands. Were not the evidences of their guilt patent to all in the hecatombs of the destroyed? Then they were charged with all the evils wrought in the houses, and on their indignant denial Harry and Tommy, each in his own home, according to their concerted scheme of action, stepped forward and relieved their minds of the deadly weight that had for long in secret borne them down. The story of each ran that time after time he had seen the butler, when he thought that nobody was looking, knocking knives together in the pantry, chairs and books and pictures in the drawing-room and study, dolls in the nursery, and plates in the kitchen. Then, indeed, was the master of each household stern and uncompromising in his demands for justice. Each butler was committed to the charge of myrmidons of the law under the double charge of drunkenness and wilful destruction of property.

Softly and sweetly slept Harry and Tommy in their little beds that night. Angels seemed to whisper to them, for they smiled as though lost in pleasant dreams. The rewards given by proud and grateful parents lay in their pockets, and in their hearts the happy consciousness of having done their duty.

Truly sweet should be the slumbers of the just.

CHAPTER VI
"Let the Dead Past Bury Its Dead."

IT MIGHT BE SUPPOSED THAT NOW THE OPERATIONS OF HARRY AND TOMMY WOULD be obliged to be abandoned.

Not so, however. The minds of these youths were of no common order, nor were their souls of such weak nature as to yield at the first summons of necessity. Like Nelson, they knew not fear; like Napoleon, they held "impossible" to be the adjective of fools; and they revelled in the glorious truth that in the lexicon of youth is no such word as "fail." Therefore on the day following the *eclaircissement* of the butlers' misdeeds, they met in the arbour to plan a new campaign.

In the hour when all seemed blackest to them, and when the narrowing walls of possibility hedged them in on every side, thus ran the deliberations of these dauntless youths:—

"We have played out the meaner things that are inanimate and inert; why not then trench on the domains of life? The dead have lapsed into the regions of the forgotten past—let the living look to themselves."

That night they met when all households had retired to balmy sleep, and naught but the amorous wailings of nocturnal cats told of the existence of life and sentience. Each bore into the arbour in his arms a pet rabbit and a piece of sticking-plaster. Then, in the peaceful, quiet moonlight, commenced awork of mystery, blood, and gloom. The proceedings began by the fixing of a piece of sticking-plaster over the mouth of each rabbit to prevent it making a noise, if so inclined. Then Tommy held up his rabbit by its scutty tail, and it hung wriggling, a white mass in the moonlight. Slowly Harry raised his rabbit holding it in the same manner, and when level with his head brought it down on Tommy's client.

But the chances had been miscalculated. The boys held firmly to the tails, but the chief portions of the rabbits fell to earth. Ere the doomed beasts could escape, however, the operators had pounced upon them, and this time holding them by the hind legs renewed the trial.

Deep into the night the game was kept up, and the Eastern sky began to show signs of approaching day as each boy bore triumphantly the dead corse of his favourite bunny and placed it within its sometime hutch.

Next night the same game was renewed with a new rabbit on each side, and for more than a week—so long as the hutches supplied the wherewithal—the battle was sustained. True that there were sad hearts and red eyes in the juveniles of Santon and Merford as one by one the beloved pets were found dead, but Harry and Tommy, with the hearts of heroes steeled to suffering and deaf to the pitiful cries of childhood, still fought the good fight on to the bitter end.

When the supply of rabbits was exhausted, other munition was not wanting, and for some days the war was continued with white mice, dormice, hedgehogs, guinea pigs, pigeons, lambs, canaries, parroqueets, linnets, squirrels, parrots, marmots, poodles, ravens, tortoises, terriers, and cats. Of these, as might be expected, the most difficult to manipulate were the terriers and the cats, and of these two classes the proportion of the difficulties in the way of terrier-hacking was, when compared with those of cat-hacking, about that which the simple *Lac* of the British Pharmacopoeia bears to water in the compound which dairymen palm off upon a too confiding public as milk. More than once when engaged in the rapturous delights of cat-hacking had Harry and Tommy wished that the silent tomb could ope its ponderous and massy jaws and engulf them, for the feline victims were not patient in their death agonies, and often broke the bonds in which the security of the artists rested, and turned fiercely on their executioners.

At last, however, all the animals available were sacrificed; but the passion for hacking still remained. How was it all to end?

CHAPTER VIII
A Cloud with Golden Lining

TOMMY AND HARRY SAT IN THE ARBOUR DEJECTED AND DISCONSOLATE. THEY WEPT like two Alexanders because there were no more worlds to conquer. At last the conviction had been forced upon them that the resources available for hacking were exhausted. That very morning they had had a desperate battle, and their attire showed the ravages of direful war. Their hats were battered into shapeless masses, their shoes were soleless and heelless and had the uppers broken, the ends of their braces, their sleeves, and their trousers were frayed, and had they indulged in the manly luxury of coat tails these too would have gone.

Truly, hacking had become an absorbing passion with them. Long and fiercely had they been swept onward on the wings of the demon of strife, and powerless at the best of times had been the promptings of good; but now, heated with combat, maddened by the equal success of arms, and with the lust for victory still unsated, they longed more fiercely than ever for some new pleasure: like tigers that have tasted blood they thirsted for a larger and more potent libation.

As they sat, with their souls in a tumult of desire and despair, some evil genius guided into the garden the twin blossoms of the tree of Bubb. Hand in hand Zacariah and Zarubbabel advanced from the back door; they had escaped from their nurses, and with the exploring instinct of humanity, advanced boldly into the great world—the *term incognita*, the *Ultima Thule* of the paternal domain.

In the course of time they approached the hedge of poplars, from behind which the anxious eyes of Harry and Tommy looked for their approach, for the boys knew that where the twins were the nurses were accustomed to be gathered together, and they feared discovery if their retreat should be cut off.

It was a touching sight, these lovely babes, alike in form, feature, size, expression, and dress; in fact, so like each other that one "might not have told either from which." When the startling similarity was recognised by Harry and Tommy, each suddenly turned, and, grasping the other by the shoulder, spoke in a keen whisper:

"Hack! They are exactly equal! This is the very apotheosis of our art!"

With excited faces and trembling hands they laid their plans to lure the unsuspecting babes within the precincts of their charnel house, and they were so successful in their efforts that in a little time the twins had toddled behind the hedge and were lost to the sight of the parental mansion.

Harry and Tommy were not famed for gentleness within the immediate precincts of their respective homes, but it would have delighted the heart of any philanthropist to see the kindly manner in which they arranged for the pleasures of the helpless babes. With smiling faces and playful words and gentle wiles they led them within the arbour, and then, under pretence of giving them some of those sudden jumps in which infants rejoice, they raised them from the ground. Tommy held Zacariah across his arm with his baby moon-face smiling up at the cobwebs on the arbour roof, and Harry, with a mighty effort, raised the cherubic Zerubbabel aloft.

Each nerved himself for a great endeavour, Harry to give, Tommy to endure a shock, and then the form of Zerubbabel was seen whirling through the air round Harry's glowing and determined face. There was a sickening crash and the arm of Tommy yielded visibly.

The pasty face of Zerubbabel had fallen fair on that of Zacariah, for Tommy and Harry were by this time artists of too great experience to miss so simple a mark. The putty-like noses collapsed, the putty-like cheeks became for a moment flattened, and when in an instant more they parted, the faces of both were dabbled in gore. Immediately the firmament was rent with a series of such yells as might have awakened the dead. Forthwith from the house of Bubb came the echoes in parental cries and footsteps. As the sounds of scurrying feet rang through the mansion, Harry cried to Tommy:

"They will be on us soon. Let us cut to the roof of the stable and draw up the ladder."

Tommy answered by a nod, and the two boys, regardless of consequences, and bearing each a twin, ascended to the roof of the stable by means of a ladder which usually stood against the wall, and which they pulled up after them.

As Ephraim Bubb issued from his house in pursuit of his lost darlings, the sight which met his gaze froze his very soul. There, on the coping of the stable roof, stood

Harry and Tommy renewing their game. They seemed like two young demons forging some diabolical implement, for each in turn the twins were lifted high in air and let fall with stunning force on the supine form of its fellow. How Ephraim felt none but a tender and imaginative father can concieve. It would be enough to wring the heart of even a callous parent to see his children, the darlings of his old age—his own beloved twins—being sacrificed to the brutal pleasure of unregenerate youths, without being made unconsciously and helplessly guilty of the crime of fratricide.

Loudly did Ephraim and also Sophonisba, who, with dishevelled locks, had now appeared upon the scene, bewail their unhappy lot and shriek in vain for aid; but by rare illchance no eyes save their own saw the work of butchery or heard the shrieks of anguish and despair. Wildly did Ephraim, mounting on the shoulders of his spouse, strive, but in vain, to scale the stable wall.

Baffled in every effort, he rushed into the house and appeared in a moment bearing in his hands a double-barrelled gun, into which he poured the contents of a shot pouch as he ran. He came anigh the stable and hailed the murderous youths:

"Drop them twins and come down here or I'll shoot you like a brace of dogs."

"Never!" exclaimed the heroic two with one impulse, and continued their awful pastime with a zest tenfold as they knew that the agonised eyes of parents wept at the cause of their joy.

"Then die!" shrieked Ephraim, as he fired both barrels, right-left, at the hackers.

But, alas! love for his darlings shook the hand that never shook before. As the smoke cleared off and Ephraim recovered from the kick of his gun, he heard a loud twofold laugh of triumph and saw Harry and Tommy, all unhurt, waving in the air the trunks of the twins—the fond father had blown the heads completely off his own offspring.

Tommy and Harry shrieked aloud in glee, and after playing catch with the bodies for some time, seen only by the agonised eyes of the infanticide and his wife, flung them high in the air. Ephraim leaped forward to catch what had once been Zacariah, and Sophonisba grabbed wildly for the loved remains of her Zerubbabel.

But the weight of the bodies and the height from which they fell were not reckoned by either parent, and from being ignorant of a simple dynamical formula each tried to effect an object which calm, common sense, united with scientific knowledge, would have told them was impossible. The masses fell, and Ephraim and Sophonisba were stricken dead by the falling twins, who were thus posthumously guilty of the crime of parricide.

An intelligent coroner's jury found the parents guilty of the crimes of infanticide and suicide, on the evidence of Harry and Tommy, who swore, reluctantly, that the inhuman monsters, maddened by drink, had killed their offspring by shooting them into the air out of a cannon—since stolen—whence like curses they had fallen on their own heads; and that then they had slain themselves *suis manibus* with their own hands.

Accordingly Ephraim and Sophonisba were denied the solace of Christian burial, and were committed to the earth with "maimed rites," and had stakes driven their their middles to pin them down in their unhallowed graves till the Crack of Doom.

Harry and Tommy were each rewarded with National honours and were knighted, even at their tender years.

Fortune seemed to smile upon them all the long after years, and they lived to a ripe old age, hale of body, and respected and beloved of all.

Often in the golden summer eves, when all nature seemed at rest, when the oldest cask was opened and the largest lamp was lit, when the chestnuts glowed in the embers and the kid turned on the spit, when their great-grandchildren pretended to mend fictional armour and to trim an imaginary helmet's plume, when the shuttles of the good wives of their grandchildren went flashing each through its proper loom, with shouting and with laughter they were accustomed to tell the tale of THE DUALITISTS; OR, THE DEATH-DOOM OF THE DOUBLE-BORN.

The Executioner

William Godwin

◆━━━◆◆━━━◆

CHAPTER I

YES, I—I AM AN EXECUTIONER—A COMMON HANGMAN!—THESE FINGERS, THAT look, as I hold them before mine eyes, as a part and parcel of humanity, have fitted the noose and strained the cord to drive forth the soul from its human mansion, and to kill the life that was within it! Oh, horror of horrors, I have stood on the public scaffold, amid the execrations of thousands, more hated than the criminal that was to die by me—more odious than the offender that tottered thither in expiation, with life half fled already—and I have heard a host of human voices join in summoning Heaven's malediction on me and my disgusting office. Well, well I deserved it; and as I listened to the piercing cry, my conscience whispered in still more penetrating accents, "Thou guilty Ambrose, did they but know all thy meed of wickedness, they would be silent—silent in mere despair of inventing curses deep enough to answer to the depth of thy offence."

What is it that prompts me to tell the history of my transgressions? Why sit I in my solitude, thinking and thinking till thought is madness, and trembling as I gaze on the white and unsoiled paper that is destined shortly to be so foully blotted with the annals of my crime and my misery? Alas, I know not why! I have no power to tell the impulse that compels me—I can only pronounce that the impulse has existence, and that it seems to me as if the sheet on which I write served me instead of a companion, and I could conjure from its fancied society a sort of sympathy in the entireness of my wretchedness.

As some men are born to greatness, so are some to misery. My evil genius, high heaven and the truth can witness, clutched me in my cradle, and never have I been free from the grasp that urged me onwards and onwards, as though the great sea of destruction was being lashed into tenfold speed and might for the sole purpose of overwhelming me.

Yes, if earliest memory may justify the phrase, from my very cradle was I fore-doomed to sin and sorrow. The first recollection that I have of those worldly incidents that marked my daily course, takes me back to a gloomy, marshy, half-sterile spot, deep seated in the fens of Lincolnshire. May I say that I lived there? Was it life to see the same dull round of nothings encompassing me day after day—to have none to speak to, or to hear speak, save an old and withered crone, who to my young compre-hension appeared to be fastened down, as it were, to the huge chimney-corner, and who seemed to exist (paradox-like) more by sleeping, than by the employment of any other function of the animal frame? The only variation of this monotonous circle of my days was the monthly arrival of my father, who used to come across the quaggy moor in a sort of farmer's cart, and on whose periodical visits we entirely depended for our provisions for the ensuing month. The parent at all times exercises mighty influence over the mind of his offspring; but were I to attempt to describe that which my father possessed over me, it would seem as if I were penning some romantic tale to make old women bless their stars and crouch nearer to the blazing Christmas log, rather than simply narrating the prime source of all those curseful events that have made me the wretch I am. Nor need I here describe his power; for each page that I have to write will more and more develope the entireness of his baneful influence over my mind, and shew how he employed it to my irretrievable undoing.

Monthly he came;—and as I grew from boyhood into the full youthtide of my blood and vigour, it seemed to me as if I only condescended to live for the recur-rence of these visits. The question in my mind was, not what day of the week, or what date of the month it was; but how many days had elapsed since my father's last visit—how many were to elapse before I should see him again. And then, after these periodical heart-aching reckonings, he would come—come but to go again, after a short tantalizing one-day stay. Once—once I ventured to press him to take me with him: my eagerness made me eloquent. I bowed to my very knees in supplication for the indulgence. But in vain—in vain; and it was then, perhaps, that I first fully ascer-tained the power that he had over my heart—ay, over my soul—my very soul of souls. Angry at my continued entreaties, he lost his temper, raged till his teeth gnashed in the fierceness of his ire, and bade me again ask to accompany him at the peril of his curse. To me, at that time, his passion was little less than so many dagger-thrusts in my bosom, and I shrank in exquisite anguish from the contest, tremblingly convinced that never again might I dare to urge the cherished desire of my imagination. When I remembered the height of his indignation, it almost seemed as if there must have been something heinous, in an unheard-of degree, in my request: my father, to my mind, was the wisest, the best, and the most judicious of mankind; how could it be otherwise, when he was the only one with whom I had ever held communication, save the crone who appeared to have slept away her brains, if she ever had any? and that wisdom, that goodness, that judiciousness, I had offended! Where, then, was the wonder that I myself cried shame upon the offence?

In this state of things I attained about my twenty-third year, as nearly as I can guess; and then, at last, a change arrived. Great heaven, what a change! Fool that I was, not to content myself with being at least as well off as the beast of the field, or the steed that is stalled and cared for, as far as nature and his appetite make demands upon him. But ignorant, restless, and morbid in my sensations, I must needs have change. It came; and I changed too—into a wretch—an outcast—a thing hated, despised, and hooted at!

It began with an ill omen! I might have foreseen that some deed of horrid circumstance was at hand.

The old woman was seated, as usual, in the chimney-corner. She had been sitting there from six in the morning till nine at night, without uttering a syllable—without tasting food, as far as I knew, though during some hours in the day she had been left to herself, while I was wandering my solitary round through the plashy fens. At length, our hour of nightly rest arrived, and I summoned her from her stationary posture. But she answered not—she moved not: I approached, and gently shook her: I took hold of her withered, wrinkled hand—it was cold and clammy:—I raised her head—it was expressionless—her eye was inanimate. She was dead!

It took some minutes for me to persuade myself that death had indeed been at work. I had thought of death—dreamed of death—pictured death; but now, for the first time, he presented himself to my outward observation, and I shrank with morbid instinct from the task of contemplation. Always a creature of passion—always a creature of waywardness and prejudice—without education, without instruction, without guidance, I had no philosophy to lead me but my own ignorance—no rule of conduct save the *ignes fatui* of my own imagination. I doubt whether at any time, or with any training, I could have taken my first lesson in mortality without an involuntary shuddering; but circumstanced as I then was, I almost instinctively tottered into a far-off corner of the room, and there, for a while, as I held my hands before my eyes, to shut out all visible presence of the corpse, I seemed as if I was gradually assuming its motionless rigour, and sharing in its cessation of existence.

It was a fearful night; and so the days and nights that followed. From the time of the old woman's decease, to the period of my father's next visit, was a fortnight. Flight from this scene of death was one of the first thoughts that presented itself to my mind—but whither? I had no one clew to guide me in my search for my parent; and to me, every thing beyond the cottage in the fens and its neighbourhood was a blank. As I debated this within myself, I tried to resolve to stay—I determined to confine myself to another room of the narrow dwelling—I called upon my energy to assist me in forgetting how nearly I was hand in hand with death. But the task was too much for me—my whole mental faculty succumbed under the attempt—and my brain felt as if it was under the utter dominion of the Prince of terrors; each hour added fresh visions of dismay to those which already appalled me; and when, after the lapse of three or four days, the odour of the decaying corpse spread itself through every portion of the cottage, the thoughts that seized upon my excited imagination became unbearable, and, without plan or project, I almost unwittingly rushed from the abode of my childhood, to face the perils of all that lay before me, unknowing and unknown.

My first steps were those of real flight, prompted by a desire of freeing myself from a sort of incubus that seemed to be urging me on to madness, as long as I remained within its influence. This feeling lent speed to my pace for nearly half the day, and then, when I began to consider the rate at which I had walked—or rather, when I was able to begin to consider any of the circumstances that attended my change, I gradually obtained the power of perceiving that I was by degrees releasing myself from the painful impulse that had hitherto been pressing me forward. But in proportion as I escaped from these sensations, others of a scarcely less dreary complexion took possession of my mind. Where was I?—What was I about?—Whither was I going?—And how was I to find my father, of whom I did not even so much as know his name?—With these and similar thoughts disturbing my imagination, I found the night fast gathering around me, while I was still vainly extending my gaze in every direction for the abode of man, or any practicable refuge for the destitute wanderer. Vainly, indeed, did I run my aching eyes along the farthest margin of the horizon. Nothing but a low marshy land, with here and there a stunted water-loving tree, was to be seen; and when I turned my glance upwards, the clouds that met my sight appeared as sullen and as gloomy as the prospect which a moment before the earth had presented. But even this was comfortable in the comparison to that which followed; for presently a chilly soaking rain commenced falling; the day completely closed; and I scarcely took a step without finding myself plunged knee-deep in some marish reservoir, or unexpected quagmire. Surrounded with evils, the best that I could do was to choose the least; and, feeling that it was hopeless to pursue my path when all was utter doubt and darkness, I resolved to take shelter in one of the stunted trees which I found scattered over the fens, and there to remain till the morning should begin to dawn. My project succeeded as far as mere rest was concerned, and with cramps and rheums for my bedfellows, I found that I might hope to pass through the tedious night. But though I thus escaped any farther trials of the treacherous footing that awaited me beneath, the thin and scanty foliage of my tree of refuge afforded no shelter from the pitiless storm, in which the wind and the rain seemed to be playing an alternate game, the one undertaking to dry me as fast as the other drenched me to the skin.

This, then, was my first introduction to the world. This was the "Go on, and prosper," that attended me on my first venturing forth from the dwelling that had hitherto sheltered me. As I sat stilted, as it were, in my dark arbour of slippery branches, amid which I felt as if couched in a morass, I could not help recalling to my mind the ominous words with which my father had, two years before, prophesied that I should most surely repent any endeavour to make the world and myself more intimately acquainted. Already did I repent! yea, even though the act of my quitting the cottage in this instance had been scarcely more than what I considered to be a sort of self-preservation.

At length morning came. It still rained—a heavy, penetrating, chilling torrent. The wind still roared, as though the northern blast was hallooing to its brother of the east to come and make dreary holyday for the nonce; a hunger, fierce and gnawing, had taken possession of me, as if that too was in cruel collusion with the elements to crush me. But still, in spite of rain, wind, and hunger, there was light—and with light came hope—with hope, a sort of artificial buoyancy and vigour, which enabled me to descend from my scrambling melancholy couch, and once again to stretch forward in search of some track of human existence.

Whither, or in what direction I wandered, I never was able to satisfy myself, though I have since, more than once, pored over the map of Lincolnshire, with a desire of tracing my first journey from the solitary cottage in the fens, to the habitation of man, and of civilized society. All that I know is, that after nearly exhausting the whole of this second day in fruitless rambling, I at length, even at the moment when I thought I must finally give up the effort, and sink in obedience to declining nature, had my heart gladdened with the sound of the barking of a dog, and by following this aural track, I was fortunate enough to reach the small village of Fairclough a little before nightfall.

How my bosom glowed as I attained this spot of human sojourn! I was like the arctic traveller, who, after wild beasts for his companions, and snow for his pillow, at last arrives, at one of those godsend hunting huts, that to his longing eyes start up in the wilderness, more brilliant than the most gorgeous palace of the East to the perverted gaze of a luxurious emir. Now, thought I, is the hour at length arrived for me to be introduced to my kindred men—now is the world of humanity before—now will every one that I meet be a brother or a sister;—and my heart, too long pent-up, and compelled to bo a self-devourer, will find an opportunity for that expansion for which it has so long been yearning.

As I thus communed with myself, I approached a cottage. The door stood invitingly open. "Hail, happy omen of the heart that reigns within," cried I; and, with an honest reverence for my own picture of human attire, I entered. The only persons that I perceived inside were a woman and a child, sickly and puling, whom the former was endeavouring to coax from its shrill crying, by the offer of a slice of bread and batter.

It was not till I had fairly crossed the threshold, and found that I was noticed by the female, that I remembered that my errand was a begging one; and the sudden recurrence of the thought threw some little embarrassment into my manner. However, I had no time for consideration; for the woman, without waiting for my address, briefly demanded—"What's your want?"

"For the sake of pity," replied I, somewhat chilled by her words, and still more by the callous manner in which she used them—"for the sake of pity, afford me some food—this is the second day that these lips have gone without a morsel."

"Food, quotha!" reiterated the woman—"hark ye, youngster, did you never hear of rent and taxes, and poor-rates to boot? It is not over much food that we get for ourselves—none that we have to give away. You had better try the overseer."

"The overseer!" returned I, somewhat puzzled as to whom he might be—"alas, I have no strength left to carry me farther! A crust of bread and half an hour's rest is all I ask." And, as I uttered these words, I sank exhausted into a chair that stood near.

"Poor fellow!" cried the occupant of the cottage, probably moved by the too apparent condition to which I was reduced:—"Well, God knows, bread is dear enough, and money is scarce enough, and supper is seldom enough; but if a crust will satisfy you, it shall not be wanting. But, harkye, you can't stay here to eat it; my husband will be here anon, and—"

Scarcely had she uttered the words—hardly was the proffered crust within my grasp, when he, of whom she spoke, made his appearance, with evident symptoms about him that he had not visited the village alehouse in vain.

"How now, Suky," cried he, as he observed my presence—"what does this chap do here?"

"Poor wretch," replied his wife, "it seems as if it were nearly over with him, what with fatigue and what with hunger, so he asked leave to sit down a bit, and rest his poor bones."

"And why the devil did you let him?" surlily demanded the man:—"I'll have no bone-resting here. Am I the lord of the manor, or squire of the village, that I can afford to take in every pauper that finds his way here?—and who gave him that bread?"

The wife seemed to shrink from the question, while I mustered resolution to reply—"She—who will be blessed for it, as long as heaven blesses charity."

"Heyday," cried the fellow, "why the chap is a Methodist parson in disguise, after all!—Harkye, Mr Parson-pauper, please to turn out.—Once a-week is quite enough for that sort of thing."

"Do not force me abroad again to-night!—I have not strength to move."

"Hoity toity," exclaimed the drunkard, "you have strength to eat, and pretty briskly too.—And who, do you suppose, is to find your lazy carcass a lodging for the night?—Turn out, I say."

"For pity's sake—"

"Pity be d———d! Turn out, I say,"—and as he spoke he seized me by the collar, and whirling me round by mere brute force, I found myself in an instant outside the cottage; while, as a token that all hope of re-entry was in vain, he slammed the door violently in my face.

This was my first introduction to the benevolence of mankind:—this was the earliest welcome that awaited the wanderer from the fens.—I groaned and tottered onwards.

But if this was my first introduction, I soon found that it was by no means a solitary specimen of what was to be presented for my acceptance. Another, and another, and another cottage was tried,—and still the same result. I was spurned by the most cruel—I was unheeded by the most humane—I was neglected by all; and one other much-begrudged crust of bread was all that my importunities were able to obtain.

With this I retired to a miserable outhouse attached to a farm at the extremity of the village, and having devoured it, I endeavoured to make myself a bed in the scattered straw that lay strewed about the ground. My hunger, though not altogether appeased, had ceased to press with such torturing pain on my very vitals; and the exhaustion of my frame speedily lulled me to sleep.

Sound and refreshing were my slumbers; and it was not till I was roused by the owner of the building that I awoke from them.

"Halloo, my fine spark!" cried he; "who gave you permission to take possession of my outhouse? Please to get up, and away; and you may think yourself well off that you escape so easily."

This was a bad omen for begging a breakfast; and I was about to part, without a syllable in reply, when it suddenly crossed my mind that I might at least solicit work. Heaven knows that it was never my desire to live on the bread of idleness, and with how much willingness I was ready to undertake the most menial or the most laborious employment to entitle myself to my daily food!

"Well!" cried the farmer, perceiving that I lingered, "will you not take my advice and disappear before I shew that I am in earnest?"

"I was hoping, sir," replied I, "that you would not take it amiss if I solicited you to give me some work. Indeed, indeed you will find me very willing; and I think I could be useful."

"Useful, youngster! In what?—Can you plough? Can you thrash? Can you reap?"

A mournful negative was my reply. "But I am ready to learn."

"And who is to pay for your teaching? Besides, a pretty hope it would be that you will ever be good for any thing, when we find a tall strapping fellow like you, who has been too idle as yet to learn to plough or to reap. No, no, thankye, we have plenty of paupers here already, and I have no fancy to add to the number, by giving you a settlement in the parish. So, good day, my friend; and when you again offer to work, see if you cannot give yourself a better character."

Again baffled in hope, and checked in spirit, I moved away, seeing but too clearly that the village of Fairclough was no resting-place for me.

"Oh, father, father!" cried I, with bitterness in my accent, as I paced slowly forward—"where am I to seek you? How am I to find you?"

It was a dreary day in March that again witnessed me—a wanderer—creeping along on my unpurposed journey, and tracking my weary way from spot to spot, as chance or early destiny might direct. The early produce of the fields afforded me a scanty, miserable breakfast; and as I looked upwards, and saw the linnet and the finch flitting with a gay carol over my head, a sort of envy of their condition seized me, and, instead of glorying in my station, as one of the master works of nature, I mourned at the shackled unhappiness of my lot. What now had become of my fancy-decked picture of the all-receiving brotherhood of mankind? Whither had flown the friendship, the kindness, the heart-in-hand welcome that I had so fondly dreamt waited my arrival in the abodes of the world? Fictions! Empty, deceitful fictions, that had betrayed me to myself, and that, for a short moment, had taken the place of the withering, frightful truth, that for the houseless, penniless wanderer there was no sympathy, no hospitable tendering to his necessities!

Thus, for many days, strayed I through the humid atmosphere of a Lincolnshire March, now and then reaping one miserable meal, or one measured draught of milk from a whole village, but more often feeding on the vegetable productions of the hedges and the fields, and trusting to the chances of the road for a nightly shelter.

Meanwhile, I felt that my heart was gradually changing within me. I had brought it into the world of men, with its offering of love and kindness, but none would accept it—none would reciprocate to it; it was the heart of a beggar, and society cried, Out upon it! I began to ask myself gloomy and frightful questions—questions that no heart ought to be forced to ask itself. As 1 laboured along in solitude, misery, and neglect, I demanded of myself a thousand times, "Why am I to have love for man, when mankind has none for me?"

At length accident conducted my steps to the little town of Okeham, the capital of Rutlandshire. There the hedges, and the other cold cheer of nature failed me, and I was compelled to beg for my very existence. It is impossible to describe the disgust with which I contemplated this necessity. The rebuffs with which, one after another, I had met, had sickened upon my soul, and I felt that the mere act of petitioning charity was like offering my cheek to be smote, or my person to be insulted. It was nothing short of utter starvation that was able to drive me to it.

But it seemed as if my evil genius was accumulating the venom of disgrace for me. It was my ill fortune to select, as my first house of trial, the abode of one of the constables of the town; and the words of imploring charity were not cold from my mouth, ere this high official burst forth in a strain that astonished even me, accustomed as I was to rebuke and reproach, for daring to announce that hunger had on me the same effect as on the rest of mankind. According to this man's creed, I was a villain, a vagabond, and a rapscallion, and I ought to go on my knees to thank him for not instantly dragging me before a magistrate, to be dealt with as the heinousness of my presumption demanded. Alas! he might have spared his wrath, for I was too well accustomed to rejection not to take the first hint, and shrink from an encounter where all power was on one side, and all irresistance on the other.

"Come with me, my poor fellow," exclaimed a gentle voice that was hardly audible amid the constabulary storm that I had raised. "Come with me, and I will afford you such poor assistance as my wretched means will allow. I am your twin-brother in misery, and my ear too well knows the cry of distress."

I looked round to see what angel it was that thus pronounced the first real words of kindness that had reached me since my secession from the cottage in the fens. He who had spoken was a thin, sickly-looking youth, about eighteen or nineteen years of age; and when his face was scanned, though only for a moment, the beholder would feel that there was no need for his confession of misery. Sorrow, and wellnigh despair, were seated there; and his thin uncoloured cheek declared the waste that grief had inflicted on his heart.

"Come with you, indeed!" cried the man of office, tauntingly. "Why, that will be rogue to rogue with a vengeance; and I suppose we shall have a pretty account by to-morrow, of some burglary to be looked after."

When I took my first glance at my new friend, it seemed to me as if nothing but art could have lent colour to his sallow countenance; but nature was more strong in him than I had imagined, and as he listened to the words that were uttered by this overbearing Dogberry, the quick blood bubbled to his cheek, and he glowed with the full fire of indignation, as he replied—"I would that the law permitted me to commit a burglary on thy wicked heart, that I might break it open, and shew mankind how foul a composition may be cased in human substance. But no matter,—I speak to iron! Come, good fellow," added he, turning to me, "we will avoid this iniquitous libel on the species, and seek another spot for farther conversation."

"Now that's just what you won't," roared his brutal opponent:—"I rather suspect what you have said amounts to a threat of assault; and I shall ask Justice Goffle about it; but at all events I know that this ragged barebones, who seems to be all at once your bosom friend, has brought himself within the vagrant act; so you may go and seek your conversation by yourself, or along with your father, who is snug in the lockup, for you know what; for as to this youngster he stirs not till Mr. Goffle has had a word or two with him; and then perhaps a month at the treadmill may put him into better condition for the high honour of your friendship."

He suited the action to the word, for before he had finished his speech I felt myself within his nervous gripe.

The youth saw that opposition was vain. For my own part I felt no inclination to struggle or contend: the one drop of liquid tempering, with which his words of sympathy had softened my heart, was again dried up and consumed by the new cruelty that attended on my destitution; and I felt a sort of bitter satisfaction that my last week's resolve of hatred against mankind had escaped the peril of being shaken by the benevolent offer of this exception to his species.

Under the watchful custody of the constable, I was speedily conveyed to the presence of Mr. Justice Goffle: my offence was too evident to admit of a moment's doubt; he who had captured me, was at once my prosecutor, my convicting witness, and my custos to lead me, according to the sentence of the law, and of Mr. Justice Goffle, to a fortnight's imprisonment and hard labour in the jail of the town. In another half hour, I was safely lodged within its gloomy walls.

The first lesson which I there learned was, that the criminal and the offender of the laws were better fed than the harmless, wretched wanderer, whose only sin was that of being hungry in obedience to nature's ordinances. I could hardly believe my senses when I had proffered to me, and without asking for it either, a substantial meal—such a one as had not gladdened my sight since I quitted the cottage in the fens: and, as I silently devoured it, I tried to account for the phenomenon, but in vain; it was too much for my philosophy. It did not, however, tend to ease the cankering hatred against mankind that was fast eating into the very core of my every sensation.

My next lesson was one still more mischievous. It was that which I received from my fellow-prisoners, and which was made up of vainglory for the enormity of their crimes that were passed, and of wily subtle resolves for the execution of those that were to come. A week before I had held all mankind to be excellent and lovely. I now deemed the whole race wicked and pernicious.

The third morning after my initiation into Okeham jail, I perceived an unusual bustle taking place: the turnkeys crossed the yard in which we were confined with more than their usual importance; and the head jailer rattled his keys with extraordinary emphasis. What to me would have been a long unravelled mystery, if left to my own lucubrations, was speedily explained by some of my companions. It was the day for the commencement of the assize—the judges were hourly expected—fresh prisoners were being brought in from the various locks-up, and every thing was in preparation for their reception. Presently a buzz went round among those that were already confined, anticipatory of a fresh arrival of colleagues in misfortune; and a minute afterwards the yard-gate was unlocked.

"Pass in Edward Foster, committed for horse-stealing," shouted one of the turnkeys, outside.

"Edward Foster passed in," echoed his brother turnkey, who stood at the yard gate; and the new prisoner, on his appearance among us, was received with a cheer by the gaping crowd of malefactors, as Lucifer might be by his kith and kin of fallen angels on his arrival at Pandemonium. After the lapse of another minute, Foster was conveyed to a solitary cell, in token of his being confined on a capital charge.

"Pass in Stephen Lockwood, king's evidence, and committed for want of sureties," again shouted the same voice, from without.

"Stephen Lockwood passed in," repeated he at the gate.

The crowd of prisoners gathered round the entry as nearly as they dared approach; and, on receiving this other new comer among them, saluted him with a threatening groan, that ran round the old walls of the jail, for the purpose of shewing their contempt of "the snivelling 'peach."

He who was thus welcomed to his dungeon, made his way as speedily as he could through the mob of jail-birds, and approached the spot where I was standing, probably so induced, from its being the least crowded part of the yard.

Eternal Heaven! what were my horror and astonishment, on perceiving that it was my father that thus drew near!

Our mutual recognition was instantaneous; but before I could speak, he muttered hastily,—"Not a word of our relationship before these wretches."

It was some time before the indignant criminals that surrounded my father, afforded us an opportunity of conversation. When at length we had an opportunity of exchanging a few words without being overheard, my parent demanded of me the circumstances that had made me the inmate of a prison. When they were recounted,—"It is well," cried he, "fate has brought us together in its own mysterious way. It is well!—it is well!—But we may yet be revenged on the world."

My eyes gleamed with delight at the sound of the word "revenge"; and I echoed it from the very bottom of my soul. It was easy for my father to understand the spirit in which I uttered it; for it had been with no cold-blooded suppression of manner that I had narrated to him my adventures since I had quitted the cottage in the fens.

"But you, my father," cried I, "why are you here?"

"Hush," whispered he, "this is no place to relate the tale of my wrongs and of my wretchedness. Your sentence of imprisonment will be over in twelve days; and till then we must restrain ourselves. I have a dreadful story for your ears."

"But how soon shall you be free?"

"In four or five days, beyond all doubt:—the trial for which I am detained is expected to come on tomorrow, after which I shall be at liberty. On the day of the expiration of your imprisonment, I will wait for you outside the jail. Meanwhile, feed your heart with thoughts of vengeance—the dearest, sweetest, only worldly solace that remains for men so undone as Stephen Lockwood and his progeny."

Dreadful was the anxiety with which I counted the hours till that of my release arrived. My father's calculation as to his own term of imprisonment proved to be correct; and for the last eight days of my confinement I was left alone to brood over my heart's wild conjectures—born of the dark and mysterious hints that he had poured into my ear.

At length the day of my restoration to liberty arrived, and, true to his word, I found my parent waiting for me in eager expectation outside the prison.

"Follow me," cried he hastily, as soon as he perceived that I was by his side:—"follow me to the fields beyond the town; for I have those things to relate that other; than you must never hear."

I obeyed in silence, for my whole soul was so completely wrapt in expectation of that which he had to communicate, that I sickened at the thought of dwelling on any less momentous subject. He, as we strode along, was equally reserved; but I could perceive that the thoughts that were raging within him were of sufficient potency to disturb the outward man, and to give a wildness of action to his demeanour that I had never before observed, save on that one occasion when I had pressed him beyond endurance to make me his companion, by releasing me from my sojourn at the cottage in the fens.

At length we arrived at a secluded spot some distance from the town we had just quitted, and where a long, blank, nearly-untrodden moor gave promise that we might escape interruption.

"It is here, Ambrose," cried my father, suddenly pausing in his progress, "it is here that we will take our stand; hateful man cannot approach us without being seen—the roaring wind cannot blab our secrecies, for none are nigh to catch the whisper it conveys—trees and darkling coverts there are none to hide our foe, or permit his stealthy footstep to creep unwarily upon us:—here, then, here we may talk truths, and cry aloud for vengeance without fear or hinderance."

I was all ear, but murmured not a sound. Like the tyro in the schools, I waited to be led to my conclusions; and with the sentiments that I entertained towards my father, his words seemed to be those of one inspired.

He himself paused as though it required some great effort to enable him to commence his tale. At length he continued—"The time is now come, Ambrose, when I have to place before you the circumstances that induced me to fix your residence in the lonely spot you have so lately quitted, in the hopes of sheltering you from the unkind treatment of that world that has used your father so bitterly. The time is come, and with it our revenge. Listen, my son, that you may learn the grudge you owe to man—that you may be taught how to resent the wrong that was inflicted on you long before you dreamt that mischief had station on the earth, or had played you false in your very earliest existence."

"Your every word, my father, reaches the very centre of my heart. I am in your hands:—mould me to your bidding."

"You will require no moulding, Ambrose. My tale will be sufficient to direct your course. Listen:—I was born of humble parents in the village of Ravenstoke; and though I had the misfortune to lose both my father and my mother almost before I knew the value of such beings, the evils that attend a child of poverty were averted by the kindly notice of the principal family of the place. The good man at its head, and who never made fall a tear till death took him from the world, early noticed me, and was pleased to think that he saw in me sufficient capacity and promise to befit me to be the companion of Edward, his only child, whose years were pretty nearly the same as my own. Thus in happiness and content passed away my youth; but it only seemed as if the demon that had marked me for his prey, was resting for the purpose of accumulating his whole force in order to crush me. In a neighbouring village, to which my walks had been frequently directed, there lived a maiden whose gentleness of disposition and beauty of person had won for her the affection of all who were blessed enough to be acquainted with her. In my eyes she was even more than my young fancy, ever too busy in picturing forth happiness and loveliness, had at any time conjured to the vision of my senses. Need I say that I loved—loved to distraction, and how more than mortally happy I deemed myself when I received from the fair lips of Ellen a half-whispered approval of my love? Oh, my Ambrose, I cannot recall those early days of fondness and affection, and prevent the hot tears coursing down my cheeks, there to stream as witnesses of my devotion, till the bitter recollection of the manner in which that devotion was abused dries up the liquid testimony at the very source, and leaves me even now, after the lapse of twenty years, the victim of a distorted faith—too fresh, too real, and too scathing, ever to be extinguished till this body is returned to moulder with the dust."

As Lockwood thus spoke, his eyes gave proof of the fulness of his feelings; and some minutes elapsed before he was able to proceed.

"I must be brief, Ambrose, with the rest of my story, for I feel that my heart will scarcely allow me words to conclude it. When Ellen had confessed her affection for me, there was nought to prevent our union, and a few weeks, therefore, saw me, as I deemed myself, the happiest of men; and our dearest hope appeared to be that we might live and die with one another. The hour of separation—fatal, fatal separation—however, arrived; and to oblige Edward, who, on the death of his father, had succeeded to the family property, which was somewhat involved, I consented to go to the East Indies for him, relative to an estate there on which he had a considerable claim. This journey, and the delay which I met with abroad, occupied two years; and it was with a heavy heart that I quitted Ellen, who, on the eve of being brought to bed, was in no condition to share with me the fatigues of a long sea voyage. Well might my heart be heavy with presentiment! Could it have anticipated all that was to happen, it would have turned to lead, and refused to obey its nature-appointed functions. At length the day of my return approached: each hour that the ship neared England I stood on the deck, counting the lazy minutes, and stretching my eyes landward, in the hope of catching the first glimpse of the white cliffs of my native land; and so, when I reached the shore, I reckoned each moment an age till the happy one should arrive that was to restore me to the arms of my wife. There was no such moment in store for me; for just as I was quitting the metropolis for Ravenstoke, I met an old village acquaintance, who felled my every hope with the intelligence that my Ellen—mine—she whom I had deemed to be the truest, the faithfullest of her sex—was living with another as his avowed mistress—acknowledged, brazen, barefaced before the whole world, and in defiance of the thousand vows in the face of God and man by which she had pledged herself mine, and mine alone. You may well start with astonishment, my son, and gaze wildly, as if in doubt of the truth of this atrocity. So started I—so doubted I—till evidence beyond evidence bore bitterest conviction to my soul. But the whole is not yet told.—Ellen's falsity came not single. He who had seduced her from her liege affections shewed with equal perjury before high Heaven. It was Edward! Yes,

Edward—my friend, my companion;—he for whom I had quitted my gentle wife and peaceful home—Edward, the monster, the traitor, the fiend begot of sin essential, had taken advantage of the opportunity, which he himself had solicited, of my friendship, and stolen from me, by double deceit and treason, the prize that I cared for more than life or any thing on earth."

"Gracious powers!" exclaimed I, overwhelmed by the dreadful incidents that had been narrated—"and am I the son of this wretched mother? Was I thus early doomed to misery?"

"It is too true," replied my father; "you are the child of whom I left Ellen pregnant when I departed on the ruinous errand besought by her seducer. When the fact of your mother's crime was made conviction to my senses, a thousand different modes of action poured in upon my brain; and, the creature more of impulse than of reason, I hurried to Ravenstoke to confront the adulterous pair. It was evening when I arrived—even such an evening as this—gloomy, dark, and cheerless,—yet in high accordance with the thoughts that urged me forward. As I hurried across the park that led to the mansion-house, a pony-chaise overtook me. I turned on its approach, and for a moment my senses forsook me at the sight of Ellen, who, with you for her only companion, was driving quickly homeward to avoid the threatening storm. My voice arrested her farther progress, as I groaned rather than uttered—'Ellen!'—'Wife!' At the summons she descended from the chaise, after wrapping you in her cloak as you lay along the seat, asleep and unconscious. What words I addressed to her I can hardly tell:—they were those which flowed at the dictation of a brain almost mad at the injury it had sustained; while her answer was none save tears and sobs of heaviness. At length she broke from the grasp with which, in my anguish, I had seized her—and then— then—Oh God, I cannot speak the words that should tell the rest!"

"For pity's sake, my father," murmured I, sunk in the fearful interest of his story,—"for pity's sake, the end in a word—the end—the end!"

"Yes, yes!—the end, the end!" he echoed fiercely:—"it is one she earned, and it is wanting to make whole the frightful tale. Ambrose,—Ambrose,—she burst from my grasp, and rushed into a copse hard by. I pursued her, but in vain; for the momentary pause I had made in wonder at her meaning, had removed her from my sight, and I followed at random, guessing the direction she had taken as nearly as I might: after thus speeding for a few minutes, I reached the side of an ornamental lake that adorned the park, and there again caught glimpse of her by the dim light of a clouded moon, as she reached the opposite bank. Ambrose,—Ambrose,—cannot you imagine the rest?"

"Oh, father, was it so indeed?—And none to save her?"

"Was not I there, boy?—Thrice I dived into the bosom of the waters, after hurrying to the bank from which she had precipitated herself into destruction—thrice did I dive to the very depth of the pool—but in vain,—I could not find her—the circuit of the lake that I had had to make had afforded too much time to her fatal intention; and the attempt to find her body was fruitless. Mad with a thousand contending emotions, I returned to the chaise, and heard your little voice crying for your mother. It was then that I remembered my child, which the crime of its parent had made me forget. I took you in my arms; and as I gazed upon your innocence, my heart softened; and I resolved to put revenge aside for a while till I had secured you from peril. It was this that made me place you under the care of the old crone at the cottage in the fens."

"But why was I kept there so long?"

"That remains yet to be told; and I shall have finished my narrative. As soon as you were safely provided for, the desire of vengeance again assumed its empire in my bosom; and I returned to Ravenstoke, hardly knowing what my purpose was, but whispering to myself, 'Revenge! Revenge!' each moment of my journey. But even revenge had then for the season forsworn me. On my arrival at the village, the man who had so deeply injured me had the audacity to have me taken into custody on the charge—hear it, Ambrose, and help me to curse the villain—on the charge of having destroyed Ellen. I destroy Ellen!—Alas, alas, it was she who had destroyed me, if the banishment of peace, and of happiness, and of joy, for ever and for ever from my bosom, can be called by so poor a name as destruction. Of course, I need not tell you that when the matter came to trial I was instantly acquitted; but the event had given me timely warning of the extent to which the seducer of Ellen was able to carry his devilish contrivance to ruin the man he had already so deeply wounded; and I resolved to keep you—my only hope—in obscure concealment till the time should have arrived when I might call on you to join me in revenging my dishonour and Ellen's unhappy fate."

"And has that time arrived?"

"It has, Ambrose!—And though we stalk on this dreary moor, the very outcasts of mankind, great and mighty is the revenge that is at hand for us."

"Let us grasp it then," cried I, fully wrought to the purpose,—"Let us grasp it then, and urge it to the quick."

"Well said, well said, my son!—Oh, what years of labour has it not cost me to bring events to their present aspect! But the labour is well repaid. For the sake of revenge,

I have consorted with villains of every description—I have sacrificed all and every thing to them, on the one sole bargain, that they should ruin my hateful foe; and well have they kept their word! The monster, a year or two after the death of Ellen, dared to marry. I was glad to the very heart when I heard of it; for I felt that the more ties he formed, the more ways there would be to pierce him to the heart. But his wife died too soon—before I had time to sacrifice her on the tomb of Ellen; and his son, the only offspring, of the marriage, has as yet eluded my vigilance. But the father, Ambrose, the father! He is fast within my clutch! My emissaries taught him the art of throwing dice, and throwing away his estates—they inoculated him with the gambler's dreadful disease; and, for the last twelve mouths, he has been a ruined man in his fortunes. Desperate have been the efforts that he has made to redeem himself; but I was at hand, though never seen; and my master-mind, fraught to the very brim with his destruction, would not allow them to succeed. At length his despair was fed to its proper pitch, and I resolved to give the final blow, for which I had waited twenty long years with that exemplary patience which revenge only could bestow. I had it proposed to him, by his most familiar blackleg, and on whom his only hopes of success rested, that they should proceed to Newmarket on a scheme, which, it was pretended, could not fail of realizing thousands. The only difficulty was, how they should get there, being at that time at Doncaster on a speculation that, through my interference, had utterly failed, and left my enemy altogether penniless; in which condition, the faithful blackleg also pretended to be. When his mind was sufficiently wrought upon by the picture of absolute and irremediable ruin that would happen, in the event of their not being able to reach Newmarket the very next evening, my agent, according to my instructions, proposed the only alternative—that of helping themselves to a horse a-piece out of the first field that afforded the opportunity, and by that means reaching the desirable spot that was to prove to them another *el Dorado*. For a long while my enemy wavered, and I almost trembled for my scheme; but at length the longed-for thousands that flitted in fancy before his eyes, gilded the danger of the means of passage, and he consented. It was then, Ambrose, that I felt that revenge at length was mine, and I almost danced and sang in the ecstasy of my delight. Pursuant to my directions, my agent informed him who was so nearly caught within my meshes, that he had a companion to take with him, who would be absolutely necessary for the prosecution of the Newmarket scheme; and when the night for departing arrived, I was introduced as this third person. I had little fear of Edward's remembering me after a lapse of twenty years, each of which had added care, sorrow, and affliction to the lineaments of my countenance;

but to guard against the possibility of danger, I muffled myself in a large cloak, and spoke the little that I uttered in a disguised voice. Every thing succeeded according to my wishes. After walking a couple of miles out of Doncaster, we came to a field where the cattle we needed were grazing; and each seizing his prize, and obtaining, with silence and caution, from the farmer's outhouse, the necessary harness, we soon found ourselves at full speed on the highway towards Newmarket. Edward was dreadfully agitated as he rode along; and once or twice I feared that he would fall from his seat—but worse evil awaited him. I will not, however, occupy our time by detailing all the minutiae of my scheme. Suffice it to say, that after giving the hint to my faithful agent to make his disappearance, I contrived that Edward and myself, on reaching the village of Stretton, should be apprehended on suspicion; and that that suspicion should be made conviction by my volunteering as king's evidence. The rest you almost know. You yourself witnessed Edward Foster's committal to jail for horse-stealing, and my detention as the chief witness against him:—and most probably have heard, that on my evidence he was nine days ago convicted, and ordered for execution."

"Conviction!—Execution!" exclaimed I. "Then our revenge is indeed complete!"

"Not quite," muttered my father; "there is one other step to make it as perfect as my sweeping desire could wish."

"Mean you a step beyond the grave? I know of none other—and only know that is impossible."

"No, Ambrose, not beyond the grave, but the step to the grave!—Ask your heart! Does it feel hatred and disgust towards the man that has made wretched one parent, and scandalous the other?—that has condemned yourself to wander fortuneless and honourless over the cheerless face of the earth?—Ay, ay, boy; your gleaming eye and flushing cheek tell me the reply that your heart has already put forth. And I ask you, would it not be revenge's most glorious consummation, to repay your dreadful debt to Foster, by yourself dealing unto him that death which the law has awarded for his crime?"

"Father, father, what words are these?"

"Milk-livered boy! Why blanches your cheek, when I hold within your clutch the very satiety of vengeance? Why clench you not the precious boon? Or are you a man but in seeming, and a puling infant in resolve?"

"Speak on, father—speak on,—it seems to me as if each word you utter burns deeper and deeper into my brain—searing, as it goes, those doubtful agitations of my soul, that would raise a trembling opposition to your bidding. But they shall not! No, no! Down, down! Your wrongs shall answer the cry of humanity—my mother's fatal end the appeals of tenderness!"

"Now," cried Lockwood, "I know you for my son. But we have talked too much—action should be doing. The death of our foe is appointed for the third day from this; and I have learned, beyond doubt, that owing to there not having been an execution in Okeham for many years, the Sheriff finds great difficulty in procuring the proper functionary. It was this that stirred me to the hope that you would volunteer to the office; and I thank you that my hope has not been deceived. You must away to the Sheriff instantly, and get appointed; that attained, I trust to be able so to instruct you, that failure in the performance will be impossible."

I obeyed—ay, I obeyed! I was successful! The honesty of human nature was scouted from my heart by the towering voice of the worst passion that ever cursed the breast of man.

The morning of execution arrived, and found me ready for my office. As the time had gradually grown nearer and nearer, my father had perceived, with dread, that misgivings, in spite of myself, shook my whole frame; and, in order to be more sure, he had kept me at carouse the whole of the previous night, in the miserable back street lodging that afforded us shelter.

The morning arrived; and, drunk with passion, vengeance, and brandy, it found me ready for my office.

The solemn tolling of the prison bell announced the hour of death to be at hand, as I awaited the coming of the prisoner in the outer cell. How I looked—how I acted— I know not; but, as well as I remember, it seems to me now as if I was awakened from a torpor of stupefaction on hearing the clanking of the chains that announced the approach of Foster; the sound reached my ear, more heart-chilling than the heavy tolling knell, that answered as if in echo; but I had not forgotten my lesson; I beat my hand against my brow, and whispered "vengeance" to the spirit that was so ill at ease within. It was at that moment, that, for the first time, I beheld Edward Foster; he was not such as my soul had depicted. I pined for him to look hateful, ferocious, and bloody; but his aspect was placid, gentle, and subdued. I could have stormed in agony at the disappointment.

My first duty was to loosen his arms from the manacles that held them, and supply their place with a cord. As I fumbled at the task, I could feel myself trembling to the very fingers' ends; and it seemed as if I could not summon strength to remove the irons. My agitation must have attracted Foster's notice; for he looked at me, and gently sighed.

Gracious God, a sigh! I could as little have believed in Foster sighing as in a tigress dandling a kid. Was it possible that he was human after all? How frightfully was I mistaken! I had imagined that I had come to officiate at the sacrifice of something more infernal than a demon!

At length, with the assistance of a turnkey, every thing was prepared, and we mounted the scaffold of death. Short shrift was there; but it seemed to me as if the scene was endless; and when I looked around on the assembled multitude, I imagined that it was to gaze on me, and not on Foster, that they had congregated.

All was prepared. With some confused recollections of my father's instructions, I had adjusted the implement of death; and the priest had arrived at his last prayer, when the dying man murmured, "I would bid farewell to my executioner." The clergyman whispered to me to put my hand within those of Foster.

I did do it! By Heaven, I did do it I But it seemed as though I were heaving a more than mountain load, and cracking my very heart-strings at the task, as I directed my hand towards his. He gently grasped it, and spoke almost in a whisper.

"Young man," said he, "I know not how this bitter duty fell to your lot—yours is no countenance for the office; and yet it comes upon my vision as a reproach. God bless you, sir! This is my world-farewelling word; and I use it to say—I forgive you, as I hope to be forgiven."

My hand, no longer held, dropped from his; and the priest resumed his praying. I could not pray! Each holy word that was uttered, seemed not for Foster, but for me—stabbing, not soothing.

At length the dread signal was given; and mechanically—it must have been, for the action of my mind seemed dead within me—mechanically I withdrew the bolt, and Foster was dead—swinging to the play of the winds—the living soul rudely dismissed, the body a lifeless mass of obliterated sensations.

A deep hoarse groan ran round the multitude—that groan was for me. It gave token of an eternal line of separation drawn between me and the boundaries of humanity.

Oh, that the groan had been all!—But there was one solitary laugh, too—dreadful and searching. It was my father that laughed, and it struck more horror to my soul than the groan of a myriad.

Oh, that the groan and the laugh had been all! As I crept away through the prison area, where each one shrank from me with disgust, I passed close to a youth deep bathed in tears, and some one whispered to another, "It is poor Foster's son!" What devil tempted me to look in his face? I know not the impulse; but I know I looked—and he looked!—Oh, consummation of wretchedness, it was Foster's son—and it was he also who had offered to share with me his slender pittance on my first arrival at Okeham! As he gazed on me, a deep heavy sob seemed as though his heart was breaking.

I rushed from the spot like one mad. In all my misery, in all my wickedness, I had fondly clung to the recollection of that youth and his goodness, as the shipwrecked mariner to the creed-born cherub that he pictures forth as the guardian of his destiny. But this blow seemed to have destroyed my only Heaven. I had not even this one poor pleasurable thought left me to feed upon. His sob thrilled in my ear, as though it would never end; and the womanly sound was more overwhelming and more excruciating than the despising groan of the mob, or the atrocious laugh of Lockwood.

CHAPTER II

MANY, MANY MONTHS HAVE ELAPSED SINCE THE DAY ON WHICH THE FRIGHTFUL EVENT I have just recorded occurred; but the vision to my senses remains as perfect as if the scene was still enacting; and instead of there being for me a morrow, and a morrow, and a morrow, it seems as though my whole life was a mere repetition of one day's existence. I am built round, and confined to one abode of sensations, as Rome's offending Vestals were encased for their unchasteness in the bondage of entombing bricks; and whatever outward events of variance occur, my heart is for ever reminding me that I am the executioner of Edward Foster. His care-worn dejected countenance flits for ever before my eyes: I meet him amid the desolateness of the far-extending moor; he walks by my side through the streets of the crowded city; and when I sleep he stalks before my fancy, dismal and enshrouded, the hero of my dreams.

But in the earlier days that followed that which ever haunts me, it was not my heart alone that reminded me of the hateful deed. I was the observed of all observers:—the rabble tracked my every footstep, and hooted me like some reptile, disgusting—not dangerous, back to my solitary den. I was the marked of men:—they almost disavowed my affinity to the species; and as I listened to their groans of execration, I began to feel as if that affinity was fast melting into air, and leaving me, in sooth, some monstrous thing that nature had created only to shew how beyond herself she had power to act.

My father very soon quitted me.—"We must part for a while," said he to me on the second morning after that which had witnessed the close of Foster's life—"We must part for a while; for I have to provide the means of subsistence for us both—and perchance even a still further revenge. Here is such money as I can spare for the present; and this day six months we will meet again on this spot, that I may make farther provision for you."

I was not sorry thus to part with him; for though he still retained his power over my mind, it was so united with fear and dread, that I rather looked upon him as a master than a friend, and felt that obedience to his will was something beyond choice or resistance. Besides, his presence was too intimately connected with the memory of my deed of death, to offer me any chance, while he remained, of being able to reject the painful burden from my mind; and I hoped that his absence would allow me to bury the hangman-image of my brain in the depths of forgetfulness.

But, as I have already said, the hope was vain. Though the author of the scene had departed, the scene itself was ever present; and after finding that I could not get rid either of my own reflections, or the insulting notice of the mob, I determined to quit Okeham, and not to return till my appointment with Lockwood demanded my reappearance there.

Once again, therefore, I became a wandering outcast, with none either to cherish or to pity me. Nay, I was in worse condition than when I first ventured to present myself to the mercy of the world on quitting the cottage in the fens. Then, though rejected by man, I had something within to support and assist in bearing me harmless against the attacks of misfortune. But now that single consolation had disappeared. I myself had struck down honesty in my heart, and had set up wickedness in its place. The death of Foster alone did not stand recorded there. The hatred of the multitude, expressed in no equivocal phrase whenever I appeared in the streets of Okeham, had driven me to the jail for refuge, where I learned to assort myself with those who set decency at defiance, and scouted morality as an intrusion upon their pleasures. I gazed upon these associates, and perceived that drink and debauchery were their prime pursuits; and when I remembered how brandy had helped me, on the night before the execution, to forget nature, and give strength to passion, I too resolved to pursue the gross luxuries taught by their brute-philosophy;—and the deeper I drank, the more firmly did I implant in my own system the wickedness of those, who, not being better, were worse than myself.

These were the changes, then, that had taken place within me since I first wandered from the cottage in the fens; and though I had not, as then, to beg for a miserable pittance, they were sufficient to make me feel that I was dragging on a useless existence with no object in view—with no remedy in prospect. I was like one of those unfortu-

nates, who, in the olden time, had the choice given them to drown by water, or to burn
at the stake; for I had but the alternative either to let the recollections of what had been
wring my very heart, or to drown them in deep intoxicating draughts, from which,
each time that I awoke from them, I was more and more hateful to myself.

The one small consolation that my departure from Okeham was intended to
afford, was that of avoiding the sight of those who knew the guilty work in which these
hands had been engaged, and who, in the exuberance of their feeling, hesitated not to
let me know that they knew it. But this consolation was not of long continuance. After
strolling for some days wherever chance directed, I reached the city of Peterborough,
wet, tired, and in deep despondency at the forlorn abandonment which seemed to
mark my destiny. It was in this state of feeling that I found myself at the door of a
mean public-house, and the sight of it reminded me that there was still the pernicious
refuge of brandy at my command. I entered, and called for liquor—drank, and called
again. The fatigue that I had undergone gave additional strength to the potations in
which I had indulged; and intoxication followed. What occurred during the stronger
influence of the liquor I know not—but on my first beginning to regain possession of
my senses, it seemed as if I had been wakened into consciousness by a severe blow on
my forehead; but I had no time to ask myself any questions, for I found that I was surrounded by a mob of the lowest rabble,—pushed from side to side, with a blow from
one and a kick from another—while universal execrations rang around. Oh, how well
did I know those sounds!—and as they reached my ear I strained my heavy eyes to see
whether some strange and unaccountable event had reconveyed me into the streets of
Okeham. But no!—The houses and the streets were utterly unknown to me—it was
the mob and their outcries alone that came familiar to my senses, and that reminded
me of the foregone scene of my insults. It was long before I could escape their fangs,
and when at last, through the humane exertions of a few, I succeeded in effecting a
retreat, I still heard, as I crossed fields and sought infrequent places, the words,—
"wretch," "villain," "hangman," echoing in my ears. Hangman!—Aye, that was the
word so uproariously dwelt upon.—Hangman!—Then I was discovered—traced!—
Even in Peterborough—miles from the scene of my fatal revenge, the mob, as it were
by instinct, had translated my character, and had joined their brethren of Okeham in
expressing their abhorrence of it.

These thoughts urged me on with fearful speed; and after creeping, noiseless and
stealthily, for another three or four days, by any path that seemed most desolate, I
arrived at Bedford. As I beheld the tall spires of the town in the distance, I shuddered,

and twice turned to avoid the place. But I was half dead with exhaustion; night was at hand; and with a kind of desperate resolution I slunk into the town, and dived into the first obscure street that presented itself. Each person that I met, I turned away my head, slouched my hat, and endeavoured to avoid his gaze. But no one seemed to notice me, and gradually I became more assured. My sinking strength warned me that I needed sustenance; and again, for the first time since my flight from Peterborough, I ventured into a public-house. Tempting brandy was at hand; I snuffed its seductive flavour as soon as I entered the place, and the recollection of its exciting, drowning, oblivious influence, infused itself with irresistible power over my spirit. Brandy was had. Glorious, destructive drink! I quaffed it, and it seemed to resuscitate me, heart and head. It was to me like the helm, and the buckler, and the coat of mail to the knight of crusade,—it armed me cap-à-pie, and I staggered beneath the power of my panoply. Fresh draughts produced fresh intoxication, and again I was lost to all recollection of what was occurring. But—horror! horror!—again I was awakened from what I deemed my bliss by a repetition of the same scene that I had undergone at Peterborough—the same insults, the same buffeting, the same execration, awakened me from my drunkenness, and forced me to fly for my life.

What could it mean? Was I pursued through all my winding paths and labyrinth of ways by some treacherous spy, that only tracked me to betray, and hold me up to the detestation of mankind? I was bewildered by the confusion of ideas that my still half-intoxicated brain presented in solution of the riddle, when a few words that dropped from one of my groaning pursuers told me all. Having launched after me a deep and ferocious shout, he exclaimed, "Beast, be wise at least in future! If you must drink, do it where there are none to hear you blab your hangman secrets."

Powers of hell, this, then, was the answer to the enigma that maddened me! I myself was the stupid spy that had discovered all, and roused the wrath of thousands against my guilty confessions. I was he that proclaimed to the world, "Ambrose is an executioner!" And what urged me to such insane disclosure? Aye, aye—brandy, brandy! The only power to which I could fly to steep me in forgetfulness of myself, played the traitor game with me of bidding flow those words that betrayed me to the rest of the world.

Farewell, then, to all refuge against myself, and my own thoughts! Farewell to all oblivion of the thing that haunted me like a demon-spectre, each day presenting itself in more frightful guise than on the last! Farewell! farewell!—the deep potations for which my aching senses yearned must be forsworn; and for the sake of hiding my sin from the gaze of men, I must be content to expose it for ever and for ever to the galling of my own conscience, and the harrowing of my own recollections.

From the day of my exposure at Bedford, I looked upon myself as one for ever doomed to live apart, not only from the intercourse of men, but even from the very sight of them; and as I wandered through the country I was ready to fly, like a frighted deer, on the first glimpse of a human figure in the distance; till the all-subduing pangs of hunger forced me to encounter man, and even then I would purchase enough to last me for days, that I might not too soon again have to face my enemy.

Thus with various wanderings over the face of England I suffered the time to elapse till the day of my appointment with my father was drawing near. I had seen it gradually approaching, as the condemned prisoner counts the gliding hours that are slipping away between him and his fate; and it was with sensations of inexpressible disgust, that I contemplated the necessity of my once again appearing in Okeham, where my face and my crime were so well known. Compulsion, however, ruled my actions with a strong arm. My money was nearly exhausted; and my heart sickened at the thought of continuing to wander in dread and misery through the byways of the world. I resolved, therefore, to meet Lockwood as he had directed; I determined to detail to him all the horrors of thought and deed that I had undergone; and to implore him, by his paternal love for me, to make some arrangement by which I might be removed to another country, where all knowledge of me would be extinct.

These thoughts somewhat lightened my heart, as I turned my steps towards Okeham; and in obedience to its suggestions, I tried to persuade myself that there was only one more painful struggle to be undergone, and that after that there might be something—if not pleasurable—at least neutral and free from torture, about to fall to my lot. The same hope made me regard, with a more kindly aspect, the prospect of my reunion with my father. It was he, indeed, that had given action to my hatred for man, by moulding it into revenge towards one individual of the species; and it was through that revenge that the last six months of misery had been inflicted. But revenge was at an end—Foster was in his grave—Ellen's manes were appeased—and I clung with inexpressible satisfaction to the hope that my father, when he should hear the details of my sufferings, would move heaven and earth to convey me from a land that seemed to have nothing but wretchedness to bestow on the most unfortunate of her children.

It was well for me that some such sensations as these stole upon me as I approached Okeham, or never should I have been able to have gathered sufficient courage within myself to enter that hated town. As it was, I lingered in the neighbourhood till the clouds of night collected thick and gloomy around, and even then did not venture amid the scenes that were too painfully inscribed on my memory ever to be forgotten, without affecting a change in my gait, and such alterations m my general appearance as seemed best calculated to spare me from recognition. At length, I arrived at the obscure lodging that had been appointed by my father for our rendezvous.—I was there to the very day,—almost to the very hour of the reckoning; and on finding that I had arrived at the goal of my expectation without discovery, or its accompanying shout of execration, such as ad farewelled me from the place, I felt as if a huge load of bitterness had been subtracted from my bosom, and whispered to myself to welcome it as the forerunner of still better tidings.

On enquiring for my father, however, I found that he was not there; but in his stead was presented to me a letter which had arrived that morning. I opened it; and these were its contents:—

"Do you remember, Ambrose, the sentiment with which we parted six months ago?—'Perchance even a still further revenge is in preparation for us!' It is that chance that I have been watching. It has arrived—but I dare not quit my victim. Come to me instantly, dear Ambrose. Come with gladness at your heart, and brightness in your eyes; for our mutual cup of vengeance will speedily be filled to the overflowing."

The letter then went on to direct me to meet him at ——. But no, no!—I have already specified too many localities to trace my wretched progress; and I will not give utterance to that which will betray my present abode, and bring the callous and the curious to my receptacle for the purpose of comparing me with my distressful story, and so feeding their depraved and unfeeling appetite.

The few lines that Lockwood had thus penned, were read by me again and again, but it was vainly that I endeavoured to interpret their meaning. What further revenge my father had in store was a mystery beyond my solution, and seemed to belong to some portion of his story with which I was unacquainted. I only knew that the very mention of vengeance struck upon my heart with a pestilential sickness, such as can only be felt when the mind itself is in a state of utter loathing. That I still hated mankind, my bosom too keenly felt to admit of any question; but the sufferings that I had undergone, in answer to my claim for revenge, had been too acute and penetrating not to excite the deepest anguish when a second scene of the same order as the first was offered to my gaze.

Yet obey his letter I must!—Wellnigh penniless—entirely friendless,—it was to him alone that I had to look!

I set out, therefore, immediately upon the journey which he had prescribed; but it was with a fearful heaviness of spirit that I prosecuted my weary way thither. The gleam of happiness that had broken in upon me for a moment, was like the fitful bursting of the sun through a deep November gloom, coming but to disappear again, and to make the traveller still more conscious of the cheerless prospect that surrounded him.

After the lapse of some days, I reached the town to which my father had summoned me; and with no little difficulty discovered the lodging to which he had directed my steps.

He received me with almost a shout of delight; and as I gazed upon his countenance, all the past events that Okeham had witnessed crowded to my imagination with a frightful verity of portraiture.

"Ambrose, Ambrose," he exclaimed, "all is now complete. The death of Foster six months since was but a stepping-stone to this—the most glorious consummation of the most glorious passion that ever filled the heart of man. But you smile not, my son! I see not that glow of fervour that was wont to cross your brow when I whispered 'revenge' in your ear, and pointed the certain road to its accomplishment."

"I cannot smile," returned I, with an inward groan, "nay, I almost feel as if to expect it of me was an insult. I am not the same Ambrose that you knew six months ago."

"Pshaw! you are a cup too low. Let us discuss a bottle of brandy, and I warrant there will be smiles enough dancing in your eyes."

"No, no, no," cried I with terror; "No brandy! I have forsworn the treacherous liquor that seduces only to betray."

"Why, that is well too," replied my father; "I scorn to do that for brandy, which I dare not do without it. Besides, we have that within which soars high above the power of any mortal draught—We have revenge!"

"We have revenge!" I echoed, and the echo was in earnest, for the mention of brandy had reminded me of Peterborough and Bedford, and my disgraces there united with my disgraces at Okeham to make callous and inhuman my heart.

My father looked at me as I repeated the word "revenge," as if he would search to my very soul for the key in which I had uttered it; and then, grasping my hand, he whispered, as if it was something too precious to be exposed to common parlance, "It is ours! it is ours!"

I returned his pressure in token that the force of his words was acknowledged. But though my grasp was firm, my heart palpitated with uncertainty. I was all in all the creature of impulse, and was waiting for its full tide to direct me. At Okeham, at

Peterborough, and at Bedford, I seemed ready to burst with hatred for the whole species; and felt as if no revenge could be sufficiently extensive to fill the measure of my
rage. But since my exposure at the latter place, I had wandered about, solitary and
unknown, now and then encountering an individual, but oftener creeping along in a
country to me as blank as the South Sea Island to the shipwrecked Crusoe. During this
time my sensations had undergone a change. The vehemence of my wrath bad been
checked for want of fuel, and the innate propensity of my bosom to love my fellow-
man had been struggling in spite of myself through the gloom of my more irritated
feelings. But the hot fit was now again fast gaining on me, and I perceived that a second
time I was about, through the intensity of my own sensations and the kindling of my
father, to be plunged into the resistless flood of hot-blooded vengeance. As the suspicion of this reached my mind, my heart beat doubtfully, as if beseeching me to avoid
that which in the end would again torture it so bitterly; but against the silent feebly-
persuasive beating of that heart there was a fearful array urging me onwards—my
father's looks and words—my now bad passions and man-hating recollections, were
all united, strong, powerful, and headlong; and I felt as if nothing short of a miracle
could save me.

I really believe that Lockwood chiefly interpreted the truth of the inward effort
my heart was making to be released from its second thraldom of revenge; for as I was
pausing after his last exclamation, he again interposed to hurry me on into the sea of
passion.

"What," cried he, "will you echo my cry of 'revenge,' and then, when I exclaim 'it
is ours,' do you desert me? Or is it true, that the fearful story of your parents' undoing,
joined to that of the thousand world-heaped insults yourself have received, needs no
further avengement? For shame, Ambrose, for shame!—Grasp that which I now offer;
let this one week make all I desire complete, and the next shall bear us away from this
cursed land for ever, to begin a new life, with new prospects and new happiness, in
some country where justice yet lives, and has a practical acknowledgment."

Yes, yes, my father must have read my thoughts; for if any thing could have confirmed me in the path that he was dictating, it was that last hope that he had presented
to me; and I exclaimed, as I listened to his words, "You have but to command, for me
to obey. Let us fly this hateful England; and let us, ere we go, make a fearful reckoning
for the injuries under which we have had to writhe."

"My own Ambrose! now you have spoken words that make me proud of my son.
It only remains to put you in possession of my meaning to make you feel in your judg-

ment, that which already has impress in your mind. When I related to you, six months since, the tale of the sufferings I had received at the hands of Foster, I was so wrapt in his crimes, that I forgot to advert to the only individual that he had made the sharer of his confidence and the upholder of his sins; for when the prime instigator of mischief is within our clutch, it is the nature of man to overlook the more humble accomplice. But no sooner had the monster suffered retribution by your hands, than my attention was directed to him, who, Foster being dead, stalked before my eyes like his ghost, mowing and chattering scornfully in my ears, as though he would say, 'Foster in me lives again—lives to spurn at Ellen's tomb—to spit at and disdain your husband-sorrows.' "

"And what has become of this wretch?" demanded I, heated almost to fury by my father's words.

"Aye, aye," replied Lockwood, "I like that question;—it bespeaks a mind panting for justice. This miserable reflector of Foster's enormities is within our power; he lies hard by in one of the dungeons of the town-prison; he, too, has been caught in the fangs of the law, and execution three days hence is to be done upon him. Ambrose, do you understand me? Three days hence he is to be hanged; and you are in the town,— nay, within one little furlong of the jail! Do you not comprehend, dear Ambrose?"

"More blood for Ambrose, wherewith to stain his soul! Oh God, my father, I cannot do it!"

"Not do it!" shouted Lockwood; "cry shame upon the puling words, and thank me for having thus a second time fostered your revenge, till it has arrived at full maturity. Think you I have worked only for myself? No; it was you that were the prime mover of all my efforts,—you, the only being in this world I have to love, to care for, or avenge. And will you now desert the glorious result that I tender ready to your hands?"

"And shall we, this accomplished, indeed quit England for evermore?"

"I swear it, Ambrose! It was for this last act alone that I have delayed our departure since Foster's death."

"Then let us go this very day," I cried. "Is it not enough that we leave the wretch in the law's all-powerful grasp, but that I must again be its executioner?"

"There lies the sum of all!" vehemently exclaimed my father. "I pine to stand below the gallows, even as I did at Okeham, and shout as I see the body of my foe swing nerveless in the air;—I long to be able to inform myself with endless repetition, 'It was Ambrose that did this good deed.' "

"No, no, no" cried I; "it will be that repetition that will kill me."

"Not when you know all!"

"Know all, my father?"

"Aye," returned he; "you have not yet heard who this fresh victim of our hatred is. Did I not tell you, when first you heard my story, that it was with joy I learned that Foster had dared to marry, that all his ties of nature might be withered by my hand? His wife, alas, escaped me by dying too early for my schemes; but the boy she left behind—Foster's only son—his dear Charles—his pride Charles!—Ha ha! it is he that is to suffer three days hence!—it is he that I call on you to immolate, for the sake of mine and your mother's wrongs!"

Oh God, how the words of Lockwood struck upon my soul! It seemed to me as if he had felled me with some mighty mental machine, and my whole brain staggered beneath the blow. Charles—the gentle, kind-hearted Charles,—he, the chosen single one of all the human race—the only being that had ever volunteered the wretched out-cast Ambrose an act of grace—was to be the victim of my butchery! I verily believe, that had the mere recollection of the youth occurred while my father had been prompting me to fresh revenge, that alone would have been sufficient to have checked his weightiest word, to have brought from my lips steady a refusal to his plans.

And I was to be this angel's executioner!

"No, no, no!"—Aye, I screamed aloud with agony, as again I uttered, "No, no, no!"

Lockwood appeared astounded at the sudden change I presented to his view. He gazed upon me as if to read my motive; and not meeting with the solution, he demanded sternly—"What now, Ambrose?—what is this, boy?"

Again I shouted, "No, no no! I would not harm a hair of Charles's head to serve myself everlastingly!"

"And our revenge—"

"Talk not of revenge, father! It will be no revenge that Charles should die. Nay, for mercy's sake, as you have plotted his death—now, at my entreaty, help to save him!"

"Save him!" exclaimed he; "I would not save him if I had ten times the power to do it. But who is to save him? He is marked for execution!"

"I will save him, if Heaven will give me strength!"

"You, Ambrose!"—and, as he spoke, Lockwood put on those looks that once, at the cottage in the fens, had so overruled my words and very thoughts. "You save him, Ambrose! Hark ye, boy; 1 know not what this Hark ye, boy; I know not what this change portends, but I command that here it cease. We have met for business, not for silly exclamations that want a meaning."

But the reign of my father's power was fast growing to an end. Impulse, that till now had been in its favour, was at last arrayed against it. Nor was I still the unknowing child I had been when he had last resorted to the same means; and even were I, the image of Charles seemed to have a supernatural power over my every sensation. I had picked him, as it were, from the rest of mankind—divested him of his mortality—and enthroned him in my heart, the very god of my admiration.

It was under this influence that I replied—"They do not want a meaning, sir. On my soul, they mean, that if a man can save Charles from execution, I will accomplish it. And you, too, must assist. When it was vengeance on Foster that you asked, I assisted you; now, that it is mercy on his son that I require, you must assist me."

Lockwood seemed wonderstruck at my manner; but the more he marvelled, the more he was enraged.

"Dog!" cried he, "do you talk of mercy when I talk of vengeance? Down, sir, down on your knees, and swear to do my bidding; or I will curse you with news that shall make your heart sicken, and the very life shrink from your bosom."

"You have curse me with news," I exclaimed, half mad; "news more bitter than aught else could conjure into mischief. But Charles shall be saved. I will go to the magistrates and tell all I know."

Lockwood absolutely foamed with passion at the audacity of my words; but at length he muttered, as though he were grinding the words between his teeth—"Yes, or no—will you do my office?"

"No, no!" I exclaimed, with a fierceness that seemed to excite him ten times more; "No, no! I will have Charles's life saved, and his course made happy."

"Then art thou utterly damned!" shouted Lockwood—"Listen, listen, while I curse you with words only exceeded in their sharpness by their truth—You are no son of mine!"

"For that I bless God," was my answer. "Say it again, that I may humble myself before Heaven in thanksgiving!"

"I do say it again; and this time I add the name of your real parent—It was Edward Foster!—Come with me, thou wretch, through the streets of this great town, that I may point out to the multitude aghast, the man that hanged his father!"

I gazed on him who had uttered these appalling words; or, rather, seemed to gaze on him; for my eyes, though there fixed, saw nothing. "All my senses flocked into my ear," which still rang with the dreadful sounds it had heard.

"Fool," continued Lockwood, "stand not staring there! But laugh—laugh, as I do, to think how deep in parricidal wickedness your soul is steeped.—Ha! ha! So the puler at last has qualms; and he who so blithely hanged his father, cannot fit the noose to his brother's neck! Well, well, poor wretch, the common hangman must do it instead; and you shall stand side by side with me below the gallows, and help me to count his dying agonies."

The very excess of anguish that these words inflicted, forced me into motion. My limbs unlocked, and my tongue loosened, as I faltered in reply—"Monster beyond belief, why has this been done? How did I ever injure you, to be exposed to misery so unutterable?"

"Can you have heard my story," replied Lockwood, "and yet ask that question? Are you not the son of Foster? and did not Foster steal Ellen from her husband?"

"Oh! Lockwood," I exclaimed, "a minute since, in the folly of my heart, I blessed Heaven when you told me that I was not your son. Now, I will bless you—nay, on my bended knees, will pray God to bless you, if you will retract those words, and once more tell me that I am yours—or only that I am not Foster's child!"

"Then should I tell a lie!" replied the fiend—"Have you not had enough of those already from me? But you shall hear all, since this has turned out to be my day of truth-telling.—Foster, by all that is sacred, is your father; as for the rest of the story, I altered it a little to allow me to call you mine. It is true, that I left Ellen for two years—not exactly on your father's business, by the by—but I left no child; and you were not born till I had been absent a year. It was this, fool, and no silly dallying of parental nonsense, that made me steal you from the pony-chaise, and take such cunning steps that Foster, with all his anxious search, could never discover your retreat. All the rest is true. I watched him till the law better provided for him; and sent you as his executioner. The solitary life that you had led, and the insults you had received in your short progress towards Okeham, rendered you ripe for my scheme, which ever was to mingle you and Charles in Foster's ruin;—and if you do not recollect the rest, it shall be my daily delight to remind you of it; to"—

"Never, never!"

"To sit by your side, and tell how Foster died!"

"Oh God, spare me!"

"To cheer your spirits, by chuckling in your ear an echo of the glad laugh that burst from me when I saw his dead body dancing in the wind!"

"Wretch!—Monster!—Devil!"

"To wake you at night with an imitation of your father's groan;—and to welcome you in the morning with a copy of the execration that has since attended you."

I could endure it no longer. I was mad—mad—mad! And, unwitting what influence ruled me, I rushed from the room, while he roared after me—"Stay, good father-killer, your brother Charles lies waiting for your further practice!"

From the moment that I thus extricated myself from the piercing words uttered by the wretch, who, under the name of father, had seduced me to my undoing, I seemed to be in that state of bewilderment, when to think would be as easy as to lift a mountain in my arms. I stalked along, without noticing aught of the outward objects that surrounded me, and was employed in the endless repetition of the words, "good father-killer." It was well that I could not think—it was well that I was so amazed and horror-struck, that my mind was incapable of reaching any conclusion; for, had it been otherwise, dreadful and instantaneous must have been the catastrophe. But, before I had really re-obtained the use of my reason, I had added to the words, "good father-killer," the rest of the demon's anathema—"your brother Charles lies waiting for your further practice." Those words, intended to curse me beyond redemption, were my salvation.—He waited for my further practice.—Yes, for him I would practise; but it should be for his life, and not for his death; and if I failed, I swore by heaven and hell, that one hour should behold the end of both.

The thought of the possibility of my being able to save Charles, made me for the moment forget the crime that I had committed at Okeham; the hope of preserving his life spread over my brain as the influence of brandy had formerly done; and it was under a sort of mental intoxication that I addressed myself to the labour.

I cannot pause to detail all that passed. Even now that I write these events, instead of enacting them, my brain is on fire, and I am ready to rend my lungs with shouts of joy, or tear my hair for maddening grief, according as the alternate picture of my brother or my father flashes across my mind.

It was Lockwood's wicked counsel that helped me in my first progress. I succeeded in getting myself appointed executioner to my brother; and, subsequently, by dint of such bribes as my slender means would allow, and large promises to the extent of the credulity of my instrument, I obtained ingress to his dungeon by favour of one of the turn-keys. It was midnight when I entered, and found him gently slumbering on his miserable pallet. As I leaned over, to watch a sleep such as I could never hope to enjoy, the mould of his features brought back to my recollection, with irresistible force, the countenance of my father, when, at the last moment of his existence, he bestowed on me his forgiveness. The thought that rushed into my mind overcame me, and I burst into a passionate flood of tears.

One of those scalding drops fell upon the cheek of my brother, and roused him from his repose. He looked up, and gently cried—"Is the hour arrived? So be it. I am ready!"

Oh, merciful Heaven! how his quiet accents ran through my blood!—I could not answer him.

As he perceived my agitation, he rose from his bed—"Who are you," he cried, "that come with tears of pity?—Let me gaze on one that speaks so comfortably to my spirit."

I had turned away my head; but his words were all-persuasive; and, forgetting that my face was already too well known to him, I turned it towards him at his bidding. A shriek, that seemed to come from the bottomn of his soul, told me how well I was recognised, and he, in his turn, averted his countenance, as if in disgust at my presence.

A minute, or perhaps more, elapsed before either of us uttered a word. But at length he cried,—"Why is this? Or is it necessary that the executioner should come to tell me that all is prepared?"

Words in seeming—daggers in sooth! The scathing scene of my father's death was again placed be fore me in all the horrid freshness of reality. But even that was softened by the influence of the errand that had brought me to my brother's dungeon; and I wept as if my heart would burst.

Charles seemed astonished; and the sound of my sobbing again induced him to turn his head towards me—"Yes, yes!" said he, after a second gaze,—"I cannot forget that face!—You do not come here to mock me?"

"To mock you, Charles?"

"Charles!"

"Dear Charles," I replied, "I have been praying that my tongue might have power to reveal to you the very truth of my soul. But it cannot be! It is beyond the reach of words; and I must be content to let my deeds stand alone. I have stolen hither to concert means by which you may be saved."

"Saved!" he exclaimed:—"Who are you? Are you not he that"—

"Mercy! mercy!" I interrupted; "do not you remind me of that, lest in my madness I should think that you were Lockwood, and forego my task."

"Lockwood!" screamed my brother; "aye, that is the villain's name, who, not content with robbing my father, stealing his child, and murdering Ellen, crowned all by a dreadful betrayal of him to the scaffold."

I staggered with horror at the words that were uttered by Charles. Great God! could this be possible, after the story that Lockwood had narrated to me? At length I mustered words to exclaim—"Again,—again,—once more;—was Lockwood that villain?"

"Too surely," replied Charles; "he was tried for breaking open my father's escritoire, and stealing money to a considerable amount. His sentence was two years' imprisonment, at the expiration of which he waylaid his wife, who, ill-used beyond endurance, had yielded in the interim to my father's addresses, and the next morning she was found drowned in the park lake. The infant that was with her could not be traced; and though Lockwood was subsequently apprehended and tried, he met with an acquittal, from the absence of a link in the circumstantial evidence, that otherwise carried with it full moral conviction of his guilt."

"And the child?"

"The child was never found! But my father to his dying day felt persuaded that the hour would arrive when he would be forthcoming; and in this belief he gave me, on his last farewell, the portrait of the mother set in diamonds, under a strict injunction to deliver it, with his blessing, to my brother, when that happy discovery should be made. Alas, alas! he has never been heard of:—and there will be no friend, no relation, to watch my last moments, when I am to undergo that death which has been unjustly awarded me."

"Unjustly?"

"Aye, sir, unjustly," returned my brother; "I cannot expect you to believe it; but as there is truth in heaven, so is the truth on my lips, when I say—unjustly! Either by some extraordinary mischance, or inhuman conspiracy, the evidence that could have proved my innocence was withheld on the trial; and an ignominious death will be the result."

"No, no!" I exclaimed;—"you shall live—live to bless—to curse your brother!"

And in very agony of spirit I clasped my hands, and sank on my knees before his feet.

He started, as if afraid to listen to my words, while I almost unconsciously ejaculated, "Brother, brother!"

"Call me not by that name," at length he said; "I would not in these last moments be at enmity with any—even you I would forgive.—But do not insult me with that appellation, lest I forget my forbearance, and spurn you as the murderer of my father."

"Yes, yes; I deserve even that—but not from you! Oh, Charles! if time permitted me to tell you how bitterly I have been deceived—how Lockwood has ever brought me up as his child, and roused me to the frightful stigma that has just escaped your lips by a thousand falsehoods, in the detail of my mother's miserable fate, you would not quite hate me, for the intervention of pity would prevent it. But the precious minutes fly! I have arranged a plan for your escape"—

At this moment our conversation was interrupted by the friendly turn-key who had admitted me, shewing himself at the door, and exclaiming, in a low whisper, "Come, come, my lad, your time is up. I dare not give you more for ten times the sum you have promised."

"One minute, and I come," I cried; and with a sort of growling assent he withdrew.

"I have not time," I continued, turning to my brother, "to explain. One word must do—sustain yourself even to the last moment; and when you get the signal from me, follow my bidding to the very letter! I shall be by your side!"

Charles looked at me doubtingly, and shook his head.

Again I kneeled—"Hear me heaven!" I exclaimed—"as I hope for mercy—as I do not expect it for the parricide—as I am a ruined, heart-riven man—I have not uttered one syllable that is not true! Farewell, dear brother—and—and do not refuse me the precious portrait of my mother, in token of your belief of my penitence."

Charles turned from me, as he muttered, "It cannot be."

"If it cannot," I replied, " I will not again ask it. I deserve no consideration; and I am too guilty to dare to press for it."

I was about to withdraw, when he called me back. His eyes were full of tears.

"I do believe your words," he said; "all of them, save those which would excite in me a hope that you can save me. Take the portrait. I am bound by my promise to our father to bestow it on you. I am more bound by the softening of my heart, which tells me that you have been the most unhappy victim of Lockwood's arts. He was wily enough to betray our father; how could your young untutored mind escape him! Brother, God bless you! If we should not meet again, remain in the assurance that that same 'God bless you,' shall be the last words these lips will utter."

How I dragged myself away from him, I know not, but, under the turnkey's guidance, I soon found myself on the outside of the prison walls. Thus set free, I went forth into the open country, where none might spy my actions, and gave myself up to the recall of the scene I had just shared with Charles. A melancholy gladness crept into my soul at the recollection of his farewell words, and at the bold resolve with which I determined to effect his escape. I pressed my mother's portrait against my bosom, as

I swore to save him, and it almost seemed to my disturbed fancy, as if the picture whispered to my heart, "Save him!"

The rest of the day was spent in maturing my plans for the next coming morning, when I was again to figure on the public scaffold as an executioner. But I had thoughts, and hopes, and expectations, to cheer me onwards, and I felt as if I could submit to a thousand disgraces for the sake of adding one iota to the chance of my being able to preserve my brother's life.

The morning came. My plans were all well laid—I felt secure of success—and my heart was lighter than it had been since the day that the execrations of the mob drove me from Okeham to wander far a-field. Yes, even in spite of the action of each minute reminding me of the part that I had there performed, my thoughts refused to be checked in their ebullition. I stood within the dreary outer cell, awaiting the appearance of my brother—but the gloom of the dungeon had not power to overcast my soul. I heard the solemn tolling of the sullen bell—but to my ear it was hopeful music that spoke of Charles's freedom. I looked around, and the eyes of all men glouted on me; yet, ere their gaze could reach me, it fell stillborn and impotent in the remembrance of the one cheering glance I was expecting from him for whom alone I lived. At length he approached from the inner prison: I heard the clanking of his chains, and the sound was welcomed by me with a smile; for I had strung my whole energies to the feat, and I was panting to be doing. But the look and the shudder of Charles, when he first beheld me with my hangman hands outstretched to knock away his fetters, nearly threw me from my balance; and I felt for a moment as if the better part of my strength had been suddenly plucked from me.

"What is this?" he murmured, as I leaned over him for the purpose of supplying the place of his irons with a cord—"What is this?—Have you spoiled my last moments and my last hope with a falsehood?—Speak, are you my brother, or are you my executioner?"

"Hush," whispered I, while my whole frame shook with emotion—"I am true, as I hope for pardon.—Keep your energies bent to their highest pitch; the rest is for me to accomplish."

He gazed on me as though he could hardly bring himself to the belief of my words; but I looked up from my odious task with such holy earnestness in my face, and his moistened eye so happily perceived that mine was ready to let fall a tear of reciprocity, that conviction in good time arrived, and I felt his tremulous fingers gently press my hand in token of his credence in my honesty.

All was arranged below; and under pretext of my office I mounted the scaffold that I might see that every thing accorded with the scheme I had previously formed in my own mind. The ascending of a score of steps placed me about ten or twelve feet above the level of the market-place, of which the jail formed one side; a narrow space of scarcely more than a yard in width, was railed off round the spot occupied by the platform for the reception of the posse comitatus, and the barriers of that division were of sufficient strength to prevent the pressure of the crowd breaking in upon the constabulary arrangement. The moment that I reached the scaffold, I cast an anxious look around to see if every thing wore the aspect that I had prefigured to myself, and on which my plans were built. Every thing was as I could wish: the constables, by means of the barrier, were prevented from suddenly mingling with the mob, and could only reach the open space by coming quite back to the wall of the jail, and so passing through a wicket that formed the termination of the railing; and even the very execrations with which my presence was hailed, were pleasant to me, for I interpreted the public hatred towards me into sympathy towards Charles; and on the sudden evolving of that sympathy much of my success depended.

Thus reassured of the favourable appearance of the market-place, I descended again to the jail for the purpose of summoning the prisoner. Together we mounted the scaffold; and the execrations with which I had previously been greeted, were changed to sounds of pity and commiseration for my brother. They vibrated like heavenly music in my ears—they made my whole blood throb with the fever of excitement. I looked back to see how far distant we were from those who had to follow us to the platform. Fortune smiled upon me. The clergyman, who should have ascended next, was elderly and decrepit, and as he placed his foot on the first step he slipped, and seemed as if he had sprained some limb; at all events he paused, while those immediately behind gathered round him as if to afford assistance.

One glance told me all this. "Now, Charles," I whispered, "this is the moment. Life or death, dear brother! Turn more towards the prison while I cut the cords that bind your hands—spring forward with a bold leap into the middle of the crowd, where you see the man with a red cap; he is placed there to make an opening for you—the multitude will be with you—they will favour your flight.—Rush through the opposite street which takes to the river, where awaits a boat—that once secured, there is none other to pursue you, and your escape to the opposite bank is certain."

My brother listened attentively, and shewed by his eye that he comprehended all. Never, never was there such a moment in the life of man as that in mine when the last coil of the rope was cut, and my brother darted forward to the leap. As I had foretold to him, the man with the cap suddenly backed, and left an open space for him on which to alight, in addition to which he extended his arms round him so as to steady his descent. That was the great moment of my agitation, for had Charles come to the ground with a shock, his flight would have been hopeless. But it was but a moment, for in another he bounded forward through the crowd, which, with exhilarating cheers, opened on every side, and pursued his way with the speed of a greyhound towards the river. Meanwhile, my own blood refused obedience to my reason, and without plan or project, I too sprang from the scaffold, unable to resist the temptation of watching him to the consummation of his escape. But, as might well be expected, my motive was utterly misunderstood, and ten thousand groans saluted me as I darted through the passage made for Charles, and which by the suddenness of my pursuit had not yet had time to close; to groans succeeded blows—to blows missiles—but still I persevered, and exerting, as it were, a more than mortal speed, I was within a yard or two of Charles by the time he reached the river. When I perceived him thus far on the sure road to liberty, I could no longer restrain myself: I absolutely screamed with ecstasy; and what with my unintelligible shouts of delight, what with the streams of mud with which I had been assailed, and which ran down me on every side, what with my bleeding lacerated face, covered with wounds from the blows that I had received, I must have looked more like a mishapen lump of chaos than aught in human shape or bearing.

But all was not yet accomplished. Charles had reached the bank, which was some two or three yards above the level of the stream, and was turning to run down the hard way that led to the boat that lay ready for him, when a man suddenly made his appearance from behind a shed that stood in the angle formed by the bank and the jetty, and shewed by his actions that he was prepared to dispute my brother's passage.

Powers of hell! it was Lockwood!

Another moment, and he would have clutched Charles in his brawny arms, towards which my brother had unconsciously been running, not having perceived him till the very last moment. At the sight, my note of joy was changed to the yell of despair. It can hardly be said that I thought! No! It was as a mere act of desperation, that, still at the height of my speed, I rushed upon the villain, who had been too intent in his observations of Charles to notice me, or to prepare himself for the tremendous shock with which I assaulted him. I was in time—yes, even to a little instant, I was in time! Full with the rage of energy and speed, I drove against him, and together we toppled over the bank into the soft and oozy mud that the low-tided river had left behind. For myself I had no care; and even while in the act of falling, I shouted to my brother, "Dear, dear Charles, to the boat—to the boat! Row with the strength of a thousand! Your demon foe is destroyed!"

Charles returned my shout with a heart-spoken blessing; and as I lay over Lockwood, who each moment, by his effort to disentangle himself from me, sank deeper and deeper into the suffocating mire, I could hear my brother ply the oars with desperate speed and vigour, while ever and anon his thanksgiving to the wicked Ambrose came on the wings of the wind, till struggling, exhaustion, and anxiety deprived me of all consciousness of existence, and left me lying senseless on the corpse of my arch-deceiver.

My story is told! My confessions are numbered! Why, I know not—but so it is; even as surely as I am now the inmate of a melancholy cell, and am counted by my fellow-men among the maniacs of the earth.—Mad! Oh no, I am not mad! Do I not remember too well the frightful scenes of Okeham—the dreadful cajolery of Lockwood, by which he has made my own thoughts my own hell?—Mad! Would I were mad; for then might these things be hidden in oblivion; and yet I would not forget all! It was I that saved the gentle Charles from execution; it was I that earned his blessings by deliverance; and though I weep when I put my hand into my bosom, and vainly seek my mother's portrait, the tears change into joyful drops when dear memory reminds me that it was to purchase his escape I sold the precious relic. No, no! I cannot be utterly mad, till I shall hear, which Heaven of mercy avert, that my brother is again within the peril of the law, as though the ghost of Lockwood, yet unsatiated, was still employed in hunting him into its toils.

The String of Pearls

OR, SWEENEY TODD, THE DEMON BARBER OF FLEET-STREET

James Malcolm Rymer

———— • ————

CHAPTER I

BEFORE FLEET-STREET HAD REACHED ITS PRESENT IMPORTANCE, AND WHEN GEORGE the Third was young, and the two figures who used to strike the chimes at old St. Dunstan's church were in all their glory—being a great impediment to errand-boys on their progress, and a matter of gaping curiosity to country people—there stood close to the sacred edifice a small barber's shop, which was kept by a man of the name of Sweeney Todd.

How it was that he came by the name of Sweeney, as a Christian appellation, we are at a loss to conceive, but such was his name, as might be seen in extremely corpulent yellow letters over his shop window, by anyone who chose there to look for it.

Barbers by that time in Fleet-street had not become fashionable, and no more dreamt of calling themselves artists than of taking the Tower by storm; moreover they were not, as they are now, constantly slaughtering fine fat bears, and yet somehow people had hair on their heads just the same as they have at present, without the aid of that unctuous auxiliary. Moreover Sweeney Todd, in common with his brethren in those really primitive sorts of times, did not think it at all necessary to have any waxen effigies of humanity in his window. There was no languishing young lady looking over the left shoulder in order that a profusion of auburn tresses might repose upon her lily neck, and great conquerors and great statesmen were not then, as they are now, held up to public ridicule with dabs of rouge upon their cheeks, a quantity of gunpowder scattered in for a beard, and some bristles sticking on end for eyebrows.

No. Sweeney Todd was a barber of the old school, and he never thought of glorifying himself on account of any extraneous circumstance. If he had lived in Henry the Eighth's palace, it would have been all the same to him as Henry the Eighth's dog-kennel, and he would scarcely have believed human nature to be so green as to pay an extra sixpence to be shaven and shorn in any particular locality.

A long pole painted white, with a red stripe curling spirally round it, projected into the street from his doorway, and on one of the panes of glass in his window was presented the following couplet:

> Easy shaving for a penny,
> As good as you will find any.

We do not put these lines forth as a specimen of the poetry of the age; they may have been the production of some young Templer; but if they were a little wanting in poetic fire, that was amply made up by the clear and precise manner in which they set forth what they intended.

The barber himself was a long, low-jointed, ill-put-together sort of fellow, with an immense mouth, and such huge hands and feet, that he was, in his way, quite a natural curiosity; and, what was more wonderful, considering his trade, there never was seen such a head of hair as Sweeney Todd's. We know not what to compare it to: probably it came nearest to what one might suppose to be the appearance of a thickset hedge, in which a quantity of small wire had got entangled. In truth, it was a most terrific head of hair; and as Sweeney Todd kept all his combs in it—some said his scissors likewise—when he put his head out of the shop-door to see what sort of weather it was, he might have been mistaken for some Indian warrior with a very remarkable head-dress.

He had a short disagreeable kind of unmirthful laugh, which came in at all sorts of odd times when nobody else saw anything to laugh at at all, and which sometimes made people start again, especially when they were being shaved, and Sweeney Todd would stop short in that operation to indulge in one those cacchinatory effusions. It was evident that the remembrance of some very strange and out-of-the-way joke must occasionally flit across him, and then he gave his hyena-like laugh, but it was so short, so sudden, striking upon the ear for a moment, and then gone, that people have been known to look up to the ceiling, and on the floor, and all round them, to know from whence it had come, scarcely supposing it possible that it proceeded from mortal lips.

Mr. Todd squinted a little to add to his charms; and so we think that by this time the reader may in his mind's eye see the individual whom we wish to present to him. Some thought him a careless enough harmless fellow, with not much sense in him, and at times they almost considered he was a little cracked; but there were others, again, who shook their heads when they spoke of him; and while they could say nothing to his prejudice, except that they certainly considered he was odd, yet, when they came to consider what a great crime and misdemeanour it really is in this world to be odd, we shall not be surprised at the ill-odour in which Sweeney Todd was held.

But for all that he did a most thriving business, and was considered by his neighbours to be a very well-to-do sort of man, and decidedly, in city phraseology, warm.

It was so handy for the young students in the Temple to pop over to Sweeney Todd's to get their chins new rasped: so that from morning to night he drove a good business, and was evidently a thriving man.

There was only one thing that seemed in any way to detract from the great prudence of Sweeney Todd's character, and that was that he rented a large house, of which he occupied nothing but the shop and parlour, leaving the upper part entirely useless, and obstinately refusing to let it on any terms whatever.

Such was the state of things, AD 1785, as regarded Sweeney Todd.

The day is drawing to a close, and a small drizzling kind of rain is falling, so that there are not many passengers in the streets, and Sweeney Todd is sitting in his shop looking keenly in the face of a boy, who stands in an attitude of trembling subjection before him.

"You will remember," said Sweeney Todd, and he gave his countenance a most horrible twist as he spoke, "you will remember, Tobias Ragg, that you are now my apprentice, that you have of me had board, washing, and lodging, with the exception that you don't sleep here, that you take your meals at home, and that your mother, Mrs. Ragg, does your washing, which she may very well do, being a laundress in the Temple, and making no end of money: as for lodging, you lodge here, you know, very comfortably in the shop all day. Now, are you not a happy dog?"

"Yes, sir," said the boy timidly.

"You will acquire a first-rate profession, and quite as good as the law, which your mother tells me she would have put you to, only that a little weakness of the headpiece unqualified you. And now, Tobias, listen to me, and treasure up every word I say."

"Yes, sir."

"I'll cut your throat from ear to ear, if you repeat one word of what passes in this shop, or dare to make any supposition, or draw any conclusion from anything you may see, or hear, or fancy you see or hear. Now you understand me—I'll cut your throat from ear to ear—do you understand me?"

"Yes, sir, I won't say nothing. I wish, sir, as I may be made into veal pies at Lovett's in Bell-yard if I as much as says a word."

Sweeney Todd rose from his seat; and opening his huge mouth, he looked at the boy for a minute or two in silence, as if he fully intended swallowing him, but had not quite made up his mind where to begin.

"Very good," he said at length, "I am satisfied, I am quite satisfied; and mark me—the shop, and the shop only, is your place."

"Yes, sir."

"And if any customer gives you a penny, you can keep it, so that if you get enough of them you will become a rich man; only I will take care of them for you, and when I think you want them I will let you have them. Run out and see what's o'clock by St. Dunstan's."

There was a small crowd collected opposite the church, for the figures were about to strike three-quarters past six; and among that crowd was one man who gazed with as much curiosity as anybody at the exhibition.

"Now for it!" he said, "they are going to begin; well, that is ingenious. Look at the fellow lifting up his club, and down it comes bang upon the old bell."

The three-quarters were struck by the figures; and then the people who had loitered to see it done, many of whom had day by day looked at the same exhibition for years past, walked away, with the exception of the man who seemed so deeply interested.

He remained, and crouching at his feet was a noble-looking dog, who looked like-wise up at the figures; and who, observing his master's attention to be closely fixed upon them, endeavoured to show as great an appearance of interest as he possibly could.

"What do you think of that, Hector?" said the man.

The dog gave a short low whine, and then his master proceeded,—

"There is a barber's shop opposite, so before I go any farther, as I have got to see the ladies, although it's on a very melancholy errand, for I have got to tell them that poor Mark Ingestrie is no more, and Heaven knows what poor Johanna will say—I think I should know her by his description of her, poor fellow. It grieves me to think now how he used to talk about her in the long night-watches, when all was still, and not a breath of air touched a curl upon his cheek. I could almost think I saw her some-times, as he used to tell me of her soft beaming eyes, her little gentle pouting lips, and the dimples that played about her mouth. Well, well, it's of no use grieving; he is dead and gone, poor fellow, and the salt water washes over as brave a heart as ever beat. His sweetheart, Johanna, though, shall have the string of pearls for all that; and if she cannot be Mark Ingestrie's wife in this world, she shall be rich and happy, poor young thing, while she stays in it, that is to say as happy as she can be; and she must just look forward to meeting him aloft, where there are no squalls or tempests. And so I'll go and get shaved at once."

He crossed the road towards Sweeney Todd's shop, and, stepping down the low doorway, he stood face to face with the odd-looking barber.

The dog gave a low growl and sniffed the air.

"Why, Hector," said his master, "what's the matter? Down, sir, down!"

"I have a mortal fear of dogs," said Sweeney Todd. "Would you mind him, sir, sitting outside the door and waiting for you, if it's all the same? Only look at him, he is going to fly at me!"

"Then you are the first person he ever touched without provocation," said the man; "but I suppose he don't like your looks, and I must confess I ain't much surprised at that. I have seen a few rum-looking guys in my time, but hang me if ever I saw such a figure-head as yours. What the devil noise was that?"

"It was only me," said Sweeney Todd; "I laughed."

"Laughed! do you call that a laugh? I suppose you caught it of somebody who died of it. If that's your way of laughing, I beg you won't do it any more."

"Stop the dog! stop the dog! I can't have dogs running into my back parlour."

"Here, Hector, here!" cried his master; "get out!"

Most unwillingly the dog left the shop, and crouched down close to the outer door, which the barber took care to close, muttering something about a draught of air coming in, and then, turning to the apprentice boy, who was screwed up in a corner, he said,—

"Tobias, my lad, go to Leadenhall-street, and bring a small bag of the thick biscuits from Mr. Peterson's; say they are for me. Now, sir, I suppose you want to be shaved, and it is well you have come here, for there ain't a shaving-shop, although I say it, in the city of London that ever thinks of polishing anybody off as I do."

"I tell you what it is, master barber: if you come that laugh again, I will get up and go. I don't like it, and there is an end of it."

"Very good," said Sweeney Todd, as he mixed up a lather. "Who are you? where did you come from? and where are you going?"

"That's cool, at all events. Damn it! what do you mean by putting the brush in my mouth? Now, don't laugh; and since you are so fond of asking questions, just answer me one."

"Oh, yes, of course: what is it, sir?"

"Do you know a Mr. Oakley, who lives somewhere in London, and is a spectacle-maker?"

"Yes, to be sure I do—John Oakley, the spectacle-maker, in Fore-street, and he has got a daughter named Johanna, that the young bloods call the Flower of Fore-street."

"Ah, poor thing! do they? Now, confound you! what are you laughing at now? What do you mean by it?"

"Didn't you say, 'Ah, poor thing?' Just turn your head a little on one side; that will do. You have been to sea, sir?"

"Yes, I have, and have only now lately come up the river from an Indian voyage."

"Indeed! where can my strop be? I had it this minute; I must have laid it down somewhere. What an odd thing that I can't see it! It's very extraordinary; what can have become of it? Oh, I recollect, I took it into the parlour. Sit still, sir. I shall not be gone a moment; sit still, sir, if you please. By the by, you can amuse yourself with the *Courier*, sir, for a moment."

Sweeney Todd walked into the back parlour and closed the door.

There was a strange sound suddenly compounded of a rushing noise and then a heavy blow, immediately after which Sweeney Todd emerged from his parlour, and, folding his arms, he looked upon *the vacant chair where his customer had been seated*, but the customer was gone, leaving not the slightest trace of his presence behind except his hat, and that Sweeney Todd immediately seized and thrust into a cupboard that was at one corner of the shop.

"What's that?" he said, "what's that? I thought I heard a noise."

The door was slowly opened, and Tobias made his appearance, saying,—

"If you please, sir, I have forgot the money, and have run all the way back from St. Paul's churchyard."

In two strides Todd reached him, and clutching him by the arm he dragged him into the farthest corner of the shop, and then he stood opposite to him glaring in his face with such a demoniac expression that the boy was frightfully terrified.

"Speak!" cried Todd, "speak! and speak the truth, or your last hour is come! How long were you peeping through the door before you came in?"

"Peeping, sir?"

"Yes, peeping; don't repeat my words, but answer me at once, you will find it better for you in the end."

"I wasn't peeping, sir, at all."

Sweeney Todd drew a long breath as he then said, in a strange, shrieking sort of manner, which he intended, no doubt, should be jocose,—

"Well, well, very well; if you did peep, what then? it's no matter; I only wanted to know, that's all; it was quite a joke, wasn't it—quite funny, though rather odd, eh? Why don't you laugh, you dog? Come, now, there is no harm done. Tell me what you thought about it at once, and we will be merry over it—very merry."

"I don't know what you mean, sir," said the boy, who was quite as much alarmed at Mr. Todd's mirth as he was at his anger. "I don't know what you mean, sir; I only just come back because I hadn't any money to pay for the biscuits at Peterson's."

"I mean nothing at all," said Todd, suddenly turning upon his heel; "what's that scratching at the door?"

Tobias opened the shop-door, and there stood the dog, who looked wistfully round the place, and then gave a howl that seriously alarmed the barber.

"It's the gentleman's dog, sir," said Tobias, "it's the gentleman's dog, sir, that was looking at old St. Dunstan's clock, and came in here to be shaved. It's funny, ain't it, sir, that the dog didn't go away with his master?"

"Why don't you laugh if it's funny? Turn out the dog, Tobias; we'll have no dogs here; I hate the sight of them; turn him out—turn him out."

"I would, sir, in a minute; but I'm afraid he wouldn't let me, somehow. Only look, sir—look; see what he is at now! did you ever see such a violent fellow, sir? why he will have down the cupboard door."

"Stop him—stop him! the devil is in the animal! stop him I say!"

The dog was certainly getting the door open, when Sweeney Todd rushed forward to stop him; but that he was soon admonished of the danger of doing, for the dog gave him a grip of the leg, which made him give such a howl, that he precipitately retreated, and left the animal to do its pleasure. This consisted in forcing open the cupboard door, and seizing upon the hat which Sweeney Todd had thrust therein, and dashing out of the shop with it in triumph.

"The devil's in the beast," muttered Todd, "he's off! Tobias, you said you saw the man who owned that fiend of a cur looking at St. Dunstan's church."

"Yes, sir, I did see him there. If you recollect, you sent me to see the time, and the figures were just going to strike three-quarters past six; and before I came away, I heard him say that Mark Ingestrie was dead, and Johanna should have the string of pearls. Then I came in, and then, if you recollect, sir, he came in, and the odd thing, you know, to me, sir, is that he didn't take his dog with him, because, you know, sir—"

"Because what?" shouted Todd.

"Because people generally do take their dogs with them, you know, sir; and may I be made into one of Lovett's pies, if I don't—"

"Hush! someone comes; it's old Mr. Grant, from the Temple. How do you do, Mr. Grant? glad to see you looking so well, sir. It does one's heart good to see a gentleman of your years looking so fresh and hearty. Sit down, sir; a little this way, if you please. Shaved, I suppose?"

"Yes, Todd, yes. Any news?"

"No, sir, nothing stirring. Everything very quiet, sir, except the high wind. They say it blew the king's hat off yesterday, sir, and he borrowed Lord North's. Trade is dull, too, sir. I suppose people won't come out to be cleaned and dressed in a misling rain. We haven't had anybody in the shop for an hour and a half."

"Lor! sir," said Tobias, "you forgot the seafaring gentleman with the dog, you know, sir."

"Ah! so I do," said Todd. "He went away, and I saw him get into some disturbance, I think, just at the corner of the market."

"I wonder I didn't meet him, sir," said Tobias, "for I came that way; and then it's so very odd leaving his dog behind him."

"Yes very," said Todd. "Will you excuse me a moment, Mr. Grant? Tobias, my lad, I just want you to lend me a hand in the parlour."

Tobias followed Todd very unsuspectingly into the parlour; but when they got there and the door was closed, the barber sprang upon him like an enraged tiger, and, grappling him by the throat, he gave his head such a succession of knocks against the wainscot, that Mr. Grant must have thought that some carpenter was at work. Then he tore a handful of his hair out, after which he twisted him round, and dealt him such a kick, that he was flung sprawling into a corner of the room, and then, without a word, the barber walked out again to his customer, and he bolted his parlour door on the outside, leaving Tobias to digest the usage he had received at his leisure, and in the best way he could.

When he came back to Mr. Grant, he apologised for keeping him waiting by saying,—

"It became necessary, sir, to teach my new apprentice a little bit of his business. I have left him studying it now. There is nothing like teaching young folks at once."

"Ah!" said Mr. Grant, with a sigh, "I know what it is to let young folks grow wild; for although I have neither chick nor child of my own, I had a sister's son to look to—a handsome, wild, harum-scarum sort of fellow, as like me as one pea is like another. I tried to make a lawyer of him, but it wouldn't do, and it's now more than two years ago he left me altogether; and yet there were some good traits about Mark."

"Mark, sir! did you say Mark?"

"Yes, that was his name, Mark Ingestrie. God knows what's become of him."

"Oh!" said Sweeney Todd; and he went on lathering the chin of Mr. Grant.

CHAPTER II

"JOHANNA, JOHANNA, MY DEAR, DO YOU KNOW WHAT TIME IT IS? JOHANNA, I SAY, my dear, are you going to get up? Here's your mother has trotted out to parson Lupin's and you know I have to go to Alderman Judd's house in Cripplegate the first thing, and I haven't had a morsel of breakfast yet. Johanna, my dear, do you hear me?"

These observations were made by Mr. Oakley, the spectacle-maker, at the door of his daughter Johanna's chamber, on the morning after the events we have just recorded at Sweeney Todd's; and presently a soft sweet voice answered him, saying,—

"I am coming, father, I am coming: in a moment, father, I shall be down."

"Don't hurry yourself, my darling, I can wait."

The little old spectacle-maker descended the staircase again and sat down in the parlour at the back of the shop where, in a few moments, he was joined by Johanna, his only and his much-loved child.

She was indeed a creature of the rarest grace and beauty. Her age was eighteen, but she looked rather younger, and upon her face she had that sweetness and intelligence of expression which almost bids defiance to the march of time. Her hair was of a glossy blackness, and what was rare in conjunction with such a feature, her eyes were of a deep and heavenly blue. There was nothing of the commanding or of the severe style of beauty about her, but the expression of her face was all grace and sweetness. It was one of those countenances which one could look at for a long summer's day, as upon the pages of some deeply interesting volume, which furnished the most abundant food for pleasant and delightful reflection.

There was a touch of sadness about her voice, which, perhaps, only tended to make it the more musical, although mournfully so, and which seemed to indicate that at the bottom of her heart there lay some grief which had not yet been spoken—some cherished aspiration of her pure soul, which looked hopeless as regards completion—

some remembrance of a former joy, which had been turned to bitterness and grief: it was the cloud in the sunny sky—the shadow through which there still gleamed bright and beautiful sunshine, but which still proclaimed its presence.

"I have kept you waiting, father," she said, as she flung her arms about the old man's neck. "I have kept you waiting."

"Never mind, my dear, never mind. Your mother is so taken up with Mr. Lupin, that you know, this being Wednesday morning, she is off to his prayer meeting, and so I have had no breakfast; and really I think I must discharge Sam."

"Indeed, father! what has he done?"

"Nothing at all, and that's the very reason. I had to take down the shutters myself this morning, and what do you think for? He had the coolness to tell me that he couldn't take down the shutter this morning, or sweep out the shop, because his aunt had the toothache."

"A poor excuse, father," said Johanna, as she bustled about and got the breakfast ready; "a very poor excuse!"

"Poor indeed! but his month is up to-day, and I must get rid of him. But I suppose I shall have no end of bother with your mother, because his aunt belongs to Mr. Lupin's congregation; but as sure as this is the 20th day of August—"

"It is the 20th day of August," said Johanna, as she sank into a chair and burst into tears. "It is, it is! I thought I could have controlled this, but I cannot, father, I cannot. It was that which made me late. I knew mother was out; I knew that I ought to be down and attending upon you, and I was praying to Heaven for strength to do so because this was the 20th of August."

Johanna spoke these words incoherently and amidst sobs, and when she had finished them she leant her sweet face upon her small hands and wept like a child.

The astonishment, not unmingled with positive dismay, of the old spectacle-maker, was vividly depicted on his countenance, and for some minutes he sat perfectly aghast, with his hands resting on his knees, and looking in the face of his beautiful child—that is to say, as much as he could see of it between those little taper fingers that were spread upon it—as if he were newly awakened from some dream.

"Good God, Johanna!" he said at length, "what is this? my dear child, what has happened? Tell me, my dear, unless you wish to kill me with grief."

"You shall know, father," she said. "I did not think to say a word about it, but considered I had strength enough of mind to keep my sorrows in my own breast, but the effort has been too much for me, and I have been compelled to yield. If you had not looked so kindly on me—if I did not know that you loved me as you do, I should easily have kept my secret, but knowing that much, I cannot."

"My darling," said the old man, "you are right, there; I do love you. What would the world be to me now without you? There was a time, twenty years ago, when your mother made up much of my happiness, but of late, what with Mr. Lupin, and psalm-singing, and tea-drinking, I see very little of her, and what little I do see is not very satisfactory. Tell me, my darling, what it is that vexes you, and I'll soon put it to rights. I don't belong to the City train-bands for nothing."

"Father, I know that your affection would do all for me that it is possible to do, but you cannot recall the dead to life; and if this day passes over and I see him not, or hear not from him, I know that, instead of finding a home for me whom he loved, he has in the effort to do so found a grave for himself. He said he would, he said he would."

Here she wrung her hands, and wept again, and with such a bitterness of anguish that the old spectacle-maker was at his wit's end, and knew not what on earth to do or say.

"My dear, my dear!" he cried, "who is he? I hope you don't mean—"

"Hush, father, hush! I know the name that is hovering on your lips, but something seems even now to whisper to me he is no more, and, being so, speak nothing of him, father, but that which is good."

"You mean Mark Ingestrie."

"I do, and if he had a thousand faults, he at least loved me. He loved me truly and most sincerely."

"My dear," said the old spectacle-maker, "you know that I wouldn't for all the world say anything to vex you, nor will I; but tell me what it is that makes this day more than any other so gloomy to you."

"I will, father; you shall hear. It was on this day two years ago that we last met; it was in the Temple-gardens, and he had just had a stormy interview with his uncle, Mr. Grant, and you will understand, father, that Mark Ingestrie was not to blame, because—"

"Well, well, my dear, you needn't say anything more upon that point. Girls very seldom admit their lovers are to blame, but there are two ways, you know, Johanna, of telling a story."

"Yes; but, father, why should Mr. Grant seek to force him to the study of a profession he disliked?"

"My dear, one would have thought that if Mark Ingestrie really loved you, and found that he might make you his wife, and acquire an honourable subsistence both for you and himself—it seems a very wonderful thing to me that he did not do so. You see, my dear, he should have liked you well enough to do something else that he did not like."

"Yes, but, father, you know it is hard, when disagreements once arise, for a young ardent spirit to give in entirely; and so from one word, poor Mark, in his disputes with his uncle, got to another, when perhaps one touch of kindness or conciliation from Mr. Grant would have made him quite pliant in his hands."

"Yes, that's the way," said Mr. Oakley; "there is no end of excuses: but go on, my dear, go on, and tell me exactly how this affair now stands."

"I will, father. It was this day two years ago then that we met, and he told me that he and his uncle had at last quarrelled irreconcilably, and that nothing could possibly now patch up the difference between them. We had a long talk."

"Ah! no doubt of that."

"And at length he told me that he must go and seek his fortune—that fortune which he hoped to share with me. He said that he had an opportunity of undertaking a voyage to India, and that if he were successful he should have sufficient to return with and commence some pursuit in London, more congenial to his thoughts and habits than the law."

"Ah, well! what next?"

"He told me that he loved me."

"And you believed him?"

"Father, you would have believed him had you heard him speak. His tones were those of such deep sincerity that no actor who ever charmed an audience with an unreal existence could have reached them. There are times and seasons when we know that we are listening to the majestic voice of truth, and there are tones which sink at once into the heart, carrying with them a conviction of their sincerity which neither time nor circumstance can alter; and such were the tones in which Mark Ingestrie spoke to me."

"And so you suppose, Johanna, that it is easy for a young man who has not patience or energy enough to be respectable at home, to go abroad and make his fortune. Is idleness so much in request in other countries, that it receives such a rich reward, my dear?"

"You judge him harshly, father; you do not know him."

"Heaven forbid that I should judge anyone harshly! and I will freely admit that you may know more of his real character than I can, who of course have only seen its surface; but go on, my dear, and tell me all."

"We made an agreement, father, that on that day two years he was to come to me or send me some news of his whereabouts; if I heard nothing of him I was to conclude he was no more, and I cannot help so concluding now."

"But the day has not yet passed."

"I know it has not, and yet I rest upon but a slender hope, father. Do you believe that dreams ever really shadow forthcoming events?"

"I cannot say, my child; I am not disposed to yield credence to any supposed fact because I have dreamt it, but I confess to having heard some strange instances where these visions of the night have come strictly true."

"Heaven knows but this may be one of them! I had a dream last night. I thought that I was sitting upon the sea-shore, and that all before me was nothing but a fathomless waste of waters. I heard the roar and the dash of the waves distinctly, and each moment the wind grew more furious and fierce, and I saw in the distance a ship—it was battling with the waves, which at one moment lifted it mountains high, and at another plunged it far down into such an abyss, that not a vestige of it could be seen but the topmost spars of the tall masts. And still the storm increased each moment in its fury, and ever and anon there came a strange sullen sound across the waters, and I saw a flash of fire, and knew that those in the ill-fated vessel were thus endeavouring to attract attention and some friendly aid. Father, from the first to the last I knew that Mark Ingestrie was there—my heart told me so: I was certain he was there, and I was helpless—utterly helpless, utterly and entirely unable to lend the slightest aid. I could only gaze upon what was going forward as a silent and terrified spectator of the scene. And at last I heard a cry come over the deep—a strange, loud, wailing cry—which proclaimed to me the fate of the vessel. I saw its masts shiver for a moment in the blackened air, and then all was still for a few seconds, until there arose a strange, wild shriek, that I knew was the despairing cry of those who sank, never to rise again, in that vessel. Oh! that was a frightful sound—it was a sound to linger on the ears, and haunt the memory of sleep—it was a sound never to be forgotten when once heard, but such as might again and again be remembered with horror and affright."

"And all this was in your dream?"

"It was, father, it was."

"And you were helpless?"

"I was—utterly and entirely helpless."

"It was very sad."

"It was, as you shall hear. The ship went down, and that cry that I had heard was the last despairing one given by those who clung to the wreck with scarce a hope, and yet because it was their only refuge, for where else had they to look for the smallest ray of consolation? where else, save in the surging waters, were they to hunt for safety? Nowhere! all was lost! all was despair! I tried to scream—I tried to cry aloud to Heaven to have mercy upon those brave and gallant souls who had trusted their dearest possession—life itself—to the mercy of the deep; and while I so tried to render so inefficient succour, I saw a small speck in the sea, and my straining eyes perceived that it was a man floating and clinging to a piece of the wreck, and I knew it was Mark Ingestrie."

"But, my dear, surely you are not annoyed at a dream?"

"It saddened me; I stretched out my arms to save him—I heard him pronounce my name, and call upon me for help. 'Twas all in vain; he battled with the waves as long as human nature could battle with them. He could do no more, and I saw him disappear before my anxious eyes."

"Don't say you saw him, my dear, say you fancy you saw him."

"It was such a fancy as I shall not lose the remembrance of for many a day."

"Well, well, after all, my dear, it's only a dream; and it seems to me, without at all adverting to anything that should give you pain as regards Mark Ingestrie, that you made a very foolish bargain; for only consider how many difficulties might arise in the way of his keeping faith with you. You know I have your happiness so much at heart that, if Mark had been a worthy man and an industrious one, I should not have opposed myself to your union; but, believe me, my dear Johanna, that a young man with great facilities for spending money, and none whatever for earning any, is just about the worst husband you could choose, and such a man was Mark Ingestrie. But come, we will say nothing of this to your mother; let the secret, if we may call it such, rest with me; and if you can inform me in what capacity and in what vessel he left England, I will not carry my prejudice so far against him as to hesitate about making what enquiry I can concerning his fate."

"I know nothing more, father; we parted, and never met again."

"Well, well! dry your eyes, Johanna, and, as I go to Alderman Judd's, I'll think over the matter, which, after all, may not be so bad as you think. The lad is a good-enough-looking lad, and has, I believe, a good ability, if he would put it to some useful purpose; but if he goes scampering about the world in an unsettled manner, you are well rid of him, and as for his being dead, you must not conclude that by any means, for somehow or another, like a bad penny, these fellows always come back."

There was more consolation in the kindly tone of the spectacle-maker than in the words he used; but, upon the whole, Johanna was well enough pleased that she had communicated the secret to her father, for now, at all events, she had someone to whom she could mention the name of Mark Ingestrie, without the necessity of concealing the sentiment with which she did so; and when her father had gone, she felt that, by the mere relation of it to him, some of the terrors of her dream had vanished.

She sat for some time in a pleasing reverie, till she was interrupted by Sam, the shop-boy, who came into the parlour and said,—

"Please, Miss Johanna, suppose I was to go down to the docks and try and find out for you Mr. Mark Ingestrie. I say, suppose I was to do that. I heard it all, and if I do find him I'll soon settle him."

"What do you mean?"

"I means that I won't stand it; didn't I tell you, more than three weeks ago, as you was the object of my infections? Didn't I tell you that when aunt died I should come in for the soap and candle business, and make you my missus?"

The only reply which Johanna gave to this was to rise and leave the room, for her heart was too full of grief and sad speculation to enable her to do now as she had often been in the habit of doing—viz., laugh at Sam's protestations of affection, so he was left to chew the cud of sweet and bitter fancy by himself.

"A thousand damns!" said he, when he entered the shop: "I always suspected there was some other fellow, and now I know it I am ready to gnaw my head off that ever I consented to come here. Confound him! I hope he is at the bottom of the sea, and eat up by this time. Oh! I should like to smash everybody. If I had my way now I'd just walk into society at large, as they calls it, and let it know what one, two, three, slap in the eye, is—and down it would go."

Mr. Sam, in his rage, did upset a case of spectacles, which went down with a tremendous crash, and which, however good an imitation of the manner in which society at large was to be knocked down, was not likely to be at all pleasing to Mr. Oakley.

"I have done it now," he said; "but never mind; I'll try the old dodge whenever I break anything; that is, I'll place it in old Oakley's way, and swear he did it. I never knew such an old goose; you may persuade him into anything; the idea, now, of his pulling down all the shutters this morning because I told him my aunt had the toothache; that was a go, to be sure. But I'll be revenged of that fellow who has took away, I consider, Johanna from me; I'll let him know what a blighted heart is capable of. He won't live long enough to want a pair of spectacles, I'll be bound, or else my name ain't Sam Bolt."

CHAPTER III

THE EARLIEST DAWN OF MORNING WAS GLISTENING UPON THE MASTS, THE CORDAGE, and the sails of a fleet of vessels lying below Sheerness.

The crews were rousing themselves from their night's repose, and to make their appearance on the decks of the vessels, from which the night-watch had just been relieved.

A man-of-war, which had been the convoy of the fleet of merchantmen through the charnel, fired a gun as the first glimpse of the morning sun fell upon her tapering masts. Then from a battery in the neighbourhood came another booming report, and that was answered by another farther off, and then another, until the whole chain of batteries that girded the coast, for it was a time of war, had proclaimed the dawn of another day.

The effect was very fine, in the stillness of the early morn, of these successions of reports; and as they died away in the distance like mimic thunder, some order was given on board the man-of-war, and, in a moment, the masts and cordage seemed perfectly alive with human beings clinging to them in various directions. Then, as if by magic, or as if the ship had been a living thing itself, and had possessed wings, which, at the mere instigation of a wish, could be spread far and wide, there fluttered out such sheets of canvas as was wonderful to see; and, as they caught the morning light, and the ship moved from the slight breeze that sprang up from the shore, she looked, indeed, as if she

Walk'd the waters like a thing of life.

The various crews of the merchantmen stood upon the decks of their respective vessels, gazing after the ship-of-war, as she proceeded upon another mission similar to the one she had just performed in protecting the commerce of the country.

As she passed one vessel, which had been, in point of fact, actually rescued from the enemy, the crew, who had been saved from a foreign prison, cheered lustily.

There wanted but such an impulse as this, and then every merchant-vessel that the man-of-war passed took up the gladsome shout, and the crew of the huge vessel were not slow in their answer, for three deafening cheers—such as had frequently struck terror into the hearts of England's enemies—awakened many an echo from the shore.

It was a proud and a delightful sight—such a sight as none but an Englishman can thoroughly enjoy—to see that vessel so proudly stemming the waste of waters. We say none but an Englishman can enjoy it, because no other nation has ever attempted to achieve a great maritime existence without being most signally defeated, and leaving us still, as we shall ever be, masters of the seas.

These proceedings were amply sufficient to arouse the crews of all the vessels, and over the taffrail of one in particular, a large-sized merchantman, which had been trading in the Indian seas, two men were leaning. One of them was the captain of the vessel, and the other a passenger, who intended leaving that morning. They were engaged in earnest conversation, and the captain, as he shaded his eyes with his hand, and looked along the surface of the river, said, in reply to some observation from his companion,—

"I'll order my boat the moment Lieutenant Thornhill comes on board; I call him Lieutenant, although I have no right to do so, because he has held that rank in the king's service, but when quite a young man was cashiered for fighting a duel with his superior officer."

"The service has lost a good officer," said the other.

"It has indeed; a braver man never stepped, nor a better officer; but you see they have certain rules in the service and everything is sacrificed to maintain them. I can't think what keeps him; he went last night and said he would pull up to the Temple-stairs, because he wanted to call upon somebody by the waterside, and after that he was going to the city to transact some business of his own, and that would have brought him nearer there, you see; and there are plenty of things coming down the river."

"He's coming," cried the other; "don't be impatient; you will see him in a few minutes."

"What makes you think that?"

"Because I see his dog—there, don't you see, swimming in the water, and coming direct towards the ship?"

"I cannot imagine—I can see the dog, certainly; but I can't see Thornhill, nor is there any boat at hand. I know not what to make of it. Do you know my mind misgives me that something has happened amiss? The dog seems exhausted. Lend a hand there to Mr. Thornhill's dog, some of you. Why, it's a hat he has in his mouth."

The dog made towards the vessel; but without the assistance of the seamen—with the whole of whom he was an immense favourite—he certainly could not have boarded the vessel; and when he reached the deck, he sank down upon it in a state of complete exhaustion, with the hat still in his grasp.

As the animal lay, panting, upon the deck, the sailors looked at each other in amazement, and there was but one opinion among them all now, and that was that something very serious had unquestionably happened to Mr. Thornhill.

"I dread," said the captain, "an explanation of this occurrence. What on earth can it mean? That's Thornhill's hat, and here is Hector. Give the dog some drink and meat directly—he seems thoroughly exhausted."

The dog ate sparingly of some food that was put before him; and then, seizing the hat again in his mouth, he stood by the side of the ship and howled piteously; then he put down the hat for a moment, and, walking up to the captain, he pulled him by the skirt of the coat.

"You understand him," said the captain to the passenger; "something has happened to Thornhill, I'll be bound; and you see the object of the dog is to get me to follow him to see what it's about."

"Think you so? It is a warning, if it be such at all, that I should not be inclined to neglect; and if you will follow the dog, I will accompany you; there may be more in it than we think of, and we ought not to allow Mr. Thornhill to be in want of any assistance that we can render him, when we consider what great assistance he has been to us. Look how anxious the poor beast is."

The captain ordered a boat to be launched at once, and manned by four stout rowers. He then sprang into it, followed by the passenger, who was a Colonel Jeffery, of the Indian army, and the dog immediately followed them, testifying by his manner great pleasure at the expedition they were undertaking, and carrying the hat with him, which he evidently showed an immense disinclination to part with.

The captain ordered the boat to proceed up the river towards the Temple-stairs, where Hector's master had expressed his intention of proceeding, and, when the faithful animal saw the direction in which they were going, he lay down in the bottom of the boat perfectly satisfied, and gave himself up to that repose, of which he was evidently so much in need.

It cannot be said that Colonel Jeffery suspected that anything of a very serious nature had happened; indeed, their principal anticipation, when they came to talk it over, consisted in the probability that Thornhill had, with an impetuosity of character they knew very well he possessed, interfered to redress what he considered some street grievance, and had got himself into the custody of the civil power in consequence.

"Of course," said the captain, "Master Hector would view that as a very serious affair, and finding himself denied access to his master, you see he has come off to us, which was certainly the most prudent thing he could do, and I should not be at all surprised if he takes us to the door of some watch-house, where we shall find our friend snug enough."

The tide was running up; and that Thornhill had not saved the turn of it, by dropping down earlier to the vessel, was one of the things that surprised the captain. However, they got up quickly, and as at that hour there was not much on the river to impede their progress, and as at that time the Thames was not a thoroughfare for little stinking steamboats, they soon reached the ancient Temple-stairs.

The dog, who had until then seemed to be asleep, suddenly sprung up, and seizing the hat again in his mouth, rushed again on shore, and was closely followed by the captain and colonel.

He led them through the Temple with great rapidity, pursuing with admirable tact the precise path his master had taken towards the entrance to the Temple in Fleet-street, opposite Chancery-lane. Darting across the road then, he stopped with a low growl at the shop of Sweeney Todd—a proceeding which very much surprised those who followed him, and caused them to pause to hold a consultation ere they proceeded further. While this was proceeding Todd suddenly opened the door, and aimed a blow at the dog with an iron bar, but the latter dexterously avoided it, and, but that the door was suddenly closed again, he would have made Sweeney Todd regret such an interference.

"We must enquire into this," said the captain; "there seems to be mutual ill-will between that man and the dog."

They both tried to enter the barber's shop, but it was fast on the inside; and after repeated knockings, Todd called from within, saying,—

"I won't open the door while that dog is there. He is mad, or has a spite against me—I don't know nor care which—it's a fact, that's all I am aware of."

"I will undertake," said the captain, "that the dog shall do you no harm; but open the door, for in we must come, and will."

"I will take your promise," said Sweeney Todd; "but mind you keep it, or I shall protect myself and take the creature's life; so, if you value it, you had better hold it fast."

The captain pacified Hector as well as he could, and likewise tied one end of a silk handkerchief round his neck, and held the other firmly in his grasp; after which Todd, who seemed to have some means from within of seeing what was going on, opened his door and admitted his visitors.

"Well, gentlemen, shaved, or cut, or dressed, I am at your service; which shall I begin with?"

The dog never took his eye off Todd, but kept up a low growl from the first moment of his entrance.

"It's rather a remarkable circumstance," said the captain, "but this is a very saga-cious dog, you see, and he belongs to a friend of ours, who has most unaccountably disappeared."

"Has he, really?" said Todd. "Tobias! Tobias!"

"Yes, sir."

"Run to Mr. Phillips's, in Cateaton-street, and get me six-penny-worth of pre-served figs, and don't say that I don't give you the money this time when you go on a message. I think I did before, but you swallowed it; and when you come back, just please remember the insight into business I gave you yesterday."

"Yes," said the boy, with a shudder, for he had a great horror of Sweeney Todd, as well he might, after the severe discipline he had received at his hands, and away he went.

"Well, gentlemen," said Todd, "what is it you require of me?"

"We want to know if anyone having the appearance of an officer in the navy came to your house?"

"Yes—a rather good-looking man, weatherbeaten, with a bright blue eye, and rather fair hair."

"Yes, yes! the same."

"Oh! to be sure, he came here, and I shaved him and polished him off."

"What do you mean by polishing him off?"

"Brushing him up a bit, and making him tidy: he said he had got somewhere to go in the city, and asked me the address of a Mr. Oakley, a spectacle-maker. I gave it him, and then he went away; but as I was standing at my door about five minutes afterwards, it seemed to me, as well as I could see the distance, that he got into some row near the market."

"Did this dog come with him?"

"A dog came with him, but whether it was that dog or not I don't know."

"And that's all you know of him?"

"You never spoke a truer word in your life," said Sweeney Todd, as he diligently stropped a razor upon his great, horny hand.

This seemed something like a complete fix; and the captain looked at Colonel Jeffery, and the colonel at the captain, for some moments, in complete silence. At length the latter said,—

"It's a very extraordinary thing that the dog should come here if he missed his master somewhere else. I never heard of such a thing."

"Nor I either," said Todd. "It is extraordinary; so extraordinary that, if I had not seen it, I would not have believed. I dare say you will find him in the next watch-house."

The dog had watched the countenance of all parties during this brief dialogue, and twice or thrice he had interrupted it by a strange howling cry.

"I'll tell you what it is," said the barber; "if that beast stays here, I'll be the death of him. I hate dogs—detest them; and I tell you, as I told you before, if you value him at all keep him away from me.

"You say you directed the person you describe to us where to find a spectacle-maker named Oakley. We happen to know that he was going in search of such a person, and, as he had property of value about him, we will go there and ascertain if he reached his destination."

"It is in Fore-street—a little shop with two windows; you cannot miss it."

The dog, when he saw they were about to leave, grew furious; and it was with the greatest difficulty they succeeded, by main force, in getting him out of the shop, and dragging him some short distance with them, but then he contrived to get free of the handkerchief that held him, and darting back, he sat down at Sweeney Todd's door, howling most piteously.

They had no resource but to leave him, intending fully to call as they came back from Mr. Oakley's; and, as they looked behind them, they saw that Hector was collecting a crowd round the barber's door, and it was a singular thing to see a number of persons surrounding the dog, while he, to all appearance, appeared to be actually making efforts to explain something to the assemblage. They walked on until they reached the spectacle-maker's, and there they paused; for they all of a sudden recollected that the mission that Mr. Thornhill had had to execute there was of a very delicate nature, and one by no means to be lightly executed, or even so much as mentioned, probably, in the hearing of Mr. Oakley himself.

"We must not be so hasty," said the colonel.

"But what am I to do? I sail tonight; at least I have got to go round to Liverpool with my vessel."

"Do not then call at Mr. Oakley's at all at present; but leave me to ascertain the fact quietly and secretly."

"My anxiety for Thornhill will scarcely permit me to do so; but I suppose I must, and if you write me a letter to the Royal Oak Hotel, at Liverpool, it will be sure to reach me, that is to say, unless you find Mr. Thornhill himself, in which case I need not by any means give you so much trouble."

"You may depend upon me. My friendship for Mr. Thornhill, and gratitude, as you know, for the great service he has rendered to us all, will induce me to do my utmost to discover him; and, but that I know he set his heart upon performing the message he had to deliver accurately and well, I should recommend that we at once go into this house of Mr. Oakley's, only that the fear of compromising the young lady—who is in the case, and who will have quite enough to bear, poor thing! of her own grief—restrains me."

After some more conversation of a similar nature, they decided that this should be the plan adopted. They made an unavailing call at the watch-house of the district, being informed there that no such person, nor anyone answering the description of Mr. Thornhill had been engaged in any disturbance, or apprehended by any of the constables; and this only involved the thing in greater mystery than ever, so they went back to try and recover the dog, but that was a matter easier to be desired and determined upon than executed, for threats and persuasions were alike ineffectual.

Hector would not stir an inch from the barber's door. There he sat, with the hat by his side, a most melancholy and strange-looking spectacle, and a most efficient guard was he for that hat, and it was evident, that while he chose to exhibit the formidable row of teeth he did occasionally, when anybody showed a disposition to touch it, it would remain sacred. Some people, too, had thrown a few copper coins into the hat, so that Hector, if his mind had been that way inclined, was making a very good thing of it; but who shall describe the anger of Sweeney Todd, when he found that he was likely to be so beleaguered?

He doubted, if, upon the arrival of the first customer to his shop, the dog might dart in and take him by storm; but that apprehension went off at last, when a young gallant came from the Temple to have his hair dressed, and the dog allowed him to pass in and out unmolested, without making any attempt to follow him. This was something, at all events; but whether or not it insured Sweeney Todd's personal safety, when he should himself come out, was quite another matter.

It was an experiment, however, which he must try. It was quite out of the question that he should remain a prisoner much longer in his own place, so, after a time, he thought he might try the experiment, and that it would be best done when there were plenty of people there, because, if the dog assaulted him, he would have an excuse for any amount of violence he might think proper to use upon the occasion.

It took some time, however, to screw his courage to the sticking-place; but, at length, muttering deep curses between his clenched teeth, he made his way to the door, and carried in his hand a long knife, which he thought a more efficient weapon against the dog's teeth than the iron bludgeon he had formerly used.

"I hope he will attack me," said Todd to himself, as he thought; but Tobias, who had come back from the place where they sold the preserved figs, heard him, and after devoutly in his own mind wishing that the dog would actually devour Sweeney, said aloud,—

"Oh dear, sir; you don't wish that, I'm sure!"

"Who told you what I wished, or what I did not? Remember, Tobias, and keep your own counsel, or it will be the worse for you, and your mother too—remember that."

The boy shrunk back. How had Sweeney Todd terrified the boy about his mother! He must have done so, or Tobias would never have shrunk as he did.

Then that rascally barber, whom we begin to suspect of more crimes than fall ordinarily to the share of man, went cautiously out of his shop-door: we cannot pretend to account for why it was so, but, as faithful recorders of facts, we have to state that Hector did not fly at him, but with a melancholy and subdued expression of countenance he looked up in the face of Sweeney Todd; then he whined piteously, as if he would have said, "Give me my master, and I will forgive you all that you have done; give me back my beloved master, and you shall see that I am neither revengeful nor ferocious."

This kind of expression was as legibly written in the poor creature's countenance as if he had actually been endowed with speech, and uttered the words themselves.

This was what Sweeney Todd certainly did not expect, and, to tell the truth, it staggered and astonished him a little. He would have been glad of an excuse to commit some act of violence, but he had now none, and as he looked in the faces of the people who were around, he felt quite convinced that it would not be the most prudent thing in the world to interfere with the dog in any way that savoured of violence.

"Where's the dog's master?" said one.

"Ah, where indeed?" said Todd; "I should not wonder if he had come to some foul end!"

"But I say, old soap-suds," cried a boy; "the dog says you did it."

There was a general laugh, but the barber was no means disconcerted, and he shortly replied,—

"Does he? he is wrong then."

Sweeney Todd had no desire to enter into anything like a controversy with the people, so he turned again and entered his own shop, in a distant corner of which he sat down, and folding his great gaunt-looking arms over his chest, he gave himself up to thought, and, if we might judge from the expression of his countenance, those thoughts were of a pleasant anticipatory character, for now and then he gave such a grim sort of smile as might well have sat upon the features of some ogre.

And now we will turn to another scene, of a widely different character.

CHAPTER IV

HARK! TWELVE O'CLOCK AT MIDDAY IS CHEERILY PROCLAIMED BY ST. DUNSTAN'S church, and scarcely have the sounds done echoing throughout the neighbourhood, and scarcely has the clock of Lincoln's-inn done chiming in with its announcement of the same hour, when Bell-yard, Temple-bar, becomes a scene of commotion.

What a scampering of feet is there, what a laughing and talking, what a jostling to be first; and what an immense number of manoeuvres are resorted to by some of the throng to distance others!

And mostly from Lincoln's-inn do these persons, young and old, but most certainly a majority of the former, come bustling and striving, although from the neighbouring legal establishments likewise there come not a few; the Temple contributes its numbers, and from the more distant Gray's-inn there come a goodly lot.

Now Bell-yard is almost choked up, and a stranger would wonder what could be the matter, and most probably stand in some doorway until the commotion was over.

Is it a fire? is it a fight? or anything else sufficiently alarming and extraordinary to excite the junior members of the legal profession to such a species of madness? No, it is none of these, nor is there a fat cause to be run for, which, in the hands of some clever practitioner, might become quite a vested interest. No, the enjoyment is purely one of a physical character, and all the pacing and racing—all this turmoil and trouble—all this pushing, jostling, laughing, and shouting, is to see who will get first to Lovett's pie-shop.

Yes, on the left-hand side of Bell-yard, going down from Carey-street, was, at the time we write of, one of the most celebrated shops for the sale of veal and pork pies that London ever produced. High and low, rich and poor, resorted to it; its fame had spread far and wide; and it was because the first batch of those pies came up at twelve o'clock that there was such a rush of the legal profession to obtain them.

Their fame had spread even to great distances, and many persons carried them to the suburbs of the city as quite a treat to friends and relations there residing. And well did they deserve their reputation, those delicious pies; there was about them a flavour never surpassed, and rarely equalled; the paste was of the most delicate construction, and impregnated with the aroma of a delicious gravy that defies description. Then the small portions of meat which they contained were so tender, and the fat and the lean so artistically mixed up, that to eat one of Lovett's pies was such a provocative to eat another, that many persons who came to lunch stayed to dine, wasting more than an hour, perhaps, of precious time, and endangering—who knows to the contrary?—the success of some law-suit thereby.

The counter in Lovett's pie-shop was in the shape of a horseshoe, and it was the custom of the young bloods from the Temple and Lincoln's-inn to sit in a row upon its edge while they partook of the delicious pies, and chatted gaily about one concern and another.

Many an appointment was made at Lovett's pie-shop, and many a piece of gossiping scandal was there first circulated. The din of tongues was prodigious. The ringing laugh of the boy who looked upon the quarter of an hour he spent at Lovett's as the brightest of the whole twenty-four, mingled gaily with the more boisterous mirth of his seniors; and oh! with what rapidity the pies disappeared!

They were brought up on large trays, each of which contained about a hundred, and from these trays they were so speedily transferred to the mouths of Mrs. Lovett's customers that it looked like a work of magic.

And now we have let out some portion of the secret. There was a Mistress Lovett; but possibly our readers guessed as much, for what but a female hand, and that female buxom, young and good-looking, could have ventured upon the production of those pies. Yes, Mrs. Lovett was all that; and every enamoured young scion of the law, as he devoured his pie, pleased himself with the idea that the charming Mrs. Lovett had made that pie especially for him, and that fate or predestination had placed it in his hands.

And it was astonishing to see with what impartiality and with tact the fair pastry-cook bestowed her smiles upon her admirers, so that none could say he was neglected, while it was extremely difficult for anyone to say he was preferred.

This was pleasant, but at the same time it was provoking to all except Mrs. Lovett, in whose favour it got up a sort of excitement that paid extraordinarily well, because some of the young fellows thought, and thought it with wisdom too, that he who consumed the most pies would be in the most likely way to receive the greatest number of smiles from the lady.

Acting upon this supposition, some of her more enthusiastic admirers went on consuming the pies until they were almost ready to burst. But there were others again, of a more philosophic turn of mind, who went for the pies only, and did not care one jot for Mrs. Lovett.

These declared that her smile was cold and uncomfortable—that it was upon her lips, but had no place in her heart—that it was the set smile of a ballet-dancer, which is about one of the most unmirthful things in existence.

Then there were some who went even beyond this, and, while they admitted the excellence of the pies, and went every day to partake of them, swore that Mrs. Lovett had quite a sinister aspect, and that they could see what a merely superficial affair her blandishments were, and that there was

a lurking devil in her eye

that, if once roused, would be capable of achieving some serious things, and might not be so easily quelled again.

By five minutes past twelve Mrs. Lovett's counter was full, and the savoury steam of the hot pies went out in fragrant clouds into Bell-yard, being sniffed up by many a poor wretch passing by who lacked the means of making one in the throng that were devouring the dainty morsels within.

"Why, Tobias Ragg," said a young man, with his mouth full of pie, "where have you been since you left Mr. Snow's in Paper-buildings? I have not seen you for some days."

"No," said Tobias, "I have gone into another line: instead of being a lawyer, and helping to shave the clients, I am going to shave the lawyers now. A twopenny pork, if you please, Mrs. Lovett. Ah! who would be an emperor, if he couldn't get pies like these—eh, Master Clift?"

"Well, they are good; of course we know that, Tobias; but do you mean to say you are going to be a barber?"

"Yes, I am with Sweeney Todd, the barber of Fleet-street, close to St. Dunstan's."

"The deuce you are! well, I am going to a party to-night, and I'll drop in and get dressed and shaved, and patronise your master."

Tobias put his mouth close to the ear of the young lawyer, and in a fearful sort of whisper said the one word—"Don't."

"Don't? what for?"

Tobias made no answer; and throwing down his two-pence, scampered out of the shop as fast as he could. He had only been sent a message by Sweeney Todd in the neighbourhood; but, as he heard the clock strike twelve, and two penny-pieces were lying at the bottom of his pocket, it was not in human nature to resist running into Lovett's and converting them into a pork pie.

"What an odd thing!" thought the young lawyer. "I'll just drop in at Sweeney Todd's now on purpose, and ask Tobias what he means. I quite forgot, too, while he was here, to ask him what all that riot was about a dog at Todd's door."

"A veal!" said a young man, rushing in; "a two-penny veal, Mrs. Lovett." When he got it he consumed it with voracity, and then, noticing an acquaintance in the shop, he whispered to him,—

"I can't stand it any more. I have cut the spectacle-maker—Johanna is faithless, and I know not what to do."

"Have another pie."

"But what's a pie to Johanna Oakley? You know, Dilki, that I only went there to be near the charmer. Damn the shutters and curse the spectacles! She loves another and I am a desperate individual! I should like to do some horrible and desperate act. Oh, Johanna, Johanna! you have driven me to the verge of what do you call it—I'll take another veal, if you please, Mrs. Lovett."

"Well, I was wondering how you got on," said his friend Dilki, "and thinking of calling upon you."

"Oh! it was all right—it was all right at first: she smiled upon me."

"You are quite sure she didn't laugh at you?"

"Sir! Mr. Dilki!"

"I say, are you sure that instead of smiling upon you she was not laughing at you?"

"Am I sure? Do you wish to insult me, Mr. Dilki? I look upon you as a puppy, sir—a horrid puppy."

"Very good; now I am convinced that the girl has been having a bit of fun at your expense.—Are you not aware, Sam, that your nose turns up so much that it's enough to pitch you head over heels? How do you suppose that any girl under forty-five would waste a word upon you? Mind, I don't say this to offend you in any way, but just quietly, by way of asking a question."

Sam looked daggers, and probably he might have attempted some desperate act in the pie-shop, if at the moment he had not caught the eye of Mrs. Lovett, and he saw by the expression on that lady's face that anything in the shape of a riot would be speedily suppressed, so he darted out of the place at once to carry his sorrows and his bitterness elsewhere.

It was only between twelve and one o'clock that such a tremendous rush and influx of visitors came to the pie-shop, for, although there was a good custom the whole day, and the concern was a money-making one from morning till night, it was at that hour principally that the great consumption of pies took place.

Tobias knew from experience that Sweeney Todd was a skilful calculator of the time it ought to take to go to different places, and accordingly, since he had occupied some portion of that most valuable of all commodities at Mrs. Lovett's, he arrived quite breathless at his master's shop.

There sat the mysterious dog with the hat, and Tobias lingered for a moment to speak to the animal. Dogs are great physiognomists; and as the creature looked into Tobias's face he seemed to draw a favourable conclusion regarding him, for he submitted to a caress.

"Poor fellow!" said Tobias. "I wish I knew what had become of your master, but it made me shake like a leaf to wake up last night and ask myself the question. You shan't starve, though, if I can help it. I haven't much for myself, but you shall have some of it."

As he spoke, Tobias took from his pocket some not very tempting cold meat, which was intended for his own dinner, and which he had wrapped up in not the cleanest of cloths. He gave a piece to the dog, who took it with a dejected air, and then crouched down at Sweeney Todd's door again.

Just then, as Tobias was about to enter the shop, he thought he heard from within a strange shrieking sort of sound. On the impulse of the moment he recoiled a step or two, and then, from some other impulse, he dashed forward at once, and entered the shop.

The first object that presented itself to his attention, lying upon a side table, was a hat with a handsome gold-headed walking-cane lying across it.

The armchair in which customers usually sat to be shaved, was vacant, and Sweeney Todd's face was just projected into the shop from the back parlour, and wearing a most singular and hideous expression.

"Well, Tobias," he said, as he advanced, rubbing his great hands together, "well, Tobias! so you could not resist the pie-shop?"

"How does he know?" thought Tobias. "Yes, sir, I have been to the pie-shop, but I didn't stay a minute."

"Hark ye, Tobias! the only thing I can excuse in the way of delay upon an errand is for you to get one of Mrs. Lovett's pies: that I can look over, so think no more about it. Are they not delicious, Tobias?"

"Yes, sir, they are; but some gentleman seems to have left his hat and stick."

"Yes," said Sweeney Todd, "he has"; and lifting the stick he struck Tobias a blow with it that felled him to the ground. "Lesson the second to Tobias Ragg, which teaches him to make no remarks about what does not concern him. You may think what you like, Tobias Ragg, but you shall say only what I like."

"I won't endure it," cried the boy; "I won't be knocked about in this way, I tell you, Sweeney Todd, I won't."

"You won't! have you forgotten your mother?"

"You say you have a power over my mother; but I don't know what it is, and I cannot and will not believe it; I'll leave you, and, come of it what may, I'll go to sea or anywhere rather than stay in such a place as this."

"Oh, you will, will you? then, Tobias, you and I must come to some explanation. I'll tell you what power I have over your mother, and then perhaps you will be satisfied. Last winter, when the frost had continued eighteen weeks, and you and your mother were starving, she was employed to clean out the chambers of a Mr. King, in the Temple, a cold-hearted, severe man, who never forgave anything in all his life and never will."

"I remember," said Tobias: "we were starving and owed a whole guinea for rent; but mother borrowed it and paid it, and after that got a situation where she now is."

"Ah, you think so. The rent was paid; but, Tobias, my boy, a word in your ear— she took a silver candlestick from Mr. King's chambers to pay it. I know it. I can prove it. Think of that, Tobias, and be discreet."

"Have mercy upon us," said the boy: "they would take her life!"

"Her life!" screamed Sweeney Todd; "ay, to be sure they would: they would hang her—hang her, I say; and now mind, if you force me, by any conduct of your own, to mention this thing, you are your mother's executioner. I had better go and be deputy hangman at once, and turn her off."

"Horrible! horrible!"

"Oh, you don't like that? indeed, that don't suit you, Master Tobias? Be discreet then, and you have nothing to fear. Do not force me to show a power which will be as complete as it is terrible."

"I will say nothing—I will think nothing."

"'Tis well; now go and put that hat and stick in yonder cupboard. I shall be absent for a short time; and if anyone comes, tell them I am called out, and shall not return for an hour or perhaps longer, and mind you take good care of the shop."

Sweeney Todd took off his apron, and put on an immense coat with huge lapels, and then, clapping a three-cornered hat on his head, and casting a strange withering kind of look at Tobias, he sallied forth into the street.

CHAPTER V

Alas! Poor Johanna Oakley—thy day has passed away and brought with it no tidings of him you love; and oh! what a weary day, full of fearful doubts and anxieties, has it been!

Tortured by doubts, hopes, and fears, that day was one of the most wretched that poor Johanna had ever passed. Not even two years before, when she had parted with her lover, had she felt such an exquisite pang of anguish as now filled her heart, when she saw the day gliding away and the evening creeping on apace, without word or token from Mark Ingestrie.

She did not herself know, until all the agony of disappointment had come across her, how much she had counted upon hearing something from him on that occasion; and when the evening deepened into night, and hope grew so slender that she could no longer rely upon it for the least support, she was compelled to proceed to her own chamber, and, feigning indisposition to avoid her mother's questions—for Mrs. Oakley was at home, and making herself and everybody else as uncomfortable as possible—she flung herself on her humble couch and gave way to a perfect passion of tears.

"Oh, Mark, Mark!" she said, "why do you thus desert me, when I have relied so abundantly upon your true affection? Oh, why have you not sent me some token of your existence, and of your continued love? the merest, slightest word would have been sufficient, and I should have been happy."

She wept then such bitter tears as only such a heart as hers can know, when it feels the deep and bitter anguish of desertion, and when the rock upon which it supposed it had built its fondest hopes resolves itself to a mere quicksand, in which becomes engulfed all of good that this world can afford to the just and the beautiful.

Oh, it is heartrending to think that such a one as she, Johanna Oakley, a being so full of all those holy and gentle emotions which should constitute the truest felicity, should thus feel that life to her had lost its greatest charms, and that nothing but despair remained.

"I will wait until midnight," she said; "and even then it will be a mockery to seek repose, and tomorrow I must myself make some exertion to discover some tidings of him."

Then she began to ask herself what that exertion could be, and in what manner a young and inexperienced girl, such as she was, could hope to succeed in her enquiries. And the midnight hour came at last, telling her that, giving the utmost latitude to the word day, it had gone at last, and she was left despairing.

She lay the whole of that night sobbing, and only at times dropping into an unquiet slumber, during which painful images were presented to her, all, however, having the same tendency, and pointing towards the presumed fact that Mark Ingestrie was no more.

But the weariest night to the weariest waker will pass away, and at length the soft and beautiful dawn stole into the chamber of Johanna Oakley, chasing away some of the more horrible visions of the night, but having little effect in subduing the sadness that had taken possession of her.

She felt that it would be better for her to make her appearance below than to hazard the remarks and conjectures that her not doing so would give rise to, so, all unfitted as she was to engage in the most ordinary intercourse, she crept down to the breakfast-parlour, looking more like the ghost of her former self than the bright and beautiful being we have represented her to the reader.

Her father understood what it was that robbed her cheek of its bloom: and although he saw it with much distress, yet he had fortified himself with what he considered were some substantial reasons for future hopefulness.

It had become part of his philosophy—it generally is a part of the philosophy of the old—to consider that those sensations of the mind that arise from disappointed affections are of the most evanescent character; and that, although for a time they exhibit themselves with violence, they, like grief for the dead, soon pass away, scarcely leaving a trace behind of their former existence.

And perhaps he was right as regards the greatest number of those passions; but he was certainly wrong when he applied that sort of worldly-wise knowledge to his daughter Johanna. She was one of those rare beings whose hearts are not won by every gaudy flatterer who may buzz the accents of admiration in their ears. No; she was qualified, eminently qualified, to love once, but only once; and, like the passion-flower, that blooms into abundant beauty once and never afterwards puts forth a blossom, she allowed her heart to expand to the soft influence of affection, which, when crushed by adversity, was gone forever.

"Really, Johanna," said Mrs. Oakley, in the true conventicle twang, "you look so pale and ill that I must positively speak to Mr. Lupin about you."

"Mr. Lupin, my dear," said the spectacle-maker, "may be all very well in his way as a parson; but I don't see what he can do with Johanna looking pale."

"A pious man, Mr. Oakley, has to do with everything and everybody."

"Then he must be the most intolerable bore in existence; and I don't wonder at his being kicked out of some people's houses, as I have heard Mr. Lupin has been."

"And if he has, Mr. Oakley, I can tell you he glories in it. Mr. Lupin likes to suffer for the faith; and if he were to be made a martyr to-morrow, I am quite certain it would give him a deal of pleasure."

"My dear, I am quite sure it would not give him half the pleasure it would me."

"I understand your insinuation, Mr. Oakley; you would like to have him murdered on account of his holiness; but, though you say these kind of things at your own breakfast-table, you won't say as much when he comes to tea this afternoon."

"To tea, Mrs. Oakley! haven't I told you over and over again that I will not have that man in my house!"

"And haven't I told you, Mr. Oakley, twice that number of times that he shall come to tea? and I have asked him now, and it can't be altered."

"But, Mrs. Oakley—"

"It's of no use, Mr. Oakley, your talking. Mr. Lupin is coming to tea, and come he shall; and if you don't like it, you can go out. There now, I am sure you can't complain, now you have actually the liberty of going out; but you are like the dog in the manger, Mr. Oakley, I know that well enough, and nothing will please you."

"A fine liberty, indeed, the liberty of going out of my own house to let somebody else into it that I don't like!"

"Johanna, my dear," said Mrs. Oakley, "I think my old complaint is coming on, the beating of the heart, and the hysterics. I know what produces it—it's your father's brutality; and just because Dr. Fungus said over and over again that I was to be kept perfectly quiet, your father seizes upon the opportunity like a wild beast, or a raving maniac, to try and make me ill."

Mr. Oakley jumped up, stamped his feet upon the floor, and, uttering something about the probability of his becoming a maniac in a very short time, rushed into his shop, and set to polishing spectacles as if he were doing it for a wager.

This little affair between her father and her mother certainly had had the effect, for a time, of diverting attention from Johanna, and she was able to assume a cheerfulness she did not feel; but she had something of her father's spirit in her as regards Mr. Lupin, and most decidedly objected to sitting down to any meal whatever with that individual, so that Mrs. Oakley was left in a minority of one upon the occasion, which, perhaps, as she fully expected, was no great matter after all.

Johanna went upstairs to her own room, which commanded a view of the street. It was an old-fashioned house, with a balcony in front, and as she looked listlessly out into Fore-street, which was far then from being the thoroughfare it is now, she saw standing in a doorway on the opposite side of the way a stranger, who was looking intently at the house, and who, when he caught her eye, walked instantly across to it, and cast something into the balcony of the first floor. Then he touched his cap, and walked rapidly from the street.

The thought immediately occurred to Johanna that this might possibly be some messenger from him concerning whose existence and welfare she was so deeply anxious. It is not to be wondered at, therefore, that with the name of Mark Ingestrie upon her lips she should rush down to the balcony in intense anxiety to hear and see if such was really the case.

When she reached the balcony she found lying in it a scrap of paper, in which a stone was wrapped up, in order to give it weight, so that it might be cast with certainty into the balcony. With trembling eagerness she opened the paper, and read upon it the following words: —

"For news of Mark Ingestrie, come to the Temple-gardens one hour before sunset, and do not fear addressing a man who will be holding a white rose in his hand."

"He lives! he lives!" she cried. "He lives, and joy again becomes the inhabitant of my bosom! Oh, it is daylight now and sunshine compared to the black midnight of despair. Mark Ingestrie lives, and I shall be happy yet."

She placed the little scrap of paper in her bosom, and then, with clasped hands and a delighted expression of countenance, she repeated the brief but expressive words it contained, adding,

"Yes, yes, I will be there; the white rose is an emblem of his purity and affection, his spotless love, and that is why his messenger carries it. I will be there. One hour before sunset, ay two hours before sunset, I will be there. Joy, joy! he lives, he lives! Mark Ingestrie lives! Perchance, too, successful in his object, he returns to tell me that he can make me his, and that no obstacle can now interfere to frustrate our union. Time, time, float onwards on your fleetest pinions!"

She went to her own apartment, but it was not, as she had last gone to it, to weep; on the contrary, it was to smile at her former fears, and to admit the philosophy of the assertion that we suffer much more from a dread of those things that never happen than we do for actual calamities which occur in their full force to us.

"Oh, that this messenger," she said, "had come but yesterday! what hours of anguish I should have been spared! But I will not complain; it shall not be said that I repine at present joy because it did not come before. I will be happy when I can; and, in the consciousness that I shall soon hear blissful tidings of Mark Ingestrie, I will banish every fear."

The impatience which she now felt brought its pains and its penalties with it, and yet it was quite a different description of feeling to any she had formerly endured, and certainly far more desirable than the absolute anguish that had taken possession of her upon hearing nothing of Mark Ingestrie.

It was strange, very strange, that the thought never crossed her mind that the tidings she had to hear in the Temple-gardens from the stranger might be evil ones, but certainly such a thought did not occur to her, and she looked forward to a meeting which she certainly had no evidence to know might not be of the most disastrous character.

She asked herself over and over again if she should tell her father what had occurred, but as often as she thought of doing so she shrank from carrying out the mental suggestion, and all the natural disposition again to keep to herself the secret of her happiness returned to her with full force.

But yet she was not so unjust as not to feel that it was treating her father but slightingly to throw all her sorrows into his lap, as it were, and then to keep from him everything of joy appertaining to the same circumstances.

This was a thing that she was not likely to continue doing, and so she made up her mind to relieve her conscience from the pang it would otherwise have had, by determining to tell him, after the interview in the Temple-gardens, what was its result; but she could not make up her mind to do so beforehand; it was so pleasant and so delicious to keep the secret all to herself, and to feel that she alone knew that her lover had so closely kept faith with her as to be only one day behind his time in sending to her, and that day, perhaps, far from being his fault.

And so she reasoned to herself and tried to wile away the anxious hours, sometimes succeeding in forgetting how long it was still to sunset, and at others feeling as if each minute was perversely swelling itself out into ten times its usual proportion of time in order to become wearisome to her.

She had said she would be at the Temple-gardens two hours before sunset instead of one, and she kept her word, for, looking happier than she had done for weeks, she tripped down the stairs of her father's house, and was about to leave it by the private staircase when a strange gaunt-looking figure attracted her attention.

This was no other than the Rev. Mr. Lupin: he was a long strange-looking man, and upon this occasion he came upon what he called horseback, that is to say, he was mounted upon a very small pony, which seemed quite unequal to support his weight, and was so short that, if the reverend gentleman had not poked his legs out at an angle, they must inevitably have touched the ground.

"Praise the Lord!" he said: "I have intercepted the evil one. Maiden, I have come here at thy mother's bidding, and thou shalt remain and partake of the mixture called tea."

Johanna scarcely condescended to glance at him; but, drawing her mantle close around her, which he actually had the impertinence to endeavour to lay hold of, she walked on, so that the reverend gentleman was left to make the best he could of the matter.

"Stop!" he cried, "stop! I can well perceive that the devil has a strong hold of you: I can well perceive—the Lord have mercy upon me! this animal hath some design against me as sure as fate."

This last ejaculation arose from the fact that the pony had flung up his heels behind in a most mysterious manner.

"I'm afraid, sir," said a lad who was no other than our old acquaintance, Sam, "I am afraid, sir, that there is something the matter with the pony."

Up went the pony's heels again in the same unaccustomed manner.

"God bless me!" said the reverend gentleman; "he never did such a thing before. I—there he goes again—murder! Young man, I pray you help me to get down; I think I know you; you are the nephew of the godly Mrs. Pump—truly this animal wishes to be the death of me!"

At this moment the pony gave such a vigorous kick up behind that Mr. Lupin was fairly pitched upon his head, and made a complete somersault, alighting with his heels in the spectacle-maker's passage; and it unfortunately happened that Mrs. Oakley at that moment, hearing the altercation, came rushing out, and the first thing she did was to fall sprawling over Mr. Lupin's feet.

Sam now felt it time to go; and as we dislike useless mysteries, we may as well explain that these extraordinary circumstances arose from the fact that Sam had bought himself from the haberdasher's opposite a halfpenny-worth of pins, and had amused himself by making a pincushion of the hind quarters of the Reverend Lupin's pony, which, not being accustomed to that sort of thing, had kicked out vigorously in opposition to the same, and produced the results we have recorded.

Johanna Oakley was some distance upon her road before the reverend gentleman was pitched into her father's house in the manner we have described, so that she knew nothing of it, nor would she have cared if she had, for her mind was wholly bent upon the expedition she was proceeding on.

As she walked upon that side of the way of Fleet-street where Sweeney Todd's house and shop were situated, a feeling of curiosity prompted her to stop for a moment and look at the melancholy-looking dog that stood watching a hat at his door.

The appearance of grief upon the creature's face could not be mistaken, and, as she gazed, she saw the shop-door gently opened and a piece of meat thrown out.

"Those are kind people," she said, "be they who they may"; but when she saw the dog turn away from the meat with loathing, and herself observed that there was a white powder upon it, the idea that it was poisoned, and only intended for the poor creature's destruction, came instantly across her mind.

And when she saw the horrible-looking face of Sweeney Todd glaring at her from the partially-opened door, she could not doubt any further the fact, for that face was quite enough to give a warrant for any amount of villainy whatever.

She passed on with a shudder, little suspecting, however, that that dog had anything to do with her fate, or the circumstances which made up the sum of her destiny.

It wanted a full hour to the appointed time of meeting when she reached the Temple-gardens, and, partly blaming herself that she was so soon, while at the same time she would not for worlds have been away, she sat down on one of the garden-seats to think over the past, and to recall to her memory, with all the vivid freshness of young Love's devotion, the many gentle words which, from time to time, had been spoken to her two summers since by him whose faith she had never doubted, and whose image was enshrined at the bottom of her heart.

CHAPTER VI

THE TEMPLE CLOCK STRUCK THE HOUR OF MEETING, AND JOHANNA LOOKED ANXIOUSLY around her for anyone who should seem to bear the appearance of being such a person as she might suppose Mark Ingestrie would choose for his messenger.

She turned her eyes towards the gate, for she thought she heard it close, and then she saw a gentlemanly-looking man, attired in a cloak, and who was looking about him, apparently in search of someone.

When his eye fell upon her he immediately produced from beneath his cloak a white rose, and in another minute they met.

"I have the honour," he said, "of speaking to Miss Johanna Oakley?"

"Yes, sir; and you are Mark Ingestrie's messenger?"

"I am; that is to say, I am he who comes to bring you news of Mark Ingestrie, although I grieve to say I am not the messenger that was expressly deputed by him to do so."

"Oh! sir, your looks are sad and serious; you seem as if you would announce that some misfortune had occurred. Tell me that it is not so; speak to me at once, or my heart will break!"

"Compose yourself, lady, I pray you."

"I cannot—dare not do so, unless you tell me he lives. Tell me that Mark Ingestrie lives, and then I shall be all patience: tell me that, and you shall not hear a murmur from me. Speak the word at once—at once! It is cruel, believe me, to keep me in this suspense."

"This is one of the saddest errands I ever came upon," said the stranger, as he led Johanna to a seat. "Recollect, lady, what creatures of accident and chance we are— recollect how the slightest circumstances will affect us, in driving us to the confines of despair, and remember by how frail a tenure the best of us hold existence."

"No more—no more!" shrieked Johanna, as she clasped her hands—"I know all now and am desolate."

She let her face drop upon her hands, and shook as with a convulsion of grief.

"Mark! Mark!" she cried, "you have gone from me! I thought not this—I thought not this. Oh, Heaven why have I lived so long as to have the capacity to listen to such fearful tidings? Lost—lost—all lost! God of Heaven! what a wilderness the world is now to me!"

"Let me pray you, lady, to subdue this passion of grief, and listen truly to what I shall unfold to you. There is much to hear and much to speculate upon; and if, from all that I have learnt, I cannot, dare not tell you that Mark Ingestrie lives, I likewise shrink from telling you he is no more."

"Speak again—say those words again! There is a hope, then—oh, there is a hope!"

"There is a hope; and better it is that your mind should receive the first shock of the probability of the death of him whom you have so anxiously expected and then afterwards, from what I shall relate to you, gather hope that it may not be so, than that from the first you should expect too much, and then have those expectations rudely destroyed."

"It is so—it is so; this is kind of you, and if I cannot thank you as I ought, you will know that it is because I am in a state of too great affliction so to do, and not from want of will; you will understand that—I am sure you will understand that."

"Make no excuses to me. Believe me. I can fully appreciate all that you would say, and all that you must feel. I ought to tell you who I am, that you may have confidence in what I have to relate to you. My name is Jeffery, and I am a colonel in the Indian army."

"I am much beholden to you, sir; but you bring with you a passport to my confidence, in the name of Mark Ingestrie, which is at once sufficient. I live again in the hope that you have given me of his continued existence, and in that hope I will maintain a cheerful resignation that shall enable me to bear up against all you have to tell me, be that what it may, and with a feeling that through much suffering there may come joy at last. You shall find me very patient, ay, extremely patient—so patient that you shall scarcely see the havoc that grief has already made here."

She pressed her hands on her breast as she spoke, and looked in his face with such an expression of tearful melancholy that it was quite heart-rending to witness it; and he, although not used to the melting-mood, was compelled to pause for a few moments ere he could proceed in the task which he had set himself.

"I will be as brief," he said, "as possible, consistent with stating all that is requisite for me to state, and I must commence by asking you if you are aware under what circumstances Mark Ingestrie went abroad?"

"I am aware of so much: that a quarrel with his uncle, Mr. Grant, was the great cause, and that his main endeavour was to better his fortunes, so that we might be happy and independent of those who looked not with an eye of favour on our projected union."

"Yes; but what I meant was, were you aware of the sort of adventure he embarked in to the Indian seas?"

"No, I know nothing further; we met here on this spot, we parted at yonder gate, and we have never met again."

"Then I have something to tell you, in order to make the narrative clear and explicit."

"I shall listen to you with an attention so profound that you shall see how my whole soul is wrapped up in what you say."

They both sat upon the garden-seat; and while Johanna fixed her eyes upon her companion's face, expressive as it was of the most generous emotions and noble feelings, he commenced relating to her the incidents which never left her memory, and in which she took so deep an interest.

"You must know," he said, "that what it was which so much inflamed the imagination of Mark Ingestrie consisted in this. There came to London a man with a well-authenticated and extremely well put together report, that there had been discovered, in one of the small islands near the Indian seas, a river which deposited an enormous quantity of gold dust in its progress to the ocean. He told his story so well, and seemed to be such a perfect master of all the circumstances connected with it, that there was scarcely room for a doubt upon the subject.

"The thing was kept quiet and secret; and a meeting was held of some influential men—influential on account of the money they possessed, among whom was one who had towards Mark Ingestrie most friendly feelings; so Mark attended the meeting with this friend of his, although he felt his utter incapacity, from want of resources, to take any part in the affair.

"But he was not aware of what his friend's generous intentions were in the matter until they were explained to him, and they consisted in this:—He, the friend, was to provide the necessary means for embarking in the adventure, so far as regarded taking a share in it, and he told Mark Ingestrie that, if he would go personally on the expedition, he would share in the proceeds with him, be they what they might.

"Now, to a young man like Ingestrie, totally destitute of personal resources, but of ardent and enthusiastic temperament, you can imagine how extremely tempting such an offer was likely to be. He embraced it at once with the greatest pleasure, and from that moment he took an interest in the affair of the closest and most powerful description. It seized completely hold of his imagination, presenting itself to him in the most tempting colours; and from the description that has been given me of his enthusiastic disposition, I can well imagine with what kindness and impetuosity he would enter into such an affair."

"You know him well," said Johanna, gently.

"No, I never saw him. All that I say concerning him is from the description of another who did know him well, and who sailed with him in the vessel that ultimately left the port of London on the vague and wild adventure I have mentioned."

"That one, be he who he may, must have known Mark Ingestrie well, and have enjoyed much of his confidence to be able to describe him so accurately."

"I believe that such was the case; and it is from the lips of that one, instead of mine, that you ought to have heard what I am now relating. That gentleman, whose name was Thornhill, ought to have made to you this communication; but by some strange accident it seems he has been prevented, or you would not be here listening to me upon a subject which would have come better from his lips."

"And he was to have come yesterday to me?"

"He was."

"Then Mark Ingestrie kept his word; and but for the adverse circumstances which delayed his messenger, I should have heard yesterday what you are now relating to me. I pray you go on, sir, and pardon the interruption."

"I need not trouble you with all the negotiations, the trouble, and the difficulty that arose before the expedition could be started fairly—suffice it to say, that at length, after much annoyance and trouble, it was started, and a vessel was duly chartered and manned for the purpose of proceeding to the Indian seas in search of the treasure, which was reported to be there for the first adventurer who had the boldness to seek it.

"It was a gallant vessel. I saw it sail many a mile from England ere it sunk beneath the waves, never to rise again."

"Sunk!"

"Yes; it was an ill-fated ship, and it did sink; but I must not anticipate—let me proceed in my narrative with regularity.

"The ship was called the *Star*; and if those who went with it looked upon it as the star of their destiny, they were correct enough, and it might be considered an evil star for them, in as much as nothing but disappointment and bitterness became their ultimate portion.

"And Mark Ingestrie, I am told, was the most hopeful man on board. Already in imagination he could fancy himself homeward-bound with the vessel, ballasted and crammed with the rich produce of that shining river.

"Already he fancied what he could do with his abundant wealth, and I have not a doubt but that, in common with many who went on that adventure, he enjoyed to the full the spending of the wealth he should obtain in imagination—perhaps, indeed, more than if he had obtained it in reality.

"Among the adventurers was one Thornhill, who had been a lieutenant in the Royal Navy, and between him and young Ingestrie there arose a remarkable friendship—a friendship so strong and powerful, that there can be no doubt they communicated to each other all their hopes and fears; and if anything could materially tend to beguile the tedium of such a weary voyage as those adventurers had undertaken, it certainly would be the free communication and confidential intercourse between two such kindred spirits as Thornhill and Mark Ingestrie.

"You will bear in mind, Miss Oakley, that in making this communication to you, I am putting together what I myself heard at different times, so as to make it for you a distinct narrative, which you can have no difficulty in comprehending, because, as I before stated, I never saw Mark Ingestrie, and it was only once, for about five minutes, that I saw the vessel in which he went upon his perilous adventure—for perilous it turned out to be—to the Indian seas. It was from Thornhill I got my information during the many weary and monotonous hours consumed in a homeward voyage from India.

"It appears that without accident or cross of any description the *Star* reached the Indian Ocean, and the supposed immediate locality of the spot where the treasure was to be found, and there she was spoken with by a vessel homeward-bound from India, called the *Neptune*.

"It was evening, and the sun had sunk in the horizon with some appearance that betokened a storm. I was on board that Indian vessel; we did not expect anything serious, although we made every preparation for rough weather, and as it turned out, it was well indeed we did, for never, within the memory of the oldest seaman, had such a storm ravished the coast. A furious gale, which it was impossible to withstand, drove us southward; and but for the utmost precautions, aided by the courage and temerity on the part of the seamen, such as I have never before witnessed in the merchant-service, we escaped with trifling damage, but we were driven at least 200 miles out of our course; and instead of getting, as we ought to have done, to the Cape by a certain time, we were an immense distance east of it.

"It was just as the storm, which lasted three nights and two days, began to abate, that towards the horizon we saw a dull red light; and as it was not in a quarter of the sky where any such appearance might be imagined, nor were we in a latitude where electric phenomena might be expected, we steered towards it, surmising what turned out afterwards to be fully correct."

"It was a ship on fire!" said Johanna.

"It was."

"Alas! alas! I guessed it. A frightful suspicion from the first crossed my mind. It was a ship on fire, and that ship was—"

"The *Star*, still bound upon its adventurous course, although driven far out of it by adverse winds and waves. After about half an hour's sailing we came within sight distinctly of a blazing vessel.

"We could hear the roar of the flames, and through our glasses we could see them curling up the cordage and dancing from mast to mast, like fiery serpents, exulting in the destruction they were making. We made all sail, and strained every inch of canvas to reach the ill-fated vessel, for distances at sea that look small are in reality very great, and an hour's hard sailing in a fair wind with every stitch of canvas set, would not do more than enable us to reach that ill-fated bark; but fancy in an hour what ravages the flames might make!

"The vessel was doomed. The fiat had gone forth that it was to be among the things that had been; and long before we could reach the spot upon which it floated idly on the now comparatively calm waters, we saw a bright shower of sparks rush up into the air. Then came a loud roaring sound over the surface of the deep, and all was still—the ship had disappeared, and the water had closed over her for ever."

"But how knew you," said Johanna, as she clasped her hands, and the pallid expression of her countenance betrayed the deep interest she took in the narration, "how knew you that ship was the *Star*? might it not have been some other ill-fated vessel that met with so dreadful a fate?"

"I will tell you: although we had seen the ship go down, we kept on our course, straining every effort to reach the spot, with a hope of picking up some of the crew, who surely had made an effort by the boats to leave the burning vessel.

"The captain of the Indiaman kept his glass at his eye, and presently he said to me,—

'There is a floating piece of wreck, and something clinging to it; I know not if there be a man, but what I can perceive seems to me to be the head of a dog.'

"I looked through the glass myself, and saw the same object; but as we neared it, we found that it was a large piece of the wreck, with a dog and a man supported by it, who were clinging with all the energy of desperation. In ten minutes more we had them on board the vessel—the man was the Lieutenant Thornhill I have before mentioned, and the dog belonged to him.

"He related to us that the ship we had seen burning was the *Star*; that it had never reached its destination, and that he believed all had perished but himself and the dog; for, although one of the boats had been launched, so desperate a rush was made into it by the crew that it had swamped, and all perished.

"Such was his own state of exhaustion, that, after he had made to us this short statement, it was some days before he left his hammock; but when he did, and began to mingle with us, we found an intelligent, cheerful companion—such a one, indeed, as we were glad to have on board, and in confidence he related to the captain and myself the object of the voyage of the *Star*, and the previous particulars with which I have made you acquainted.

"And then, during a night-watch, when the soft and beautiful moonlight was more than usually inviting, and he and I were on the deck, enjoying the coolness of the night, after the intense heat of the day in the tropics, he said to me,—

'I have a very sad mission to perform when I get to London. On board our vessel was a young man named Mark Ingestrie; and some time before the vessel in which we were went down, he begged of me to call upon a young lady named Johanna Oakley, the daughter of a spectacle-maker in London, providing I should be saved and he perish; and of the latter event, he felt so strong a presentiment that he gave me a string of pearls, which I was to present to her in his name; but where he got them I have not the least idea, for they are of immense value.'

"Mr. Thornhill showed me the pearls, which were of different sizes, roughly strung together, but of great value; and when we reached the river Thames, which was only three days since, he left us with his dog, carrying his string of pearls with him, to find out where you reside."

"Alas! he never came."

"No; from all the enquiries we can make, and all the information we can learn, it seems that he disappeared somewhere about Fleet-street."

"Disappeared!"

"Yes; we can trace him to the Temple-stairs, and from thence to a barber's shop, kept by a man named Sweeney Todd; but beyond there no information of him can be obtained."

"Sweeney Todd!"

"Yes; and what makes the affair more extraordinary, is that neither force nor persuasion will induce Thornhill's dog to leave the place."

"I saw it—I saw the creature, and it looked imploringly, but kindly, in my face; but little did I think, when I paused a moment to look upon that melancholy but faithful animal, that it held a part in my destiny. Oh! Mark Ingestrie, Mark Ingestrie, dare I hope that you live when all else have perished?"

"I have told you all that I can tell you, and according as your own judgement may dictate to you, you can encourage hope, or extinguish it for ever. I have kept back nothing from you which can make the affair worse or better—I have added nothing; but you have it simply as it was told to me."

"He is lost—he is lost!"

"I am one, lady, who always thinks certainty of any sort preferable to suspense; and although, while there is no positive news of death, the continuance of life ought fairly to be assumed, yet you must perceive from a review of all the circumstances, upon how very slender a foundation all your hopes must rest."

"I have no hope—I have no hope—he is lost to me for ever! It were madness to think he lived. Oh! Mark, Mark! and is this the end of all our fond affection? did I indeed look my last upon that face, when on this spot we parted?"

"The uncertainty," said Colonel Jeffery, wishing to withdraw as much as possible from a consideration of her own sorrows, "the uncertainty, too, that prevails with the regard to the fate of poor Mr. Thornhill, is a sad thing. I much fear that those precious pearls he had have been seen by someone who has not scrupled to obtain possession of them by his death."

"Yes, it would seem so indeed; but what are pearls to me? Oh! would that they had sunk to the bottom of that Indian sea, from whence they had been plucked. Alas, alas! it has been their thirst for gain that has produced all these evils. We might have been poor here, but we should have been happy. Rich we ought to have been, in contentment; but now all is lost, and the world to me can present nothing that is to be desired, but one small spot large enough to be my grave."

She leant upon the arm of the garden-seat, and gave herself up to such a passion of tears that Colonel Jeffery felt he dared not interrupt her.

There is something exceedingly sacred about real grief, which awes the beholder, and it was with an involuntary feeling of respect that Colonel Jeffery stepped a few paces off, and waited until that burst of agony had passed away.

It was during those few brief moments that he overheard some words uttered by one who seemed likewise to be suffering from that prolific source of all affliction, disappointed affection. Seated at some short distance was a maiden, and one not young enough to be called a youth, but still not far enough advanced in existence to have had all his better feelings crushed by an admixture with the cold world, and he was listening while the maiden spoke.

"It is the neglect," she said, "which touched me to the heart. But one word spoken or written, one message of affection, to tell me that the memory of a love I thought would be eternal, still lingered in your heart, would have been a world of consolation; but it came not, and all was despair."

"Listen to me," said her companion, "and if ever in this world you can believe that one who truly loves can be cruel to be kind, believe that I am that one. I yielded for a time to the fascination of a passion which should never have found a home within my heart; but yet it was far more of a sentiment than a passion, inasmuch as never for one moment did an evil thought mingle with its pure aspirations.

"It was a dream of joy, which for a time obliterated a remembrance that ought never to have been forgotten; but when I was rudely awakened to the fact that those whose opinions were of more importance to your welfare and your happiness knew nothing of love, but in its grossest aspect, it became necessary at once to crush a feeling which, in its continuance, could shadow forth nothing but evil.

"You may not imagine, and you may never know, for I cannot tell the heart-pangs it has cost me to persevere in a line of conduct which I felt was due to you—whatever heart-pangs it might cost me. I have been content to imagine that your affection would turn to indifference, perchance to hatred; that a consciousness of being slighted would arouse in your defence all a woman's pride, and that thus you would be lifted above regret. Farewell for ever! I dare not love you honestly and truly; and better is it thus to part than to persevere in a delusive dream that can but terminate in degradation and sadness."

"Do you hear those words?" whispered Colonel Jeffery to Johanna. "You perceive that others suffer, and from the same cause, the perils of affection."

"I do. I will go home, and pray for strength to maintain my heart against this sad affliction."

"The course of true love never yet ran smooth; wonder not, therefore, Johanna Oakley, that yours has suffered such a blight. It is the great curse of the highest and noblest feelings of which humanity is capable, that while, under felicitous circumstances, they produce an extraordinary amount of happiness, when anything adverse occurs, they are most prolific sources of misery. Shall I accompany you?"

Johanna felt grateful for the support of the colonel's arm towards her own home, and as they passed the barber's shop they were surprised to see that the dog and the hat were gone.

CHAPTER VII

IT IS NIGHT AND A MAN, ONE OF THE MOST CELEBRATED LAPIDARIES IN LONDON, BUT yet a man frugal withal, although rich, is putting up the shutters of his shop.

This lapidary is an old man; his scanty hair is white, and his hands shake as he secures the fastenings, and then, over and over again, feels and shakes each shutter, to be assured that his shop is well secured.

This shop of his is in Moorfields, then a place very much frequented by dealers in bullion and precious stones. He was about entering his door, just having cast a satisfied look upon the fastenings of his shop, when a tall, ungainly-looking man stepped up to him. This man had a three-cornered hat, much too small for him, perched upon the top of his great, hideous-looking head, while the coat he wore had ample skirts enough to have made another of ordinary dimensions.

Our readers will have no difficulty in recognising Sweeney Todd, and well might the little old lapidary start as such a very unprepossessing-looking personage addressed him.

"You deal," he said, "in precious stones."

"Yes, I do," was the reply; "but it's rather late. Do you want to buy or sell?"

'To sell."

"Humph! Ah, I dare say it's something not in my line; the only order I get is for pearls, and they are not in the market."

"And I have nothing but pearls to sell," said Sweeney Todd; "I mean to keep all my diamonds, my garnets, topazes, brilliants, emeralds, and rubies."

"The deuce you do! Why, you don't mean to say you have any of them? Be off with you! I am too old to joke with, and am waiting for my supper."

"Will you look at the pearls I have?"

"Little seed-pearls, I suppose; they are of no value, and I don't want them; we have plenty of those. It's real, genuine, large pearls we want. Pearls worth thousands."

"Will you look at mine?"

"No; good night!"

"Very good; then I will take them to Mr. Coventry up the street. He will, perhaps, deal with me for them if you cannot."

The lapidary hesitated. "Stop," he said; "what's the use of going to Mr. Coventry? he has not the means of purchasing what I can present cash for. Come in, come in; I will, at all events, look at what you have for sale."

Thus encouraged, Sweeney Todd entered the little, low, dusky shop, and the lapidary having procured a light, and taken care to keep his customer outside the counter, put on his spectacles, and said,—

"Now, sir, where are your pearls?"

"There," said Sweeney Todd, as he laid a string of twenty-four pearls before the lapidary.

The old man's eye opened to an enormous width, and he pushed his spectacles right up upon his forehead, as he glared in the face of Sweeney Todd with undisguised astonishment. Then down he pulled his spectacles again, and taking up the string of pearls, he rapidly examined every one of them, after which he exclaimed,—

"Real, real, by Heaven! All real!"

Then he pushed his spectacles up again to the top of his head and took another long stare at Sweeney Todd.

"I know they are real," said the latter. "Will you deal with me or will you not?"

"Will I deal with you? Yes; I am quite sure that they are real. Let me look again. Oh, I see, counterfeits; but so well done, that really, for the curiosity of the thing, I will give £50 for them."

"I am fond of curiosities," said Sweeney Todd, "and, as they are not real, I'll keep them; they will do for a present to some child or other."

"What! give those to a child? you must be mad—that is to say, not mad, but certainly indiscreet. Come, now, at a word, I'll give you £100 for them."

"Hark ye," said Sweeney Todd, "it neither suits my inclination nor my time to stand here chaffing with you. I know the value of the pearls, and, as a matter of ordinary and every-day business, I will sell them to you so that you may get a handsome profit."

"What do you call a handsome profit?"

"The pearls are worth £12,000, and I will let you have them for ten. What do you think of that for an offer?"

"What odd noise was that?"

"Oh, it was only I who laughed. Come, what do you say, at once; are we to do business or are we not?"

"Hark ye, me friend, since you do know the value of your pearls, and this is to be a downright business transaction, I think I can find a customer who will give £11,000 for them, and if so, I have no objection to give you £8,000."

"Give me the £8,000," said Sweeney Todd, "and let me go. I hate bargaining."

"Stop a bit; there are some rather important things to consider. You must know, my friend, that a string of pearls of this value are not to be bought like a few ounces of old silver of anybody who might come with it. Such a string of pearls as these are like a house, or an estate, and when they change hands, the vendor of them must give every satisfaction as to how he came by them, and prove how he can give to the purchaser a good right and title to them."

"Psha!" said Sweeney Todd, "who will question you, who are well known to be in the trade, and to be continually dealing in such things?"

"That's all very fine; but I don't see why I should give you the full value of an article without evidence as to how you came by it."

"In other words, you mean, you don't care how I came by them, provided I sell them to you at a thief's price, but if I want their value you mean to be particular."

"My good sir, you may conclude what you like. Show me you have a right to dispose of the pearls, and you need go no further than my shop for a customer."

"I am not disposed to take that trouble, so I shall bid you good night, and when you want any pearls again, I would certainly advise you not to be so wonderfully particular where you get them."

Sweeney Todd strode towards the door, but the lapidary was not going to part with him so easy, for springing over his counter with an agility one would not have expected from so old a man, he was at the door in a moment, and shouted at the top of his lungs,—

"Stop thief! Stop thief! Stop him! There he goes! The big fellow with the three-cornered hat! Stop thief! Stop thief!"

These cries, uttered with great vehemence, as they were, could not be totally ineffective, but they roused the whole neighbourhood, and before Sweeney Todd had proceeded many yards a man made an attempt to collar him, but was repulsed by such a terrific blow in his face, that another person, who had run half-way across the road with a similar object, turned and went back again, thinking it scarcely prudent to risk his own safety in apprehending a criminal for the good of the public.

Having thus got rid of one of his foes, Sweeney Todd, with an inward determination to come back someday and be the death of the old lapidary, looked anxiously about for some court down which he could plunge, and so get out of sight of the many pursuers who were sure to attack him in the public streets.

His ignorance of the locality, however, was a great bar to such a proceeding, for the great dread he had was, that he might get down some blind alley, and so be completely caged, and at the mercy of those who followed him.

He pelted on at a tremendous speed, but it was quite astonishing to see how the little old lapidary ran after him, falling down every now and then, and never stopping to pick himself up, as people say, but rolling on and getting on his feet in some miraculous manner, that was quite wonderful to behold, particularly in one so aged, and so apparently unable to undertake any active exertion.

There was one thing, however, he could not continue doing, and that was to cry "stop thief!" for he had lost his wind, and was quite incapable of uttering a word. How long he would have continued the chase is doubtful, but his career was suddenly put an end to, as regards that, by tripping his foot over a projecting stone in the pavement, and shooting headlong down a cellar which was open.

But abler persons than the little old lapidary had taken up the chase, and Sweeney Todd was hard pressed; and, although he ran very fast, the provoking thing was, that in consequence of the cries and shouts of his pursuers, new people took up the chase, who were fresh and vigorous, and close to him.

There is something awful in seeing a human being thus hunted by his fellows; and although we can have no sympathy with a man such as Sweeney Todd, because, from all that has happened, we begin to have some very horrible suspicions concerning him, still, as a general principle, it does not decrease the fact that it is a dreadful thing to see a human being hunted through the streets.

On he flew at the top of his speed, striking down whoever opposed him, until at last many who could have outrun him gave up the chase, not liking to encounter the knock-down blow which such a hand as his seemed capable of inflicting.

His teeth were set, and his breathing came short and laborious, just as a man sprung out at a shop-door and succeeded in laying hold of him.

"I have got you, have I?" he said.

Sweeney Todd uttered not a word, but, putting forth an amount of strength that was perfectly prodigious, he seized the man by a great handful of his hair and by his clothes behind, and flung him through the shop-window, smashing glass, frame-work, and everything in his progress.

The man gave a shriek, for it was his own shop, and he was a dealer in fancy goods of the most flimsy texture, so that the smash with which he came down among his stock-in-trade, produced at once what the haberdashers are so delighted with in the present day, a ruinous sacrifice.

This occurrence had a great effect upon Sweeney Todd's pursuers; it taught them the practical wisdom of not interfering with a man possessed evidently of such tremendous powers of mischief, and consequently, as just about this period the defeat of the little lapidary took place, he got considerably the start of his pursuers.

But he was by no means yet safe. The cry of "stop thief!" still sounded in his ears, and on he flew, panting with the exertion he made, until he heard a man behind him say,—

"Turn into the second court on your right and you will be safe. I'll follow you. They shan't nab you, if I can help it."

Sweeney Todd had not much confidence in human nature—it was not likely he would; but, panting and exhausted as he was, the voice of anyone speaking in friendly accents was welcome, and, rather impulsively than from reflection, he darted down the second court to his right.

CHAPTER VIII

IN A VERY FEW MINUTES SWEENEY TODD FOUND THAT THIS COURT HAD NO thoroughfare, and therefore there was no outlet or escape; but he immediately concluded that something more was to be found than was at first sight to be seen, and, casting a furtive glance beside him in the direction in which he had come, rested his hand upon a door which stood close by.

The door gave way, and Sweeney Todd hearing, as he imagined, a noise in the street, dashed in and closed the door, and then he, heedless of all consequences, walked to the end of a long, dirty passage, and, pushing open a door, descended a short flight of steps, to the bottom of which he had scarcely got, when the door which faced him at the bottom of the steps opened by some hand, and he suddenly found himself in the presence of a number of men seated round a large table.

In an instant all eyes were turned towards Sweeney Todd, who was quite unprepared for such a scene, and for a minute he knew not what to say; but, as indecision was not Sweeney Todd's characteristic, he at once advanced to the table and sat down.

There was some surprise evinced by the persons who were seated in that room, of whom there were many more than a score, and much talking was going on among them, which did not appear to cease on his entrance.

Those who were near him looked hard at him, but nothing was said for some minutes, and Sweeney Todd looked about to understand, if he could, how he was placed, though it could not be much of a matter of doubt as to the character of the individuals present.

Their looks were often an index to their vocations, for all grades of the worst of characters were there, and some of them were by no means complimentary to human nature, for there were some of the most desperate characters that were to be found in London.

They were dressed in various fashions, some after the manner of the city—some more gay, and some half military, while not a few wore the garb of country-men; but there was in all that an air of scampish, offhand behaviour, not unmixed with brutality.

"Friend," said one, who sat near him, "how came you here; are you known here?"

"I came here, because I found the door open, and I was told by someone to come here, as I was pursued."

"Pursued!"

"Ay, someone running after me, you know."

"I know what being pursued is," replied the man, "and yet I know nothing of you."

"That is not at all astonishing," said Sweeney, "seeing that I never saw you before, nor you me; but that makes no difference. I'm in difficulties, and I suppose a man may do his best to escape the consequences."

"Yes, he may, yet there is no reason why he should come here; this is the place for free friends, who know and aid one another."

"And such I am willing to be; but at the same time I must have a beginning. I cannot be initiated without someone introducing me. I have sought protection, and I have found it; if there be any objection to my remaining here any longer, I will leave."

"No, no," said a tall man on the other side of the table, "I have heard what you said, and we do not usually allow any such things; you have come here unasked, and now we must have a little explanation, our own safety may demand it; at all events we have our customs, and they must be complied with."

"And what are your customs?" demanded Todd.

"This: you must answer the questions which we shall propound unto you; now answer truly what we shall ask of you."

"Speak," said Todd, "and I will answer all that you proposed to me if possible."

"We will not tax you too hardly, depend upon it: who are you?"

"Candidly, then," said Todd, "that's a question I do not like to answer, nor do I think it is one that you ought to ask. It is an inconvenient thing to name oneself—you must pass by *that* enquiry."

"Shall we do so?" enquired the interrogator of those around him, and, gathering his cue from their looks, he after a brief pause continued,—

"Well, we will pass over that, seeing it is not necessary; but you must tell us what you are, cutpurse, footpad, or what not?"

"I am neither."

"Then tell us in your own words," said the man, "and be candid with us. What are you?"

"I am an artificial pearl-maker—or a sham pearl-maker, whichever way you please to call it."

"A sham pearl-maker! that may be an honest trade for all we know, and that will hardly be your passport to our house, friend sham pearl-maker!"

"That may be as you say," replied Todd, "but I will challenge any man to equal me in my calling. I have made pearls that would pass with almost a lapidary, and which would pass with nearly all the nobility."

"I begin to understand you, friend; but I would wish to have some proof of what you say: we may hear a very good tale, and yet none of it shall be true; we are not the men to be made dupes of, besides, there are enough to take vengeance, if we desire it."

"Ay, to be sure there is," said a gruff voice from the other end of the table, which was echoed from one to the other, till it came to the top of the table.

"Proof! proof! proof!" now resounded from one end of the room to the other.

"My friends," said Sweeney Todd, rising up, and advancing to the table, and thrusting his hand into his bosom, and drawing out the string of twenty-four pearls, "I challenge you or anyone to make a set of artificial pearls equal to these: they are my make, and I'll stand to it in any reasonable sum that you cannot bring a man who shall beat me in my calling."

"Just hand them to me," said the man who had made himself interrogator.

Sweeney Todd threw the pearls on the table carelessly, and then said,—

"There, look at them well, they'll bear it, and I reckon, though there may be some good judges 'mongst you, that you cannot any of you tell them from real pearls, if you had not been told so."

"Oh, yes, we know pretty well," said the man, "what these things are: we have now and then a good string in our possession, and that helps us to judge of them. Well, this is certainly a good imitation."

"Let me see it," said a fat man; "I was bred a jeweller, and I might say born, only I couldn't stick to it; nobody likes working for years upon little pay, and no fun with the gals. I say, hand it here!"

"Well," said Todd, "if you or anybody ever produced as good an imitation, I'll swallow the whole string; and, knowing there's poison in the composition, it would certainly not be a comfortable thing to think of."

"Certainly not," said the big man, "certainly not; but hand them over, and I'll tell you all about it."

The pearls were given into his hands; and Sweeney Todd felt some misgivings about his precious charge, and yet he showed it not, for he turned to the man, who sat beside him, saying,—

"If he can tell true pearls from them, he knows more than I think he does, for I am a maker, and have often had the true pearl in my hand."

"And I suppose," said the man, "you have tried your hand at putting the one for the other, and so doing your confiding customers."

"Yes, yes, that is the dodge, I can see very well," said another man, winking at the first; "and a good one too, I have known them do so with diamonds."

"Yes, but never with pearls; however, there are some trades that it is desirable to know."

"You're right."

The fat man now carefully examined the pearls, and set them down on the table, and looked hard at them.

"There now, I told you I could bother you. You are not so good a judge that you would not have known, if you had not been told they were sham pearls, but what they were real."

"I must say, you have produced the best imitations I have ever seen. Why, you ought to make your fortune in a few years—a handsome fortune."

"So I should, but for one thing."

"And what is that?"

"The difficulty," said Todd, "of getting rid of them; if you ask anything below their value, you are suspected, and you run the chance of being stopped and losing them at the least, and perhaps, entail a prosecution."

"Very true; but there is risk in everything; we all run risks; but then the harvest."

"That may be," said Todd, "but this is peculiarly dangerous. I have not the means of getting introductions to the nobility themselves, and if I had I should be doubted, for they would say a workman cannot come honestly by such valuable things, and then I must concoct a tale to escape the Mayor of London!"

"Ha!—ha!—ha!"

"Well, then, you can take them to a goldsmith."

"There are not many of them who would do so; they would not deal in them; and, moreover, I have been to one or two of them; as for a lapidary, why, he is not so easily cheated."

"Have you tried?"

"I did, and had to make the best of my way out, pursued as quickly as they could run, and I thought at one time I must have been stopped, but a few lucky turns brought me clear, when I was told to turn up this court, and I came in here."

"Well," said one man, who had been examining the pearls, "and did the lapidary find out they were not real?"

"Yes, he did; and he wanted to stop me and the string altogether, for trying to impose upon him; however I made a rush at the door, which he tried to shut, but I was the stronger man, and here I am."

"It has been a close chance for you," said one.

"Yes, it just has," replied Sweeney, taking up the string of pearls, which he replaced in his clothes, and continued to converse with some of those around him.

Things now subsided into their general course; and little notice was taken of Sweeney. There was some drink on the board, of which all partook. Sweeney had some, too, and took the precaution of emptying his pockets before them all, and gave a share of his money to pay their footing.

This was policy, and they all drank to his success, and were very good companions. Sweeney, however, was desirous of getting out as soon as he could, and more than once cast his eyes towards the door; but he saw there were eyes upon him, and dared not excite suspicion, for he might undo all that he had done.

To lose the precious treasure he possessed would be maddening; he had succeeded to admiration in inducing the belief that what he showed them was merely a counterfeit; but he knew so well that they were real, and that a latent feeling that they were humbugged might be hanging about; and that at the first suspicious movement he would be watched, and some desperate attempt would be made to make him give them up.

It was with no small violence to his own feelings that he listened to their conversation, and appeared to take an interest in their proceedings.

"Well," said one, who sat next him, "I'm just off for the north-road."

"Any fortune there?"

"Not much; and yet I mustn't complain: these last three weeks the best I have had has been two sixties."

"Well, that would do very well."

"Yes, the last man I stopped was a regular looby Londoner; he appeared like a don, complete tip-top man of fashion; but Lord! when I came to look over him, he hadn't as much as would carry me twenty-four miles on the road."

"Indeed! don't you think he had any hidden about him? they do so now."

"Ah, ah!" returned another, "well said, old fellow; 'tis a true remark that we can't always judge a man from appearances. Lor! bless me, now, who'd a-thought your swell cove proved to be out of luck! Well, I'm sorry for you; but you know 'tis a long lane that has no turning, as Mr. Somebody says—so, perhaps, you'll be more fortunate another time. But come, cheer up, whilst I relate an adventure that occurred a little time ago; 'twas a slice of good luck, I assure you, for I had no difficulty in bouncing my victim out of a good swag of tin; for you know farmers returning from market are not always too wary and careful, especially as the lots of wine they take at the market dinners make the cosy old boys ripe and mellow for sleep. Well, I met one of these jolly gentlemen, mounted on horseback, who declared he had nothing but a few paltry guineas about him; however, that would not do—I searched him, and found a hundred and four pounds secreted about his person."

"Where did you find it?"

"About him. I tore his clothes to ribands. A pretty figure he looked upon horse-back, I assure you. By Jove, I could hardly help laughing at him; in fact, I did laugh at him, which so enraged him, that he immediately threatened to horsewhip me, and yet he dared not defend his money; but I threatened to shoot him, and that soon brought him to his senses."

"I should imagine so. Did you ever have a fight for it?" inquired Sweeney Todd.

"Yes, several times. Ah! it's by no means an easy life, you may depend. It is free, but dangerous. I have been fired at six or seven times."

"So many?"

"Yes. I was near York once, when I stopped a gentleman; I thought him an easy conquest, but not so he turned out, for he was a regular devil."

"Resisted you?"

"Yes, he did. I was coming along when I met him, and I demanded his money.

"'I can keep it myself,'" he said, "'and do not want any assistance to take care of it.'"

"'But I want it,'" said I; "your money or your life.'"

"'You must have both, for we are not to be parted,'" he said, presenting his pistol at me; and then I had only time to escape from the effect of the shot. I struck the pistol up with my riding-whip, and the bullet passed by my temples, and almost stunned me.

"I cocked and fired; he did the same, but I hit him, and he fell. He fired, however, but missed me. I was down upon him; he begged hard for life."

"Did you give it him?"

"Yes; I dragged him to one side of the road, and then left him.

"Having done so much I mounted my horse, and came away as fast as I could, and then I made for London, and spent a merry day or two there.

"I can imagine you must enjoy your trips into the country, and then you must have still greater relish for the change when you come to London—the change is so great and so entire."

"So it is; but have you never any run of luck in your line? I should think you must at times succeed in tricking the public."

"Yes, yes," said Todd, "now and then we—but I tell you it is only now and then; and I have been afraid of doing too much. To small sums I have been a gainer; but I want to do something grand. I tried it on, but at the same time I have failed."

"That is bad; but you may have more opportunities by and by. Luck is all chance."

"Yes," replied Todd, "that is true, but the sooner the better, for I am growing impatient."

Conversation now went on; each man speaking of his exploits, which were always some species of rascality and robbery accompanied by violence generally; some were midnight robbers and breakers into people's houses; in fact, all the crimes that could be imagined.

This place was, in fact, a complete home or rendezvous for thieves, cutpurses, highwaymen, footpads, and burglars of every grade and description—a formidable set of men of the most determined and desperate appearance.

Sweeney Todd knew hardly how to rise and leave the place, though it was now growing very late, and he was most anxious to get safe out of the den he was in; but how to do that was a problem yet to be solved.

"What is the time?" he muttered to the man next to him.

"Past midnight," was the reply.

"Then I must leave here," he answered, "for I have work that I must be at in a very short time, and I shall not have too much time."

So saying he watched his opportunity, and rising, walked up to the door, which he opened, and went out; after that he walked up the five steps that led to the passage, and this latter had hardly been gained when the street-door opened, and another man came in at the same moment, and met him face to face.

"What do you here?"

"I am going out," said Sweeney Todd.

"You are going back: come back with me."

"I will not," said Todd. "You must be a better man than I am, if you make me do my best to resist your attack, if you intend to make one."

"That I do," replied the man; and he made a determined rush upon Sweeney, who was scarcely prepared for such a sudden onslaught, and was pushed back till he came to the head of the stairs, where a struggle took place, and both rolled down the steps. The door was immediately thrown open, and everyone rushed out to see what was the matter, but it was some moments before they could make it out.

"What does he do here?" said the first, as soon as he could speak, and pointing to Sweeney Todd.

"It's all right."

"All wrong, I say."

"He's a sham pearl-maker, and has shown us a string of sham pearls that are beautiful."

"Psha!"

"I will insist on seeing them; give them to me," he said, "or you do not leave this place."

"I will not," said Sweeney.

"You must. Here, help me—but I don't want help, I can do it by myself."

As he spoke, he made a desperate attempt to collar Sweeney and pull him to the earth, but he had miscalculated his strength when he imagined that he was superior to Todd, who was by far the more powerful man of the two, and resisted the attack with success.

Suddenly, by an herculean effort, he caught his adversary below the waist, and lifting him up, he threw him upon the floor with great force; and then, not wishing to see how the gang would take this —whether they would take the part of their companion or of himself he knew not—he thought he had an advantage in the distance, and he rushed upstairs as fast as he could, and reached the door before they could overtake him to prevent him.

Indeed, for more than a minute they were irresolute what to do; but they were somehow prejudiced in favour of their companion, and they rushed up after Sweeney just as he got to the door.

He would have had time to escape them; but, by some means, the door became fast, and he could not open it, exert himself how he would.

There was no time to lose; they were coming to the head of the stairs, and Sweeney had hardly time to reach the stairs, to fly upwards, when he felt himself grasped by the throat.

This he soon released himself from; for he struck the man who seized him a heavy blow, and he fell backwards, and Todd found his way up to the first floor, but he was closely pursued.

Here was another struggle; and again Sweeney Todd was the victor, but he was hard pressed by those who followed him—fortunately for him there was a mop left in a pail of water, this he seized hold of, and, swinging it over his head, he brought it full on the head of the first man who came near him.

Dab it came, soft and wet, and splashed over some others who were close at hand.

It is astonishing what an effect a new weapon will sometimes have. There was not a man among them who would not have faced danger in more ways than one, that would not have rushed headlong upon deadly and destructive weapons, but who were quite awed when a heavy wet mop was dashed into their faces.

They were completely paralysed for a moment; indeed, they began to look upon it something between a joke and a serious matter, and either would have been taken just as they might be termed.

"Get the pearls!" shouted the man who had first stopped him; "seize the spy! seize him—secure him—rush at him! You are men enough to hold one man!"

Sweeney Todd saw matters were growing serious, and he plied his mop most vigorously upon those who were ascending, but they had become somewhat used to the mop, and it had lost much of its novelty, and was by no means a dangerous weapon.

They rushed on, despite the heavy blows showered by Sweeney, and he was compelled to give way stair after stair.

The head of the mop came off, and then there remained but the handle, which formed an efficient weapon, and which made fearful havoc of the heads of the assailants; and despite all that their slouched hats could do in the way of protecting them, yet the staff came with a crushing effect.

The best fight in the world cannot last for ever; and Sweeney again found numbers were not to be resisted for long; indeed, he could not have physical energy enough to sustain his own efforts, supposing he had received no blows in return.

He turned and fled as he was forced back to the landing, and then came to the next stair-head, and again he made a desperate stand.

This went on for stair after stair, and continued for more than two or three hours.

There were moments of cessation when they all stood still and looked at each other.

"Fire upon him!" said one.

"No, no; we shall have the authorities down upon us, and then all will go wrong."

"I think we had much better have let it alone in the first place, as he was in, for you may be sure this won't make him keep a secret; we shall all be split upon as sure as fate."

"Well, then, rush upon him and down with him. Never let him out! On to him! Hurrah!"

Away they went, but they were resolutely met by the staff of Sweeney Todd, who had gained new strength by the short rest he had had.

"Down with the spy!"

This was shouted out by the men, but as each of them approached, they were struck down, and at length finding himself on the second floor landing, and being fearful that someone was descending from above, he rushed into one of the inner rooms.

In an instant he had locked the doors, which were strong and powerful.

"Now," he muttered, "for means to escape."

He waited a moment to wipe the sweat from his brow, and then he crossed the floor to the windows, which were open.

They were the old-fashion bag-windows, with the heavy ornamental work which some houses possessed, and overhung the low doorways, and protected them from the weather.

"This will do," he said, as he looked down to the pavement—"this will do. I will try this descent, if I fall."

The people on the other side of the door were exerting all their force to break it open, and it had already given one or two ominous creaks, and a few minutes more would probably let them into the room.

The streets were clear—no human being was moving about, and there were faint signs of the approach of morning. He paused a moment to inhale the fresh air, and then he got outside of the window.

By means of the sound oaken ornaments, he contrived to get down to the drawing-room balcony, and then he soon got down into the street.

As he walked away, he could hear the crash of the door, and a slight cheer, as they entered the room; and he could imagine to himself the appearance of the faces of those who entered, when they found the bird had flown, and the room was empty.

Sweeney Todd had not far to go; he soon turned into Fleet-street, and made for his own house. He looked about him, but there was none near him; he was tired and exhausted, and right glad was he when he found himself at his own door.

Then stealthily he put the key into the door, and slowly entered his house.

CHAPTER IX

Johanna Oakley would not allow Colonel Jeffery to accompany her all the way home, and he, appreciating the scruples of the young girl, did not press his attention on her, but left her at the corner of Fore-street, after getting a half promise that she would meet him again on that day week, at the same hour, in the Temple-gardens.

"I ask this of you, Johanna Oakley," he said, "because I have resolved to make all the exertion in my power to discover what has become of Mr. Thornhill, in whose fate I am sure I have succeeded in interesting you, although you care so little for the string of pearls, which he has in trust for you."

"I do, indeed, care little for them," said Johanna, "so little, that it might be said to amount to nothing."

"But still they are yours, and you ought to have the option of disposing of them as you please. It is not well to despise such gifts of fortune; for if you can yourself do nothing with them, there are surely some others whom you may know, upon whom they would bestow great happiness."

"A string of pearls, great happiness?" said Johanna, inquiringly.

"Your mind is so occupied by your grief that you quite forget such strings are of great value. I have seen those pearls, Johanna, and can assure you that they are in themselves a fortune."

"I suppose," she said sadly, "it is too much for human nature to expect two blessings at once. I had the fond, warm heart that loved me without the fortune, that would have enabled us to live in comfort and affluence; and now, when that is perchance within my grasp, the heart that was by far the most costly possession, and the richest jewel of them all, lies beneath the wave, with its bright influences, and its glorious and romantic aspirations, quenched for ever."

"You will meet me then, as I request of you, to hear if I have any news for you?"

"I will endeavour to do so. I have all the will; but Heaven knows if I may have the power."

"What mean you, Johanna?"

"I cannot tell what a week's anxiety may do; I know not but that a sick bed may be my resting-place, until I exchange it for the tomb. I feel even now my strength fail me, and I am scarcely able to totter to my home. Farewell, sir! I owe you my best thanks, as well for the trouble you have taken, as for the kindly manner in which you have detailed to me what has passed."

"Remember!" said Colonel Jeffery, "that I bid you adieu, with the hope of meeting you again."

It was thus they parted, and Johanna proceeded to her father's house. Who now that had met her and chanced not to see that sweet face, which could never be forgotten, would have supposed her to be the once gay and sprightly Johanna Oakley? Her steps were sad and solemn, and all the juvenile elasticity of her frame seemed to be gone. She seemed like one prepared for death; and she hoped that she would be able to glide, silently and unobserved, to her own little bed-chamber—that chamber where she had slept since she was a little child, and on the little couch, on which she had so often laid down to sleep, that holy and calm slumber, which such hearts as hers can only know.

But she was doomed to be disappointed, for the Rev. Mr. Lupin was still there, and as Mrs. Oakley had placed before that pious individual a great assortment of creature comforts, and among the rest some mulled wine, which seemed particularly to agree with him, he showed no disposition to depart.

It unfortunately happened that this wine of which the reverend gentleman partook with such a holy relish, was kept in a cellar, and Mrs. Oakley had had occasion twice to go down to procure a fresh supply, and it was on a third journey for the same purpose that she encountered poor Johanna, who had just let herself in at the private door.

"Oh! you have come home, have you?" said Mrs. Oakley, "I wonder where you have been to, gallivanting; but I suppose I may wonder long enough before you will tell me. Go into the parlour, I want to speak to you."

Now poor Johanna had quite forgotten the very existence of Mr. Lupin—so, rather than explain to her mother, which would beget more questions, she wished to go to bed at once, notwithstanding it was an hour before the usual time for so doing. She walked unsuspectingly into the parlour, and as Mr. Lupin was sitting, the slightest movement of his chair closed the door, so she could not escape.

Under any other circumstances probably Johanna would have insisted upon leaving the apartment; but a glance at the countenance of the pious individual was quite sufficient to convince her he had been sacrificing sufficiently to Bacchus to be capable of any amount of effrontery, so that she dreaded passing him, more especially as he swayed his arms about like the sails of a windmill.

She thought at least that when her mother returned she would rescue her; but in that hope she was mistaken, and Johanna had no more idea of the extent to which religious fanaticism will carry its victim, than she had of the manners and customs of the inhabitants of the moon.

When Mrs. Oakley did return, she had some difficulty in getting into the apartment, inasmuch as Mr. Lupin's chair occupied so large a portion of it; but when she did obtain admission, and Johanna said, "Mother, I beg of you to protect me against this man, and allow me a free passage from the apartment," Mrs. Oakley affected to lift up her hands in amazement as she said,—

"How dare you speak so disrespectfully of a chosen vessel. How dare you, I say, do such a thing—it's enough to drive anyone mad to see young girls nowadays!"

"Don't snub her—don't snub the virgin," said Mr. Lupin; "she don't know the honour yet that's intended her."

"She don't deserve it," said Mrs. Oakley, "she don't deserve it."

"Never mind, madam—never mind; we—we—we don't get all what we deserve in this world."

"Take a drop of something, Mr. Lupin; you have got the hiccups."

"Yes; I—I rather think I have a little. Isn't it a shame that anybody so intimate with the Lord should have the hiccups? What a lot of lights you have got burning, Mrs. Oakley!"

"A lot of lights, Mr. Lupin! Why, there is only one; but perhaps you allude to the lights of the gospel?"

"No; I—I don't, just at present; damn the lights of the gospel—that is, I mean damn all backsliders! But there is a lot of lights, and no mistake, Mrs. Oakley. Give us a drop of something, I'm as dry as dust."

"There is some more mulled wine, Mr. Lupin; but I am surprised that you think there is more than one light."

"It's a miracle, madam, in consequence of my great faith. I have faith in s-s-s-six lights, and here they are."

"Do you see that, Johanna?" exclaimed Mrs. Oakley, "are you not convinced now of the holiness of Mr. Lupin?"

"I am convinced of his drunkenness, mother, and entreat of you to let me leave the room at once.

"Tell her of the honour," said Mr. Lupin—"tell her of the honour."

"I don't know, Mr. Lupin; but don't you think it would be better to take some other opportunity?"

"Very well, then, this is the opportunity."

"If it's your pleasure, Mr. Lupin, I will. You must know, then, Johanna, that Mr. Lupin has been kind enough to consent to save my soul on condition that you marry him, and I am quite sure you can have no reasonable objection; indeed, I think it's the least you can do, whether you have any objection or not."

"Well put," said Mr. Lupin, "excellently well put."

"Mother," said Johanna, "if you are so far gone in superstition as to believe this miserable drunkard ought to come between you and heaven, I am not so lost as not to be able to reject the offer with more scorn and contempt than ever I thought I could have entertained for any human being; but hypocrisy never, to my mind, wears so disgusting a garb as when it attires itself in the outward show of religion."

"This conduct is unbearable," cried Mrs. Oakley; "am I to have one of the Lord's saints insulted under my own roof?"

"If he were ten times a saint, mother, instead of being nothing but a miserable drunken profligate, it would be better that he should be insulted ten times over, than that you should permit your own child to have passed through the indignity of having to reject such a proposition as that which has just been made. I must claim the protection of my father; he will not suffer one, towards whom he has ever shown his affection, the remembrance of which sinks deep into my heart, to meet with so cruel an insult beneath his roof."

"That's right, my dear," cried Mr. Oakley, at that moment pushing open the parlour-door. "That's right, my dear; you never spoke truer words in your life."

A faint scream came from Mrs. Oakley, and the Rev. Mr. Lupin immediately seized upon the fresh jug of mulled wine, and finished it at a draught.

"Get behind me, Satan," he said. "Mr. Oakley, you will be damned if you say a word to me."

"It's all the same, then," said Mr. Oakley; "for I'll be damned if I don't. Then, Ben, Ben, come—come in, Ben."

"I'm a-coming," said a deep voice, and a man about six feet four inches in height, and nearly two-thirds of that amount in width, entered the parlour. "I'm a-coming, Oakley, my boy. Put on your blessed spectacles, and tell me which is the fellow."

"I could have sworn it," said Mrs. Oakley, as she gave the table a knock, with her fist—"I could have sworn, when you came in, Oakley—I could have sworn, you little snivelling, shrivelled-up wretch. You'd no more have dared to come into this parlour as never was with those words in your mouth than you'd have dared to have flown, if you hadn't had your cousin, Big Ben, the beef-eater from the Tower, with you."

"Take it easy, ma'am," said Ben, as he sat down in a chair, which immediately broke all to pieces with his weight. "Take it easy, ma'am; the devil—what's this?"

"Never mind, Ben," said Mr. Oakley; "it's only a chair; get up."

"A cheer," said Ben; "do you call that a cheer? but never mind—take it easy."

"Why, you big, bullying, idle, swilling and guttling ruffian!"

"Go on, ma'am, go on."

"You good-for-nothing lump of carrion; a dog wears his own coat, but you wear your master's, you great stupid overgrown, lurking hound. You parish brought-up wild beast, go and mind your lions and elephants in the Tower, and don't come into honest people's houses, you cut-throat, bullying, pickpocketing wretch."

"Go on, ma'am, go on."

This was a kind of dialogue that could not last, and Mrs. Oakley sat down exhausted, and then Ben said,—

"I tell you what, ma'am, I considers you—I looks upon you, ma'am, as a female variety of that ere animal as is very useful and sagacious, ma'am."

There was no mistake in this allusion, and Mrs. Oakley was about to make some reply, when the Rev. Mr. Lupin rose from his chair, saying,—

"Bless you all! I think I'll go home."

"Not yet, Mr. Tulip," said Ben; "you had better sit down again—we've got something to say to you.

"Young man, young man, let me pass. If you do not, you will endanger your soul."

"I ain't got none," said Ben; "I'm only a beef-eater, and don't pretend to such luxuries."

"The heathen!" exclaimed Mrs. Oakley, "the horrid heathen! but there's one consolation, and that is, that he will be fried in his own fat for everlasting."

"Oh, that's nothing," said Ben; "I think I shall like it, especially if it's any pleasure to you. I suppose that's what you call a Christian consolation. Will you sit down, Mr. Tulip?"

"My name ain't Tulip, but Lupin; but if you wish it, I don't mind sitting down, of course."

The beef-eater, with a movement of his foot, kicked away the reverend gentleman's chair, and down he sat with a dab upon the floor.

"My dear," said Mr. Oakley to Johanna, "you go to bed, and then your mother can't say you have anything to do with this affair. I intend to rid my house of this man. Good night, my dear, good night."

Johanna kissed her father on the cheek, and then left the room, not at all sorry that so vigorous a movement was being made for the suppression of Mr. Lupin.

When she was gone, Mrs. Oakley spoke, saying, "Mr. Lupin, I bid you good night, and of course after the rough treatment of these wretches, I can hardly expect you to come again. Good night, Mr. Lupin, good night."

"That's all very well, ma'am," said Ben, "but before this ere wild beast of a parson goes away, I want to admonish him. He don't seem to be wide awake, and I must rouse him up."

Ben took hold of the reverend gentleman's nose, and gave it such an awful pinch that when he took his finger and thumb away, it was perfectly blue.

"Murder, oh murder! my nose! my nose!" shrieked Mr. Lupin, and at that moment Mrs. Oakley, who was afraid to attack Ben, gave her husband such an open-handed whack on the side of his head, that the little man reeled again, and saw a great many more lights than the Rev. Mr. Lupin had done under the influence of the mulled wine.

"Very good," said Ben, "now we are getting into the thick of it."

With this Ben took from his pocket a coil of rope, one end of which was a noose, and that he dexterously threw over Mrs. Oakley's head.

"Murder!" she shrieked. "Oakley, are you going to see me murdered before your eyes?

"There is such a singing in my ears," said Mr. Oakley, "that I can't see anything."

"This is the way," said Ben, "we manages the wild beastesses when they shuts their ears to all sorts of argument. Now, ma'am, if you please, a little this way."

Ben looked about until he found a strong hook in the wall, over which, in consequence of his great height, he was enabled to draw the rope, and then the other end of it he tied securely to the leg of a heavy secretaire that was in the room, so that Mrs. Oakley was well secured.

"'Murder!" she cried. "Oakley, are you a man, that you stand by and see me treated in this way by a big brute?"

"I can't see anything," said Mr. Oakley; "there is such a singing in my ears; I told you so before—I can't see anything."

"Now, ma'am, you may just say what you like," said Ben; "it won't matter a bit, any more than the grumbling of a bear with a sore head; and as for your Mr. Tulip, you'll just get down on your knees, and beg Mr. Oakley's pardon for coming and drinking his tea without his leave, and having the infernal impudence to speak to his daughter."

"Don't do it, Mr. Lupin," cried Mrs. Oakley—"don't do it."

"You hear," said Ben, "what the lady advises. Now, I am quite different; I advise you to do it—for, if you don't, I shan't hurt you; but it strikes me I shall be obliged to fall on you and crush you."

"I think I will," said Mr. Lupin; "the saints were always forced to yield to the Philistines."

"If you call me any names," said Ben, "I'll just wring your neck."

"Young man, young man, let me exhort you. Allow me to go, and I will put up prayers for your conversion."

"Confound your impudence! what do you suppose the beasts in the Tower would do, if I was converted? Why, that 'ere tiger we have had lately, would eat his own tail, to think I had turned out such an ass. Come, I can't waste any more of my precious time; and if you don't get down on your knees directly, we'll see what we can do."

"I must," said Mr. Lupin, "I must, I suppose"; and down he flopped on his knees.

"Very good; now repeat after me.—I am a wolf that stole sheep's clothing."

"Yes; I am a wolf that stole sheep's clothing—the Lord forgive me."

"Perhaps he may, and perhaps he mayn't. Now go on—all that's wirtuous is my loathing."

"Oh dear, yes—all that's wirtuous is my loathing."

"Mr. Oakley; I have offended."

"Yes; I am a miserable sinner, Mr. Oakley, I have offended."

"And ask his pardon, on my bended—'

'Oh dear, yes—I asks his pardon on my bended—The Lord have mercy on us miserable sinners."

"Knees—I won't do so more."

"Yes—knees, I won't do so more."

"As sure as I lies on this floor."

"Yes—as sure as I lies on this floor. —Death and the devil, you've killed me!"

Ben took hold of the reverend gentleman by the back of the neck, and pressed his head down upon the floor, until his nose, which had before been such a sufferer, was nearly completely flattened with his face.

"Now; you may go," said Ben.

Mr. Lupin scrambled to his feet; but Ben followed him into the passage, and did not yet let him go, until he had accelerated his movements by two hearty kicks. And then the victorious beef-eater returned to the parlour.

"Why, Ben," said Mr. Oakley, "you are quite a poet."

"I believe you, Oakley, my boy," said Ben, "and now let us be off, and have a pint round the corner."

"What!" exclaimed Mrs. Oakley, "and leave me here, you wretches?"

"Yes," said Ben, "unless you promises never to be a female variety of the useful animal again, and begs pardon of Mr. Oakley, for giving him all this trouble; as for me, I'll let you off cheap, you shall only have to give me a kiss, and say you loves me."

"If I do, may I be—"

"Damned, you mean."

"No, I don't; choked I was going to say."

"Then you may be choked, for you have nothing to do but to let your legs go from under you, and you will be hung as comfortable as possible—come along; Oakley."

"Mr. Oakley—stop—stop—don't leave me here. I am sorry."

"That's enough," said Mr. Oakley; "and now, my dear, bear in mind one thing from me. I intend from this time forward to be master in my own house. If you and I are to live together, we must do so on very different terms to what we have been living, and if you won't make yourself agreeable, Lawyer Hutchins tells me that I can turn you out and give you a maintenance; and, in that case, I'll have home my sister Rachel to mind house for me; so now you know my determination, and what you have to expect. If you wish to begin, well do so at once, by getting something nice and tasty for Ben's supper."

Mrs. Oakley made the required promise, and being released, she set about preparations for the supper in real earnest; but whether she was really subdued or not, we shall, in due time, see.

CHAPTER X

COLONEL JEFFERY WAS NOT AT ALL SATISFIED WITH THE STATE OF AFFAIRS, AS regarded the disappearance of Mr. Thornhill, for whom he entertained a very sincere regard, both on account of the private estimation in which he held him, and on account of actual services rendered by Thornhill to him.

Not to detain Johanna Oakley in the Temple-gardens, he had stopped his narrative, completely at the point when what concerned her had ceased, and had said nothing of much danger which the ship *Neptune* and its crew and passengers has gone through, after Mr. Thornhill had been taken on board with his dog.

The fact is, the storm which he had mentioned was only the first of a series of gales of wind that buffeted the ship for some weeks, doing it much damage, and enforcing almost the necessity of putting in somewhere for repairs.

But a glance at the map will be sufficient to show, that situated as the Neptune was, the nearest port at which they could at all expect assistance, was the British colony, at the Cape of Good Hope; but such was the contrary nature of the winds and waves, that just upon the evening of a tempestuous day, they found themselves bearing down close in shore, on the eastern coast of Madagascar.

There was much apprehension that the vessel would strike on a rocky shore; but the water was deep, and the vessel rode well; there was a squall, and they let go both anchors to secure the vessel, as they were so close in shore, lest they should be driven in and stranded.

It was fortunate they had so secured themselves, for the gale while it lasted blew half a hurricane, and the ship lost some of her masts, and some other trifling damage, which, however, entailed upon them the necessity of remaining there a few days, to cut timber to repair their masts, and to obtain a few supplies.

There is but little to interest a general reader in the description of a gale. Order after order was given until the masts and spars went one by one, and then the orders for clearing the wreck were given.

There was much work to be done, and but little pleasure in doing it, for it was wet and miserable while it lasted, and there was the danger of being driven upon a lee shore, and knocked to pieces upon the rocks.

This danger was averted, and they anchored safe at a very short distance from the shore in comparative safety and security.

"We are safe now," remarked the captain, as he gave his second in command charge of the deck, and approached Mr. Thornhill and Colonel Jeffery.

"I am happy it is so," replied Jeffery.

"Well, captain," said Mr. Thornhill, "I am glad we have done with being knocked about; we are anchored, and the water here appears smooth enough."

"It is so, and I dare say it will remain so; it is a beautiful basin of deep water—deep and good anchorage; but you see it is not large enough to make a fine harbour."

"True; but it is rocky."

"It is; and that may make it sometimes dangerous, though I don't know that it would be so in some gales. The sea may beat in at the opening, which is deep enough for anything to enter—even Noah's ark would enter there easily enough."

"What will you do now?"

"Stay here for a day or so, and send boats ashore to cut some pine trees, to refit the ship with masts."

"You have no staves, then?"

"Not enough for such a purpose; and we never do go out stored with such things."

"You obtain them wherever you may go to."

"Yes, any part of the world will furnish them in some shape or other."

"When you send ashore, will you permit me to accompany the boat's crew?" said Jeffery.

"Certainly; but the natives of this country are violent and intractable, and, should you get into any row with them, there is every probability of your being captured, or some bodily injury done you."

"But I will take care to avoid that."

"Very well, colonel, you shall be welcome to go."

"I must beg the same permission," said Mr. Thornhill, "for I should much like to see the country, as well as to have some acquaintance with the natives themselves."

"By no means trust yourself alone with them," said the captain, "for if you live you will have cause to repent it—depend upon what I say."

"I will," said Thornhill; "I will go nowhere but where the boat's company goes."

"You will be safe then."

"But do you apprehend any hostile attack from the natives?" inquired Colonel Jeffery.

"No, I do not expect it; but such things have happened before today, and I have seen them when least expected, though I have been on this coast before, and yet I have never met with any ill-treatment; but there have been many who have touched on this coast, who have had a brush with the natives and come off second best, the natives generally retiring when the ship's company muster strong in number, and calling out the chiefs, who come down in great force that we may not conquer them."

The next morning the boats were ordered out to go ashore with crews, prepared for cutting timber, and obtaining such staves as the ship was in want of.

With these boats old Thornhill and Colonel Jeffery went both of them on board, and after a short ride, they reached the shore of Madagascar.

It was a beautiful country, and one in which vegetables appeared abundant and luxuriant, and the party in search of timber, for ship-building purposes, soon came to some lordly monarchs of the forest, which would have made vessels of themselves.

But this was not what was wanted; but where the trees grew thicker and taller, they began to cut some tall pine trees down.

This was the wood they most desired; in fact it was exactly what they wanted; but they hardly got through a few such trees, when the natives came down upon them, apparently to reconnoitre.

At first they were quiet and tractable enough, but anxious to see and inspect everything, being very inquisitive and curious.

However, that was easily borne, but at length they became more numerous, and began to pilfer all they could lay their hands upon, which, of course, brought resentment, and after some time a blow or two was exchanged.

Colonel Jeffery was forward and endeavouring to prevent some violence being offered to one of the woodcutters; in fact, he was interposing himself between the two contending parties, and tried to restore order and peace, but several armed natives rushed suddenly upon him, secured him, and were hurrying him away to death before anyone could stir in his behalf.

His doom appeared certain, for, had they succeeded, they would have cruelly and brutally murdered him.

However, just at that moment aid was at hand, and Mr. Thornhill, seeing how matters stood, seized a musket from one of the sailors, and rushed after the natives who had Colonel Jeffery.

There were three of them, two others had gone on to apprise, it was presumed, the chiefs. When Mr. Thornhill arrived, they had thrown a blanket over the head of Jeffery; but Mr. Thornhill in an instant hurled one with a blow from the butt-end of his musket, and the second met the same fate, as he turned to see what was the matter.

The third seeing the colonel free, and the musket levelled at his own head, immediately ran after the other two, to avoid any serious consequences to himself. "Thornhill, you have saved my life," said Colonel Jeffery, excitedly.

"Come away, don't stop here—to the ship!—to the ship!" And as he spoke, they hurried after the crew; and they succeeded in reaching the boats and the ship in safety; congratulating themselves not a little upon so lucky an escape from a people quite warlike enough to do mischief, but not civilised enough to distinguish when to do it.

When men are far away from home, and in foreign lands, with the skies of other climes above them, their hearts become more closely knit together in those ties of brotherhood which certainly ought to actuate the whole universe, but which as certainly do not do so, except in very narrow circumstances.

One of these instances, however, would probably be found in the conduct of Colonel Jeffery and Mr. Thornhill, even under any circumstances, for they were most emphatically what might be termed kindred spirits; but when we come to unite to that fact the remarkable manner in which they had been thrown together, and the mutual services that they had had it in their power to render to each other, we should not be surprised at the almost romantic friendship that arose between them.

It was then that Thornhill made the colonel's breast the repository of all his thoughts and all his wishes, and a freedom of intercourse and a community of feeling ensued between them, which, when it does take place between persons of really congenial dispositions, produces the most delightful results of human companionship.

No one who has not endured the tedium of a sea voyage can at all be aware of what a pleasant thing it is to have someone on board in the rich stores of whose intellect and fancy one can find a never-ending amusement.

The winds might now whistle through the cordage, and the waves toss the great ship on their foaming crests; still Thornhill and Jeffery were together, finding, in the midst of danger, solace in each other's society, and each animating the other to the performance of deeds of daring that astonished the crew.

The whole voyage was one of the greatest peril, and some of the oldest seamen on board did not scruple, during the continuance of their night watches, to intimate to their companions that the ship, in their opinion, would never reach England, and that she would founder somewhere along the long stretch of the African coast.

The captain, of course, made every possible exertion to put a stop to such prophetic sayings, but when once they commenced, in short time there is no such thing as completely eradicating them; and they, of course, produced the most injurious effect, paralysing the exertions of the crew in times of danger, and making them believe that they are in a doomed ship, and, consequently, all they can do is useless.

Sailors are extremely superstitious on such matters, and there cannot be any reasonable doubt but that some of the disasters that befell the *Neptune* on her homeward voyage from India may be attributable to this feeling of fatality getting hold of the seamen, and inducing them to think that, let them try what they might, they could not save the ship.

It happened that after they had rounded the Cape, a dense fog came on, such as had not been known on that coast for many a year, although the western shore of Africa, at some seasons of the year, is subject to such a species of vaporous exhalation.

Every object was wrapped in the most profound gloom, and yet there was a strong eddy or current of the ocean, flowing parallel with the land, and as the captain hoped, rather off than on the shore.

In consequence of this fear, the greatest anxiety prevailed on board the vessel, and lights were left burning on all parts of the deck, while two men were continually engaged making soundings. It was about half-an-hour after midnight, as the barometer indicated a storm, that suddenly the men, who were on watch on the deck, raised a loud cry of alarm.

They had suddenly seen, close to the larboard bow, lights, which must belong to some vessel that, like the *Neptune*, was encompassed in the fog, and a collision was quite inevitable, for neither ship had time to put about.

The only doubt, which was a fearful and an agonising one to have solved, was whether the stronger vessel was of sufficient bulk and power to run them down, or they it; and that fearful question was one which a few moments must settle.

In fact, almost before the echo of that cry of horror, which had come from the men, had died away, the vessels met. There was a hideous crash—one shriek of dismay and horror, and then all was still. The *Neptune*, with considerable damage, and some of the bulwarks stove in, sailed on; but the other ship went with a surging sound, to the bottom of the sea.

Alas! nothing could be done. The fog was so dense, that, coupled, too, with the darkness of the night, there could be no hope of rescuing one of the ill-fated crew of the ship; and the officers and seamen of the *Neptune*, although they shouted for some time, and then listened, to hear if any of the survivors of the ship that had been run down were swimming, no answer came to them; and when, in about six hours more they sailed out of the fog into a clear sunshine, where there was not so much as a cloud to be seen, they looked at each other like men newly awakened from some strange and fearful dream.

They never discovered the name of the ship they had run down, and the whole affair remained a profound mystery. When the *Neptune* reached the port of London, the affair was repeated, and every exertion made to obtain some information concerning the ill-fated ship that had met with so fearful a doom.

Such were the circumstances which awakened all the liveliest feelings of gratitude on the part of Colonel Jeffery towards Mr. Thornhill; and hence it was that he was in

London, and had the necessary leisure so to do, to leave no stone unturned to discover what had become of him.

After deep and anxious thought, and feeling convinced that there was some mystery which it was beyond his power to discover, he resolved upon asking the opinion of a friend, likewise in the army, a Captain Rathbone, concerning the whole of the facts.

This gentleman, and a gentleman he was in the fullest acceptation of the term, was in London; in fact, he had retired from active service, and inhabited a small but pleasant house in the outskirts of the metropolis.

It was one of those old-fashioned cottage residences, with all sorts of odd places and corners about it, and a thriving garden full of fine old wood, such as are rather rare near to London, and which are daily becoming more rare, in consequence of the value of the land immediately contiguous to the metropolis not permitting large pieces to remain attached to small residences.

Captain Rathbone had an amiable family about him, such as he was and might well be proud of, and was living in as great a state of domestic felicity as this world could very well afford him.

It was to this gentleman, then, that Colonel Jeffery resolved upon going to lay all the circumstances before him concerning the possible and probable fate of poor Thornhill.

This distance was not so great but that he could walk it conveniently, and he did so, arriving towards the dusk of the evening, on the day following that which had witnessed his deeply interesting interview with Johanna Oakley in the Temple-gardens.

There is nothing on earth so delightfully refreshing, after a dusty and rather a long country walk, as to suddenly enter a well-kept and extremely verdant garden; and this was the case especially to the feelings of Colonel Jeffery, when he arrived at Lime Tree Lodge, the residence of Captain Rathbone.

He was met with a most cordial and frank welcome—a welcome which he expected, but which was none the less delightful on that account; and after sitting awhile with the family in the house, he and the captain strolled into the garden, and then Colonel Jeffery commenced with his revelation.

The captain, with very few interruptions, heard him to the end; and when he concluded by saying, "And now I have come to ask your advice upon all these matters," the captain immediately replied, in his warm, off-hand manner,—

"I'm afraid you won't find my advice of much importance; but I offer you my active co-operation in anything you think ought to be done or can be done in this affair, which,

I assure you, deeply interests me, and gives me the greatest possible impulse to exertion. You have but to command me in the matter, and I am completely at your disposal."

"I was quite certain you would say as much. But notwithstanding the manner in which you shrink from giving an opinion, I am anxious to know what you really think with regard to what are, you will allow, most extraordinary circumstances."

"The most natural thing in the world," said Captain Rathbone, "at the first flush of the affair, seemed to be that we ought to look for your friend Thornhill at the point where he disappeared."

"At the barber's in Fleet-street?"

"Precisely. Did he leave, or did he not?"

"Sweeney Todd says that he left him, and proceeded down the street towards the city, in pursuance of a direction he had given to Mr. Oakley, the spectacle-maker, and that he saw him get into some sort of disturbance at the end of the market; but to put against that, we have the fact of the dog remaining by the barber's door, and his refusing to leave it on any amount of solicitation. Now the very fact that a dog could act in such a way proclaims an amount of sagacity that seems to tell loudly against the presumption that such a creature could make any mistake."

"It does. What say you, now, to going into town tomorrow morning, and making a call at the barber's, without proclaiming we have any special errand except to be shaved and dressed? Do you think he would know you again?"

"Scarcely, in plain clothes; I was in my undress uniform when I called with the captain of the *Neptune*, so that his impression of me must be decidedly of a military character; and the probability is, that he would not know me at all in the clothes of a civilian. I like the idea of giving a call at the barber's."

"Do you think your friend Thornhill was a man likely to talk about the valuable pearls he had in his possession?"

"Certainly not."

"I merely ask you, because they might have offered a great temptation; and if he has experienced any foul play at the hands of the barber, the idea of becoming possessed of such a valuable treasure might have been the inducement."

"I do not think it probable, but it has struck me that, if we obtain any information whatever of Thornhill, it will be in consequence of these very pearls. They are of great value, and not likely to be overlooked; and yet, unless a customer be found for them, they are of no value at all; and nobody buys jewels of that character but from the personal vanity of making, of course, some public display of them."

"That is true; and so, from hand to hand, we might trace those pearls until we come to the individual who must have had them from Thornhill himself, and who might be forced to account most strictly for the manner in which they came into his possession."

After some more desultory conversation upon the subject, it was agreed that Colonel Jeffery should take a bed there for the night at Lime Tree Lodge, and that, in the morning, they should both start for London, and, disguising themselves as respectable citizens, make some attempts, by talking about jewels and precious stones, to draw out the barber into a confession that he had something of the sort to dispose of; and, moreover, they fully intended to take away the dog, with the care of which, Captain Rathbone charged himself.

We may pass over the pleasant, social evening which the colonel passed with the amiable family of the Rathbones, and skipping likewise a conversation of some strange and confused dreams which Jeffery had during the night concerning his friend Thornhill, we will presume that both the colonel and the captain have breakfasted, and that they have proceeded to London and are at the shop of a clothier in the neighbourhood of the Strand, in order to procure coats, wigs, and hats, that should disguise them for their visit to Sweeney Todd.

Then, arm-in-arm, they walked towards Fleet-street, and soon arrived opposite the little shop within which there appears to be so much mystery.

"The dog you perceive is not here," said the colonel; "I had my suspicions, however, when I passed with Johanna Oakley that something was amiss with him, and I have no doubt but that the rascally barber has fairly compassed his destruction."

"If the barber be innocent," said Captain Rathbone, "you must admit that it would be one of the most confoundedly annoying things in the world to have a dog continually at his door assuming such an aspect of accusation, and in that case I can scarcely wonder at his putting the creature out of the way.

"No, presuming upon his innocence, certainly; but we will say nothing about all that, and remember we must come in as perfect strangers, knowing nothing whatever of the affair of the dog, and presuming nothing about the disappearance of anyone in this locality."

"Agreed, come on; if he should see us through the window, hanging about at all or hesitating, his suspicions will be at once awakened, and we shall do no good."

They both entered the shop and found Sweeney Todd wearing an extraordinary singular appearance, for there was a black patch over one of his eyes, which was kept in its place by a green riband that went round his head, so that he looked more fierce and diabolical than ever; and having shaved off a small whisker that he used to wear, his countenance, although to the full as hideous as ever, certainly had a different character of ugliness to that which had before characterised it, and attracted the attention of the colonel.

That gentleman would hardly have known him again anywhere but in his own shop, and when we come to consider Sweeney Todd's adventures of the preceding evening, we shall not feel surprised that he saw the necessity of endeavouring to make as much change in his appearance as possible for fear he should come across any of the parties who had chased him, and who, for all he knew to the contrary, might, quite unsuspectingly, drop in to be shaved in the course of the morning, perhaps to retail at that acknowledged mart for all sorts of gossip—a barber's shop—some of the very incidents which he was so well qualified himself to relate.

"Shaved and dressed, gentlemen," said Sweeney Todd, as his customers made their appearance.

"Shaved only," said Captain Rathbone, who had agreed to be the principal spokesman, in case Sweeney Todd should have any reminiscence of the colonel's voice, and so suspect him.

"Pray be seated," said Sweeney Todd to Colonel Jeffery. "I'll soon polish off your friend, sir, and then I'll begin upon you. Would you like to see the morning paper, sir? I was just looking myself, sir, at a most mysterious circumstance, if it's true, but you can't believe, you know, all that is put in the papers."

"Thank you—thank you," said the colonel.

Captain Rathbone sat down to be shaved, for he had purposely omitted that operation at home, in order that it should not appear a mere excuse to get into Sweeney Todd's shop.

"Why, sir," continued Sweeney Todd, "as I was saying, it is a most remarkable circumstance."

"Indeed!"

"Yes, sir, an old gentleman of the name of Fidler had been to receive a sum of money at the west-end of the town, and has never been heard of since; that was only yesterday, sir, and there is a description of him in the papers of to-day."

"'A snuff-coloured coat, and velvet smalls—black velvet, I should have said— silk stockings, and silver shoe-buckles, and a golden-headed cane, with W. D. F. upon it, meaning William Dumpledown Fidler'—a most mysterious affair, gentlemen."

A sort of groan came from the corner of the shop, and, on the impulse of the moment, Colonel Jeffery sprang to his feet, exclaiming—

"What's that—what's that?"

"Oh, it's only my apprentice, Tobias Ragg. He has got a pain in his stomach from eating too many of Lovett's pork pies. Ain't that it, Tobias, my bud?"

"Yes, sir," said Tobias, with another groan.

"Oh, indeed," said the colonel, "it ought to make him more careful for the future."

"It's to be hoped it will, sir; Tobias, do you hear what the gentleman says: it ought to make you more careful in future. I am too indulgent to you, that's the fact. Now, sir, I believe you are as clean shaved as ever you were in your life."

"Why, yes," said Captain Rathbone, "I think that will do very well, and now, Mr. Green,"—addressing the colonel by that assumed name—"and now, Mr. Green, be quick, or we shall be too late for the duke, and so lose the sale of some of our jewels."

"We shall indeed," said the colonel, "if we don't mind. We sat too long over our breakfast at the inn, and his grace is too rich and too good a customer to lose—he don't mind what price he gives for things that take his fancy, or the fancy of his duchess."

"Jewel merchants, gentlemen, I presume," said Sweeney Todd.

"Yes, we have been in that line for some time; and by one of us trading in one direction, and the other in another, we manage extremely well, because we exchange what suits our different customers, and keep up two distinct connexions."

"A very good plan," said Sweeney Todd. "I'll be as quick as I can with you, sir. Dealing in jewels is better than shaving."

"I dare say it is."

"Of course it is, sir; here have I been slaving for some years in this shop, and not done much good—that is to say, when I talk of not having done much good, I admit I have made enough to retire upon, quietly and comfortably, and I mean to do so very shortly. There you are, sir, shaved with celerity you seldom meet with, and as clean as possible, for the small charge of one penny. Thank you, gentlemen—there's your change; good morning."

They had no recourse but to leave the shop; and when they had gone, Sweeney Todd, as he stropped the razor he had been using upon his hand, gave a most diabolical grin, muttering,—

"Clever—very ingenious—but it wouldn't do. Oh dear no, not at all! I am not so easily taken in—diamond merchants, ah! ah! and no objection, of course, to deal in pearls—a good jest that, truly a capital jest. If I had been accustomed to be so defeated, I had not now been here a living man. Tobias, Tobias, I say!"

"Yes, sir," said the lad, dejectedly.

"Have you forgotten your mother's danger in case you breathe a syllable of anything that has occurred here, or that you think has occurred here, or so much as dream of?"

"No," said the boy, "indeed I have not. I never can forget it, if I were to live a hundred years."

"That's well, prudent, excellent, Tobias. Go out now, and if those two persons who were here last waylay you in the street, let them say what they will, and do you reply to them as shortly as possible; but be sure you come back to me quickly, and report what they do say. They turned to the left, towards the city—now be off with you."

"It's of no use," said Colonel Jeffery to the captain; "the barber is either too cunning for me, or he is really innocent of all participation in the disappearance of Thornhill."

"And yet there are suspicious circumstances. I watched his countenance when the subject of jewels was mentioned, and I saw a sudden change come over it; it was but momentary, but still it gave me a suspicion that he knew something which caution alone kept within the recesses of his breast. The conduct of the boy, too, was strange; and then again, if he has the string of pearls, their value would give him all the power to do what he says he is about to do—viz., to retire from business with an independence."

"Hush! there did you see the lad?"

"Yes; why it's the barber's boy."

"It is the same lad he called Tobias—shall we speak to him?"

"Let's make a bolder push, and offer him an ample reward for any information he may give us."

"Agreed, agreed."

They both walked up to Tobias, who was listlessly walking along the streets, and when they reached him, they were both struck with the appearance of care and sadness that was upon the boy's face.

He looked perfectly haggard, and care-worn—an expression sad to see upon the face of one so young, and, when the colonel accosted him in a kindly tone he seemed so unnerved that tears immediately darted to his eyes, although at the same time he shrank back as if alarmed.

"My lad," said the colonel, "you reside, I think, with Sweeney Todd, the barber. Is he not a kind master to you that you seem so unhappy?"

"No, no, that is, I mean yes, I have nothing to tell. Let me pass on."

"What is the meaning of this confusion?"

"Nothing, nothing."

"I say, my lad, here is a guinea for you, if you will tell us what became of the man of a seafaring appearance, who came with a dog to your master's house, some days since to be shaved."

"I cannot tell you," said the boy, "I cannot tell you, what I do not know."

"But, you have some idea, probably. Come, we will make it worth your while, and thereby protect you from Sweeney Todd. We have the power to do so, and all the inclination; but you must be quite explicit with us, and tell us frankly what you think, and what you know concerning the man in whose fate we are interested."

"I know nothing, I think nothing," said Tobias. "Let me go, I have nothing to say, except that he was shaved, and went away."

"But how came he to leave his dog behind him?"

"I cannot tell. I know nothing."

"It is evident that you do know something, but hesitate either from fear or some other motive to tell it; as you are inaccessible to fair means, we must resort to others, and you shall at once come before a magistrate, which will force you to speak out."

"Do with me what you will," said Tobias, "I cannot help it. I have nothing to say to you, nothing whatever. Oh, my poor mother, if it were not for you—"

"What, then?"

"Nothing! nothing! nothing!"

It was but a threat of the colonel to take the boy before a magistrate, for he really had no grounds for so doing; and if the boy chose to keep a secret, if he had one, not all the magistrates in the world could force words from his lips that he felt not inclined to utter; and so, after one more effort, they felt that they must leave him.

"Boy," said the colonel, "you are young, and cannot well judge of the consequences of particular lines of conduct; you ought to weigh well what you are about, and hesitate long before you determine keeping dangerous secrets; we can convince you that we have the power of completely protecting you from all that Sweeney Todd could possibly attempt. Think again, for this is an opportunity of saving yourself perhaps from much future misery that may never arise again."

"I have nothing to say," said the boy, "I have nothing to say."

He uttered these words with such an agonised expression of countenance, that they were both convinced he had something to say, and that, too, of the first importance—a something which would be valuable to them in the way of information, extremely valuable probably, and yet which they felt the utter impossibility of wringing from him.

They were compelled to leave him, and likewise with the additional mortification, that, far from making any advance in the matter, they had placed themselves and their cause in a much worse position, in so far as they had awakened all Sweeney Todd's suspicions if he were guilty, and yet advanced not one step in the transaction.

And then to make matters all the more perplexing, there was still the possibility that they might be altogether upon a wrong scent, and that the barber of Fleet-street had no more to do with the disappearance of Mr. Thornhill than they had themselves.

CHAPTER XI

TOWARDS THE DUSK OF THE EVENING IN THAT DAY, AFTER THE LAST BATCH OF PIES AT Lovett's had been disposed of, there walked into the shop a man most miserably clad, and who stood for a few moments staring with weakness and hunger at the counter before he spoke.

Mrs. Lovett was there, but she had no smile for him, and instead of its usual bland expression, her countenance wore an aspect of anger, as she forestalled what the man had to say, by exclaiming,—

"Go away, we never give to beggars."

There came a flash of colour, for a moment, across the features of the stranger, and then he replied,—

"Mistress Lovett, I do not come to ask alms of you, but to know if you can recommend me to any employment?"

"Recommend you! recommend a ragged wretch like you!"

"I am a ragged wretch, and, moreover, quite destitute. In better times I have sat at your counter, and paid cheerfully for what I have wanted, and then one of your softest smiles has been ever at my disposal. I do not say this as a reproach to you, because the cause of your smile was well-known to be a self-interested one, and when that cause has passed away, I can no longer expect it; but I am so situated that I am willing to do anything for a mere subsistence."

"Oh, yes, and then when you have got into a better case again, I have no doubt but you have quite sufficient insolence to make you unbearable; besides, what employment can we have but pie-making, and we have a man already who suits us very well with the exception that he, as you would do if you were to exchange with him, has grown insolent, and fancies himself master of the place."

"Well, well," said the stranger, "of course there is always sufficient argument against the poor and destitute to keep them so. If you will assert that my conduct would be of the nature you describe it, it is quite impossible for me to prove the contrary."

He turned and was about to leave the shop, when Mrs. Lovett called after him, saying—"Come in again in two hours."

He paused a moment or two, and then, turning his emaciated countenance upon her, said—"I will if my strength permits me—water from the pumps in the streets is but a poor thing for a man to subsist upon for twenty-four hours."

"You may take one pie."

The half-famished, miserable-looking man seized upon a pie, and devoured it in an instant.

"My name," he said, "is Jarvis Williams: I'll be here, never fear, Mrs. Lovett, in two hours; and notwithstanding all you have said, you shall find no change in my behaviour because I may be well-kept and better clothed; but if I should feel dissatisfied with my situation, I will leave it and no harm done."

So saying, he walked from the shop, and after he was gone, a strange expression came across the countenance of Mrs. Lovett, and she said in a low tone to herself.— "He might suit for a few months, like the rest, and it is clear we must get rid of the one we have; I must think of it."

There is a cellar of vast extent, and of dim and sepulchral aspect—some rough red tiles are laid upon the floor, and pieces of flint and large jagged stones have been hammered into the earthen walls to strengthen them; while here and there rough huge pillars made by beams of timber rise perpendicularly from the floor, and prop large flat pieces of wood against the ceiling, to support it.

Here and there gleaming lights seem to be peeping out from furnaces, and there is a strange, hissing, simmering sound going on, while the whole air is impregnated with a rich and savoury vapour.

This is Lovett's pie manufactory beneath the pavement of Bell-yard, and at this time a night-batch of some thousands is being made for the purpose of being sent by carts the first thing in the morning all over the suburbs of London.

By the earliest dawn of the day a crowd of itinerant hawkers of pies would make their appearance, carrying off a large quantity to regular customers who had them daily, and no more thought of being without them than of forbidding the milkman or the baker to call at their residences.

It will be seen and understood, therefore, that the retail part of Mrs. Lovett's business, which took place principally between the hours of twelve and one, was by no means the most important or profitable portion of a concern which was really of immense magnitude, and which brought in a large yearly income.

To stand in the cellar when this immense manufacture of what, at first sight, would appear such a trivial article was carried on, and to look about as far as the eye could reach, was by no means to have a sufficient idea of the extent of the place; for there were as many doors in different directions, and singular low-arched entrances to different vaults, which all appeared as black as midnight, that one might almost suppose the inhabitants of all the surrounding neighbourhood had, by common consent, given up their cellars to Lovett's pie factory.

There is but one miserable light, except the occasional fitful glare that comes from the ovens where the pies are stewing, hissing, and spluttering in their own luscious gravy.

There is but one man, too, throughout all the place, and he is sitting on a low three-legged stool in one corner, with his head resting upon his hands, and gently rocking to and fro, as he utters scarcely audible moans.

He is but lightly clad; in fact, he seems to have but little on him except a shirt and a pair of loose canvas trousers. The sleeves of the former are turned up beyond his elbows, and on his head he has a white night-cap.

It seems astonishing that such a man, even with the assistance of Mrs. Lovett, could make so many pies as are required in a day; but the system does wonders, and in those cellars there are various mechanical contrivances for kneading the dough, chopping up the meat, &c., which greatly reduce the labour.

But what a miserable object is this man—what a sad and soul-stricken wretch he looks! His face is pale and haggard, his eyes deeply sunken; and, as he removes his hands from before his visage, and looks about him, a more perfect picture of horror could not have been found.

"I must leave to-night," he said, in coarse accents—"I must leave to-night. I know too much—my brain is full of horrors. I have not slept now for five nights, nor dare I eat anything but the raw flour. I will leave tonight if they do not watch me too closely. Oh! if I could but get into the streets—if I could but once again breathe the fresh air! Hush! what's that? I thought I heard a noise."

He rose, and stood trembling and listening; but all was still, save the simmering and hissing of the pies, and then he resumed his seat with a deep sigh.

"All the doors fastened upon me," he said, "what can it mean? It's very horrible, and my heart dies within me. Six weeks only have I been here—only six weeks. I was starving before I came. Alas, alas! how much better to have starved! I should have been dead before now, and spared all this agony!"

"Skinner!" cried a voice, and it was a female one—"Skinner, how long will the ovens be?"

"A quarter of an hour," he replied, "a quarter of an hour, Mrs. Lovett. God help me!"

"What is that you say?"

"I said, God help me! surely a man may say that without offence."

A door slammed shut, and the miserable man was alone again.

"How strangely," he said, "on this night my thoughts go back to early days, and to what I once was. The pleasant scenes of my youth recur to me. I see again the ivy-mantled porch, and the pleasant green. I hear again the merry ringing laughter of my playmates, and there, in my mind's eye, appears to me, the bubbling stream, and the ancient mill, the old mansion-house, with its tall turrets, and its air of silent grandeur. I hear the music of the birds, and the winds making rough melody among the trees. 'Tis very strange that all these sights and sounds should come back to me at such a time as this, as if just to remind me what a wretch I am."

He was silent for a few moments, during which he trembled with emotion; then he spoke again, saying,—

"Thus the forms of those whom I once knew, and many of whom have gone already to the silent tomb, appear to come thronging round me. They bend their eyes momentarily upon me, and, with settled expressions, show acutely the sympathy they feel for me.

"I see her, too, who first, in my bosom, lit up the flame of soft affection. I see her gliding past me like the dim vision of a dream, indistinct, but beautiful; no more than a shadow—and yet to me most palpable. What am I now—what am I now?"

He resumed his former position, with his head resting upon his hands; he rocked himself slowly to and fro, uttering those moans of a tortured spirit, which we have before noticed.

But see, one of the small arch doors opens, in the gloom of those vaults, and a man, in a stooping posture, creeps in—a half-mask is upon his face, and he wears a cloak; but both his hands are at liberty. In one of them he carries a double-headed hammer, with a powerful handle, of about ten inches in length.

He has probably come out of a darker place than the one into which he now so cautiously creeps, for he shades the light from his eyes, as if it was suddenly rather too much for him, and then he looks cautiously round the vault, until he sees the crouched-up figure of the man whose duty it is to attend to the ovens.

From that moment he looks at nothing else; but advances towards him, steadily and cautiously. It is evident that great secrecy is his object, for he is walking on his stocking soles only; and it is impossible to hear the slightest sound of his footsteps. Nearer and nearer he comes, so slowly, and yet so surely towards him, who still keeps up the low moaning sound, indicative of mental anguish. Now he is close to him, and he bends over him for a moment, with a look of fiendish malice. It is a look which, despite his mask, glances full from his eyes, and then, grasping the hammer tightly in both hands, he raises it slowly above his head, and gives it a swinging motion through the air.

There is no knowing what induced the man that was crouching upon the stool to rise at that moment; but he did so, and paced about with great quickness.

A sudden shriek burst from his lips, as he beheld so terrific an apparition before him; but, before he could repeat the word, the hammer descended, crushing into his skull, and he fell lifeless without a moan.

"And so Mr. Jarvis Williams, you have kept your word," said Mrs. Lovett to the emaciated, care-worn stranger, who had solicited employment of her, "and so Mr. Jarvis Williams, you have kept your word, and come for employment."

"I have, madam, and hope that you can give it to me: I frankly tell you that I would seek for something better, and more congenial to my disposition if I could; but who would employ one presenting such a wretched appearance as I do? You see that I am all in rags, and I have told you that I have been half starved, and therefore it is only some common and ordinary employment that I can hope to get, and that made me come to you."

"Well, I don't see why we should not make a trial of you, at all events, so if you like to go down into the bakehouse, I will follow you, and show you what you have to do. You remember that you have to live entirely upon the pies, unless you like to purchase for yourself anything else, which you may do if you can get the money. We give none, and you must likewise agree never to leave the bake-house."

"Never to leave it?"

"Never, unless you leave it for good, and for all; if upon those conditions you choose to accept the situation, you may, and if not you can go about your business at once, and leave it alone."

"Alas, madam, I have no resource; but you spoke of having a man already."

"Yes; but he has gone to some of his very oldest friends, who will be quite glad to see him, so now say the word:—Are you willing or are you not, to take the situation?"

"My poverty and my destitution consent, if my will be adverse, Mrs. Lovett; but, of course, I quite understand that I leave when I please."

"Oh, of course, we never think of keeping anybody many hours after they begin to feel uncomfortable. If you are ready, follow me."

"I am quite ready, and thankful for a shelter. All the brightest visions of my early life have long since faded away, and it matters little or, indeed, nothing what now becomes of me; I will follow you, madam, freely upon the condition you have mentioned."

Mrs. Lovett lifted up a portion of the counter which permitted him to pass behind it, and then he followed her into a small room, which was at the back of the shop. She then took a key from her pocket, and opened an old door which was in the wainscoting, and immediately behind which was a flight of stairs.

These she descended, and Jarvis Williams followed her, to a considerable depth, after which she took an iron bar from behind another door, and flung it open, showing to her new assistant the interior of that vault which we have already very briefly described.

"These," she said, "are the ovens, and I will proceed to show you how you can manufacture the pies, feed the furnaces, and make yourself generally useful. Flour will be always let down through a trap-door from the upper shop, as well as everything required for making the pies but the meat, and that you will always find ranged upon shelves either in lumps or steaks, in a small room through this door, but it is only at particular times you will find the door open; and whenever you do so, you had better always take out what meat you think you will require for the next batch."

"I understand all that, madam," said Williams, "but how does it get there?"

"That's no business of yours; so long as you are supplied with it, that is sufficient for you; and now I will go through the process of making one pie, so that you may know how to proceed, and you will find with what amazing quickness they can be manufactured if you set about them in the proper manner."

She then showed how a piece of meat thrown into a machine became finely minced up, by merely turning a handle; and then how flour and water and lard were mixed up together, to make the crusts of the pies, by another machine, which threw out the paste, thus manufactured, in small pieces, each just large enough for a pie.

Lastly, she showed him how a tray, which just held a hundred, could be filled, and, by turning a windlass, sent up to the shop, through a square trapdoor, which went right up to the very counter.

"And now," she said, "I must leave you. As long as you are industrious, you will get on very well, but as soon as you begin to be idle, and neglect the orders that are sent to you by me, you will get a piece of information which will be useful, and which, if you are a prudent man, will enable you to know what you are about."

"What is that? you may as well give it to me now."

"No; we but seldom find there is occasion for it at first, but, after a time, when you get well fed, you are pretty sure to want it."

So saying, she left the place, and he heard the door, by which he had entered, carefully barred after her. Suddenly then he heard her voice again, and so clearly and distinctly, too, that he thought she must have come back again; but, upon looking up at the door, he found that that arose from the fact of her speaking through a small grating at the upper part of it, to which her mouth was closely placed.

"Remember your duty," she said, "and I warn you that any attempt to leave here will be as futile as it will be dangerous."

"Except with your consent, when I relinquish the situation."

"Oh, certainly—certainly, you are quite right there, everybody who relinquishes the situation, goes to his old friends, whom he has not seen for many years, perhaps."

"What a strange manner of talking she has!" said Jarvis Williams to himself, when he found he was alone. "There seems to be some singular and hidden meaning in every word she utters. What can she mean by a communication being made to me, if I neglect my duty! It is very strange, and what a singular-looking place this is! I think it would be quite unbearable if it were not for the delicious odour of the pies, and they are indeed delicious—perhaps more delicious to me, who has been famished so long, and has gone through so much wretchedness; there is no one here but myself, and I am hungry now—frightfully hungry, and whether the pies are done or not, I'll have half a dozen of them at any rate, so here goes."

He opened one of the ovens, and the fragrant steam that came out was perfectly delicious, and he sniffed it up with a satisfaction such as he had never felt before, as regarded anything that was eatable.

"Is it possible," he said, "that I shall be able to make such delicious pies? at all events one can't starve here, and if it is a kind of imprisonment, it's a pleasant one. Upon my soul, they are nice, even half-cooked—delicious! I'll have another half-dozen, there are lots of them—delightful! I can't keep the gravy from running out of the corners of my mouth. Upon my soul, Mrs. Lovett, I don't know where you get your meat, but it's all as tender as young chickens, and the fat actually melts away in one's mouth. Ah, these are pies, something like pies!—they are positively fit for the gods!"

Mrs. Lovett's new man ate twelve threepenny pies, and then he thought of leaving off. It was a little drawback not to have anything to wash them down with but cold water, but he reconciled himself to this. "For," as he said, "after all it would be a pity to take the flavour of such pies out of one's mouth—indeed, it would be a thousand pities, so I won't think of it, but just put up with what I have got and not complain. I might have gone further and fared worse with a vengeance, and I cannot help looking upon it as a singular piece of good fortune that made me think of coming here in my deep distress to try and get something to do. I have no friends, and no money; she whom I loved is faithless, and here I am, master of as many pies as I like, and to all appearance monarch of all I survey; for there really seems to be no one to dispute my supremacy.

"To be sure, my kingdom is rather a gloomy one; but then I can abdicate it when I like, and when I am tired of those delicious pies, if such a thing be possible, which I really very much doubt, I can give up my situation and think of something else.

"If I do that I will leave England for ever; it's no place for me after the many disappointments I have had. No friend left me, my girl false, not a relation but who would turn his back upon me! I will go somewhere where I am unknown and can form new connections, and perhaps make new friendships of a more permanent and stable character than the old ones, which have all proved so false to me; and, in the meantime, I'll make and eat pies as fast as I can."

CHAPTER XII

THE BEAUTIFUL JOHANNA—WHEN IN OBEDIENCE TO THE COMMAND OF HER FATHER she left him, and begged him (the beef-eater) to manage matters with the Rev. Mr. Lupin—did not proceed directly upstairs to the apartment, but lingered on the staircase to hear what ensued; and if anything in her dejected state of mind could have given her amusement, it would certainly have been the way in which the beef-eater exacted a retribution from the reverend personage, who was not likely again to intrude himself into the house of the spectacle-maker.

But when he was gone, and she heard that a sort of peace had been patched up with her mother—a peace which, from her knowledge of the high-contracting parties, she conjectured would not last long—she returned to her room, and locked herself in; so that if any attempt was made to get her down to partake of the supper, it might be supposed she was asleep, for she felt herself totally unequal to the task of making one in any party, however much she might respect the individual members that composed it.

And she did respect Ben the beef-eater; for she had a lively recollection of much kindness from him during her early years, and she knew that he had never come to the house when she was a child without bringing her some token of his regard in the shape of a plaything, or some little article of doll's finery, which at that time was very precious.

She was not wrong in her conjecture that Ben would make an attempt to get her downstairs, for her father came up at the beef-eater's request, and tapped at her door. She thought the best plan, as indeed it was, would be to make no answer, so that the old spectacle-maker concluded at once what she wished him to conclude, namely that she had gone to sleep; and he walked quietly down the stairs again, glad that he had not disturbed her, and told Ben as much.

Now feeling herself quite secure from interruption for the night, Johanna did not attempt to seek repose, but set herself seriously to reflect upon what had happened. She almost repeated to herself, word for word, what Colonel Jeffery had told her; and, as she revolved the matter over and over again in her brain, a strange thought took possession of her, which she could not banish, and which, when once it found a home within her breast, began to gather probability from every slight circumstance that was in any way connected with it. This thought, strange as it may appear, was that the Mr. Thornhill, of whom Colonel Jeffery spoke in terms of such high eulogium, was no other than Mark Ingestrie himself.

It is astonishing, when once a thought occurs to the mind, that makes a strong impression, how, with immense rapidity, a rush of evidence will appear to come to support it. And thus it was with regard to this supposition of Johanna Oakley.

She immediately remembered a host of little things which favoured the idea, and among the rest, she fully recollected that Mark Ingestrie had told her he meant to change his name when he left England; for that he wished her and her only to know anything of him, or what had become of him; and that his intention was to baffle enquiry, in case it should be made, particularly by Mr. Grant, towards whom he felt a far greater amount of indignation, than the circumstances at all warranted him in feeling.

Then she recollected all that Colonel Jeffery had said with regard to the gallant and noble conduct of this Mr. Thornhill, and, girl-like, she thought that those high and noble qualities could surely belong to no one but her own lover, to such an extent; and that, therefore, Mr. Thornhill and Mark Ingestrie must be one and the same person.

Over and over again, she regretted she had not asked Colonel Jeffery for a personal description of Mr. Thornhill, for that would have settled all her doubts at once, and the idea that she had it still in her power to do so, in consequence of the appointment he had made with her for that day week, brought her some consolation.

"It must have been he," she said. "His anxiety to leave the ship, and get here by the day he mentions, proves it; besides, how improbable it is, that at the burning of the ill-fated vessel, Ingestrie should place in the hands of another what he intended for me, when that other was quite as likely, and perhaps more so, to meet with death as Mark himself."

Thus she reasoned, forcing herself each moment into a stronger belief of the identity of Thornhill with Mark Ingestrie, and so certainly narrowing her anxieties to a consideration of the fate of one person instead of two.

"I will meet Colonel Jeffery," she said, "and ask him if his Mr. Thornhill had fair hair, and a soft and pleasing expression about the eyes, that could not fail to be remembered. I will ask him how he spoke, and how he looked; and get him, if he can, to describe to me, even the very tones of his voice; and then I shall be sure, without the shadow of a doubt, that it is Mark. But then, oh! then comes the anxious question, of what has been his fate?"

When poor Johanna began to consider the multitude of things that might have happened to her lover during his progress from Sweeney Todd's, in Fleet-street, to her father's house, she became quite lost in a perfect maze of conjecture, and then her thoughts always painfully reverted back to the barber's shop where the dog had been stationed; and she trembled to reflect for a moment upon the frightful danger to which that string of pearls might have subjected him.

"Alas, alas!" she cried, "I can well conceive that the man whom I saw attempting to poison the dog would be capable of any enormity. I saw his face but for a moment, and yet it was one never again to be forgotten. It was a face in which might be read cruelty and evil passions; besides, the man who would put an unoffending animal to a cruel death shows an absence of feeling, and a baseness of mind, which makes him capable of any crime he thinks he can commit with impunity. What can I do—oh! what can I do to unravel this mystery?"

No one could have been more tenderly and more gently brought up than Johanna Oakley, but yet, inhabitive of her heart was a spirit and a determination which few indeed could have given her credit for, by merely looking on the gentle and affectionate countenance which she ordinarily presented.

But it is no new phenomenon in the history of the human heart to find that some of the most gentle and loveliest of human creatures are capable of the highest efforts of perversion; and when Johanna Oakley told herself, which she did, she was determined to devote her existence to a discovery of the mystery that enveloped the fate of Mark Ingestrie, she likewise made up her mind that the most likely means for accomplishing that object should not be rejected by her on the score of danger, and she at once set to work considering what those means should be.

This seemed an endless task, but still she thought that if, by any means whatever, she could get admittance to the barber's house, she might be able to come to some conclusion as to whether or not it was there where Thornhill, whom she believed to be Ingestrie, had been stayed in his progress.

"Aid me Heaven," she cried, "in the adoption of some means of action on the occasion. Is there anyone with whom I dare advise? Alas! I fear not, for the only person in whom I have put my whole heart is my father, and his affection for me would prompt him at once to interpose every possible obstacle to my proceeding, for fear danger should come of it. To be sure, there is Arabella Wilmot, my old school fellow and bosom friend, she would advise me to the best of her ability, but I much fear she is too romantic and full of odd, strange notions, that she has taken from books, to be a good adviser; and yet what can I do? I must speak to someone, if it be but in case of any accident happening to me, my father may get news of it, and I know of no one else whom I can trust but Arabella."

After some little more consideration, Johanna made up her mind that on the following morning she would go immediately to the house of her old school friend, which was in the immediate vicinity, and hold a conversation with her.

"I shall hear something," she said, "at least of a kindly and consoling character; for what Arabella may want in calm and steady judgement, she fully compensates for in actual feeling; and what is most of all, I know I can trust her word implicitly, and that my secret will remain as safely locked in her breast as if it were in my own."

It was something to come to a conclusion to ask advice, and she felt that some portion of her anxiety was lifted from her mind by the mere fact that she had made so firm a mental resolution, that neither danger nor difficulty should deter her from seeking to know the fate of her lover.

She retired to rest now with a greater hope, and while she is courting repose, notwithstanding the chance of the discovered images that fancy may present to her in her slumbers, we will take a glance at the parlour below, and see how far Mrs. Oakley is conveying out the pacific intention she had so tacitly expressed, and how the supper is going forward, which, with not the best grace in the world, she is preparing for her husband, who for the first time in his life had begun to assert his rights, and for Big Ben, the beefeater, whom she as cordially disliked as it was possible for any woman to detest any man.

Mrs. Oakley by no means preserved her taciturn demeanour, for after a little while she spoke, saying—"There is nothing tasty in the house; suppose I run over the way to Waggarge's, and get some of those Epping sausages with the peculiar flavour."

"Ah, do," said Mr. Oakley, "they are beautiful, Ben, I can assure you."

"Well, I don't know," said Ben, the beef-eater, "sausages are all very well in their way, but you need such a plagued lot of them; for if you only eat them one at a time, how soon will you get through a dozen or two?"

"A dozen or two," said Mrs. Oakley; "why, there are only five to a pound."

"Then," said Ben, making a mental calculation, "then, I think, ma'am, you ought not to get more than nine pounds of them, and that will be a matter of forty-five mouthfuls for us."

"Get nine pounds of them," said Mr. Oakley, "if they are wanted; I know Ben has an appetite."

"Indeed," said Ben, "but I have fell off lately, and don't take to my wittals as I used; you can order, missus, if you please, a gallon of half-and-half as you go along. One must have a drain of drink of some sort; and mind you don't be going to any expense on my account, and getting anything but the little snack I have mentioned, for ten to one I shall take supper when I get to the Tower; only human nature is weak, you know, missus, and requires something to be a continually a-holding of it up."

"Certainly," said Mr. Oakley, "certainly have what you like, Ben; just say the word before Mrs. Oakley goes out, is there anything else?"

"No, no," said Ben, "oh dear no, nothing to speak of; but if you should pass a shop where they sells fat bacon, about four or five pounds, cut into rashers, you'll find, missus, will help down the blessed sausages."

"Gracious Providence," said Mrs. Oakley, "who is to cook it?"

"Who is to cook it, ma'am? why, the kitchen fire, I suppose; but mind ye if the man ain't got any sausages, there's a shop where they sells biled beef at the corner, and I shall be quite satisfied if you brings in about ten or twelve pounds of that. You can make it up into about half a dozen sandwiches."

"Go, my dear, go at once," said Mr. Oakley, "and get Ben his supper. I am quite sure he wants it, and be as quick as you can."

"Ah," said Ben, when Mrs. Oakley was gone, "I didn't tell you how I was sarved last week at Mrs. Harvey's. You know they are so precious genteel there that they won't speak above their blessed breaths for fear of wearing themselves out; and they sits down in a chair as if it was balanced only on one leg, and a little more one way or t'other would upset them. Then, if they sees a crumb a-laying on the floor they rings a bell, and a poor half-starved devil of a servant comes and says, 'Did you ring, ma'am?' and then they says, 'Yes, bring a dust shovel and a broom, there is a crumb a-laying there,' and then says I—'Damn you all,' says I, 'bring a scavenger's cart, and a half-dozen birch brooms, there's a cinder just fell out of the fire.'

"Then in course they gets shocked, and looks as blue as possible, and arter that when they sees as I ain't a-going, one of them says, 'Mr. Benjamin Blummergutts, would you like to take a glass of wine?' 'I should think so,' says I. Then he says, says he, 'Which would you prefer, red or white?' says he.

"'White,' says I, 'while you are screwing up your courage to pull out the red,' so out they pull it; and as soon as I got hold of the bottle, I knocked the neck of it off over the top of the fireplace, and then drank it all up.

"'Now, damn ye,' says I, 'you thinks as all this is mighty genteel and fine, but I don't, and consider you to be the blessedest set of humbugs ever I set eyes on; and, if you ever catch me here again, I'll be genteel too, and I can't say more than that. Go to the devil, all of ye.' So out I went, only I met with a little accident in the hall, for they had got a sort of lamp hanging there, and, somehow or 'nother, my head went bang into it; and I carried it out round my neck; but, when I did get out, I took it off, and shied it slap in at the parlour window. You never heard such a smash in all your life. I dare say they all fainted away for about a week, the blessed humbugs."

"Well, I should not wonder," said Mr. Oakley. "I never go near them, because I don't like their foolish pomposity and pride, which, upon very slender resources, tries to ape what it don't at all understand; but here is Mrs. Oakley with the sausages, and I hope you will make yourself comfortable, Ben."

"Comfortable! I believe ye. I rather shall. I means it, and no mistake."

"I have brought three pounds," said Mrs. Oakley, "and told the man to call in a quarter of an hour, in case there is more wanted."

"The devil you have; and the bacon, Mrs. Oakley, the bacon!"

"I couldn't get any—the man had nothing but hams."

"Lor', ma'am, I'd a put up with a ham, cut thick, and never have said a word about it. I am an angel of a temper, if you did but know it! Hilloa, look, is that the fellow with the half-and-half?"

"Yes, here it is—a pot."

"A what!"

"A pot, to be sure."

"Well, I never; you are getting genteel, Mrs. Oakley. Then give us a hold of it."

Ben took the pot, and emptied it at a draught, and then he gave a tap at the bottom of it with his knuckles, to signify he had accomplished that feat, and then he said, "I tells you what, ma'am, if you takes me for a baby, it's a great mistake, and anyone would think you did, to see you offering me a pot merely; it's a insult, ma'am."

"Fiddle-de-de," said Mrs. Oakley; "it's a much greater insult to drink it all up, and give nobody a drop."

"Is it? I wants to know how you are to stop it, ma'am, when you gets it to your mouth? that's what I axes you—how are you to stop it, ma'am? You didn't want me to spew it back again, did you, eh, ma'am?"

"You low, vile wretch."

"Come, come, my dear," said Mr. Oakley, "you know our cousin Ben don't live among the most refined society, and so you ought to be able to look over a little of—of—his—I may say, I am sure without offence, roughness, now and then;—come, come, there is no harm done, I'm sure. Forget and forgive, say I. That's my maxim; and always has been, and will always be."

"Well," said the beef-eater, "it's a good one to get through the world with, and so there's an end of it. I forgives you, Mother Oakley."

"You forgive—"

"Yes, to be sure. Though I am only a beef-eater, I supposes as I may forgive people for all that—eh, Cousin Oakley?"

"Oh, of course, Ben, of course. Come, come, wife, you know as well as I that Ben has many good qualities, and that take him for all in all as the man in the play says, we shan't in a hurry look upon his like again."

"And I'm sure I don't want to look upon his like again," said Mrs. Oakley; "I'd rather by a good deal keep him a week than a fortnight. He's enough to breed a famine in the land, that he is."

"Oh, bless you, no," said Ben, "that's amongst your little mistakes, ma'am, I can assure you. By-the-by, what a blessed long time that fellow is coming with the rest of the beer and the other sausages—why, what's the matter with you, Cousin Oakley—eh, old chap, you look out of sorts?"

"I don't feel just the thing, do you know, Ben."

"Not—the thing—why—why now you come to mention it, I somehow feel as if all my blessed inside was on a turn and a twist. The devil—I—don't feel comfortable at all, I don't."

"And I am getting very ill," gasped Mr. Oakley.

"And I'm getting iller," said the beef-eater, manufacturing a word for the occasion. "Bless my soul! there's something gone wrong in my inside. I know there's murder—there's a go—oh, Lord! it's a-doubling me up, it is."

"I feel as if my last hour had come," said Mr. Oakley—"I'm a—a—dying, man—I am—oh, good gracious, there was a twinge!"

Mrs. Oakley, with all the coolness in the world, took down her bonnet from behind the parlour-door where it hung, and, as she put it on, said,—

"I told you both that some judgement would come over you, and now you see it has. How do you like it? Providence is good, of course, to its own, and I have—'

"What—what—?"

"*Pisoned* the half-and-half."

Big Ben, the beef-eater, fell off his chair with a deep groan, and poor Mr. Oakley sat glaring at his wife, and shivering with apprehension, quite unable to speak, while she placed a shawl over her shoulder, as she added, in the same tone of calmness she had made the terrific announcement concerning the poisoning,—

"Now, you wretches, you see what a woman can do when she makes up her mind for vengeance. As long as you all live, you'll recollect me; but if you don't, that won't much matter, for you won't live long, I can tell you, and now I'm going to my sister's, Mrs. Tiddiblow."

So saying, Mrs. Oakley turned quickly round, and, with an insulting toss of her head, and not at all caring for the pangs and sufferings of her poor victims, she left the place, and proceeded to her sister's house, where she slept as comfortably as if she had not by any means committed two diabolical murders.

But has she done so, or shall we, for the honour of human nature, discover that she went to a neighbouring chemist's, and only purchased some dreadfully powerful medicinal compound, which she placed in the half-and-half, and which began to give those pangs to Big Ben, the beef-eater, and to Mr. Oakley, concerning which they were so eloquent?

This must have been the case; for Mrs. Oakley could not have been such a fiend in human guise as to laugh as she passed the chemist's shop. Oh no! she might not have felt remorse, but that is a very different thing, indeed, from laughing at the matter, unless it were really laughable and not serious, at all.

Big Ben and Mr. Oakley must have at length found out how they had been hoaxed, and the most probable thing was that the before-mentioned chemist himself told them; for they sent for him in order to know if anything could be done to save their lives.

Ben from that day forthwith made a determination that he would not visit Mr. Oakley, and the next time they met he said,

"I tell you what it is, that old hag your wife is one too many for us, that's a fact; she gets the better of me altogether—so, whenever you feels a little inclined for a gossip about old times, just you come down to the Tower."

"I will, Ben."

"Do; we can always find you something to drink, and you can amuse yourself, too, by looking at the animals. Remember feeding time is two o'clock; so, now and then, I shall expect to see you, and, above all, be sure you let me know if that canting parson, Lupin, comes any more to your house."

"I will, Ben."

"Ah, do; and I'll give him another lesson if he should, and I'll tell you how I'll do it. I'll get a free admission to the wild *beastesses* in the Tower, and when he comes to see 'em, for them 'ere sort of fellows always goes everywhere they can go for nothing, I'll just manage to pop him into a cage along of some of the most *cantankerous* creatures as we have."

"But would that not be dangerous?"

"Oh dear no! we has a laughing hyena as would frighten him out of his wits; but I don't think as he'd bite him much, do you know. He's as playful as a kitten, and very fond of standing on his head."

"Well, then, Ben, I have, of course, no objection, although I do think that the lesson you have already given to the reverend gentleman will and ought to be fully sufficient for all purposes, and I don't expect we shall see him again."

"But how does Mrs. O. behave to you?" asked Ben.

"Well, Ben, I don't think there's much difference; sometimes she's a little civil, and sometimes she ain't; it's just as she takes into her head."

"Ah! all that comes of marrying."

"I have often wondered, though, Ben, that you never married."

Ben gave a chuckle as he replied,—

"Have you, though, really? Well, Cousin Oakley, I don't mind telling you, but the real fact is, once I was very near being served out in that sort of way."

"Indeed!"

"Yes. I'll tell you how it was: there was a girl called Angelina Day, and a nice-looking enough creature she was as you'd wish to see, and didn't seem as if she'd got any claws at all; leastways, she kept them in, like a cat at meal times."

"Upon my word, Ben, you have a great knowledge of the world."

"I believe you, I have! Haven't I been brought up among the wild beasts in the Tower all my life? That's the place to get a knowledge of the world in, my boy. I ought to know a thing or two, and in course I does."

"Well, but how was it, Ben, that you did not marry this Angelina you speak of?"

"I'll tell you; she thought she had me as safe as a hare in a trap, and she was as amiable as a lump of cotton. You'd have thought, to look at her, that she did nothing but smile; and, to hear her, that she said nothing but nice, mild, pleasant things, and I really began to think as I had found the proper sort of animal."

"But you were mistaken?"

"I believe you, I was. One day I'd been there to see her, I mean, at her father's house, and she'd been as amiable as she could be; I got up to go away, with a determination that the next time I got there I would ask her to say yes, and when I had got a little way out of the garden of the house where they lived—it was out of town some distance—I found I had left my little walking-cane behind me, so I goes back to get it, and when I got into the garden, I heard a voice."

"Whose voice?"

"Why Angelina's to be sure; she was a-speaking to a poor little dab of a servant they had; and oh, my eye! how she did rap out, to be sure! Such a speech as I never heard in all my life. She went on for a matter of ten minutes without stopping, and every other word was some ill name or another, and her voice—oh, gracious! it was like a bundle of wire all of a tangle—it was."

"And what did you do, then, upon making such a discovery as that in so very odd and unexpected a manner?"

"Do? What do you suppose I did?"

"I really cannot say, as you are rather an eccentric fellow."

"Well then, I'll tell you. I went up to the house, and just popped in my head, and says I, 'Angelina, I find out that all cats have claws after all; good-evening, and no more from your humble servant, who don't mind the job of taming a wild animal, but a woman'; and then off I walked, and I never heard of her afterwards."

"Ah, Ben, it's true enough! You never know them beforehand; but, after a little time, as you say, then out come the claws."

"They does—they does."

"And I suppose you since then made up your mind to be a bachelor for the rest of your life, Ben?"

"Of course I did. After such experience as that I should have deserved all I got, and no mistake, I can tell you; and if you ever catches me paying any attention to a female woman, just put me in mind of Angelina Day, and you'll see how I shall be off at once like a shot."

"Ah!" said Mr. Oakley, with a sigh, "everybody, Ben, ain't born with your good luck, I can tell you. You are a most fortunate man, Ben, and that's a fact. You must have been born under some lucky planet I think, Ben, or else you never would have had such a warning as you have had about the claws. I found 'em out, Ben, but it was a deal too late; so I had to put up with my fate, and put the best face I could upon the matter."

"Yes, that's what learned folks call—what's its name—fill—fill—something."

"Philosophy, I suppose you mean, Ben."

"Ah, that's it—you must put up with what you can't help, it means, I take it. It's a fine name for saying you must grin and bear it."

"I suppose that is about the truth, Ben."

It cannot, however, be exactly said that the little incident connected with Mr. Lupin had no good effect upon Mrs. Oakley, for it certainly shook most alarmingly her confidence in that pious individual.

In the first place, it was quite clear that he shrank from the horrors of martyrdom; and, indeed, to escape any bodily inconvenience was perfectly willing to put up with any amount of degradation or humiliation that he could be subjected to; and that was, to the apprehension of Mrs. Oakley, a great departure from what a saint ought to be.

Then again, her faith in the fact that Mr. Lupin was such a chosen morsel as he had represented himself, was shaken from the circumstance that no miracle in the shape of a judgement had taken place to save him from the malevolence of Big Ben, the beef-eater; so that, taking one thing in connection with another, Mrs. Oakley was not near so religious a character after that evening as she had been before it, and that was something gained.

Then circumstances soon occurred, of which the reader will very shortly be fully aware, which were calculated to awaken all the feelings of Mrs. Oakley, if she really had any feelings to awaken, and to force her to make common cause with her husband in an affair that touched him to the very soul, and did succeed in awakening some feelings in her heart that had lain dormant for a long time, but which were still far from being completely destroyed.

These circumstances were closely connected with the fate of one in whom we hope that, by this time, the reader has taken a deep and kindly interest—we mean Johanna— that young and beautiful, and artless creature, who seemed to have been created to be so very happy, and yet whose fate had become so clouded by misfortune, and who appears now to be doomed through her best affections to suffer so great an amount of sorrow, and to go through so many sad difficulties.

Alas, poor Johanna Oakley! Better had you loved someone of less aspiring feelings, and of less ardent imagination, than him to whom you have given your heart's young affections.

It is true that Mark Ingestrie possessed genius, and perhaps it was the glorious light that hovers around that fatal gift which prompted you to love him. But genius is not only a blight and a desolation to its possessor, but it is so to all who are bound to the gifted being by the ties of fond affection.

It brings with it that unhappy restlessness of intellect which is ever straining after the unattainable, and which is never content to know the end and ultimatum of earthly hopes and wishes; no, the whole life of such persons is spent in one long struggle for a fancied happiness, which like the *ignis-fatuus* of the swamp glitters but to betray those who trust to its delusive and flickering beams.

CHAPTER XIII

ALAS! POOR JOHANNA, THOU HAST CHOSEN BUT AN INDIFFERENT CONFIDANTE IN THE person of that young and inexperienced girl to whom it seems good to thee to impart thy griefs.

Not for one moment do we mean to say, that the young creature to whom the spectacle-maker's daughter made up her mind to unbosom herself was not all that anyone could wish as regards honour, goodness, and friendship. But she was one of those creatures who yet look upon the world as a fresh green garden, and have not yet lost that romance of existence which the world and its ways soon banish from the breasts of all.

She was young, almost to girlhood, and having been the idol of her family circle, she knew just about as little of the great world as a child.

But while we cannot but to some extent regret that Johanna should have chosen such a confidante and admirer, we with feelings of great freshness and pleasure proceed to accompany her to that young girl's house.

Now, a visit from Johanna Oakley to the Wilmots was not so rare a thing, that it should excite any unusual surprise, but in this case it did excite unusual pleasure because she had not been there for some time.

And the reason she had not may well be found in the peculiar circumstances that had for a considerable period environed her. She had a secret to keep which, although it might not proclaim what it was most legibly upon her countenance, yet proclaimed that it had an existence, and as she had not made Arabella a confidante, she dreaded the other's friendly questions of the young creature.

It may seem surprising that Johanna Oakley had kept from one whom she so much esteemed, and with whom she had made such a friendship, the secret of her affections; but that must be accounted for by a difference of ages between them to a sufficient extent in that early period of life to show itself palpably.

That difference was not quite two years, but when we likewise state, that Arabella was of that small, delicate style of beauty which makes her look like a child, when even upon the verge of womanhood, we shall not be surprised that the girl of seventeen hesitated to confide a secret of the heart to what seemed but a beautiful child.

The last year, however, had made a great difference in the appearance of Arabella, for although she still looked a year or so younger than she really was, a more staid and thoughtful expression had come over her face, and she no longer presented, except at times when she laughed, that child-like expression, which had been as remarkable in her as it was delightful.

She was as different looking from Johanna as she could be, for whereas Johanna's hair was of a rich and glossy brown, so nearly allied to black that it was commonly called such, the long waving ringlets that shaded the sweet countenance of Arabella Wilmot were like amber silk blended to a pale beauty.

Her eyes were really blue, and not that pale grey, which courtesy calls of that celestial colour, and their long, fringing lashes hung upon a cheek of the most delicate and exquisite hue that nature could produce.

Such was the young, lovable, and amiable creature who had made one of those girlish friendships with Johanna Oakley that, when they do endure beyond the period of almost mere childhood, endure for ever, and become one among the most dear and cherished sensations of the heart.

The acquaintance had commenced at school, and might have been of that evanescent character of so many school friendships, which, in after life, are scarcely so much remembered as the most dim visions of a dream; but it happened that they were congenial spirits, which, let them be thrown together under any circumstances whatever, would have come together with a perfect and a most endearing confidence in each other's affections.

That they were school companions was the mere accident that brought them together, and not the cause of their friendship.

Such, then, was the being to whom Johanna Oakley looked for counsel and assistance; and notwithstanding all that we have said respecting the likelihood of that counsel being of an inactive and girlish character, we cannot withhold our meed of approbation to Johanna that she had selected one so much in every way worthy of her honest esteem.

The hour at which she called was such as to insure Arabella being within, and the pleasure which showed itself upon the countenance of the young girl, as she welcomed her old playmate, was a feeling of the most delightful and unaffecting character.

"Why, Johanna," she said, "you so seldom call upon me now, that I suppose I must esteem it as a very special act of grace and favour to see you."

"Arabella," said Johanna, "I do not know what you will say to me when I tell you that my present visit to you is because I am in a difficulty, and want your advice."

"Then you could not have come to a better person, for I have read all the novels in London, and know all the difficulties that anybody can possibly get into, and, what is more important, I know all the means of getting out of them, let them be what they may."

"And yet, Arabella, scarcely in your novel reading will you find anything so strange and so eventful as the circumstances, I grieve to say, it is in my power to record to you. Sit down, and listen to me, dear Arabella, and you shall know all."

"You surprise and alarm me by the serious countenance, Johanna."

"The subject is a serious one. I love."

"Oh! is that all? So do I; there's young Captain Desbrook in the King's Guards. He comes here to buy his gloves; and if you did but hear him sigh as he leans over the counter, you would be astonished."

"Ah! but, Arabella, I know you well. Yours is one of those fleeting passions that, like the forked lightning, appear for a moment, and ere you can say behold is gone again. Mine is deeper in my heart, so deep, that to divorce it from it would be to destroy its home for ever."

"But why so serious, Johanna? You do not mean to tell me that it is possible for you to love any man without his loving you in return?"

"You are right there, Arabella. I do not come to speak to you of a hopeless passion—far from it; but you shall hear. Lend me, my dear friend, your serious attention, and you shall hear of such mysterious matters."

"Mysterious? then I shall be in my very element. For know that I quite live and exult in mystery, and you could not possibly have come to anyone who would more welcomely receive such a commission from you; I am all impatience."

Johanna then, with great earnestness, related to her friend the whole of the particulars connected with her deep and sincere attachment to Mark Ingestrie. She told her how, in spite of all circumstances which appeared to have a tendency to cast a shadow and a blight upon their young affection, they had loved and loved truly; how Ingestrie, disliking, both from principle and distaste, the study of the law, had quarrelled with his uncle, Mr. Grant, and then how, as a bold adventurer, he had gone to seek his fortunes in the Indian seas, fortunes which promised to be splendid; but which might end in disappointment and defeat, and they had ended in such calamities most deeply and truly did she mourn to be compelled to state. And now she concluded by saying,—

"And now, Arabella, you know all I have to tell you. You know how truly I have loved, and how after teaching myself to expect happiness, I have met with nothing but despair; and you may judge for yourself, how sadly the fate of Mark Ingestrie must deeply affect me, and how lost my mind must be in all kinds of conjecture concerning him."

The hilarity of spirits which had characterised Arabella, in the earlier part of their interview, entirely left her, as Johanna proceeded in her mournful narration, and by the time she had concluded, tears of the most genuine sympathy stood in her eyes.

She took the hands of Johanna in both her own, and said to her,—

"Why, my dear Johanna, I never expected to hear from your lips so sad a tale. This is most mournful, indeed very mournful; and although I was half inclined before to quarrel with you for this tardy confidence—for you must recollect that it is the first I have heard of this whole affair—but now the misfortunes that oppress you are quite sufficient, Heaven knows, without me adding to them by the shadow of a reproach."

"They are indeed, Arabella, and believe me if the course of my love ran smoothly, instead of being, as it has been, full of misadventure, you should have had nothing to complain of on the score of want of confidence; but I will own I did hesitate to inflict upon you my miseries, for miseries they have been and alas! miseries they seem destined to remain."

"Johanna, you could not have used an argument more delusive than that. It is not one which should have come from your lips to me."

"But surely it was a good motive, to spare you pain?"

"And did you think so lightly of my friendship that it was to be entrusted with nothing but what wore a pleasant aspect? True friendship is surely best shown in the encounter of difficulty and distress. I grieve, Johanna, indeed, that you have so much mistaken me."

"Nay, now you do me an injustice: it was not that I doubted your friendship for one moment, but that I did indeed shrink from casting the shadow of my sorrows over what should be, and what I hope is, the sunshine of your heart. That was the respect which deterred me from making you aware of what I suppose I must call this ill-fated passion."

"No, not ill-fated, Johanna. Let us believe that the time will come when it will be far otherwise than ill-fated."

"But what do you think of all that I have told you? Can you gather from it any hope?"

"Abundance of hope, Johanna. You have no certainty of the death of Ingestrie."

"I certainly have not, as far as regards the loss of him in the Indian sea; but, Arabella, there is one supposition which, from the moment it found a home in my breast, has been growing stronger and stronger, and that supposition is, that this Mr. Thornhill was no other than Mark Ingestrie himself."

"Indeed! Think you so? That would be a strange supposition. Have you any special reasons for such a thought?"

"None—further than a something which seemed ever to tell my heart from the first moment that such was the case, and a consideration of the improbability of the story related by Thornhill. Why should Mark Ingestrie have given him the string of pearls and the message to me, trusting to the preservation of this Thornhill, and assuming, for some strange reason, that he himself must fall?"

"There is good argument in that, Joanna."

"And moreover Mark Ingestrie told me he intended altering his name upon the expedition."

"It is strange; but now you mention such a supposition, it appears, do you know, Johanna, each moment more probable to me. Oh, that fatal string of pearls."

"Fatal, indeed! for if Mark Ingestrie and Thornhill be one and the same person, the possession of those pearls has been the temptation to destroy him."

"There cannot be a doubt upon that point, Johanna, and so you will find in all the tales of love and romance, that jealousy and wealth have been the sources of all the abundant evils which fond and attached hearts have from time to time suffered."

"It is so; I believe, it is so, Arabella; but advise me what to do, for truly I am myself incapable of action. Tell me what you think it is possible to do, under these disastrous circumstances, for there is nothing which I will not dare attempt."

"Why, my dear Johanna, you must perceive that all the evidence you have regarding this Thornhill follows him up to that barber's shop in Fleet-street, and no farther."

"It does, indeed."

"Can you not imagine, then, that there lies the mystery of his fate, and, from what you have yourself seen of that man, Todd, do you think he is one who would hesitate even at a murder?"

"Oh, horror! my own thoughts have taken that dreadful turn, but I dreaded to pronounce the word which would embody them. If, indeed, that fearful-looking man fancied that by any deed of blood he could become possessed of such a treasure as that which belonged to Mark Ingestrie, unchristian and illiberal as it may sound, the belief clings to me, that he would not hesitate to do it."

"Do not, however, conclude, Johanna, that such is the case. It would appear, from all you have heard and seen of these circumstances, that there is some fearful mystery; but do not, Johanna, conclude hastily, that that mystery is one of death."

"Be it so or not," said Johanna, "I must solve it, or go distracted. Heaven have mercy upon me; for even now I feel a fever in my brain, that precludes almost the possibility of rational thought."

"Be calm, be calm, we will think the matter over, calmly and seriously; and who knows but that, mere girls as we are, we may think of some adventitious mode of arriving at a knowledge of the truth; and now I am going to tell you something, which your narrative has recalled to my mind."

"Say on, Arabella, I shall listen to you with deep attention."

"A short time since, about six months, I think, an apprentice of my father, in the last week of his servitude, was sent to the west-end of the town to take a considerable sum of money; but he never came back with it, and from that day to this we have heard nothing of him, although from enquiry that my father made, he ascertained that he received the money, and that he met an acquaintance in the Strand, who parted from him at the corner of Milford-lane, and to whom he said he intended to call at Sweeney Todd, the barber's, in Fleet-street, to have his hair dressed, because there was to be a regatta on the Thames, and he was determined to go to it, whether my father liked or not."

"And he was never heard of?"

"Never. Of course, my father made every enquiry upon the subject, and called upon Sweeney Todd for the purpose, but, as he declared that no such person had ever called at his shop, the inquiry there terminated."

" 'Tis very strange."

"And most mysterious; for the friends of the youth were indefatigable in their searches for him; and, by subscribing together for the purpose, they offered a large reward to anyone who could or would give them information regarding his fate."

"And was it all in vain?"

"All; nothing could be learned whatever: not even the remotest clue was obtained, and there the affair has rested, in the most profound of mysteries."

Johanna shuddered, and for some few moments the two young girls were silent. It was Johanna who broke that silence, by exclaiming, "Arabella, assist me with what advice you can, so that I may go about what I purpose with the best prospect of success and the least danger; not that I shrink on my own account from risk; but if any misadventure were to occur to me, I might thereby be incapacitated from pursuing that object to which I will now devote the remainder of my life."

"But what can you do, my dear Johanna? It was but a short time since there was a placard in the barber's window to say that he wanted a lad as an assistant in his business, but that has been removed, or we might have procured someone to take the situation, for the express purpose of playing the spy upon the barber's proceedings."

"But, perchance, there still may be an opportunity of accomplishing something in that way, if you knew of anyone that would undertake the adventure."

"There will be no difficulty, Johanna, in discovering one willing to do so, although we might be long in finding one of sufficient capacity that we could trust: but I am adventurous, Johanna, as you know, and I think I could have got my cousin Albert to personate the character, only that he's rather a giddy youth, and scarcely to be trusted with a mission of so much importance."

"Yes, and a mission likewise, Arabella, which, by a single false step, might be made frightfully dangerous."

"It might, indeed."

"Then it would be unfair to place it upon anyone but those who feel most deeply for its success."

"Johanna, the enthusiasm with which you speak awakens in me a thought which I shrank from expressing to you, and which, I fear, perhaps more originates from a certain feeling of romance, which, I believe, is a besetting sin, than from any other cause."

"Name it, Arabella; name it."

"It would be possible for you or I to accomplish the object, by going disguised to the barber's, and accepting such a situation, if it were vacant, for a period of about twenty-four hours, in order that during that time, some opportunity might be taken of searching in his house for some evidence upon the subject nearest to your heart."

"It is a happy thought," said Johanna, "and why should I hesitate at encountering any risk or toil or difficulty for him who has risked so much for me? What is there to hinder me from carrying out such a resolution? At any moment, if great danger should beset me, I can rush into the street, and claim protection from the passers-by."

"And, moreover, Johanna, if you went on with such a mission, remember you go with my knowledge, and that consequently I would bring you assistance, if you appeared not in the specified time for your return."

"Each moment, Arabella, the plan assumes to my mind a better shape. If Sweeney Todd be innocent of contriving anything against the life and liberty of those who seek his shop, I have nothing to fear; but if, on the contrary he be guilty, danger to me would be the proof of such guilt, and that is a proof which I am willing to chance encountering for the sake of the great object I have in view; but how am I to provide myself with the necessary means?"

"Be at rest upon that score. My cousin Albert and you are as nearly of a size as possible. He will be staying here shortly, and I will secrete from his wardrobe a suit of clothes, which I am certain will answer your purpose. But let me implore you to wait until you have had your second interview with Colonel Jeffery."

"That is well thought of. I will meet him, and question him closely as to the personal appearance of this Mr. Thornhill; besides, I shall hear if he has any confirmed suspicion on the subject."

"That is well, you will soon meet him, for the week is running on, and let me implore you, Johanna, to come to me the morning after you have met him, and then we will again consult upon this plan of operations, which appears to us feasible and desirable."

Some more conversation of a similar character ensued between these young girls; and, upon the whole, Johanna Oakley felt much comforted by her visit, and more able to think calmly as well as seriously upon the subject which engrossed her whole thoughts and feelings; and when she returned to her own home, she found that much of the excitement of despair, which had formerly had possession of her, had given way to hope, and with that natural feeling of joyousness, and that elasticity of mind which belongs to the young, she began to build in her imagination some airy fabrics of future happiness.

Certainly, these suppositions went upon the fact that Mark Ingestrie was a prisoner, and not that his life had been taken by the mysterious barber; for although the possibility of his having been murdered had found a home in her imagination, still to her pure spirit it seemed by far too hideous to be true, and she scarcely could be said really and truly to entertain it as a matter which was likely to be true.

CHAPTER XIV

PERHAPS ONE OF THE MOST PITIABLE OBJECTS NOW IN OUR HISTORY IS POOR TOBIAS, Sweeney Todd's boy, who certainly had his suspicions aroused in the most terrific manner, but who was terrified by the threats of what the barber was capable of doing against his mother, from making any disclosures.

The effect upon his personal appearance of this wear and tear of his intellect was striking and manifest. The hue of youth and health entirely departed from his cheeks, and he looked so sad and care-worn, that it was quite a terrible thing to look upon a young lad so, as it were, upon the threshold of existence, and in whom anxious thoughts were making such war upon the physical energies.

His cheeks were pale and sunken; his eyes had an unnatural brightness about them, and, to look upon his lips, one would think that they had never parted in a smile for many a day, so sadly were they compressed together.

He seemed ever to be watching likewise for something fearful, and even as he walked the streets, he would frequently turn, and look enquiringly round him with a shudder, and in his brief interview with Colonel Jeffery and his friend the captain, we can have a tolerably good impression of the state of his mind.

Oppressed with fears and all sorts of dreadful thoughts, panting to give utterance to what he knew and to what he suspected, and yet terrified into silence for his mother's sake, we cannot but view him as signally entitled to the sympathy of the reader, and as, in all respects, one sincerely to be pitied for the cruel circumstances in which he was placed.

The sun is shining brightly, and even that busy region of trade and commerce, Fleet-street, is looking gay and beautiful; but not for that poor spirit-stricken lad are any of the sights and sounds which used to make up the delight of his existence, reaching his eyes or ears now with their accustomed force.

He sits moody and alone, and in the position which he always assumes when Sweeney Todd is from home—that is to say, with his head resting on his hands, and looking the picture of melancholy abstraction.

"What shall I do," he said to himself, "what will become of me! I think if I live here any longer, I shall go out of my senses. Sweeney Todd is a murderer—I am quite certain of it, and I wish to say so, but I dare not for my mother's sake. Alas! alas! the end of it will be that he will kill me, or that I shall go out of my senses, and then I shall die in some mad-house, and no one will care what I say."

The boy wept bitterly after he had uttered these melancholy reflections, and he felt his tears something of a relief to him, so that he looked up after a little time, and glanced around him.

"What a strange thing," he said, "that people should come into this shop, to my certain knowledge, who never go out of it again, and yet what becomes of them I cannot tell."

He looked with a shuddering anxiety towards the parlour, the door of which Sweeney Todd took care to lock always when he left the place, and he thought that he should like much to have a thorough examination of that room.

"I have been in it," he said, "and it seems full of cupboards and strange holes and corners, such as I never saw before, and there is an odd stench in it that I cannot make out at all; but it's out of the question thinking of ever being in it above a few minutes at a time, for Sweeney Todd takes good care of that."

The boy rose, and opened a cupboard that was in the shop. It was perfectly empty.

"Now, that's strange," he said; "there was a walking-stick with an ivory top to it here just before he went out, and I could swear it belonged to a man who came in to be shaved. More than once—ah! and more than twice, too, when I have come in suddenly, I have seen people's hats, and Sweeney Todd would try and make me believe that people go away after being shaved and leave their hats behind them."

He walked up to the shaving-chair, as it was called, which was a large old-fashioned piece of furniture, made of oak, and carved; and as the boy threw himself into it, he said,—

"What an odd thing it is that this chair is screwed so tight to the floor! Here is a complete fixture, and Sweeney Todd says that it is so because it's in the best possible light, and if he were not to make it fast in such a way, the customers would shift it about from place to place, so that he could not conveniently shave them; it may be true, but I don't know."

"And you have your doubts," said the voice of Sweeney Todd, as that individual, with a noiseless step, walked into the shop—"you have your doubts, Tobias? I shall have to cut your throat, that is quite clear."

"No, no; have mercy upon me; I did not mean what I said."

"Then it's uncommonly imprudent to say it, Tobias. Do you remember our last conversation? Do you remember that I can hang your mother when I please, because, if you do not, I beg to put you in mind of that pleasant little circumstance."

"I cannot forget—I do not forget."

"'Tis well; and mark me, I will not have you assume such an aspect as you wear when I am not here. You don't look cheerful, Tobias; and notwithstanding your excellent situation, with little to do, and the number of Lovett's pies you eat, you fall away."

"I cannot help it," said Tobias. "Since you told me what you did concerning my mother, I have been so anxious that I cannot help—'

"Why should you be so anxious? Her preservation depends upon yourself, and upon yourself wholly. You have but to keep silent, and she is safe; but if you utter one word that shall be displeasing to me about my affairs, mark me, Tobias, she comes to the scaffold; and if I cannot conveniently place you in the same mad-house where the last boy I had was placed, I shall certainly be under the troublesome necessity of cutting your throat."

"I will be silent—I will say nothing, Mr. Todd. I know I shall die soon, and then you will get rid of me altogether, and I don't care how soon that may be, for I am quite weary of my life—I shall be glad when it is over."

"Very good," said the barber; "that's all a matter of taste. And now, Tobias, I desire that you look cheerful and smile, for a gentleman is outside feeling his chin with his hand, and thinking he may as well come in and be shaved. I may want you, Tobias, to go to Billingsgate, and bring me a pennyworth of shrimps."

"Yes," thought Tobias with a groan—"yes, while you murder him."

CHAPTER XV

Now that there was a great object to be gained by a second interview with Colonel Jeffery, the anxiety of Johanna Oakley to have it became extremely great, and she counted the very hours until the period should arrive when she could again proceed to the Temple-gardens with something like a certainty of finding him.

The object, of course, was to ask him for a description of Mr. Thornhill, sufficiently accurate to enable her to come to something like a positive conclusion, as to whether she ought to call him to her own mind as Mark Ingestrie or not.

And Colonel Jeffery was not a bit the less anxious to see her, than she was to look upon him; for, although in diverse lands he had looked upon many a fair face, and heard many a voice that had sounded soft and musical to his ears, he had seen none that, to his mind, was so fair, and had heard no voice that he had considered really so musical and charming to listen to as Johanna Oakley's.

A man of more admirable and strict sense of honour than Colonel Jeffery could not have been found, and therefore it was that he allowed himself to admire the beautiful, under any circumstances, because he knew that his admiration was of no dangerous quality, but that, on the contrary, it was one of those feelings which might exist in a bosom such as his, quite undebased by a meaner influence.

We think it necessary, however, before he has his second interview with Johanna Oakley, to give such an explanation of his thoughts and feelings as is in our power.

When first he met her, the purity of her mind, and the genuine and beautiful candour of all she said, struck him most forcibly, as well as her great beauty, which could not fail to be extremely manifest.

After that he began to reason with himself as to what ought to be his feelings with regard to her—namely, what portion of these ought to be suppressed, and what ought to be encouraged.

If Mark Ingestrie were dead, there was not a shadow of interference or dishonour in him, Colonel Jeffery, loving the beautiful girl, who was surely not to be shut out of the pale of all affections, because the first person to whom her heart had warmed, with a pure and holy passion, was no more.

"It may be," he thought, "that she is incapable of feeling a sentiment which can at all approach that which once she felt; but still she may be happy and serene, and may pass many joyous hours as the wife of another."

He did not positively make these reflections, as applicable to himself, although they had a tendency that way, and he was fast verging on a state of mind which might induce him to give them a more actual application.

He did not tell himself that he loved her—no, the word "admiration" took the place of the more powerful term; but then, can we not doubt that, at this time, the germ of a very pure and holy affection was lighted up in the heart of Colonel Jeffery, for the beautiful creature, who had suffered the pangs of so much disappointment, and who loved one so well, who, we almost fear, if he was living, was scarcely the sort of person fully to requite such an affection.

But we know so little of Mark Ingestrie, and there appears to be so much doubt as to whether he be alive or dead, that we should not prejudge him upon such very insufficient evidence.

Johanna Oakley did think of taking Arabella Wilmot with her to this meeting with Colonel Jeffery, but she abandoned the idea, because it really looked as if she was either afraid of him, or afraid of herself, so she resolved to go alone; and when the hour of appointment came, she was there walking upon that broad, gravelled path, which has been trodden by some of the best, and some of the most eminent, as well as some of the worst of human beings.

It was not likely that with the feelings of Colonel Jeffery towards her, he should keep her waiting. Indeed, he was there a good hour before the time, and his only great dread was, that she might not come.

He had some reason for this dread, because it will be readily recollected by the reader, that she had not positively promised to come; so that all he had was a hope that way tending and nothing farther.

As minute after minute had passed away, she came not, although the time had not really arrived; his apprehension that she would not give him the meeting, had grown in his mind, almost to a certainty, when he saw her timidly advancing along the garden walk.

He rose to meet her at once, and for a few moments after he had greeted her with kind civility she could do nothing but look enquiringly in his face, to know if he had any news to tell her of the object of her anxious solicitude.

"I have heard nothing, Miss Oakley," he said, "that can give you any satisfaction, concerning the fate of Mr. Thornhill, but we have much suspicion—I say we, because

I have taken a friend into my confidence—that something serious must have happened to him, and that the barber, Sweeney Todd, in Fleet-street, at whose door the dog so mysteriously took his post, knows something of that circumstance, be it what it may."

He led her to a seat as he spoke, and when she had recovered sufficiently the agitation of her feelings to speak, she said in a timid, hesitating voice,—

"Had Mr. Thornhill fair hair, and large, clear, grey eyes?"

"Yes, he had such; and, I think, his smile was the most singularly beautiful I ever beheld in a man."

"Heaven help me!" said Johanna.

"Have you any reason for asking that question regarding Thornhill?"

"God grant, I had not; but alas! I have indeed. I feel that, in Thornhill, I must recognise Mark Ingestrie himself."

"You astonish me."

"It must be so, it must be so; you have described him to me, and I cannot doubt it; Mark Ingestrie and Thornhill are one; I knew that he was going to change his name when he went upon that wild adventure to the Indian sea. I was well aware of that fact."

"I cannot think, Miss Oakley, that you are correct in that supposition. There are many things which induce me to think otherwise; and the first and foremost of them is, that the ingenuous character of Mr. Thornhill forbids the likelihood of such a thing occurring. You may depend it is not—cannot be, as you suppose."

"The proofs are too strong for me, and I find I dare not doubt them. It is so, Colonel Jeffery, as time, perchance, may show; it is sad, very sad, to think that it is so, but I dare not doubt it, now that you have described him to me exactly as he lived."

"I must own, that in giving an opinion on such a point to you, I may be accused of arrogance and assumption, for I have had no description of Mark Ingestrie, and never saw him; and although you never saw certainly Mr. Thornhill, yet I have described him to you, and therefore you are able to judge from that description something of him."

"I am indeed, and I cannot—dare not doubt. It is horrible to be positive on this point to me, because I do fear with you that something dreadful has occurred, and that the barber in Fleet-street could unravel a frightful secret, if he chose, connected with Mark Ingestrie's fate."

"I do sincerely hope from my heart that you are wrong; I hope it, because I tell you frankly, dim and obscure as is the hope that Mark Ingestrie may have been picked up from the wreck of his vessel, it is yet stronger than the supposition that Thornhill has escaped the murderous hands of Sweeney Todd, the barber."

Johanna looked in his face so imploringly, and with such an expression of hope-lessness, that it was most sad indeed to see her, and quite involuntarily he exclaimed,—

"If the sacrifice of my life would be to you a relief, and save you from the pangs you suffer, believe me, it should be made."

She started as she said, "No, no; Heaven knows enough has been sacrificed already—more than enough, much more than enough. But do not suppose that I am ungrateful for the generous interest you have taken in me. Do not suppose that I think any the less of the generosity and nobility of soul that would offer a sacrifice, because it is one I would hesitate to accept. No, believe me, Colonel Jeffery, that among the few names that are enrolled in my breast—and such to me will ever be honoured—remem-ber yours will be found while I live, but that will not be long—but that will not be long."

"Nay, do not speak so despairingly."

"Have I not cause for despair?"

"Cause have you for great grief, but yet scarcely for despair. You are young yet, and let me entertain a hope that even if a feeling of regret may mingle with your future thoughts, time will achieve something in tempering your sorrow, and if not great hap-piness, you may know great serenity."

"I dare not hope it, but I know your words are kindly spoken, and most kindly meant."

"You may well assure yourself that they are so."

"I will ascertain his fate, or perish."

"You alarm me by those words, as well as by your manner of uttering them. Let me implore you, Miss Oakley, to attempt nothing rash; remember how weak and inef-ficient must be the exertions of a young girl like yourself, one who knows so little of the world, and can really understand so little of its wickedness."

"Affection conquers all obstacles, and the weakest and most inefficient girl that ever stepped, if she have strong within her that love which, in all its sacred intensity, knows no fear, shall indeed accomplish much. I feel that in such a cause, I could shake off all girlish terrors and ordinary alarms; and if there be danger, I would ask, what is life to me without all that could adorn it, and make it beautiful?"

"This, indeed, is the very enthusiasm of affection, when believe me, it will lead you to some excess—to some romantic exercise of feeling, such as will bring great danger in its train, to the unhappiness of those who love you."

"Those who love me—who is there to love me now?"

"Johanna Oakley, I dare not and will not utter words that come thronging to my lips, but which I fear might be unwelcome to your ears; I will not say that I can answer the questions you have asked, because it would sound ungenerous at such a time as this, when you have met me to talk of the fate of another. Oh! forgive me, that hurried away by the feeling of a moment, I have uttered these words, for I meant not to utter them."

Johanna looked at him in silence, and it might be that there was the slightest possible tinge of reproach in her look, but it was very slight, for one glance at that ingenuous countenance would be sufficient to convince the most sceptical of the truth and single-mindedness of its owner: of this, there could be no doubt whatever, and if anything in the shape of a reproach was upon the point of coming from her lips, she forbore to utter it.

"May I hope," he added, "that I have not lowered myself in your esteem, Miss Oakley, by what I have said?"

"I hope," she said gently, "you will continue to be my friend."

She laid an emphasis on the word "friend," and he fully understood what she meant to imply thereby, and after a moment's pause said,—

"Heaven forbid, that ever by word, or by action, Johanna, I should do aught to deprive myself of that privilege. Let me be your friend, since—"

He left the sentence unfinished, but if he had added the words—"since I can do no more," he could not have made it more evident to Johanna that those were the words he intended to utter.

"And now," he added, "that I hope and trust we understand each other better than we did, and you are willing to call me by the name of friend, let me once more ask you, by the privilege of such a title, to be careful of yourself, and not to risk much in order that you may perhaps have some remote chance of achieving very little."

"But can I endure this dreadful suspense?"

"It is, alas! too common an affliction on human nature, Johanna. Pardon me for addressing you as Johanna."

"Nay, it requires no excuse. I am accustomed so to be addressed by all who feel a kindly interest for me. Call me Johanna if you will, and I shall feel a greater assurance of your friendship and your esteem."

"I will then avail myself of that permission, and again and again I will entreat you to leave to me the task of making what attempts may be made to discover the fate of Mr. Thornhill. There must be danger even in enquiring for him, if he has met with any foul play, and therefore I ask you to let that danger be mine."

Johanna asked herself if she should or not tell him of the scheme of operations that had been suggested by Arabella Wilmot, but, somehow or another, she shrank most wonderfully from so doing, both on account of the censure which she concluded he would be likely to cast upon it, and the romantic, strange nature of the plan itself, so she said, gently and quickly,—

"I shall attempt nothing that shall not have some possibility of success attending it. I will be careful, you may depend, for many considerations. My father, I know, centres all his affections in me, and for his sake I will be careful."

"I shall be content then, and now may I hope that this day week I may see you here again, in order that I may tell you if I have made any discovery, and that you may tell me the same; for my interest in Thornhill is that of a sincere friend, to say nothing of the deep interest in your happiness which I feel, and which has now become an element in the transaction of the highest value."

"I will come," said Johanna, "if I can come."

"You do not doubt?"

"No, no. I will come, and I hope to bring you some news of him in whom you are so much interested. It shall be no fault of mine if I come not."

He walked with her from the gardens, and together they passed the shop of Sweeney Todd, but the door was close shut, and they saw nothing of the barber, or that of the poor boy, his apprentice, who was so much to be pitied.

He parted with Johanna near to her father's house, and he walked slowly away with his mind so fully impressed with the excellence and beauty of the spectacle-maker's daughter, that it was quite clear, as long as he lived, he would not be able to rid himself of the favourable impression she had made upon him.

"I love her," he said; "I love her, but she seems in no respect willing to enchain her affections. Alas! how sad it is for me that the being whom, above all others, I could wish to call my own, instead of being a joy to me, I have only encountered that she might impart a pang to my heart. Beautiful and excellent Johanna, I love you, but I can see that your own affections are withered for ever."

CHAPTER XVI

IT WOULD SEEM AS IF SWEENEY TODD, AFTER HIS ADVENTURE IN TRYING TO DISPOSE of the string of pearls which he possessed, began to feel a little doubtful about his chances of success in that matter, for he waited patiently for a considerable period, before he again made the attempt, and then he made it after a totally different fashion.

Towards the close of night on that same evening when Johanna Oakley had met Colonel Jeffery for the second time, in the Temple-gardens, and while Tobias sat alone in the shop in his usual deep dejection, a stranger entered the place, with a large blue bag in his hand, and looked enquiringly about him.

"Hilloa, my lad!" said he. "Is this Mr. Todd's?"

"Yes," said Tobias; "but he is not at home. What do you want?"

"Well, I'll be hanged," said the man, "if this don't beat everything; you don't mean to tell me he is a barber, do you?"

"Indeed I do; don't you see?"

"Yes, I see, to be sure; but I'll be shot if I thought of it beforehand. What do you think he has been doing?"

"Doing," said Tobias, with animation; "do you think he will be hung?"

"Why, no, I don't say it is a hanging matter, although you seem as if you wished it was; but I'll just tell you now we are artists at the west-end of the town."

"Artists! Do you mean to say you draw pictures?"

"No, no, we make clothes; but we call ourselves artists now, because tailors are out of fashion."

"Oh, that's it, is it?"

"Yes, that's it; and you would scarcely believe it, but he came to our shop actually, and ordered a suit of clothes, which were to come to no less a sum than thirty pounds, and told us to make them up in such a style that they were to do for any nobleman, and he gave his name and address, as Mr. Todd, at this number in Fleet-street, but I hadn't the least idea that he was a barber; if I had, I am quite certain that the clothes would not have been finished in the style they are, but quite the reverse."

"Well," said Tobias, "I can't think what he wants such clothing for, but I suppose it's all right. Was he a tall, ugly-looking fellow?"

"As ugly as the very devil. I'll just show you the things, as he is not at home. The coat is of the finest velvet, lined with silk, and trimmed with lace. Did you ever, in all your life, see such a coat for a barber?"

"Indeed, I never did; but it is some scheme of his, of course. It is a superb coat."

"Yes, and all the rest of the dress is of the same style; what on earth can he be going to do with it I can't think, for it's only fit to go to court in."

"Oh, well, I know nothing about it," said Tobias, with a sigh, "you can leave it or not as you like, it is all one to me."

"Well, you seem to be the most melancholy wretch ever I came near; what's the matter with you?"

"The matter with me? Oh, nothing. Of course, I am as happy as I can be. Ain't I Sweeney Todd's apprentice, and ain't that enough to make anybody sing all day long?"

"It may be for all I know, but certainly you don't seem to be in a singing humour; but, however, we artists cannot waste our time, so just be so good as to take care of the clothes, and be sure you give them to your master; and so I wash my hands of the transaction."

'Very good, he shall have them; but, do you mean to leave such valuable clothes without getting the money for them?"

"Not exactly, for they are paid for."

"Oh! that makes all the difference—he shall have them."

Scarcely had this tailor left the place, when a boy arrived with a parcel, and, looking around him with undisguised astonishment, said,—"Isn't there some other Mr. Todd in Fleet-street?"

"Not that I know of," said Tobias. "What have you got there?"

"Silk stockings, gloves, lace, cravats, ruffles, and so on."

"The deuce you have; I dare say it's all right."

"I shall leave them; they are paid for. This is the name, and this is the number."

"Now, stupid!"

This last exclamation arose from the fact that this boy, in going out, ran up against another who was coming in.

"Can't you see where you're going?" said the new arrival.

"What's that to you? I have a good mind to punch your head."

"Do it, and then come down to our court, and see what a licking I'll give you."

"Will you? Why don't you? Only let me catch you, that's all."

They stood for some moments so close together that their noses very nearly touched; and then after mutual assertions of what they would do if they caught each other—although, in either case, to stretch out an arm would have been quite sufficient to have accomplished that object—they separated, and the last corner said to Tobias, in a tone of irritation, probably consequent upon the misunderstanding he had just had with the hosier's boy,—

"You can tell Mr. Todd that the carriage will be ready at half-past seven precisely."

And then he went away, leaving Tobias in a state of great bewilderment as to what Sweeney Todd could possibly be about with such an amount of finery as that which was evidently coming home for him.

"I can't make it out," he said. "It's some villainy of course, but I can't make out what it is; I wish I knew; I might thwart him in it. He is a villain, and neither could nor would project anything good; but what can I do? I am quite helpless in this, and will just let it take its course. I can only wish for a power of action I will never possess. Alas, alas! I am very sad, and know not what will become of me. I wish that I was in my grave, and there I am sure I shall be soon, unless something happens to turn the tide of all this wretched evil fortune that has come upon me."

It was in vain for Tobias to think of vexing himself with conjectures as to what Sweeney Todd was about to do with so much finery, for he had not the remotest foundation to go upon in the matter, and could not for the life of him imagine any possible contingency or chance which should make it necessary for the barber to deck himself in such gaudy apparel.

All he could do was to lay down in his own mind a general principle as regarded Sweeney Todd's conduct, and that consisted in the fact, that whatever might be his plans, and whatever might be his objects, they were for no good purpose; but, on the contrary, were most certainly intended for the accomplishment of some great evil which that most villainous person intended to perpetrate.

"I will observe all I can," thought Tobias to himself, "and do what I can to put a stop to his mischiefs; but I fear it will be very little he will allow me to observe, and perhaps still less that he will allow me to do; but I can but try, and do my best."

Poor Tobias's best, as regarded achieving anything against Sweeney Todd, we may well suppose would be little indeed, for that individual was not the man to give anybody an opportunity of doing much; and possessed as he was of the most consummate art, as well as the greatest possible amount of unscrupulousness, there can be very little doubt but that any attempt poor Tobias might make would recoil upon himself.

In about another half hour the barber returned, and his first question was, "Have any things been left for me?"

"Yes, sir," said Tobias, "here are two parcels, and a boy has been to say that the carriage will be ready at half-past seven precisely."

"'Tis well," said the barber, "that will do; and Tobias, you will be careful, whilst I am gone, of the shop. I shall be back in half an hour, mind you, and not later; and be sure I find you here at your post. But you may say, if anyone comes here on business, that there will be neither shaving nor dressing tonight. You understand me?"

"Yes, sir, certainly."

Sweeney Todd then took the bundles which contained the costly apparel, and retired into the parlour with them; and, as it was then seven o'clock, Tobias correctly enough supposed that he had gone to dress himself, and he waited with a considerable amount of curiosity to see what sort of an appearance the barber would cut in his fine apparel.

Tobias had not to control his impatience long, for in less than twenty minutes out came Sweeney Todd, attired in the very height of fashion for the period. His waistcoat was something positively gorgeous, and his fingers were loaded with such costly rings that they quite dazzled the sight of Tobias to look upon; then, moreover, he wore a sword with a jewelled hilt, but it was one which Tobias really thought he had seen before, for he had a recollection that a gentleman had come in to have his hair dressed, and had taken it off, and laid just such a sword across his hat during the operation.

"Remember," said Sweeney Todd, "remember your instructions; obey them to the letter, and no doubt you will ultimately become happy and independent."

With these words, Sweeney Todd left the place, and poor Tobias looked after him with a groan, as he repeated the words "happy and independent. Alas! what a mockery it is of this man to speak to me in such a way—I only wish that I were dead!"

But we will leave Tobias to his own reflections, and follow the more interesting progress of Sweeney Todd, who, for some reason best known to himself, was then playing so grand a part, and casting away so large a sum of money. He made his way to a livery-stables in the immediate neighbourhood, and there, sure enough, the horses were being placed to a handsome carriage; and all being very soon in readiness, Sweeney Todd gave some whispered directions to the driver, and the vehicle started off westward.

At that time Hyde Park Corner was very nearly out of town, and it looked as if you were getting a glimpse of the country, and actually seeing something of the peasantry of England, when you got another couple of miles off, and that was the direction in which Sweeney Todd went; and as he goes, we may as well introduce to the reader the sort of individual whom he was going to visit in so much state, and for whom he thought it necessary to go to such great expense.

At that period the follies and vices of the nobility were somewhere about as great as they are now, and consequently extravagance induced on many occasions troublesome sacrifice of money, and it was found extremely convenient to apply to a man of the name of John Mundel, an exceedingly wealthy person, a Dutchman by extraction, who was reported to make immense sums of money by lending to the nobility and others what they required on emergencies, at enormous rates of interest.

But it must not be supposed that John Mundel was so confiding as to lend his money without security. It was quite the reverse, for he took care to have the jewels, some costly plate, or the title deeds of an estate, perchance, as security, before he would part with a single shilling of his cash.

In point of fact, John Mundel was nothing more than a pawnbroker on a very extensive scale, and, although he had an office in town, he usually received his more aristocratic customers at his private residence, which was about two miles off, on the Uxbridge Road.

After this explanation, it can very easily be imagined what was the scheme of Sweeney Todd, and that he considered if he borrowed from John Mundel a sum equal in amount to half the real value of the pearls he should be well rid of a property which he certainly could not sufficiently well account for the possession of, to enable him to dispose of it openly to the highest bidder.

We give Sweeney Todd great credit for the scheme he proposes. It was eminently calculated to succeed, and one which in the way he undertook it was certainly set about in the best possible way.

During his ride, he revolved in his mind exactly what he should say to John Mundel, and from what we know of him we may be well convinced that Sweeney Todd was not likely to fail from any amount of bashfulness in the transaction; but that, on the contrary, he was just the man to succeed in any scheme which required great assurance to carry it through; for he was certainly master of great assurance, and possessed of a kind of diplomatic skill, which, had fortune placed him in a more elevated position of life, would no doubt have made a great man of him, and gained him great political reputation.

John Mundel's villa, which was called, by-the-by, Mundel House, was a large, handsome, and modern structure, surrounded by a few acres of pleasure gardens, which however the money-lender never looked at, for his whole soul was too much engrossed by his love for cash to enable him to do so; and, if he derived any satisfaction at all from it, that satisfaction must have been entirely owing to the fact that he had wrung mansion, grounds, and all the costly furnishing of the former from an improvident debtor, who had been forced to fly the country, and leave his property wholly in the hands of the money-lender and usurer.

It was but a short drive with the really handsome horses that Sweeney Todd had succeeded in hiring for the occasion, and he soon found himself opposite the entrance gates of Mundel House.

His great object now was that the usurer should see the equipage which he had brought down; and he accordingly desired the footman, who had accompanied him, at once to ring the bell at the entrance-gate, and to say that a gentleman was waiting in his carriage to see Mr. Mundel.

This was done; and when the money-lender's servant reported to him that the equipage was a costly one, and that, in his opinion, the visitor must be some nobleman of great rank, John Mundel made no difficulty about the matter, but walked down to the gate at once, where he immediately mentally subscribed to the opinion of his servant, by admitting to himself that the equipage was faultless, and presumed at once that it did belong to some person of great rank.

He was proportionally humble, as such men always are, and advancing to the side of the carriage, he begged to know what commands his lordship—for so he called him at once—had for him.

"I wish to know," said Sweeney Todd, "Mr. Mundel, if you are inclined to lay under an obligation a rather illustrious lady, by helping her out of a little pecuniary difficulty."

John Mundel glanced again at the equipage, and he likewise saw something of the rich dress of his visitor, who had not disputed the title which had been applied to him, of lord; and he made up his mind accordingly, that it was just one of the transactions that would suit him, provided the security that would be offered was of a tangible nature. That was the only point upon which John Mundel had the remotest doubt, but, at all events, he urgently pressed his visitor to alight, and walk in.

CHAPTER XVII

As Sweeney Todd's object, as far as the money-lender's having seen the carriage, was fully answered, he had no objection to enter the house, which he accordingly did at once, being preceded by John Mundel, who became each moment more and more impressed with the fact, as he considered it, that his guest was some person of very great rank and importance in society.

He ushered him into a splendidly-furnished apartment, and after offering him refreshments, which Sweeney Todd politely declined, he waited with no small degree of impatience for his visitor to be explicit with regard to the object of his visit.

"I should," said Sweeney Todd, "have myself accommodated the illustrious lady with the sum of money she requires, but as I could not do so without encumbering some estates, she positively forbade me to think of it."

"Certainly," said Mr. Mundel, "she is a very illustrious lady, I presume?"

"Very illustrious indeed, but it must be a condition of this transaction, if you at all enter into it, that you are not to enquire precisely who she is, nor are you to enquire precisely who I am."

"It's not my usual way of conducting business, but if everything else be satisfactory, I shall not cavil at that."

"Very good; by everything else being satisfactory I presume you mean the security offered?"

"Why, yes, that is of great importance, my lord."

"I informed the illustrious lady that as the affair was to be wrapped up in something of a mystery, the security must be extremely ample."

"That's a very proper view to take of the matter, my lord."

"I wonder," thought John Mundel, "if he is a duke; I'll call him your grace next time and see if he objects to it."

"Therefore," continued Sweeney Todd, "the illustrious lady placed in my hands security to a third greater amount than she required."

"Certainly, certainly, a very proper arrangement, your grace; may I ask the nature of the proffered security?"

"Jewels."

"Highly satisfactory and unexceptionable security; they go into a small space, and do not deteriorate in value."

"And if they do," said the barber, "deteriorate in value, it would make no difference to you, for the illustrious person's honour will be committed to their redemption."

"I don't doubt that, your grace, in the least; I merely made the remark incidentally, quite incidentally."

"Of course, of course; and I trust, before going further, that you are quite in a position to enter into this subject."

"Certainly I am, and, I am proud to say, to any amount. Show me the money's worth, your grace, and I will show you the money—that's my way of doing business; and no one can say that John Mundel ever shrunk from a matter that was brought fairly before him, and that he considered worth his going into."

"It was by hearing such a character of you that I was induced to come to you. What do you think of that?"

Sweeney Todd took from his pocket, with a careless air, the string of pearls, and cast them down before the eyes of the money-lender, who took them up and ran them rapidly through his fingers for a few seconds before he said,—

"I thought there was but one string like this in the kingdom, and that those belonged to the Queen."

"Well!" said Sweeney Todd.

"I humbly beg your grace's pardon. How much money does your grace require on these pearls?"

"Twelve thousand pounds is their current value, if a sale of them was enforced; eight thousand are required of you on their security."

"Eight thousand is a large sum. As a general thing I lend but half the value upon anything; but in this case, to oblige your grace and the illustrious personage, I do not of course hesitate for one moment, but shall for one month lend the required amount."

"That will do," said Sweeney Todd, scarcely concealing the exultation he felt at getting so much more from John Mundel than he expected, and which he certainly would not have got if the money-lender had not been most fully and completely impressed with the idea that the pearls belonged to the Queen, and that he had actually at length majesty itself for a customer.

He did not suppose for one moment that it was the Queen who wanted the money; but his view of the case was, that she had lent the pearls to this nobleman to meet some exigency of his own, and that of course they would be redeemed very shortly.

Altogether a more pleasant transaction for John Mundel could not have been imagined. It was just the sort of thing he would have looked out for, and had the greatest satisfaction in bringing to a conclusion, and he considered it was opening the door to the highest class of business in his way that he was capable of doing.

"In what name, your grace," he said, "shall I draw a check upon my banker?"

"In the name of Colonel George."

"Certainly, certainly; and if your grace will give me an acknowledgement for £8,000, and please to understand that at the end of a month from this time the transaction will be renewed if necessary, I will give you a cheque for £7,500."

"Why £7,500 only, when you mentioned £8,000?"

"The £500 is my little commission upon the transaction. Your grace will perceive that I appreciate highly the honour of your grace's custom, and consequently charge the lowest possible price. I can assure your grace I could get more for my money by a great deal, but the pleasure of being able to meet your grace's views is so great, that I am willing to make a sacrifice, and therefore it is that I say £500, when really I ought to say £1,000, taking into consideration the great scarcity of money at the present juncture; and I can assure your grace that—"

"Peace, peace," said Sweeney Todd; "give me the money, and if it be not convenient to redeem the jewels at the end of a month from this time, you will hear from me most assuredly."

"I am quite satisfied of that," said John Mundel, and he accordingly drew a check for £7,500, which he handed to Sweeney Todd, who put it in his pocket, not a little delighted that at last he had got rid of his pearls, even at a price so far beneath their real value.

"I need scarcely urge upon you, Mr. Mundel," he said, "the propriety of keeping this affair profoundly secret."

"Indeed, you need not, your grace, for it is part of my business to be discreet and cautious. I should very soon have nothing to do in my line, your grace may depend, if I were to talk about it. No, this transaction will for ever remain locked up in my own breast, and no living soul but your grace and I need know what has occurred."

With this, John Mundel showed Sweeney Todd to his carriage, with abundance of respect, and in two minutes more he was travelling along towards town with what might be considered a small fortune in his pocket.

We should have noticed earlier that Sweeney Todd had, upon the occasion of his going to sell the pearls to the lapidary, in the city, made some great alterations in his appearance, so that it was not likely he should be recognised again to a positive certainty. For example,—having no whiskers whatever of his own, he had put on a large black pair of false ones, as well as moustachios, and he had given some colour to his cheeks likewise, which had so completely altered his appearance, that those who were most intimate with him would not have known him except by his voice, and that he took great care to alter in his intercourse with John Mundel, so that it should not become a future means of detection.

"I thought that this would succeed," he muttered to himself, as he went towards town, "and I have not been deceived. For three months longer, and only three, I will carry on the business in Fleet-street, so that any sudden alteration in my fortunes may not give rise to suspicion."

He was then silent for some minutes, during which he appeared to be revolving some very knotty question in his brain, and then he said, suddenly,—

"Well, well, as regards Tobias, I think it will be safer, unquestionably, to put him out of the way by taking his life than to try to dispose of him in a mad-house, and I think there are one or two more persons whom it will be highly necessary to prevent being mischievous, at all events at present. I must think—I must think."

When such a man as Sweeney Todd set about thinking, there could be no possible doubt but that some serious mischief was meditated, and anyone who could have watched his face during that ride home from the money-lender's would have seen by its expression that the thoughts which agitated him were of a dark and a desperate character, and such as anybody but himself would have shrunk from, aghast.

But he was not a man to shrink from anything, and, on the contrary, the more a set of circumstances presented themselves in a gloomy and a terrific aspect, the better they seemed to suit him, and the peculiar constitution of his mind.

There can be no doubt but that the love of money was the predominant feeling in Sweeney Todd's intellectual organisation and that, by the amount it would bring him, or the amount it would deprive him of, he measured everything.

With such a man, then, no question of morality or ordinary feeling could arise, and there can be no doubt but that he would quite willingly have sacrificed the whole human race, if, by doing so, he could have achieved any of the objects of his ambition.

And so on his road homeward, he probably made up his mind to plunge still deeper into criminality; and perchance to indulge in acts that a man not already so deeply versed in iniquity would have shrunk from with the most positive terror.

And by a strange style of reasoning, such men as Sweeney Todd reconcile themselves to the most heinous crimes upon the ground of what they call policy.

That is to say, that having committed some serious offence, they are compelled to commit a great number more for the purpose of endeavouring to avoid the consequences of the first lot; and hence the continuance of criminality becomes a matter necessary to self-defence, and an essential ingredient in their consideration of self-preservation.

Probably Sweeney Todd had been, for the greater part of his life, aiming at the possession of extensive pecuniary resources, and, no doubt, by the aid of a superior intellect, and a mind full of craft and design, he had managed to make others subservient to his views, and now that those views were answered, and that his underlings and accomplices were no longer required, they became positively dangerous.

He was well aware of that cold-blooded policy which teaches that it is far safer to destroy than to cast away the tools, by which a man carves his way to power and fortune.

"They shall die," said Sweeney Todd, "dead men tell no tales, nor women nor boys either, and they shall all die, after which there will, I think, be a serious fire in Fleet-street. Ha! ha! it may spread to what mischief it likes, always provided it stops not short of the entire destruction of my house and premises.

"Rare sport—rare sport will it be to me, for then I will at once commence a new career, in which the barber will be forgotten, and the man of fashion only seen and remembered, for with this last addition to my means, I am fully capable of vying with the highest and the noblest, let them be who they may."

This seemed a pleasant train of reflections to Sweeney Todd, and as the coach entered Fleet-street, there sat such a grim smile upon his countenance that he looked like some fiend in human shape, who had just completed the destruction of a human soul.

When he reached the livery stables to which he directed them to drive, instead of to his own shop, he rewarded all who had gone with him most liberally, so that the coachman and footman who were both servants out of place, would have had no objection for Sweeney Todd every day to have gone on some such an expedition, so that they should receive as liberal wages for the small part they enacted in it as they did upon that occasion.

He then walked from the stables towards his own house, but upon reaching there, a little disappointment awaited him, for he found to his surprise that no light was burning; and when he placed his hand upon the shop-door, it opened, but there was no trace of Tobias, although he, Sweeney Todd, called loudly upon him the moment he set foot within the shop.

Then a feeling of great apprehension crept across the barber, and he groped anxiously about for some matches, by the aid of which he hoped to procure a light, and then an explanation of the mysterious absence of Tobias.

But in order that we may in its proper form relate how it was that Tobias had had the daring, thus in open contradiction of his master, to be away from the shop, we must devote to Tobias a chapter which will plead his extenuation.

CHAPTER XVIII

TOBIAS GUESSED, AND GUESSED RIGHTLY, TOO, THAT WHEN SWEENEY TODD SAID HE would be away half an hour, he only mentioned that short period of time, in order to keep the lad's vigilance on the alert, and to prevent him from taking advantage of a more protracted absence.

The very style and manner in which he had gone out precluded the likelihood of it being for so short a period of time; and that circumstance set Tobias seriously thinking over a situation which was becoming more intolerable every day.

The lad had the sense to feel that he could not go on much longer as he was going on, and that in a short time such a life would destroy him.

"It is beyond endurance," he said, "and I know not what to do; and since Sweeney Todd has told me that the boy he had before went out of his senses, and is now in the cell of a mad-house, I feel that such will be my fate, and that I, too, shall come to that dreadful end, and then no one will believe a word I utter, hut consider everything to be mere raving."

After a time, as the darkness increased, he lit the lamp which hung in the shop, and which, until it was closed for the night, usually shed a dim ray from the window. Then he sat down to think again, and he said to himself,—

"If I could but summon courage to ask my mother about this robbery which Sweeney Todd imputes to her, she might assure me it was false, and that she never did such a deed; but then it is dreadful for me to ask her such a question, because it may be true; and then how shocking it would be for her to be forced to confess to me, her own son, such a circumstance."

These were the honourable feelings which prevented Tobias from questioning his mother as regarded Todd's accusation of her—an accusation too dreadful to believe implicitly, and yet sufficiently probable for him to have a strong suspicion that it might be true after all.

It is to be deeply regretted that Tobias's philosophy did not carry him a little further, and make him see, the moment the charge was made, that he ought unquestionably to investigate it to the very utmost.

But, still, we could hardly expect from a mere boy that acute reasoning and power of action, which depends so much on the knowledge of the world, and an extensive practice in the usages of society.

It was sufficient if he felt correctly—we could scarcely expect him to reason so. But upon this occasion above all other, he seemed completely overcome by the circumstances which surrounded him; and from his excited manner, one might almost have imagined that the insanity he himself predicted at the close of his career was really not far off.

He wrung his hands, and he wept, every now and then, in sad speech, bitterly bemoaning his situation, until at length, with a sudden resolution, he sprang to his feet, exclaiming,—

"This night shall end it. I can endure it no more. I will fly from this place, and seek my fortune elsewhere. Any amount of distress, danger, or death itself even, is preferable to the dreadful life I lead."

He walked some paces towards the door, and then he paused, as he said to himself in a low tone,—

"Todd will surely not be home yet for awhile, and why should I then neglect the only opportunity I may ever have of searching this house to satisfy my mind as regards any of the mysteries it contains."

He paused over this thought, and considered well its danger, for dangerous indeed it was to no small extent, but he was desperate; and with a resolution that scarcely could have been expected from him, he determined upon taking that first step above all others, which Todd was almost certain to punish with death.

He closed the shopdoor, and bolted it upon the inside, so that he could not be suddenly interrupted, and then he looked round him carefully for some weapon by the aid of which he should be able to break his way into the parlour, which the barber always kept closed and locked in his absence. A weapon that would answer the purpose of breaking any lock, if Tobias chose to proceed so roughly to work, was close at hand in the iron bar, which, when the place was closed at night, secured a shutter to the door.

Wrought up as he was to almost frenzy, Tobias seized this bar, and advancing towards the parlour-door, he with one blow smashed the lock to atoms, and the door soon yielded.

The moment it did so, there was a crash of glass, and when Tobias entered the room he saw that upon its threshold lay a wineglass shattered to atoms, and he felt certain it had been placed in some artful position by Sweeney Todd as a detector, when he should return, of any attempt that had been made upon the door of the parlour.

And now Tobias felt that he was so far committed that he might as well go on with his work, and accordingly he lit a candle, which he found upon the parlour table, and then proceeded to make what discoveries he could.

Several of the cupboards in the room yielded at once to his hands, and in them he found nothing remarkable, but there was one that he could not open; so, without a moment's hesitation, he had recourse to the bar of iron again, and broke its lock, when the door swung open, and to his astonishment there tumbled out of this cupboard such a volley of hats of all sorts and descriptions, some looped with silver, some three-cornered, and some square, that they formed quite a museum of that article of attire, and excited the greatest surprise in the mind of Tobias, at the same time that they

tended very greatly to confirm some other thoughts and feelings which he had concerning Sweeney Todd.

This was the only cupboard which was fast, although there was another door
which looked as if it opened into one; but when Tobias broke that down with the bar of
iron, he found it was the door which led to the staircase conducting to the upper part
of the house, that upper part which Sweeney Todd with all his avarice would never let,
and of which the shutters were kept continually closed, so that the opposite neighbours
never caught a glimpse into any of the apartments.

With cautious and slow steps, which he adopted instantaneously, although he
knew that there was no one in the house but himself, Tobias ascended the staircase.

"I will go to the very top rooms first," he said to himself, "and so examine them all
as I come down, and then if Todd should return suddenly, I shall have a better chance
of hearing him than if I began below and went upwards."

Acting upon this prudent scheme, he went up to the attics, all the doors of which
were swinging open, and there was nothing in any one of them whatever.

He descended to the second floor with the like result, and a feeling of great disappointment began to creep over him at the thought that, after all, the barber's house
might not repay the trouble of examination.

But when he reached the first floor he soon found abundant reason to alter his
opinion. The doors were fast, and he had to burst them open; and, when he got in,
he found that those rooms were partially furnished, and that they contained a great
quantity of miscellaneous property of all kinds and descriptions.

In one corner was an enormous quantity of walking-sticks, some of which were of
a very costly and expensive character, with gold and silver chased tops to them, and in
another corner was a great number of umbrellas—in fact at least a hundred of them.

Then there were boots and shoes, lying upon the floor, partially covered up, as
if to keep them from dirt; there were thirty or forty swords of different styles and
patterns, many of them appearing to be very firm blades, and in one or two cases the
scabbards were richly ornamented.

At one end of the front and larger of the two rooms was an old-fashioned-looking
bureau of great size, and with as much woodwork in it as seemed required to make at
least a couple of such articles of furniture.

This was very securely locked, and presented more difficulties in the way of opening it, than any of the doors had done, for the lock was of great strength and apparent
durability. Moreover it was not so easily got at, but at length by using the bar as a sort

of lever, instead of as a mere machine to strike with, Tobias succeeded in forcing this bureau open, and then his eyes were perfectly dazzled with the amount of jewellery and trinkets of all kinds and descriptions that were exhibited to his gaze.

There was a great number of watches, gold chains, silver and gold snuff-boxes, and a large assortment of rings, shoe-buckles, and brooches.

These articles must have been of great value, and Tobias could not help exclaiming aloud,—

"How could Sweeney Todd come by these articles, except by the murder of their owners?"

This, indeed, seemed but too probable a supposition, and the more especially so, as in a further part of this bureau a great quantity of apparel was found by Tobias.

He stood with a candle in his hand, looking upon these various objects for more than a quarter of an hour, and then as a sudden and a natural thought came across him of how completely a few of them even would satisfy his wants and his mother's for a long time to come, he stretched forth his hand towards the glittering mass, but he drew it back again with a shudder, saying,—

"No, no, these things are the plunder of the dead. Let Sweeney Todd keep them to himself, and look upon them if he can with the eyes of enjoyment. I will have none of them: they would bring misfortune along with every guinea that they might be turned into."

As he spoke, he heard St. Dunstan's clock strike nine, and he started at the sound, for it let him know that already Sweeney Todd had been away an hour beyond the time he said he would be absent, so that there was a probability of his quick return now, and it would scarcely be safe to linger longer in his home.

"I must be gone, I must be gone, I should like to look upon my mother's face once more before I leave London for ever perhaps. I may tell her of the danger she is in from Todd's knowledge of her secret; no, no, I cannot speak to her of that, I must go, and leave her to those chances which I hope and trust will work favourable for her."

Flinging down the iron bar which had done him such good service, Tobias stopped not to close any of those receptacles which contained the plunder that Sweeney Todd had taken most probably from murdered persons, but he rushed downstairs into the parlour again, where the boots that had fallen out of the cupboard still lay upon the floor in wild disorder.

It was a strange and sudden whim that took him, rather than a matter of reflection, that induced him instead of his own hat to take one of those which were lying so indiscriminately at his feet; and he did so.

By mere accident it turned out to be an exceedingly handsome hat, of rich work-manship and material, and then Tobias, feeling terrified lest Sweeney Todd should return before he could leave the place, paid no attention to anything, but turned from the shop, merely pulling the door after him, and then darting over the road towards the Temple like a hunted hare; for his great wish was to see his mother, and then he had an undefined notion that his best plan for escaping the clutches of Sweeney Todd would be to go to sea.

In common with all boys of his age, who know nothing whatever of the life of a sailor, it presented itself in the most fascinating colours.

A sailor ashore and a sailor afloat are about as two different things as the world can present; but, to the imagination of Tobias Ragg, a sailor was somebody who was always dancing hornpipes, spending money, and telling wonderful stories. No wonder, then, that the profession presented itself under such fascinating colours to all such per-sons as Tobias; and, as it seemed, and seems still, to be a sort of general understanding that the real condition of a sailor should be mystified in every possible way and shape both by novelist and dramatist, it is no wonder that it requires actual experience to enable those parties who are in the habit of being carried away by just what they hear, to come to a correct conclusion.

"I will go to sea!" ejaculated Tobias. "Yes, I will go to sea!"

As he spoke those words, he passed out of the gate of the Temple, leading into Whitefriars, in which ancient vicinity his mother dwelt, endeavouring to eke out a liv-ing as best she might.

She was very much surprised (for she happened to be at home) at the unexpected visit of her son Tobias, and uttered a faint scream as she let fall a flat-iron very nearly upon his toe.

"Mother," he said, "I cannot stay with Sweeney Todd any longer, so do not ask me."

"Not stay with a respectable man?"

"A respectable man, mother! Alas, alas, how little you know of him! But what am I saying? I dare not speak! Oh, that fatal, fatal candlestick!"

"But how are you to live, and what do you mean by a fatal candlestick?"

"Forgive me—I did not mean to say that! Farewell, mother! I am going to sea."

"To see what, my dear?" said Mrs. Ragg, who was much more difficult to talk to than even Hamlet's grave-digger. "You don't know how much I am obliged to Sweeney Todd."

"Yes, I do. And that's what drives me mad to think of. Farewell, mother, perhaps for ever! If I can, of course, I will communicate with you, but now I dare not stay."

"Oh! what have you done, Tobias—what have you done?"

"Nothing—nothing! but Sweeney Todd is—"

"What—what?"

"No matter—no matter! Nothing—nothing! And yet at this last moment I am almost tempted to ask you concerning a candlestick."

"Don't mention that," said Mrs. Ragg; "I don't want to hear anything said about it."

"It is true, then?"

"Yes; but did Mr. Todd tell you?"

"He did—he did. I have now asked the question I never thought could have passed my lips. Farewell, mother, for ever farewell!"

Tobias rushed out of the place, leaving old Mrs. Ragg astonished at his behaviour, and with a strong suspicion that some accession of insanity had come over him.

"The Lord have mercy upon us!" she said, "what shall I do? I am astonished at Mr. Todd telling him about the candlestick; it's true enough, though, for all that. I recollect it as well as if it were yesterday; it was a very hard winter, and I was minding a set of chambers, when Todd came to shave the gentleman, and I saw him with my own eyes put a silver candlestick in his pocket. Then I went over to his shop and reasoned with him about it, and he gave it me back, and I brought it to the chambers, and laid it down exactly on the spot where he took it from.

"To be sure," said Mrs. Ragg, after a pause of a few moment, "to be sure he has been a very good friend to me ever since, but that I suppose is for fear I should tell, and get him hung or transported. But, however, we must take the good with the bad, and when Tobias comes to think of it, he will go back again to his work, I dare say, for, after all, it's a very foolish thing for him to trouble his head whether Mr. Todd stole a silver candlestick or not."

CHAPTER XIX

ABOUT THIS TIME, AND WHILE THESE INCIDENTS OF OUR MOST STRANGE AND EVENTFUL narrative were taking place, the pious frequenters of old St. Dunstan's church began to perceive a strange and most abominable odour throughout that sacred edifice.

It was in vain that old women who came to hear the sermons, although they were too deaf to catch a third part of them, brought smelling-bottles, and other means of stifling their noses; still that dreadful charnel-house sort of smell would make itself most painfully and most disagreeably apparent.

And the Rev. Joseph Stillingport, who was the regular preacher, smelt it in the pulpit; and had been seen to sneeze in the midst of a most pious discourse indeed, and to hold to his pious mouth a handkerchief, in which was some strong and pungent essence, for the purpose of trying to overcome the terrible effluvia.

The organ-blower and the organ-player were both nearly stifled, for the horrible odour seemed to ascend to the upper part of the church; although those who sat in what may be called the pit by no means escaped it.

The churchwardens looked at each other in their pews with contorted countenances, and were almost afraid to breathe; and the only person who did not complain bitterly of the dreadful odour in St. Dunstan's church, was an old woman who had been a pew-opener for many years; but then she had lost the faculties of her nose, which, perhaps, accounted satisfactorily for that circumstance.

At length, however, the nuisance became so intolerable, that the beadle, whose duty it was in the morning to open the church-doors, used to come up to them with the massive key in one hand, and a cloth soaked in vinegar in the other, just as the people used to do in the time of the great plague of London; and when he had opened the doors, he used to run over to the other side of the way.

"Ah, Mr. Blunt!" he used to say to the bookseller, who lived opposite—"ah, Mr. Blunt! I is obligated to cut over here, leastways, till the *aty-monspheric* air is mixed up all along with the *stinkifications* which come from the church."

By this, it will be seen that the beadle was rather a learned man, and no doubt went to some mechanics' institution of those days, where he learned something of everything but what was calculated to be of some service to him.

As might be supposed from the fact that this sort of thing had gone on for a few months, it began to excite some attention with a view to a remedy; for, in the great city of London, a nuisance of any sort of description requires to become venerable by age before anyone thinks of removing it; and after that, it is quite clear that that becomes a good argument against removing it at all.

But at last, the churchwardens began to have a fear that some pestilential disease would be the result, if they for any longer period of time put up with the horrible stench; and that they might be among its first victims, so they began to ask each other what could be done to obviate it.

Probably, if this frightful stench, being suggestive, as it was, of all sorts of horrors, had been graciously pleased to confine itself to some poor locality, nothing would have been heard of it; but when it became actually offensive to a gentleman in a metropolitan pulpit, and when it began to make itself perceptible to the sleepy faculties of the churchwardens of St. Dunstan's church, in Fleet-street, so as to prevent them even from dozing through the afternoon sermon, it became a very serious matter indeed.

But what it was, what could it be, and what was to be done to get rid of it—these were the anxious questions that were asked right and left, as regarded the serious nuisance, without the nuisance acceding any reply.

But yet one thing seemed to be generally agreed, and that was, that it did come, and must come, somehow or other, out of the vaults from beneath the church.

But then, as the pious and hypocritical Mr. Batterwick, who lived opposite, said,—

"How could that be, when it was satisfactorily proved by the present books that nobody had been buried in the vault for some time, and therefore it was a very odd thing that dead people, after leaving off smelling and being disagreeable, should all of a sudden burst out again in that line, and be twice as bad as ever they were at first."

And on Wednesdays sometimes, too, when pious people were not satisfied with the Sunday's devotion, but began again in the middle of the week, the stench was positively terrific.

Indeed, so bad was it, that some of the congregation were forced to leave, and have been seen to slink into Bell-yard, where Lovett's pie-shop was situated, and then and there relieve themselves with a pork or a veal pie, in order that their mouths and noses should be full of a delightful and agreeable flavour, instead of one most peculiarly and decidedly the reverse.

At last there was a confirmation to be held at St. Dunstan's church, and so great a concourse of persons assembled, for a sermon was to be preached by the bishop, after the confirmation; and a very great fuss indeed was to be made about really nobody knew what.

Preparations, as newspapers say, upon an extensive scale, and regardless of expense, were made for the purpose of adding lustre to the ceremony, and surprising the bishop when he came with a good idea that the authorities of St. Dunstan's church were somebodies and really worth confirming.

The confirmation was to take place at twelve o'clock, and the bells ushered in the morning with their most pious tones, for it was not every day that the authorities of St. Dunstan's succeeded in catching a bishop, and when they did so, they were determined to make the most of him.

And the numerous authorities, including churchwardens, and even the very beadle, were in an uncommon fluster, and running about and impeding each other, as authorities always do upon public occasions.

But of those who only look to the surface of things, and who come to admire what was grand and magnificent in the preparations, the beadle certainly carried away the palm, for that functionary was attired in a completely new cocked hat and coat, and certainly looked very splendid and showy upon the occasion. Moreover, the beadle had been well and judiciously selected, and the parish authorities made no secret of it, when there was an election for beadle, that they threw all their influence into the scale of that candidate who happened to be the biggest, and, consequently, who was calculated to wear the official costume with an air that no smaller man could possibly have aspired to on any account.

At half-past eleven o'clock the bishop made his gracious appearance, and was duly ushered into the vestry, where there was a comfortable fire, and on the table in which, likewise, were certain cold chickens and bottles of rare wines; for confirming a number of people, and preaching a sermon besides, was considered no joke, and might, for all they knew, be provocative of a great appetite in the bishop.

And with a bland and courtly air the bishop smiled as he ascended the steps of St. Dunstan's church. How affable he was to the church-wardens, and he actually smiled upon a poor, miserable charity boy, who, his eyes glaring wide open, and his muffin cap in his hand, was taking his first stare at a real live bishop.

To be sure, the beadle knocked him down directly the bishop had passed, for having the presumption to look at such a great personage, but then that was to be expected fully and completely, and only proved that the proverb which permits a cat to look at a king, is not equally applicable to charity boys and bishops.

When the bishop got to the vestry, some very complimentary words were uttered to him by the usual officiating clergyman, but, somehow or another, the bland smile had left the lips of the great personage, and, interrupting the vicar in the midst of a fine flowing period, he said,—

"That's all very well, but what a terrible stink there is here!"

The churchwardens gave a groan, for they had flattered themselves, that perhaps the bishop would not notice the dreadful smell, or that, if he did, he would think it was accidental and say nothing about it; but now, when he really did mention it, they found all their hopes scattered to the winds, and that it was necessary to say something.

"Is this horrid charnel-house sort of smell always here?"

"I am afraid it is," said one of the churchwardens.

"Afraid!" said the bishop, "surely you know; you seem to me to have a nose."

"Yes," said the churchwarden, in great confusion, "I have that honour, and I have the pleasure of informing you, my lord bishop—I mean I have the honour of informing you, that this smell is always here."

The bishop sniffed several times, and then he said—

"It is very dreadful; and I hope that by the next time I come to St. Dunstan's you will have the pleasure and the honour, both, of informing me that it has gone away."

The churchwarden bowed, and got into an extreme corner, saying to himself,—

"This is the bishop's last visit here, and I don't wonder at it, for as if out of pure spite, the smell is ten times worse than ever to-day."

And so it was, for it seemed to come up through all the crevices of the flooring of the church with a power and perseverance that was positively dreadful.

"Isn't it dreadful?—did you ever before know the smell in St. Dunstan's so bad before?" and everybody agreed that they had never known it anything like so bad, for that it was positively awful—and so indeed it was.

The anxiety of the bishop to get away was quite manifest, and if he could decently have taken his departure without confirming anybody at all, there is no doubt but that he would have willingly done so, and left all the congregation to die and be—something or another.

But this he could not do, but he could cut it short, and he did so. The people found themselves confirmed before they almost knew where they were, and the bishop would not go into the vestry again on any account, but hurried down the steps of the church and into his carriage, with the greatest precipitation in the world, thus proving that holiness is no proof against a most abominable stench.

As may be well supposed, after this, the subject assumed a much more serious aspect, and on the following day a solemn meeting was held of all the church authorities, at which it was determined that men should be employed to make a thorough and searching examination of all the vaults of St. Dunstan's, with the view of discovering, if possible, from whence particularly the abominable stench emanated.

And then it was decided that the stench was to be put down, and that the bishop was to be apprised it was put down, and that he might visit the church in perfect safety.

CHAPTER XX

We left the barber in his own shop, much wondering that Tobias had not responded to the call which he had made upon him, but yet scarcely believing it possible that he could have ventured upon the height of iniquity, which we know Tobias had really been guilty of.

He paused for a few moments, and held up the light which he had procured, and gazed around him with enquiring eyes, for he could, indeed, scarcely believe it possible that Tobias had sufficiently cast off his dread of him, Sweeney Todd, to be enabled to achieve any act for his liberation. But when he saw that the lock of the parlour-door was open, positive rage obtained precedence over every other feeling.

"The villain!" he cried, "has he dared really to consummate an act I thought he could not have dreamt of for a moment? Is it possible that he can have presumed so far as to have searched the house?"

That Tobias, however, had presumed so far, the barber soon discovered, and when he went into his parlour and saw what had actually occurred, and that likewise the door which led to the staircase and the upper part of the house had not escaped, he got perfectly furious, and it was some time before he could sufficiently calm himself to reflect upon the probable and possible amount of danger he might run in consequence of these proceedings.

When he did, his active mind at once told him that there was not much to be dreaded immediately, for that, most probably, Tobias, still having the fear before his eyes of what he might do as regarded his mother, had actually run away; and, "In all likelihood," muttered the barber, "he has taken with him something which would allow me to fix upon him the stigma of robbery: but that I must see to."

Having fastened the shop-door securely, he took the light in his hands, and ascended to the upper part of his house—that is to say, to the first floor, where alone anything was to be found.

He saw at once the open bureau with all its glittering display of jewels, and as he gazed upon the heap he muttered,—

"I have not so accurate a knowledge of what is here, as to be able to say if anything be extracted or not, but I know the amount of money, if I do not know the precise number of jewels which this bureau contains."

He opened a small drawer which had entirely evaded the scrutiny of Tobias, and proceeded to count a large number of guineas which were there.

"These are correct," he said, when he had finished his examination, "these are correct, and he has touched none of them."

He then opened another drawer, in which were a great many packets of silver done up in paper, and these likewise he carefully counted and was satisfied they were right.

"It is strange," he said, "that he has taken nothing, but yet perhaps it is better that it should be so, inasmuch as it shows a wholesome fear of me. The slightest examination would have shown him these hoards of money; and since he has not made that slight examination, nor discovered any of them, it seems to my mind decisive upon the subject, that he has taken nothing, and perchance I shall discover him easier than I imagine."

He repaired to the parlour again and carefully divested himself of everything which had enabled him so successfully to impose upon John Mundel, and replaced them by his ordinary costume, after which he fastened up his house and sallied forth, taking his way direct to Mrs. Ragg's humble home, in the expectation that there he would hear something of Tobias, which would give him a clue where to search for him, for to search for him he fully intended; but what were his precise intentions perhaps he could hardly have told himself, until he actually found him.

When he reached Mrs. Ragg's house, and made his appearance abruptly before that lady, who seemed somehow or another always to be ironing and always to drop the iron when anyone came in very near their toes, he said,—"Where did your son Tobias go after he left you to-night?"

"Lor! Mr. Todd, is it you? you are as good as a conjurer, sir, for he was here; but bless you, sir, I know no more where he is gone to than the man in the moon. He said he was going to sea, but I am sure I should not have thought it, *that* I should not."

"To sea! then the probability is that he would go down to the docks, but surely not to-night. Do you not expect him back here to sleep?"

"Well, sir, that's a very good thought of yours, and he may come back here to sleep, for all I know to the contrary."

"But you do not know it for a fact."

"He didn't say so; but he may come, you know, for all that."

"Did he tell you his reason for leaving me?"

"Indeed no, sir; he really did not, and he seemed to me to be a little bit out of his senses."

"Ah! Mrs. Ragg," said Sweeney Todd, "there you have it. From the first moment that he came into my service, I knew and felt confident that he was out of his senses. There was a strangeness of behaviour about him, which soon convinced me of that fact, and I am only anxious about him, in order that some effort may be made to cure him of such a malady, for it is a serious, and a dreadful one, and one which, unless taken in time, will yet be the death of Tobias."

These words were spoken with such solemn seriousness, that they had a wonderful effect upon Mrs. Ragg, who, like most ignorant persons, began immediately to confirm that which she most dreaded.

"Oh, it's too true," she said, "it's too true. He did say some extraordinary things tonight, Mr. Todd, and he said he had something to tell which was too horrid to speak of. Now the idea, you know, Mr. Todd, of anybody having anything at all to tell, and not telling it at once, is quite singular."

"It is; and I am sure that his conduct is such as you never would be guilty of, Mrs. Ragg; but hark! what's that?"

"It's a knock, Mr. Todd."

"Hush, stop a moment, what if it be Tobias?"

"Goodness gracious! it can't be him, for he would have come in at once."

"No; I slipped the bolt of the door, because I wished to talk to you without observation; so it may be Tobias you perceive, after all; but let me hide somewhere, so that I may hear what he says, and be able to judge how his mind is affected. I will not hesitate to do something for him, let it cost me what it may."

"There's the cupboard, Mr. Todd. To be sure there is some dirty saucepans and a frying-pan in it, and of course it ain't a fit place to ask you to go into."

"Never mind that—never mind that; only you be careful, for the sake of Tobias's very life, to keep secret that I am here."

The knocking at the door increased each moment in vehemence, and just as Sweeney Todd had succeeded in getting into the cupboard along with Mrs. Ragg's pots and pans, and thoroughly concealing himself, she opened the door; and, sure enough, Tobias, heated, tired, and looking ghastly pale, staggered into the room.

"Mother," he said, "I have taken a new thought, and have come back to you."

"Well, I thought you would, Tobias; and a very good thing it is that you have."

"Listen to me: I thought of flying from England for ever, and of never setting foot upon its shores, but I have altered that determination completely, and I feel now that it is my duty to do something else."

"To do what, Tobias?"

"To tell all I know—to make a clean breast, mother, and, let the consequences be what they may, to let justice take its course."

"What do you mean, Tobias?"

"Mother, I have come to a conclusion that what I have to tell is of such vast importance, compared with any consequences that might arise from the petty robbery of the candlestick, which you know of, that I ought not to hesitate a moment in revealing everything."

"But, my dear Tobias, remember that is a dreadful secret, and one that must be kept."

"It cannot matter—it cannot matter; and, besides, it is more than probable that by revealing what I actually know, and which is of such great magnitude, I may, mother, in a manner of speaking, perchance completely exonerate you from the consequences of that transaction. Besides, it was long ago, and the prosecutor may have mercy; but be that how it may, and be the consequences what they may, I must and will tell what I now know."

"But what is it, Tobias, that you know?"

"Something too dreadful for me to utter to you alone. Go into the Temple, mother, to some of the gentlemen whose chambers you attend to, and ask them to come to me, and listen to what I have got to say. They will be amply repaid for their trouble, for they will hear that which may, perhaps, save their own lives."

"He is quite gone," thought Mrs. Ragg, "and Mr. Todd is correct; poor Tobias is as mad as he can be! Alas, alas, Tobias, why don't you try to reason yourself into a better state of mind! You don't know a bit what you are saying any more than the man in the moon."

"I know I am half mad, mother, but yet I know what I am saying well; so do not fancy that it is not to be relied upon, but go and fetch someone at once to listen to what I have to relate."

"Perhaps," thought Mrs. Ragg, "if I were to pretend to humour him, it would be as well, and while I am gone, Mr. Todd can speak to him."

This was a bright idea of Mrs. Ragg's, and she forthwith proceeded to carry it into execution, saying,—

"Well, my dear, if it must be, it must be; and I will go; but I hope while I have gone, somebody will speak to you, and convince you that you ought to try to quiet yourself."

These words Mrs. Ragg uttered aloud, for the special benefit of Sweeney Todd, who, she considered, would have been there, to take the hint accordingly.

It is needless to say he did hear them, and how far he profited by them, we shall quickly perceive.

As for poor Tobias, he had not the remotest idea of the close proximity of his arch enemy; if he had, he would quickly have left that spot, where he ought well to conjecture so much danger awaited him; for although Sweeney Todd under the circumstances probably felt, that he dare not take Tobias's life, still he might exchange something that could place it in his power to do so shortly, without the least personal danger to himself.

The door closed after the retreating form of Mrs. Ragg, and as considering the mission she was gone upon, it was very clear some minutes must elapse before she could return, Sweeney Todd did not feel there was any very particular hurry in the transaction.

"What shall I do?" he said to himself. "Shall I await his mother's coming again, and get her to aid me, or shall I of myself adopt some means which will put an end to trouble on this boy's account?"

Sweeney Todd was a man tolerably rapid in thought, and he contrived to make up his mind that the best plan unquestionably would be to lay hold on poor Tobias at once, and so prevent the possibility of any appeal to his mother becoming effective.

Tobias, when his mother left the place, as he imagined, for the purpose of procuring someone to listen to what he considered to be Sweeney Todd's delinquencies, rested his face upon his hands, and gave himself up to painful and deep thought.

He felt that he had arrived at quite a crisis in his history, and that the next few hours cannot but surely be very important to him in their results; and so they were indeed, but not certainly exactly in the way that he had all along anticipated, for he thought of nothing but of the arrest and discomfiture of Todd, little expecting how close was his proximity to that formidable personage.

"Surely," thought Tobias, "I shall by disclosing all that I know about Todd, gain some consideration for my mother, and after all she may not be prosecuted for the robbery of the candlestick; for how very trifling is that affair compared to the much more dreadful things which I more than suspect Sweeney Todd to be guilty of. He is, and must be, from all that I have seen, and heard, a murderer—although how he disposes of his victims is involved in the most complete mystery; and it is to me a matter past all human power of comprehension. I have no idea even upon that subject whatever."

This indeed was a great mystery, for even admitting that Sweeney Todd was a murderer, and it must be allowed that as yet we have only circumstantial evidence of that fact, we can form no conclusion from such evidence as to how he perpetrated the deed, or how afterwards he disposed of the body of his victim.

This great and principal difficulty in the way of committing murder with impunity—namely, the disposal of a corpse, certainly did not seem at all to have any effect on

Sweeney Todd; for if he made corpses, he had some means of getting rid of them with the most wonderful expedition as well as secrecy.

"He is a murderer," thought Tobias. "I know he is, although I have never seen him do the deed, or seen any appearance in the shop of a deed of blood having been committed. Yet, why is it that occasionally when a better dressed person than usual comes into the shop he sends me out on some errand to a distant part of the town?"

Tobias did not forget, too, that on more than one occasion he had come back quicker doubtless than he had been expected, and that he had caught Sweeney Todd in some little confusion, and seen the hat, the stick, or perhaps the umbrella of the last customer quietly waiting there, although the customer had gone; and, even if the glaring improbability of a man leaving his hat behind him in a barber's shop was got over, why did he not come back for it?

This was a circumstance which was entitled to all the weight which Tobias during his mental cogitation could give to it, and there could be but one possible explanation of a man not coming back for his hat, and that was that he had not the power to do so.

"His house will be searched," thought Tobias, "and all those things which must of course have belonged to so many different people will be found, and then they will be identified, and he will be required to say how he came by them, which, I think, will be a difficult task indeed for Sweeney Todd to accomplish. What a relief it will be to me, to be sure, when he is hanged, as I think he is tolerably sure to be!"

"What a relief!" muttered Sweeney Todd, as he slowly opened the cupboard-door unseen by Tobias—"what a relief it will be to me when this boy is in his grave, as he really will be soon, or else I have forgotten all my moral learning, and turned chicken-hearted—neither of them very likely circumstances."

CHAPTER XXI

Sweeney Todd paused for a moment at the cupboard-door, before he made up his mind as to whether he should pounce on poor Tobias at once, or adopt a more creeping, cautious mode of operation.

The latter course was by far the more congenial to him, and so he adopted it in another moment or so, and stole quietly from his place of concealment, and with so little noise, that Tobias could not have the least suspicion anyone was in the room but himself.

Treading as if each step might involve some fearful consequences, he thus at length got completely behind the chair on which Tobias was sitting, and stood with folded arms, and such a hideous smile upon his face, that they together formed no inept representation of the Mephistopheles of the German drama.

"I shall at length," murmured Tobias, "be free from my present dreadful state of mind by thus accusing Todd. He is a murderer—of that I have no doubt; it is but a duty of mine to stand forward as his accuser."

Sweeney Todd stretched out his two brawny hands, and clutched Tobias by the head, which he turned round till the boy could see him, and then he said,—

"Indeed, Tobias, and did it never strike you that Todd was not so easily to be overcome as you would wish him, eh, Tobias?"

The shock of this astonishing and sudden appearance of Sweeney Todd was so great, that for a few moments Tobias was deprived of all power of speech or action, and with his head so strangely twisted as to seem to threaten the destruction of his neck, he glared in the triumphant and malignant countenance of his persecutor, as he would into that of the arch enemy of all mankind, which probably he now began to think the barber really was.

If aught more than another was calculated to delight such a man as Todd, it certainly was to perceive what a dreadful effect his presence had upon Tobias, who remained about a minute and a half in this state before he ventured upon uttering a shriek, which, however, when it did come almost frightened Todd himself.

It was one of those cries which can only come from a heart in its utmost agony—a cry which might have heralded the spirit to another world, and proclaimed as it very nearly did, the destruction of the intellect for ever.

The barber staggered back a pace or two as he heard it, for it was too terrific even for him, but it was for a very brief period that it had that stunning effect upon him, and then, with a full consciousness of the danger to which it subjected him, he sprang upon poor Tobias as a tiger might be supposed to do upon a lamb, and clutched him by the throat, exclaiming,—

"Such another cry, and it is the last you ever live to utter, although it cover me with difficulties to escape the charge of killing you. Peace! I say, peace!"

This exhortation was quite needless, for Tobias could not have uttered a word, had he been ever so much inclined to do so; the barber held his throat with such an iron clutch, as if it had been in a vice.

"Villain," growled Todd, "villain, so this is the way in which you have dared to disregard my injunctions. But no matter, no matter! you shall have plenty of leisure to reflect upon what you have done for yourself. Fool to think that you could cope with me, Sweeney Todd. Ha! ha!"

He burst into a laugh, so much more hideous, more than his ordinary efforts in that way, that, had Tobias heard it—which he did not, for his head had dropped upon his breast, and he had become insensible—it would have terrified him almost as much as Sweeney Todd's sudden appearance had done.

"So," muttered the barber, "he has fainted, has he? Dull child, that is all the better—for once in a way, Tobias, I will carry you, not to oblige you, but to oblige myself—by all that's damnable it was a lively thought that brought me here tonight, or else I might, by the dawn of the morning, have had some very troublesome inquiries made of me."

He took Tobias up as easily as if he had been an infant, and strode from the chambers with him, leaving Mrs. Ragg to draw whatever inference she chose from his absence, but feeling convinced that she was too much under his control to take any steps of a nature to give him the smallest amount of uneasiness.

"The woman," he muttered to himself, "is a double distilled ass, and can be made to believe anything, so that I have no fear whatever of her. I dare not kill Tobias, because it is necessary, in case of the matter being at any other period mentioned, that his mother shall be in a position to swear that she saw him after this night alive and well."

The barber strode through the Temple, carrying the boy, who seemed not at all in a hurry to recover from the nervous and partial state of suffocation into which he had fallen.

As they passed through the gate, opening into Fleet-street, the porter, who knew the barber well by sight, said,—

"Hilloa, Mr. Todd, is that you? Why, who are you carrying?"

"Yes, it's I," said Todd, "and I am carrying my apprentice boy, Tobias Ragg, poor fellow."

"Poor fellow! why, what's the matter with him?"

"I can hardly tell you, but he seems to me and to his mother to have gone out of his senses. Good-night to you, good-night. I'm looking for a coach."

"Good-night, Mr. Todd; I don't think you'll get one nearer than the market—what a kind thing now of him to carry the boy! It ain't every master would do that; but we must not judge of people by their looks, and even Sweeney Todd, though he has a face that one would not like to meet in a lonely place on a dark night, may be a kind-hearted man."

Sweeney Todd walked rapidly down Fleet-street, towards old Fleet Market, which was then in all its glory, if that could be called glory which consisted in all sorts of filth enough to produce a pestilence within the city of London.

When there he addressed a large bundle of great coats, in the middle of which was supposed to be a hackney coachman of the regular old school, and who was lounging over his vehicle, which was as long and lumbering as a city barge.

"Jarvey," he said, "what will you take me to Peckham Rye for?"

"Peckham Rye—you and the boy—there ain't any more of you waiting round the corner are there, 'cos, you know, that won't be fair."

"No, no, no."

"Well, don't be in a passion, master, I only asked, you know, so you need not be put out about it; I will take you for twelve shillings, and that's what I call remarkable cheap, all things considered."

"I'll give you half the amount," said Sweeney Todd, "and you may consider yourself well paid."

"Half, master! that is cutting it low; but howsoever, I suppose I must put up with it, and take you. Get in, I must try and make it up by some better fare out of somebody else."

The barber paid no heed to these renewed remonstrances of the coachman, but got into the vehicle, carrying Tobias with him, apparently with great care and consideration; but when the coach door closed, and no one was observing him, he flung him down among the straw that was at the bottom of the vehicle, and resting his immense feet upon him, he gave one of his disagreeable laughs, as he said,—

"Well, I think I have you now, Master Tobias; your troubles will soon be over. I am really very much afraid that you will die suddenly, and then there will be an end of you altogether, which will be a very sad thing, although I don't think I shall go into mourning, because I have an opinion that that only keeps alive the bitterness of regret, and that it's a great deal better done without, Master Tobias."

The hackney coach swung about from side to side in the proper approved manner of hackney coaches in the olden times, when they used to be called bone shakers, and to be thought wonderful if they made a progress of three miles and a half an hour.

This was the sort of vehicle then in which poor Tobias, still perfectly insensible, was rumbled over Blackfriars-bridge, and so on towards Peckham, which Sweeney Todd announced to be his place of destination.

Going at the rate they did, it was nearly two hours before they arrived upon Peckham Rye; and any one acquainted with that locality is well aware that there are two roads, the one to the left, and the other to the right, both of which are pleasantly enough studded with villa residences. Sweeney Todd directed the coachman to take the road to the left, which he accordingly did, and they pursued it for a distance of about a mile and a half.

It must not be supposed that this pleasant district of country was then in the state it is now, as regards inhabitants or cultivation. On the contrary, it was rather a wild spot, on which now and then a serious robbery had been committed; and which had witnessed some of the exploits of those highwaymen, whose adventures, in the present day, if one may judge from the public patronage they may receive, are viewed with a great amount of interest.

There was a lonely, large, rambling old-looking house by the wayside, on the left. A high wall surrounded it, which only allowed the topmost portion of it to be visible, and that presented great symptoms of decay, in the dilapidated character of the chimney-pots, and the general appearance of discomfort which pervaded it.

Then Sweeney Todd directed the coachman to stop, and when the vehicle, after swinging to and fro for several minutes, did indeed at last resolve itself into a state of repose, Sweeney Todd got out himself, and rang a bell, the handle of which hung invitingly at the gate.

He had to wait several minutes before an answer was given to this summons, but at length a noise proceeded from within, as if several bars and bolts were being withdrawn; and presently the door was opened, and a huge, rough-looking man made his appearance on the threshold.

"Well! what is it now?" he cried.

"I have a patient for Mr. Fogg," said Sweeney Todd. "I want to see him immediately."

"Oh! well, the more the merrier; it don't matter to me a bit. Have you got him with you and is he tolerably quiet?"

"It's a mere boy, and he is not violently mad, but very decidedly so as regards what he says."

"Oh! that's it, is it? He can say what he likes here, it can make no difference in the world to us. Bring him in—Mr. Fogg is in his own room."

"I know the way: you take charge of the lad, and I will go and speak to Mr. Fogg about him. But stay, give the coachman these six shillings, and discharge him."

The doorkeeper of the lunatic asylum, for such it was, went out to obey the injunctions of Sweeney Todd, while that rascally individual himself walked along a wide passage to a door which was at the further extremity of it.

CHAPTER XXII

WHEN THE PORTER OF THE MAD-HOUSE WENT OUT TO THE COACH, HIS FIRST impression was that the boy, who was said to be insane, was dead; for not even the jolting ride to Peckham had been sufficient to arouse him to a consciousness of how he was situated; and there he lay still at the bottom of the coach alike insensible to joy or sorrow.

"Is he dead?" said the man to the coachman.

"How should I know?" was the reply; "he may be or he may not, but I want to know how long I am to wait here for my fare."

"There is your money, be off with you. I can see now that the boy is all right, for he breathes, although it's after an odd fashion that he does so. I should rather think he has had a knock on the head, or something of that kind."

As he spoke, he conveyed Tobias within the building, and the coachman, since he had no further interest in the matter, drove away at once, and paid no more attention to it whatever.

When Sweeney Todd reached the door at the end of the passage, he tapped at it with his knuckles, and a voice cried,—

"Who knocks—who knocks? Curses on you all, who knocks?"

Sweeney Todd did not make any verbal reply to this polite request, but opening the door he walked into the apartment, which is one that really deserves some description.

It was a large room with a vaulted roof, and in the centre was a superior oaken table, at which sat a man considerably advanced in years, as was proclaimed by his grizzled locks that graced the sides of his head, but whose herculean frame and robust constitution had otherwise successfully resisted the assaults of time.

A lamp swung from the ceiling, which had a shade over the top of it, so that it kept a tolerably bright glow upon the table below, which was covered with books and papers, as well as glasses and bottles of different kinds, which showed that the mad-house keeper was, at all events, as far as he himself was concerned, not at all indifferent to personal comfort.

The walls, however, presented the most curious aspect, for they were hung with a variety of tools and implements, which would have puzzled anyone not initiated into the matter even to guess at their uses.

These were, however, in point of fact, specimens of the different kinds of machinery which were used for the purpose of coercing the unhappy persons whose evil destiny made them members of that establishment.

Those were what is called the good old times, when all sorts of abuses flourished in perfection, and when the unhappy insane were actually punished, as if they were guilty of some great offence. Yes, and worse than that were they punished, for a criminal who might have injustice done to him by any who were in authority over him, could complain, and if he got hold of a person of higher power, his complaints might be listened to, but no one heeded what was said by the poor maniac, whose bitterest accusations of his keepers, let their conduct have been to him what it might, was only listened to and set down as a further proof of his mental disorder.

This was indeed a most awful and sad state of things, and, to the disgrace of this country, it was a social evil allowed until very late years to continue in full force.

Mr. Fogg, the mad-house keeper, fixed his keen eyes, from beneath his shaggy brows, upon Sweeney Todd, as the latter entered his apartment, and then he said,—

"Mr. Todd, I think, unless my memory deceives me."

"The same," said the barber, making a hideous face. "I believe I am not easily forgotten."

"True," said Mr. Fogg, as he reached for a book, the edges of which were cut into a lot of little slips, on each of which was a capital letter, in the order of the alphabet— "True, you are not easily forgotten, Mr. Todd."

He then opened the book at the letter T, and read from it:—

"Mr. Sweeney Todd, Fleet-street, London, paid one year's keep and burial of Thomas Simkins, aged 13, found dead in his bed, after a residence in the asylum of 14 months and 4 days. I think, Mr. Todd, that was our last little transaction: what can I do now for you, sir?"

"I am rather unfortunate," said Todd, "with my boys. I have got another here, who has shown such decided symptoms of insanity, that it has become absolutely necessary to place him under your care."

"Indeed! does he rave?"

"Why, yes, he does, and it's the most absurd nonsense in the world he raves about; for, to hear him, one would really think that, instead of being one of the most humane of men, I was in point of fact an absolute murderer."

"A murderer, Mr. Todd!"

"Yes, a murderer—a murderer to all intents and purposes; could anything be more absurd than such an accusation?—I, that have the milk of human kindness flowing in every vein, and whose very appearance ought to be sufficient to convince anybody at once of my kindness of disposition."

Sweeney Todd finished his speech by making such a hideous face, that the mad-house keeper could not for the life of him tell what to say to it; and then there came one of those short, disagreeable laughs which Todd was such an adept in, and which, somehow or another, never appeared exactly to come from his mouth, but always made people look up at the walls and ceiling of the apartment in which they were, in great doubt as to whence the remarkable sound came.

"For how long," said the mad-house keeper, "do you think this malady will continue?"

"I will pay," said Sweeney Todd, as he leaned over the table, and looked into the face of his questioner, "I will pay for twelve months; but I don't think, between you and I, that the case will last anything like so long—I think he will die suddenly."

"I shouldn't wonder if he did. Some of our patients do die very suddenly, and somehow or another, we never know exactly how it happens; but it must be some sort of fit, for they are found dead in the morning in their beds, and then we bury them privately and quietly, without troubling anybody about it at all, which is decidedly the best way, because it saves a great annoyance to friends and relations, as well as prevents any extra expenses which otherwise might be foolishly gone to."

"You are wonderfully correct and considerate," said Todd, "and it's no more than what I expected from you, or what anyone might expect from a person of your great experience, knowledge, and acquirements. I must confess I am quite delighted to hear you talk in so elevated a strain."

"Why," said Mr. Fogg, with a strange leer upon his face, "we are forced to make ourselves useful, like the rest of the community; and we could not expect people to send their mad friends and relatives here, unless we took good care that their ends and views were answered by so doing. We make no remarks, and we ask no questions. Those are the principles upon which we have conducted business so successfully and so long; those are the principles upon which we shall continue to conduct it, and to merit, we hope, the patronage of the British public."

"Unquestionably, most unquestionably."

"You may as well introduce me to your patient at once, Mr. Todd, for I suppose, by this time, he has been brought into this house."

"Certainly, certainly, I shall have great pleasure in showing him to you."

The mad-house keeper rose, and so did Mr. Todd, and the former, pointing to the bottles and glasses on the table, said, "When this business is settled, we can have a friendly glass together."

To this proposition Sweeney Todd assented with a nod, and then they both proceeded to what was called a reception-room in the asylum, and where poor Tobias had been conveyed and laid upon a table, when he showed slight symptoms of recovering from the state of insensibility into which he had fallen, and a man was sluicing water on his face by the assistance of a hearth broom, occasionally dipped into a pailful of that fluid.

"Quite young," said the mad-house keeper, as he looked upon the pale and interesting face of Tobias.

"Yes," said Sweeney Todd, "he is young—more's the pity—and, of course, we deeply regret his present situation."

"Oh, of course, of course; but see, he opens his eyes, and will speak directly."

"Rave, you mean, rave!" said Todd; "don't call it speaking, it is not entitled to the name. Hush,—listen to him."

"Where am I?" said Tobias, "where am I—Todd is a murderer. I denounce him."

"You hear—you hear," said Todd.

"Mad indeed," said the keeper.

"Oh, save me from him, save me from him," said Tobias, fixing his eyes upon Mr. Fogg. "Save me from him, it is my life he seeks, because I know his secrets—he is a murderer—and many a person comes into his shop who never leaves it again in life, if at all."

"You hear him," said Todd, "was there anybody so mad?"

"Desperately mad," said the keeper. "Come, come, young fellow, we shall be under the necessity of putting you in a straight waistcoat, if you go on in that way. We must do it, for there is no help in such cases if we don't."

Todd slunk back into the darkness of the apartment, so that he was not seen, and Tobias continued, in an imploring tone.

"I do not know who you are, sir, or where I am; but let me beg of you to cause the house of Sweeney Todd, the barber, in Fleet-street, near St. Dunstan's church, to be searched, and there you will find that he is a murderer. There are at least a hundred hats, quantities of walking-sticks, umbrellas, watches and rings, all belonging to unfortunate persons who, from time to time, have met with their deaths through him."

"How uncommonly mad!" said Fogg.

"No, no," said Tobias, "I am not mad; why call me mad, when the truth or false-hood of what I say can be ascertained so easily? Search his house, and if those things be not found there, say that I am mad, and have but dreamed of them. I do not know how he kills the people. That is a great mystery to me yet, but that he does kill them I have no doubt—I cannot have a doubt."

"Watson," cried the mad-house keeper, "hilloa! here, Watson."

"I am here, sir," said the man, who had been dashing water upon poor Tobias's face.

"You will take this lad, Watson, as he seems extremely feverish and unsettled. You will take him, and shave his head, Watson, and put a straight waistcoat upon him, and let him be put in one of the dark, damp cells. We must be careful of him, and too much light encourages delirium and fever."

"Oh! no, no!" cried Tobias; "what have I done that I should be subjected to such cruel treatment? What have I done that I should be placed in a cell? If this be a mad-house, I am not mad. Oh, have mercy upon me, have mercy upon me!"

"You will give him nothing but bread and water, Watson, and the first symptoms of his recovery, which will produce better treatment, will be his exonerating his master from what he has said about him, for he must be mad so long as he continues to accuse such a gentleman as Mr. Todd of such things; nobody but a mad man or a mad boy would think of it."

"Then," said Tobias, "I shall continue mad, for if it be madness to know and to aver that Sweeney Todd, the barber, of Fleet-street, is a murderer, mad am I, for I know it, and aver it. It is true, it is true."

"Take him away, Watson, and do as I desired you. I begin to find that the boy is a very dangerous character, and more viciously mad than anybody we have had here for a considerable time."

The man named Watson seized upon Tobias, who again uttered a shriek some-thing similar to the one which had come from his lips when Sweeney Todd clutched hold of him in his mother's room. But they were used to such things at that mad-house, and cared little for them, so no one heeded the cry in the least, but poor Tobias was carried to the door half maddened in reality by the horrors that surrounded him.

Just as he was being conveyed out, Sweeney Todd stepped up to him, and putting his mouth close to his ear, he whispered,

"Ha! ha! Tobias! how do you feel now? Do you think Sweeney Todd will be hung, or will you die in the cell of a mad-house?"

CHAPTER XXIII

FROM WHAT WE HAVE ALREADY HAD OCCASION TO RECORD ABOUT MRS. LOVETT'S NEW cook, who ate so voraciously in the cellar, our readers will no doubt be induced to believe that he was a gentleman likely enough soon to tire of his situation.

To a starving man, and one who seemed completely abandoned even by hope, Lovett's bake-house, with an unlimited leave to eat as much as possible, must of course present itself in the most desirable and lively colours; and no wonder, therefore, that banishing all scruple, a man so pleased, would take the situation with very little inquiry.

But people will tire of good things; and it is a remarkably well-authenticated fact that human nature is prone to be discontented.

And those persons who are well acquainted with the human mind, and who know well how little value people soon set upon things which they possess, while those which they are pursuing, and which seem to be beyond their reach, assume the liveliest colours imaginable, adopt various means of turning this to account.

Napoleon took good care that the meanest of his soldiers should see in perspective the possibility of grasping a marshal's baton.

Confectioners at the present day, when they take a new apprentice, tell him to eat as much as he likes of those tempting tarts and sweetmeats, one or two of which before had been a most delicious treat.

The soldier goes on fighting away, and never gets the marshal's baton. The confectioner's boy crams himself with Banbury cakes, gets dreadfully sick, and never touches one afterwards.

And now, to revert to our friend in Mrs. Lovett's bake-house.

At first everything was delightful, and, by the aid of the machinery, he found that it was no difficult matter to keep up the supply of pies by really a very small amount of manual labour. And that labour was such a labour of love, for the pies were delicious; there could be no mistake about that. He tasted them half cooked, he tasted them wholly cooked, and he tasted them overdone; hot and cold, pork and veal with seasoning, and without seasoning, until at last he had had them in every possible way and shape; and when the fourth day came after his arrival in the cellar, he might have been seen sitting in rather a contemplative attitude with a pie before him.

It was twelve o'clock: he heard that sound come from the shop. Yes, it was twelve o'clock, and he had eaten nothing yet; but he kept his eyes fixed upon the pie that lay untouched before him.

"The pies are all very well," he said, "in fact of course they are capital pies; and now that I see how they are made, and know that there is nothing wrong in them, I of course relish them more than ever, but one can't live always upon pies; it's quite impossible one can subsist upon pies from one end of the year to the other, if they were the finest pies the world ever saw, or ever will see. I don't say anything against the pies—I know they are made of the finest flour, the best possible butter, and that the meat, which comes from God knows where, is the most delicate-looking and tender I ever ate in my life."

He stretched out his hand and broke a small portion of the crust from the pie that was before him, and he tried to eat it.

He certainly did succeed, but it was a great effort; and when he had done, he shook his head, saying,—

"No, no! damn it, I cannot eat it, and that's the fact—one cannot be continually eating pie; it is out of the question, quite out of the question, and all I have to remark is, damn the pies! I really don't think I shall be able to let another one pass my lips."

He rose and paced with rapid strides the place in which he was, and then suddenly he heard a noise, and, looking up, he saw a trap-door in the roof open, and a sack of flour begin gradually to come down.

"Hilloa, hilloa!" he cried, "Mrs. Lovett, Mrs. Lovett!"

Down came the flour, and the trap-door was closed.

"Oh, I can't stand this sort of thing," he exclaimed. "I cannot be made into a mere machine for the manufacture of pies. I cannot, and will not endure it—it is past all bearing."

For the first time almost since his incarceration, for such it really was, he began to think that he would take an accurate survey of the place where this tempting manufacture was carried on.

The fact was, his mind had been so intensively occupied during the time he had been there in providing merely for his physical wants, that he had scarcely had time to think or reason upon the probabilities of a uncomfortable termination of his career; but now, when he had become quite surfeited with the pies, and tired of the darkness and gloom of the place, many unknown fears began to creep across him, and he really trembled, as he asked himself what was to be the end of all.

It was with such a feeling as this that he now set about taking a careful and accurate survey of the place, and, taking a little lamp in his hand, he resolved to peer into every corner of it, with a hope that surely he should find some means by which he should effect an escape from what otherwise threatened to be an intolerable imprisonment.

The vault in which the ovens were situated was the largest; and although a number of smaller ones communicated with it, containing the different mechanical contrivances for the pie-making, he could not from any one of them discover an outlet.

But it was to the vault where the meat was deposited upon stone shelves, that he paid the greatest share of attention, for to that vault he felt convinced there must be some hidden and secret means of ingress, and therefore of egress likewise, or else how came the shelves always so well stocked with meat as they were?

This vault was larger than any of the other subsidiary ones, and the roof was very high, and, come into it when he would, it always happened that he found meat enough upon the shelves, cut into large lumps and sometimes into slices, to make a batch of pies with.

When it got there was not so much a mystery to him as how it got there; for of course, as he must sleep sometimes, he concluded, naturally enough, that it was brought in by some means during the period that he devoted to repose.

He stood in the centre of this vault with the lamp in his hand, and he turned slowly round, surveying the walls and the ceiling with the most critical and marked attention, but not the smallest appearance of an outlet was observable.

In fact, the walls were so entirely filled up with the stone shelves, that there was no space left for a door; and, as for the ceiling, it seemed to be perfectly entire.

Then the floor was of earth; so that the idea of a trap door opening in it was out of the question, because there was no one on his side of it to place the earth again over it, and give it its compact and usual appearance.

"This is most mysterious," he said; "and if ever I could have been brought to believe that anyone had the assistance of the devil himself in conducting human affairs, I should say that by some means Mrs. Lovett had made it worth the while of that elderly individual to assist her; for, unless the meat gets here by some supernatural agency, I really cannot see how it can get here at all. And yet here it is, so fresh, and pure, and white-looking, although I never could tell the pork from the veal myself, for they seemed to me both alike."

He now made a still narrower examination of this vault, but he gained nothing by that. He found that the walls at the backs of the shelves were composed of flat pieces of stone, which, no doubt, were necessary for the support of the shelves themselves; but beyond that he made no further discovery, and he was about leaving the place, when he fancied he saw some writing on the inner side of the door.

. A closer inspection convinced him that there were a number of lines written with lead pencil, and after some difficulty he deciphered them as follows:—

Whatever unhappy wretch reads these lines may bid adieu to the world and all hope, for he is a doomed man! He will never emerge from these vaults with life, for there is a hideous secret connected with them so awful and so hideous, that to write it makes one's blood curdle, and the flesh to creep upon my bones. That secret is this—and you may be assured, whoever is reading these lines, that I write the truth, and that it is as impossible to make that awful truth worse by any exaggeration, as it would be by a candle at midday to attempt to add lustre to the sunbeams.

Here, most unfortunately, the writing broke off, and our friend, who, up to this point, had perused the lines with the most intense interest, felt great bitterness of disappointment, from the fact that enough should have been written to stimulate his curiosity to the highest possible point, but not enough to gratify it.

"This is, indeed, most provoking," he exclaimed; "what can this most dreadful secret be, which it is impossible to exaggerate? I cannot, for a moment, divine to what it can allude."

In vain he searched over the door for some more writing—there was none to be found, and from the long straggling pencil mark which followed the last word, it seemed as if he who had been then writing had been interrupted, and possibly met the fate that he had predicted, and was about to explain the reason of.

"This is worse than no information. I had better have remained in ignorance than have so indistinct a warning; but they shall not find me an easy victim, and, besides, what power on earth can force me to make pies unless I like, I should wish to know."

As he stepped out of the place in which the meat was kept into the large vault where the ovens were, he trod upon a piece of paper that was lying upon the ground, and which he was quite certain he had not observed before. It was fresh and white, and clean too, so that it could not have been long there, and he picked it up with some curiosity.

That curiosity was, however, soon turned to dismay when he saw what was written upon it, which was to the following effect, and well calculated to produce a considerable amount of alarm in the breast of anyone situated as he was, so entirely friendless and so entirely hopeless of any extraneous aid in those dismal vaults, which he began, with a shudder, to suspect would be his tomb:—

> You are getting dissatisfied, and therefore it becomes necessary to explain to you your real position, which is simply this:—you are a prisoner, and were such from the first moment that you set foot where you now are; and you will find that, unless you are resolved upon sacrificing your life, your best plan will be to quietly give in to the circumstances in which you find yourself placed. Without going into any argument or details upon the subject, it is sufficient to inform you that so long as you continue to make the pies, you will be safe; but if you refuse, then the first time you are caught sleeping your throat will be cut.

This document was so much to the purpose, and really had so little of verbosity about it, that it was extremely difficult to doubt its sincerity.

It dropped from the half-paralysed hands of that man who, in the depth of his distress, and urged on by great necessity, had accepted a situation that he would have given worlds to escape from, had he been possessed of them.

"Gracious Heavens!" he exclaimed, "and am I then indeed condemned to such a slavery? Is it possible that even in the very heart of London I am a prisoner, and without the means of resisting the most frightful threats that are uttered against me? Surely, surely, this must all be a dream! It is too terrific to be true!"

He sat down upon that low stool where his predecessor had sat before, receiving his death wound from the assassin who had glided in behind him, and dealt him that terrific crashing blow, whose only mercy was that it at once deprived the victim of existence.

He could have wept bitterly, wept as he there sat, for he thought over days long passed away, of opportunities let go by with the heedless laugh of youth; he thought over all the chances and misfortunes of his life, and now to find himself the miserable inhabitant of a cellar, condemned to a mean and troublesome employment, without even the liberty of leaving that to starve if he chose, upon pain of death—a frightful death which had been threatened him—was indeed torment!

No wonder that at times he felt himself unnerved, and that a child might have conquered him, while at other moments such a feeling of despair would come across him, that he called aloud to his enemies to make their appearance, and give him at least the chance of a struggle for his life.

"If I am to die," he cried, "let me die with some weapon in my hand, as a brave man ought, and I will not complain, for there is little indeed in life now which should induce me to cling to it; but I will not be murdered in the dark."

He sprang to his feet, and running up to the door, which opened from the house into the vaults, he made a violent and desperate effort to shake it.

But such a contingency as this had surely been looked forward to and provided against, for the door was of amazing strength, and most effectually resisted all his efforts, so that the result of his endeavours was but to exhaust himself, and he staggered back, panting and despairing, to the seat he had so recently left.

Then he heard a voice, and upon looking up he saw that the small square opening in the upper part of the door, through which he had been before addressed, was open, and a face there appeared, but it was not the face of Mrs. Lovett.

On the contrary, it was a large and hideous male physiognomy, and the voice that came from it was croaking and harsh, sounding most unmusically upon the ears of the unfortunate man, who was then made a victim to Mrs. Lovett's pies' popularity.

"Continue at your work," said the voice, "or death will be your portion as soon as sleep overcomes you, and you sink exhausted to that repose which you will never awaken from, except to feel the pangs of death, and to be conscious that you are weltering in your blood.

"Continue at your work and you will escape all this—neglect it and your doom is sealed."

"What have I done that I should be made such a victim of? Let me go, and I will swear never to divulge the fact that I have been in these vaults, so I cannot disclose any of their secrets, even if I knew them."

"Make pies," said the voice, "eat them and be happy. How many a man would envy your position—withdrawn from all the struggles of existence, amply provided with board and lodging, and engaged in a pleasant and delightful occupation. It is astonishing how you can be dissatisfied!"

Bang! went the little square orifice at the top of the door, and the voice was heard no more. The jeering mockery of those tones, however, still lingered upon the ear of the unhappy prisoner, and he clasped his head in his hands with a fearful impression upon his brain that he surely must be going mad.

"He will drive me to insanity," he cried; "already I feel a sort of slumber stealing over me for want of exercise, and the confined air of these vaults hinders me from taking regular repose; but now, if I close an eye, I shall expect to find the assassin's knife at my throat."

He sat for some time longer, and not even the dread he had of sleep could prevent a drowsiness creeping over his faculties, and this weariness would not be shaken off by any ordinary means, until at length he sprang to his feet, and shaking himself roughly like one determined to be wide awake, he said to himself mournfully,—

"I must do their bidding or die; hope may be a delusion here, but I cannot altogether abandon it, and not until its faintest image has departed from my breast can I lie down to sleep and say—Let death come in any shape it may, it is welcome."

With a desperate and despairing energy he set about replenishing the furnaces of the oven, and when he had got them all in a good state he commenced manufacturing a batch of one hundred pies, which, when he had finished and placed upon the tray and set the machine in motion which conducted them up to the shop, he considered to be a sort of price paid for his continued existence, and flinging himself upon the ground, he fell into a deep slumber.

CHAPTER XXIV

When Sweeney Todd had with such diabolical want of feeling whispered the few words of mockery which we have recorded in Tobias's ear, when he was carried out of Mr. Fogg's reception-room to be taken to a cell, the villainous barber drew back and indulged in rather a longer laugh than usual.

"Mr. Todd," said Mr. Fogg, "I find that you still retain your habit of merriment, but yours ain't the most comfortable laugh in the world, and we seldom hear anything to equal it, even from one of our cells."

"No!" said Sweeney Todd, "I don't suppose you do, and for my part I never heard of a cell laughing yet."

"Oh! you know what I mean, Mr. Todd, well enough."

"That may be," said Todd, "but it would be just as well to say it for all that. I think, however, as I came in, you said something about refreshment?"

"I certainly did; and if you will honour me by stepping back to my room, I think I can offer you, Mr. Todd, a glass of as nice wine as the king himself could put on his table, if he were any judge of that commodity, which I am inclined to think he is not."

"What do you expect," said Sweeney Todd, "that such an idiot should be a judge of; but I shall have great pleasure in tasting your wine, for I have no hesitation in saying that my work to-night has made me thirsty."

At this moment a shriek was heard, and Sweeney Todd shrank away from the door.

"Oh! it's nothing, it's nothing," said Mr. Fogg: "if you had resided here as long as I have, you would get accustomed to hearing a slight noise. The worst of it is, when half a dozen of the mad fellows get shrieking against each other in the middle of the night. That, I grant, is a little annoying."

"What do you do with them?"

"We send in one of the keepers with the lash, and soon put a stop to that. We are forced to keep the upper hand of them, or else we should have no rest. Hark! do you hear that fellow now? he is generally pretty quiet, but he has taken it into his head to be outrageous today; but one of my men will soon put a stop to that. This way, Mr. Todd, if you please, and as we don't often meet, I think when we do we ought to have a social glass."

Sweeney Todd made several horrible faces as he followed the mad-house keeper, and he looked as if it would have given him quite as much pleasure, and no doubt it would, to brain that individual, as to drink his wine, although probably he would have preferred doing the latter process first, and executing the former afterwards, and at his leisure.

They soon reached the room which was devoted to the use of Mr. Fogg and his friends, and which contained the many little curiosities in the way of mad-house discipline, that were in that age considered indispensable in such establishments.

Mr. Fogg moved away with his hands a great number of the books and papers which were on the table, so as to leave a vacant space, and then drawing the cork of a bottle he filled himself a large glass of its contents, and invited Sweeney Todd to do the same, who was by no means slow in following his example.

While these two villains are carousing, and caring nothing for the scene of misery with which they are surrounded, poor Tobias, in conformity with the orders that had been issued with regard to him, was conveyed along a number of winding passages and down several staircases towards the cells of the establishment.

In vain he struggled to get free from his captor—as well might a hare have struggled in the fangs of a wolf—nor were his cries at all heeded; although, now and then, the shriek he uttered was terrible to hear, and enough to fill anyone with dismay.

"I am not mad," said he, "indeed I am not mad—let me go, and I will say nothing—not one word shall ever pass my lips regarding Mr. Todd—let me go, oh, let me
go, and I will pray for you as long as I live."

Mr. Watson whistled a lively tune.

"If I promise—if I swear to tell nothing, Mr. Todd will not wish me kept here—
all he wants is my silence, and I will take any oath he likes. Speak to him for me,
I implore you, and let me go."

Mr. Watson commenced the second part of his lively tune, and by that time he
reached a door, which he unlocked, and then, setting down Tobias upon the threshold,
he gave him a violent kick, which flung him down two steps on to the stone floor of
a miserable cell, from the roof of which continual moisture was dripping, the only
accommodation it possessed being a truss of damp straw flung into one corner.

"There," said Mr. Watson, "my lad, you can stay there and make yourself comfortable till somebody comes to shave your head, and after that you will find yourself
quite a gentleman."

"Mercy! mercy!—have mercy on me!"

"Mercy! what the devil do you mean by mercy? Well, that's a good joke; but I can
tell you, you have come to the wrong shop for that, we don't keep it in stock here, and
if we wanted ever so little of it, we should have to go somewhere else for it."

Mr. Watson laughed so much at his own joke, that he felt quite amiable, and
told Tobias that if he were perfectly quiet, and said "thank you" for everything,
he wouldn't put him in the straight waistcoat, although Mr. Fogg had ordered it;
"for," added Mr. Watson, "so far as that goes, I don't care a straw what Mr. Fogg
says or what he does; he can't do without me, damn him! because I know too many
of his secrets."

Tobias made no answer to this promise, but he lay upon his back on the floor of
his cell wringing his hands despairingly, and feeling that almost the very atmosphere
of the place seemed pregnant with insanity, and giving himself up for lost entirely.

"I shall never—never," he said, "look upon the bright sky and the green fields
again. I shall be murdered here, because I know too much; what can save me now? Oh,
what an evil chance it was that brought me back again to my mother, when I ought
to have been far, far away by this time, instead of being, as I know I am, condemned
to death in this frightful place. Despair seizes upon me! What noise is that—a shriek?
Yes, yes, there is some other blighted heart beside mine in this dreadful house. Oh,
Heaven! what will become of me? I feel already stifled and sick, and faint with the air

of this dreadful cell. Help, help, help! have mercy upon me, and I will do anything, promise anything, swear anything!"

If poor Tobias had uttered his complaints on the most desolate shore that ever a shipwrecked mariner was cast upon, they could not have been more unheeded than they were in that house of terror.

He screamed and shrieked for aid. He called upon all the friends he had ever known in early life, and at that moment he seemed to remember the name of everyone who had ever uttered a kind word to him; and to those persons who, alas! could not hear him, but were far enough removed away from his cell, he called for aid in that hour of his deep distress.

At length, faint, wearied and exhausted, he lay a mere living wreck in that damp, unwholesome cell, and felt almost willing that death should come and relieve him, at least from the pang of constantly expecting it!

His cries, however, had had the effect of summoning up all the wild spirits in that building; and, as he now lay in the quiet of absolute exhaustion, he heard from far and near smothered cries and shrieks and groans, such as one might expect would fill the air of the infernal regions with dismal echoes.

A cold and clammy perspiration broke out upon him, as these sounds each moment more plainly fell upon his ear, and as he gazed upon the profound darkness of the cell, his excited fancy began to people it with strange, unearthly beings, and he could suppose that he saw hideous faces grinning at him, and huge misshapen creatures crawling on the walls, and floating in the damp, pestiferous atmosphere of the wretched cell.

In vain he covered his eyes with his hands; these creatures of his imagination were not to be shut out from the mind, and he saw them, if possible, more vividly than before, and presenting themselves with more frightfully tangible shapes. Truly, if such visions should continue to haunt him, poor Tobias was likely enough to follow the fate of many others who had been held in that establishment perfectly sane, but in a short time exhibited in it as raving lunatics.

"A nice clear cool glass of wine," said Sweeney Todd, as he held up his glass between him and the light, "and pleasant drinking; so soft and mild in the mouth, and yet gliding down the throat with a pleasant strength of flavour."

"Yes," said Mr. Fogg, "it might be worse. You see, some patients, who are low and melancholy mad, require stimulants, and their friends send them wine. This is some that was so sent."

"I should certainly, Mr. Fogg, not expect such an act of indiscretion from you, knowing you as I do to be quite a man of the world."

"Thank you for the compliment. This wine, now, was sent for an old gentleman who had turned so melancholy, that he not only would not take food enough to keep life and soul together, but he really terrified his friends so by threatening suicide that they sent him here for a few months; and, as stimulants were recommended for him, they sent this wine, you see; but I stimulated him without it quite as well, for I drink the wine myself and give him such an infernal good kick or two every day, and that stimulates him, for it puts him in such a devil of a passion that I am quite sure he doesn't want any wine.

"A good plan," said Sweeney Todd, "but I wonder you don't contrive that your own private room should be free from the annoyance of hearing such sounds as those that have been coming upon my ears for then last five or ten minutes."

"It's impossible; you cannot get out of the way if you live in the house at all; and you see, as regards these mad fellows, they are quite like a pack of wolves, and when once one of them begins howling and shouting, the others are sure to chime in, in full chorus, and make no end of a disturbance till we stop them, as I have already told you we do, with a strong hand."

"While I think of it," said Sweeney Todd, as he drew from his pocket a leathern bag, "while I think of it, I may as well pay you the year's money, for the lad I have brought you; you see, I have not forgot the excellent rule you have of being paid in advance. There is the amount."

"Ah, Mr. Todd," said the mad-house keeper, as he counted the money, and then placed it in his pocket, "it's a pleasure to do business with a thorough business man like yourself. The bottle stands with you, Mr. Todd, and I beg you will not spare it. Do you know, Mr. Todd, this is a line of life which I have often thought would have suited you; I am certain you have a genius for such things."

"Not equal to you," said Todd; "but as I am fond, certainly, of what is strange and out of the way, some of the scenes and characters you come across would, I have no doubt, be highly entertaining to me."

"Scenes and characters, I believe you! During the course of a business like ours, we come across all sorts of strange things; and if I chose to do it, which, of course, I don't, I could tell a few tales which would make some people shake in their shoes; but I have no right to tell them, for I have been paid, and what the deuce is it to me?"

"Oh, nothing, of course, nothing. But just while we are sipping our wine, now, couldn't you tell me something that would not be betraying anybody else's confidence?"

"I could, I could; I don't mean to say that I could not, and I don't much care if I do to you."

CHAPTER XXV

AFTER A SHORT PAUSE, DURING WHICH MR. FOGG APPEARED TO BE REFERRING TO THE cells of memory, with the view of being refreshed in a matter that had long since been a bygone, but which he desired to place as clearly before his listener as he could, in fact, to make if possible that relation real to him, and to omit nothing during its progress that should be told; or possibly that amiable individual was engaged in considering if there were any salient points that might incriminate himself, or give even a friend a handle to make use of against him, but apparently there was nothing of the kind, for, after a loud "hem!" he filled the glasses, saying,—

"Well, now, as you are a friend, I don't mind telling you how we do business here—things that have been done, you know, by others; but I have had my share as well as others—I have known a thing or two, Mr. Todd, and I may say I have done a thing or two, too."

"Well, we must all live and let live," said Sweeney Todd, "there's no going against that, you know; if all I have done could speak, why—but no matter, I am listening to you—however, if deeds could speak, one or two clever things would come out, rather, I think."

"Ay, 'tis well they don't," said Mr. Fogg, with much solemnity, "if they did, they would constantly be speaking at times when it would be very inconvenient to hear them, and dangerous besides."

"So it would," said Sweeney, "a still tongue makes a wise head—but, then the silent system would bring no grist to the mill, and we must speak when we know we are right and among friends."

"Of course," said Fogg, "of course, that's the right use of speech, and one may as well be without it as to have it and not use it; but come—drink, and fill again before I begin, and then to my tale. But we may as well have sentiment. Sentiment, you know," continued Fogg, "is the very soul of friendship. What do you say to 'The heart that can feel for another'?"

"With all my soul," said Sweeney Todd; "it's very touching—very touching indeed. 'The heart that can feel for another!' " and as he spoke, he emptied the glass, which he pushed towards Fogg to refill.

"Well," said Fogg, as he complied, "we have had the sentiment, we may as well have the exemplification."

"Ha! ha! ha!" said Todd, "very good, very good indeed; pray go on, that will do capitally."

"I may as well tell you the whole matter, as it occurred; I will then let you know all I know, and in the same manner. None of the parties are now living, or, at least, they are not in this country, which is just the same thing, so far as I am concerned."

"Then that is an affair settled and done with," remarked Sweeney Todd parenthetically.

"Yes, quite:—Well, it was one night—such a one as this, and pretty well about the same hour, perhaps somewhat earlier than this. However, it doesn't signify a straw about the hour; but it was quite night, a dark and wet night too, when a knock came at the street door—a sharp double knock—it was. I was sitting alone, as I might have been now, drinking a glass or two of wine; I was startled, for I was thinking about an affair I had on hand at that very moment, of which there was a little stir.

"However, I went to the door, and peeped through a grating that I had there, and saw only a man; he had drawn his horse inside the gate, and secured him; he wore a large Whitney riding-coat with a cape that would have thrown off a deluge.

"I fancied, or I thought I could tell, that he meant no mischief; so I opened the door at once and saw a tall gentlemanly man, but wrapped up so, that you could not tell who or what he was; but my eyes are sharp, you know, Mr. Todd: we haven't seen so much of the world without learning to distinguish what kind of person one has to deal with."

"I should think not," said Todd.

" 'Well,' said I, 'what is your pleasure, sir?' "

"The stranger paused a moment or two before he made any reply to me.

" 'Is your name Fogg?' he said.

" 'Yes, it is,' said I, 'my name is Fogg,—what is your pleasure, sir?'

" 'Why,' said he, after another pause, during which he fixed his eye very hard upon me—'why, I wish to have a little private conversation with you, if you can spare so much time, upon a very important matter which I have in hand.'

"'Walk in, sir,' said I, as soon as I heard what it was he wanted, and he followed me in. 'It is a very unpleasant night, and it's coming on to rain harder: I think it is fortunate you have got housed.'

"He came into this very parlour, and took a seat before the fire, with his back to the light, so that I couldn't see his face very well.

"However, I was determined that I would be satisfied in these particulars, and so, when he had taken off his hat, I stirred up the fire, and made a blaze that illuminated the whole room, and which showed me the sharp, thin visage of my visitor, who was a dark man with keen grey eyes that were very restless,—

"'Will you have a glass of wine?' said I; 'the night is cold as well as wet.'

"'Yes, I will,' he replied; 'I am cold with riding. You have a lonely place about here; your house, I see, stands alone too. You have not many neighbours.'

"'No, sir,' said I; 'we hadn't need, for when any of the poor things set to scream-ing, it would make them feel very uncomfortable indeed.'

"'So it would; there is an advantage in that both to yourself as well as to them. It would be disagreeable to you to know that you were disturbing your neighbours, and they would feel equally uncomfortable in being disturbed, and yet you must do your duty.'

"'Ay! to be sure,' said I; 'I must do my duty, and people won't pay me for letting madmen go, though they may for keeping them; and besides that, I think some on 'em would get their throats cut if I did.'

"'You are right—quite right,' said he; 'I am glad to find you of that mind, for I came to you about an affair that requires some delicacy about it, since it is a female patient.'

"'Ah!' said I, 'I always pay a great attention, very great attention, and I don't rec-ollect a case, however violent it may be, but what I can overcome. I always make 'em acknowledge me, and there's much art in that.'

"'To be sure, there must be.'

"'And moreover, they wouldn't so soon crouch and shrink away from me, and do what I tell 'em, if I did not treat them with kindness, that is, as far as is consistent with one's duty, for I mustn't forget that.'

"'Exactly,' he replied; 'those are my sentiments, exactly.'

"'And now, sir, will you inform me in what way I can serve you?'

"'Why, I have a relative—a female relative, who is unhappily affected with a brain disease; we have tried all we can do, without any effect. Do what we will, it comes to the same thing in the end.'

"'Ah!' said I; 'poor thing—what a dreadful thing it must be to you or any of her friends, who have the charge of her, to see her day by day an incurable maniac. Why, it is just as bad as when a friend or relative was dead, and you were obliged to have the dead body constantly in your house before your eyes.'

"'Exactly, my friend,' replied the stranger, 'exactly, you are a man of discernment, Mr. Fogg. I see that is truly the state of the case. You may then guess at the state of our feelings, when we have to part with one beloved by us.'

"As he spoke, he turned right round, and faced me, looking very hard into my face.

"'Well,' said I, 'yours is a hard case; but to have one afflicted about you in the manner the young lady is, is truly distressing: it is like having a perpetual lumbago in your back.'

"'Exactly,' said the stranger. 'I tell you what, you are the very man to do this thing for me.'

"'I am sure of it,' said I.

"'Then we understand each other, eh?' said the stranger. 'I must say I like your appearance; it is not often such people as you and I meet.'

"'I hope it will be to our mutual advantage,' said I, 'because such people don't meet every day, and we oughtn't to meet to no purpose; so, in anything delicate and confidential, you may command me.'

"'I see you are a clever man,' said he; 'well, well, I must pay you in proportion to your talents. How do you do business—by the job, or by the year?'

"'Well,' said I, 'where it's a matter of some nicety it may be both—but it entirely depends upon circumstances. I had better know exactly what it is I have to do.'

"'Why, you see, it is a young female about eighteen, and she is somewhat troublesome, takes to screaming and all that kind of thing. I want her taken care of, though you must be very careful she neither runs away, nor suddenly commits any mischief, as her madness does not appear to me to have any particular form, and would, at times, completely deceive the best of us, and then suddenly she will break out violently, and snap or fly at anybody with her teeth.'

"'Is she so bad as that?'

"'Yes, quite. So, it is quite impossible to keep her at home; and I expect it will be a devil of a job to get her here. I tell you what you shall have; I'll pay you your yearly charge for board and care, and you'll come and assist me in securing her, and bringing her down. It will take some trouble.'

"'Very well,' said I, 'that will do; but you must double the note and make it twenty, if you please; it will cost something to come and do the job well.'

"'I see—very well—we won't disagree about a ten-pound note; but you'll know how to dispose of her if she comes here.'

"'Oh, yes—very healthy place.'

"'But I don't know that health is a very great blessing to anyone under such circumstances; indeed, who would begrudge an early grave to one severely afflicted?'

"'Nobody ought,' said I; 'if they know what mad people went through, they would not, I'm sure.'

"'That is very true again, but the fact is, they don't, and they only look at one side of the picture; for my own part, I think that it ought to be so ordained, that when people are so afflicted, nature ought to sink under the affliction, and so insensibly to revert to the former state of nonentity.'

"'Well,' said I, 'that may be as you please, I don't understand all that; but I tell you what, I hope if she were to die much sooner than you expect, you would not think it too much trouble to afford me some compensation for my loss.'

"'Oh dear no! and to show you that I shall entertain no such illiberal feeling, I will give you two hundred pounds, when the certificate of her burial can be produced. You understand me?'

"'Certainly.'

"'Her death will be of little value to me, without the legal proof,' said the stranger; 'so she must die at her own pleasure, or live while she can.'

"'Certainly,' said I.

"'But what terrifies me,' said the stranger, 'most is, her terror-stricken countenance, always staring us in our faces; and it arose from her being terrified; indeed, I think if she were thoroughly frightened, she would fall dead. I am sure, if any wickedly disposed person were to do so, death would no doubt result.'

"'Ah!' said I, 'it would be a bad job; now tell me where I am to see you, and how about the particulars.'

"'Oh, I will tell you; now, can you be at the corner of Grosvenor-street, near Park-lane?'

"'Yes,' I replied, 'I will.'

"'With a coach, too. I wish you to have a coach, and one that you can depend upon, because there may be a little noise. I will try to avoid it, if possible, but we cannot always do what we desire; but you must have good horses.'

"'Now, I tell you what is my plan; that is, if you don't mind the damages, if any happen."

"'What are they?'

"'This: suppose a horse falls, and is hurt, or an upset—would you stand the racket?'

"'I would, of course.'

"'Then listen to me; I have had more of these affairs than you have, no doubt. Well, then, I have had experience which you have not. Now, I'll get a trotting-horse, and a covered cart or chaise—one that will go along well at ten miles an hour, and no mistake about it.'

"'But will it hold enough?'

"'Yes, four or five or six, and upon a push, I have known eight to cram in it; but then you know we were not particular how we were placed; but still it will hold as many as a hackney coach, only not so conveniently; but then we have nobody in the affair to drive us, and there can't be too few.'

"'Well, that is perhaps best; but have you a man on whom you can depend, because if you could, why, I would not be in the affair at all.'

"'You must,' said I; 'in the first place, I can depend upon one man best; him I must leave here to mind the place; so if you can manage the girl, I will drive, and know the road as well as the way to my own mouth; I would rather have as few in it as possible.'

"'Your precaution is very good, and I think I will try and manage it, that there shall be only you and I acquainted with the transaction; at all events, should it become necessary, it will be time enough to let some other person into the secret at the moment their services are required. That, I think, will be the best arrangement that I can come to; what do you say?'

"'That will do very well—when we get her here, and when I have seen her a few days, I can tell you what to do with her.'

"'Exactly; and now, goodnight—there is the money I promised, and now again, good-night! I shall see you at the appointed time.'

"'You will,' said I—'one glass more, it will do you good, and keep the rain out.'

"He took off a glass of wine, and then pulled his hat over his face, and left the house.

"It was a dark, wet night, and the wind blew, and we heard the sound of his horse's hoofs for some time; however, I shut the door and went in, thinking over in my own mind what would be the gain of my own exertions.

"Well, at the appointed hour, I borrowed a chaise cart, a covered one, with what you call a head to it, and I trotted to town in it. At the appointed time, I was at the corner of Grosvenor-street; it was late, and yet I waited there an hour or more before I saw any one.

"I walked into a little house to get a glass of spirits to keep up the warmth of the body, and when I came out again, I saw someone standing at my horse's head. I immediately went up.

" 'Oh, you are here,' he said.

" 'Yes, I am,' said I, 'I have been here the Lord knows how long. Are you ready?'

" 'Yes, I am come,' said he, as he got into the cart, 'come to the place I shall tell you—I shall only get her into the cart, and you must do the rest.'

" 'You'll come back with me: I shall want help on the road, and I have no one with me.'

" 'Yes, I will come with you, and manage the girl, but you must drive, and take all the casualties of the road, for I shall have enough to do to hold her, and keep her from screaming, when she does awake.'

" 'What! is she asleep?'

" 'I have given her a small dose of laudanum, which will cause her to sleep comfortably for an hour or two, but the cold air and disturbance will most probably awaken her first.'

" 'Throw something over her, and keep her warm, and have something ready to thrust into her mouth, in case she takes to screaming, and then you are all right.'

" 'Good,' he replied: 'now wait here. I am going to yon house. When I've entered, and disappeared several minutes, you may quietly drive up, and take your station on the other side of the lamp-post.'

"As he spoke he got out, and walked to a large house which he entered softly, and left the door ajar; and after he had gone in, I walked the horse quietly up to the lamp-post, and as I placed it, the horse and front of the cart were completely in the dark.

"I had scarcely got up to the spot, when the door opened, and he looked out to see if anybody was passing. I gave him the word, and out he came, leaving the door, and came with what looked like a bundle of clothes, but which was the young girl and some clothes he had brought with him.

" 'Give her to me,' said I, 'and jump up and take the reins; go on as quickly as you can.'

"I took the girl in my arms, and handed her into the back part of the chaise, while he jumped up, and drove away. I placed the young girl in an easy position upon some hay, and stuffed the clothes under her, so as to prevent the jolting from hurting her.

" 'Well,' said I, 'you may as well come back here, and sit beside her: she is all right. You seem rather in a stew.'

" 'Why, I have run with her in my arms, and altogether it has flurried me.'

" 'You had better have some brandy,' said I.

" 'No, no! don't stop.'

" 'Pooh, pooh!' I replied, pulling up, 'here is the last house we shall come to, to have a good stiff tumbler of hot brandy-and-water. Come, have you any change, about a sovereign will do, because I shall want change on the road? Come, be quick.'

"He handed me a sovereign, saying,—

" 'Don't you think it's dangerous to stop—we may be watched, or she may wake."

" 'Not a bit of it. She snores too loudly to wake just yet, and you'll faint without the cordial; so keep a good look-out upon the wench, and you will recover your nerves again.'

"As I spoke, I jumped out, and got two glasses of brandy and water, hot, strong, and sweet. I had in about two minutes made out of the house.

" 'Here,' said I, 'drink—drink it all up—it will bring the eyes out of your head.'

"I spoke the truth, for what with my recommendation and his nervousness and haste, he drank about half of it at a gulp.

"I shall never forget his countenance. Ha! ha! ha! I can't keep my mirth to myself. Just imagine the girl inside a covered cart, all dark, so dark that you could hardly see the outlines of the shadow of a man—and then imagine, if you can, a pair of keen eyes, that shone in the dark like cat's eyes, suddenly give out a flash of light, and then turn round in their sockets, showing the whites awfully, and then listen to the fall of the glass, and see him grasp his throat with one hand, and thrust the other hand into his stomach.

"There was a queer kind of voice came from his throat, and then something like a curse and a groan escaped him.

" 'Damn it,' said I; 'what is the matter now—you've supped all the liquor—you are very nervous—you had better have another dose.'

" 'No more—no more,' he said, faintly and huskily, 'no more, for God's sake no more. I am almost choked, my throat is scalded, and my entrails on fire.'

"'I told you it was hot,' said I.

"'Yes, hot, boiling—go on. I'm mad with pain—push on.'

"'Will you have any water or anything to cool your throat?' said I.

"'No, no—go on.'

"'Yes,' said I, 'but the brandy-and-water is hot; however, it's going down very fast now—very fast indeed, here is the last mouthful'; and as I said so, I gulped it down, returned with the one glass, and then paid for the damage.

"This did not occupy five minutes, and away we came along the road at a devil of a pace, and we were all right enough; my friend behind me got over his scald, though he had a very sore gullet, and his intestines were in a very uncomfortable state; but he was better.

"Away we rattled, the ground rattling to the horse's hoofs and the wheels of the vehicle, the young girl still remaining in the same state of insensibility in which she had first been brought out.

"No doubt she had taken a stronger dose of the opium than she was willing to admit. That was nothing to me, but made it all the better, because she gave the less trouble, and made it safer.

"We got here easy enough, drove slap up to the door, which was opened in an instant, jumped out, took the girl, and carried her in.

"When once these doors are shut upon anyone, they may rest assured that it is quite a settled thing, and they don't get out very easy, save in a wooden surtout; indeed, I never lost a boarder by any other means; we always keep one connection, and they are usually so well satisfied, that they never take anyone away from us.

"Well, well! I carried her indoors, and left her in a room by herself on a bed. She was a nice girl—a handsome girl, I suppose people would call her, and had a low, sweet and plaintive voice. But enough of this!

"'She's all right,' said I, when I returned to this room. 'It's all right—I have left her.'

"'She isn't dead?' he enquired, with much terror.

"'Oh! no, no!—she is only asleep, and has not woke up yet from the effects of the laudanum. Will you now give me one year's pay in advance?'

"'Yes,' he replied, as he handed the money, and the remainder of the bonds. 'Now, how am I to do about getting back to London to-night?'

"'You had better remain here.'

"'Oh, no! I should go mad too, if I were to remain here; I must leave here soon.'

" 'Well, will you go to the village inn?'

" 'How far is that off?'

" 'About a mile—you'll reach it easy enough; I'll drive you over for the matter of that, and leave you there. I shall take the cart there.'

" 'Very well, let it be so; I will go. Well, well, I am glad it is all over, and the sooner it is over for ever, the better. I am truly sorry for her, but it cannot be helped. It will kill her, I have no doubt; but that is all the better; she will escape the misery consequent upon her departure, and release us from a weight of care.'

" 'So it will,' said I, 'but come, we must go at once, if going you are.'

" 'Yes, yes,' he said hurriedly.

" 'Well, then, come along; the horse is not yet unharnessed, and if we do not make haste, we shall be too late to obtain a lodging for the night.'

" 'That is very good,' he said, somewhat wildly; 'I am quite ready—quite.'

"We left the house, and trotted off to the inn at a good rate, where we arrived in about ten minutes or less, and then I put up the horse, and saw him in the inn, and came back as quick as I could on foot. 'Well, well,' I thought, 'this will do, I have had a good day of it—paid well for business, and haven't wanted for sport on the road.'

"Well, I came to the conclusion that if the whole affair was to speedily end, it would be more in my pocket than if she were living, and she would be far happier in heaven than here, Mr. Todd."

"Undoubtedly," said Mr. Sweeney Todd, "undoubtedly that is a very just observation of yours."

"Well, then I set to work to find out how the matter could be managed, and I watched her until she awoke. She looked around her, and seemed much surprised, and confused, and did not seem to understand her position, while I remained near at hand.

"She sighed deeply, and put her hand to her head, and appeared for a time quite unable to comprehend what had happened to her, or where she was.

"I sent some tea to her, as I was not prepared to execute my purpose, and she seemed to recover, and asked some questions, but my man was dumb for the occasion, and would not speak, and the result was, she was very much frightened. I left her so for a week or two, and then, one day, I went into her cell. She had greatly altered in appearance, and looked very pale.

" 'Well,' said I, 'how do you find yourself now?'

"She looked up into my face, and shuddered; but she said in a calm voice, looking round her,—

" 'Where am I?'

" 'You are here!' said I, 'and you'll be very comfortable if you only take on kindly, but you will have a straight waistcoat put on you if you do not.'

" 'Good God!' she exclaimed, clasping her hands, 'have they put me here—in—in—'

"She could not finish the sentence, and I supplied the word which she did not utter, until I had done so, and then she screamed loudly,—

" '*A mad-house*!'

" 'Come,' said I, 'this will never do; you must learn to be quiet, or you'll have fearful consequences.'

" 'Oh, mercy, mercy! I will do no wrong! What have I done that I should be brought here—what have I done? They may have all I have if they will let me live in freedom. I care not where or how poor I may be. Oh! Henry, Henry!—if you knew where I was, would you not fly to my rescue? Yes, you would, you would!'

" 'Ah,' said I, 'there is no Henry here, and you must be content to do without one.'

" 'I could not have believed that my brother would have acted such a base part. I did not think him wicked; although I knew him to be selfish, mean and stern, yet I did not think he intended such wickedness; but he thinks to rob me of all my property—yes, that is the object he has in sending me here.'

" 'No doubt,' said I.

" 'Shall I ever get out?' she enquired in a pitiful tone; 'do not say my life is to be spent here.'

" 'Indeed it is,' said I; 'while he lives, you'll never leave these walls.'

" 'He shall not attain his end, for I have deeds about me that he will never be able to obtain; indeed he may kill me, but he cannot benefit by my death.'

" 'Well,' said I, 'it serves him right. And how did you manage that matter—how did you contrive to get the deeds away?'

" 'Never mind that; it is a small deed, and I have secured it. I did not think he would have done this thing, but he may yet relent. Will you aid me? I shall be rich, and can pay you well.'

" 'But your brother?' said I.

" 'Oh, he is rich without mine, but he is over-avaricious; but say you will help me—only help me to get out, and you shall be no loser by the affair.'

" 'Very well,' said I. 'Will you give me this deed as a security that you will keep your word?'

" 'Yes,' she replied, drawing forth the deed—a small parchment from her bosom. 'Take it, and now let me out; you shall be handsomely rewarded.'

" 'Ah!' said I, 'but you must allow me first to settle this matter with my employers. You must really be mad. We do not hear of young ladies carrying deeds and parchments about them when they are in their senses.'

" 'You do not mean to betray me?" she said, springing up wildly, and running towards the deed, which I carefully placed in my breast-coat-pocket.

" 'Oh dear no! but I shall retain the deed, and speak to your brother about this matter.'

" 'My God! my God!' she exclaimed, and then she sank back on her bed, and in another moment she was covered with blood. She had burst a blood vessel.

"I sent for a surgeon and physician, and they both gave it as their opinion that she could not be saved, and that a few hours would see the last of her.

"That was the fact. She was dead before another half hour, and then I sent to the authorities for the purpose of burial; and, producing the certificate of the medical men, I had no difficulty, and she was buried all comfortably without any trouble."

" 'Well,' thought I, 'this is a very comfortable affair, but it will be more profitable than I had any idea of, and I must get my first reward first; and if there should be any difficulty, I have the deed to fall back upon.'

"He came down next day, and appeared with rather a long face.

" 'Well,' said he, 'how do matters go here?'

" 'Very well,' said I; 'how is your throat?'

"I thought he cast a malicious look at me, as much as to imply he laid it all to my charge.

" 'Pretty well,' he replied; 'but I was ill for three days. How is the patient?'

" 'As well as you could possibly wish,' said I.

" 'She takes it kindly, eh? Well, I hardly expected it—but no matter. She'll be a long while on hand, I perceive. You haven't tried the frightening system yet, then?'

" 'Hadn't any need,' I replied, putting the certificate of her burial in his hand, and he jumped as if he had been stung by an adder, and turned pale; but he soon recovered, and smiled complaisantly as he said—

"Ah! well, I see you have been diligent; but I should have liked to have seen her, to have asked her about a missing deed, but no matter."

" 'Now, about the two hundred pounds,' said I.

"'Why,' said he, 'I think one will do when you come to consider what you have received, and the short space of time and all: you have had a year's board in advance.'

"'I know I had; but because I have done more than you expected, and in a shorter time, instead of giving me more, you have the conscience to offer me less.'

"'No, no, not the—the—what did you call it?—we'll have nothing said about that—but here is a hundred pounds, and you are well paid.'

"'Well,' said I, taking the money, 'I must have £500 at any rate, and unless you give it me, I will tell other parties where a certain deed is to be found.'

"'What deed?'

"'The one you were alluding to. Give me £400 more, and you shall have the deed.'

"After much conversation and trouble he gave it to me, and I gave him the deed, with which he was well pleased, but looked hard at the money, and seemed to grieve at it very much.

"Since that time I have heard that he was challenged by his sister's lover, and they went out to fight a duel, and he fell—and died. The lover went to the continent, where he has since lived."

"Ah," said Sweeney Todd, "you had decidedly the best of this affair: nobody gained anything but you."

"Nobody at all that I know of, save distant relations, and I did very well; but then you know I can't live upon nothing: it costs me something to keep my house and cellar, but I stick to business, and so I shall as long as business sticks to me."

CHAPTER XXVI

IF WE WERE TO SAY THAT COLONEL JEFFERY WAS SATISFIED WITH THE STATE OF affairs as regarded the disappearance of his friend Thornhill, or that he had made up his mind now contentedly to wait until chance, or the mere progress of time, blew something of a more defined nature in his way, we should be doing that gentleman a very great injustice indeed.

On the contrary, he was one of those chivalrous persons who, when they do commence anything, take the most ample means to bring it to a conclusion, and are not satisfied that they have made one great effort, which, having failed, is sufficient to satisfy them.

Far from this, he was a man who, when he commenced any enterprise, looked forward to but one circumstance that could possibly end it, and that was its full and complete accomplishment in every respect; so that in this affair of Mr. Thornhill, he certainly did not intend by any means to abandon it.

But he was not precipitate. His habits of military discipline, and the long life he had led in camps, where anything in the shape of hurry and confusion is much reprobated, made him pause before he decided upon any particular course of action; and this pause was not one contingent upon a belief, or even a surmise, in the danger of the course that suggested itself, for such a consideration had no effect whatever upon him; and if some other mode had suddenly suggested itself, which, while it placed his life in the most imminent peril, would have seemed more likely to accomplish his object, it would have been at once most gladly welcomed.

And now, therefore, he set about thinking deeply over what could possibly be done in a matter that as yet appeared to be involved in the most profound of possible mysteries.

That the barber's boy, who had been addressed by him, and by his friend, the captain, knew something of an extraordinary character, which fear prevented him from disclosing, he had no doubt, and, as the colonel remarked,—

"If fear keeps that lad silent upon the subject, fear may make him speak; and I do not see why we should not endeavour to make ourselves a match for Sweeney Todd in such a matter."

"What do you propose, then?" said the captain.

"I should say that the best plan would be, to watch the barber's shop, and take possession of the boy, as we may find an opportunity of so doing."

"Carry him off!"

"Yes, certainly; and as in all likelihood his fear of the barber is but a visionary affair; after all, it can really, when we have him to ourselves, be dispelled; and then when he finds that we can and will protect him, we shall hear all he has to say."

After some further conversation, the plan was resolved upon; and the captain and the colonel, after making a careful *reconnaissance*, as they called it, of Fleet-street, found that by taking up a station at the window of a tavern, which was very nearly opposite to the barber's shop, they should be able to take such effectual notice of whoever went in and came out, that they would be sure to see the boy sometime during the course of the day.

This plan of operations would no doubt have been greatly successful, and Tobias would have fallen into their hands, had he not, alas! for him, poor fellow, already been treated by Sweeney Todd, as we have described, by being incarcerated in that fearful mad-house on Peckham Rye, which was kept by so unscrupulous a personage as Fogg.

And we cannot but consider that it was most unfortunate, for the happiness of all those persons in whose fate we take so deep an interest, and in whom we hope, as regards the reader, we have likewise awakened a feeling of great sympathy—if Tobias had not been so infatuated as to make the search he did of the barber's house, but had waited even for twenty-four hours before doing so, in that case, not only would he have escaped the dreadful doom which awaited him, but Johanna Oakley would have been saved from much danger, which afterwards befell her.

But we must not anticipate; and the fearful adventures which it was her doom to pass through, before she met with the reward of her great virtue, and her noble perseverance will speak for themselves, trumpet-tongued indeed.

It was at a very early hour in the morning that the two friends took up their station at the public house so nearly opposite to Sweeney Todd's, in Fleet-street; and then, having made an arrangement with the landlord of the house, that they were to have undisturbed possession of the room for as long as they liked, they both sat at the window, and kept an eye upon Todd's house.

It was during the period of time there spent, that Colonel Jeffery first made the captain acquainted with the fact of his great affection for Johanna, and that, in her he thought he had at last fixed his wandering fancy, and found, really, the only being with whom he thought he could, in this world, taste the sweets of domestic life, and know no regret.

"She is all," he said, "in beauty that the warmest imagination can possibly picture, and along with these personal charms, which certainly are most peerless, I have seen enough of her to feel convinced that she has a mind of the purest order that ever belonged to any human being in the world."

"With such sentiments and feelings towards her, the wonder would be," said the captain, "if you did not love her, as you now avow you do."

"I could not be insensible to her attractions. But, understand me, my dear friend, I do not on account of my own suddenly-conceived partiality for this young and beautiful creature, intend to commit the injustice of not trying might and main, and with heart and hand, to discover, if she supposes it be true, that Thornhill and Mark Ingestrie be one and the same person; and when I tell you that I love her with a depth and a sincerity of affection that makes her happiness of greater importance to me than my own—you know, I think, enough of me to feel convinced that I am speaking only what I really feel."

"I can," said the captain; "and I do give you credit for the greatest possible amount of sincerity, and I feel sufficiently interested myself in the future fate of this fair young creature to wish that she may be convinced her lover is no more, and may so much better herself as I am quite certain she would, by becoming your wife; for all we can hear of this Ingestrie seems to prove that he is not the most stable-minded of individuals the world ever produced, and perhaps not exactly the sort of man to make such a girl as Johanna Oakley happy; however, of course she may think to the contrary, and he may in all sincerity think likewise."

"I thank you for the kind feeling towards me, my friend, which has dictated that speech, but—"

"Hush!" said the captain, suddenly, "hush! look at the barber!"

"The barber? Sweeney Todd?"

"Yes, yes, there he is; do you not see him? There he is, and he looks as if he had come off a long journey. What can he have been about, I wonder? He is draggled in mud."

Yes, there was Sweeney Todd, opening his shop from the outside with a key that, after a vast amount of fumbling, he took from his pocket; and, as the captain said, he did indeed look as if he had come off a long journey, for he was draggled with mud, and his appearance altogether was such as to convince anyone that he must have fallen during the early part of the morning upon London and its suburbs.

And this was just the fact, for after staying with the mad-house keeper in the hope that the bad weather which had set in would be alleviated, he had been compelled to give up all chance of such a thing, and as no conveyance of any description was to be had, he enjoyed the pleasure, if it could be called such, of walking home up to his knees in the mud of that dirty neighbourhood.

It was, however, some satisfaction to him to feel that he had got rid of Tobias, who, from what he had done as regarded the examination of the house, had become extremely troublesome indeed, and perhaps the most serious enemy that Sweeney Todd had ever had.

"Ha!" he said, as he came within sight of his shop in Fleet-street,—"ha! Master Tobias is safe enough; he will give me no more trouble, that is quite clear. What a wonderfully convenient thing it is to have such a friend as Fogg, who for a consideration will do so much towards ridding one of an uncomfortable encumbrance. It is possible enough that that boy might have compassed my destruction. I wish I dared, with the means I now have from the string of pearls, joined to my other resources, to leave the business, and so not be obliged to run the risk and have the trouble of another boy."

Yes, Sweeney Todd would have been glad now to shut up his shop in Fleet-street at once and for ever, but he dreaded that when John Mundel found that his customer did not come back to him to redeem the pearls, that he, John Mundel, would proceed to sell them, and that then their beauty, and their great worth would excite much attention, and someone might come forward who knew much more about their early history than he did.

"I must keep quiet," he thought, "I must keep quiet; for although I think I was pretty well disguised, and it is not at all likely that anyone—no, not even the acute John Mundel himself—would recognise in Sweeney Todd, the poor barber of Fleet-street, the nobleman who came from the Queen to borrow £8,000 upon a string of pearls, yet there is a remote possibility of danger, and should there be a disturbance about the precious stones, it is better that I should remain in obscurity until that disturbance is completely over."

This was no doubt admirable policy on the part of Todd, who, although he found himself a rich man, had not, as many people do when they make that most gratifying and interesting discovery, forgotten all the prudence and tact that had made him one of that most envied class of personages.

He was some few minutes before he could get the key to turn in the lock of his street-door, but at length he effected that object and disappeared from before the eyes of the colonel and his friend into his own house, and the door was instantly again closed upon him.

"Well," said Colonel Jeffery, "what do you think of that?"

"I don't know what to think, further than that your friend Todd has been out of town, as the state of his boots abundantly testifies."

"They do indeed; and he has the appearance of having been a considerable distance, for the mud that is upon his boots is not London mud."

"Certainly not; it is of quite a different character altogether. But see, he is coming out again."

Sweeney Todd strode out of his house, bare-headed now, and proceeded to take down the shutters of his shop, which, there being but three, he accomplished in a few seconds of time, and walked in again with them in his hand, along with the iron bar which had secured them, and which he had released from the inside.

This was all the ceremony that took place at the opening of Sweeney Todd's shop, and the only surprise our friends, who were at the public house window, had upon the subject was, that having a boy, he, Todd, should condescend to make himself so useful as to open his own shop. And nothing could be seen of the lad, although the hour, surely, for his attendance must have arrived; and Todd, equally surely, was not the sort of man to be so indulgent to a boy, whom he employed to make himself generally useful, as to allow him to come when all the dirty work of the early morning was over.

But yet such to all appearances would seem to be the case, for presently Todd appeared with a broom in his hand, sweeping out his shop with a rapidity and a vengeance which seemed to say, that he did not perform that operation with the very best grace in the world.

"Where can the boy be!" said the captain. "Do you know, little reason as I may really appear to have for such a supposition, I cannot help in my own mind connecting Todd's having been out of town, somehow, with the fact of that boy's non-appearance this morning."

"Indeed! the coincidence is curious, for such was my own thought likewise upon the occasion, and the more I think of it the more I feel convinced that such must be the case, and that our watch will be a fruitless one completely. Is it likely—for possible enough it is—that the villain has found out that we have been asking questions of the boy, and has thought proper to take his life?"

"Do not let us go too far," said the captain, "in mere conjecture; recollect that as yet, let us suspect what we may, we know nothing, and that the mere fact of our not being able to trace Thornhill beyond the shop of this man will not be sufficient to found an accusation upon."

"I know all that, and I feel how very cautious we must be; and yet to my mind the whole of the circumstances have been day by day assuming a most hideous air of probability, and I look upon Todd as a murderer already."

"Shall we continue our watch?"

"I scarcely see its utility. Perchance we may see some proceedings which may interest us; but I have a powerful impression that we certainly shall not see the boy we want. But, at all events, the barber, you perceive, has a customer already."

As they looked across the way, they saw a well-dressed-looking man, who, from a certain air and manner which he had, could be detected not to be a Londoner. He had rather resembled some substantial yeoman, who had come to town to pay or receive money, and, as he came near to Sweeney Todd's shop, he might have been observed to stroke his chin, as if debating in his mind the necessity or otherwise of a shave.

The debate, if it were taking place in his mind, ended by the ayes having it, for he walked into Todd's shop, being most unquestionably the first customer which he had had that morning.

Situated as the colonel and his friend were, they could not see into Todd's shop, even if the door had been opened, but they saw that after the customer had been in for a few moments, it was closed, so that, had they been close to it, all the interior of the shaving establishment would have been concealed.

They felt no great degree of interest in this man, who was a commonplace personage enough, who had entered Sweeney Todd's shop; but when an unreasonable time had elapsed, and he did not come out, they did begin to feel a little uneasy. And when another man went in and was only about five minutes before he emerged shaved, and yet the first man did not come, they knew not what to make of it, and looked at each other for some moments in silence. At length the colonel spoke—saying,—

"My friend, have we waited here for nothing now? What can have become of that man whom we saw go into the barber's shop; but who, I suppose we feel ourselves to be in a condition to takes our oaths never came out?"

"I could take my oath; and what conclusion can we come to?"

"None, but that he has met his death there; and that, let his fate be what it may, is the same which poor Thornhill has suffered. I can endure this no longer. Do you stay here, and let me go alone."

"Not for worlds—you would rush into an unknown danger: you cannot know what may be the powers of mischief that man possesses. You shall not go alone, colonel, you shall not indeed; but something must be done."

"Agreed; and yet that something surely need not be of the desperate character you meditate."

"Desperate emergencies require desperate remedies."

"Yes, as a general principle I will agree with you there, too, colonel; and yet I think that in this case everything is to be lost by precipitation, and nothing is to be gained. We have to do with one who to all appearance is keen and subtle, and if anything is to be accomplished contrary to his wishes, it is not to be done by that open career which for its own sake, under ordinary circumstances, both you and I would gladly embrace."

"Well, well," said the colonel, "I do not and will not say but what you are right."

"I know I am—I am certain I am; and now hear me: I think we have gone quite far enough unaided in this transaction, and that it is time we drew some others into the plot."

"I do not understand what you mean."

"I will soon explain. I mean, that if in the pursuit of this enterprise, which grows each moment to my mind more serious, anything should happen to you and me, it is absolutely frightful to think that there would then be an end of it."

"True, true; and as for poor Johanna and her friend Arabella, what could they do?"

"Nothing, but expose themselves to great danger. Come, come now, colonel, I am glad to see that we understand each other better about this business; you have heard, of course, of Sir Richard Blunt?"

"Sir Richard Blunt—Blunt—oh, you mean the magistrate?"

"I do; and what I propose is, that we have a private and confidential interview with him about the matter—that we make him possessed of all the circumstances, and take his advice what to do. The result of placing the affair in such hands will at all events be, that, if, in anything we may attempt, we may be by force or fraud overpowered, we shall not fall wholly unavenged."

"Reason backs your proposition."

"I knew it would, when you came to reflect. Oh, Colonel Jeffery, you are too much a creature of impulse."

"Well," said the colonel, half jestingly, "I must say that I do not think the accusation comes well from you, for I have certainly seen you do some rather impulsive things, I think."

"We won't dispute about that; but since you think with me upon the matter, you will have no objection to accompany me at once to Sir Richard Blunt's?"

"None in the least; on the contrary, if anything is to be done at all, for Heaven's sake let it be done quickly. I am quite convinced that some fearful tragedy is in progress, and that, if we are not most prompt in our measures, we shall be too late to counteract its dire influence upon the fortunes of those in whom we have become deeply interested."

"Agreed, agreed! Come this way, and let us now for a brief space, at all events, leave Mr. Todd and his shop to take care of each other, while we take an effectual means of circumventing him. Why do you linger?"

"I do linger. Some mysterious influence seems to chain me to the spot."

"Some mysterious fiddlestick! Why, you are getting superstitious, colonel."

"No, no! Well, I suppose I must come along with you. Lead the way, lead the way; and believe me that it requires all my reason to induce me to give up a hope of making some important discovery by going to Sweeney Todd's shop."

"Yes, you might make an important discovery, and only suppose that the discovery you did make was that he murdered some of his customers. If he does so, you may depend that such a man takes good care to do the deed effectually, and you might make the discovery just a little too late. You understand that?"

"I do, I do. Come along, for I positively declare that if we see anybody else going into the barber's, I shall not be able to resist rushing forward at once, and giving an alarm."

It was certainly a good thing that the colonel's friend was not quite as enthusiastic as he was, or from what we happen actually to know of Sweeney Todd, and from what we suspect, the greatest amount of danger might have befallen Jeffery, and instead of being in a position to help others in unravelling the mysteries connected with Sweeney Todd's establishment, he might be himself past all help, and most absolutely one of the mysteries.

But such was not to be.

CHAPTER XXVII

We cannot find it in our hearts to force upon the mind of the reader the terrible condition of poor Tobias.

No one, certainly, of all the *dramatis personae* of our tale, is suffering so much as he; and, consequently, we feel it to be a sort of duty to come to a consideration of his thoughts and feelings as he lay in that dismal cell, in the mad-house at Peckham Rye.

Certainly Tobias Ragg was as sane as any ordinary Christian need wish to be, when the scoundrel, Sweeney Todd, put him in the coach, to take him to Mr. Fogg's establishment; but if by any ingenious process the human intellect can be toppled from its throne, certainly that process must consist in putting a sane person into a lunatic asylum.

To the imagination of a boy, too, and that boy one of vivid imagination, as was poor Tobias, a mad-house must be invested with a world of terrors. That enlarged experience which enables persons of more advanced age to shake off much of the unreal, which seemed so strangely to take up its abode in the mind of the young Tobias, had not reached him; and no wonder, therefore, that to him his present situation was one of acute and horrible misery and suffering.

He lay for a long time in the gloomy dungeon-like cell, into which he had been thrust, in a kind of stupor, which might or might not be the actual precursor of insanity, although, certainly, the chances were all in favour of its being so. For many hours he moved neither hand nor foot, and as it was a part of the policy of Mr. Fogg to leave well alone, as he said, he never interfered, by any intrusive offers of refreshment, with the quiet or the repose of his patients.

Tobias, therefore, if he had chosen to remain as still as an Indian fakir, might have died in one position, without any remonstrances from anyone.

It would be quite a matter of impossibility to describe the strange visionary thoughts and scenes that passed through the mind of Tobias during this period. It seemed as if his intellect was engulphed in the charmed waters of some whirlpool, and that all the different scenes and actions which, under ordinary circumstances, would have been clear and distinct, were mingled together in inextricable confusion.

In the midst of all this, at length he began to be conscious of one particular impression or feeling, and that was, that someone was singing in a low, soft voice, very near to him.

This feeling, strange as it was in such a place, momentarily increased in volume, until at length it began, in its intensity, to absorb almost every other; and he gradually awakened from the sort of stupor that had come over him. Yes, someone was singing. It was a female voice, he was sure of that; and as his mind became more occupied with that one subject of thought, and his perceptive faculties became properly exercised, his intellect altogether assumed a healthier tone.

He could not distinguish the words that were sung, but the voice itself was very sweet and musical; as Tobias listened, he felt as if the fever of his blood was abating, and that healthier thoughts were taking the place of those disordered fancies that had held sway within the chambers of his brain.

"What sweet sounds!" he said. "Oh, I do hope that singing will go on. I feel happier to hear it; I do so hope it will continue. What sweet music! Oh, mother, mother, if you could but see me now!"

He pressed his hands over his eyes, but he could not stop the gush of tears that came from them, and which would trickle through his fingers. Tobias did not wish to weep, but those tears, after all the horrors of the night, did him a world of good, and he felt wonderfully better after they had been shed. Moreover, the voice continued singing without intermission.

"Who can it be," thought Tobias, "that don't tire with so much of it?"

Still the singer continued; but now and then Tobias felt certain that a very wild note or two was mingled with the ordinary melody; and that bred a suspicion in his mind, which gave him a shudder to think of, namely, that the singer was mad.

"It must be so," said he. "No one in their senses could or would continue to sing for so long a period of time such strange snatches of song. Alas! alas, it is someone who is really mad, and confined for life in this dreadful place; for life do I say, and am I not too confined for life here? Oh! help, help, help!"

Tobias called out in so loud a tone, that the singer of the sweet strains that had for a time lulled him to composure, heard him, and the strains which had before been redolent of the softest and sweetest melody, suddenly changed to the most terrific shrieks that can be imagined.

In vain did Tobias place his hands over his ears to shut out the horrible sounds. They would not be shut out, but ran, as it were, into every crevice of his brain, nearly driving him distracted by their vehemence.

But hoarser tones came upon his ears, and he heard the loud, rough voice of a man say,—

"What, do you want the whip so early this morning? The whip, do you understand that?"

These words were followed by the lashing of what must have been a heavy carter's whip, and then the shrieks died away in deep groans, every one of which went to the heart of poor Tobias.

"I can never live amid all these horrors," he said. "Oh, why don't they kill me at once? It would be much better, and much more merciful. I can never live long here. Help, help, help!"

When he shouted this word "help," it was certainly not with the most distant idea of getting any help, but it was a word that came at once uppermost to his tongue; and so he called it out with all his might, that he should attract the attention of someone, for the solitude, and the almost total darkness of the place he was in, were beginning to fill him with new dismay.

There was a faint light in the cell, which made him know the difference between day and night; but where that faint light came from, he could not tell, for he could see no grating or opening whatever; but yet that was in consequence of his eyes not being fully accustomed to the obscurity of the place; otherwise he would have seen that close up to the roof there was a narrow aperture, certainly not larger than anyone could have passed a hand through, although of some four or five feet in length; and from a passage beyond that, there came the dim borrowed light, which made darkness visible in Tobias's cell.

With a kind of desperation, heedless of what might be the result, Tobias continued to call aloud for help, and after about a quarter of an hour, he heard the sound of a heavy footstep.

Someone was coming; yes, surely someone was coming, and he was not to be left to starve to death. Oh, how intently he now listened to every sound, indicative of the nearer approach of whoever it was who was coming to his prison-house.

Now he heard the lock move, and a heavy bar of iron was let down with a clanging sound.

"Help, help!" he cried again, "help, help!" for he feared that whoever it was might even yet go away again, after making so much progress to get at him.

The cell door was flung open, and the first intimation that poor Tobias got of the fact of his cries having been heard, consisted in a lash with a whip which, if it had struck him as fully as it was intended to do, would have done him serious injury.

"So, do you want it already?" said the same voice he had before heard.

"Oh, no, mercy, mercy," said Tobias.

"Oh, that's it now, is it? I tell you what it is, if we have any more disturbance here, this is the persuader to silence that we always use: what do you think of that as an argument, eh?"

As he spoke, the man gave the whip a loud smack in the air, and confirmed the truth of the argument by reducing poor Tobias to absolute silence; indeed the boy trembled so that he could not speak.

"Well, now, my man," added the fellow, "I think we understand each other. What do you want?"

"Oh, let me go," said Tobias, "let me go. I will tell nothing. Say to Mr. Todd that I will do what he pleases, and tell nothing, only let me go out of this dreadful place. Have mercy upon me—I'm not at all mad—indeed I am not."

The man closed the door, as he whistled a lively tune.

CHAPTER XXVIII

THIS SUDDEN RETREAT OF THE MAN WAS UNEXPECTED BY TOBIAS, WHO AT LEAST thought it was the practice to feed people, even if they were confined to such a place; but the unceremonious departure of the keeper, without so much as mentioning

anything about breakfast, began to make Tobias think that the plan by which he was
to be got rid of was starvation; and yet that was impossible, for how easy it was to kill
him if they felt so disposed! 'Oh, no, no," he repeated to himself, "surely they will not
starve me to death."

As he uttered these words, he heard the plaintive singing commence again; and he
could not help thinking that it sounded like some requiem for the dead, and that it was
a sort of signal that his hours were numbered.

Despair again began to take possession of him, and despite the savage threats of
the keeper, he would again have called loudly for help, had he not become conscious
that there were footsteps close at hand.

By dint of listening most intently he heard a number of doors opened and shut,
and sometimes when one was opened, there was a shriek, and the lashing of the whips,
which very soon succeeded in drowning all other noises. It occurred to Tobias, and
correctly too, for such was the fact, that the inmates of that most horrible abode were
living like so many wild beasts, in cages fed. Then he thought how strange it was that
even for any amount of money human beings could be got to do the work of such an
establishment. And by the time Tobias had made this reflection to himself, his own
door was once more opened upon its rusty hinges.

There was the flash of a light, and then a man came in with a water-can in his
hand, to which there was a long spout, and this he placed to the mouth of Tobias,
who fearing that if he did not drink then he might be a long time without, swallowed
some not over-savoury ditch-water, as it seemed to him, which was thus brought
to him.

A coarse, brown-looking hard loaf was then thrown at his feet, and the party was
about to leave his cell, but he could not forbear speaking, and, in a voice of the most
supplicating earnestness, he said,—

"Oh, do not keep me here. Let me go, and I will say nothing of Todd. I will go to sea
at once if you will let me out of this place, indeed I will, but I shall go really mad here."

"Good, that, Watson, ain't it?" said Mr. Fogg, who was of the party.

"Very good, sir. Lord bless you, the cunning of 'em is beyond anything in the
world, sir; you'd be surprised at what they say to me sometimes."

"But I am not mad, indeed I am not mad," cried Tobias.

"Oh," said Fogg, "it's a bad case, I'm afraid; the strongest proof of insanity, in my
opinion, Watson, is the constant reiteration of the statement that he is not mad on the
part of a lunatic. Don't you think it is so, Watson?"

"Of course, sir, of course."

"Ah! I thought you would be of that opinion; but I suppose as this is a mere lad we may do without chaining him up; besides, you know that to-day is inspection-day, when we get an old fool of a superannuated physician to make us a visit."

"Yes, sir," said Watson, with a grin, "and a report that all is well conducted."

"Exactly. Who shall we have this time, do you think? I always give a ten guinea fee."

"Why, sir, there's old Dr. Popplejoy, he's 84 years old, they say, and sand-blind; he'll take it as a great compliment, he will, and no doubt we can humbug him easily."

"I dare say we may! I'll see to it; and we will have him at twelve o'clock, Watson. You will take care to have everything ready, of course, you know; make all the usual preparations."

Tobias was astonished that before him they chose thus to speak so freely, but despairing as he was, he little knew how completely he was in the power of Mr. Fogg, and how utterly he was shut out from all human sympathy.

Tobias said nothing; but he could not help thinking that however old and stupid the physician whom they mentioned might be, surely there was a hope that he would be able to discover Tobias's perfect sanity.

But the wily Mr. Fogg knew perfectly well what he was about, and when he retired to his own room, he wrote the following note to Dr. Popplejoy, who was a retired physician, who had purchased a country house in the neighbourhood. The note will speak for itself, being as fine a specimen of hypocrisy as we can ever expect to lay before our readers:

The Asylum, Peckham

SIR—Probably you may recognise my name as that of the keeper of a lunatic asylum in this neighbourhood. Consistent with a due regard for the safety of that most unhappy class of the community submitted to my care, I am most anxious, with the blessing of Divine Providence, to ameliorate as far as possible, by kindness, that most shocking of all calamities—insanity. Once a year it is my custom to call in some experienced, able, and enlightened physician to see my patients (I enclose a fee)—a physician who has nothing to do with the establishment, and therefore cannot be biased.

If you, sir, would do me the favour, at about twelve o'clock to-day, to make a short visit of inspection, I shall esteem it a great honour, as well as a great favour.

Believe me to be, sir, with the most profound respect, your most obedi-
ent and humble servant,

To Dr. Popplejoy, &c.   O.D. FOGG

This note, as might be expected, brought old, purblind, superannuated Dr.
Popplejoy to the asylum, and Mr. Fogg received him in due form, and with great
gravity, saying, almost with tears in his eyes,—

"My dear sir, the whole aim of my existence now is to endeavour to soften the
rigours of the necessary confinement of the insane, and I wish this inspection of my
establishment to be made by you in order that I may thus for a time stand clear with
the world—with my own conscience I am of course always clear; and if your report
be satisfactory about the treatment of the unhappy persons I have here, not the slightest breath of slander can touch me."

"Oh, yes, yes," said the garrulous old physician; "I—I—very good—oh yes—
eugh, eugh—I have a slight cough."

"A very slight one, sir. Will you, first of all, take a look at one of the sleeping
chambers of the insane?"

The doctor agreed, and Mr. Fogg led him into a very comfortable sleeping-
room, which the old gentleman declared was very satisfactory indeed, and when they
returned to the apartment in which they had already been, Mr. Fogg said,—

"Well, then, sir, all we have to do is bring in the patients, one by one, to you as
fast as we can, so as not to occupy more of your valuable time than necessary; and any
questions you may ask will, no doubt, be answered and I, being by, can give you the
heads of any case that may excite your especial notice."

"Exactly, exactly. I—I—quite correct. Eugh—Eugh!

The old man was placed in a chair of state, reposing on some very comfortable
cushions; and, take him altogether, he was so pleased with the ten guineas and the flat-
tery of Mr. Fogg, for nobody had given him a fee for the last fifteen years, that he was
quite ready to be the foolish tool of the mad-house keeper in almost any way that he
chose to dictate to him.

We need not pursue the examination of the various unfortunates who were
brought before old Dr. Popplejoy; it will suffice for us if we carry the reader through
the examination of Tobias, who is our principal care, without, at the same time,
detracting from the genial sympathy we must feel for all who, at that time, were subject to the tender mercies of Mr. Fogg.

At about half-past twelve the door of Tobias's cell was opened by Mr. Watson, who, walking in, laid hold of the boy by the collar, and said,—

"Hark you, my lad! you are going before a physician, and the less you say the better. I speak to you for your own sake; you can do yourself no good, but you can do yourself a great deal of harm. You know we keep a cart-whip here. Come along."

Tobias said not a word in answer to this piece of gratuitous advice, but he made up his mind that if the physician was not absolutely deaf, he should hear him.

Before, however, the unhappy boy was taken into the room where old Dr. Popplejoy was waiting, he was washed and brushed down generally, so that he presented a much more respectable appearance than he would have done had he been ushered in in his soiled state, as he was taken from the dirty mad-house cell.

"Surely, surely," thought Tobias, "the extent of cool impudence can go no further than this; but I will speak to the physician, if my life should be sacrificed in so doing. Yes, of that I am determined."

In another minute he was in the room, face to face with Mr. Fogg and Dr. Popplejoy.

"What—what? eugh! eugh!" coughed the old doctor; "a boy, Mr. Fogg, a mere boy. Dear me! I—I—eugh! eugh! eugh! My cough is a little troublesome, I think, today—eugh! eugh!"

"Yes, sir," said Mr. Fogg with a deep sigh, and making a pretence to dash a tear from his eye; "here you have a mere boy. I am always affected when I look upon him, doctor. We were boys ourselves once, you know, and to think that the divine spark of intelligence has gone out in one so young, is enough to make any feeling heart throb with agony. This lad, though, sir, is only a monomaniac. He has a fancy that someone named Sweeney Todd is a murderer, and that he has discovered his bad practices. On all other subjects he is sane enough; but upon that, and upon his presumed freedom from mental derangement, he is furious."

"It is false, sir, it is false!" said Tobias, stepping up. "Oh, sir, if you are not one of the creatures of this horrible place, I beg that you will hear me, and let justice be done."

"Oh, yes—I—I—eugh! Of course—I—eugh!"

"Sir, I am not mad, but I am placed here because I have become dangerous to the safety of criminal persons."

"Oh, indeed! Ah—oh—yes."

"I am a poor lad, sir, but I hate wickedness, and because I found out that Sweeney Todd is a murderer, I am placed here."

"You hear him, sir," said Fogg; "just as I said."

"Oh, yes, yes. Who is Sweeney Todd, Mr. Fogg?"

"Oh, sir, there is no such person in the world."

"Ah, I thought as much—I thought as much—a sad case, a very sad case indeed. Be calm, my little lad, and Mr. Fogg will do all that can be done for you, I'm sure."

"Oh, how can you be as foolish, sir," cried Tobias, "as to be deceived by that man, who is making a mere instrument of you to cover his own villainy? What I say to you is true, and I am not mad!"

"I think, Dr. Popplejoy," said Fogg with a smile, "it would take rather a cleverer fellow than I am to make a fool of you; but you perceive, sir, that in a little while the boy would get quite furious, that he would. Shall I take him away?"

"Yes, yes—poor fellow."

"Hear me—oh, hear me," shrieked Tobias. "Sir, on your deathbed you may repent this day's work—I am not mad—Sweeney Todd is a murderer—he is a barber in Fleet-street—I am not mad!"

"It's melancholy, sir, is it not?" said Fogg, as he again made an effort to wipe away a tear from his eye. "It's very melancholy."

"Oh! very, very."

"Watson, take away poor Tobias Ragg, but take him very gently, and stay with him a little in his nice comfortable room, and try to soothe him; speak to him of his mother, Watson, and get him round if you can. Alas, poor child! my heart quite bleeds to see him. I am not fit exactly for this life, doctor, I ought to be made of sterner stuff, indeed I ought."

"Well," said Mr. Watson, as he saluted poor Tobias with a furious kick outside the door, "what a deal of good you have done!"

The boy's patience was exhausted; he had borne all that he could bear, and this last insult maddened him. He turned with the quickness of thought, and sprang at Mr. Watson's throat.

So sudden was that attack, and so completely unprepared for it was that gentleman, that down he fell in the passage, with such a blow of his head against the stone floor that he was nearly insensible; and before anybody could get to his assistance, Tobias had pummelled and clawed his face, that there was scarcely a feature discernible, and one of his eyes seemed to be in fearful jeopardy.

The noise of this assault soon brought Mr. Fogg to the spot, as well as old Dr. Popplejoy, and the former tore Tobias from his victim, whom he seemed intent upon murdering.

CHAPTER XXIX

THE ADVICE WHICH HIS FRIEND HAD GIVEN TO COLONEL JEFFERY WAS CERTAINLY the very best that could have been tendered to him; and, under the whole of these circumstances, it would have been something little short of absolute folly to have ventured into the shop of Sweeney Todd without previously taking every possible precaution to ensure the safety of so doing.

Sir Richard was within when they reached his house, and, with the acuteness of a man of business, he at once entered into the affair.

As the colonel, who was the spokesman in it, proceeded, it was evident that the magistrate became deeply interested, and when Jeffery concluded by saying,—

"You will thus, at all events, perceive that there is great mystery somewhere," he replied,—

"And guilt, I should say."

"You are of that opinion, Sir Richard?"

"I am, most decidedly."

"Then what would you propose to do? Believe me, I do not ask out of any idle curiosity, but from a firm faith, that what you set about will be accomplished in a satisfactory manner."

"Why, in the first place, I shall certainly go and get shaved at Todd's shop."

"You will venture that?"

"Oh, yes; but do not fancy that I am so headstrong and foolish as to run any unnecessary risks in the matter—I shall do no such thing: you may be assured that I will do all in my power to provide for my own safety; and if I did not think I could do that most effectually, I should not be at all in love with the adventure, but, on the contrary, carefully avoid it to the best of my ability. We have before heard something of Mr. Todd."

"Indeed! and of a criminal character?"

"Yes; a lady once in the street took a fancy to a pair of shoe-buckles in imitation diamonds that Todd had on, when he was going to some city entertainment; she screamed out, and declared that they had belonged to her husband, who had gone out one morning, from his house in Fetter-lane, to get himself shaved. The case came before me, but the buckles were of too common a kind to enable the lady to persevere in her statement; and Todd, who preserved the most imperturbable coolness throughout the affair, was of course discharged."

"But the matter left a suspicion upon your mind?"

"It did, and more than once I have resolved in my own mind what means could be adopted of coming at the truth; other affairs, however, of more immediate urgency, have occupied me, but the circumstances you detail revive all my former feelings upon the subject; and I shall now feel that the matter has come before me in a shape to merit immediate attention."

This was gratifying to Colonel Jeffery, because it not only took a great weight off his shoulders, but it led him to think, from the well-known tact of the magistrate, that something would be accomplished, and that very shortly too, towards unravelling the secret that had as yet only appeared to be more complicated and intricate the more it was enquired into. He made the warmest acknowledgements to the magistrate for the courtesy of his reception, and then took his leave.

As soon as the magistrate was alone, he rang a small hand-bell that was upon the table, and the summons was answered by a man, to whom he said, —

"Is Crotchet here?"

"Yes, your worship."

"Then tell him I want him at once, will you?"

The messenger retired, but he presently returned, bringing with him about as rough a specimen of humanity as the world could have produced. He was tall and stout, and his face looked as if, by repeated injuries, it had been knocked out of all shape, for the features were most strangely jumbled together indeed, and an obliquity of vision, which rendered it always a matter of doubt who and what he was looking at, by no means added to his personal charms.

"Sit down, Crotchet," said the magistrate, "and listen to me without a word of interruption."

If Mr. Crotchet had no other good quality on earth, he still had that of listening most attentively, and he never opened his mouth while the magistrate related to him what had just formed the subject matter of Mr. Jeffery's communication; indeed, Crotchet seemed to be looking out of the window all the while; but then Sir Richard knew the little peculiarities of his visual organs.

When he had concluded his statement, Sir Richard said,—

"Well, Crotchet, what do you think of all that? What does Sweeney Todd do with his customers?"

Mr. Crotchet gave a singular and peculiar kind of grin as he said, still looking apparently out of the window, although his eyes were really fixed upon the magistrate,—

"He *smugs* 'em."

"What?"

"Uses 'em up, your worship; it's as clear to me as mud in a wineglass, that it is. Lor' bless you! I've been thinking he does that 'ere sort of thing a deuce of a while, but I didn't like to interfere too soon, you see."

"What do you advise, Crotchet? I know I can trust to your sagacity in such a case."

"Why, your worship, I'll think it over a bit in the course of the day, and let your worship know what I think . . . It's an awkward job, rather, for a wariety of reasons, but howsomdever, there's always a something to be done, and if we don't do it, I'll be hung if I know who can, that's all!"

"True, true, you are right there, and perhaps, before you see me again, you will walk down Fleet-street, and see if you can make any observations that will be of advantage in the matter. It is an affair which requires great caution indeed."

"Trust me, your worship: I'll do it, and no mistake. Lor' bless you, it's easy for anybody now to go lounging about Fleet-street, without being taken much notice of; for the fact is, the whole place is agog about the horrid smell, as has been for never so long in the old church of St. Dunstan."

"Smell, smell, in St. Dunstan's church! I never heard of that before, Crotchet."

"O Lor' yes, it's enough to pison the devil himself, Sir Richard; and t'other day, when the blessed bishop went to 'firm a lot of people, he as good as told 'em they might all be damned first, afore he 'firm nobody in such a place."

The magistrate was in deep thought for a few minutes, and then he said suddenly,—

"Well, well, Crotchet, you turn the matter over in your mind and see what you can make of it; I will think it over, likewise. Do you hear? mind you are with me at six this evening punctually; I do not intend to let the matter rest, you may depend, but from that moment will give it my greatest attention."

"Wery good, yer worship, wery good indeed. I'll be here, and something seems to strike me uncommon forcible that we shall unearth this very soon, yer worship."

"I sincerely hope so."

Mr. Crotchet took his leave, and when he was alone the magistrate rose and paced his apartment for some time with rapid strides, as if he were much agitated by the reflections that were passing through his mind. At length he flung himself into a chair with something like a groan, as he said,—

"A horrible idea forces itself upon my consideration, most horrible! most horrible! most horrible! Well, well, we shall see, we shall see. It may not be so; and yet what a hideous probability stares me in the face! I will go down at once to St. Dunstan's and see what they are really about. Yes, yes, I shall not get much sleep, I think now, until some of these mysteries are developed. A most horrible idea, truly!"

The magistrate left some directions at home concerning some business calls which he fully expected in the course of the next two hours, and then he put on a plain, sad-coloured cloak and a hat destitute of all ornament, and left his house with a rapid step.

He took the most direct route towards St. Dunstan's church, and finding the door of the sacred edifice yielded to the touch, he at once entered it; but he had not advanced many steps before he was met and accosted by the beadle, who said, in a tone of great dignity and authority,—

"This ain't Sunday, sir; there ain't no service here today."

"I don't suppose there is," replied the magistrate; "but I see you have workmen here. What is it you are about?"

"Well, of all the impudence that ever I came near this is the *worstest*—to ask a beadle what he is about. I beg to say, sir, this here is quite private, and there's the door."

"Yes, I see it, and you may go out at it just as soon as you think proper."

"Oh, *conwulsions*! oh, *conwulsions*! This to a beadle."

"What is all this about?" said a gentlemanly-looking man, stepping forward from a part of the church where several masons were employed in raising some of the huge flag-stones with which it was paved. "What disturbance is this?"

"I believe, Mr. Antrobus, you know me," said the magistrate.

"Oh, Sir Richard, certainly. How do you do?"

"Gracious!" said the beadle, "I've put my blessed foot in it. Lor' bless us, sir, how should I know as you was Sir Richard? I begs as you won't think nothing o' what I said. If I had a knowed you, in course I shouldn't have said it, you may depend, Sir Richard—I humbly begs your pardon."

"It's of no consequence, I ought to have announced myself; and you are perfectly justified in keeping strangers out of the church, my friend."

The magistrate walked up the aisle with Mr. Antrobus, who was one of the churchwardens; and as he did so, he said, in a low, confidential tone of voice,—

"I have heard some strange reports about a terrible stench in the church. What does it mean? I suppose you know all about it, and what it arises from?"

"Indeed I do not. If you have heard that there is a horrible smell in the church after it has been shut up some time, and upon the least change in the weather, from dry to wet, or cold to warm, you know as much as we know upon the subject. It is a most serious nuisance, and, in fact, my presence here today is to try and make some discovery of the cause of the stench; and you see we are going to work our way into some of the old vaults that have not been opened for some time, with a hope of finding out the cause of this disagreeable odour."

"Have you any objection to my being a spectator?"

"None in the least."

"I thank you. Let us now join the workmen, and I can only now tell you that I feel the strongest possible curiosity to ascertain what can be the meaning of all this, and shall watch the proceedings with the greatest amount of interest."

"Come along, then; I can only say, for my part, that, as an individual, I am glad you are here, and as a magistrate, likewise, it gives me great satisfaction to have you."

CHAPTER XXX

THE RAGE INTO WHICH MR. FOGG WAS THROWN BY THE ATTACK WHICH THE DESPERATE Tobias had made upon his representative Mr. Watson, was so great that, had it not been for the presence of stupid old Dr. Popplejoy in the house, no doubt he would have taken some most exemplary revenge upon him. As it was, however, Tobias was thrown into his cell with a promise of vengeance as soon as the coast was clear.

These were the kind of promises which Mr. Fogg was pretty sure to keep, and when the first impulse of his passion had passed away, poor Tobias, as well indeed he might, gave himself up to despair.

"Now all is over," he said; "I shall be half murdered! Oh, why do they not kill me at once? There would be some mercy in that. Come and murder me at once, you wretches! You villains, murder me at once!"

In his new excitement, he rushed to the door of the cell, and banged it with his fists, when to his surprise it opened, and he found himself nearly falling into the stone corridor from which the various cell doors opened. It was evident that Mr. Watson thought he had locked him in, for the bolt of the lock was shot back but had missed its hold—a circumstance probably arising from the state of rage and confusion Mr. Watson was in, as a consequence of Tobias's daring attack upon him.

It almost seemed to the boy as if he had already made some advance towards his freedom, when he found himself in the narrow passage beyond his cell-door, but his heart for some minutes beat so tumultuously with the throng of blissful associations connected with freedom that it was quite impossible for him to proceed.

A slight noise, however, in another part of the building roused him again, and he felt that it was only now by great coolness and self-possession, as well as great courage, that he could at all hope to turn to account the fortunate incident which had enabled him, at all events, to make that first step towards liberty.

"Oh, if I could but get out of this dreadful place," he thought; "if I could but once again breathe the pure fresh air of heaven, and see the deep blue sky, I think I should ask for no other blessings."

Never do the charms of nature present themselves to the imagination in more lovely guise than when someone with an imagination full of such beauties and a mind to appreciate the glories of the world is shut up from real, actual contemplation. To Tobias now the thought of green fields, sunshine and flowers, was at once rapture and agony.

"I must," he said, "I must—I will be free."

A thorough determination to do anything, we are well convinced, always goes a long way towards its accomplishment; and certainly Tobias now would cheerfully have faced death in any shape, rather than he would again have been condemned to the solitary horrors of the cell, from which he had by such a chance got free.

He conjectured the stupid old Dr. Popplejoy had not left the house by the unusual quiet that reigned in it, and he began to wonder if, while that quiet subsisted, there was the remotest chance of his getting into the garden, and then scaling the wall, and so reaching the open common.

While this thought was establishing itself in his mind, and he was thinking that he would pursue the passage in which he was until he saw where it led to, he heard the sound of footsteps, and he shrank back.

For a few seconds they appeared as if they were approaching where he was; and he began to dread that the cell would be searched, and his absence discovered, in which there would be no chance for him but death. Suddenly, however, the approaching foot-steps paused, and then he heard a door banged shut.

It was still, even now, some minutes before Tobias could bring himself to traverse the passage again, and when he did, it was with a slow and stealthy step.

He had not, however, gone above thirty paces, when he heard the indistinct murmur of voices, and being guided by the sound, he paused at a door on his right hand, which he thought must be the one he had heard closed but a few minutes previously.

It was from the interior of the room which that was the door of, that the sound of voices came, and as it was a matter of the very first importance to Tobias to ascertain in what part of the house his enemies were, he placed his ear against the panel, and listened attentively.

He recognised both the voices: they were those of Watson and Fogg.

It was a very doubtful and ticklish situation that poor Tobias was now in, but it was wonderful how, by dint of strong resolution, he had stilled the beating of his heart, and the general nervousness of his disposition. There was but a frail door between him and his enemies, and yet he stood profoundly still and listened.

Mr. Fogg was speaking.

"You quite understand me, Watson: I think," he said, "as concerns that little viper Tobias Ragg, he is too cunning, and much too dangerous, to live long. He almost staggered old superannuated Popplejoy."

"Oh, confound him!" replied Watson, "and he quite staggered me."

"Why, certainly your face is rather scratched."

"Yes, the little devil! but it's all in the way of business that, Mr. Fogg, and you never heard me grumble at such little matters yet; and I'll be bound never will, that's more."

"I give you credit for that, Watson; but between you and I, I think the disease of that boy is of a nature that will carry him off very suddenly."

"I think so too," said Watson, with a chuckle.

"It strikes me forcibly that he will be found dead in his bed some morning, and I should not in the least wonder if that was tomorrow morning: what's your opinion, Watson?"

"Oh, damn it, what's the use of all this round-about nonsense between us? the boy is to die, and there's an end of it, and die he shall, during the night—I owe him a personal grudge of course now."

"Of course you do—he has disfigured you."

"Has he? Well, I can return the compliment, and I say, Mr. Fogg, my opinion is, that it's very dangerous having these medical inspections you have such a fancy for."

"My dear fellow, it is dangerous, that I know as well as you can tell me, but it is from that danger we gather safety. If anything in the shape of a disturbance should arise about any patient, you don't know of what vast importance a report from such a man as old Dr. Popplejoy might be."

"Well, well, have it your own way. I shall not go near Master Tobias for the whole day, and shall see what starvation and solitude does towards taming him down a bit."

"As you please; but it is time you went your regular rounds."

"Yes, of course."

Tobias heard Watson rise. The crisis was a serious one. His eye fell upon a bolt that was outside the door, and, with the quickness of thought, he shot it into its socket, and then made his way down the passage towards his cell, the door of which he shut close.

His next movement was to run to the end of the passage and descend some stairs. A door opposed him, but a push opened it, and he found himself in a small, dimly-lighted room, in one corner of which, upon a heap of straw, lay a woman, apparently sleeping.

The noise which Tobias made in entering the cell, for such it was, roused her up, and she said,—

"Oh! no, no, not the lash! not the lash! I am quiet. God, how quiet I am, although the heart within is breaking. Have mercy upon me!"

"Have mercy upon me," said Tobias, "and hide me if you can."

"Hide you! hide you! God of Heavens, who are you?"

"A poor victim, who has escaped from one of the cells, and I—"

"Hush!" said the woman; and she made Tobias shrink down in the corner of the cell, cleverly covering him up with the straw, and then lying down herself in such a position that he was completely screened. The precaution was not taken a moment too soon, for by the time it was completed, Watson had burst open the door of the room which Tobias had bolted, and stood in the narrow passage.

"How the devil," he said, "came that door shut, I wonder?"

"Oh! save me," whispered Tobias.

"Hush! hush! He will only look in," was the answer. "You are safe. I have been only waiting for someone who could assist me, in order to attempt an escape. You must remain here until night, and then I will show you how it may be done. Hush!—he comes." Watson did come, and looked into the cell, muttering an oath, as he said,—

"Oh, you have enough bread and water till tomorrow morning, I should say; so you need not expect to see me again till then."

"Oh! we are saved! we shall escape," said the poor creature, after Watson had been gone some minutes.

"Do you think so?"

"Yes, yes! Oh, boy, I do not know what brought you here, but if you have suffered one-tenth part of the cruelty and oppression I have suffered, you are indeed to be pitied."

"If we are to stay here," said Tobias, "till night, before making any attempt to escape, it will, perhaps, ease your mind, and beguile the time, if you were to tell me how you came here."

"God knows! it might—it might!"

Tobias was very urgent upon the poor creature to tell her story, to beguile the tedium of the time of waiting, and after some amount of persuasion she consented to do so.

The Mad Woman's Tale

You shall now hear (she said to Tobias), if you will listen, such a catalogue of wrongs, unredressed and still enduring, that would indeed drive any human being mad; but I have been able to preserve so much of my mental faculties as will enable me to recollect and understand the many acts of cruelty and injustice I have endured here for many a long and weary day.

My persecutions began when I was very young—so young that I could not comprehend their cause, and used to wonder why I should be treated with greater rigour or with greater cruelty than people used to treat those who were really disobedient and wayward children.

I was scarcely seven years old when a maiden aunt died; she was the only person whom I remember as being uniformly kind to me, though I can only remember her indistinctly, yet I know she was kind to me. I know also I used to visit her, and she used to look upon me as her favourite, for I used to sit at her feet upon a stool, watching her as she sat amusing herself by embroidering, silent and motionless sometimes, and then I asked her some questions which she answered.

This is the chief feature of my recollection of my aunt: she soon after died, but while she lived, I had no unkindness from anybody; it was only after that that I felt the cruelty and coldness of my family.

It appeared that I was a favourite with my aunt above all others whether in our family or any other; she loved me, and promised that, when she died, she would leave me provided for, and that I should not be dependent upon any one.

Well, I was, from the day after the funeral, an altered being. I was neglected, and no one paid any attention to me whatsoever; I was thrust about, and nobody appeared to care even if I had the necessaries of life.

Such a change I could not understand. I could not believe the evidence of my own senses; I thought it must be something that I did not understand; perhaps my poor aunt's death had caused this distress and alteration in people's demeanour to me.

However, I was a child, and though I was quick enough at noting all this, yet I was too young to feel acutely the conduct of my friends.

My father and mother were careless of me, and let me run where I would; they cared not when I was hurt, they cared not when I was in danger. Come what would, I was left to take my chance.

I recollect one day when I had fallen from the top to the bottom of some stairs and hurt myself very much; but no one comforted me; I was thrust out of the drawing-room, because I cried. I then went to the top of the stairs, where I sat weeping bitterly for some time.

At length, an old servant came out of one of the attics, and said, "Oh! Miss Mary, what has happened to you, that you sit crying so bitterly on the stair-head? Come in here!"

I arose and went into the attic with her, when she set me on a chair, and busied herself with my bruises, and said to me, "Now, tell me what you are crying about, and why did they turn you out of the drawing-room, tell me now?"

"Ay," said I, "they turned me out because I cried when I was hurt. I fell all the way down stairs, but they don't mind."

"No, they do not, and yet in many families they would have taken more care of you than they do here!"

"And why do you think they would have done so?" I inquired.

"Don't you know what good fortune has lately fallen into your lap? I thought you knew all about it."

"I don't know anything, save they are very unkind to me lately."

"They have been very unkind to you, child, and I am sure I don't know why, nor can I tell you why they have not told you of your fortune."

"My fortune," said I; "what fortune?"

"Why, don't you know that when your poor aunt died you were her favourite?"

"I know my aunt loved me," I said; "she loved me, and was kind to me; but since she has been dead, nobody cares for me."

"Well, my child, she has left a will behind her which says that all her fortune shall be yours: when you are old enough you shall have all her fine things; you shall have all her money and her house."

"Indeed!" said I; "who told you so?"

"Oh, I have heard of it from those who were present at the reading of the will that you were, when you are old enough, to have all. Think what a great lady you will be then! You will have servants of your own."

"I don't think I shall live till then."

"Oh yes, you will—or, at least, I hope so."

"And if I should not, what will become of all those fine things that you have told me of? Who'll have them?"

"Why, if you do not live till you are of age, your fortune will go to your father and mother, who take all."

"Then they would sooner I die than live."

"What makes you think so?" she inquired.

"Why," said I, "they don't care anything for me now, and they would have my fortune if I were dead—so they don't want me."

"Ah, my child," said the old woman, "I have thought of that more than once; and now you can see it. I believe that it will be so. There has many a word been spoken truly enough by a child before now, and I am sure you are right—but do you be a good child, and be careful of yourself, and you will always find that Providence will keep you out of any trouble."

"I hope so," I said.

"And be sure you don't say who told you about this."

"Why not?" I inquired; "why may I not tell who told me about it?"

"Because," she replied, "if it were known that I told you anything about it, as you have not been told by them they might discharge me, and I should be turned out."

"I will not do that," I replied; "they shall not learn who told me, though I should like to hear them say the same thing."

"You may hear them do so one of these days," she replied, "if you are not impatient: it will come out one of these days—two may know of it."

"More than my father and mother?"

"Yes, more—several."

No more was said then about the matter; but I treasured it up in my mind. I resolved that I would act differently, and not have anything to do with them—that is, I would not be more in their sight than I could help—I would not be in their sight at all, save at meal times—and when there was any company there I always appeared.

I cannot tell why; but I think it was because I sometimes attracted the attention of others, and I hoped to be able to hear something respecting my fortune; and in the end I succeeded in doing so, and then I was satisfied—not that it made any alteration in my conduct, but I felt I was entitled to a fortune.

How such an impression became imprinted upon a girl of eight years old, I know not; but it took hold of me, and I had some kind of notion that I was entitled to more consideration than I was treated to.

"Mother," said I one day to her.

"Well, Mary, what do you want to tease me about now?"

"Didn't Mrs. Carter the other day say my aunt left me a fortune?"

"What is the child dreaming about?" said my mother. "Do you know what you are talking about, child?—you can't comprehend."

"I don't know, mother, but you said it was so to Mrs. Carter."

"Well, then, what if I did, child?"

"Why, you must have told the truth or a falsehood."

"Well, Miss Impudence!—I told the truth, what then?"

"Why, then, I am to have a fortune when I grow up, that's all I mean, mother, and then people will take care of me. I shall not be forgotten, but everything will be done for me, and I shall be thought of first."

My mother looked at me very hard for a moment or two, and then, as if she was actuated by remorse, she made an attempt to speak, but checked herself, and then anger came to her aid, and she said,—

"Upon my word, miss! what thoughts have you taken into your fancy now? I suppose we shall be compelled to be so many servants to you! I am sure you ought to be ashamed of yourself—you ought, indeed!"

"I didn't know I had done wrong," I said.

"Hold your tongue, will you, or I shall be obliged to flog you!" said my mother, giving me a sound box on the ears that threw me down. "Now hold your tongue and go upstairs, and give me no more insolence."

I arose and went upstairs, sobbing as if my heart would break. I can recollect how many bitter hours I spent there, crying by myself—how many tears I shed upon this matter, and how I compared myself to other children, and how much my situation was worse than theirs by a great deal.

They, I thought, had their companions—they had their hours of play. But what companions had I—and what had I in the way of relaxation? What had I to do save to pine over the past, and present, and the future?

My infantile thoughts and hours were alike occupied by the sad reflections that belonged to a more mature age than mine; and yet I was so.

Days, weeks, and months passed on—there was no change, and I grew apace; but I was always regarded by my family with dislike, and always neglected. I could not account for it in any way than they wished me dead.

It may appear dreadful—very dreadful indeed—but what else was I to think? The old servant's words came upon my mind full of their meaning—if I died before I was one-and-twenty, they would have all my aunt's money.

"They wish me to die," I thought, "they wish me to die; and I shall die—I am sure I shall die! But they will kill me—they have tried it by neglecting me, and making me sad. What can I do—what can I do?"

These thoughts were the current matter of my mind, and how often do they recur to my recollection now I am in this dull, dreadful place! I can never forget the past. I am here because I have rights elsewhere, which others can enjoy, and do enjoy.

However, that is an old evil. I have thus suffered long. But to return.

After a year had gone by—two, I think, must have passed over my head—before I met with anything that was at all calculated to injure me. I must have been nearly ten years old, when, one evening, I had no sooner got into bed, than I found I had been put into damp—I may say wet sheets.

They were so damp that I could not doubt but this was done on purpose. I am sure no negligence ever came to anything so positive, and so abominable in all my life. I got out of bed, and took them off, and then wrapped myself up in the blankets, and slept till morning, without wakening anyone.

When morning came, I inquired who put the sheets there?

"What do you mean, minx?" said my mother.

"Only that somebody was bad and wicked enough to put positively wet sheets in the bed; it could not have been done through carelessness—it must have been done though sheer wilfulness. I'm quite convinced of that."

"You will get yourself well thrashed if you talk like that," said my mother. "The sheets are not damp; there are none in the house that are damp."

"These are wet."

This reply brought her hand down heavily upon my shoulder, and I was forced upon my knees. I could not help myself, so violent was the blow.

"There," added my mother, "take that, and that, and answer me if you dare."

As she said this she struck me to the ground, and my head came into violent contact with the table, and I was rendered insensible.

How long I continued so I cannot tell. What I first saw when I awoke was the dreariness of the attics into which I had been thrust, and thrown upon a small bed without any furniture. I looked around and saw nothing that indicated comfort, and upon looking at my clothes, there were traces of blood. This, I had no doubt, came from myself.

I was hurt, and upon putting my hand to my head found that I was much hurt, as my head was bound up.

At that moment the door was opened, and the old servant came in.

"Well, Miss Mary," she said, "and so you have come round again? I really began to be afraid you were killed. What a fall you must have had!"

"Fall," said I; "who said it was a fall?"

"They told me so."

"I was struck down."

"Struck, Miss Mary? Who could strike you? And what did you do to deserve such a severe chastisement? Who did it?"

"I spoke to my mother about the wet sheets."

"Ah! what a mercy you were not killed! If you had slept in them, your life would not have been worth a farthing. You would have caught cold, and you would have died of inflammation, I am sure of it. If anybody wants to commit murder without being found out, they have only to put them into damp sheets."

"So I thought, and I took them out."

"You did quite right—quite right."

"What have you heard about them?" said I.

"Oh! I only went into the room in which you sleep, and I at once found how damp they were, and how dangerous it was; and I was going to tell your mamma, when I met her, and she told me to hold my tongue, but to go down and take you away, as you had fallen down in a fit, and she could not bear to see you lying there."

"And she didn't do anything for me?"

"Oh, no, not as I know of, because you were lying on the floor bleeding. I picked you up, and brought you here."

"And she has not enquired after me since?"

"Not once."

"And don't know whether I am yet sensible or not?"

"She does not know that yet."

"Well," I replied, "I think they don't care much for me, I think not at all, but the time may come when they will act differently."

"No, Miss, they think, or affect to think, that you have injured them; but that cannot be, because you could not be cunning enough to dispose your aunt to leave you all, and so deprive them of what they think they are entitled to."

"I never could have believed half so much."

"Such, however, is the case."

"What can I do?"

"Nothing, my dear, but lie still till you get better, and don't say any more; but sleep, if you can sleep, will do you more good than anything else now for an hour or so, so lie down and sleep."

The old woman left the room, and I endeavoured to compose myself to sleep; but could not do so for some time, my mind being too actively engaged in considering what I had better do, and I determined upon a course of conduct by which I thought I should escape much of my present persecution.

It was some days, however, before I could put it in practice, and one day I found my father and mother together, and said to her,—

"Mother, why do you not send me to school?"

"You—send you to school! did you mean you, Miss?"

"Yes, I meant myself, because other people go to school to learn something, but I have not been sent at all."

"Are you not contented?"

"I am not," I answered, "because other people learn something; but at the same time, I should be more out of your way, since I am more trouble to you, as you complain of me; it would not cost more than living at home."

"What is the matter with the child?" asked my father.

"I cannot tell," said my mother.

"The better way will be to take care of her, and confine her to some part of the house, if she does not behave better."

"The little minx will be very troublesome."

"Do you think so?"

"Yes, decidedly."

"Then we must adopt some more active measures, or we shall have to do what we do not wish. I am amused at her asking to be sent to school! Was ever there heard such wickedness? Well, I could not have believed such ingratitude could have existed in human nature."

"Get out of the room, you huzzy," said my mother; "go out of the room, and don't let me hear a word from you more.

I left the room terrified at the storm I had raised up against me. I knew not that I had done wrong, and went up crying to my attic alone, and found the old servant, who asked what was the matter. I told her all I had said, and what had been the result, and how I had been abused.

"Why, you should let things take their own course, my dear."

"Yes, but I can learn nothing."

"Never mind; you will have plenty of money when you grow older, and that will cure many defects; people who have money never want for friends."

"But I have them not, and yet I have money."

"Most certainly—most certainly, but you have it not in your power, and you are not old enough to make use of it, if you had it."

"Who has it?" I inquired.

"Your father and mother."

No more was said at that time, and the old woman left me to myself, and I recollect I long and deeply pondered over this matter, and yet I could see no way out of it, and resolved that I would take things as easily as I could; but I feared that I was not likely to have a very quiet life; indeed, active cruelty was exercised against me.

They would lock me up in a room a whole day at a time, so that I was debarred the use of my limbs. I was even kept without food, and on every occasion I was knocked about, from one to the other, without remorse—everyone took a delight in tormenting me, and in showing me how much they dared to do.

Of course servants and all would not treat me with neglect and harshness if they did not see it was agreeable to my parents.

This was shocking cruelty; but yet I found that this was not all. Many were the little contrivances made and invented to cause me to fall down stairs—to slip— to trip, to do anything that might have ended in some fatal accident, which would have left them at liberty to enjoy my legacy, and no blame would be attached to them for the accident, and I should most likely get blamed for what was done, and from which I had been the sufferer—indeed, I should have been deemed to have suffered justly.

On one occasion, after I had been in bed some time, I found it was very damp, and upon examination I found the bed itself had been made quite wet, with the sheet put over it to hide it.

This I did not discover until it was too late, for I caught a violent cold, and it took me some weeks to get over it, and yet I escaped eventually, though after some months' illness. I recovered, and it evidently made them angry because I did live.

They must have believed me to be very obstinate; they thought me obdurate in the extreme—they called me all the names they could imagine, and treated me with every indignity they could heap upon me.

Well, time ran on, and in my twelfth year I obtained the notice of one or two of our friends, who made some inquiries about me.

I always remarked that my parents disliked anyone to speak to, or take any notice of me. They did not permit me to say much—they did not like my speaking; and on one occasion, when I made some remark respecting school, she replied,—

"Her health is so bad that I have not yet sent her, but shall do so by and by, when she grows stronger.

There was a look bent upon me that told me at once what I must expect if I persisted in my half-formed resolve of contradicting all that had been said.

When the visitor went I was well aware of what kind of a life I should have had, if I did not absolutely receive some serious injury. I was terrified, and held my tongue.

Soon after that I was seized with violent pains and vomiting. I was very ill, and the servant being at home only, a doctor was sent for, who at once said I had been poisoned, and ordered me to be taken care of.

I know how it was done; I had taken some cake given me—it was left out for me; and that was the only thing I had eaten, and it astonished me, for I had not had such a thing given me for years, and that is why I believe the poison was put in the cake, and I think others thought so too.

However I got over that after a time, though I was a long while before I did so; but at the same time I was very weak, and the surgeon said that had I been a little longer without assistance, or had I not thrown it up, I must have sunk beneath the effects of a violent poison.

He advised my parents to take some measures to ascertain who it was that had administered the poison to me; but though they promised compliance, they never troubled themselves about it—but I was for a long time very cautious of what I took, and was in great fear of the food that was given to me.

However, nothing more of that character took place, and at length I quite recovered, and began to think in my own mind that I ought to take some active steps in the matter, and that I ought to seek an asylum elsewhere.

I was now nearly fifteen years of age, and could well see how inveterate was the dislike with which I was regarded by my family: I thought that they ought to use me better, for I could remember no cause for it. I had given no deadly offence, nor was there any motive why I should be treated thus with neglect and disdain.

It was, then, a matter of serious consideration with me as to whether I should not go and throw myself upon the protection of some friend, and beg their interference in my behalf; but then there was no one whom I felt would do so much for me—no one from whom I expected so great an act of friendship.

It was hardly to be expected from anyone that they should interfere between me and my parents; they would have had their first say, and I should have contradicted all said, and should have appeared in a very bad light indeed.

I could not say they had neglected my education—I could not say that, because there I had been careful myself, and I had assiduously striven when alone to remedy this defect, and had actually succeeded; so that, if I were examined, I should have denied my own assertions by contrary facts, which would injure me. Then again, if I were neglected, I could not prove any injury, because I had all the means of existence; and all I could say would be either attributed to some evil source, or it was entirely false—but at the same time I felt I had great cause of complaint, and none of gratitude.

I could hold no communion with anyone—all alike deserted me, and I knew none who could say aught for me if I requested their good will.

I had serious thoughts of possessing myself of some money, and then leaving home, and staying away until I had arrived at age; but this I deferred doing, seeing that there was no means, and I could not do more than I did then—that is, to live on without any mischief happening, and wait for a few years more.

I contracted an acquaintance with a young man who came to visit my father— he came several times, and paid me more civility and attention than anyone else ever did, and I felt that he was the only friend I possessed.

It is no wonder I looked upon him as being my best and my only friend. I thought him the best and the handsomest man I ever beheld.

This put other thoughts into my head. I did not dress as others did, much less had I the opportunity of becoming possessed of many of those little trinkets that most young women of my age had.

But this made no alteration in the good opinion of the young gentleman, who took no notice of that, but made me several pretty presents.

These were treasures to me, and I must say I gloated over them, and often, when alone, I have spent hours in admiring them; trifling as they were, they made me happier. I knew now one person who cared for me, and a delightful feeling it was too. I shall never know it again—it is quite impossible.

Here among the dark walls and unwholesome cells we have no cheering ray of life or hope—all is dreary and cold; a long and horrible imprisonment takes place, to which there is no end save with life, and in which there is not one mitigating circumstance—all is bad and dark. God help me!

However, my dream of happiness was soon disturbed. By some means my parents had got an idea of this, and the young man was dismissed the house, and forbidden to come to it again. This he determined to do, and more than once we met, and then in secret I told him all my woes.

When he had heard all I had said, he expressed the deepest commiseration, and declared I had been most unjustly and harshly treated, and thought that there was not a harder or harsher treatment than that which I had received.

He then advised me to leave home.

"Leave home," I said; "where shall I fly? I have no friend."

"Come to me, I will protect you, I will stand between you and all the world; they shall not stir hand or foot to your injury."

"But I cannot, dare not do that; if they found me out, they would force me back with all the ignominy and shame that could be felt from having done a bad act; not any pity would they show me."

"Nor need you; you would be my wife, I mean to make you my wife."

"You?"

"Yes! I dreamed not of anything else. You shall be my wife; we will hide ourselves, and remain unknown to all until the time shall have arrived when you are of age—when you can claim all your property, and run no risk of being poisoned or killed by any other means."

"This is a matter," said I, "that ought to be considered well before adopting anything as violent or so sudden."

"It is; and it is not one that I think will injure by being reflected upon by those who are the principal actors; for my own part my mind is made up, and I am ready to perform my share of the engagement."

I resolved to consider the matter well in my own mind, and felt every inclination to do what he proposed, because it took me away from home, and because it would give me one of my own.

My parents had become utterly estranged from me; they did not act as parents, they did not act as friends, they had steeled my heart against them; they never could have borne any love to me, I am sure of it, who could have committed such great crimes against me.

As the hour drew near, that in which I was likely to become an object of still greater hatred and dislike to them, I thought I was often the subject of their private thoughts, and often when I entered the room my mother, and father, and the rest, would suddenly leave off speaking, and look at me, as if to ascertain if I had ever heard them say anything. On one occasion I remember very well I heard them conversing in a low tone. The door happened to have opened of itself, the hasp not having been allowed to enter the mortice; I heard my name mentioned: I paused and listened.

"We must soon get rid of her," said my mother.

"Undoubtedly," he replied; "if we do not, we shall have her about our ears: she'll get married, or some infernal thing, and then we shall have to refund."

"We could prevent that."

"Not if her husband was to insist upon it, we could not; but the only plan I can now form is what I told you of already."

"Putting her in a mad-house?"

"Yes: there, you see, she will be secured, and cannot get away. Besides, those who go there die in a natural way before many years."

"But she can speak."

"So she may; but who attends to the ravings of a mad woman? No, no; depend upon it that is the best plan: send her to a lunatic asylum—a private mad-house. I can obtain all that is requisite in a day or two."

"Then we will consider that settled."

"Certainly."

"In a few days, then?"

"Before next Sunday; because we can enjoy ourselves on that day without any restraint, or without any uncomfortable feelings of uncertainty about us."

I waited to hear no more: I had heard enough to tell me what I had to expect. I went back to my own room, and having put on my bonnet and shawl I went out to see the individual to whom I have alluded, and saw him.

I then informed him of all that had taken place, and heard him exclaim against them in terms of rising indignation.

"Come to me," he said; "come to me at once."

"Not at once.

"Don't stop a day."

"Hush!" said I; "there's no danger: I will come the day after tomorrow; and then I will bid adieu to all these unhappy moments, to all these persecutions; and in three years' time I shall be able to demand my fortune, which will be yours.

We were to meet the next day but one, early in the morning—there were not, in fact, to be more than thirty hours elapse before I was to leave home—if home I could call it—however there was no time to be lost. I made up a small bundle and had all in readiness, before I went to bed, and placed in security, intending to rise early and let myself out and leave the house.

That, however, was never to happen. While I slept, at a late hour of the night, I was awakened by two men standing by my bedside, who desired me to get up and follow them. I refused, and they pulled me rudely out of bed.

I called out for aid, and exclaimed against the barbarity of their proceedings.

"It is useless to listen to her," said my father, "you know what a mad woman will say!"

"Ay, we do," replied the men, "they are the cunningest devils we ever heard. We have seen enough of them to know that."

To make the matter plain, I was seized, gagged, and thrust into a coach, and brought here, where I have remained ever since.

CHAPTER XXXI

THERE WAS SOMETHING EXTREMELY TOUCHING IN THE TONE, AND APPARENTLY IN the manner, in which the poor persecuted one detailed the story of her wrongs, and she had the tribute of a willing tear from Tobias.

"After the generous confidence you have had in me," he said, "I ought to tell you something of myself."

"Do so," she replied, "we are companions in misfortune."

"We are indeed."

Tobias then related to her at large all about Sweeney Todd's villainies, and how at length he, Tobias, had been placed where he was, for the purpose of silencing his testimony of the evil and desperate practices of the barber. After that, he related to her what he had overheard about the intention to murder him that night, and he concluded by saying,—

"If you have any plan of escape from this horrible place, let me implore you to tell it to me, and let us put it into practice tonight, and if we fail, death is at any time preferable to continued existence here."

"It is—it is—listen to me."

"I will indeed," said Tobias; "you will say you never had such attention as I will now pay to you."

"You must know, then, that this cell is paved with flag-stones, as you see, and that the wall here at the back forms likewise part of the wall of an old wood-house in the garden, which is never visited."

"Yes, I understand."

"Well, as I have been here so long, I managed to get up one of the flag-stones that forms the flooring here, and to work under the wall with my hands—a slow labour, and one of pain, until I managed to render a kind of excavation, one end of which is here, and the other in the wood-house."

"Glorious!" said Tobias, "I see—I see—go on."

"I should have made my escape if I could, but the height of the garden wall has always been the obstacle. I thought of tearing this miserable quilt into strips, and making a sort of rope of it; but then how was I to get it on the wall? You, perhaps, will, with your activity and youth, be able to accomplish that."

"Oh, yes, yes! you're right enough there; it is not a wall that shall stop me."

They waited until, from a church clock in the vicinity, they heard ten strike, and then they began operations. Tobias assisted his new friend to raise the stone in the cell, and there, immediately beneath, appeared the excavation leading to the wood-house, just sufficiently wide for one person to creep through.

It did not take long to do that, and Tobias took with him a piece of work, upon which he had been occupied for the last two hours, namely, the quilt torn up into long pieces, twisted and tied together, so that it formed a very tolerable rope, which Tobias thought would sustain the weight of his companion.

The wood-house was a miserable-looking hole enough, and Tobias at first thought that the door of it was fastened, but by a little pressure it came open; it had only stuck through the dampness of the woodwork at that low point of the garden.

And now they were certainly both of them at liberty, with the exception of surmounting the wall, which rose frowningly before them in all its terrors.

There was a fine cool fresh air in the garden, which was indeed most grateful to the senses of Tobias, and he seemed doubly nerved for anything that might be required of him after inhaling that delicious cool, fresh breeze.

There grew close to the wall one of those beautiful mountain-ash trees, which bend over into such graceful foliage, and which are so useful in the formation of pretty summerhouses. Tobias saw that if he ascended to the top of this tree, there would not be much trouble in getting from there to the wall.

"We shall do it," he said, "we shall succeed."

"Thank God, that I hear you say so," replied his companion.

Tobias tied one end of the long rope they had made of the quilt to his waist, so that he might carry it up with him, and yet leave him free use of hands and feet, and then he commenced, with great activity, ascending the tree. In three minutes he was on the wall.

The moon shone sweetly. There was not a tree or house in the vicinity that was not made beautiful now, in some portions of it, by the sweet, soft light that poured down upon them.

Tobias could not resist pausing a moment to look around him upon the glorious scene: but the voice of her for whom he was bound to do all that was possible, aroused him.

"Oh, Tobias!" she said, "quick, quick—lower the rope; oh, quick!"

"In a moment—in a moment," he cried.

The top of the wall was here and there armed with iron spikes, and some of these formed an excellent grappling place for the torn quilt. In the course of another minute Tobias had his end of it secure.

"Now," he said, "can you climb up by it, do you think? Don't hurry about it. Remember, there is no alarm, and for all we know we have hours to ourselves yet."

"Yes, yes—oh, yes—thank God!" he heard her say.

Tobias was not where he could, by any exertion of strength, render her now the least assistance, and he watched the tightening of the frail support by which she was gradually climbing to the top of the wall with the most intense and painful interest that can be imagined.

"I come—I come," she said, "I am saved."

"Come slowly—for God's sake do not hurry."

"No, no."

At this moment Tobias heard the frail rope giving way: there was a tearing sound—it broke, and she fell.

Lights, too, at that unlucky moment, flashed from the house, and it was now evident an alarm had been given. What could he do? if two could not be saved, one could be saved.

He turned, and flung his feet over the wall, he hung by his hands, as low as he could, and then he dropped the remainder of the distance.

He was hurt, but in a moment he sprang to his feet, for he felt that safety could only lie in instant and rapid flight.

The terror of pursuit was so strong upon him that he forgot his bruises.

"Thank Heaven," exclaimed Tobias, "I am at last free from that horrible place. Oh, if I can but reach London now, I shall be safe; and as for Sweeney Todd, let him beware, for a day of retribution for him cannot be far off."

So saying, Tobias turned his steps towards the city, and at a hard trot, soon left Peckham Rye far behind him as he pursued his route.

CHAPTER XXXII

HAVING THUS FAR TRACED TOBIAS'S CAREER, WE ARE THE BETTER ENABLED TO TURN now our exclusive attention to the proceedings of Johanna Oakley, who, we cannot help thinking, is about to commence a most dangerous adventure.

The advice which had been given to her by her romantic young friend, Arabella Wilmot, had from the first taken a strong hold upon her imagination; and the more she had thought it over, and the more she found the others failed, in procuring any tidings of her lost lover, the more intent she was upon carrying it out.

"Yes," she said, "yes, true love will accomplish very great wonders; and what force or ability will fail at, confident affection even of a mere girl may succeed in.

"Tis true I risk my life; but what is life to me without what made it desirable? What is continued existence to me, embittered with the constant thought that such a dreadful mystery hangs over the fate of Mark Ingestrie?"

So it will be seen it was partly despair, and partly a kind of presentiment she had that success would attend her enterprise, that induced her to go to Sweeney Todd's.

There was a placard in Todd's window, which bore the following announcement:

Wanted: a lad. One of strict religious principles preferred.
Apply within.

The fact is, as we have said, although Sweeney Todd now, from the sale of the string of pearls, had the means of retiring from his avocations, and fully meant to do so, he did not think it prudent to hurry over such a step, and was resolved to wait until all noise and enquiry, if any were made, about the pearls had subsided; and therefore was it that he found it necessary to provide himself with a new boy, who, for all he cared, might share the fate of poor Tobias—that fate which Sweeney Todd considered certain, but concerning which the reader is better informed.

"Ah," muttered Todd to himself, "I like boys of a religious turn. They are much easier managed, for the imagination in such cases has been cultivated at the expense of the understanding. Hilloa, who have we here?"

Todd was stropping a razor, and peering out into the street while he spoke, and he saw a decent-looking young lad of remarkably handsome exterior, stop at the window, and read the tempting announcement. The lad advanced a step towards the door, hesitated, retreated, and then advanced again, as if he wished to apply for the vacant situation, and yet dreaded to do so.

"Who can he be?" said Todd, as he looked curiously at him. "He don't seem the likely sort to apply for the situation of barber's boy."

Todd was right enough there, for this seeming lad was no other than Johanna Oakley; and little, indeed, did she seem as if she belonged to the rough class from whom Sweeney Todd, the barber, might be supposed to find a lad for his shop.

In another moment she entered the shop, and was face to face with the man whom she might fairly consider to be the bane of her young existence, if what was suspected of him were true.

Todd fixed his strange glance upon her; but he was silent, for it was no rule of his to speak first, and Johanna felt constrained to commence the rather embarrassing conversation.

"You are in want of a lad, sir," she said, "to mind your shop, I suppose?"

"Yes."

Johanna had certainly hoped for a longer answer; but as Todd was silent, she had now no recourse but to go on.

"I shall be glad to take the situation."

"Who are you? You don't seem likely to want such a place. Who and what are you?"

Johanna had her story ready, for of course she had anticipated questions being asked of her; so she replied, with a readiness that did not seem at all forced,—

"I am an orphan, I was left in the care of a mother-in-law; I don't like her, she was cruel to me, and I ran away."

"Where from?"

"Oxford."

"Oxford, Oxford," muttered Todd; "then nobody knows you in London, I suppose, my little lad?"

"No one. I have come to town comfortably enough, in a wagon; but, if I don't get something to do, I shall have to go back, which I don't like the idea of at all. I'd rather be anything in London, than go back to Mrs. Green."

"Green, and what's your name?"

"Charley Green, of course; you sees my name's the same as hers, because she married my father."

"Oh, you won't suit me; you ain't the sort of boy I want."

"Sorry I troubled you, sir," said Johanna, as she turned carelessly and left the shop without making the least attempt to move the barber's determination, or even looking behind her.

"Pshaw!" exclaimed Todd, as he flung down the razor he had commenced sharpening again, "how foolishly suspicious I am. I shall wait a while, I think, before I get anyone to suit me as this lad will. In London alone, without friends, an orphan, nobody to enquire after him—the very thing."

Sweeney Todd was at his door in an instant. "Hoi! hoi!" he called. Johanna looked back, and saw him beckon to her; with new hope she returned, and was again in the shop.

"Hark ye, my lad," said Todd; "I feel disposed to take you on account of your friendless condition. I feel for you, I'm an orphan myself, that's a fact." Here he made one of those hideous grimaces he was in the habit of indulging in when he thought he said anything particularly racy. "Yes, I'm a poor orphan myself, with nothing but my strong sense of religion to support me. I'll take you on trial."

"I am much beholden to you, sir."

"Oh, don't mention that; your duties will consist of minding the shop if I happen to be absent. You will have sixpence a day, but nothing else from me; for out of that, you provide yourself with food; and the cheapest and the best thing you can do is, to go always to Lovett's, in Bell-yard, and have a pie for your dinner; you will sleep at night here in the shop, run messages, see and hear much, but if you gossip about me and my affairs, I'll cut your throat."

"You may depend upon me, sir; I'm only too happy in being taken into the service of such a respectable gentleman."

"Respectable gentleman!" repeated Todd, as he finished stropping the razor. "Respectable"; and then he gave one of his hideous laughs, which thrilled through the very heart of Johanna, as she thought that it might have been the last noise that sounded in the ears of Mark Ingestrie in this world. Todd turned very suddenly round, and said,—

"Did you groan?"

"I groan!" replied Johanna; "what for?"

"Oh, I only thought you did, Master Charley, that's all. See if that water on the fire is hot, and if so, bring it to me. Ha! a customer."

As Todd uttered these words, two persons entered the shop; they looked like substantial countrymen, farmers perhaps, in a good way of business; and one of them said,—

"Now, Mr. Barber, for a clean shave, if you please," while the other stood at the door, as if to wait for his companion.

"Certainly, sir," said Todd. "Pray sit down here if you please, sir; a nice day for the time of year; come from the country, sir, I suppose?"

"Yes, me and my cousin; we don't know much of London, yet."

"Indeed, sir, you ought not to leave it soon, then, I'm sure, for there is much to see, and that can't be seen quickly; and if you live far off, it's better to take the opportunity while you are here. Give me that soap dish, Charley."

"Yes, sir."

"Ah, to be sure," replied the countryman, "it is; but we have brought up to the London market a number of beasts, which having sold well, we have too much money about us to risk in going to see sights."

"Indeed! you are prudent. Would you like your whiskers trimmed?"

"A little, but not quite off."

There was now a pause of some moments' duration, after which Sweeney Todd said, in a very offhand manner—"I suppose you have seen the two figures at St. Dunstan's church strike the hour?"

"Two figures?" said the one who was not being shaved, for the other would have had a mouthful of lather if he had spoken; "two figures? No—what may they be all about?"

"Well," resumed Todd, with the most indifferent air and manner in the world, "if you have not seen them, it's quite a shame that you should not; and while I am shaving your friend, as it now only wants about five minutes to eleven, you have a good opportunity of going and getting back in time when your friend is—disposed of—what do you say to that? Charley, go with the gentleman, and show him the figures striking the hour at St. Dunstan's. You must cross over to the other side of the way, you know, to see them properly and effectually. Don't hurry, sir."

"Very much obliged," said the disengaged grazier, for such he seemed to be; "but I would rather go with my friend here, when he is shaven. You can't think what cynical remarks he makes at anything he has not seen before, so that to go with him is really always to me half the treat."

"Very good and very right," said Todd; "I shall soon be done. I have just about finished you off, now, sir. That will do."

There was no disappointment at all visible in Todd's manner, and the grazier rose and wiped his face on the jack-towel, that hung from a roller for the use of those whom it might concern, paid his money, and with a civil good-day to the barber, left the shop along with his friend.

An awfully diabolical look came across the countenance of Sweeney Todd, as he muttered to himself,—

"Curses on them both! I may yet have one of them though."

"What did you say, sir?" asked Johanna.

"What is that to you, you young imp?" roared Todd. "Curse you! I'll pull out your teeth by degrees, with red-hot pincers, if you presume to listen to what I say! I'll be the death of you, you devil's cub."

Johanna shrank back, alarmed, and then Todd walked across his shop to the back-parlour, the door of which he carefully double-locked, after which, turning to Johanna, he said,—

"You will mind the shop till I return, and if anybody comes, you can tell them that they need not wait, for I shall probably be some time gone. All you have to do is mind the place, and, hark you, no peeping nor prying about; sit still, and touch nothing, for if you do, I shall most assuredly discover it, and your punishment will be certain and perhaps terrible."

"I will be careful, sir."

"Do so, and you will be rewarded. Why, the last lad I had served me so well that I have had him taken care of for life, in a fine handsome country house, with grounds attached, a perfect villa, where he is waited upon by attendants, in the most attentive manner."

"How kind," said Johanna, "and is he happy?"

"Very, very—notwithstanding the general discontent of human nature, he is quite happy, as a matter of course. Mind my instructions, and in due time you will no doubt yourself share as amiable a fate."

Todd put on his hat, and with a horrible and strange leer upon his countenance, left the shop, and Johanna found herself in the situation she had coveted, namely, to be alone in the shop of Sweeney Todd, and able to make what examination of it she pleased, without the probability of much interruption.

"Heaven be my aid," she cried, "for the sake of truth."

CHAPTER XXXIII

"Well, Sir Richard," remarked the beadle of St. Dunstan's to the magistrate, after the ponderous stone was raised in the centre of the church, upon which the workmen had been busy, "don't you smell nothink now?"

The magistrate, churchwardens, and, indeed, everyone present, shrank back from the horrible stench that saluted them, now that the stone was fairly removed.

"Why, good God!" exclaimed the senior churchwarden; "have we been sitting and hearing sermons with such a charnel-house under? I always understood that none of the vaults exactly underneath the church had been used for many years past."

"Hush!" said the magistrate. "The enquiry we are upon is, perhaps, a more important one than you imagine, sir."

"More important! How can that be? Didn't the bishop smell it when he came to confirm the people, and didn't he say in the vestry that he could not confirm anybody while such a smell was in the church, and didn't we tell him that it would be a sad thing if he didn't? and then he did confirm the people in such a twinkling, that they didn't know what they were confirmed in at all."

"Hush! my good sir, hush, and hear me. Will you, now that you have got up this great stone, and opened, as I see, the top of a stone staircase, by so doing, send away the workmen, and, indeed, all persons but yourself and me?"

"Well, but—but you don't mean us to go down, sir, do you?"

"I mean to go, you may depend. Send away the men at once, if you please. I have ample warrant for all I am about to do, I assure you. I suspect I shall be well able to free St. Dunstan's church from the horrible stench that has been infesting it for some time past."

"You think so, sir? Bless you, then, I'll do just whatever you like."

The workmen were not sorry to be dismissed from the uncomfortable employment, but the beadle who was holding his nose, and who having overheard what Sir Richard had said, was extremely anxious upon the subject, put in his claim to stay, on the ground of being one of the officials of the church; and he was accordingly permitted to stay.

"This seems to lead to the vaults," remarked Sir Richard, as he looked down the chasm, which the removal of the stone had left.

"Yes," replied the churchwarden, "it does, and they have, as I say, been unused for a long time; but how that dreadful smell can come from bodies that have been forty or fifty years there, I can't think."

"We must be careful of the foul air," remarked the magistrate. "Get a torch, Mr. Beadle, if you please, and we will lower it into the vault. If that lives, we can: and if you please go first to the door of the church, and take this silk handkerchief with you, and hold it up in your hand; and upon that signal, four persons will come to you. They are officers of mine, and you will bring them to me."

"Oh, dear, yes, certainly," said the beadle, who was quite happy at the thoughts of such a reinforcement. "I'll do it, sir, and as for a torch, there is some famous links in the vestry cupboard, as I'll get in a minute. Well, I do think the smell is a little better already; don't you, sir? I'm a going. Don't be impatient, sir. I'm going like a shot, I am."

To give the beadle his due, he certainly executed his orders quickly. The four officers, sure enough, obeyed the signal of the handkerchief, and in a few minutes more, a torchlight was lowered by a rope down the gloomy aperture. All watched the light with great interest as it descended; but, although it certainly burnt dimmer than before, yet it showed no signs of going out, and the magistrate said,—

"We may safely descend. The air that will support flame will likewise support animal life; therefore we need be under no sort of apprehension. Follow me."

He commenced a careful descent of the stone steps, and was promptly followed by his four men, and much more slowly by the beadle and the churchwarden, neither of whom seemed much to relish the adventure, although their curiosity prompted them to continue it.

The stone steps consisted of about twenty, and when the bottom was gained, it was found to be covered with flag-stones of considerable size, upon which sawdust was strewn, but not sufficiently thickly to cover them in all places completely.

There was a death-like stillness in the place, and the few crumbling coffins which were in niches in the walls were, with their tenants, evidently too old to give forth that frightful odour of animal decomposition which pervaded the place.

"You will see, Sir Richard," said the churchwarden, producing a piece of paper, "that, according to the plans of the vault I have here, this one opens into a passage that runs halfway round the church, and from that passage opens a number of vaults, not one of which has been used for years past."

"I see the door is open."

"Yes, it is as you say. That's odd, Sir Richard, ain't it? Oh! gracious!—just put your head out into the passage, and won't you smell it then!"

They all tried the experiment, and found, indeed, that the smell was horrible. Sir Richard took a torch from one of the constables, and advanced into the passage. He could see nothing but the doors of some of the vaults open: he crossed the threshold of one of them, and was away about a minute; after which he came back, saying,—

"I think we will all retire now: we have seen enough to convince us all about it."

"All about it, sir!" said the churchwarden, "what about it?"

"Exactly, that will do—follow me, my men."

The officers, without the slightest questions or remarks, followed Sir Richard, and he began rapidly, with them at his heels, to ascend the stone staircase into the church again.

"Hilloa!" cried the beadle—"I say, stop. O lord! don't let me be lost—Oh, don't! I shall think something horrible is coming up after me, and going to lay hold of my heels: don't let me be lost! oh dear!"

"You can't be lost," said one of the officers; "you know if anything is going to lay hold of your heels. Take it easy; it's only a ghost at the most, you know."

By the time the beadle got fairly into the church, he was in that state of perspiration and fright, that he was obliged to sit down upon a tomb to recover himself; and the magistrate took that opportunity of whispering to the churchwarden,—

"I want to speak to you alone; come out with me—order the church to be locked up, as if we meditated no further search in the vaults."

"Yes, oh, yes! I knew there was some secret."

"There is a horrible one!—such a one as all London will ring with in twenty-four hours more—such a secret as will never be forgotten in connection with old St. Dunstan's church, while it is in existence."

There was a solemnity about the manner in which the magistrate spoke, which quite alarmed the churchwarden, and he turned rather pale as they stood upon the church threshold.

"Do you know one Sweeney Todd?" asked the magistrate.

"Oh, yes—a barber."

"Good. Incline your ear to me while we walk down to Downing-street. I am going to call upon the Secretary of State for the Home Department, and before we get there, I shall be able to tell you why and what sort of assistance I want of you."

The churchwarden did incline his ear most eagerly, but before they had got half way down the Strand, he was compelled to go into a public-house to get some brandy, such an overpowering effect had the horrible communication of the magistrate upon him. What that communication was we shall very soon discover; but it is necessary that we follow Mr. Todd a little in his proceedings after he left Johanna in charge of his shop.

Todd walked briskly on, till he came nearly to Pickett-street, in the Strand, and then he went into a chemist's shop that was there, in which only a lad was serving.

"You recollect," said Todd, "serving me with some rat poison?"

"Oh, yes, yes—Mr. Todd, I believe."

"The same. I want some more; for the fact is, that owing to the ointments I have in my shop for the hair, the vermin are attracted, and I have now as many as ever. It was only last night I awakened, and saw one actually lapping up hair-oil, and another drinking some rose-water that they had upset, and broken a bottle of, so I will thank you to give me some liquid poison, if you please, as they seem so fond of drink."

"Exactly, sir, exactly," said the lad, as he took down a bottle, and made up a potion; "exactly, sir. If you put a few drops only of this in half a pint of liquid, it will do."

"A couple of drops? This must be powerful."

"It is—a dozen drops, or about half a teaspoonful, would kill a man to a certainty, so you will be careful of it, Mr. Todd. Of course, we don't sell such things to strangers, you know, but you being a neighbour alters the case."

"True enough. Thank you. Goodday. I think we shall have rain shortly, do you know."

Todd walked away with the poison in his pocket, and when he had got a few yards from the chemist's door, he gave such a hideous chuckle that an old gentleman, who was close before him, ran like a lamp-lighter in his fright, and put himself quite out of breath.

"This will do," muttered Todd; "I must smooth the path to my retirement from business. I know well that if I were to hint at such a thing in a certain quarter, it would be considered a certain proof that I had made enough to be worth dividing, and that is a process I don't intend exactly to go through. No, no, Mrs. Lovett, no, no."

Todd marched slowly towards his own house, but when he got to the corner of Bell-yard, and heard St. Dunstan's strike twelve, he paused a moment, and then muttered,—

"I'll call and see her—yes, I'll call, and see her. The evening will answer better my present purpose."

He then walked up Bell-yard, until he came to the fascinating Mrs. Lovett's pie-shop. He paused a moment at the window, and leered in at two lawyer's clerks who were eating some of yesterday's pies. The warm day batch had not yet come up. "Happy youths!" he chuckled, and walked into the shop.

Mrs. Lovett received him graciously as an acquaintance, and invited him into the parlour, while the two limbs of the law continued eating and praising the pies.

"Delicious, ain't they?" said one.

"Oh, I believe you," replied the other; "and such jolly lots of gravy, too, ain't there? I wonder how she does make 'em. Lor' bless you, I almost live upon 'em. You know, I used to take all my meals with my fat old uncle, Marsh, but since he disappeared one day, I live on Lovett's pies, instead of the old buffer."

CHAPTER XXXIV

FOR SOME TIME AFTER TODD HAD LEFT THE SHOP, JOHANNA COULD SCARCELY BELIEVE that she was sufficiently alone to dare to look about her; but as minute after minute passed away, and no sound indicative of his speedy return fell upon her ears, she gathered more courage.

"Yes," she said, "I am at last alone, in the place where my suspicions have always pointed as the death place of poor Mark. O Heavens, grant that it may not be so, and that, in unravelling the evident mystery of this man's life, I may hail you living, my dear Mark, and not have to mourn you dead! And yet, how can I, even for a moment, delude myself with such false hopes? No, no, he has fallen a victim to this ruthless man."

For a few minutes, as Johanna gave way to this violent burst of grief, she wrung her hands and wept; but then, as a thought of the danger she would be in should Todd return and see signs of emotion crossed her mind, she controlled her tears, and managed to bear the outward semblance of composure.

She then began to look about her in the same way that poor Tobias had done; but she could find nothing of an explanatory character, although her suspicions made almost everything into grounds of suspicion. She looked into the cupboard, and there she saw several costly sticks and some umbrellas, and then she narrowly examined all the walls, but could see nothing indicative of another opening, save the door, visible and apparent. As she moved backwards, she came against the shaving chair, which she found was a fixture, as, upon examination, she saw that the legs of it were firmly secured to the floor. What there could be suspicious in such a circumstance she hardly knew, and yet it did strike her as such.

"If I had but time," she thought, "I would make an attempt to go into that parlour; but I dare not yet. No, no, I must be more sure of the continued absence of Todd, before I dare make any such attempt."

As she uttered these words, someone opened the door cautiously, and, peeping in, said, "Is Mr. Todd at home?"

"No," replied Johanna.

"Oh, very good. Then you are to take this letter, if you please, and read it. You will find, I dare say, whom it's from, when you open it. Keep it to yourself though, and if Mr. Todd should come in, hide it, mind, whatever you do."

Before Johanna could make any reply, the man disappeared, and great was her astonishment to read upon the outside of the letter that had been put into her hands, her own proper name. With trembling fingers she opened it, and read as follows:

From Sir Richard Blunt, magistrate, to Miss Oakley:—
Miss Johanna Oakley, you have with great chivalry of spirit embarked in a very dangerous enterprise—an enterprise which, considering your youth and your sex, should

have been left to others; and it is well that others are in a position to watch over you and ensure your safety.

Your young friend, Arabella Wilmot, after giving so much romantic advice, and finding that you followed it, became herself alarmed at its possible consequences, and very prudently informed one who brought the intelligence to me, so that you are now well looked after; and should any danger present itself to you, you have but to seize any article that comes within your reach and throw it through a pane of glass in the shop window, when assistance will immediately come to you. I tell you this in order that you should feel quite at ease.

As, however, you have placed yourself in your present position in Todd's shop, it is more than likely you will be able to do good service in aiding to unmask that villain. You will, therefore, be good enough, towards the dusk of the evening, to hold yourself in readiness to do anything required of you by anyone who shall pronounce to you the password of "St. Dunstan."

From your Friend (mentioned above)

Johanna read this letter, certainly, with most unmitigated surprise, and yet there was a glow of satisfaction in her mind as she perused it, and the difference in her feelings, now that she was assured of protection, was certainly something wonderful and striking. To think that she had but to seize any one of the numerous stray articles that lay about and fling it through the window, in order to get assistance, was a most consolatory idea, and she felt nerved for almost any adventure.

She had just hidden the letter, when Sweeney Todd made his appearance.

"Anybody been?" he asked.

"Yes, one man, but he would not wait."

"Ah, wanted to be shaved, I suppose; but no matter—no matter; and I hope you have been quiet, and not been attempting to indulge your curiosity in any way, since I have been gone. Hush! there's somebody coming. Why, it's old Mr. Wrankley, the tobacconist, I declare. Good-day to you, sir—shaved, I suppose; I'm glad you have come, sir, for I have been out till this moment. Hot water, Charley, directly, and hand me that razor."

Johanna, in handing Todd the razor, knocked the edge of it against the chair, and it being uncommonly sharp, cut a great slice of the wood off one of the arms of it.

"What shameful carelessness," said Todd; "I have half a mind to lay the strop over your back, sir; here, you have spoilt a capital razor—not a bit of edge left upon it."

"Oh, excuse him, Mr. Todd—excuse him," said the old gentleman; "he's only a little lad, after all. Let me intercede for him."

"Very good, sir; if you wish me to look over it, of course I will, and, thank God, we have a stock of razors, of course, always at hand. Is there any news stirring, sir?"

"Nothing that I know of, Mr. Todd, except it's the illness of Mr. Cummings, the overseer. They say he got home about twelve to his own house, in Chancery-lane, and ever since then he has been sick as a dog, and all they can get him to say is, "Oh, those pies—oh, those pies!"'

"Very odd, sir."

"Very. I think Mr. Cummings must be touched in the upper storey, do you know, Mr. Todd. He's a very respectable man, but, between you and I, was never very bright."

"Certainly not—certainly not. But it's a very odd case. What pies can he possibly mean, sir? Did you call when you came from home?"

"No. Ha, ha! I can't help laughing; but ha, ha! I have come away from home on the sly, you see. The fact is, my wife's cousin, Mr. Mundel—hilloa!—I think you have cut me."

"No, no; we can't cut anybody for three-halfpence, sir."

"Oh, very good—very good. Well, as I was saying, my wife's cousin, Mr. Mundel, came to our house last night, and brought with him a string of pearls, you see. He wanted me to go to the City, this morning, with them, to Round and Bridget, the court jewellers', and ask them if they had ever seen them before."

"Were they beauties?"

"Yes, they are brilliant ones. You see, Mundel lends money, and he didn't like to go himself, so he asked me to go, as Mr. Round knows me very well; for between you and me, Mr. Todd, my wife's cousin, Mr. Mundel, thinks they belonged, once upon a time, to some lady."

"Oh, indeed!"

"Yes; and as it won't do to say too much to women, I told my wife I was going over the water, you see, and just popped out. Ha, ha, ha! and I've got the pearls in my pocket. Mundel says they are worth £12,000 at the least, ha, ha!"

"Indeed, sir, £12,000? A pretty sum that, sir—a very pretty sum. No doubt Mr. Mundel lent £7,000 or £8,000 upon the pearls. I think I will just give you another lather, sir, before I polish you off; and so you have the pearls with you, well, how odd things come round, to be sure."

"What do you mean?"

"This shaving-brush is just in a good state now. Always as a shaving-brush is on the point of wearing out, it's the best. Charley, you will go at once to Mr. Cummings's, and ask if he is any better; you need not hurry, that's a good lad, I am not at all angry with you now; and so, sir, they think at home that you have gone after some business over the water, do they, and have not the least idea that you have come here to be shaved—there, be off, Charley—shut the door, that's a good lad, bless you."

When Johanna came back, the tobacconist was gone.

"Well," said Sweeney Todd, as he sharpened a razor, very leisurely; "how is Mr. Cummings?"

"I found out his house, sir, with some difficulty, and they say he is better, having gone to sleep."

"Oh, very good! I am going to look over some accounts in the parlour, so don't choose to be disturbed, you understand; and for the next ten minutes, if anybody comes, you will say I am out."

Sweeney Todd walked quite coolly into the parlour, and Johanna heard him lock the door on the inside; a strange, undefined sensation of terror crept over her, she knew not why, and she shuddered, as she looked around her. The cupboard door was not close shut, and she knew not what prompted her to approach and peep in. On the first shelf was the hat of the tobacconist: it was a rather remarkable one, and recognised in a moment.

"What has happened? Good God! what can have happened?" thought Johanna, as she staggered back, until she reached the shaving-chair, into which she cast herself for support. Her eyes fell upon the arm which she had taken such a shaving off with the razor, but all was perfectly whole and correct; there was not the least mark of the cut that so recently had been given to it; and, lost in wonder, Johanna, for more than a minute, continued looking for the mark of the injury she knew could not have been, by any possibility, effaced.

And yet she found it not, although there was the chair, just as usual, with its wide spreading arms and its worn, tarnished paint and gilding. No wonder that Johanna rubbed her eyes, and asked herself if she were really awake.

What could account for such a phenomenon? The chair was a fixture too, and the others in the shop were of a widely different make and construction, so it could not have been changed.

"Alas, alas!" mourned Johanna, "my mind is full of horrible surmise, and yet I can form no rational conjecture. I suspect everything, and know nothing. What can I do?

What ought I to do, to relieve myself from this state of horrible suspense? Am I really in a place where, by some frightful ingenuity, murder has become bold and familiar, or can it all be a delusion?"

She covered her face with her hands for a time, and when she uncovered them, she saw that Sweeney Todd was staring at her with looks of suspicion from the inner room.

The necessity of acting her part came over Johanna, and she gave a loud scream.

"What the devil is all this about?" said Todd, advancing with a sinister expression. "What's the meaning of it? I suspect——"

'Yes, sir," said Johanna, "and so do I; I must tomorrow have it out."

'Have what out?'

"My tooth, sir, it's been aching for some hours; did you ever have the toothache? If you did, you can feel for me, and not wonder that I lean my head upon my heads and groan."

CHAPTER XXXV

Todd was but half satisfied with this excuse of Master Charley's, and yet it was one he could not very well object to, and might be true; so, after looking at Johanna for some moments suspiciously, he thought he might take it upon trust.

"Well, well," he said, "no doubt you will be better tomorrow. There's your six-pence for today; go and get yourself some dinner; and the cheapest thing you can do is to go to Lovett's pie-shop with it."

"Thank you, sir."

Johanna was aware as she walked out of the shop, that the eyes of Sweeney Todd were fixed upon her, and that if she betrayed, by even the remotest gesture, that she had suspicions of him, probably he would yet prevent her exit; so she kept herself seemingly calm, and went out very slowly; but it was a great relief to gain the street, and feel that she was not under the same roof with that dreadful and dreaded man.

Instead of going to Lovett's pie-shop, Johanna turned into a pastry-cook's near at hand, and partook of some refreshments; and while she is doing so, we will go back again, and take a glance at Sweeney Todd as he sat in his shop alone.

There was a look of great triumph upon his face, and his eyes sparkled with an unwonted brilliance. It was quite clear that Sweeney Todd was deeply congratulating himself upon something; and, at length, diving his hand into the depths of a huge pocket, he produced the identical string of pearls for which he had already received so large a sum from Mr. Mundel.

"Truly," he said, "I must be one of Fortune's prime favourites, indeed. Why, this string of pearls to me is a continued fortune; who could have for one moment dreamed of such a piece of rare fortune? I need not now be at all suspicious or troubled concerning John Mundel. He has lost his pearls, and lost his money. Ha, ha, ha! That is glorious; I will shut up shop sooner than I intended by far, and be off to the Continent. Yes, my next sale of the string of pearls shall be in Holland."

With the pearls in his hand, Todd now appeared to fall into a very distracted train of thought, which lasted him about ten minutes, and then some accidental noise in the street, or the next house, jarred upon his nerves, and he sprang to his feet, exclaiming,—

"What's that—what's that?"

All was still again, and he became reassured.

"What a fool I get," he muttered to himself, "That every casual sound disturbs me, and causes this tremor. It is time, now that I am getting nervous, that I should leave England. But first, I must dispose of one whose implacable disposition I know well, and who would hunt me to the farthest corner of the earth, if she were not at peace in the grave. Yes, the peace of the grave must do for her. I can think of no other mode of silencing so large a claim."

As he spoke those words, he took from his pocket the small packet of poison that he had purchased, and held it up between him and the light with a self-satisfied expression. Then he rose hastily, for he had again seated himself, and walked to the window, as if he were anxious for the return of Johanna, in order that he might leave the place. As he waited, he saw a young girl approach the shop, and having entered it, she said,—

"Mrs. Lovett's compliments, Mr. Todd, and she has sent you this note, and will be glad to see you at eight o'clock this evening."

"Oh, very well, very well. Why, Lucy, you look prettier than ever."

"It's more than you do, Mr. Todd," said the girl, as she left, apparently in high indignation that so ugly a specimen of humanity as Sweeney Todd should have taken it upon himself to pay her a compliment.

Todd only gave a hideous sort of a grin, and then he opened the letter which had been brought to him. It was without signature, and contained the following words: —

The new cook is already tired of his place, and you must tonight make another vacancy. He is the most troublesome one I have had, because the most educated. He must be got rid of—you know how. I am certain mischief will come of it.

"Indeed!" said Todd, when he finished this epistle, "this is quick; well, well, we shall see, we shall see. Perhaps we shall get rid of more than one person, who otherwise would be troublesome tonight. But here comes my new boy; he suspects nothing."

Johanna returned, and Todd asked somewhat curiously about the toothache; however, she made him so apparently calm and cool a reply, that he was completely foiled, and fancied that his former suspicions must surely have had no real foundation, but had been provoked merely by his fears.

"Charley," he said, "you will keep an eye on the door, and when anyone wants me, you will pull that spring, which communicates with a bell that will make me hear. I am merely going to my bedroom."

"Very well, sir."

Todd gave another suspicious glance at her, and then left the shop. She had hoped that he would have gone out, so that there would have been another opportunity, and a better one than the last, of searching the place, but in that she was disappointed; and there was no recourse but to wait with patience.

The day was on the decline, and a strong impression came over Johanna's mind, that something in particular would happen before it wholly passed away into darkness. She almost trembled to think what that something could be, and that she might be compelled to be a witness to violence, from which her gentle spirit revolted; and had it not been that she had determined nothing should stop her from investigating the fate of poor Mark Ingestrie, she could even then have rushed into the street in despair.

But as the soft daylight deepened into the dim shadows of evening, she grew more composed, and was better able, with a calmer spirit, to await the progress of events.

Objects were but faintly discernible in the shop when Sweeney Todd came downstairs again; and he ordered Johanna to light a small oil lamp which shed but a very faint and sickly ray around it, and by no means facilitated the curiosity of anyone who might wish to peep in at the window.

"I am going out," he said, "I shall be gone an hour, but not longer. You may say so to anyone who calls."

"I will, sir."

"Be vigilant, Charley, and your reward is certain."

"I pray to Heaven it may be," said Johanna, when she was again alone; but scarcely had the words passed her lips, when a hackney coach drove up to the door; and then alighted someone who came direct into the shop. He was a tall, gentlemanly-looking man, and before Johanna could utter a word, he said,—

"The watchword, Miss Oakley, is St. Dunstan; I am a friend."

Oh, how delightful it was to Johanna, to hear such words, oppressed as she was by the fearful solitude of that house; she sprang eagerly forward, saying,—

"Yes, yes; oh, yes! I had the letter."

"Hush! there is no time to lose. Is there any hiding-place here at all?"

"Oh yes! a large cupboard."

"That will do; wait here a moment while I bring in a friend of mine, if you please, Miss Oakley. We have got some work to do to-night."

The tall man, who was as cool and collected as anyone might be, went to the door, and presently returned with two persons, both of whom, it was found, might with very little trouble be hidden in the cupboard. Then there was a whispered consultation for a few minutes, after which the first comer turned to Johanna, and said,—

"Miss Oakley, when do you expect Todd to return?"

"In an hour."

"Very well. As soon as he does return, I shall come in to be shaved, and no doubt you will be sent away; but do not go further than the door, whatever you do, as we may possibly want you. You can easily linger about the window."

"Yes, yes! But why is all this mystery? Tell me what it is that you mean by all this. Is there any necessity for keeping me in the dark about it?"

"Miss Oakley, there is nothing exactly to tell you yet, but it is hoped that this night will remove some mysteries, and open your eyes to many circumstances that at present you cannot see. The villainy of Sweeney Todd will be espied, and if there be any hope of your restoration to one in whom you feel a great interest, it will be by such means.

"You mean Mark Ingestrie?"

"I do. Your history has been related to me."

"And who are you—why keep up to me a disguise if you are a friend?"

"I am a magistrate, and my name is Blunt; so you may be assured that all that can be done shall be done."

"But, hold! you spoke of coming here to be shaved. If you do, let me implore you not to sit in that chair. There is some horrible mystery connected with it, but what it is, I cannot tell. Do not sit in it."

"I thank you for your caution, but it is to be shaved in that very chair that I came. I know there is a mystery connected with it, and it is in order that it should be no longer a mystery that I have resolved upon running what, perhaps, may be considered a little risk. But our further stay here would be imprudent. Now, if you please."

These last words were uttered to the two officers that the magistrate had brought with him, and it was quite wonderful to see with what tact and precision they managed to wedge themselves into the cupboard, the door of which they desired Johanna to close upon them, and when she had done so and turned round, she found that the magistrate was gone.

Johanna was in a great state of agitation, but still it was some comfort to her now to know that she was not alone, and that there were two strong and no doubt well-armed men ready to take her part, should anything occur amiss; she was much more assured of her own safety, and yet she was much more nervous than she had been.

She waited for Sweeney Todd, and strove to catch the sound of his returning footstep, but she heard it not; and, as that gentleman went about some rather important business, we cannot do better than follow him, and see how he progressed with it.

When he left his shop, he went direct to Bell-yard, although it was a little before the time named for his visit to Mrs. Lovett.

CHAPTER XXXVI

IT WOULD HAVE BEEN CLEAR TO ANYONE, WHO LOOKED AT SWEENEY TODD AS HE took his route from his own shop in Fleet-street to Bell-yard, Temple-bar, that it was not to eat pies he went there.

No; he was on very different thoughts indeed intent, and as he neared the shop of Mrs. Lovett, where those delicacies were vended, there was such a diabolical expression upon his face that, had he not stooped like grim War to "Smooth his wrinkled form," ere he made his way into the shop, he would, most unquestionably, have excited the violent suspicions of Mrs. Lovett, that all was not exactly as it should be, and that the mysterious bond of union that held her and the barber together was not in that blooming state that it had been.

When he actually did enter the shop, he was all sweetness and placidity.

Mrs. Lovett was behind the counter, for it seldom happened that the shop was free of customers, for when the batches of hot pies were all over, there usually remained some which were devoured cold with avidity by the lawyers' clerks, from the offices and chambers in the neighbourhood.

But at nine o'clock, there was a batch of hot pies coming up, for of late Mrs. Lovett had fancied that between half-past eight and nine, there was a great turn-out of clerks from Lincoln's-inn, and a pie became a very desirable and comfortable prelude to half-price at the theatre, or any other amusements of the three hours before midnight.

Many people, too, liked them as a relish for supper, and took them home quite carefully. Indeed, in Lincoln's-inn, it may be said, that the affections of the clerks oscillated between Lovett's pies and sheep's heads; and it frequently so nicely balanced in their minds, that the two attractions depended upon the toss-up of a halfpenny, whether to choose "sang amary Jameses" from Clare Market, or pies from Lovett's.

Half-and-half washed both down equally well.

Mrs. Lovett, then, may be supposed to be waiting for the nine o'clock batch of pies, when Sweeney Todd, on this most eventful evening, made his appearance.

Todd and Mrs. Lovett met now with all the familiarity of old acquaintance.

"Ah, Mr. Todd," said the lady, "how do you do? Why, we have not seen you for a long time."

"It has been some time; and how are you, Mrs. Lovett?"

"Quite well, thank you. Of course, you will take a pie?"

Todd made a horrible face, as he replied,—

"No, thank you; it's very foolish, when I knew I was going to make a call here, but I have just had a pork chop."

"Had it the kidney in it, sir?" asked one of the lads who were eating cold pies.

"Yes, it had."

"Oh, that's what I like! Lor' bless you, I'd eat my mother, if she was a pork chop, done brown and crisp, and the kidney in it; just fancy it, grilling hot, you know, and just popped on a slice of bread, when you are cold and hungry."

"Will you walk in, Mr. Todd?" said Mrs. Lovett, raising a portion of the counter, by which an opening was made, that enabled Mr. Todd to pass into the sacred precincts of the parlour.

The invitation was complied with by Todd, who remarked that he hadn't above a minute to spare, but that he would sit down while he could stay, since Mrs. Lovett was so kind as to ask him.

This extreme suavity of manner, however, left Sweeney Todd when he was in the parlour, and there was nobody to take notice of him but Mrs. Lovett; nor did she think it necessary to wreathe her face in smiles, but with something of both anger and agitation in her manner, she said, "And when is all this to have an end, Sweeney Todd?

you have been now for these six months providing me such a division of spoil as shall enable me, with an ample independence, once again to appear in the salons of Paris. I ask you now when is this to be?"

"You are very impatient!"

"Impatient, impatient? May I not well be impatient? do I not run a frightful risk, while you must have the best of the profits? It is useless your pretending to tell me that you do not get much. I know you better, Sweeney Todd; you never strike, unless for profit or revenge."

"Well?"

"Is it well, then, that I should have no account? Oh God! if you had the dreams I sometimes have!"

"Dreams?"

She did not answer him, but sank into a chair, and trembled so violently that he became alarmed, thinking she was very, very unwell. His hand was upon a bell rope, when she motioned him to be still, and then she managed to say in a very faint and nearly inarticulate voice,—

"You will go to that cupboard. You will see a bottle. I am forced to drink, or I should kill myself, or go mad, or denounce you; give it to me quick—quick, give it to me: it is brandy. Give it to me, I say: do not stand gazing at it there, I must, and I will have it. Yes, yes, I am better now, much better now. It is horrible, very horrible, but I am better; and I say, I must, and I will have an account at once. Oh. Todd, what an enemy you have been to me!"

"You wrong me. The worst enemy you ever had is in your head."

"No, no, no! I must have that to drown thought!"

"Indeed! can you be so superstitious? I presume you are afraid of your reception in another world."

"No, no—oh no! you and I do not believe in a hereafter, Sweeney Todd; if we did, we should go raving mad, to think what we had sacrificed. Oh, no—no, we dare not, we dare not!"

"Enough of this," said Todd, somewhat violently, "enough of this; you shall have an account tomorrow evening; and when you find yourself in possession of £20,000, you will not accuse me of having been unmindful of your interests; but now, there is someone in the shop who seems to be enquiring for you."

Mrs. Lovett rose, and went into the shop. The moment her back was turned, Todd produced the little bottle of poison he had got from the chemist's boy, and emptied it into the brandy decanter. He had just succeeded in this manoeuvre, and concealed the bottle again, when she returned, and flung herself into a chair.

"Did I hear you aright," she said, "or is this promise but a mere mockery; £20,000—is it possible that you have so much? oh, why was not all this dreadful trade left off sooner? Much less would have been done. But when shall I have it—when shall I be enabled to fly from here for ever? Todd, we must live in different countries; I could never bear the chance of seeing you."

"As you please. It don't matter to me at all; you may be off tomorrow night, if you like. I tell you your share of the last eight years' work shall be £20,000. You shall have the sum tomorrow, and then you are free to go where you please; it matters not to me one straw where you spend your money. But tell me now, what immediate danger do you apprehend from your new cook?"

"Great and immediate; he has refused to work—a sign that he has got desperate, hopeless and impatient; and then only a few hours ago, I heard him call to me, and he said he had thought better of it, and would bake the nine o'clock batch, which, to my mind, was saying, that he had made up his mind to some course which gave him hope, and made it worth his while to temporise with me for a time, to lull suspicion."

"You are a clever woman. Something must and shall be done. I will be here at midnight, and we shall see if a vacancy cannot be made in your establishment."

"It will be necessary, and it is but one more."

"That's all—that's all, and I must say you have a very perfect and philosophic mode of settling the question; avoid the brandy as much as you can, but I suppose you are sure to take some between now and the morning?"

"Quite sure. It is not in this house that I can wean myself of such a habit. I may do so abroad, but not here."

"Oh, well, it can't matter; but, as regards the fellow downstairs, I will, of course, come and rid you of him. You must keep a good lookout now for the short time you will be here, and a good countenance. There, you are wanted again, and I may as well go likewise."

Mrs. Lovett and Todd walked from the parlour to the shop together, and when they got there, they found a respectable-looking woman and a boy, the latter of whom carried a bundle of printed papers with him; the woman was evidently in great distress of mind.

"Cold pie, marm?" said Mrs. Lovett.

"Oh dear no, Mrs. Lovett," said the woman; "I know you by sight, mem, though you don't know me. I am Mrs. Wrankley, mem, the wife of Mr. Wrankley, the tobacconist, and I've come to ask a favour of you, Mrs. Lovett, to allow one of these bills to be put in your window?"

"Dear me," said Mrs. Lovett, "what's it about?"

Mrs. Wrankley handed her one of the bills and then seemed so overcome with grief, that she was forced to sink into a chair while it was read, which was done aloud by Mrs. Lovett, who, as she did so, now and then stole a glance at Sweeney Todd, who looked as impenetrable and destitute of all emotion as a block of wood.

"Missing!—Mr. John Wrankley, tobacconist, of 92 Fleet-street. The above gentleman left his home to go over the water, on business, and has not since been heard of. He is supposed to have had some valuable property with him, in the shape of a string of pearls. The said Mr. John Wrankley is five feet four inches high, full face, short thick nose, black whiskers, and what is commonly called a bullet-head; thickset and skittle-made, not very well upon his feet; and whoever will give any information of him at 92 Fleet-street, shall be amply rewarded."

"Yes, yes," said Mrs. Wrankley, when the reading of the bill was finished, "that's him to a T, my poor, dear, handsome Wrankley! oh, I shall never be myself again; I have not eaten anything since he went out."

"Then buy a pie, madam," said Todd, as he held one close to her. "Look up, Mrs. Wrankley, lift off the top crust, madam, and you may take my word for it you will soon see *something* of Mr. Wrankley."

The hideous face that Todd made during the utterance of these words quite alarmed the disconsolate widow, but she did partake of the pie for all that. It was very tempting—a veal one, full of coagulated gravy—who could resist it? Not she, certainly, and besides, did not Todd say she would see something of Wrankley? There was hope in his words, at all events, if nothing else.

"Well," she said, "I will hope for the best; he may have been taken ill, and not have had his address in his pocket, poor dear soul! at the time."

"And at all events, madam," said Todd, "you need not be cut up about it, you know; I dare say you will know what has become of him some-day, soon."

CHAPTER XXXVII

MRS. LOVETT WAS A WOMAN OF JUDGEMENT, AND WHEN SHE TOLD SWEENEY TODD that the prisoner was getting impatient in the lower regions of that house which was devoted to the manufacture of the delicious pies, she had guessed rightly his sensations with regard to his present state and future prospects.

We last left that unfortunate young man lying upon the floor of the place where the steaming and tempting manufacture was carried on; and for a time, as a very natural consequence of exhaustion, he slept profoundly.

That sleep, however, if it rested him bodily, likewise rested him mentally; and when he again awoke it was but to feel more acutely the agony of his most singular and cruel situation. There was a clock in the place by which he had been enabled to accurately regulate the time that the various batches of pies should take in cooking, and upon looking up to that he saw that it was upon the hour of six, and consequently it would be three hours more before a batch of pies was wanted.

He looked about him very mournfully for some time, and then he spoke.

"What evil destiny," he said, "has placed me here? Oh, how much better it would have been if I had perished, as I have been near perishing several times during the period of my eventful life, than that I should be shut up in this horrible den and starved to death, as in all human probability I shall be, for I loathe the pies. Damn the pies!"

There was a slight noise, and upon his raising his eyes to that part of the place near the roof where there were some iron bars and between which Mrs. Lovett was wont to give him some directions, he saw her now detested face.

"Attend," she said; you will bake an extra batch to-night, at nine precisely."

"What?"

"An extra batch, two hundred at least; do you understand me?"

"Hark ye, Mrs. Lovett. You are carrying this sort of thing too far; it won't do, I tell you, Mrs. Lovett; I don't know how soon I may be numbered with the dead, but, as I am a living man now, I will make no more of your detestable pies."

"Beware!"

"Beware yourself! I am not one to be frightened at shadows. I say I will leave this place, whether you like it or not; I will leave it; and perhaps you will find your power insufficient to keep me here. That there is some frightful mystery at the bottom of all the proceedings here, I am certain, but you shall not make me the victim of it!"

"Rash fool!"

"Very well, say what you like, but remember I defy you."

"Then you are tired of your life, and you will find, when too late, what are the consequences of your defiance. But listen to me: when I first engaged you, I told you you might leave when you were tired of the employment."

"You did, and yet you keep me a prisoner here. God knows I'm tired enough of it. Besides, I shall starve, for I cannot eat pies eternally; I hate them."

"And they so admired!"

"Yes, when one ain't surfeited with them. I am now only subsisting upon baked flour. I cannot eat the pies."

"You are strangely fantastical."

"Perhaps I am. Do you live upon pies, I should like to know, Mrs. Lovett?"

"That is altogether beside the question. You shall, if you like, leave this place tomorrow morning, by which time I hope to have got someone else to take over your situation, but I cannot be left without anyone to make the pies."

"I don't care for that, I won't make another one."

"We shall see," said Mrs. Lovett. "I will come to you in an hour, and see if you persevere in that determination. I advise you as a friend to change, for you will most bitterly repent standing in the way of your own enfranchisement."

"Well, but—she is gone, and what can I do? I am in her power, but shall I tamely submit? No, no, not while I have my arms at liberty, and strength enough to wield one of these long pokers that stir the coals in the ovens. How foolish of me not to think before that I had such desperate weapons, with which perchance to work my way to freedom."

As he spoke, he poised in his hand one of the long pokers he spoke of, and, after some few minutes spent in consideration, he said to himself, with something of the cheerfulness of hope,—

"I am in Bell-yard, and there are houses right and left of this accursed pie-shop, and those houses must have cellars. Now surely with such a weapon as this, a willing heart, and an arm that has not yet quite lost all its powers, I may make my way from this abominable abode."

The very thought of thus achieving his liberty lent him new strength and resolution, so that he felt himself to be quite a different man to what he had been, and he only paused to consider in which direction it would be best to begin his work.

After some reflection upon that head, he considered that it would be better to commence where the meat was kept—that meat of which he always found abundance, and which came from—he knew not where; since, if he went to sleep with little or none of it upon the shelves where it was placed for use, he always found plenty when he awoke.

"Yes," he said, "I will begin there, and work my way to freedom."

Before, however, he commenced operations, he glanced at the clock, and found that it wanted very little now to seven, so that he thought it would be but common prudence to wait until Mrs. Lovett had paid him her promised visit, as then, if he said he would make the pies she required, he would, in all probability, be left to himself for two hours, and, he thought, if he did not make good progress in that time towards his liberty, it would be strange indeed.

He sat down, and patiently waited until seven o'clock.

Scarcely had the hour sounded, when he heard the voice of his tormentor and mistress at the grating.

"Well," she said, "have you considered?"

"Oh, yes, I have. Needs must, you know, Mrs. Lovett, when a certain person drives. But I have a great favour to ask of you, madam."

"What is it?"

"Why, I feel faint, and if you could let me have a pot of porter, I would undertake to make a batch of pies superior to any you have ever had, and without any grumbling either."

Mrs. Lovett was silent for a few moments, and then said,—

"If you are supplied with porter, will you continue in your situation?"

"Well, I don't know that; but perhaps I may. At all events, I will make you the nine o'clock batch, you may depend."

"Very well. You shall have it."

"She disappeared at these words, and in about ten minutes, a small trap-door opened in the roof, and there was let down by a cord a foaming pot of porter.

"This is capital," cried the victim of the pies, as he took half of it at a draught. "This is nectar for the gods. Oh, what a relief, to be sure. It puts new life into me."

And so it really seemed, for shouldering the poker, which was more like a javelin than anything else, he at once rushed into the vault where the meat was kept.

"Now," he said, "for a grand effort at freedom, and if I succeed I promise you, Mrs. Lovett, that I will come round to the shop, and rather surprise you, madam. Damn the pies!"

We have before described the place in which the meat was kept, and we need now only say that the shelves were very well stocked indeed, and that our friend, in whose progress we have a great interest, shovelled off the large pieces with celerity from one of the shelves, and commenced operations with the poker.

He was not slow in discovering that his work would not be the most easy in the world, for every now and then he kept encountering what felt very much like a plate of iron; but he fagged away with right good will, and succeeded after a time in getting down one of the shelves, which was one point gained at all events.

"Now for it," he said. "Now for it; I shall be able to act—to work upon the wall itself, and it must be something unusually strong to prevent me making a breach through it soon."

In order to refresh himself, he finished the porter, and then using his javelin-like poker as a battering ram, he banged the wall with the end of it for some moments, without producing any effect, until suddenly a portion of it swung open just like a door, and he paused to wonder how that came about.

All was darkness through the aperture, and yet he saw that it was actually a little square door that he had knocked open; and the idea then recurred to him that he had found how the shelves were supplied with meat, and he had no doubt that there was such a little square door opening at the back of every one of them.

"So," he said, "that mystery is solved; but what part of Mrs. Lovett's premises have I got upon now? We shall soon see."

He went boldly into the large cellar, and procured a light—a flaming torch, made of a piece of dry wood, and returning to the opening he had made in the wall, he thrust his head through it, and projected the torch before him.

With a cry of horror he fell backwards, extinguishing the torch in his fall, and he lay for a full quarter of an hour insensible upon the floor. What dreadful sight had he seen that had so chilled his young blood, and frozen up the springs of life?

When he recovered, he looked around him in the dim, borrowed light that came from the other vault, and he shuddered as he said,—

"Was it a dream?"

Soon, however, as he rose, he gave up the idea of having been the victim of any delusion of the imagination, for there was the broken shelf, and there the little square opening, through which he had looked and seen what had so transfixed him with horror.

Keeping his face in that direction, as if it would be dreadful to turn his back for a moment upon some frightful object, he made his way into the larger cellar where the ovens were, and then he sat down with a deep groan.

"What shall I do? Oh, what shall I do?" he muttered. "I am doomed—doomed."

"Are the pies doing?" said the voice of Mrs. Lovett. "It's eight o'clock."

"Eight, is it?"

"Yes, to be sure, and I want to know if you are bent upon your own destruction or not? I don't hear the furnaces going, and I'm quite sure you have not made the pies."

"Oh, I will keep my word, madam, you may depend. You want two hundred pies at nine o'clock, and you will see that they shall come up quite punctually to the minute."

"Very good. I am glad you are better satisfied than you were."

"I am quite satisfied now, Mrs. Lovett. I am quite in a different mood of mind to what I was before. I can assure you, madam, that I have no complaints to make, and I think the place has done me some good; and if at nine o'clock you let down the platform, you shall have two hundred pies up, as sure as fate, and something else, too," he added to himself, "or I shall be of a very different mind to what I now am."

We have already seen that Mrs. Lovett was not deceived by this seeming submission on the part of the cook, for she used that as an argument with Todd, when she was expatiating upon the necessity of getting rid of him that night.

But the cleverest people make mistakes at times, and probably, when the nine o'clock batch of pies makes its appearance, something may occur at the same time which will surprise a great many more persons than Mrs. Lovett and the reader.

But we must not anticipate, merely saying with the eastern sage, what will be will be, and what's impossible don't often come to pass; certain it is that the nine o'clock batch of two hundred pies were made and put in the ovens; and equally certain is it that the cook remarked, as he did so,—

"Yes, I'll do it—it may succeed; nay, it must succeed; and if so, woe be to you, Mrs. Lovett, and all who are joined with you in this horrible speculation, at which I sicken."

CHAPTER XXXVIII

JOHANNA IS STILL ALONE IN THE BARBER'S SHOP. HER HEAD IS RESTING UPON HER hands, and she is thinking of times gone past, when she had hoped for happiness with Mark Ingestrie. When we say alone, we must not be presumed to have forgotten the two officers who were so snugly packed in the cupboard. But Johanna, as her mind wandered back to her last interview with him whom she had loved so well, and clung to so fondly, and so constantly, almost for a time forgot where she was and that there was such a person as Sweeney Todd in existence.

"Alas, alas!" she said, "it seems likely enough that by the adoption of this disguise, so unsuited to me, I may achieve vengeance, but nothing more. Where are you, Mark Ingestrie? Oh, horror! something seems to tell me that no mortal voice can answer me."

Tears came trickling to her relief; and as she felt them trickling through her fingers, she started as she thought that the hour which Todd had said would expire before he returned must have nearly gone.

"I must control these thoughts," she said, "and this emotion. I must seem that which I am not."

She rose, and ceased weeping; she trimmed the little miserable lamp, and then she was about to go to the door to look for the return of Todd, when that individual, with a slow and sneaking footstep, made his appearance, as if he had been hiding just within the door-way.

Todd hung his hat upon a peg, and then turning his eyes enquiringly upon Johanna, he said,—

"Well, has anyone been?"

"Yes."

"Who? Speak, speak out. Confound you, you mumble so, I can hardly hear you."

"A gentleman to be shaved, and he went away again. I don't know what puts you in such a passion, Mr. Todd; I'm sure nothing—'

"What is it to you? Get out of my way, will you, and you may begin to think of shutting up, I think, for we shall have no more customers tonight. I am tired and weary. You are to sleep under the counter, you know."

"Yes, sir, you told me so. I dare say I shall be very comfortable there."

"And you have not been peeping and prying about, have you?"

"Not at all."

"Not looking even into that cupboard, I suppose, eh? It's not locked, but that's no reason why you should look into it—not that there is any secret in it, but I object to peeping and prying upon principle."

Todd, as he spoke, advanced towards the cupboard, and Johanna thought that in another moment a discovery would undoubtedly take place of the two officers who were there concealed; and probably that would have been the case had not the handle of the shop-door been turned at that moment and a man presented himself, at which Todd turned quickly, and saw that he was a substantial-looking farmer with dirty top boots, as if he had just come off a journey.

"Well, master," said the visitor, "I wants a clean shave."

"Oh," said Todd, not in the best of humours, "it's rather late. I suppose you would not like to wait till morning, for I don't know if I have any hot water?"

"Oh, cold will do."

"Cold, oh dear, no; we never shave in cold water; but if you must, you must; so sit down, sir, and we will soon settle the business."

'Thank you, thank you, I can't go to bed comfortable without a clean shave, do you see? I have come up from Braintree with beasts on commission, and I'm staying at the Bull's Head, you see."

"Oh, indeed," said Todd, as he adjusted the shaving cloth, "the Bull's Head."

"Yes, master; why I brought up a matter o' 220 beasts, I did, do you see, and was on my *pooney*, as good a stepper as you'd wish to see; and I sold 'em all, do you see, for 550 *pun*. Ho, ho! good work, that, do you see, and only forty-two on 'em was my beasts, do you see; I've got a missus at home, and a daughter; my girl's called Johanna—ahem!"

Up to this point, Johanna had not suspected that the game had begun, and that this was the magistrate who had come to put an end to the malpractices of Sweeney Todd; but his marked pronunciation of her name at once opened her eyes to the fact, and she knew that something interesting must soon happen.

"And so you sold them all," said Todd.

"Yes, master, I did, and I've got the money in my pocket now, in bank-notes; I never leaves my money about at inns, do you see, master; safe bind, safe find, you see; I carries it about with me."

"A good plan, too," said Todd; "Charley, some hot water; that's a good lad— and—and, Charley."

"Yes, sir."

"While I am just finishing off this gentleman, you may as well just run to the Temple to Mr. Serjeant Toldrunis and ask for his wig; we shall have to do it in the morning, and may as well have it the first thing in the day to begin upon, and you need not hurry, Charley, as we shall shut up when you come back."

"Yes, sir."

Johanna walked out, but went no further than the shop window, close to which she placed her eyes so that, between a pomatum jar and a lot of hair brushes, she could clearly see what was going on.

"A nice-looking little lad, that," said Todd's customer.

"Very, sir; an orphan boy; I took him out of charity, poor little fellow; but there, we ought to try to do all the good we can."

"Just so; I'm glad I have come to be shaved here. Mine's a rather strong beard, I think, do you see."

"Why, sir, in a manner of speaking," replied Todd, "it is a strong beard. I suppose you didn't come to London alone, sir?"

"Oh, yes, quite alone; except the drovers, I had no company with me; why do you ask?"

"Why, sir, I thought if you had any gentleman with you who might be waiting at the Bull's Head, you would recommend him to me if anything was wanting in my way, you know, sir; you might have just left him, saying you were going to Todd, the barber's, to have a clean shave, sir."

"No, not at all; the fact is, I did not come out to have a shave, but a walk, and it wasn't till I gave my chin a stroke, and found what a beard I had, that I thought of it, and then passing your shop, in I popped, do you see."

"Exactly, sir, I comprehend; you are quite alone in London?"

"Oh, quite, but when I come again, I'll come to you to be shaved, you may depend, and I'll recommend you too."

"I'm very much obliged to you," said Todd, as he passed his hand over the chin of his customer. "I'm very much obliged; I find I must give you another lather, sir, and I'll get another razor with a keener edge, now that I have taken off all the rough as one may say in a manner of speaking."

"Oh, I shall do."

"No, no, don't move, sir, I shall not detain you a moment; I have my other razors in the next room, and will polish you off now, sir, before you will know where you are; you know, sir, you have promised to recommend me, so I must do the best I can with you."

"Well, well, a clean shave is a comfort, but don't be long, for I want to get back, do you see."

"Not a moment, not a moment."

Sweeney Todd walked into his back-parlour, conveying with him the only light that was in the shop, so that the dim glimpse that, up to this time, Johanna from the outside had contrived to get of what was going on, was denied to her; and all that met her eyes was impenetrable darkness.

Oh, what a world of anxious agonising sensations crossed the mind of the young and beautiful girl at that moment. She felt as if some great crisis in her history had arrived, and that she was condemned to look in vain into the darkness to see of what it consisted.

We must not, however, allow the reader to remain in the same state of mysti-fication, which came over the perceptive faculties of Johanna Oakley; but we shall proceed to state clearly and distinctly what did happen in the barber's shop, while he went to get an uncommonly keen razor in his back-parlour.

The moment his back was turned, the seeming farmer who had made such a good thing of his beasts, sprang from the shaving-chair, as if he had been electrified; and yet he did not do it with any appearance of fright, nor did he make any noise. It was only astonishingly quick, and then he placed himself close to the window, and waited patiently with his eyes fixed upon the chair, to see what would happen next.

In the space of about a quarter of a minute, there came from the next room a sound like the rapid drawing of a heavy bolt, and then in an instant the shaving-chair disap-peared beneath the floor; and the circumstances by which Sweeney Todd's customers disappeared was evident.

There was a piece of the flooring turning upon a centre, and the weight of the chair when a bolt was withdrawn, by means of a simple leverage from the inner room, weighed down upon one end of the top, which, by a little apparatus, was to swing completely round, there being another chair on the under surface, which thus became the upper, exactly resembling the one in which the unhappy customer was supposed to be "polished off."

Hence was it that in one moment, as if by magic, Sweeney Todd's visitors disap-peared, and there was the empty chair. No doubt, he trusted to a fall of about twenty feet below, on to a stone floor, to be the death of them, or, at all events, to stun them until he could go down to finish the murder, and—*to cut them up for Mrs. Lovett's pies!* after robbing them of all money and valuables they might have about them.

In another moment, the sound as of a bolt was again heard, and Sir Richard Blunt, who had played the part of the wealthy farmer, feeling that the trap was closed again, seated himself in the new chair that had made its appearance with all the nonchalance in life, as if nothing had happened.

It was a full minute before Todd ventured to look from the parlour into the dark-ened shop, and then he shook so that he had to hold by the door to steady himself.

"That's done," he said. "That's the last, I hope. It is time I finished; I never felt so nervous since the first time. Then I did quake a little. How quiet he went; I have sometimes had a shriek ringing in my ears for a whole week."

It was a large high-backed piece of furniture, that shaving-chair, so that, when Todd crept into the shop with the light in his hand, he had not the remotest idea it was tenanted; but when he got round it, and saw his customer calmly waiting with the lather upon his face, the cry of horror that came gargling and gushing from his throat was horrible to hear.

"Why, what's the matter?" said Sir Richard.

"O God, the dead! the dead! O God!" cried Todd, "this is the beginning of my punishment. Have mercy, Heaven! oh, do not look upon me with those dead eyes!"

"Murderer!" shouted Sir Richard, in a voice that rang like the blast of a trumpet through the house.

In an instant he sprang upon Sweeney Todd, and grappled him by the throat. There was a short struggle, and they were down upon the floor together, but Todd's wrists were suddenly laid hold of, and a pair of handcuffs were scientifically put upon him by the officers, who, at the word "murderer," that being a preconcerted signal, came from the cupboard where they had been concealed.

"Secure him well, my men," said the magistrate, "and don't let him lay violent hands upon himself. Ah! Miss Oakley, you are in time. This man is a murderer. I found out all the secret about the chair last night, after twelve, by exploring the vaults under the old church. Thank God, we have stopped his career."

CHAPTER XXXIX

IT WANTS FIVE MINUTES TO NINE, AND MRS. LOVETT'S SHOP IS FILLING WITH persons anxious to devour or to carry away one or more of the nine o'clock batch of savoury, delightful, gushing gravy pies.

Many of Mrs. Lovett's customers paid her in advance for the pies, in order that they might be quite sure of getting their orders fulfilled when the first batch should make its gracious appearance from the depths below.

"Well, Jiggs," said one of the legal fraternity to another. "How are you to-day, old fellow? What do you bring it in?"

"Oh! I ain't very blooming. The fact is the count and I, and a few others, made a night of it last evening, and, somehow or another, I don't think whiskey and water, half-and-half, and tripe go together."

"I should wonder if they did."

"And so I've come for a pie just to settle my stomach; you see, I'm rather delicate."

"Ah! you are just like me, young man, there," said an elderly personage; "I have a delicate stomach, and the slightest thing disagrees with me. A mere idea will make me quite ill."

"Will it, really?"

"Yes; and my wife, she—"

"Oh! bother your wife. It's only five minutes to nine, don't you see? What a crowd there is, to be sure. Mrs. Lovett, you charmer, I hope you have ordered enough pies to be made to-night. You see what a lot of customers you have."

"Oh! there will be plenty."

"That's right. I say, don't push so; you'll be in time, I tell you; don't be pushing and shoving in that sort of way—I've got ribs."

"And so have I. Last night, I didn't get to bed at all, and my old woman is in a certain condition, you see, gentlemen, and won't fancy anything but one of Lovett's veal pies, so I've come all the way from Newington to get one for—"

"Hold your row, will you? and don't push."

"For to have the child marked as a pie as its—"

"Behind there, I say; don't be pushing a fellow as if it was half-price at a theatre."

Each moment added some new comers to the throng, and at last any strangers who had known nothing of the attractions of Mrs. Lovett's pie-shop, and had walked down Bell-yard, would have been astonished at the throng of persons there assembled—a throng, that was each moment increasing in density, and becoming more and more urgent and clamorous.

One, two, three, four, five, six, seven, eight, nine! Yes, it is nine at last. It strikes by old St. Dunstan's church clock, and in weaker strains the chronometrical machine at the pie-shop echoes the sound. What excitement there is now to get at the pies when they shall come! Mrs. Lovett lets down the square, moveable platform that goes upon pulleys into the cellar; some machinery, which only requires a handle to be turned, brings up a hundred pies in a tray. These are eagerly seized by parties who have previously paid, and such a smacking of lips ensues as never was known.

Down goes the platform for the next hundred, and a gentlemanly man says,—

"Let me work the handle, Mrs. Lovett, if you please; it's too much for you, I'm sure."

"Sir, you are very kind, but I never allow anybody on this side of the counter but my own people, sir; I can turn the handle myself, sir, if you please, with the assistance of this girl. Keep your distance, sir, nobody wants your help."

How the waggish young lawyers' clerks laughed as they smacked their lips, and sucked in the golopshious gravy of the pies, which, by-the-by, appeared to be all delicious veal this time, and Mrs. Lovett worked the handle of the machine all the more vigorously, that she was a little angry with the officious stranger. What an unusual trouble it seemed to be to wind up those forthcoming hundred pies! How she toiled, and how the people waited; but at length there came up the savoury steam, and then the tops of the pies were visible.

They came up upon a large tray, about six feet square, and the moment Mrs. Lovett ceased turning the handle, and let a catch fall that prevented the platform receding again, to the astonishment and terror of everyone, away flew all the pies, tray and all, across the counter, and a man, who was lying crouched down in an exceedingly flat state under the tray, sprang to his feet.

Mrs. Lovett shrieked, as well she might, and then she stood trembling, and looking as pale as death itself. It was the doomed cook from the cellars, who had adopted this mode of escape.

The throngs of persons in the shop looked petrified, and after Mrs. Lovett's shriek, there was an awful stillness for about a minute, and then the young man who officiated as cook spoke.

"Ladies and Gentlemen—I fear that what I am going to say will spoil your appetites; but the truth is beautiful at all times, and I have to state that Mrs. Lovett's pies are made of *human flesh!*"

How the throng of persons recoiled—what a roar of agony and dismay there was! How frightfully sick about forty lawyers' clerks became all at once, and how they spat out the gelatinous clinging portions of the rich pies they had been devouring. "Good gracious!—oh, the pies!—confound it!"

"'Tis false!" screamed Mrs. Lovett.

"You are my prisoner, madam," said the man who had obligingly offered to turn the handle of the machine that wound up the pies, at the same time producing a constable's staff.

"Prisoner!"

"Yes, on a charge of aiding and abetting Sweeney Todd, now in custody, in the commission of many murders."

Mrs. Lovett staggered back, and her complexion turned a livid colour.

"I am poisoned," she said. "Good God! I am poisoned," and she sank insensible to the floor.

There was now some confusion at the door of the shop, for several people were effecting an entrance. These consisted of Sir Richard Blunt, Colonel Jeffery, Johanna Oakley and Tobias Ragg, who, when he escaped from the mad-house at Peckham Rye, went direct to a gentleman in the Temple, who took him to the magistrate.

"Miss Oakley," said Sir Richard, "you objected to coming here, but I told you I had a particular reason for bringing you. This night, about half an hour since, I made an acquaintance I want to introduce you to."

"Who—oh, who?"

"There's an underground communication all the way from Sweeney Todd's cellar to the ovens of this pie-shop; and I found there Mrs. Lovett's cook, with whom I arranged this little surprise for his mistress. Look at him, Miss Oakley, do you know him? Look up, Master Cook."

"Mark—Mark Ingestrie!" shrieked Johanna, the moment she glanced at the person alluded to.

"Johanna!"

In another moment she was in his arms, and clasped to his heart.

"Oh, Mark, Mark—you are not dead."

"No, no—I never was. And you, Johanna, are not in love with a fellow, in military undress, you met in the Temple."

"No, no, I never was."

When Mrs. Lovett was picked up by the officers, she was found to be dead. The poison which Sweeney Todd had put into the brandy she was accustomed to solace herself with, when the pangs of conscience troubled her, and of which she always took some before the evening batch of pies came up, had done its work.

That night Todd passed in Newgate, and in due time a swinging corpse was all that remained of the barber of Fleet-street. Mr. Fogg's establishment, at Peckham Rye, was broken up, and that gentleman persuaded to emigrate, for which the government kindly paid all expenses. Tobias went into the service of Mark Ingestrie, and, at the marriage of Mark with his beautiful bride, Big Ben, the beef-eater, did some extraordinary things, which space and opportunity will not permit us to chronicle in these pages.

The youths who visited Lovett's pie-shop, and there luxuriated upon those delicacies, are youths no longer. Indeed, the grave has closed over all but one, and he is very, very old, but even now, as he thinks of how he enjoyed the flavour of the "veal," he shudders, and has to take a drop of brandy.

Beneath the old church of St. Dunstan were found the heads and bones of Todd's victims. As little as possible was said by the authorities about it; but it was supposed that some hundreds of persons must have perished in the frightful manner we have detailed.

Our tale is over, and the only seeming mystery that has to be explained consists in settling the point with regard to who Thornhill was, and what became of him.

He was just what he represented himself to be, the friend of Mark Ingestrie, to whom had been, by Mark, entrusted the care of the string of pearls; but he fell a victim to the awful criminality of Sweeney Todd, who was in league with Mrs. Lovett, and who robbed his murdered customers, while she sold them for pies.

Mark Ingestrie, after many dangers and hardships, had reached London; but he did so, unfortunately, only just in time to follow Johanna to the Temple-gardens, in one of her innocent ramblings with Colonel Jeffery, but believing from that circumstance that she was false to him, and hearing nothing of his friend Thornhill, he, in a moment of despair, took the desperate situation of cook at Mrs. Lovett's far-famed pie-shop, from where he so narrowly escaped with his life.

Johanna and Mark Ingestrie lived long and happily together, enjoying all the comforts of an independent existence; but they never forgot the strange and eventful circumstances connected with the String of Pearls.

Original Sources

———◆———

Alcott, Louisa May. "Lost in a Pyramid; or, The Mummy's Curse," *The New World*, January 16, 1869.

Anonymous. "The Apparition of Lord Tyrone to Lady Beresford," *The Terrific Register*. London: Sherwood, Jones, and Co., 1825.

———. "A Night in the Grave; or, The Devil's Receipt," *Legends of Terror! and Tales of the Wonderful and Wild*. London: Sherwood, Gilbert, and Piper, 1826.

Collins, Wilkie. "The Dream-Woman," *The Queen of Hearts*. London: Hurst and Blackett, 1859.

Cram, Ralph Adams. "In Kropfsburg Keep," *Black Spirits and White*. Chicago: Stone and Kimball, 1895.

Doyle, Arthur Conan. "The Case of Lady Sannox," *The Idler*, November 1893.

Galt, John. "The Buried Alive," *Blackwood's*, October 1825.

Godwin, William. "The Executioner," *Blackwood's*, February 1832.

Hoffmann, E.T.A. (trans. Alexander Ewing). "Aurelia," *The Serapion Brethren*. London: George Bell & Sons, 1892.

Hogg, James. "George Dobson's Expedition to Hell," *Blackwood's*, May 1827.

Irving, Washington. "The Adventure of the German Student," *Tales of a Traveller*. London: John Murray, 1824.

Maupassant, Guy de. "The Diary of a Madman," *The Complete Short Stories of Guy de Maupassant*. New York: Blue Ribbon Books, Inc., 1903.

Poe, Edgar Allan. "The Pit and the Pendulum," *The Gift: A Christmas and New Year's Present for 1842*. Philadelphia: Carey & Hart, 1842.

Rymer, James Malcolm. "The String of Pearls," *The People's Periodical and Family Library*, November 21, 1846–March 20, 1847.

Shelley, Mary. *Frankenstein; or, The Modern Prometheus*. London: Lackington, Hughes, Harding, Mavor, & Jones, 1818.

Stevenson, Robert Louis. *Strange Case of Dr. Jekyll and Mr. Hyde*. London: Longman's, Green, and Co., 1886.

Stoker, Bram. "The Dualitists; or, The Death-Doom of the Double-Born," *The Theatre Annual*, Christmas 1887.

Thomson, Richard. "The Wehr-Wolf: A Legend of the Limousin," *Tales of an Antiquary: Chiefly Illustrative of the Manners, Traditions, and Remarkable Localities of Ancient London*. London: H. Colburn, 1828.

Tieck, Ludwig. "Wake Not the Dead!; or The Bride of the Grave," *Legends of Terror! and Tales of the Wonderful and Wild*. London: Sherwood, Gilbert, and Piper, 1826.

Whitehead, Charles. "Sawney Beane: The Man Eater," *Lives and Exploits of the Most Noted Highwaymen, Robbers and Murderers, of All Nations, Drawn from the Most Authentic Sources and Brought Down to Present Times*. Hartford, CT: Ezra Strong, 1836.